SU

Two Dominants.
One a Navy SEAL.
One a Mistress facing a hell she can't escape.
Luckily, hell is just another day at the office for a SEAL...

Abigail Rose is CFO for Thomas Rose Associates, a successful New Orleans marketing firm she runs with her best friend Rosalinda Thomas, and their three fellow executives, Cyn, Vera and Skye.

Since all five are Dommes, they work *and* play together. However, Abby has lived with the threat of a severe mental illness for most of her life, and now the monster has come out of the shadows. Everything that defines her--including her control as a Mistress--is shattering.

Neil Shepherd is so calm under pressure, his SEAL teammates know he'll hold the line, no matter what goes down on a mission. At home, he finds his peace navigating the waters of the Louisiana bayou. As a Dom himself, he shouldn't be attracted to Abby, but Fate doesn't consult the power exchange playbook when it comes to who is meant to be together. From the first time they meet, he knows he wants her. Even the shadows that are trying to claim her won't stop him.

AT HER SERVICE

A Mistresses of the Board Room Novel

JOEY W. HILL

At Her Service

Mistresses of the Board Room Novel - Book #2

A spin-off series set in the award winning Knights of the Board Room world.

Copyright © 2021 Joey W. Hill

ALL RIGHTS RESERVED

Cover design by W. Scott Hill

SWP Digital & Print Edition publication November 2021 by Story Witch Press, 452 Mattamushkeet Dr., Little River, South Carolina 29566, USA

This book may not be reproduced or used in whole or in part by any means existing without written permission from the publisher, Story Witch Press, 452 Mattamushkeet Drive, Little River, SC 29566.

Warning: The unauthorized reproduction or distribution of this copyrighted work is illegal. No part of this book may be scanned, uploaded or distributed via the Internet or any other means, electronic or print, without the publisher's permission. Criminal copyright infringement, including infringement without monetary gain, is investigated by the FBI and is punishable by up to 5 years in federal prison and a fine of $250,000. (http://www.fbi.gov/ipr/). Please purchase only authorized electronic or print editions and do not participate in or encourage the electronic piracy of copyrighted material. Your support of the author's rights is appreciated.

This book is a work of fiction and any resemblance to persons, living or dead, or places, events or locales is purely coincidental. The characters are productions of the author's imagination and used fictitiously.

The publisher and author(s) acknowledge the trademark status and trademark ownership of all trademarks, service marks and word marks mentioned in this book.

The following material contains graphic sexual content meant for mature readers. Reader discretion is advised.

Digital ISBN: 978-1-951544-16-4

Print ISBN: 978-1-951544-17-1

ACKNOWLEDGMENTS

In researching paranoid schizophrenia and mental illness, one thing became clear. There are a lot of treatment options, and discussions on how best to respect a patient's will and decision-making ability. Abby's experience as a schizophrenic is her journey, prompted by my research and where the story took us. It will therefore not match in every respect how other professionals, patients and families choose to address it, though there will be overlap (if I did my research right). There is no one-size-fits-all reaction to schizophrenia.

Good recommendations guided me to excellent resources on this topic. I also had the profoundly important input of a reader whose husband deals with a closely related mental illness. Traci beta read the book to offer her (and his) thoughts on it. Considering the emotional effort it took for them to do that, when they're already living it in so many ways, I can never thank them enough.

One of my regular beta readers is also a therapist, and that professional perspective was equally invaluable. Thank you, Gabriela!

Because the book is still, at its heart, a love story, and an erotic romance, I doubt I have captured in its total form how difficult schizophrenia is for the person suffering it, or those who love them. Regardless, I hope I have at least honored the enormous struggle a person with schizophrenia faces, along with their loved ones and expert caregivers.

I write love stories because I never give up on the idea that, even when life becomes a never-ending series of storms, there are always days where the sun shines. Love carries a person through the storm and gives us someone to connect and share with on the sunny days. One thing I can say with certainty, after researching this illness, is that love, and the will to grasp it, hold onto it, is essential to quality of life.

As it is to all of us, no matter what we weather.

Thank you so much to everyone who helped me on this topic - those who recommended sources, the source authors themselves, Traci and her husband, Gabriela, and the rest of my wonderful beta readers.

Also, my great thanks to Lynn, my longstanding source on SEAL information, for the additional details and refreshers she provided for me about Neil. Note: For the purposes of the short time range this story covers, I made Neil's "work schedule" as a SEAL a little different from the norm. According to my sources, deployments from the States and training times are usually more scheduled and prolonged. I ask the forgiveness of those who know better for "Hollywoodizing" that aspect of SEAL life, and offer once again my respect and admiration for what our armed forces handle and face.

As ever, any mistakes I have made on any of the above are entirely mine.

At the end of Neil and Abby's journey, be sure and check my Postscript Acknowledgment for a delightful "behind the scenes" commentary on the epilogue. I don't want to offer any spoilers, but I will give a tremendous thanks here to Kristin H, for her important contribution to that closing chapter.

CHAPTER ONE

When she saw Neil's truck, Abby told herself to turn around and leave. Instead, she bypassed that lot, following curved roads through the forested section of the city park until she reached the soccer fields. Parking there, the option farthest from his vehicle, should eliminate the chances of her seeing him. It was a big park, with extensive running trails.

He'd told her about it because he knew it was her cardio workout of choice. That was why she was here.

Though if she'd *really* wanted to avoid all chance of seeing him, she wouldn't have come here early afternoon. That was the time he'd told her he preferred. The New Orleans humidity and nine-to-five job schedules made it a less appealing time for anyone. But he was a Navy SEAL. Seeking out less-than-optimal weather conditions was part of his conditioning.

She wasn't a Navy SEAL. She ran as the sun was coming up. At that hour the air held onto the fading possibility of coolness. Even more importantly, she witnessed the reassuring way the light pushed back the shadows. The voices in her head needed the shadows' cover to torment her.

At least so far.

She might get heat stroke, running at this hour of the day, but she had no complaint with the brightness. As she locked her Lexus, the silver color flashed with sunlight. Heat soaking into her skin aided her warm-up stretches. She tightened her ponytail, bounced on her toes, running in place as she closed her eyes, got into the zone. She was going to push herself today. She was here to work out, not bump into him "by accident."

Still, she indulged a vision of his tall frame in shorts that showed muscled calves, his impossibly firm ass. Maybe a loose tank shirt...or no shirt at all.

Unlike her, he didn't need the "gonna push myself today" pep talk before his workout. It was his default mode. His life, the lives of his team, depended on his level of fitness, mentally, physically. She approved of that discipline and dedication.

She remembered the strength of his hands, the piercing regard of his slate-colored eyes. When shadowed by his bill cap, the irises were purple-tinged gray. Light made them bluer. The last time she'd seen him, the cap he'd worn had been frayed along the bill, with a white mesh in the back. The cap bore an embroidered patch of a large-mouthed bass, some kind of outfitter store logo. He looked like what he was; a Louisiana good old boy, from the strong jaw covered by a gleaming soft brown beard, clipped short, to the tips of his thick tread shoes designed for all sorts of outdoorsman type activities.

It was a cosmic tragedy that there wasn't a submissive bone in that tall, lean body. Taking his deep commitment to service down roads that could make a different kind of sweat sheen upon his skin? In the solitude of her bed, the desire had fueled her fantasies, given her a blissful break from the pre-dawn worries that made sleep elude her.

She chose the six-mile trail. It circled the park, but also included an auxiliary loop around the more heavily wooded adjacent utility station property.

He'd mentioned those woods occasionally offered wildlife sightings. Deer, foxes. A young black bear. Even an alligator venturing out of the marshy areas.

Watch out for snakes. They won't bug you if you don't bug them, but if you startle one on the path, he might get cranky. Don't run that utility loop without a partner. It's pretty isolated. When I'm home, I run there regularly.

The advice had been given at a cookout at Dale and Athena's, mutual friends, and the first place she and Neil had spent time together socially. The half-smile on Neil's lips as he lifted his beer to his mouth, that steady look in his appealing gaze, told her he was more than willing to be that running partner.

Some of the other things he'd said to her that day had been far more direct. But so was her firm assertion that them getting together wasn't a possibility. She'd used the simplest explanation. She was a Domme. That was how she liked to enjoy men. He was not a sub.

"I don't need you to be what you're not," she'd told him.

"Maybe being what you need is what I am," he'd responded. *"Have you thought of that?"*

She needed to pace herself, but to drive away those thoughts, she lengthened her stride and increased her speed. She focused on her form, becoming mindful of her muscles, the way her body moved.

Thankfully, by the time she'd reached the turn onto the utility loop, her mind had dropped her into that zone. As she took the path, the forest became thicker along the sides. At least until the utility station and its outbuildings came into view on her left. Then a thinner buffer of foliage separated the path from the chain link fence that enclosed the structures and equipment.

Because she kept her gaze trained on the denser vegetation to her right, she saw the flash of a fox's red coat and sharp nose, a plethora of squirrels scuttling along tree branches. Plus at least one snake, a long, gleaming brown and black Eastern garter. He crossed the path well ahead of her, so there was no need for either of them to get cranky.

As she reached a rise in the trail, she had a view of it a quarter mile ahead, where it sloped down and along the other side of the utility station, following the fencing. Through the dispersal of trees on that side, she caught a flash of movement. Two men running side by side.

The impression was brief, the trees and bushes swallowing them again. No way to tell anything about them except they were men. Yet every muscle in her body tightened, and her breath shortened. One of them was him. She knew it.

He was right. There were all kinds of animals to be seen on this trail, including those that quickened a woman's pulse.

Why did he hold her attention like this? She had another, far more critical reason for discouraging him, but the one she'd given him had plenty of merit on its own. Every man she'd enjoyed, every lover she'd taken, had come with that minimum requirement.

That he wanted to serve a Mistress.

Outside of regular sessions in a BDSM club, it had been years since she'd allowed a man into her life, beyond a friendly coffee, meal or social gathering. Things where boundaries were as defined as within the scene itself.

Sexual pleasure, the intense intimacy that a BDSM session could create, the warm friendship that could exist outside it when you chose right—she had all that with her small select group of male partners.

She was halfway through the utility station loop. If she back-tracked, she calculated she'd complete a four-mile run. Plenty for today's workout.

Instead she kept going. Her stride lengthened. The men had looked similar in height, suggesting he was running with Max, a friend and fellow SEAL. She'd have to push herself to catch up with those two sets of long, strong legs. But the sun was shining, she was feeling good, and something playful took hold of her.

Something urgent and playful.

When she closed the distance, it was at a straightaway on the north side. The trail opened up and widened as it headed back toward the park.

Surprising two trained special operators was an accomplishment. But this was familiar, non-threatening ground. The gust of wind that had the trees sighing, creating cover for her approach, also aided her half-baked plan. As she offered a runner's courtesy, she managed, mostly, to keep the exultance out of her voice.

"Coming up on your left," she called. Then, lungs and muscles burning, she dug out a burst of speed to sprint past Max. As two handsome heads turned to mark her, she shot them both a grin. "Kind of dragging today, aren't you, boys?"

She glimpsed surprise and a man's pleasure as Neil recognized her. It charged her with another spurt of energy, and then it was on. She laughed as she heard them increase their pace. She wasn't going to have the advantage long, but she enjoyed it while she had it—all of eight seconds, and that was because the trail twisted in a couple sharp curves easier for one lone woman to navigate, versus two tall men running side by side.

They rejoined the main park path, which had ample room for the two of them to draw abreast, Neil closest to her side. With a suppressed smile, she noted that meant he and Max had changed places. She tossed a smile in their direction, but had no breath to speak. She did have the energy to appreciate Neil's sweaty muscles, concentrated expression, and tendrils of short, damp hair clinging to his nape. He was wearing a gray T-shirt with NAVY posted on the front in blue block letters, the fabric clinging to his upper body. Max wore a muscle tank open on the sides.

Both of them had on the clingier exercise shorts that held everything securely, things that didn't appreciate the constant jostling of a hard run. The fabric extended a few inches below the loose pairs of shorts they had pulled over the top. She would have preferred the men run in the clingy shorts alone, but Nature would demand a woman give that view her undivided attention. The inevitable collisions with inanimate objects made that option inadvisable.

Preferable, but inadvisable.

They didn't leave her behind, as they could easily do. But she was reaching the critical point where her laboring lungs needed an oxygen break. Fortunately, an approaching workout station gave her a graceful exit excuse. She didn't intend to disrupt their workout intensity, and there was no way she could keep up with them indefinitely.

Plus it would highlight the vital subtext. She wasn't here to meet up with anyone. This had merely been a pleasurable coincidence.

The irony of her choosing to play games with her own head wasn't lost on her.

"We do interval training here," Neil said before she could gasp out a friendly farewell. He and Max didn't even seem winded. Super-soldier maniacs. "Why don't you take a break while we run through the stations?"

"I'll just keep going." At least until she got around the next curve, where she could drop to a staggering cooldown walk with her dignity intact. She let the corners of her mouth tip up. "I was just passing by. Literally. I'm impressed you kept up."

His return smile held something heated and dangerous. "Going to make me chase you down?"

Max had already started on the chin up bar. Abby jogged in place. Neil was doing the same, though his movements seemed to rotate around a still and intense core of energy, ready to surge into action.

The sweat of a good workout was drying on her skin, the wicking mesh fabric of her top offering her coolness. She felt strong, alive. Foolishly optimistic. Foolish enough to flirt with a man she shouldn't flirt with. His expression held the same hazards as the very first time their gazes had met. He wanted more than she'd ever be able to give him.

"You think you could catch up to me after you did the whole circuit of stations?" She bounced from foot to foot. It gave the impression she was getting ready to resume her run, though she was slowing her pace, bringing her heart rate down. Optimistic her mind might be about it, but her body was a hardcore realist.

"He's supposed to do three rounds," Max called out.

"Three. Wow. So probably not."

Neil shot Max a narrow look, but then his gaze returned and swept over her. Among the obvious signs of male interest, a blatant appreciation of her curves, was also a concern for her well-being. Care and desire. A heady combination. "Want to find out?" he asked. "After you take a water break?"

She did, actually. She wanted to test him, push him. Play with him. "Maybe," she said. "But the water break is as much of an advantage as I'll give you."

The corner of his mouth lifted again, and he headed for the stations, breaking into a graceful run and lunge onto the jump pad. From there, he hooked his hands into the underside of a net suspended in the air, swinging along its length. Max had left the chin up bar and was traversing the uneven balance beams. Barely looking at his feet, he leaped over to the jump pad after Neil and launched himself at the net just as Neil finished it and moved to the chin up bar. He began to lift himself up and down with seemingly effortless upper body strength.

One armed. Left, then right.

She was circling the stations at a slow jog, sipping her water. In a gym, a person's peripheral vision might be trained on whomever he or she hoped was watching as they showed off their rippling muscles, toned bodies, their feats of dexterity, strength or endurance. This wasn't that. With how much energy and speed they were applying, any loss of focus and they'd end up with broken limbs. She was watching two men in top fighting form, dedicated to keeping it that way.

While they couldn't afford distractions, she had no such boundaries. Any woman who denied herself the delight of watching this needed a lesson in self-care. She transitioned from a jog to a swift walk, which allowed her to keep her heartrate up but offered a better view of their move from station to station.

Max's open-sided shirt gave her a trove of anatomical splendor, in smooth rolling muscle. Though Neil's shirt didn't offer as much of a view, it stretched over his shoulders and biceps. Plus, with the intensity of the workout, even the loose covering shorts couldn't hide the intriguing display of flexing haunches and thigh muscles.

Max completed the other stations, dropped to his feet and returned to the trail. Tipping his dark blond head to her, he sent her a friendly look. "Gotta get to work. Don't let him slack off. Crack the whip if you have to."

The amused gray eyes said it was a deliberate tease. Max was in a deep and committed relationship with Janet, a Mistress whom Abby knew. A former SEAL, Max worked security as head limo driver at Kensington & Associates in New Orleans. Janet was executive admin to the CEO there, Matt Kensington.

Noticing Max was headed the way they'd come, she realized he was going to run the same distance back, instead of the shorter length remaining to complete the loop. He might be a former SEAL, but he still trained like he was on active duty.

Neil was on his second circuit of the ten stations, working his way over parallel bars. The short sleeves of his T-shirt revealed the scar from the shrapnel wound he had taken on one of his most recent missions. The day of Dale and Athena's barbecue, he'd just received a thumbs up that he was fit for duty again. Which meant he could be called back at any time to Virginia Beach. *VA Beach*, he'd called it, *VA* rhyming with *Ah*.

As in *Ah, shit.*

Max's teasing comment reminded her that, if Neil knew Janet was a Mistress, Abby's reason for keeping him at arm's length had lost some of its starch. He had a close-at-hand example of a power exchange incompatibility that hadn't hampered two people pursuing a relationship.

Especially when the interest between the two people in question ran this strong.

Every time she saw the scar, she had the most irritating need to lay her fingers on it, ensure herself of his durability. Admonish him in a purely Mistress-driven way to take better care of what she absurdly felt possessive about.

Him.

They hadn't even kissed. But it had been a very close thing that day.

"I just love your fucking mouth. I've dreamed of it. Am I in your dreams at all, Abby?"

The memory sent her a small burst of revived energy. He was halfway through the second circuit. It should give her enough time to make her escape.

Not escape, she primly corrected herself. Well-timed exit. But she'd dallied in perilous waters long enough. Once out of his sight, she'd finish out the rest of the run at a cooldown pace. She considered herself pretty fit, but she was going to have to go home and let a hot shower and aspirin do what they could to minimize the sore muscles she'd have later.

But it had been worth it.

"You've got one circuit to go after this one," she called out, waiting until he landed on the opposite side of a cargo net he'd just scaled. "Max says no cheating or cutting it short."

"He's such a mom," Neil grunted. He ran through the high step blocks, though at the end of it, his gaze flicked toward her, calculating. Telling her he knew what she was planning.

"He's got an outstanding set of pecs to complement his maternal side," she noted casually. "Good ass, too."

She tried not to make the smile she tossed him challenging, but she couldn't seem to stop herself, or the words that came out of her mouth. "I don't expect to see you again today."

"Would you like to?" He stopped on the peg bridge, held the resistance moment as he kept himself off the ground, hands clasped around the pegs, elbows bent. The view was enough to give a woman multiple eye-gasms.

She let the yearning grab and hold her, the way her gaze did his. "Impress me."

His intent smile grabbed her at every level. "Yes, ma'am."

She nimbly leaped back onto the path and took off. Her heart might burst in her chest, but if she kept the pace, she had a chance of reaching her car before he caught up.

Maybe.

Every time her body begged her to slow down, she refused it. She could be as much of a hardass with it as she was with her subs. SEALs weren't the only ones with extreme self-discipline.

This was a mating dance, but not the mating dance of a female coyly slowing her pace or cloaking her strengths to reel in male prey. She meant it. She wanted to be impressed. She wanted a man to work his ass off for her, because everything in the world worth having was earned.

What she could give a man would reward the effort.

When she couldn't do that anymore, then her days of making a man work for it, gratifying that Mistress side of her, would gracefully come to an end.

She was fair and kind to the men who pleased her.

Her body had found a second wind. She lengthened her stride, the knowledge of the pursuit fueling her adrenaline. She passed a couple male joggers braving the heat, aware that they tried to increase their pace as she blasted by them.

It was an erotic game, but beneath it was the call of nature, the male proving he was strong and fast enough to protect a female, keep her safe, drive or hold off an attacker.

Something about Neil suggested he could do that in the battleground of her mind. Though she'd locked away the thought, it kept coming back, a reminder of how foolish her interest in him was. Delusions came in a lot of insidious, subtle forms. If she let the conscious ones get a foothold, the unconscious ones might break through all the faster.

She enjoyed outpacing the other men, wasn't offended by the wolf whistle she heard follow her. She had no false modesty about her appeal. Her slender waist, fabulous legs and generous curves were what actresses busted their asses to get. Her red hair, long and wavy, framed a face with fair skin, catlike hazel eyes, lush lips.

In a public venue, she had the looks that would cause a fire hazard if she pulled out a cigarette, because of the small army of lighters that would be whipped out of male pockets. Fortunately, she didn't smoke.

Beauty had its time and place. She enjoyed the male attention while knowing how little it meant for what she sought and needed from a man. She found that in his eyes, had developed a knack for recognizing and cultivating it. Being an experienced Domme came with a shitload of well-earned privileges.

Which was why her pull toward Neil made no damn sense at all. Playtime was over. She needed to abandon this. Not soon, but now. She was coming up on a shortcut. If she took it, he wouldn't know she'd left the main trail. She'd most certainly make it to her car before him. She could head for a shower.

She'd put in her time at work this morning, but there was more she could do at home.

She hesitated, kangarooing it in place, her ponytail swinging against her shoulders. She weighed what made sense against what a far more deep-seated part of her wanted.

Then she glanced over her shoulder, and her heart stuttered, leaped. She could see him through the trees, coming.

Coming fast.

He'd also stripped off his T-shirt, because she caught a glimpse of his upper body, tanned, muscled, furred flesh. From the pool party at Dale and Athena's, she knew he had a nice layer of chest hair, gleaming brown.

He turned his head, and even through the trees and the winding path's distance, she knew he'd seen her. She shot off the main trail onto the shortcut. It went through denser woods and was narrower.

She was a good runner, and she was competitive. What moved her feet now wasn't only the desire to make him earn the prize. It was to prove she could keep the upper hand.

Nothing would stop her. Sexual awareness kicked in to add to that adrenaline reservoir. When she tripped on a root and went down, she rolled, came back up and hit her stride again with barely a pause, ignoring the pain singing through her scraped knee.

She was giving her all, and he was closing the gap. *Yes.* She wouldn't look back, sacrificing precious seconds. But she could feel him. When the trail widened out and rejoined the main one again, she saw the soccer fields and parking lot where she'd left her car.

He was ten feet behind her.

She sprinted across the lot, but in the open flat terrain, his longer legs had the distinct advantage. She dodged right, but one arm snaked out, circled her waist. Laughter bubbled from her as he swung her toward him. Her feet brushed the ground, and then he had her back braced against her Lexus. Despite their speed, the energy that propelled them, the movement was controlled, careful of her.

But there was a quiver in the muscled arm, and the light in his slate-colored eyes was a windstorm, whipping away her gasping breath.

He'd tied the T-shirt around his waist. Still holding her, he tugged it free, mopped it over his damp chest so he didn't coat her in sweat, a consideration that just intensified her desire to get closer. Her hands were clutched over his slick biceps. She was aching, staring up at him.

A kiss would be so easy to take, to give, but in this stretched out, erotically charged moment, neither of them wanted easy. She wanted that suspended blink where nothing could be claimed or denied, wild and undefined as the power of nature. Since a beginning started the journey toward an end, she wanted no beginning. Just this, the power and anticipation of an impending storm.

He backed off. Not to let her go, but to let his hand slide to her hip as he dropped to a knee. He pressed the T-shirt to her leg, which was trickling blood down into her ankle sock. She'd scraped it when she fell and he'd noticed.

"So did Max really have to get to work?" she said, gazing down at his bent head.

"Nope. He said he had an urgent snipe hunt."

Her heart rate was dizzyingly high. He rose to his feet, his eyes on hers, his chest expanding and contracting. When she offered her water bottle, he took it, their hands brushing. Watching his throat work as he took a couple swallows had her reaching up, letting her fingertips glide over it, curve. His gaze locked back on her, and when he lowered the bottle, her touch went to his jaw.

"You work out hard. Your focus...it's intense." Her gaze slid over him, attempting to convey practical interest. "You don't have a soft spot on you. How do you make sure you work out every muscle group equally?"

She didn't care about his answer. She was just giving herself time to consider her options.

"To get every muscle group in the right shape, you have to isolate it in your mind," he said. "Even if the rest of your body is moving, you're focused on that one set of muscles, targeting them, asking everything from them and closing out the rest. So you can get the maximum effort from them, and the maximum gain as a result."

Though his tone seemed as casual as the question, his eyes never left hers. She needed to look away, but she didn't know how.

"You give care and attention to each group," he continued. "Let it know how vital it is, alone as well as part of the whole. When you need them all, they'll come together the way they're supposed to, give you everything, every part responsive."

Her lips curved, showing appreciation for the cleverness, the shades of meaning. But then his gaze became more serious. "I've been dreaming about you," he said.

The words weren't calculated charm. There was bemusement in them.

"Was it a nightmare?"

"Hardly." A half smile tinged with regret. "I head back to VA Beach tomorrow."

Though sharp disappointment gripped her, it was tempered with relief. The temptation he presented, the mistake any prolonged involvement would herald, was mitigated by his job. While he had a pilot's license and apparent access to a plane that allowed him to fly to and from New Orleans whenever he had a few days, his work *was* based out of Virginia Beach. Anything she indulged with him would have clear start and end times. Not too different from having regular sessions with subs.

Except he wasn't a sub.

It didn't stop her from wanting to play with him like one, though. She let it loose, cocking her head, giving him a bolder look. "So this dream. Did you wake up with your hand on yourself?" Her gaze dipped pointedly.

She'd eased back from his hold and crossed her arms under her breasts. Leaning against her car, she hooked her ankle around her other leg. Though measured in inches, it established distance between them.

"In a manner of speaking." Though his attention was on her like a target, his lips twitched. "In my dream, it wasn't my hand. So when I woke, I preferred to keep thinking of it that way."

"Was it my hand? Or my mouth?" She moistened her lips, drawing his attention there. "Or regions further south?"

"It was your breasts. They were slick with an oil that smelled like honey." He braced a hand on the top of the car to her right, and fired a shot as brazen as her own. "You were working my cock between them, nipples tight as they rubbed against my thighs. I had my hand wrapped up in your gorgeous hair, trying not to hold so tight, but there was something in your eyes, wanting me to make it hurt."

He took another swallow of the water, lowered the bottle, stared at her. "It's easier for you, isn't it? Me not being here all the time. Keeps it contained."

Contained wasn't the word she'd apply to anything about him, particularly after he'd expanded on his dream. She'd dug her nails into her biceps. But he'd also just confirmed and reminded her what he was —exactly what she was herself. A sexual Dominant.

"Is keeping it contained a problem for you?" she said, even.

"Not yet." He'd noted the pressure of her nails. It eased the set of his jaw, but not the flint in his gaze. He set the water bottle on the ground and squared off with her. "So what's your optimal scenario here? I'm not looking for high level analysis. I mean right here, right now."

He'd kept it simple. She responded in kind. "I want to touch you how I like, and not have you touch me back. Not unless I say so."

She didn't expect him to take that with good grace. But he leaned forward, braced his arms on either side of her. He had an extraordinary capacity for maintaining continuous eye contact. She thought the slow blink he gave her now was the first he'd done since the conversation started.

Looking someone in the eyes for more than a second or two was getting increasingly difficult for her, but today was a good day. She held the lock.

His arms were caging her against the car but not touching her, his palms flat against the window frame. He'd complied with her request in a way that sent an entirely different message. Not submission. Not compliance. A sensual lure.

"Go for it," he said.

Though this was a quieter part of the park, particularly this time of day, there were still people around. A group of young men were playing on the soccer field. The occasional walker emerged along the path bordering the parking lot. But she could indulge herself and stay within public decency laws.

Mostly.

He'd dropped his shirt on the hood of her car. She retrieved it, placed it against his chest, over his heart, feeling the thud through the thin cotton. He'd swiped it over that part of himself, but he hadn't done his shoulders, neck, arms. She did the arms and shoulders first. She'd topped men in amazing shape, but this...even if he was stripped naked, he was conditioned to be a weapon.

Her stroke slowed over that mark on his upper arm. It was the freshest scar, but not the only one.

His shoulders looked as if they could carry the weight of another man. If she ducked under his arm and circled him, she'd see that same development in his back, down to the defined waist and sculpted buttocks, upper thighs. Every inch of him was taut to the touch.

She was deliberately keeping the shirt as a thin barrier between her palm and his skin, though his heat penetrated it. She was in the shelter of his body, feeling his breath as she touched him how she wanted.

She moved the shirt to the back of his neck. It required her to straighten from the car, lean her body further into his. Still without touching him, but so close the temptation to wind his arms around her, erase that last distance between them, would be growing.

Too easy. He could pass a test like that.

She glanced around them. Thanks to her proximity to him and the car behind her, she had a couple sure moments of privacy. She wore the mesh sports bra under a gray tank, paired with crimson red leggings. Leaving the T-shirt draped on his shoulder, she reached beneath the tank, hooked the elastic of the sports bra and pulled it above her breasts, still mostly concealed beneath the loose tank.

"Eyes up, sailor," she murmured.

Tucking the tank into that band of elastic over her breasts, she leaned in, pressing her unbound nipples to his bare chest. She reclaimed his T-shirt, reached under his arm to run it up the damp valley of his spine, in between his shoulder blades. Then down that valley again to his lower back, her fingertips pressing against the upper rise of his buttocks.

She spoke in a quiet whisper. "Did my nipples feel like that in your dream?"

"Fucking hell," he muttered. In her peripheral vision, she saw his arms flex, his palms press harder against the car. But he held, and kept his gaze on her face.

She eased back, smoothly pulling the tank and sports bra back into position. The T-shirt rested against his chest, her hand clutched in it. She wanted to keep it. A trophy. She wouldn't, because this was a race she couldn't win. She wouldn't take what she hadn't earned.

As an experienced Mistress, she'd had the privilege and pleasure of having a man belong to her entirely, give her a full surrender. An act of trust and willing submission. When it was over, if it was a particularly intense scene, she drank a single glass of wine to mitigate the Dom-drop she'd experience at leaving that state of heady intensity, the return to reality.

If Neil belonged to her, she wondered if that state would ever recede. If even the simplest kiss exchanged would waft that feeling over her, leave her knees weak and heart pounding.

"So you leave tomorrow," she said. It broke the moment. Somewhat. She was staring at her hand, his chest, feeling the thud of his heart.

Slowly, he straightened. He wasn't touching her or physically providing support, but when his hands left the car and the boundary of his arms no longer existed, she swayed. His hands were on her then, resting on her waist, her hips, a steadying touch, but more than that as well. Her skin reacted as if firecrackers had gone off all along the nerve endings.

"When I kiss you for the first time, you're going to ask for it," he said.

"And you needed to say that, why?"

He touched her face, a light thing, but when his hand lingered there, she turned her cheek against it, holding. Wanting to close her eyes. When he said his next words, she did.

"Because that's the threshold, bébé. The real starting line. We both know it."

Shit.

She moved away from him, an awkward jerk, restoring her personal space. Fishing her car key out of her pocket gave her a moment to collect herself, regain control of the situation. She hit the unlock button, heard the chirp. She didn't look at him. "When will you be back?"

A pause. "Don't know. Hard to say when we're down range."

Down range. The term SEALs used for unknown corners of the world, where dangers far beyond the quiet of this New Orleans park waited.

"Where—" She stopped herself, sent him a humorless half smile. "I know that's a question you can't answer."

"No. But here's one I can." He opened her car door for her, leaned on it. "I'll be thinking about you. A lot. And looking forward to the next time I can get back here."

"Do me a favor. Don't be thinking about me when you should be thinking about staying alive."

His gaze was a wandering caress, on her lips, her cheeks, her brow. "I thought a Mistress didn't ask for favors," he observed. "She just laid it out and said how it's going to be."

She pressed her lips together. With a decisive movement, she put her hand on his side, under his shirt. "Don't move."

As her unmistakable command, the mixed blue-gray of his eyes went to a deeper hue. He didn't lift a hand to touch her, though she could feel his natural inclination to do so.

Sliding her hand down, she caressed his waist beneath the elastic, molding her hand over his hip bone, her thumb doing a stroke of the intriguing inguinal muscle that arrowed toward his groin. She held there, knowing she had his full attention. Her touch rested in an intimate spot, not an inappropriate one, but close enough it was all within tempting reach.

"Watch your ass," she said evenly. "That's the only thing you should be thinking about. Not mine."

His smile was quick and feral. Fearless. "There are some things that even survival instinct can't override," he said. "The tides, the rising of the sun, and me thinking about your ass."

He put his hand on her face, his thumb caressing her jaw, her lips. He hadn't waited for permission, and she knew it was deliberate.

Everything he'd done had been calculated, things he'd accepted and allowed. Just as she had. No submission involved. They were two dominant personalities, dancing around the inevitable crash and burn, too attracted by the flame to have any sense about it.

"I'll see you soon, dream girl," he said. "Count on it."

CHAPTER TWO

"What do you want, Tiger?"

"To kneel at your feet, Mistress."

"What else?"

"I want to put my mouth on you. Give you pleasure. Watch you ride the wave."

She'd described it that way to Tiger. *It's like a wave that rises, and I'm skimming along the top, feeling the rush of the water, the wind. Sun on my face, my skin.*

"What do you want in return?" she demanded.

"That *is* what I want, Mistress. That's the gift you're giving me, permission to do that."

Abby rose from her seat, walked around him. He was standing. Kneeling was also a privilege. From the quiver that ran along his muscles as she passed so close to him, she knew how he ached for it. He wanted to give her the honor of going to his knees.

She rested a hand on his back, watched the muscles react, felt the heat of his skin. Everything tonight was so vivid, every detail precise. She found a clarity doing this that made other things irrelevant, kept them at bay. Things that didn't make sense, buried in a fog of uncertainty, things that fear wanted to destroy for her. They belonged outside.

What happened to her when she was in this room connected to all the things that made her life worth living. This was her baseline. As long as she had this, she knew everything was still okay.

"I love you, Tiger." She said it in a Mistress's voice. The declaration belonged only in this space. He understood that. Truth, unguarded, unfettered, unconcealed.

Uncomplicated.

"I love what you give to me," she added. "How you give it with your whole heart and soul. You are everything a Mistress could want."

"You humble me, Mistress. Please...let me kneel to you. For you."

"Very well." She stayed behind him, watched his big body lower, the athletic ease he demonstrated as he went to one knee, bare back curving. Her fingertips slid over his skin as she followed the motion. She'd had him keep on his jeans, remove shirt and shoes. The black gleaming chest hair matched what was sprinkled over his forearms. His dark blue eyes, set jaw and shape of his face was a mix between Mark Wahlberg and John Cena. He exuded the salt-of-the-earth, blue collar male he was. His nicked and rough hands, the mechanic's grease permanently embedded under the nails, were the proud badge of his career path.

They'd known one another long enough, closely enough, that she was aware Tiger was his given name, not just his scene one. He ran a body shop that provided excellent service and reasonable prices. Two of the five mechanics he employed were women. One was a submissive who had a membership at a club in Baton Rouge.

When Abby had brought her car to his shop the first time, she'd discovered a garden of metal sculptures in the back scrap yard. They'd been created mostly out of car parts. Tiger was the craftsman, something he did in his spare time, purely as a hobby. He'd give one to anyone who asked, if they agreed to put at least a twenty in a donation jar on his front counter. The jar was always for a local cause, like helping out the parents of a kid with cancer, or raising money for school band uniforms.

Tiger was a lot of interesting things. What he became in this room was one of them.

She ran her fingertips over his close shorn hair. It smelled like bergamot, pomegranate and cucumber, the fragrances of the shampoo he used. She had a bottle of it at home, because she'd become fond of the scent and asked him what it was. When she inhaled it, it balanced and centered her the way their sessions did.

In this room, she used very few props, and the number kept dropping. Most of the stimulation centered around what she called from him, and that was more than enough.

She traced the tattoo on one broad shoulder. It was a mix of colors, a jungle with creatures hidden in the design. As the thought crossed her mind, she drew her hand away, stepped back. But she wasn't quick enough.

They will jump out and kill you. Creep up on you when you're not looking.

Tiger had his head bowed, but when her back hit the wall, her leg tangling with the chair there, making it scrape against the cool tile floor, he tilted his chin in her direction. Then his head came all the way up, his blue eyes narrowed in concern. "Mistress?"

She had her fists clenched, her heart pounding in her chest. A physical fight wasn't the best way. But sometimes, when in danger of drowning, the body overrode the mind. And if the mind was broken...

She thrashed around in there, found the image she needed. An oak. Like the one she'd planted in her yard and then transferred its soul into her mind. It was growing, putting on new leaves. Roots getting deeper by the day. Steady.

Steady as a pair of slate-colored eyes.

The thought came with the memory of his hand on her hip, the caress of his fingers, sending sensation spiraling out like a starburst wish.

The way "dream girl" sounded on his lips.

Was he dreaming of her still? It had been three and a half weeks. In VA Beach, he could video call her. Text. He hadn't. Maybe he understood the diabolical power of deprivation the way she did, and was equally good at exercising it.

Or he was no longer in VA Beach, but in some other part of the world.

She could tell herself the oak visual was what steadied her, but *why* was not as important as managing *what*. *Why* was unquestionably the one-way road to madness.

Maybe because of that realization, those who battled insanity learned an important truth far sooner than the rest of the human race. Life was a fucked-up problem that couldn't be solved. They might as well fight the rising of the sun. All you could do was meet the day, lift your face to the light. Whether it burned, warmed, or offered nothing, you carried on.

Good thing her childhood had been a test run of that hard-earned knowledge.

Only five seconds had passed. She'd counted out the beats. "It's all right," she said, for herself as well as Tiger.

She was okay. She'd set this session later in the evening than she normally did, but she could manage the mild things that came out of the shadows. Nothing different than any other day. Except those whispers had never spoken at that volume. As if they were getting closer.

Shrugging that off, she returned to his side with precise steps, heels punctuating her progress on the tile. She dropped the robe, feeling it slip off her skin. The heat of a man's gaze covered what she exposed.

"Did I give you permission to look, Tiger?"

"No, Mistress." She heard his bit-back curse. Tiger was an alpha, so sometimes he forgot to rein back that nature, keep it within the lines she drew him.

She needed to ride that building wave, but she wouldn't let this pass. Penance was required for balance. It was also something she particularly enjoyed exacting.

She settled in the chair, a silver framed creation with a seat upholstered in red vinyl. With its heart-shaped top, it looked inspired by the queen in *Alice in Wonderland*. Tiger's eyes were properly lowered again, his knuckles pressed into the floor. She had a mat for his knees. A mechanic's life was tough on the body. Tiger was almost forty. He appreciated the cushion for his routinely abused joints.

As she looked at his hand, curled against the floor, she imagined his heated, firm lips upon her cunt, his tongue sliding deep. He was good at oral, playing over her labia, sucking on her clit, his tongue gliding over it with thorough precision before thrusting inside her. He'd nuzzle and caress her with his sandpaper jaw and cheeks, bringing all her nerve endings onto the crest of that wave.

She sighed, a shuddering thing that caught his attention. The fine muscles bridging his shoulders became a taut line. His lips pressed together. She rarely kissed any of her subs. While she couldn't remember the last time she'd kissed a man on the mouth, she remembered the last time she'd wanted to do so.

Vividly.

When he kisses you, he'll stick a knife in your stomach. You'll slide down to his feet bleeding.

The low moan broke from her before she could stop herself. Fortunately, she was able to modify the note of anguish, dampen it into a sensual sound. Since she'd begun to stroke her upper thigh, play around the areas she was fantasizing about, that helped cover the stumble.

She told herself the words hadn't forced themselves into her mind. Anxiety was conjuring them, a self-fulfilling prophecy. If the voice was real, she wouldn't be able to push it away as she did now, putting it in the proper perspective, discarding it as fantasy. Not reality.

Steadier with the thought, she spoke with soft urgency. "Tiger, come here."

He moved forward, stopping between her spread knees. She curved the sole of her foot over his shoulder. "You may kiss my arch and the top of my foot. Only there."

He turned his head, his mouth twisting ribbons of sexual response up her leg, through her core. She moved her fingers fully between her legs, sighed again as the two stimuli collided, made her hips lift, seeking more. She propped her other foot on his thigh, curled her toes so he could feel the coital rise and fall movement she was allowing herself.

Tiger growled, but moved tongue and lips with exquisite care, exercising a dedicated sub's concentration on her foot. He treated it as if it was her sex, which was being stroked so close to his body her arm moved against his side.

Every erogenous zone of her body felt his desire to put his mouth where her fingers were. But for his infraction, looking at her without permission, stepping over that line, he'd be limited to this, while she brought herself to climax.

If the only reward she gave him after that was placing a heated wet cloth against her to clean away her release, he would accept that. No matter how much his powerful body showed its raging need for more, with hot eyes coal dark, mouth firm with dangerous, leashed intent, and his erection straining against the jeans.

Holding back a powerful sub until his desire and nature might break the strongest chain he could impose on himself was an edge she loved to walk. It took concentration, full immersion, and coordination between two sets of desires, with multiple layers. Which should sound complex, overwhelming, but it wasn't. No more than walking a tight rope. A lot of things had to be kept balanced to make it happen, but there was only one overriding goal. One that kept everything ordered toward survival.

Low number of variables, one concentrated stimulus. A perfect combination.

Over the years, she'd realized—or hoped--what she was doing in these rooms would train her mind, prepare it for when things became more complicated.

The war looming on the horizon.

Her sex was wet, her fingers sliding easily over labia, making her clitoris slippery, then dipping inside, coming back out. Her feet pressed against his shoulder and thigh, toes curling, small gasps coming from her.

She stroked fingertips over his short hair. "Tiger, have you paid for your infraction?"

"That's for my Mistress to say," he said, his mouth still resting on her foot. His gaze slid along the inside of her extended forearm like a stroke of that tender skin. "Mercy and forgiveness are her gifts to give, if she feels like I've earned them."

The casual world outside these doors was an awkward one. So much left to misinterpretation, so much left unsaid, because the words would sound out of place and time. Artificial mockery.

That world didn't exist in this space; something far deeper, more beautiful and memorable did. This was its place, where such poetic language, ways of communicating, could still thrive.

She caressed his jaw, applied pressure to reinforce her response. "Take me where I want to go, Tiger. At the pace I want to get there."

His gaze gleamed with a blaze of satisfaction. But male lust didn't overtake his desire to serve. Experience, discipline under the hand of a Mistress, had taught him the marriage of the two was where the true reward lay.

"Yes, ma'am."

Neil had apparently ruined the ability of any other man to call her *ma'am*, without it conjuring him into the room. She saw those purple-blue-gray eyes again, Neil's mouth. He and Tiger had different body types. Tiger was broad, big. Neil was leaner, more tightly muscled, but just as strong.

The oak planting roots in her mind. Her soul.

She'd tell Tiger not to use the address again. Later.

He settled between her legs, those rough cheeks above the line of his short beard scraping her tender inner thighs. She stroked his shoulders, his nape, the short hair over his skull. Then curled her fingers around the rope looped over his shoulder, an unspoken reinforcement that he was there to serve her.

Earlier in the night, when she'd been in the public area with her Domme friends, socializing, Cyn had crafted a rope harness over Tiger's upper body. They'd decided to leave him in it. Abby liked having the ability to tug on it without it restricting his movements. She preferred ropes that didn't bind, but reminded him of their significance.

Only her words, not the rope, restrained him.

When Tiger's mouth touched her, she let out a throaty hum. The first wave of pleasure washed over her. Her body lifted and fell, the rhythm building.

She'd worn a light chemise under her robe, no panties. She'd dropped those over a chair earlier, sliding out of them beneath the concealment of the robe. As she arched up into the workings of his mouth, she gripped the back of the chair, her upper body twisting. Full breasts rose over the chemise's loose neckline, silk slithering across her nipples. His eyes went to them as his mouth seduced her slick flesh, and she relished the lust she glimpsed before he shuttered them again and behaved.

She'd let him suckle her nipples when he was done. Perhaps bring her to another climax before she'd put him back on his knees at her feet. She'd order him to open his jeans, fist his thick length and spurt to a climax while she had her feet pressed to the tops of his thighs, her knees spread. She'd brought a pair of stilettos in her toy bag and would slip those on, press the sharp heels against his muscles. The stilettos had tiny chains running across the upper.

"Ah..." That rise and fall feeling was bringing her closer to the wave she wouldn't be able to resist catching, a thundering, wild ride.

Her hand tightened on the rope over his shoulder. She was lifting, about to fly...

In that intuitive way he had about him, Tiger slid his hands under her thighs, held her steady as she writhed and bucked. He spoke his husky appreciation against her with his warm, wet mouth. Drove her on, higher, wanting to take her as high as he could.

Groans ripped from her, her hands clutched, her body bucked, and then the wave slowly, slowly flattened. It brought her in slow, the water slipping away as her overwhelmed body vibrated on shore.

She touched his jaw, passing her fingers over his damp lips that would smell like her. Slowly, she straightened in the chair. "Show me," she ordered, her voice thick.

He sat back on his heels reluctantly, but his eyes were feverish as he unfastened the jeans, and scooped out the heavy weight of his testicles. His cock was a thick, blood-filled column over them. His thumb rested at the base, holding it upright, displayed for her.

"All for you, Mistress," he said, his voice hoarse. "Yours to command."

At his rough fervency, a little aftershock pulsed through her. She put two fingers inside herself, a slow swirling in the wet heat. Then, withdrawing them, she leaned forward and offered the slick digits. "Stroke yourself to climax while sucking on my fingers, Tiger. Don't stop. If you stop sucking, you have to stop stroking. You do that well, I'll let you suck my nipples until I climax again."

His mouth closed over her fingers, giving her a hint of teeth that made her smile. He was a very good bad boy. Then her gaze lowered, to indulge in a full female appreciation of how he handled himself. Even now, he was conscious of her pleasure, not getting right down to it like a quick pump in his shower. He stroked himself, squeezed his balls, ran his thumb over the frenulum, making his hips jerk and exposed thighs flex.

His mouth and tongue worked her fingers, pulling. Tiger was as straight as they came, but he could get off on her homoerotic fantasies, as she imagined him sucking off another man, just as powerful.

He thrust into his hand, and his hips moved in that fucking rhythm, finding his own wave to ride. She imagined being wrapped up in a man's arms, his body flesh to flesh with her, cock penetrating, driving deep.

Stabbing. Stabbing. They want to hurt you.

"Mistress, may I—"

"Yes," she said sharply, slicing that curtain to ribbons, the one threatening to cover her mind. She dug her nails into his shoulder.

It wasn't real, she told herself again. Nighttime, particularly this late hour, made her vulnerable to her worries, to a premonition so dreaded it could assume a life of its own.

Tiger climaxed into the condom he'd donned, and she watched the tip fill, the splash of semen against the latex. Wanting free, but contained inside, viscous life.

Contained. She held onto the word, the reminder. Habit had her acting in his interest, moving to handle his aftercare as he came down. The vital need to watch over him helped her find her center again, hold her panic at bay.

She let him lay his head on her knees, stroked his bare back and shoulders as she curved over him. When his gaze eventually slid up toward her breasts, a reminder of what she'd offered, she caressed his lips, accepting the kiss he put on her knuckles.

"Next time," she said. The two words she sometimes used to end the scene. It was abrupt for her, and she'd need to smooth that over. Then her gaze slid to his shoulder, and her chest squeezed in on itself. "You're bleeding."

She rose on wobbly legs, moved to the cabinet that held basic first aid supplies. When she returned, Tiger had tucked himself back into his jeans and was glancing at the spot. "It's all right, Mistress."

She cleaned and dressed the wound, the four crescent-shaped deep cuts, unmistakably the bite of a woman's nails.

She didn't do sessions with attached men whose significant female others weren't brought into the loop. Which for her meant a face-to-face with the woman, no secondhand "yeah, my girlfriend knows about this" or "me and my wife have an open relationship" bullshit.

She wasn't worried about that. Tiger wasn't attached. But crossing a limit was a serious matter to her.

"I apologize, Tiger." As she closed the first aid box, she fought to keep her voice even. "I know blood play is a hard limit for you."

"Intentional blood play, Mistress. This kind of mark, we'll call it a soft limit." His eyes smiled, but they also held concern. "Are you all right?"

"Death comes to us all," she replied. "Sometimes before death. It comes out of the shadows and smells like my mother's soap. And alcohol."

She laughed and the sound of her voice was strained. "Irish spring, just the thing. All clean, no need to scream."

Terror gripped her. The words were pebbles thrown against a rusty train car, left in an overgrown field to rot.

Which was more random, disconnected imagery she should squelch. A florid imagination was not her friend. The words' meaning reflected what she intended, but not how she'd intended to say them.

She'd discuss the limit thing with him next time. Smooth it over. Right now, she had to get the hell out of here.

Fortunately, she shared Tiger, tag team style, with Skye, and Skye was about to arrive. Abby could relinquish him to her close friend and fellow Domme.

She'd allowed him a release tonight, but other times she worked him up to a near frenzy, holding him on the edge until Skye took over. Skye might choose to pull him back from that edge, then take him to it several more times before she finally let him go over. Prolonged orgasm deprivation turned his submission into a thing of intense beauty.

Even though Abby had allowed him one release, Skye would still demand enough from him to drive any worries out of his head. That was good.

It was happening at last. The beginning of the end.

No, it wasn't.

Yes, it was.

How much was she rationalizing? How much was she concealing, so that the choices she made could belong to herself alone? Or, as she kept telling herself, was she so obsessed with something happening, she was playing mind tricks on herself?

Or had the anxiety of waiting for the axe to fall called the reality to her? A desire to be done with it, while she could still manage a straight line from beginning to end, the way she'd intended?

The world loved to fuck with a straight line. Sometimes doing confusing shit to wash portions of it away, so the map was no longer clear.

"On your knees," she said. "Waiting submissive posture."

She was so relieved the words came out as she intended that she placed a hand against the wall to steady herself. Tiger laced his hands behind his head, back straight, knees spread, eyes down. It pressed the rope harness into his flexed muscles. She checked to make sure it wasn't inhibiting pressure points or blood flow. She didn't anticipate it was, because Cyn excelled at rope work. But movement, sweat, all those things could impact the stretch or contraction of the fibers.

Tiger kept his eyes lowered, except for one more uncertain look, laced with the same concern. When she summoned an appropriately warm and approving expression to answer it, it faded. He offered a tentative half smile and a quiet, "Thank you, Mistress."

She laid her hand on his shoulder, gripped briefly, a silent acknowledgement and praise, before she moved to the door. Skye slid into the room.

The boutique marketing firm of Thomas Rose Associates had been the brainchild of herself and Rosalinda Thomas, Abby's best friend. Three other accomplished women had been recruited to share the executive management responsibilities of the firm, and more than business interests connected them. All five of them were Dommes, and over the years, the friendship had morphed into the unbreakable bonds of family, a sisterhood.

Skye was their IT and communications manager. Since a childhood accident had left her mute, it seemed ironic, but Skye's proficiency with technology and language to expand her methods of communicating was impressive. When she utilized the voice software on her devices, her flying fingers could produce insights as quickly and eloquently as a Greek orator. She had one voice she claimed as her own, a mild Southern accent with a musical feminine hum threaded through it, decisive and pleasant. However, she routinely employed recognizable celebrity voices to reflect her moods and amuse.

She was also fluent in signing, as were the four of them. They'd wanted to be able to understand her, if ever her other means of communicating weren't accessible. Plus it came in handy for exchanging information about a sub in front of him.

Abby wanted Tiger to hear her right now, though. Particularly the note of praise. "He's done very well tonight. I'm headed out."

She usually stayed to watch from a viewing room, or joined the others in the socializing area until Skye rejoined them for the recap. Not tonight. She needed to go home.

They will follow you. They're watching you. She knows. She can see it.

Skye touched her arm, signed at her. *You okay?*

Abby tried to maintain a friendly, normal expression. Things swam in between her and Skye like a fog, and she had to shift her gaze to the wall. Her heart was thundering up into her throat. No, no, *no*.

She remembered that day in the park with Neil. Sun shining. Everything clear and fun. Exciting. Trying to outrun Max and Neil. The world turned on a fucking dime. Fucking dime, out of time...out of time.

"Enjoy him," she told Skye. Then she fled the room.

Neil paused at the corner, listening. He drew the Glock from the back of his jeans. They'd had to go into this job with just small arms, in order to blend with the local population. He was severely missing his night vision goggles, but there was no easy way to carry those concealed. He'd turned his cap around, so the bill didn't obscure his vision from any direction, including the tops of the buildings flanking the narrow alley. In front of him were Cedrick and Dodge, with Billy as point man, all four aware of one another and everything else. The rest of their eight-man team was positioning itself to be their backup. They'd run through this scenario several dozen times during training.

However, one unexpected variable could fuck up an op.

They approached the ingress point and Billy knocked off the door lock, pocketed it. When they eased inside and headed down the hallway of the seemingly vacant building, everything was quiet. According to their intel, the access to the tunnels and bunker beneath this first floor level was through a trap door, hidden underneath an old steamer trunk. The trunk was supposed to be in a room that looked like an abandoned office.

When they found it, the room was empty, just a desk and a few chairs. One crooked picture on the wall, a paddle boat headed down a river. No file cabinet. Everything of value was going to be below. Billy moved to the trunk to check for wires, any evidence of booby trapping, then he and Cedrick eased the trunk back while Neil and Dodge watched their six. The trap door was there.

Great, but fuck, they all hated tunnels.

The door *was* wired, but it was simple, intended to eliminate the casual snoop, not trained operators. Still, Billy did a thorough check after deactivation. They couldn't pull the steamer trunk back over the door as they went below, but they did adjust it, so it was between the opening and the door to the office space. It could give them some flimsy cover when they emerged, and the position made it possible that someone just passing by wouldn't see the trunk had been moved off the door it concealed.

Down the ladder they went, Billy in front, Dodge and Cedrick still in the middle and Neil bringing up the rear.

"Cause you're so fucking tall, no one can see over you," Dodge had told him during the practice runs. "I can't see what's ahead."

"He's such a backseat driver," Billy said.

"True," Neil had rejoined. "But with my tall ass blocking the rear, they have to shoot through me to get to him."

"That's just an added benefit." Dodge had grinned. As their team leader, he could bust their balls when necessary, but didn't go hardass when it wasn't needed.

Upon reaching the bottom of the ladder, they found themselves in the usual warren. This was when an operator had to have faith in the intel, because if it was wrong, or someone had double crossed the agents who'd gathered it, it could all go bad.

Not something they spent time thinking about, not once the op was in play. Didn't do any good, and no one lived forever.

The first guard they came upon had his back to them. He was playing a video game on his phone, gun propped against the wall next to him. Billy slid up behind him, dispatched him silently with his knife, let him ease down to the floor. They stepped over him. Neil didn't look at his face and neither did the others.

That didn't do any good either. An enemy assigned shit guard duty was often barely more than a teenager. But if he saw them first, he'd kill them. That was his job. They all had their jobs to do, choices to make, even if they were shitty choices.

A couple crates of Russian grade weapons were stacked up on the wall, next to a battered file cabinet and a table holding a computer. The computer geek hadn't heard them, absorbed by his screen. Cedrick knocked him out. They knew his haunts, and he'd be picked up once they had the laptop back to base. Then the spooks would try to flip him, get more intel about his group's plans.

Cedrick slid into the chair, scanned what the guy had been doing, and then closed the laptop down. He put it into his Kevlar-lined and waterproof bag. As he began to rifle through the file cabinet, Neil and the others marked a flicker of shadows along the wall of another tunnel leading out of this room, heard the echo of carried voices.

Cedrick was up and ready, all of them positioned as the three men stepped into view. They were carrying what looked like takeout from one of the nearby restaurants. Bringing food for their compatriots.

Everybody had to eat.

Two of them drew handguns, but the one in the middle had an assault rifle. Before he could swing the muzzle up, Neil had put a bullet through his forehead.

A nine-millimeter against an assault weapon meant the guy with the nine-mil had to shoot first and make it count. But hell, with no chance to resolve it hand-to-hand, they'd just alerted anyone else in these tunnels to their presence.

As he dropped, Billy dispatched the guy to his left, Dodge handling the other before he could make a run for it. Neil glanced down at the dropped food. There'd been apple pie. The guys who claimed to hate everything about Americans liked their unofficial national dessert.

It was a fucked-up world.

They dragged the bodies into the room, the file cabinet providing a semi-decent screen for them. They left the way they came, pausing at every turn in the tunnel system to scope what was ahead. They were getting close to their ladder exit without further incident, but Neil knew better than to assume that meant anything good.

When almost home free, a team of idiots would decide it had all gone to plan because they were just that good.

Billy brought them to a halt with a raised fist. As he flattened against the wall, they followed suit, alternating pattern, Dodge and Cedrick on the opposite side, Neil same side as Billy.

Urgent, sharp tones. As expected, the gunfire had drawn attention. Their planned exit was cut off.

The group of men, dressed in camouflage pants and beige T-shirts, filed around the corner. The tunnel width at this point allowed several men to walk abreast. Neil's eyes met those of one in the middle. Brawny, thick beard, dark hair and startled expression.

A blink of time, a suspended moment. Dodge fired as the bearded guy and his companions brought their weapons into position, even as the others jockeyed for a clear spot where they wouldn't shoot one another in their own crossfire.

Nothing worse than a close quarters firefight. Plus gunfire in a small space made the eardrums scream. A strangled curse, and Billy went down. Neil took out two of the other shooters as Cedrick dragged their fallen teammate back. Neil's targets dropped as their fired bullets were still sending up rock dust off the tunnel walls. Neil advanced with Dodge while Cedrick held in front of Billy to protect him. But another enemy going down with a scream, his knee ripped open by a bullet, told them Billy might be down, but he was still in the game.

It became a hand-to-hand struggle, knives thrust into flesh, guns now used to bludgeon. Dust, shouts, the smell of gunpowder. Over in seconds. Dodge and Cedrick seized Billy and pulled him over fallen bodies, Neil covering their six. In another few minutes, they'd reached the ladder. The men they'd just faced could have left reinforcements in the room above, but going back into the warren wasn't an option.

Dodge went up one-handed, one of the assault weapons he'd grabbed held at the ready. Neil had snagged another and situated it the same way, holding Billy up with his other hand.

Dodge reached down, signifying things were clear, and Neil hoisted Billy into his grasp. The agony of the gut shot twisted Billy's features. The adrenaline shooting through his veins would keep him moving, but it wouldn't last.

As Neil reached the top of the ladder after Cedrick, Dodge yanked him to the ground, bringing him down next to Billy and Ced, already prone. Bullets peppered the thin walls and the door.

"This day just got a lot more fucking interesting," Dodge snarled between gritted teeth. "Comms not working."

Which meant they didn't know the status of their backup. Neil kept his hand on Billy, ready to haul him up as soon as the reload moment happened. Just as he'd feared, the kid's eyes were starting to show shock and some disorientation.

Neil met Dodge's gaze. "Butch Cassidy and Sundance time," the team leader said.

"I was hoping for something more Star Trek," Neil said. "Beam us out of here, chief."

Cedrick laughed and spat. The gunfire stopped and they were up in one coordinated movement, headed for the door. *Slow is smooth and smooth is fast.* They weren't going to have enough time between reloads, but it was the one chance they had. They knew the layout outside the door, and they might be able to choose another place with better cover.

More gunfire staccatoed before they breached the threshold. It wasn't aimed at them. The rest of their eight-man team had arrived.

"Let's get out there." Billy coughed against Neil's shoulder. "Can't let them have...all the fun."

~

They'd made it to rendezvous and the helicopter had lifted them out. It carried them to the plane that flew them back to base in Germany.

Neil packed ice on the side of his face, covering the ugly bruise swelling there. Compliments of a weighted slapper one of his opponents had wielded. Fortunately, it hadn't cracked his cheekbone. The follow up fist to his kidney hadn't been bad enough to have him pissing blood, but it ached like a son of a bitch.

Billy's gut shot was a bad one. They'd been able to stabilize him on the flight, but they were all aware the clock was ticking on getting him to the help he needed. His vitals remaining stable made them tentatively optimistic that he might be okay if he could avoid a post-op complication or infection. As he stood next to the gurney, Dodge told Billy what he needed to hear.

"Even if it gets infected, you've had worse from a Ukraine brothel," he declared.

Billy managed a weak grin. He fumbled off his oxygen mask long enough to fire off a response before Mike, Dodge's second-in-command, gently eased it back in place.

"She was worth it. Gorgeous, big titties. Sweet smile. And she cooked me dinner after she blew me."

Once back in Germany, Billy was transported to the hospital, and the rest of them that needed it were checked out by on-base medical. While Dodge disappeared to handle the aftermath report with the higher ups, Neil found a shower and changed into clean clothes.

He went to his preferred decompression spot, a crate set up against the back wall of one of base outbuildings. It faced the tarmac where the planes landed. Beyond that was a tall chain link fence, a field and a line of trees. The breeze was good, the night sky was clear.

As he sipped a beer, he was aware of every sound, everything amplified. No flickering shadow, no matter how small, escaped his notice, whether from personnel cutting across the path of myriad ground lights, or the stray camp dog nosing about. Even the flutter of the American flag, snapping in the fitful breeze, was noted, logged.

He raised his beer to it. Then he turned over his other wrist. He'd left his watch off after his shower, so the cross tattooed there, a solid black design no bigger than a quarter, was visible to his gaze. He brushed his lips over it, bent his head in a silent, brief prayer of gratitude. He prayed for Billy. He asked the forgiveness of those whose lives he'd taken. Bearded Guy's startled eyes and the video game kid he hadn't looked at too closely went through his mind.

Then he let them go. He settled against the wall again, returned his attention to the comfort food taste of beer.

"You know, I watch for you to do that at the end of every mission," Dodge said. "We all witness one another's rituals, make sure we all do them. Superstitious bunch of bastards that we are."

"We're Navy." Every one of them had his thing, a tradition Neil suspected connected the seafarers of centuries ago to the special forces operators on the front line now.

He'd heard Dodge coming, parsing his chief's familiar tread from the other camp sounds. A cohesive team had a pack sense, a familiar energy that helped them recognize one another even before they were seen. Part of the same instincts that made hair rise on the back of his neck when something not familiar or so friendly was approaching.

"Before the op, you kiss the cross, salute the flag," Dodge noted. "Afterward, it's salute the flag and kiss the cross."

"Faith is the alpha and the omega," Neil said. "Beginning and end.

But the order is always the same in my head. Faith first, country second, family always and forever."

The ritual kept him clear. A reminder of what the job was and wasn't, what the path should and shouldn't be.

He kept a place in VA Beach, because training or deployments made it necessary. However, when he had a couple days to pilot the Cessna home to New Orleans, he usually went off into the bayou on his own to fish. Or he'd spend time with Max, Lawrence and Dale. Former team guys who understood that necessary transition time, to recognize he was home, that those around him were friendlies.

Women helped with that, because the air around them stateside was different from what lingered on any women he encountered here, friendly or otherwise. Scent was the one thing that always told him when he was home. It was a big part of why he went into the bayou. That marsh odor, the plants, animals and salt water, life cycles and natural decay.

Nothing smelled like home except home.

Dodge sat down next to him. Since he'd expected him, and eventually the other members of their team, Neil nudged the full cooler toward him. Dodge took a beer, clinked off the top and stretched out his legs, stacking his booted feet on another crate. "The spooks are tickled as Elmo about the intel we got. We'll need to act on it quick. Probably going back out soon."

"Yeah. Figured."

"Where are Mount and Cedrick?" Dodge asked. "Mike headed for the showers after helping me with the briefing."

"Cedrick's video chatting with his wife and sons. I left Mount cleaning his gun and talking about hitting the showers, too." Neil adjusted his head to a new angle against the wall.

"Face hurt?"

"Not bad."

Dodge took another swallow. "The others will be here before long. They know you always have beer after an op." Dodge's half smile creased his lined face, but his gaze on Neil was speculative. "You may have the most level head I've ever seen on a frogman, Twizz."

A shortened form of Twizzler, a nickname he'd earned when he was a skinny but tough beanpole, and had caught a bad sunburn at BUD/S training.

"Which means I notice when there's something giving you a bit of a tilt," Dodge continued. "Like looking at your phone more often when we're on base. Can I see her?"

Neil had a damn good poker face, but the chief did, too. After matching deadpan stares for a beat, Neil ruefully fished out his phone, scrolled and selected the close-up before he handed it over for Dodge's viewing.

Lawrence had sent him several shots, all of them snapped at Dale and Athena's barbecue. While Lawrence had merely titled the half dozen files, "BBQ pics," Neil had noted they all contained good shots of Abby.

Team members, even former ones, didn't miss much.

Lawrence confirmed it when the little asshole shortly thereafter sent Neil crops of two of the photos, accompanied by the text, "Always good to isolate the target."

One of those crops was Abby in a two-piece swimsuit. She was coming out of the pool, her skin glistening with water, including those high, generous breasts and slim thighs. Even a casual shot of her stunning beauty made her look like it should be in a sports mag spread.

His dick fucking loved that photo, enough to routinely beg him to jerk off to it. He'd managed so far to shut that down. But thinking about it took him back to the park, those cat eyes so close, her pursed moist lips asking about his dreams. How she'd rubbed her nipples across his chest. The gentle friction had left an impression in his mind, on his flesh, as indelible as that wrist tattoo.

If he got wood thinking about her right now, Dodge was not going to let him live it down.

Yeah, he liked the hell out of that one, even as he intended to give Lawrence shit about the crop. But despite the lust it inspired, the picture Neil looked at the most was the one he showed Dodge.

The pre-cropped version showed her sitting in a circle with the other women, all of them chatting. She had her head turned in the direction of the conversation, her hand resting on the arm of her chair. Her fabulous legs were crossed, revealed by a pair of classy, tailored shorts. A scoop-necked top which had gold and green melted colors drew the eye to her slender throat and gentle swell of her breasts.

The women sitting closest to her were her female power set, the four women she worked with at Thomas Rose Associates, including her closest friend and the CEO, Rosalinda Thomas.

Ros was Lawrence's Mistress. Neil didn't refer to their relationship that way publicly, but in his own head it was too obvious to call it anything but what it was. They hadn't talked marriage yet, but the commitment was already there. Lawrence belonged to Ros, heart and soul. From the way Ros acted toward him, that was a two-way street. Every direction a street could go led back to the two of them together, now and always.

Neil was glad for his friend. He deserved that kind of all-encompassing, supportive love. Ros was protective of Lawrence, caring, dedicated to his well-being. Something Lawrence sure as hell hadn't gotten in his previous eight-year relationship with an alcoholic girlfriend.

The cropped version of the pic focused on Abby's face. Her lips were slightly parted, her hazel eyes attentive. Though it was far less revealing physically than the bikini picture, Neil had hesitated before handing it over. She was listening to the conversation, but somehow seemed cut off from it. Something going on in her mind indicated a private struggle, carefully concealed unless the viewer could study her expression more closely. Which made the captured moment feel private, personal.

He'd seen the look before. Informants keeping so much buried below the surface, they maintained a relentless alertness, almost never lowering their guard.

When she'd lowered hers in the park, the power behind it had staggered him. Intriguing, but also disturbing. It was a message, something he needed to understand, something that was key to what connected them.

"Wow. That woman is beyond any mortal man's grasp." Dodge shot Neil a wicked smile. "Thank God propaganda and our abs of steel have romanticized us into superheroes."

Neil sent him a wry look. "Yeah. Since most of us are dysfunctional fucks no female in her right mind would want to keep."

But her heart... He thought her heart ached to be held in one man's hands. The one who could protect it...from something. Or give her a center, when her own didn't hold.

She was strong as hell, no wilting flower. He'd seen it. But sometimes when he was around her, he got that hair-raising dread he felt when an op was about to go wrong.

It inspired a kneejerk desire to surround her with a fortress, but since he had nothing to substantiate it, he kept the compulsion firmly locked down. No strong woman welcomed a man treating her like a damsel in distress. At least not as anything more than the occasional and properly timed romantic indulgence.

And treating a Domme that way? He might as well send her an engraved invitation to rip his balls off.

"That's poetic," Dodge handed him back the phone. "Particularly the dysfunctional fuck part." He sent Neil a meaningful look. "If you're that particular about another guy looking at her picture, then I expect you feel pretty strong about her. She feel the same?"

"I think so. But she thinks there are things that don't work between us."

"You don't think so."

"No."

"Hmm. God help her. Keep me in the loop when she takes out a restraining order on you."

They drank in companionable silence, and then Dodge shifted, signaling a subject change. A significant one, based on how he seemed to be gathering his thoughts. Neil knew what it was. The change had been on the horizon for awhile.

"In a few more months, Mike will be taking over the team. They're almost ready to make it official."

"Yeah, we're still trying to figure out ways to keep your ass here."

Dodge shook his head. "I'm reaching my twenty-year point, Neil. Those that call the shots are always changing how we fight what's out here, and way too often it has to do with someone's bullshit agenda or ambition, not an actual understanding of what we're facing. I'm tired of dealing with the whiplash." A shadow crossed his gaze. "I've done my part. I'm ready to go fish, hang out with my nieces and nephews."

While he didn't think it would be quite that simple for Dodge to leave it behind—it hadn't been for Lawrence or Max—Neil got it.

"You're the first choice to step into Mike's shoes when he takes my place," Dodge continued. "Are you interested?"

"Could be." Since he'd suspected it had been coming, he'd already been giving it extensive thought. There was no reason not to say yes, since he wanted to be as useful as his skillset could offer. But, even so... "When you need a definite answer, ask me then."

Since so often they had to make decisions in the space of a heartbeat, when given the luxury of it, Neil would give one the actual time it deserved. He knew Dodge understood that.

"Okay then." He nudged Neil, an approving thump that managed to avoid any bruised places.

"Any beer left, or did Dodge guzzle it all down?" Mike asked, joining them and pulling up a crate.

"I saved you some backwash," Dodge told him.

As Mount, Cedrick and the others wandered in behind him, Neil passed out the beers. Once they were all there, there was a pause. They raised the bottles, all eyes moving to Dodge. Time for one more ritual.

Dodge's wife was an avid reader, always sending him quotes. Funny things, inspirational, tender. He saved the appropriate ones for the first shared beer after an op. Or in this case, a key stage in it.

"'Be men or be more than men. Be steady to your purpose and firm as a rock.'"

They clinked the necks of the bottles as Mount winked and reached down to give his crotch a quick squeeze. "Always, boss. That's what your wife tells me."

After the obligatory round of insulting banter, Neil cocked a brow. "What's that from?"

"*Frankenstein.* Cheryl says the character was a total fuck up, but the quote was sound."

"All the more appropriate for us, then," Cedrick noted with a grin.

The conversation turned to the day's op, and an update on Billy, who was holding his own. They'd be able to see him later, though not likely before they had to go back out. Cedrick talked about a science project his kid had done in school.

Normal stuff, but from the subtle twitching of muscles, the alert body language, Neil knew they were all staying mentally prepped.

The mission wasn't done yet.

CHAPTER THREE

When Dodge eventually told them to go grab some sack time, Neil didn't disagree, but took a short walk around the base first. He was scoping out a spot, and eventually found it. Putting his back to one of the sturdy poles framing a supply tent, he sat down in its shadow. It was decently private here, unlike the room he shared with Ced.

He pulled out his phone and studied Abby's picture again. One of the things he didn't like about touch screens was the inability to run a fingertip over someone's face, like with a print photo. Maybe he'd make a wallet size of this one to carry. He hadn't carried a woman's picture on him since his early twenties, and not just because training and habit kept him from carrying a lot of personal items.

He turned the phone over in his hands. He'd told himself he'd hold off calling or texting her. Carrot and stick. It was a game they both recognized. Deprivation and denial. But he only played games when they were fun for both parties involved. He was carrying Billy in his head, in his gut. He needed something different tonight.

It was nearly one in the morning here, which meant early evening where she was. She might be working late. But Lawrence had mentioned a couple things that suggested she was recently opting to work more afternoons from home, preferring to do morning hours at the office. TRA's success had been growing, such that they'd been really busy this year with new clients. Since Abby was their numbers cruncher and CFO, maybe she got more done working remotely.

He chose a video call option. She'd have the choice of audio only, if she was in curlers or green goo face mask. The thought made him smile, even as he finger-combed his own hair and stroked his hand over his beard, to make sure he looked decent enough to call on a woman he cared about.

She'd added his personal number to her phone a while back, when they were dealing with issues involving Ros's run-in with a local gang member. Abby could have deleted his number after that was over, so that she wouldn't recognize his caller ID.

He could have tested that theory with a text at any time, but again, it was the nature of the game. Him calling straight out like this would indicate something deeper. Thinking of that look in her eyes, protecting something within from the threat of exposure, he wondered if that alone might cause her not to answer.

Two rings. Three. It went to her voicemail. He clicked off before it reached the beep.

She could be in the shower. Mowing her yard. If she had a yard. He knew where she lived, but he hadn't driven by the place. He'd thought about it, plenty of times.

Dodge might be right about that restraining order.

He stood, suppressing the disappointment. Probably just as well. They hadn't had time to enjoy the fun and games part nearly long enough. It was a good place to linger, not rush it. This call hadn't been motivated by casual flirtation, or even the more intense power exchange flirt.

Yeah, she thought the Domme versus Dom thing was a deal breaker for the long term. She probably thought his unwillingness to see that was because he didn't understand, because he wasn't active in the "lifestyle" as they called it.

What she didn't realize was he *had* been exposed to the club scene, and had made a choice that fit his preferences.

He understood her concern, though, and didn't dismiss it. Two personalities firmly in the Dom camp didn't necessarily make for an easy fit. But a wolf pack had an alpha breeding pair. He assumed they hunted, ran the pack together, a thing as right and natural as any other kind of pairing that was meant to be.

He had cut around the corner of the tent, intending to head back to his assigned quarters for some sleep, when his phone vibrated. Seeing who it was, he pivoted, returned to the pole he'd used as a back brace, and accepted the video option. He'd had ops where he didn't move as fast.

And there she was.

As he slid down to his heels, he gazed at her face. He expected men reacted to her beauty routinely with tongue-tied idiocy or attempts to act cool around her. She probably handled all of it with grace and charm. Kindness if needed, but without encouragement.

He saw her beauty, same as any man with eyes and a halfway working dick, but God, there was something more about her. He was a cliché, one of those wild animals who found his mate and was done, with that very first dance around her. It was a feeling in his gut, far deeper than his reaction to her gorgeous body, the lustrous thickness of her deep red hair, the way it framed her features, the catlike eyes. Eyes that possessed a full measure of *come-hitherness*—but only if she backed it up with a verbal command or permission.

He saw that reserve he'd just been thinking about, telegraphing her wariness about the two of them. But he also saw the softness of her mouth, the light in her eyes. She was glad he'd called.

He understood the value of that gift, a genuine connection between two people. In all the crazy brutality of the world, those moments still happened. If they were acknowledged, savored, they could spread out in the soul, rest there a spell, long after time ticked onward.

Right now, seeing something that didn't look like it belonged on a military base, his reaction to her was as clear to him as knowing he was hungry or thirsty.

Looking at her, he was both.

They had gazed at one another for a full ten seconds without saying anything, he realized, reinforcing his thoughts like a punch to the solar plexus. Then she backed away from it.

"Well, hey there, sailor," she said. "What? Got tired of being on hold for 1800-See-My-Boobs?"

"I maxed out my credit card." He smiled at her, warm and lazy. Did she know the maple syrup in her voice drizzled straight over his cock and set up camp everywhere else that mattered?

She'd arched a brow, but then it lowered, lines of concern appearing above it as she took a closer look at him. She tapped her face, pointing out the swelling bump on his own. "Didn't I say watch your ass?"

He made a show of half-rolling to a hip and looking down. "Ass is all good. Someone thought they could make me less stubborn by hitting me in the head."

"I expect the recoil from the unyielding nature of the target did far more damage to them."

"Clever. What were you doing when I called? It'd be nice to hear something happening...that's not like here." Thoughts of Billy came back into his mind. How the day had gone, or could have gone.

The concern didn't leave her expression, but understanding joined it. When she responded, she did so without shining a light on the change of subject or tone.

"Transplanting one of my azaleas. It wasn't thriving where it had been planted. It was an older one, so it took some work and patience to dig it out without hurting the major roots."

He recognized smudges of dirt on the T-shirt, a sprinkling of particles along her nape and cheek. "That's a big job. I could have helped when I got back."

"I liked the workout." Her gaze passed over his face and shoulders, touching his eyes only briefly. "It was a tough day, wasn't it? I'm not asking for details. Just want to offer...acknowledgment."

He lifted a shoulder. "Just my usual workday. I wanted to talk to you. You have time for a conversation?"

She glanced to the left, where he assumed there was a clock. While disappointment spiked in his gut at the evidence she had somewhere to be, the genuine regret in her expression gave him something.

"For about fifteen minutes. Then I have to get a shower and change. But you've got me until then." Her teasing look sent a small lick of flame through him. "As long as you make it interesting. I'm not much on small talk."

"Makes two of us. Where you headed tonight?"

"Club Progeny. I meet up with Ros and the others there once a week."

He knew she'd thrown it out there on purpose. Not to screw with him—nothing about her suggested she had that kind of meanness to her—but to see how he'd handle it. *This is who I am*, her frank look said. *Take it or leave it.*

Well, she'd said she didn't care for small talk.

"How did you get started with the Domme stuff?" Points for him, he didn't snarl the question. While he couldn't quell his very territorial *fuck that* reaction to her announcement of her evening plans, he managed to keep it off screen. He even acted as if it were entirely normal for a woman who'd captured his interest to tell him she was headed off to a club to top some willing guy, one he'd later imagine breaking into bite-sized pieces for the camp dogs to eat.

She gave him a studied look that suggested he might not have been as successful as he'd thought, but then she settled back in her chair and answered his question. As she did, she lifted her arms to pull her gorgeous fire-touched hair off her neck, bundle it under her barrette to keep it that way. It lifted her upper body, made her breasts move sweetly under the T-shirt. His gaze lingered on her exposed neck, the brush of her fingers as she gathered up the thick locks.

"I met Ros during my first year in college. I grew up in Alabama, but went to NYU. She'd come to college late, same as I had, so we were more adult than a lot of our fellow students. We clicked, along with another friend, Laurel. Laurel was from this area. They were both Dommes. Ros invited me to sit in on one of her sessions, then help out with it, two Dommes topping one sub."

"How'd you do?"

"She'd prepped me already, so I wasn't a total round-eyed newbie, but that night I figured out just how real the desire was for me." Her gaze wandered off screen again, he assumed as she turned her mind toward her memories.

"I had a shit childhood. No father, and in a lot of ways, I was my mother's caretaker. But I was good at it. I had a knack for it, an inclination of sorts, that went beyond the norm. Ros talked me into the session by asking how I'd like to care for someone who was caring for me right back. A closed circle rather than an open-ended storm drain."

She hadn't tried to sugar coat a difficult childhood or wallow in it. It was just information, her tone matter-of-fact.

"What took you from Alabama to New York?"

"A friend. Cassandra Moira. Now Adler. Lucas's wife."

Lucas Adler was Kensington & Associates CFO, someone Max knew well. Neil had occasionally seen Lucas at their poker games. His wife, Cassandra, was a successful corporation negotiator with Piedmont Consulting and another knockout. If Abby's looks had been as obvious in her college days, he expected traffic pileups had happened when Cass and Abby hung out together.

"Her mom...had a similar situation," Abby continued. "Cass encouraged me to apply to NYU, get completely away, into a whole different city. That's where I met Ros. She was everything I wasn't used to--a confident woman in full control of her life, who didn't need anyone to take care of her. And she liked topping men. She showed me how nourishing it was, for both sides, when it was done right." A thoughtful gaze crossed her face. "And I was deeply in need of nourishment."

He saw her recognize that was perhaps a deeper insight than she'd intended to offer, but he took the advantage it provided. "I'd like to understand more about that."

He was interested in everything about her. Every thought, dream or plan she might have. Even if some of it didn't make him all that comfortable.

She'd shifted her gaze off screen again, but he could see her thinking about it. "My mother projected helplessness," she said at last. "Resignation and helplessness. She didn't teach me confidence. I had to claim it, my power as a person, bit by bit. As a Domme, every scrap of that I'd gathered came together, became something. A whole. When I have a man at my feet, one who wants to honor my power, worship it, revel in it...it's so different."

She set her chin. A quick glance back at him. "I'm not a rescuer. The men I top are healthy, strong men with normal hang-ups. They're mostly past that struggle with identity about being a male sub. They know they want a Mistress, and they'll work to earn the privilege of serving."

She stopped. "You hate that I'm heading to a club to do this."

"It doesn't thrill me," he said honestly. "But that's a reaction that doesn't fit in that world. I get that. It's like fear management. Fear has a role in what I do, but it can't ever hold the upper hand. Not if I want to fully understand the situation, or succeed at accomplishing the mission. Some impulses are good. Some get in the way."

He lifted a shoulder. Her gaze coursed over it, then up to linger on his mouth, his brow and bearded jaw. It reminded him of her fingers there, stroking.

He leaned in. Oddly, she drew back as if he was physically in front of her, her gaze shifting away again. But the tilt of her head, the stillness of her body, suggested he had her full attention, so he spoke that way. Intently.

"I respect who you are, what you are. I'm hearing that topping a sub is important. I also understand you require zero validation from me on it. You touching another guy, him having his hands, eyes or any other part of him focused on you, makes me want to do a lot of pretty violent things. I don't mind telling you that, one, because I know it won't change a thing about how you spend your night, and two, because I want to tell you the truth."

He paused. "Mostly I just wish I was there with you, right now, and that you didn't have to end the conversation."

She pressed her lips together. He imagined he was touching them, her face.

"Want to take a shower with me?" she said at last. She had her hand up on her throat, was lightly stroking the base, and her mouth had softened.

"You read my mind."

With a serious smile, she rose, carrying the phone. As they went up some steps, she let him see the surroundings as if he were walking with her. She'd remembered he wanted to feel like he was somewhere else. Someplace where a co-worker getting gut shot wasn't a normal day.

The stairs were old wood, in good condition and polished. They creaked as she went up them, but she wasn't wearing any shoes, because he didn't hear her steps. Three paintings were mounted along the wall. She liked those Impressionist-style things, that muted softness that provided details at a distance and a multi-hued cloud of shifting colors up close. It was a blurry style he thought suggested a dream state.

One was a landscape, with twisted trees and an ocean in the background. The second was a field, where the feathered tops of meadow grass were punctuated by wildflowers. The final one was a pond, with lily pads.

They'd reached a landing and moved toward a bedroom, passing a guest room and a bathroom on the way. In her bedroom he saw a double bed, the comforter white, with small flowers embroidered on it. It picked up the style of the two wall paintings, each displaying a single small drawn flower against a backdrop of white space.

The dresser held only a vase of flowers. He saw no TV, but expected it was inside the large wardrobe. The room had a huge bank of windows. If it was east facing, some heavy curtains would be needed for sleep-in mornings. Instead, the windows had white blinds, pulled all the way up top, the strings wrapped around the end of the accordioned slats.

She carried him into the bathroom and propped the phone on the counter. Here she had a spacious open shower, cobbled with smooth and round earth-toned rock. Suspended over the area was a wide rectangular fixture, one of those that simulated rain.

Though her home was embellished with a light touch, the quality choices were a reminder she made good money doing what she did. She lived in one of the older sections of New Orleans' Garden District, not far from where Ros lived.

She stepped toward the shower. "Can you see enough of me?"

"I don't think that's possible."

Her lips did that sweet curve again. "I won't be able to hear you in the shower, so if you need to click off before I'm out, I'll assume you got called away."

She was really going to take a shower in front of him. She might intend to keep pushing him away, holding him at arm's length, but her intentions and her needs, that connection, were saying something entirely different to him.

He closed a hand on his knee. "You're showing a lot of trust here. What if I invite the team to watch?"

She chuckled. "You won't. You just told me you don't like to share."

"I am kind of a jerk that way."

She took out her barrette. The glory of all that gold-tinged red hair cascading over her shoulders had his breath tying itself in a hard knot just above his breastbone. His muscles tightened as she gripped the hem of her soil-stained T-shirt and pulled it over her head. Since she was turned partially away from him, his gaze clung to the graceful undulation of her shoulders, rib cage, hips. Reaching back, she unclipped her black bra, let it slide down her arms.

He'd certainly seen a woman undress. He wasn't sure he'd ever watched it with this level of intensity, absorbed the true intimacy of it. Nothing else in the world was more important to him than capturing every detail.

The bra tumbled off her finely boned wrists before she opened her jeans, toed off her shoes. As she skimmed denim off her hips, she revealed panties in the same dark color. Nothing lacy or provocative, but every inch of her, the shape of her ass, the contrast between her pale skin and the dark fabric, her long hair tumbling forward over bare shoulders, did things to him he would never be able to put into words.

If she'd been doing this in session, she would be showing a sub what she could offer him when she was in the mood to do so. This was similar but different. He wanted to come up behind her, push all her hair over one shoulder, feel its thick softness over his scraped knuckles. He'd put his mouth on her shoulder, her throat. As he closed his hands over her breasts, pressed his body up against hers, she'd feel so full of life, peace. A wonder of nature imbued with that unforgettable feminine scent of home.

The distance between this moment and what he'd been doing a few hours ago was Grand Canyon vast.

All the things he was thinking and feeling...it answered the questions about why he did what he did, why he fought and killed. It didn't answer the questions about why people were crazy enough to fight and kill at all, when they could reach for this instead. But if life ever made any kind of sense, he knew those answers wouldn't be found in human nature.

She'd activated the rain fixture, and he could hear the water hitting the stone. When she slipped off the panties, she was still partially turned away, but she tilted her head in his direction. He watched, waiting. After a moment, she dipped her chin, a little nod, and stepped into the shower. No curtain, no door.

He thought about that pause, realized it was a very Domme thing to do. She wasn't a pay-by-the-minute porno site, asking the viewer if he wanted to watch her scrub this, reveal that. He had been granted a very distinct privilege; to watch a Mistress bathe.

If he were a sub, respectful behavior would ensure he got the full privilege. He'd be ordered to kneel outside the shower. As long as he didn't succumb to the unsightly urge to drool like a hungry dog—Neil could imagine the sultry tease in her voice as she said that—he might not be ordered to keep his eyes turned toward the floor.

Since she struck him as a careful, compassionate Domme, the sub would have a folded towel under his knees.

He wasn't a sub, but Neil remained quiet, because he was watching her a different way. The way a Dom would.

If he was there, he'd be straddling a chair a few feet away. Propping his elbows on it as he watched every move she made, the dip of her head, the turn of her body, how water rolled over her skin. How she closed her eyes as she turned her face up to the falling rain and pressed her lips together.

When she finally stepped out, he would have the towel in hand. He would dry her with slow strokes and gentle pats, squeeze the moisture out of her hair. He'd have her stand there, then, shivering not from cold, but from him placing his lips on every treasured, damp inch of her skin he'd studied. He'd know what was happening to her body and in her mind—if she was uncertain, pleased, aroused... He'd give her everything she needed, so she'd know she could rely on him for that.

She could rely on her Dom, her Master, for everything.

What would Abby say if she heard those thoughts? She'd probably offer that dry, brittle laugh and say he'd just offered proof of their incompatibility.

But silently following their own paths, yet wanting to be together while they did so, featuring one another in those mental scenarios, didn't feel incompatible at all.

She'd say virtual sex games allowed more latitude. He'd call her a liar, but it wasn't a lie. Abigail's brick wall of practicality was his biggest obstacle. He could attribute it to her being a number cruncher, an accounting expert, CFO of a successful company, but he suspected it was more than that. He felt her deep-seated desire. She wanted this, but she didn't think it could work.

Certain encounters with reality could imprison a soul. They happened on the worst kinds of battlefields, places where hope was lost. Living life with purpose and pleasure was still possible afterwards, but never again without studied effort, a continual vigilance against the past that would always be there, waiting to close in.

Was it from dealing with whatever issue her mother had? He assumed it had been some form of substance abuse, taking a serious toll on Abby's childhood.

He could contemplate the puzzle of how such truth touched her, affected her decisions, when he was in his bunk. Right now, he put that away and tuned in a hundred percent to the Mistress's gift being offered. Having seen her in a bikini at Dale and Athena's barbecue, he knew how appealing her body was. But to see her palm her breasts, the weight and generous shape of the curves, particularly as she soaped them, tugged on the nipples, it was as if she'd closed her hand around his cock and done the same to it. He wanted to put her up against the wall of the shower, drive into her as the rain beat down on both of them.

She turned, washing her shoulders, the lengths of her arms. Rinsing them. Shampooing her hair. When wet, the tresses were dark, the bathroom light catching flashes of the red-gold color, like the horizon soon after the sun went down. As she lifted the hair to rinse it, combed through it, his fingers twitched as if he were the one doing that.

She propped a foot on the shower bench to soap the length of her leg, bringing the soap high on her thigh and running it over her buttock. When she'd teased him earlier, he'd thought of giving her ass a good smack. How would she react to that? As a Domme, she might not get a thing out of that, just give him an indifferent look.

Or demand quid pro quo.

He hadn't asked for specifics on what she did with her subs, but when the time was right, he needed to have that discussion. Then he'd have to decide what to do with that.

The stiffness of his cock felt damn good, evidence of being alive and virile, ready to plow into a woman's wet, willing folds. This woman. If he'd been there right now, he was pretty sure they wouldn't have sex, though. They weren't there yet, but that would be okay. He'd put his nose to the tender part of her scalp, inhale, slide his hands over her, see how she reacted to his touch, to being held.

To that kiss he was determined she would ask him for.

She shut off the shower, reached for the towel. When she patted it over herself, and wrapped it around her, tucking it in over her breasts, she came back to the phone, picked it up. "Want to help me choose what to wear?" she asked.

"I'm not sure you're going to want my advice. I've worn the same brand of jeans for nearly two decades. If I want to impress a woman, I find an excuse to wear my uniform."

"That tells me you don't obsess over your own appearance, as long as you're clean enough to show respect to the woman on your arm. I suspect you'd put far more thought into what you'd want a woman to wear."

Interesting wording. "You want me to pick out what you're wearing."

"Yes." Her eyes gleamed as she walked him back into the bedroom. "I wouldn't mind seeing you in that uniform, though."

"I'll have to make sure our relationship is ready for that. The uniform has the power to make women instantly drop their panties and bend over."

She chuckled, that sultry, cock-teasing sound again. "Sounds like wishful thinking from the man wearing it."

As she entered a walk-in closet, he noted garments arranged with neat, even spacing, organized by color and possibly type of outfit. She didn't have as many as he would have expected. Organization seemed to trump quantity.

Putting the phone on a shelf even with her face, she stepped back, combing her fingers through her hair again. As her attention skimmed over the clothes, he thought he detected a slight tension in her. Maybe about offering him the choice, so he spoke before she could change her mind.

"What look are you going for?"

She responded so smoothly, he thought he might have been mistaken. "Soft and pretty, but in charge. Makes him want to touch, but the look says no touching. Not until I say he's earned it."

"Do they ever earn it?"

"Depends on if that's the path we're taking that night."

"Going to have his mouth on you?" he said, with deceptive mildness.

"Not tonight." Her hazel eyes flashed a challenge that said his tone still wasn't fooling her. "I'll do most of the touching."

"What's different about tonight?"

"It's just better if I have him keep his hands and mouth to himself."

He was on board with that idea, no argument, but he wondered about the slight pause before she spoke the words, as if she was weighing her feelings about it with more caution than usual.

She turned to a set of built-in cedar drawers which contained a frothy pile of underwear. As she fished in there, she shifted a Hitachi wand out of the way.

"I see you have your 'who-needs-a-man' backup."

She chuckled. "Intimidated?"

"No," he said truthfully. "When I was in my early twenties, I was lucky enough to date a woman about ten years older than me. She told me a man should never resent a woman's vibrator."

"Really? Why so?"

"She said it gives a woman time to fantasize on her own, explore herself, understand the scope of her desires. But she also said a man should never be outperformed by one." He paused, remembering. "He should find out what those fantasies are, meet them. Help her explore and discover deeper ones. Not just the surface things. She said intimacy is a fantasy that can be explored in a million ways."

He smiled. "That's a quote. I memorized it. She said a smart man keeps material in reserve."

"For when the uniform option isn't available."

"Exactly."

When she glanced toward the phone, an amused and interested hazel eye glittered at him from behind strands of her damp hair. But he also noted her hand had tightened on the silky fabrics in the drawer as he spoke.

He wanted to see her wear each one, a fashion show just for him. He'd relish how she stretched them across her backside, adjusted them over the folds between her legs. Or hooked her fingers in the straps, silk and lace, shimmying out of them to try on another.

"Neil..." The tension was back in her voice.

"Don't hang up," he said quietly. "Show me that silver thing about two or three hangers to your left."

She paused a long moment. Tapped the edge of the drawer with her free hand in a quick, nervous rhythm that didn't seem entirely like her. But before he could decide how to address it, she reached for the garment he'd indicated. It was a sleeveless top. Translucent lace would reveal the shoulders and probably a nice amount of cleavage. A white silk liner concealed the rest of the front. The back was fully lace.

"Put that with the black slacks you wore the day Dale and I came to your office," he said.

The slacks had flowed like a skirt, a gauze layer over the opaque legs. She retrieved them, held them up with the lace top. "You going to be throwing a whip? Something where you need more stability on your feet?"

Curious speculation in her gaze said she hadn't expected him to think of that. "If I do, I'll step out of my shoes."

"Wear your favorite high heels, then. Work your hair up on top of your head. If you have any dangly earrings that caress your neck when you turn your head, that'll be the finishing touch. You'll have what you're looking for. Soft and touchable, but also tough and in charge."

She hung the two items up so she could run her fingers over them. As she spread out the slacks to take a closer look at them, he expected she was doing it to present a profile that matched her forced casual tone.

"Is that what you'd want me to wear if you were with me?"

"No. But it'll make the guy kneeling at your feet lose his mind." He paused. "You already have him picked out."

"I have a couple regulars. It will be one of those. I'll be right back. I can still hear you, if you want to keep talking."

She stepped out of view, taking the clothes. He expected she might have gone to do some private, post-bathing things she didn't want him to see. Lotions, sprays, things that added to her haunting scent.

"So what do you usually want from them?" he asked. "Your subs. Oral? Sex? Service?"

With Club Progeny being a private club, and one that offered private rooms, any of those things could be on the table. Even if it changed—and he was all too aware that it could—he was relieved she'd stated her intent wasn't to go too far down those roads tonight. He'd restrained his more primal behaviors up until now, but he wasn't sure how well he'd maintain if she tested that leash.

"Never sex." Her voice reached him, a little muffled. "Oral on occasion. Usually I let him finish himself while I watch, after I've given him the privilege of watching me. Though sometimes I'll force them to release and then punish them."

She returned. She'd donned the outfit, had her wet hair combed and wrapped up in a twist like he'd suggested. She'd probably blow it out and rearrange it after they hung up. She did a graceful turn, showing off the lace top over the slacks. Glossy silver heels gave a tempting tilt to her backside, an arch to her back that displayed her breasts. Her earrings were a fall of tiny crescent shaped wires tipped with glittering stones that caressed her neck as he'd described. It made him want even more to put his mouth on her throat.

Yeah, he'd asked the question, but now seeing what another man was going to appreciate, and putting that together with what she'd described, brought him to an edge he knew wasn't a good place.

"I wanted you to see the full effect."

Goddamn, she was determined to push him over it. He saw the awareness in her eyes. Despite that, he couldn't keep the edge out of his frank reaction.

"Mission accomplished, Mistress. Everyone with a dick will lose his train of thought the second you walk in."

"There it is," she said. "Drop the civilized veneer, Neil. What kind of Dom are you?"

Her hazel gaze locked with his for only a couple blinks, but the demand in it, the challenge, hooked that façade and ripped it away. Fine. He was ready to show her what was beneath it.

"The kind that wants to lay a woman out on her bed, spread her out and feast on her," he said. "Look at me."

He sharpened his tone, because her gaze had shifted away again. Her hand was at her neck, one finger tapping the base of her throat. She shook her head, her eyes back to staring toward the left of the screen. What the hell was over there?

"Go on," she said, voice throaty. "Tell me. Talk. Drown everything else out."

"I'd make her so hot, pull her right to the edge so she'd scream and claw at me, begging for release. I wouldn't let her up until I'd made a full course meal out of her, putting my mark on her in every way possible." He had the phone in a tight grip. The kind he'd like to have on her. Her hair, her ass, as he drove into her.

"When she's worn out from the orgasms, I'd put myself inside her one more time. Where I'd been ruthless before, now I'd pull her legs up around me with gentle hands."

He paused, finding the steadiness. Pulling on the invaluable lesson that long ago lover had taught him. "I'd whisper, tell her to stare into my gaze while I fuck her one more time. It'd be a deep rock, in and out, until she's rising to me like an ocean wave."

Abby nodded, her standing body moving in a slight rhythm, as if emulating his words. That tapping on her throat was increasing.

"Abby..."

"Keep going," she said urgently.

"I'd come inside her then, take her to climax once more. Then I'd tend to her, curl her up in my arms, stroke her hair. I'd listen to her make those soft noises, those low hums you women do, that language that tells me we've given each other what we both need."

Her rocking slowed as he put the emotion that went with that aftermath in his voice. The care. He sensed she needed to hear it. She tapped the base of her throat, three times. Two times. Back to three. Then five. Like a personal code of some type.

"Abby."

A quick glance at him, her gaze like shards of glass. "If we had gone to the club together tonight, what would *you* have wanted me to wear, Neil? Tell me."

He ran his fingers along the perimeter of the phone, wanting to touch her so much it hurt. "I saw a picture of you in a magazine. It was from a couple years ago, when you were at a benefit ball. You were wearing a black dress. It had a strap on one shoulder and the other shoulder was bare. From the top of your shoulder to under the other arm had short silver rods sewn into it."

She moved to the back of the closet. She pulled the dress out, covered by the transparent film of a dry-cleaning service. "This one. Why?"

"Because it was short and tight enough to get my blood up." He gave her a male smile. "I liked looking at you in it, though I didn't like any other guy getting the chance."

She hung the dress up, so it was flat against the other clothes, like she had her current outfit. "What did you think about when you looked at me? Did you imagine us together?"

When he didn't immediately speak, her hands moved under the plastic to stroke and grip the fabric. She stayed silent, waiting for him to fill that void.

"I imagined I was at that benefit with you," he said at last. "And during the evening we found a private room, a library with a grand piano."

A slight smile touched her beautiful face. "Because those places always have a room like that."

"Yeah. I laid you down on your front on the top of it, had you stretch out your arms while I pushed the skirt up in back. When I put myself inside, it was fucking heaven, finding all that honey that had been slicking up your thighs, because of the things you knew I wanted to do to you."

"I see." Her lips parted. Her voice was throaty. "I want there to be someone playing the piano. A man, a sub. He's blindfolded, required to stay that way while he plays, so he can't see us. Only hear us, feel our vibration as we move against the piano."

"I'll go with that. He'd play something classical. Classy. But something with fire to it, and an edge. Like the woman I'm buried inside. Abby."

She tilted her head toward him, almost as if the imperative behind her name was a physical touch, his palm cupping the side of her face, fingertips caressing her hair. He'd pull that lace top off her shoulder, tease her bra strap with his fingers, her skin with his mouth. He'd told her to put her hair up, and the delicate line of her throat, begging for his mouth, his teeth, tortured him.

"I don't want any damn man in the world touching you but me. I want to be there with you right now, so I can fuck you all night long. I want to hold you while you sleep."

Her eyes closed, her fingers tightening on the dress.

"Abby." He was going to keep saying her name until she looked at him.

But she shook her head again, opened her eyes and hung the dress up again. She turned her chin in his direction. "It upsets me, to see that someone hurt you, bruised your face," she said. "But it was worse than that. Your eyes are more bruised than the rest of you. Are your people okay, Neil? Can you tell me that?"

The shift in topics told him he'd maybe spooked her, taken this too far. But hell, when she'd pushed him to let loose, she'd matched that desire, kept pace with the fantasy.

It didn't matter. He read the signals. He reined himself back from the passion that had overtaken him, that made him ready to rip through the laws of physics to somehow dive into his phone and emerge from hers, into her closet with her.

She waited him out until he found that balance. She stood motionless in her closet, head tilted in his direction.

"One of them, not so much," he said carefully. "But we think he'll be all right."

"Good. I'll hope for that."

She took a breath, and he could almost hear the spell break. "I should go. I'm already going to be late."

Now at last she looked his way. Though the eye contact was still brief, everything he saw there rocked through him, hard. "You are a fascinating man. But you're still not a sub."

"I don't think that's relevant."

"Agree to disagree."

"We can make it work, Abby," he said. "I think tonight says that."

She pressed her lips together. "It's more than both of us needing to be in charge, Neil. If you could keep it at the club with me, keep it structured, maybe...but you can't. Everything about you says you want more. Limitless, bottomless, ceiling-less more."

"We don't have to define it by anyone's rules but our own," he countered. "You didn't tell me to rip off the veneer to prove that to me, Abby. It was what you wanted, too."

Her expression closed up. "Wanting is irrelevant. You probably wanted your friend not to be hurt, but it wouldn't have changed a thing about what you did for him to end up that way, right? Because you know some things must be done. That's what I know about my life and yours, Neil. They must stay separate."

He was too far away to turn this into a fight, even though that was exactly what the feelings rising in him wanted.

"You going to tell me why?" He strove for an even tone.

"Maybe eventually. Not now. I need to go." She paused. Her hand hovered over the screen, as if she was tracing his face without touching it. "Please stay safe," she said softly.

The frustration died back. He heard the genuine care in her voice, the wanting and desire. Whatever games were fucking with her head, or his, they'd figure it out. Another time. When they were back together again.

"You too," he managed. "Make sure that sub treats you right. Else I'll have to kick his ass. I might do it anyway."

Her hazel eyes were as mysterious as the universe itself. "Good night, Neil."

~

Abby cut the connection. Took off the clothes, put on her nightshirt. Brushed out her hair, dried it, then braided it for bedtime. Sat down and prepared for a night of facing the shadows.

Though this *was* the normal night for her to meet up with Ros and the rest at Progeny, she'd taken a pass. However, she'd figured pretending she was going, bringing it up like that, would provoke a reaction in Neil that would make it clear how wrong they were for one another, no matter their off-the-charts sexual chemistry.

Instead, an interesting mix of their two power exchange styles had occurred. Her body was still vibrating from the impact of it, from wanting what he could offer. He'd watched her shower silently, almost like a sub but not. She'd responded to his choices for her wardrobe in a similar way. Like a sub, but not.

He confused her without upsetting her, the conflicts a pleasant, winding path, not a quagmire. At least until the end, when she'd poisoned the exchange with her anxiety. She wished she hadn't done that.

She wished praying would help. She did believe in it; she just didn't believe anyone listened to hers, so she'd stopped, a long time ago. She'd learned to rely on herself, chart out her path with precision and determination.

She might be headed for hell and chaos, but by God, she'd take the scenic route, as long as she had the ability to control the wheel. On that thought—along with more thoughts of Neil—she returned to the closet, closed her hand over the Hitachi wand. Tonight, she knew exactly who would be in the car with her.

CHAPTER FOUR

"Abby, I have a problem."

"You're a control freak with a terrible temper, you have no tact, and you should adjust the hem of your slacks for those new ice pick heels."

"I plan to use one of them to stab you through your cold heart. Multiple times. When they question me, the police will never realize I'm wearing the murder weapon."

As Abby saved and closed the document she'd been composing, she glanced toward her office doorway. Cynbad Marigold, their senior account manager, stood there, looking fabulous, no matter her hem line. Cyn was built like a lean female warrior in a gritty post-apocalyptic video game. Her sleek biceps, B-cup breasts and toned ass were well represented by her sleeveless red shot silk shirt and tailored brown slacks. She also had an artfully tousled mane of shoulder-length brown hair and the wide liquid eyes of a deer. If Bambi had the unwavering focus of a serial killer.

The combination was indicative of what kind of businesswoman Cyn was. She was direct with clients, sometimes brutally so. Sentiment wasn't her thing, but she was so dedicated to exceeding their goals that even those customers she pissed off at the beginning of the relationship quickly became slavish fans.

She had a similar effect on her subs. Cyn was extreme and demanding, a full immersion experience that sometimes walked the line with outright sadism. Though she had no interest in being a pro-Domme, Ros and the others joked she'd be a self-made millionaire if she hung out her shingle.

"A pro-Domme has to be about what the sub wants," Cyn always said in tart response. "When I'm topping, it's about giving me what I want, and finding the sub who's the best match for that. Giving me what I want *is* what he needs."

She didn't want an easy capitulation. She wanted the ones who liked to fight it, who took the extremes of pain, snarled, and dared her to give them more.

As she got lost in recalling some of Cyn's more memorable scenes, Abby realized she was still too much in the grip of what had happened last night on the phone with Neil. Cyn was talking again, telling her what she needed. Abby held up a hand.

"Sorry, start over."

Cyn shot her an impatient look. "Hon, this meeting starts in a half hour. The client needs a recalculation of his project costs if we go for an international marketing scheme that includes India and Germany, because..."

Abby fought to keep pace with the flow of the words, but they got suspended in the air, spinning. She couldn't keep her gaze from following them, wandering away from Cyn and passing over the clock on the wall. She paused there. It was after two. She worked from home Tuesday and Thursday afternoons, but she'd had too much to do this morning, and time had gotten away from her. Had she eaten lunch? She couldn't remember.

"Got it," she said, when Cyn ran down. "I can pull together some high-level projections for the meeting. Tell him he'll have more precise numbers by the week's end."

"That'll work," Cyn relieved her by saying. "He'll re-tweak during the meeting, which will impact the finals. You okay?"

Cyn was looking at her too closely. A wet clicking noise to Abby's left was making her shoulder twitch. She had to turn that way. Had to. Cyn looked that way, too.

She's in on it. They're all in on it.

No. No, they're not. Your mind is fucking with you.

"Yes, I'm fine." Abby cleared her throat to cover the brittle sound of her strained voice. "I'll shoot the data to your computer in a few minutes. Close my door, would you?"

They had an open-door policy at TRA, so if the door was closed, that meant the person was in a meeting, or working on a deadline that shouldn't be interrupted unless it was critical. This would qualify.

Cyn had gone. The door was closed. A shadow fell across her desk, making Abby start. It was just the time of day, she told herself. The sun that shone through the bank of her office windows throughout the morning and early afternoon had passed over. The TRA office was a refitted ten-thousand square foot historic home in the Garden District, the building designed by the architect Henry Howard. It was surrounded by large live oaks that would wrap their arms around it at this time of day, shutting off all light.

Squeezing it, until the house crumbled in on itself. Then the crabs would come. With their clicking, wet claws, coming in the darkness. Out of the shadows.

They wanted her brain. Needed it. All those numbers. They'd shake them out, carry them away. Everyone knew it, was in on it.

She closed her eyes, counted. Primes. Forty-three, fifty-three. Seventy-three. Eighty-three. She opened her eyes and punched the mouse, calling up the client's project documents. Click, click, click. A different kind of clicking, the right kind. She was good at this.

But Cyn needed the numbers now. Time pressure. Urgency, creeping up the back of her neck. Double click, when she meant to single click. She cursed, counted another set of primes. Divisible only by one and itself. No other numbers could crowd in on them.

It helped her re-focus on the data. Cross-checking, pulling up tables. She pushed herself in that zone, like taffy, stretched, and stretched.

Some part of her deep inside was weeping.

It was a race, her hands and mind moving as fast as possible, the spin cycle on the washer. Washing it away, leaving it the way it should be. Sparkling clean.

That was the dishwasher. No, the dishwasher didn't have a spin cycle. Or did it?

She stared at the numbers on the screen. They started to dissolve, slide down into the ones below, forming an avalanche that pooled at the bottom of her screen, trickled out onto her desk, moving toward her fingers.

She jerked her hands back. *It's not real. It's not real. It makes no sense, so it's not real.*

She put her hands back on the keyboard, making little fearful gasps as the words crawled over her fingers. "It's not real, it's not real." She kept chanting it, finally saved the document to Cyn's folder in the shared files and sent her an alert to let her know it was there. The second she hit the enter button, she jerked her hands away from the keyboard and stood up. The movement was violent enough to send her chair back, knock it into her credenza.

The whispering grew louder. Ignoring the quaking in her belly, she collected her purse and keys. Put her tablet in her briefcase. When she opened her office door, she saw Ros headed down the hall. Her destination was likely the conference room. She'd drop into Cyn's meeting, do the CEO thing, as she did whenever a client came to the office. Whether a big-money client or a burgeoning entrepreneur, she conveyed that they, and their needs, were important. She'd assure them they were in excellent hands before turning them over to Cyn and her support staff.

Since coming to New Orleans, Ros had softened her crisp corporate New York edges, but she knew which clients responded to her Upper East side look, and today's visitor was one of them. Her white-blond hair, dark at the tips, was curled fashionably over her shoulders, and she was clad in a trim power suit. It was black with thin purple pinstripes, and she'd paired it with a purple blouse, accessorized with silver jewelry. Ros loved her shoes, and these were open-toed black pumps with bits of purple trim and artful silver pieces arranged along the sides.

Whether it was an astonishingly successful boutique marketing firm or a takeover of the Western world, she looked capable of handling anything.

It made Abby smile, even as that weeping deep inside her increased.

Ros detoured to her. "Thanks for running those numbers. You could have finished those data reports from home, though. You should have been out of here already."

"It's all right. I think I'm going to head to Indiana for a few days.

See if I can get a couple maintenance things done for the fall while I'm up there. Contractors can back up if I wait too long."

The home on Monroe Lake she'd inherited from her great-uncle was a haven for her. The fully updated get-away space was also a good location for her to work remotely.

"Okay." Ros gazed at her with the same shrewdness Cyn had. They already knew too much about one another, but on top of that, all four executive staff members had exceptional intuition. A Domme thing, a businesswoman thing, a personal close friend thing. Like called to like.

The five of them defied the assumption that successful, beautiful women collected less successful, less beautiful women around them to make them look better. Every one of them was a fiercely burning star in the sky, not afraid of the competition of anyone else's light.

In their case, they'd learned combining that light meant they could outshine their competition in all the right ways.

"You haven't called me at night in a while," Ros said. "That's good, right?"

"Yes." When she'd crossed into her thirties, Abby's worries about her future had evolved into nightmares about the impending shadows. The first time her fear exceeded her good sense and she'd called Ros in the middle of the night, Ros had proven why she was Abby's best friend. She'd talked Abby past her terrors, re-linked her to her usual practicality. The voices weren't really there. Yet. The nightmares were fueled by her dread of the hourglass running out of sand.

Ros gripped her hand with firm, caring fingers. If Abby jumped a little before settling into the familiar contact, Ros didn't react to it. "You look tired, Abigail. Go home and forget about this place for the rest of the day. Stop and grab Freak for pet therapy if you want his company for the night."

"No. It's all right, but thanks." Abby found a genuine smile at the thought of Ros's precocious three-legged feline. While devoted to Ros, Freak allowed himself to be time-shared with Abby, treating her place like his second home. "There's a red-eye flight that can take me up to Indianapolis tonight. I'll check into a hotel there and be at the lake house by lunch tomorrow. You can reach me on my phone."

"Text me when you get there."

"Always. Give Lawrence my best."

"Not a chance. I have to make sure he knows I'm the only woman in the world."

"Have you seen how he looks at you?" Abby nudged her, glad for the surge of warm amusement. "To him, you are. 'Property of Rosalinda Thomas' may be stamped on that custom dog tag you had made for him, but even without it, it's stamped all over him."

The softer look in Ros's jewel blue eyes acknowledged the simple truth. She felt just as deeply about the former SEAL. Now she cocked her head, those shrewd eyes playful. "Are you and Neil still doing the 'who'll blink first' thing?"

"He called me the other night," Abby said before she could stop herself. She needed to go. But she enjoyed the way Ros's face lit up.

"You cagey bitch. Details."

"You have no time for details." Abby nodded toward Lacey, who'd poked her head out of the conference room. Lacey was Cyn's right hand.

"Ms. Thomas, Bastion says Mr. Corley and his people have arrived. He's bringing them up."

Ros waved at her in acknowledgement, but still kept Abby in her gun sights. "Quick, high level. Was there phone or video sex? Male nudity?"

"It was interesting. I'm still wrapping my mind around what it was." Abby sobered. "He'd had a rough day, I think. One of his team got injured, and he had a bad bruise on his face. He was moving stiff. But he was okay."

Ros squeezed Abby's hand again. "Lawrence and Dale say he's one of the best operators there is," she said staunchly. "Since they were top-tier SEALs, too, that means something."

"Yes. True." But you could be the best at what you do, and the numbers would still dissolve and run down the screen.

"Did he say when he'll be back?"

Abby shook her head. "He wasn't calling from Virginia Beach, I know that much."

Abby heard Bastion's deep voice responding to Alfred Corley's comments as they crested the stairs. An unlikely looking but incredibly efficient office manager, Bastion Lake was six feet tall, with brown eyes and dark hair tied back in a neat tail. His slacks and dress shirt combo were worn with masculine flare on a powerful body that would attract the attention of men or women alike. Which worked for Bastion, since he played either side of that fence with equal enthusiasm.

"Have a safe trip. Reach out if you need me." When Ros's attention moved to the client, she spoke out of the side of her mouth like a conspirator in a bank robbery. "Slide out the back staircase so you don't get caught in the schmoozing."

Covering Abby's escape, Ros turned and clicked away on her heels to meet the client halfway, the cloth of her slacks rustling, the purple and silver of her shoes glinting.

Grateful, Abby slipped into the back stairwell that had been used in other eras as a servants' passageway. When she emerged into the little courtyard outside a side door, she looked up into the interlaced branches of those live oaks. The ones that would wrap around the house and squeeze it, kill everyone.

No, they wouldn't. The sunlight filtered through, offering sparkles like on Ros's shoes, only golden, not silver.

"Time to go," Abby murmured. "Into the sun, wax melting like words. Falling to earth."

She thought of Neil's hands. Though she couldn't always see them during their call, she suspected there'd been tension in those long, sensitive fingers, a desire to touch. She'd wanted to reach through the screen, overlap, lace her own with them, tight. Like a binding that would never be released, until the rope cut into the flesh, promising to leave a scar that would never fade.

Time to go.

"You look like the center of a spinning world," a voice intruded on her thoughts.

Damn it all.

Veracity Morgan sat on one of the concrete benches, a tablet balanced on her knee as she tapped a pen against the seat next to her, probably the beat to some song going through her mind. The bench had ornate cherub faces on the support pieces, nature spirits appropriate here among the froth of azaleas that were scattered around the seating area.

Vera headed up their HR and Legal department. Ros dryly referred to her as TRA's priestess, because of her spiritual nature and tough love demeanor.

"Needed a change of venue?" Abby wished it had been one of the interns or a lower-ranked staff member, where it would be acceptable for her to nod, absently smile and hurry away. She needed to go. Not in a few minutes. Now. The tree branches had gotten closer. Any moment they'd reach down like claws, toward Vera. Grab her. Abby gripped her laptop case hard, bit her tongue so she wouldn't tell Vera to move. To move *now*.

It doesn't make sense. Not real. Not real. The clicking noise was coming from somewhere to her left. Always left. She was a practical person. Left was her dominant hand. It had something to do with her brain, her shattering brain. She told herself that, even as she imagined her feet in concrete. She would *not* spin around, try to locate the sound.

"When I have a plethora of forms to file, coming out here seems preferable to staying in my office," Vera said. "If my brain explodes from idiotic government bureaucracy, the gray matter won't stain the carpet and wallpaper. Actually, idiotic isn't the right word. It takes diabolical genius and dedication to make a process this confusing."

"The same thought I have every time I handle our taxes," Abby returned. Voice stilted but making sense, because Vera didn't indicate the words had come out wrong. Abby located an unfiltered patch of sunlight and shifted into it. Vera's head was not going to explode. She was joking. Just joking.

Vera chuckled at Abby's comment, though now Abby couldn't remember what she'd just said to her. "I didn't realize you were still here," the HR manager said. "You're usually home by now on a Tuesday."

"Got bogged down. Headed that way, and then I'm off to Indiana for a few days."

Abby started moving away, keeping to a swift walk. The wind picked up and the branches creaked, making her want to break into a terrified run. With effort, she managed to throw something over her shoulder that sounded normal. "Text if Ros needs anything she won't bother me with. She pisses me off when she does that."

Vera said something. The clicking noise drowned it out. From the sparkle in Vera's eyes, she'd probably said something teasing about Ros and Abby's sisterly relationship. Abby lifted a hand in farewell, pulled off a normal smile, and headed for the back parking lot.

When she reached the safety of her car, doors closed and locked, she closed her eyes. Thoroughly considered if she could drive. She should have done her morning run to the office. It wouldn't be the first time she'd done that, taken a quick shower in one of the full baths. She kept a set or two of clothes here for that purpose.

Walls pushed in on her. Walls of information, questions, people talking, none of it easy to filter or quiet. She needed to get home.

Then to Indiana. Where no one else could see her.

The idea of coordinating all that, booking a plane, a hotel, a car...it was too much. She'd take a nap first, then think about it. Maybe she'd leave tomorrow.

~

Twenty minutes later, Ros stepped out of the conference room, leaving Alfred in Cyn's capable hands. Normally she'd enjoy staying a little longer, just to watch Cyn handle him. Corley was a formidable, older Italian businessman who usually required some bullying to prove to him they knew what they were doing. Since they'd been his marketing firm for three years, she suspected he indulged in being recalcitrant just for the pleasure of crossing swords with Cyn, and having her routinely prove hers was bigger.

Ros had plenty more on her plate before she could call it a day, but what held priority didn't relate to work at all. When she stopped in the doorway to Vera's office, her HR executive was finishing up a phone call. As she set down the receiver, she read Ros's face in her usual intuitive way.

"She looked a little rough to me, too. But you know she has days like that."

"More lately. I'm going to talk to Bastion. Make sure he knows that whatever it takes, she doesn't get held up here like she did today. She does better when she works from home in the afternoons. I'm going to encourage her to do it whenever she wants, not just Tuesdays and Thursdays. She can handle almost anything from home she handles here. Her staff can manage the office-dependent work."

At least for now. Over the past several months, Ros had been letting Abby ease out of the high-pressure meetings, as well as many of the face-to-faces with their customers. Though Ros was always glad for Abby's way of balancing her sharper edges, what made things easier for Ros didn't matter at all when it came to this.

"Think she'll resist it?" Vera asked.

"I think she's hanging on by her fucking fingernails." Ros was about done with abiding by Abby's wish to pretend the truth wasn't about to land on her like a ton of bricks. The reality ached under Ros's breastbone, like those bricks had landed there first. "The fact she hasn't noticed the subtle ways we've upped the mother hen factor is a big flag. Six months ago she would have set me back on my fabulous heels if I suggested she work from home more often. Now I think she's on the brink of suggesting it herself."

Helen Mirren's crisp British voice broke into the conversation. "Because our busy office is becoming overwhelming," she said.

Ros glanced over at Skye, who'd approached from her office and offered the input through the phone she held. Each of them knew when a pow-wow was needed. If Cyn wasn't in a meeting, Ros had no doubt she'd have joined them at Vera's door.

Before Ros had left the meeting, her senior account manager, dark eyes troubled, had confirmed it with a murmured comment. "Abby's struggling today."

When she shared that, Vera nodded, and Skye reinforced it. "You can tell when you talk to her, or if you're firing too many things at her at once," her Helen-voice continued. "She starts to fidget and look away after a few seconds."

"If the symptoms of the illness are truly starting to manifest," Vera noted, "it's past time for her to be evaluated and diagnosed, so she can review her treatment options."

"Something that should have been done a long time ago," Ros said bluntly. "But if I push, she shuts me down. Shuts me out. Tries harder to cover in front of us, and she's already too damn good at that. I don't want to give her more reasons to practice."

"All of which isolates her further," Vera said. "We have to keep trying."

"I didn't say I'm giving up, damn it," Ros retorted. "I just have to work on the timing."

She sighed, sent Vera an apologetic look. Skye touched Ros's shoulder, a reassurance.

"We'll get through it together." She'd changed the voice to the one she used as "herself," a Southern-accented musical tone. "Like we do everything else."

Ros wanted to agree, but she had firsthand knowledge of what happened when solidarity failed, spectacularly enough that it left a friend-sized hole in her life. A sister, a family member. If she lost Abby...

Soon she'd have to let all of them in on the deeper, darker areas of the path Abby was following. When she did, Ros knew they'd wonder why Ros or Abby hadn't told them earlier. They'd be angry. Particularly Cyn. But tied up with Ros's respect for Abby's wishes had been her own futile wish, overly reliant on Abby's desperate hope, that they'd never reach this point in the road.

Abby was still functioning, she reminded herself. Struggling, but she was coming to work. The off things they noticed about her came and went frequently enough that Ros sometimes doubted whether they were really becoming a problem or not. Abby seemed to be managing things.

That might be evidence of superb masking, but without Abby's willingness to approach things differently, nothing could be done but what they were doing. Pulling her mind away from that, Ros chose a different path. "Neil called her."

Two female faces brightened, eyes sharpening. "How did that go?" Vera asked.

"It seemed to be occupying her mind, which I'm going to take as a promising sign. I hope he can get back here soon. Lawrence says he's beyond smitten, and not likely to be deterred by anything less than a full rejection. From the way she was acting, that definitely wasn't the vibe she was giving him on the phone."

"But how exactly will that work?" Skye was back to using Helen's brisk British cadence. "The whole Dom squared thing. Because active in the club scene or not, when he's around a woman, he full-on prefers to be in charge."

"I've no idea, and honestly, I don't give a shit," Ros said. "He interests her. Whatever keeps her engaged works. Even if it eventually crashes and burns, maybe she'll consider a proper treatment plan while it's still candlelight and roses. Stop playing this bullshit avoidance game."

The anger had surged up, the worry not as tamped down as she'd hoped. "Ros," Vera said softly.

Ros waved a hand. "I won't let the way I feel spill over on her, but it makes me so furious with her. For her." Pain gripped her. "She may be handling it, but it's reached the point we can see it coming. No matter how much farther down the road it is, it's no longer a hypothetical, and she knows it. It's harder to go after her, push her to deal with it, when she's already being knocked to her knees."

"How about that psychotherapist Max recommended through his sister's treatment contacts?" Vera asked. "Maureen Whisnant."

"Abby won't—"

Vera shook her head. "For us. As a group. *We* meet with her. We've all done what we can to learn about what she's facing from credible research sources, but if she's starting to display debilitating symptoms, maybe it's time to arm ourselves with more specifics. Meet with someone who can answer our questions, guide us on additional ways to support her."

Personally and professionally, Ros recognized the ping when the right course had been identified. The advantage of being surrounded by smart people who looked at problems from different angles. The slight easing of the jagged band around her insides was just an additional perk. "I'll reach out, see if she'll schedule a consultation with us."

"Maybe that, and whatever happens with Neil, will present us with better ways to support her," Vera said.

"Should he be warned?" Skye's voice once more.

Ros met the IT manager's troubled, brown-eyed gaze, peering through bangs of spiky dyed blond and black hair.

"Lawrence asked me the same thing. It would be easy to let him give Neil some kind of heads up. But..." Ros shook her head. She'd wrestled with the question herself, all the layers to it. "We're the people she trusts most. If we have to bring Neil into the loop against her wishes, I'd strongly prefer if she could be told it's going to happen before it happens, and why we're doing it. Give her a chance to be part of that decision, even if she objects to it."

"What do you think he'll do?" Vera asked.

"Depends on how invested he is when it happens. If he decides to keep going with her, that's when I'll ask Lawrence to talk to him.

Make sure he understands the difference between testosterone-driven stubbornness or romantic idealism, and what she's actually facing."

"Most of the SEALs we know, like Max and Dale, seem pretty grounded in reality," Vera observed. "When the time comes, I hope Neil keeps his hand in. In the meantime, *my* tactical suggestion is lots of prayer. No matter what we each believe, it focuses intent. Sometimes that can adjust the rudder, show us the best way to go."

Vera's irises were the light color of water touched by sunlight. In the depths of those eyes, Ros saw she understood just how bad this could get, an empathy as reassuring as a hard hug. It was reflected in the emotion Vera wrapped around her next words and handed to her.

"We love her, Ros. Love her and you, so very much."

The feeling was mutual. Cyn, Skye and Vera were her family as much as her blood relations. Lawrence had become part of her heart and soul, with a depth and scope she never would have anticipated.

But before any of them, there'd been Abby and Laurel. She'd met them in college. They'd clicked almost immediately, become a trinity, inseparable.

Then she'd lost Laurel to an abusive husband. And not right away, no. Instead, it had happened after a soul-shredding effort that came to nothing. That outcome had nearly destroyed Ros.

Without Abby, she wouldn't have gotten through it, found a way to heal her heart so that she could love the way she'd found with Lawrence.

That kind of love could give a woman the strength to pick up shield and sword, ready to fight the battles that before had seemed unwinnable.

Vera was right. Neil might just provide the key wildcard. Yes, his personality broadcast a marching drumbeat of *Dom, Dom, Dom*. But he'd engaged Abby's attention, and Ros would unapologetically make use of every ally for her friend's benefit.

Ros knew Vera was right about Abby's sense of isolation. Even as her closest friends, they still had an outsider's view of the future that had threatened Abby her entire life. But now that it was on the horizon, there was one thing Ros knew for certain.

Paranoid schizophrenia was an opponent that would test the will of whoever came up against it.

CHAPTER FIVE

As Neil pulled into the driveway of Abby's house, he asked himself again what he was doing here. Bastion, the deep-voiced guardian of the gate at the TRA offices, had told him she was out of town. A personal trip, to her great-uncle's place in Indiana.

He'd intended to surprise her, so had been disappointed, since he wouldn't be here long. But that was the personal life suck factor of being a SEAL. A biblical miracle was easier than keeping a predictable schedule. He'd reconciled himself to that some time ago. But he'd also never had a relationship serious enough to make it chafe like this.

That was changing, evident by his urgent need to see Abby. Yeah, okay, maybe a booty call had crossed his mind, but not in that shallow way. More like a hunger for a woman he wasn't in the mood to put off seeing a second longer than necessary.

Thirteen hours after grabbing that intel from the tunnels, they'd been sent back out. Because of the size of the op, a second team had coordinated with them. They'd breached the hideout of the high value target, secured him alive, and now the spooks had him. Twenty-four hours later, they were on their way back to VA Beach, Dodge telling them they had three days of down time, unless anything changed.

Which was why he loved having a pilot's license. Plus rich friends with access to a small fleet of planes. Matt Kensington had given him access to the Cessna single engine piston whenever he needed a quick trip home. It could get him to New Orleans in about an hour.

Peter Winston, the operations manager of Kensington & Associates, was the friend who'd made that happen. A National Guard captain who'd done tours in the Middle East, Peter liked giving back to his fellow servicemen.

Plus, Neil had had several really good nights at the poker table with him and Matt. Though in hindsight, Neil thought Matt might have put the offer on the table and let Neil win. The CEO of the successful global manufacturing company wasn't the type to have a losing hand that bad. But Max worked for him, too, and Matt had a close relationship with Ros, which meant Lawrence was on his radar. Matt Kensington took care of his people—and their friends.

With Abby absent, Neil had decided the next best thing was driving by her house and gathering external details about her. He figured he could locate the azalea she'd been talking about, see how it was doing. If it was in her backyard and she had an open gate, well, he might take a glance. She probably wouldn't mind that. Not too stalk-erish. Breaking into her house, smelling her clothes, lying in her bed; that would be stalking.

Truth, he just wanted to brush up against some sense of her while he was here, something to keep expanding the pictures he had of her in his mind. The nip of her waist and line of her back as she leaned forward to turn on the rain fixture, locks of her glossy red hair falling over her bare shoulder. The hint of her breast under her arm as she'd turned toward the phone. The way her toes pointed, and the glimpsed arch of her foot as she stepped into the shower.

Her smile, sweet or sexy. Tight, faint. Changing with whatever emotions passed through her gaze, like pages of a book he couldn't read fast enough, even as he wanted to slow it down, absorb every word.

He'd thought a whole lot about that mouth of hers. It was steadily becoming a test of wills, who'd ask for that kiss first. Without a word, she'd turned the tables on him. Those cat-like eyes held so much awareness of what went through a man's mind when he was thinking about a woman. Wanting a woman.

He wished he could fly up to Indiana. He'd played with that idea, particularly when Bastion had been so surprisingly forthcoming. Whether it was Lawrence's connection to Ros, and Neil's connection to Lawrence, or something else was happening, Neil seemed to have the blessing of the staff to spend time with Abby. No matter where she stood on it.

Which was a little odd, knowing how protective the women were of each other. Lawrence had told him a man didn't screw with any of those females, unless he wanted the whole flock to peck him to death.

I'm talking raptors, not chickens, bro. The kind that will rip off your tender bits and eat them in front of you while you're still alive.

Neil didn't know what he'd done to earn their stamp of approval, but he'd take it as one less hurdle to get what he wanted with her.

A fair chance.

She'd given him a couple slim openings, which made him more certain the Dom/sub stumbling block was a smoke screen. If that was all there was to it, their intriguing give-and-take dance would keep her in the game. They were both adults and responsible for their own feelings. If they hit a dead-end road, it would be only after they'd taken it as far as they were obviously interested in going.

A confident woman might put up certain defenses to be sure a man was earning her attention, or wasn't going to be a dick if she let him get skin close. He had limited leisure time, but he was always willing to give her that kind of assurance. Up until now, though, he hadn't had a lot of interest in getting deeper into a woman's head. But Abby's confusing signals had become a mystery he wanted to solve.

Without being stalkerish, he reminded himself. He didn't want his tender parts pecked, ripped *or* shredded.

She lived in a lower Garden District home, close to Coliseum Square. The pretty two-story was about twenty-five hundred square feet, built in the late 1800s. White clapboard, tall windows flanked by black shutters and crown molding. Ancient live oaks had moss and lichen-furred branches curving out twenty feet or more from their thick trunks, which were flanked by wild growing azaleas.

She took care of the house, but had preserved the aged look. She also didn't clutter it up. From his parked spot in the driveway, he saw a couple pots of red flowers resting on the step. The porch had a swing and two black painted rockers. The porch boards were painted gray, which gleamed in a way that told him they'd been done recently. The second story porch had a decorative iron railing between the large pillars that rose from the lower porch to support the brick-colored tinned roof.

A crumbling fountain was in the small front yard, a cherub with an upturned face perched on the bowl's edge. Since the fountain part no longer functioned, it served as a natural bird bath. Several mockingbirds were there, enjoying the collection from recent rains.

Her car was parked on the side of the house. It and a perimeter of those uninhibited azaleas partially screened an iron barred back fence. She must have taken a taxi to the airport.

As he parked behind the car and left his truck, he acted like he belonged here. He'd infiltrated far more difficult places than a gentrified New Orleans neighborhood, so wasn't worried about that.

The gate had metal scrollwork decorating the top. Through it and the screen of more azaleas he saw a slice of back porch. The gate didn't have a lock on it.

He'd put his hand on the latch, intending to take a quick glimpse of her backyard, find that azalea, when he caught movement through a side window. The thump of feet from within reached his ears before the back porch screen door creaked open. Something metal, with loose parts, landed on the porch with a resounding, clanking thump. The screen door closed with a free fall thud.

Maybe she was having some work done while she was gone. But where was the worker's vehicle, evidence of his tools or equipment? He could call Bastion and find out. Or he could ask the interloper himself, make sure it wasn't somebody trying to rob her place.

Since the attendees at that routine poker game often included a seasoned Baton Rouge police sergeant, Leland Keller, Neil had plenty of info on how thieves in the area might operate. The person in Abby's house could have an accomplice who'd dropped him off, so as not to attract attention. He'd toss the house, depositing his finds on the back porch. When ready, he'd text his partner in crime to return with a vehicle so they could load up.

Neil let himself in through the gate, cursing the inevitable squeak, but whoever had made the deposit on the back porch was back inside. He slid cautiously around the bushes. His gun had been in a holster inside his waistband, concealed by his loose T-shirt, but he had it drawn, held at his side where it wouldn't incite alarm if he merely discovered a maid service. One who'd ridden the trolley here, all the cleaning supplies provided in the house.

The raised hairs on his neck said differently. Something wasn't right.

Her neighbors were close, their upper story windows looking down into her backyard, but their blinds were closed, those subtle courtesies observed by those who lived on small lots in the coveted historic district.

He could hear static. As he eased forward and gained a wider view of the back porch, what he saw didn't provide him clear answers. Only more questions.

A pile of appliances. A toaster, blender. Mixer and bread maker. Not the kind of things someone risked a prison sentence to steal. He found the source of the static, a boombox. It was turned way up, but it wasn't playing music. The rush of noise was broken by the occasional blurted syllable as a station tried to break through.

Footsteps returning, uneven, then a female back pressed to the screen door as she used her body to open it. Her arms were full of a movie popcorn maker, the big rectangular kind with a bright red frame. She let it tumble out of her hands so it crashed to the porch boards, coming to a rest against the toaster with a discordant ring of metal meeting metal.

"Abby?"

He holstered his weapon and stepped from his concealment. As soon as he'd recognized her, he'd considered returning to the front porch and ringing the bell, so he didn't startle her. But she didn't seem startled. What she seemed was far more unsettling.

She'd turned slowly, almost shuffling. Looked at him. He saw no recognition in her expression. "It's a long way to say," she said. Her gaze roved briefly over his face, drifted away, then snapped down to the boombox.

Dropping to her knees next to it, she put her hands on either side of the machine. Rather than lifting it, she crouched down, bringing her ear to the side of the device. An easier look crossed her face. "There you are," she said. "You sent him to kill me, but he can't. I have you in the box. You can't get out."

She moved back onto her heels, looked at him again with a wary triumph. He could feel fear beneath the look. Her hand remained on the boombox, as if that was the key to keeping him and whatever she thought was inside it at bay.

Her hair was scraped into a tail, and looked lank, unwashed and unbrushed. No makeup. She wore an oversized T-shirt and old jeans, spattered liberally with dried mud. A short silk robe, the pretty floral thing he'd seen hanging up in her closet, was shrugged on over the T-shirt like an old car coat.

A smear of dried blood was on one of her bare feet. Probably from the slice on her arm, what looked like a nasty though fortunately superficial cut. It had congealed, but he could follow the track where the blood had dripped down, because it had stained her clothes and knuckles.

Those hazel eyes abruptly became laser focused. As she stared at him, he felt like she was sorting something. When she spoke, he realized it was his identity.

"Neil." She gave him a puzzled look. "You aren't here."

"I am," he said. "I got back to VA Beach yesterday and had a couple days, so I came home."

"Home." She looked around her. "Where is home?"

He was going to explain where he lived, but she continued, telling him her question hadn't been for him.

"Home is here, there, nowhere. No place to run and hide, Neil." For the first time she looked at him square on, and anguish was in her eyes, as if she were a prisoner staring at him from behind bars. "Run and hide, Neil. Go now."

She pivoted and was back in the house, the screen door slapping the frame. He heard her running feet, an ungainly stride. It sounded like she was heading up the stairs to the second level. She was also singing in a discordant, harsh tone, a tune he didn't recognize, but loud enough to drown out anything else. She mixed it up with odd words, bursts of sound amid the music.

He sure as fuck wasn't going anywhere, but it was clear help and reinforcements were needed. His heart was beating high in his chest, his throat was tight, and he had light perspiration on his back. Signs an op was headed in a seriously bad direction. He took out his phone.

He didn't call unless he needed something right away, so Lawrence answered. "Hey, amigo. You home?"

Based on the words Abby had just spoken, that question intensified his heart's painful drumbeat.

"In a sense. I'm at Abby's."

"She's in Indiana." Lawrence's regretful though mildly amused words said he deduced Neil had called to ask him Abby's whereabouts.

"No. She's not. She's here, and something's off with her." *A goddamn understatement.* He studied the pile of appliances. "Do you know what's up?"

Lawrence's pause spiked his blood pressure. Neil's hand tightened on the phone. "Tell me."

"It's not my information to give," Lawrence said.

"Fuck that, man. She's altered, talking like she's out of her head. She's got half her kitchen on the back porch, and looks like hell." Neil kept his voice flat. His *don't screw with me* tone. "She's not okay. Give me what I need to help her."

"Hold on." Lawrence's manner became as terse as Neil's. "I'm texting Ros. She and the rest of the TRA team are in a meeting in Baton Rouge. It may take her a second to respond, but I can have her pulled out of the meeting if she's shut off her phone. Is Abby okay for a couple minutes?"

"I'm with her. I'll make sure of it. I just need to know what I'm facing. Do I need to call an ambulance—"

"*No!*"

For all that she'd charged through the house like a marching army, she'd apparently crept back down the stairs like a ninja and had been listening. She came flying at the screen door, her eyes fierce as lightning bolts. She slammed the wooden door, locked the dead bolt and brandished the key at him through one of the narrow windows flanking the entryway. She was still yelling as he cautiously came up on the porch, stepping over the toaster and breadmaker.

"No white and red. Blood on the walls. No...hospital." She thrust out the last word with effort, glared with the victory. Only she wasn't looking at him. Her gaze was moving wildly over the porch, as if there was a team of doctors standing there, waiting with a net. "Do not pass go," she snarled. "Go home. You're not getting in. They're not getting out. I won't let them. I can't go. You can't kill me. It's trapped. It can't get out. I can't go."

She spun around and disappeared, feet pounding back through the house, up the stairs once again.

"Christ." Lawrence sounded startled. "Was that her?"

"Yeah. Shit. She's locked me out."

"Can you get in?"

"Is that a real question?"

"Sorry. Ros is responding, hold on... Confirming she thought Abby was in Indiana, too. She's getting out of the meeting now. She'll call me as soon as she's in the car."

It told Neil that Lawrence's text had properly conveyed the urgency of the situation, but he needed more. "You got thirty seconds to tell me what I can use to help Abby, and then I'm breaking into her house to get to her."

"Fucking hell." Lawrence blew out a breath. "Abby is probably in the prodromal stage of paranoid schizophrenia. She's suffering beginning symptoms, occasional hints of psychosis."

What the fuck?

Down range, Neil took the unexpected and catastrophic in stride. Getting hit with it at home was different. Lawrence's words spun up like a cyclone in his head, scattering everything else there.

Fortunately, he hadn't been home long enough to get out of that mission mindset. While it took several beats to manage the personal reaction, get it under control, the top priority asserted itself.

She needed help. That was the bite-sized piece, the way to start. Reflection would come later. As well as a serious-assed discussion with his friend, who'd obviously been aware of the situation.

Neil's gaze slid over the boombox that had "captured" the voices. "This isn't a hint of psychosis. This is a neon billboard. Is she on any meds?"

"I'll follow up with Ros. I'm not sure. When you go in, go easy and don't crowd her. Try to distract her from whatever she's obsessing over, figure out what might help calm her."

"Has she done this before?"

"No. But you remember what Leland said?"

Speak of the devil. The Baton Rouge PD sergeant he'd been thinking of only moments before.

"The training he took for psych-related calls." Lawrence continued, talking fast, even. Giving Neil what he needed. "Said it was mainly figuring out what was freaking the person out, getting them to calm down, while keeping them and those around them safe."

He heard another thump inside. She didn't seem inclined to leave the house, but he wouldn't discount that she might try another exit.

"Okay. Tell Ros to drive safe. Abby'll be fine until she gets here. I'll make sure of it."

"I'm out at the rec center, but soon as the other coach gets here, I'll head your way. I'll keep you posted on everything. Do the same when you can."

"Roger that." Neil pocketed the phone. It sure as hell filled in some missing puzzle pieces on her reluctance to get close to him. They'd deal with that. Only one thing mattered right now. Her well-being. How he felt about that told him just how much Abby already meant to him.

It was a standard dead bolt on a wooden door that opened inward. Aiming for the sweet spot to the left of the knob, he gave it the short, powerful kick that would force the deadbolt against the soft wood on the inside and shove through it.

The door opened with a sharp pop. He'd repair it for her.

Though he'd heard her go back up the stairs, he recalled how she'd snuck back to overhear his comment about an ambulance. As a result, he didn't make assumptions about her whereabouts. He was just glad she wasn't in the kitchen, because he didn't want him forcing the door to scare her.

As he moved into the living area, he gathered snapshots of his surroundings. Lots of warm colors, soft fabrics. A couple paintings in key spots. Very few knickknacks. Simple and uncluttered, matching the rooms he'd already seen.

The night of their call, it had seemed like she kept a clean house. That wasn't the case right now.

The area rug had been folded back. The mud he'd seen on her legs and clothes was also on a wide section of the pine floor. It looked as if she'd been using dirt dug out of her yard to mortar the hairline thin cracks between the boards.

A pet bed rested on one of the chairs. Lawrence had mentioned that Freak, Ros's cat, sometimes came to stay with Abby. Neil saw no evidence the cat was here, and hoped that was because he was at Ros's, not accidentally let out. Both women loved the eccentric feline.

He'd reached the steps. The dark wood matched the trim around the interior doors and windows. He stopped at the bottom stair, because he'd found her.

She was sitting on the step midway between the upper and lower floors. Her arms were wrapped around herself, and she was rocking, her head doing a light tattoo against the beadboard below the chair railing. She rested on it as she turned her gaze to him.

Oh, Abby. Only moments ago, he'd been recalling images of the woman who'd flirted with him, her eyes lit with the fires of sexual suggestion, confidence and pleasure.

But this was the same woman, and she was under attack. Just because it wasn't an enemy he could shoot didn't change the need to defuse the threat. The aching thought of what she was dealing with, all the implications of it, for her and for both of them, for her friends who loved her, wanted to push into his head and fuck with it.

He knew how to shut that out, take everything out of the equation that didn't help. He decided the best course of action was one used with jacked-up innocents caught in the crossfire, torn between siding with the enemy or his team.

"Can I come sit with you?" he asked.

At the sound of his voice, her attention moved up the walls, down, like she was following a fly's track. She picked at the cracks between the bead board slats. The only place her gaze didn't go was to him, to meet his eyes. But after a long moment, she nodded. "The floor is stable here," she said. "The walls thick. No cracks." She reached up, flattened her palm against it, next to her head, just above where her temple pressed to the beadboard and chair rail. "They can't get in. If they get out, they can't get in."

He came up the steps, moving slow and careful, and took a seat on the stair just below her, bracing his back against the balustrades.

His team had talked about his propensity for quiet. Not silence. Quiet. They were two different things. He didn't need words most the time. Didn't clutter his head with a lot of ponderings. Which meant, when he did need words, what made the most sense to say came to him easier than most.

On one operation, he'd been trapped in a room with a suicide bomber, one of those you-can't-make-this-shit-up things where the door accidentally got barricaded from the outside, locking them in together. They were there for two hours. The man was currently an informant for them, with hopes to live in America, away from the violent life he'd once thought was his only choice.

"I saw the mud you used to mortar the floor cracks. Was some of that left over from transplanting the azalea?"

Pause. Blink. Pause. "Yes." Her voice had a flat sonorous quality. "Nothing can come through the cracks now."

"Smart. I didn't get a chance to see the azalea. Maybe you can give me a tour of the yard later."

His phone buzzed, and she drew up her legs, cringed back. "The voices come through the machines," she said. "They'll get in if you let them."

"This is my phone, and it's secured," he said easily. "I'm a SEAL, remember?"

Her expression cleared, then she seemed to relax a little. "You mind if I read this text?" he asked. "It's probably from Lawrence."

"Will you tell me what it says? Or will you hide, run and hide."

"I'll show it to you." He glanced down at the text. *Bottle of meds in her nightstand. Offer two pills. Ros says Abby put it there as backup, in case this happened. 30 min for effect to kick in. If it works.*

He offered her the phone and she cringed away from it again, shuddering. Tucking it away, he kept the same even tone. "Lawrence says you put a medicine in your nightstand to help you feel better. Do you want me to get you a glass of water so you can take it?"

She gazed down at her hands. Her eyes moved past him, up, down, then straight ahead. At the park, she'd seemed to take pleasure in locking gazes with him. But not that night on the phone. He'd thought it was just evidence of her struggle against giving him too much encouragement. There'd also been a couple pauses that hadn't made total sense, echoes of the much longer ones she was doing now.

Hell. She'd already been showing symptoms then, and he hadn't known. He wanted to tear Lawrence a new one for leaving him out of the loop. But Ros and Lawrence's reaction to her being here instead of in Indiana suggested they hadn't realized things had gotten this bad, either. Whenever Abby had given Ros that info about the pills, Neil wondered how she'd managed to do it without arousing Ros's suspicions about what Neil suspected Abby had already seen coming.

"The magic pill. No red lights. Only a red haze. Red lights or red haze. Still blood leaking out my ears." She rose. When she swayed, he was on his feet in an instant, reaching out, bracing his foot on the step next to her, a block to keep her from tumbling down the stairs. She stumbled up one step, staring at the outstretched hand as if it were a striking snake.

He quelled the reflex to draw back, instead holding it in the air between them. "I wanted to steady you. Have you eaten?"

"My brain. Something ate my brain. It must have been me, because I'm not hungry." She laughed then, with such a note of despair, he had to clench his fists not to draw her to him. But then she reached out carefully, pinched his hand between her thumb and forefinger. He kept it still, passive, as she turned it over, looked at it closely, then interlaced their fingers. Her hand was cold, dry. Mud in the creases of her palm rubbed against his, but he was glad for the ability to have a grip on her.

"Good fit. Knot tied. Ready to fly."

She turned and headed up the stairs, keeping their hands clasped so that it turned her arm across her body. He kept his other hand open and poised behind her, since she was treading heavily, her weight rocking forward and to the side, like a chair with one leg shorter than the other.

The things she was saying, while unusual in their presentation, made some sense. Maybe she knew what she was trying to say, and was working around her altered mind to communicate it.

As they reached the landing, she stopped. "Mohammed reached the top of the mountain," she informed the walls. "The journey was where he lost his map."

Testing his theory, he spoke the reminder. "We're going to your bedroom to get the medicine you left there."

That stillness, a delay in response. Processing, he realized. Like a computer with an overload of data to sift. She dropped his hand and turned toward the bedroom, shuffling. She was muttering to herself again.

When she reached the doorway, she abruptly pivoted and shoved at him, both hands smacking his chest. He didn't grab at her, held his arms out to his sides, but before he finished the no-harm gesture, she'd darted inside the bedroom and slammed the door.

He could have put his foot inside the threshold before she managed that. But with her obvious need to feel safe, a different way might be better. While he could open this door with a slim piece of plastic if needed, he held off, keeping his ear tuned to what was going on.

Muttering. She was by the door, and a familiar staccato beat told him she was doing that rocking and gentle beat of her head against it again. A rustle and he was pretty sure she'd slid down to sit against it.

He settled himself on the other side. "I've missed you, Abby," he said. "I'm glad to see you."

A pause. He glanced down at a movement and saw three of her fingers sliding into view, under the crack of the door. He put his own next to them, stroked one of hers lightly. It twitched, but she didn't pull away. "Hey there," he said. "Do you want a cup of water to take your medicine?"

"No. A pebble dropped in a tornado becomes a bullet."

His heart twisted at the weariness in her voice. "Can you let me in, Abby? I want to help."

Another pause, a rustle. He rose as the doorknob twisted, the panel opening a few inches. She was moving away from it, so he pushed it open. She sat down on her bed, next to the nightstand. Stared at the drawer.

He came across the room, opened it, watching her to gauge her reaction to his movements. She crossed her arms over herself and rocked.

Inside the drawer, he saw a pill bottle in the corner. It was flanked by a couple paperbacks, a gull's feather tied with a blue ribbon, and a pair of police issue handcuffs.

He took out the bottle, heard the rattle. There were no dosage instructions, so it was a good thing Lawrence had been specific. He shook two out in his hand.

"Sure you don't want water?"

She glanced at him and, after an expectant pause, where she stared at his shoulder as if she'd answered him, he realized she maybe thought she had. Interpreting it as a *yes*, he went into her bathroom. She had an insulated plastic cup by the sink, blue sparkling water and tiny floating fish figures caught inside the insulation for decoration.

He filled the cup with water and returned to her. She'd stopped rocking, but was tapping a foot, her palm moving back and forth over the bedspread. Though her gaze remained on her hand, she drew back again at his approach, telling him she was tracking him in her peripheral vision. He placed the water on the nightstand, the pills next to it.

"Just as the Mistress ordered," he said.

That got a response. Her gaze flickered, and he dropped to a knee in front of her, the nightstand and its contents to his left. Since he had his hand resting on the nightstand, her attention followed his arm to the cup and pills.

When it lingered there, he picked up the pills, extended them to her in an open palm. She cupped his hand in both of hers like it was a bowl. Slowly, she brought it up to her face, closed her lips over the medication, the softness of her flesh pressed against his rough palm. He had to resist the overwhelming urge to lift his other hand, cup it over her skull in a gesture of protective comfort, give in to his need to touch her, hold her.

She lifted her head, dropped it back. His gaze slid over her throat as she swallowed.

Only then did she take the water. She drank several swallows, paused, then drank the rest, thirstily. Her body had recognized what it needed, and confirmed what he'd thought from her hollow-eyed look. She was dehydrated.

She left the bed, crossed the room. Paced it three times, then set the cup on the floor. Folding herself down next to it on her side, she curled around the cup, tapping the glass to make the sparkles and fish in the trapped blue water move.

Picking up a stool next to the bed, he brought it near her. As he sat down on it, she scooted into a different position, still curved around the cup. While it put her back toward him, it also put her closer to him.

After a moment, she lifted herself to a sitting position. A slight shift put her between his knees. A quiet sigh, and she dropped her head on his thigh. Surprised, he tentatively began to stroke her hair, with more confidence as she let out a little hum, blew out another exhausted breath.

"Long road. Long row. Short life." She sounded more herself, but he thought it was too soon for the meds to kick in. She was rocking against him again, self-comfort.

"I'm here," he said. "We're here, Abby. You're not alone."

"The shadows won't go away now. They think I don't know they're there all the time. I'm smarter than them. Not stronger, though. Not faster. And there are a lot more of them. Hopeless, really."

She didn't seem to want to say anything else. When he leaned forward enough to see her face, he saw her eyes were closed, shrouded by locks of limp hair that had fallen forward along her cheek. She started muttering again as she rocked, but she seemed less agitated. Perhaps the action of taking the pills had calmed her some, even before they took effect. Offering some sense of control.

As he kept stroking her hair, her shoulder, he glanced around, drew in additional details. More dark wood molding and trim around the windows, white plaster walls. The historic house scent mixed with fresh laundry smell from her linens, an undercurrent he associated with her normal female fragrance.

The tiny flowers on the white comforter were blue and yellow, matching those two drawings on the wall. She'd put a fresh bouquet of wildflowers in the dresser vase. All normal things, until one noted the wardrobe. It had been padlocked with a thick chain. Since there was dirt on the floor beneath the padlock, and the chain was rusty, oversized for the job, he suspected she'd dug it out of her garden shed. The wardrobe was probably an entertainment center, with TV and other electronics.

Her walk-in closet was closed. A metal chair he recognized from the outdoor patio set was propped beneath the doorknob.

He moved his touch to her shoulder, massaged slowly, his thumb passing over her nape beneath the curtain of unwashed hair. Hair that normally smelled like sunshine and that lavender laundry smell.

"When you feel better," he said, "I'm going to take you out in the bayou on my boat. Let you meet a couple of my friends. It's quiet there, and sunny. I think you'd like it."

She paused the rocking. Slowly, her fingers curled over his knee. Uncurled. Curled. "Maybe, baby. I'll have you."

His throat tightened at the singsong tone, but he managed a smile. "Yeah, you might. Buddy Holly." He hummed the next words, giving her back more of the same. "Think it over."

"Let me know. Don't be slow."

"You're full of surprises, dream girl. Let's dance."

She lifted her head, gazed at him. Her eyes shifted away in a blink, but it was the first time she'd made any real eye contact with him. He rose, grasping her hand, lifting her up. She felt too insubstantial. He wanted to feed her, get more fluids in her, but when she went along with his crazy idea to dance, he decided not to rush it. He'd settle for believing they'd made a step forward.

He held her secure in his arms, and she leaned against him as he swayed. He crooned the lyrics to "Maybe Baby" in her ear, and she began to hum along with him. As he turned them in slow circles, she buried her nose in his shirt. While she mumbled the occasional word, eventually she started matching more of them, bringing together full lyrics, cycling through them, a slowly turning circle around a point that was becoming more fixed.

"Do me a favor?" he murmured.

She nodded against his chest. She'd responded more quickly that time, less of a processing pause. "When your head clears," he said, "don't pull away from me, okay? No need for that kind of nonsense between us."

He wasn't sure if it penetrated, but her hands were scraping against his arm, still doing some of that repetitive motion thing, but it was halting every once in a while, before starting back up again.

"Lay down Sally."

"Clapton's vocal skills are a little beyond my range," he said, but he understood. He guided her to the bed, and she wilted onto it. She refused the covers, but pulled one of the pillows against her so she could hug it to her body. Her gaze touched him once more, lingered an additional second, then the hazel eyes closed, and she turned her face to the pillow.

He pulled a chair close and watched over her. As her breath became even, her body seemed to melt further into the mattress. All that rigid energy disappeared, exhausted.

When he heard the door open downstairs, he rose. As he left the room, he gave his charge one more look. He knew it might be a few days before she'd be okay seeing him again. He'd probably have to push for it.

He could do that. He'd told her he'd take her out on his boat, and she hadn't said no. So he'd proceed as if that had been a yes. But he had some thinking to do, for sure. And he needed more info.

Leaving the room, he headed downstairs to get it.

CHAPTER SIX

Getting that information proved more difficult than expected. Lawrence wasn't unwilling to provide it, but he wanted to wait for Ros. Then, when Ros arrived, she rightly insisted on going upstairs to check in with Abby before having any substantive conversation.

Upon her return, she stood on the bottom step and reported Abby was already demonstrating more normal behavior. Enough that she'd asked Ros to thank Neil—and tell him to leave.

"She's issuing orders," Lawrence said with careful amiability. "Proof she's coming back to herself."

"I thought so," Ros agreed, though her gaze didn't leave Neil's frozen expression.

No. He wanted to stay close in case she needed his protection and care. And to assure himself she was okay.

It didn't take a genius to interpret the reaction. Alpha male plus woman he cared about in distress. But it also didn't take a genius to understand Abby's demand, which Ros indicated had been adamant. Urgent.

Hell, he'd recognized it himself earlier. They'd barely started a relationship—she hadn't even acknowledged it was one. Him staying when she'd made it clear she didn't want him witnessing her struggle to put herself back together wasn't going to help it progress. This was hell and gone past showing up and surprising her in her pajamas and fuzzy slippers, with uncombed hair and no makeup.

Her best friend was here, with Lawrence for backup. The episode was passing. Even so, Neil sent Ros a resolute look.

"I'll be back. She's not going to shut me out."

"That's up to her." Ros's met him look for look, her own reflecting her Domme side, as well as the kickass CEO. She also didn't hold back on the brutal honesty. "But whatever decisions are yours, Neil, be sure you mean them. It's early enough that no one's feelings are too involved. After this, she's going to push back against you hard, and she'll mean that, a hundred percent. Spend some time thinking about how far you want to take this."

"Are you pulling for me?" It was a stupid question; he knew it as soon as the words left his mouth. Ros's response was no surprise.

"I'm pulling for her." But then she sighed. "Later this week, we'll be meeting a psychotherapist. The whole team, and Lawrence. Abby is unaware of the meeting."

She raised a hand, stopping his reaction before she explained. "It was my hope to inform her ahead of time, but because of this and other factors I'm not prepared to discuss right now, I'm not going to. I *will* tell her after the fact, but it's specifically for us, those of us trying to support and help her in the best way possible."

"Asking forgiveness, not permission."

"Yes. We need professional guidance at this stage, and we're not making any decisions for Abby herself at the meeting. That's how I'm rationalizing it." Her expression slipped, showing her personal struggle with it. "This woman comes highly recommended. I hope like hell it's warranted."

She met Neil's gaze. "If you want to be there, to listen, to help you make your own decisions, you're welcome. Lawrence will text you the time and date."

Ros and her people, Abby's *de facto* family, were one thing. He had mixed feelings about him being there without her knowledge. But if nothing was pending for his team, he could wrangle another day or two out of Dodge. "Do you think having me in her life will hurt her?" He wouldn't let himself shrink from asking the question.

"Only if you're not the kind of man I think you are." Her half smile was pained, though. "Everything can hurt her, Neil. She's said it's like being in a tornado. Never knowing what's going to hit you or where it's going to take you."

A pebble in a tornado becomes a bullet. She'd said that about her meds.

Ros turned to go back up the steps. Stopped on the second one, leaning over the banister to Lawrence to have one of those wordless conversations that bonded couples did. He closed his hand over hers, kissed her knuckles as she put her other palm on his jaw. The pain Ros was carrying showed starkly in her gaze, but it didn't change the resolve Neil saw there. If he wanted a warrior in Abby's corner, he was looking at proof that Abby had more than one.

"Ros." He drew her attention. "I told her I was going to take her out on my boat. Tomorrow too soon?"

"That's up to her, too. But my opinion? Day after would probably be better. It'll give her more time to raise walls between you, but I expect you can handle those. Just like doors." With a rueful smile, she glanced toward the kitchen. "She'll be expecting you to pay for the repairs."

"Done and covered. I'm a good handyman."

That same tight smile, and she started up the stairs. "Lawrence will keep you in the loop. You and she can take it from there."

Lawrence's gaze followed her. Neil knew he was logging everything about his Mistress's state of mind as she dealt with this. Most of his life, Neil hadn't needed that kind of close bond with a woman. He'd had plenty other priorities. He wasn't opposed to it; he just believed such a thing came to a man at its own pace.

His interactions with Abby had been few in actual number, but every one of them had included an exceptional level of intensity. Sexual, emotional. Spiritual.

Some people might scoff at talk of destiny, but he wasn't one of them. He'd had his ass saved too many times by unlikely combinations of fate, timing and luck.

As Ros reached the top of the stairs, Neil bit back the impulse to remind her that Abby needed fluids and food. If she wanted to bathe, Abby would need to sit on one of those benches in her big shower, have someone watch over her. She wasn't steady on her feet.

Ros had powers of observation, same as he did.

If it had been up to him, he would have been in the shower with Abby, letting her lean against him as he washed her hair, stroked his fingers through it. He'd hope that the care, the contact, would be reassuring. She could close her eyes, let the tension slip out of her muscles as she gave herself over to his hands.

Given her current feelings about him being here, she'd probably be horrified by the idea. It would take a lot of perseverance to convince her otherwise.

He had plenty of that to give to her. Whereas he had zero patience for staying down here, standing on the sidelines. Fortunately, his former teammate knew him pretty well.

"Come on, brother." Lawrence nudged him away from the stairs. "Abby's got some scrap lumber in her garden shed. Let's fix the door so our ladies are safe, then we'll head over to the DH, have a beer. It's close enough we'll be near if Ros or Abby needs us. Okay?"

It wasn't a request, but Neil appreciated that Lawrence made it sound that way.

"Okay."

~

The DH was short for Dale's house, but it also had a couple other names. Decompression hut or "down home." The opposite of down range.

Dale lived with his wife Athena at the home she and her late husband had shared, a sprawling mansion compound on the outskirts of New Orleans. However, before they'd met, Dale's needs had been met by a matchbox-sized house in a poor New Orleans neighborhood, inhabited by elements who routinely boosted the city's monthly crime stats. A retired Master Chief, Dale had preferred being a stable force in an often unstable area.

After he and Athena married, he'd kept the little house. It had become an informal gathering space for cookouts, poker games. A place for an active SEAL like Neil to hang out with others who understood the transition that had to happen from active duty to down time.

Normally after taking the plane from VA Beach, he'd go home, take a few hours out on his boat to remind himself where he was and let the differences in his environment sink in. But if he'd had a particularly rough time down range, he'd come here first, meet with

Lawrence, Max, Dale, whoever was available, just hang out some. Then go do the boat thing.

Max's woman, Janet, referred to it as a SEAL club house, teasing them about secret passwords, junk food and a stack of girlie magazines.

While there were no girlie magazines or passwords, the fridge always had beer in a variety of flavors, and the cabinets overflowed with snacks and quick meals. Since Dale's marriage, the offerings had expanded. Athena now handled the pantry stocking, her way of showing her deep fondness for Dale's former teammates.

When Neil and Lawrence arrived, they snagged a beer and headed out to the back porch. The brightly painted metal chairs rocked on their bases, helping a man having trouble sitting still adopt a more relaxed rhythm of motion.

The decision to go to her before anywhere else meant he'd arrived on her doorstep in a mindset capable of handling a crisis situation. But now, the post-mission restlessness was hitting him, mixed with a WTF revelation about a woman he had serious feelings for. He wasn't in the mood for relaxation.

He sat forward, elbows on his knees, his beer dangling from his fingertips as he gazed at Dale's small but well-tended backyard. A crop of wooden birdhouses was planted in the beds of mixed flowers and ornamentals. An avid woodworker, Dale always had a few extras to give away to neighbors who wanted them.

It was only early afternoon, the sun brightly shining. He wondered if the shadows that deviled Abby so intently had shut out his own awareness of the light until he'd emerged from her house.

He wanted to be back by her side. But it wasn't about what he wanted.

When they'd arrived at the DH, two kids had been playing in the front yard. They knew Dale's was a safe space, even when he wasn't there. Though frequent visits from friends like Neil, Max and Lawrence reinforced it, Dale was a scary fucker when you crossed him. Plus he had cameras on all approaches to the house. If someone stepped on his lawn with bad intentions, they'd regret it.

Another reason the house was considered a refuge was the cook-outs he routinely held here, so well attended that they spilled out into the street out front. He invited members of the NOLA PD to the events, increasing community outreach between law enforcement and the residents.

Some things were tough problems but had solutions. Those solutions might require building trust, figuring out how to connect different personalities, but that was doable, as long as people were willing to make the effort.

The scenario they'd left at Abby's house wasn't so straightforward.

Waiting out Neil's thought process, Lawrence had said almost nothing. As he sipped his beer, he had his foot braced on one of the cinder blocks stacked around the patio, probably intended for some other project Dale was doing. A placid-looking toad rested inside the opening of the block.

"So." Neil kept his gaze on the birdhouses as he spoke. A finch of some kind emerged, darted off. "Back when I got interested in Abby, Max and Dale egged me on. But you seemed reserved about it. This was why."

"Yeah." Regret briefly gripped Lawrence's features. "Rosalinda knew I was going to tell you when you got home this time, if Abby didn't, because of how things seemed to be changing. But before then, I couldn't. It didn't seem right, and she asked me not to, to respect Abby's privacy."

Neil was irritated, but he understood the logic. "How'd Ros feel about you telling me this time?"

"She listened, agreed. You pissed?"

"I would have preferred not to be broadsided by it," Neil said. "But this obviously took you two by surprise, too. This hasn't happened before, has it?"

"Far as we know." Lawrence's troubled green gaze was a reminder this wasn't happening to just Abby and Ros. The five women who made up the executive management of TRA were family, and Lawrence was part of that family now.

"I'm sorry, Munch."

Lawrence had earned the nickname in the teams, thanks to his shorter stature and compact musculature. The height often misled opponents, who realized too late he was as difficult to stop as a tank.

Lawrence's expression tightened. "Abby doesn't deserve this shit."

"No. She doesn't." Neil leaned back and adjusted the chair so he was half turned toward Lawrence, an ankle resting on the opposite knee. "Give me what details you can."

Unlike Ros, Lawrence didn't ask him if his intentions toward Abby warranted a full read-in. Neil wouldn't ask the question otherwise.

"Abby's mom had it. So did her grandmother. Abby took care of her mom through hers, when she was still a kid."

From her vague but brutal assessment of her childhood, Neil had assumed addiction. He'd missed the mark. "Shit."

"Yeah. Her mom took care of her grandmother through the same thing. A late onset like this, without much in the way of early indicators, is really rare. For all three of them, it started in their thirties. Both mom and grandma were resistant to the meds available at the time. Even when a paranoid schizophrenic isn't resistant to meds, it takes a while to figure out the best combination, and that can change over time. Abby's mom didn't help by balancing hers with alcohol and recreational drugs."

Okay, so not completely off the mark. "Sounds like you've been studying up."

"Ros has been keeping herself on top of the latest research for a while. She hoped it would never happen, that it would skip Abby, but she didn't want to be behind the curve if it didn't. I brought myself up to speed."

"When did they start noticing...what did you call it?"

"The prodromal stuff." A shadow crossed Lawrence's face. "A while back, Abby started having nightmares, where she thought voices were talking to her from the shadows. Together she and Ros were able to realize—at least at that time—they were just nightmares, caused by Abby's fear of the disease taking hold. Once she woke up, turned on the lights, everything was okay."

Lawrence ran a hand along the back of his corded neck, kneaded tense muscles. "They happened pretty regularly once she passed her mother's onset age and headed toward her grandmother's. Then Abby stopped calling. Ros assumed that meant she was handling them better, or having less of them."

Lawrence sighed. "Now she believes Abby realized when they crossed the line, from fear of the delusion into the delusion itself. She chose to conceal the change as long as she could."

Neil gripped the bottle in a tense hand. "I thought she was putting me off because of the Domme thing."

"She was, initially." Lawrence dipped his head. "Being a Domme is something she really loves. It feeds her soul. And man, the way she handles a sub at Progeny is a work of art."

Though he was dedicated to his Mistress, Lawrence let his honest appreciation of it show. "Abby realized right off she felt something deeper for you, so it set off both concerns. First, that you two wouldn't be able to work out the Dom stuff, and second, that she'd pull you down a path she's determined not to take anyone. Not past a certain point."

Lawrence took another swallow of his beer. "Ros has tried to convince her to get officially diagnosed. Once that's done, she can look at different meds and psychotherapy options, but so far she's having none of it."

"So how did she get the meds I gave her?" Neil frowned.

"When Abby told Ros about them, as a backup measure, she told her she had a source, and that it was a med that sort of worked for her mom. She wouldn't say anything more about it, though."

"Christ. And Ros was okay with that?"

"What do you think?" Lawrence gave him a sharp look. "If Ros pushes too hard on any of this, Abby shuts her down, shuts her out. Ros already thinks that's why she's hidden some of this stuff from her."

His gaze locked with Neil's, held. "It's hard to be with someone who has a serious problem, Neil. If that person won't get help, it becomes worse than that."

Neil pulled himself back from the emotions Lawrence had provoked, studied his friend. "That's another reason why you didn't want to push me toward Abby. You were thinking of Valentina."

The eight years Lawrence had spent with her had been an exercise in despair. She'd get better for a time, then fall right back into her alcoholism. It hadn't helped that, like many addicts, she'd had a manipulative personality that became a toxic mix with Lawrence's determination to help. To fix.

Even when he'd managed at last to end the romantic part of their relationship, his SEAL brothers had feared he'd lost a piece of his heart and soul he'd never get back. Instead, he'd found those pieces with Rosalinda Thomas, and become whole again. Seeing him heal under the respect and love of a Mistress who adored him meant Ros had earned the steadfast loyalty of Lawrence's teammates.

Even if Neil and Ros clashed over other things, that wouldn't change.

"Bringing you into the loop about Abby, it doesn't mean you really understand it," Lawrence said. "It's like saying you know what a war zone is like from reading a book."

"It's different from Valentina," Neil said.

"Alcoholism is a disease. So is schizophrenia."

"Both can be managed." Though Neil knew he was talking out his ass, because he'd never even read an Internet synopsis of the illness.

Lawrence didn't point out that obvious fact, but he did point out another even less welcome one. "No matter how tough the road is, an addict who gets their addiction under control can eventually manage their own life, have a degree of independence without too much oversight. You look at the statistics on schizophrenics, and under fifty percent can live independently. The more unpredictable or resistant the patient is, mentally or physically, to the meds or the treatment plans, the lower that percentage gets. And if Abby's mom and grandmother are an indication, then her chances of falling in that range are damn high."

"You're still trying to talk me out of this. Why?"

Lawrence leaned forward, stared at the backyard. "No, I'm not. Not exactly. I just don't want you to jump off the cliff before you know everything. There are a couple other things I'm still not telling you."

Neil stared him down. "Any reason you're holding back?"

Lawrence's green eyes were serious. "Ros hasn't told the others, either. She will at the psychotherapist meet. She wants you to hear it all, figure out how you feel after that." Though his expression was still tense, he bumped a closed fist lightly on the top of Neil's leg before leaning back and returning his foot to the cinderblock.

"I'm not being an asshole. This is a lot already, and it gets worse. Go out on your boat, think it over. When a relationship turns into a shitshow, most people have already invested enough time they're willing, for better or worse, to risk their lives, their heart and soul, to defend what they hold dear. Doing something that matters for the long haul takes a full commitment from all three of those things."

Lawrence exchanged a knowing look with him. "You and I know that. Better than most."

~

Since he couldn't do anything else for now, Neil took Lawrence's advice. He drove to the parish where he lived, about forty-five minutes outside New Orleans. Stopped at the contract post office to pick up his mail, got to his place, threw some clothes in the wash. Then he sat on his weathered dock, drinking a Pepsi he'd picked up at the bait shop on his way in.

He cleared his mind, listened to the familiar swamp creatures warble, click, buzz and chirp. At length, he got up, threw the lines off his battered aluminum fishing boat, started up the reasonably quiet, well-maintained motor, and headed into the estuaries formed by the Mississippi delta.

As he steered through the tranquil gloom of a cypress forest, past the lazy eyes of gators resting on piles of fallen branches and foliage, he let the reality of the place sink into him. This wasn't a safe place, but because he knew how to react and anticipate his environment, he could find peace here. If a man had the right information and experience, could plan ahead, he could usually manage any situation. Even the outright suckfests.

Like what she was facing.

He wondered if Abby would be angry that Ros had let Lawrence tell him what he had. She might be, but no matter what, Neil was sure of one thing. If he did nothing further, she'd shut him out of her life, as abruptly as she'd slammed that door in his face.

Should he let her?

He expected the automatic roar of denial, his very core offended that his mind had suggested the question. That was the reaction of any male who'd ever wanted to play the hero to a woman he cared about. But this wasn't helping a woman change a flat tire, or rescuing her from the overly pushy drunken guy in the bar who didn't understand the words "not interested."

He didn't know jack about the details of paranoid schizophrenia, but he knew it was something no one wanted to hear a doctor say to them. A severe, lifelong mental illness.

She needed friends, a strong support network. What she didn't need was a guy dicking with her heart and libido. She'd tried to warn him, push him away, probably for that very reason. But as strong and practical a woman as she was, she hadn't managed to completely convince herself to close that door.

When everything else was going to shit, wouldn't it be nice to have one person who kept pursuing her as a desirable woman? Maybe.

There was a more important question. Was he up for this? Was anyone?

Did it make a difference?

He wasn't asking the right questions.

Shutting off the boat and letting it drift, he did something he never did while he was out here. He took out his phone to surf the Net. Typing with one thumb, he hit search.

Paranoid schizophrenia.

While skimming online articles wasn't going to give him everything he needed, it was a place to start.

A fragmenting of the brain...

It was a disease that scuttled brilliant minds, derailed lives. Artists, mathematicians. Rich, poor. It didn't give a shit. Some people experienced visual hallucinations, but mostly it was auditory. The illness disrupted the brain's normal communication pathways, turning words into seeming gibberish. Concentrating on daily tasks, everything from a busy job to basic daily hygiene, could become challenging. Overwhelming.

Low stimulation, an easy pace, taking things a moment at a time, one thing at a time, helped a person suffering from schizophrenia stay away from or head off psychotic episodes, though it didn't always prevent them.

He looked at the quiet world around him, devoid of people, work, everything but a drifting peace. Maybe she could find that here, too.

A shadow that had been hanging over her for most of her life had arrived. Was it like facing the death of a beloved family member, only in this case, it was her sense of herself that was dying? Slipping through her fingers.

Denial, anger, bartering, depression, acceptance. Normal human reactions to almost every fucked-up thing life could throw at a person. If he could be part of what got her past those, maybe she'd seek the assistance that could help her manage this shit. And accept the support she needed from the people who cared about her.

But if he was going to help, he had to get her past any bullshit hang-ups about him having seen what he had. To get her to go out on his boat with him, he had to treat her as she'd want to be treated.

He just had to figure out what that meant to her.

Lawrence had said she loved being a Domme, and Neil had picked up on that himself, when he asked her questions about it. Maybe...

Stopping, he realized he wasn't doing what Lawrence had suggested. Look into his own heart, and see if this was a road Neil really wanted to go down. Or if he should back off.

Problem was, he'd looked into his heart and found her. That was its own answer. The first and most important one.

The morning after her episode, Abby proved to Ros she was okay. Fighting off the fatigue that felt like a dump truck had dropped a pile of manure on her, she made them breakfast. Nothing more complicated than toast and scrambled eggs, yes, but she did it. Then she handed Ros her briefcase and told her to get her ass to work.

"Someone has to run the place," she told her friend. "I'll work from home, send the numbers for tomorrow's staff meeting. I'll take it easy. It's okay."

Ros gave her a searching look. The previous night, after she'd gotten Abby in the shower, bullied her into eating something, she'd returned to her broken record lecture. All the things Abby should be considering. Psychotherapy, drug regimens, an openness to all the improvements and advancements in the treatment of schizophrenia.

Nothing could tune out Ros when she was determined. She'd prodded Abby for input. *What do you think of trying this? Of doing that?*

Because she'd put them through a day of hell, and she didn't have the strength for it, Abby hadn't argued with her. She'd simply kept shaking her head, stared out the window. The world was spinning a little, her mouth was dry. Waves of nausea came and went. Side effects of the drug she'd taken, she knew, nothing too awful. At least the voices were back to muttering in the shadows, and when she talked, her words came out in strings of coherent dialogue.

Eventually, Ros stopped talking. She sat on the couch next to her, stroked her hair. Abby stretched out, laid her head on her friend's thigh, closed her eyes, and let the world spin off as she gave in to exhaustion. Ros sighed, put her arm over her, and Abby felt her lips brush her crown. As well as the tremble of frustration and pain in the gesture.

"Goddamn stubborn bitch."

"Pot. Kettle." Eyes still closed, Abby squeezed Ros's leg. Her heart ached, another symptom of the force battering her mind and soul. She was tearing her friend apart, but she wouldn't deviate from the track she'd long ago realized she had to follow.

"You lied to me," Ros said. "You knew it had changed."

"I lied to myself," Abby corrected. "I didn't want it to be true, and telling you would have made it more true."

One good thing about having a friend who knew her so well was the understanding. Ros hadn't said anything else. Just stroked Abby's shoulder and let her drift.

Now, as Ros stood before her, giving her that penetrating look, Abby leaned in, held her briefly. "It's okay," she repeated. "Really. Please go to work."

Ros set her jaw, her blue eyes worried. "Text me every couple hours. Every hour would be preferable."

"Don't lose your shit and send in the National Guard if I don't. I might take a long nap after I do the numbers."

"Text me that when you do. I'll bring dinner tonight."

"Fine. But it'll be a drop off. Afterward, you go home. I'm not keeping you from Lawrence two nights in a row."

"You didn't." Ros moved toward the back door. "He slept on the couch last night. He headed to work from here." Lawrence worked as a coach at the local youth recreation center.

"That's not the same as being with him at home."

"It was better." Ros shot her a look. "We had the most intense scene in your living room that any club dungeon has ever seen. Sex so incendiary we left scorch marks on your walls."

"Uh-huh." Abby tried to smile to acknowledge the effort. But the shadows under Ros's eyes were from a different kind of sleepless night.

Her friend put down the briefcase, came back over. Ros coming at her with such a determined stride was startling, but Abby managed to contain the flinch, settling when Ros captured and squeezed her hand once more, hard.

"See you in a bit."

"Yeah." Abby watched her pick up the case and depart, close the repaired door. The molding would need painting, but otherwise it was good as new. Neil and Lawrence were a good handyman team.

As Ros headed down the steps to her Mercedes, Abby moved to the side window and waved like a normal person while her friend backed out. Then she sidled over to the door and put her hand on the door frame. Was her palm resting on a place Neil had been the last to touch?

That thought wouldn't help anything. Returning to the counter, she poured her third cup of coffee, then made herself go straight to her computer. Just walking there was tiring, a warning. Depression closed in after a psychotic episode. In a few hours she'd likely lose the motivation to do anything.

Yes, the numbers kept sliding off the screen and falling onto her desk, but she took another dose of the meds, made them return to their proper place, and got through it. Before she sent the file to the office, she checked the numbers three times to be sure she hadn't fucked them up.

After that, she put her head down on the desk and took a nap to give her the energy to get out of the chair, make it back to the couch. On her way there, she remembered she needed to text Ros, tell her she was diving into that nap.

She discovered she had a handful of texts. From Vera, Cyn and Skye. Bastion. A couple from Neil. She didn't read any of them. The letters weren't behaving any better than the numbers, and watching them move made her queasy again.

She did text her source for the unprescribed meds, since Abby calculated she'd need at least one more bottle. It was the only medication that had worked with any level of success for her own mother. If Abby had the same issue, it wouldn't be effective for long.

But then, it didn't have to be.

She fell asleep staring into the kitchen, at the broken wood around her deadbolt. Imagining Neil doing the action hero thing was kind of stirring. She blocked the reason he'd done it, because the embarrassment was too deep.

As predicted, she slept long and deep. She woke an hour before Ros arrived with dinner, so she had time to brush her hair, apply some makeup, look like she had her shit together. She faked feeling okay. Ros didn't really buy it, but Abby placated her enough to get her to go home.

Her life as she'd defined it had ended. Through the long night, she paced the rooms of her house, trailing her fingers along the walls. The voices in the shadows stayed low, like a murmur of sound through a radio. They didn't get out, though, didn't come for her. Ros had asked her if she wanted the stuff on the porch brought back in. She'd said no, she'd do it herself. Eventually. Thank God she hadn't tossed her computer out there during her electronics purge.

A lot of thoughts needed thinking about, but she let them drift through and past her. Disappeared them into the walls, through her fingertips.

She had a limited core set of tasks she had to protect, to hold close with every ounce of will she had.

Until it was time to let go.

~

Chirp, chirp.

Abby stared upward, counting the swirled brush strokes in the white paint that gave her bedroom ceiling its texturized look.

He'd sent her five texts total. She'd assigned the cricket sound to them, so she could differentiate his from other texts she was receiving.

She still hadn't read them. She liked knowing they were there, but as long as she didn't read them, she could imagine the way he felt about her—saw her—was no different from how it had been in the park. Or on his phone call. She didn't want to think about the distorted flashes of other things. Him stepping over her appliances. His careful way of talking to her on the stairwell. She didn't recall his expressions, wasn't sure if she'd looked at his face while he was here, or if she was making up his reactions.

Dismay, shock. Pity.

She kept going back to when she'd put her fingers under the door, and felt him touch them. She didn't know why she'd done it. Her mind had been screaming. *Don't put your fingers in the hole. They'll bite them off. They'll take them, and chew them. They won't give them back.*

But he'd been talking. *He'll wrap his voice around them and protect them.*

It was morning again. She'd responded to Ros's *are you okay* text. She hoped to go into work tomorrow morning. Today was the project status meeting, where each department reported on their accounts. She imagined the interns, the regular staff, all of them—Cyn, Vera, Skye and Ros—talking, joking. Marketing was a marriage between art and business. Abby had always been the numbers and business side, but she enjoyed the hell out of watching her accomplished friends and their staff come up with creative marketing solutions to satisfy their customers, people with dreams for their own companies.

Blissfully normal lives. People talked about that being a myth, that no one truly had a normal life. She supposed that depended on how they defined normal.

She pushed herself up, glanced at the note on her side table. *Shower, brush teeth, get dressed.* She'd done all of that. The aftermath of the meds had been like a hangover, but she'd come out of it clear. Just sad and tired. Scared. But mostly sad and tired.

Another cricket chirp. With a sigh, she picked up the phone. The most recent text wasn't a text at all, but a video. The frozen picture showed the bow of a boat, cutting through tan and green waters. Interested, she pressed play.

It set the boat into motion. It felt like she was sitting in it, watching the water flow past. She heard bird calls, warbles of frogs, the raspy sawing noises of bugs. The color of the water, the hints of greenery in the distance, an occasional branch intersecting the screen, suggested the boat was drifting along an estuary in the extensive bayou system.

He'd said something about his boat, hadn't he? It came back to her, just the word, repeated over and over, a male murmur near her ear.

The video went on for a couple minutes, but she could replay it, and did, four times. It was soothing. Light played on the water, making her imagine sunlight on her skin. If her face didn't feel so weighted down, she would have smiled.

But no. On top of everything else, there was no reason she had to put herself through facing him. Or witness the awkward struggle of him realizing what she knew. The pleasure of what had gone before was just that. Gone.

All she had to do was send him a text. *Good-bye. Thank you.* She'd block his number, and send Lawrence a request to tell Neil not to contact her again.

Her fingers hovered, then dropped to rest on the pillow next to her. She played the video again. For the first time in two days, something had captured her interest.

When her mother fell into depression after an episode, she would take to her bed. Abby would set up camp there, devising things to entertain her, interest her. Cooking her a food she liked, going through a fashion magazine together. Coaxing her to sit up and notice the birds outside. The sun always drew her. If Abby could get her out on their small porch, to sit in the light, her mother found the energy to claw her way back to functional again.

Abby buried her head in her hands. The sound of the water in the video helped absorb the whispers in the shadows. As she recognized that, her head came up.

Coliseum Park had a fountain, and it was within walking distance. She could sit next to it. Though her body still weighed a thousand pounds, she pulled herself to her feet. She could catch a trolley. They were less crowded this time of day. Maybe she'd take one all the way to the Aquarium. She could walk along the riverfront, lean far out over the railing, let the wakes against the bulkheads from the passing boats drown out the voices further.

It took time to organize it in her head. Dig out and pocket exact change for the trolley pass. Take her phone. Check that she was fully dressed, matching socks and shoes. The effort almost defeated her, sent her back to bed, but every time she played that video again, she found another ounce of energy.

Finally, she went out the back, took one step and turned around. *Lock the door.*

As she pocketed the key, she ran it through her head again, what she had with her, if she'd remembered everything. If she had left anything running, turned on.

She leaned her forehead against the door, hand still on the knob. Fortunately, it was the time of early morning where the angle of the sun allowed fingertips of warmth to reach the porch. Feeling the hint of that warmth on her shoulders, she squared them, pivoted away from the door, and headed down the steps.

Then came up short, because Neil was sitting on her backyard swing, watching her.

He had a bag from her favorite bagel place next to him. She might have reacted more negatively to his presence, but he had coffee. The wind favored him, bringing the scent of strong caffeine. It drew her toward him as magnetically as the man himself.

He had on the worn jeans that molded his lower body in such a mouthwatering way. His T-shirt showed off shoulders and biceps that made a Mistress want to touch, hold. His bill cap was pulled low on his brow, a dangerous look that was unplanned, since Neil didn't need fashion choices to make him look lethal. He had on canvas boat shoes with no socks, and the shoes were broken in, a frayed small hole in the side of one of them.

She'd purposefully not looked at his face. The expression she found there would determine what would happen next, and she dreaded it. She'd have to walk away, tell him to leave her alone.

She couldn't handle another fight.

He rose. She saw him drop his hat next to the bagels, and he was moving toward her. She still had her keys, clutched in her hand almost like a weapon. He'd almost reached her when her gaze rose, an automatic reaction. She glimpsed his firm mouth, strong features. A momentary impression before he closed his hand over her wrist, turned that clutched fist outward, but only so he could slide his other arm around her, bring her close and lift her off her feet.

Her gaze snapped upward to his slate-colored eyes.

Nothing there but clean, hot desire.

The flames roared through her, burning away embarrassment, worry, doubt and dread. When his mouth hovered over hers, her lips were already parted, her hands sliding up his chest. The keys had been dropped, forgotten. The weight she'd felt on her like a boulder, holding her down, was gone, a bird freed to fly. The whispers became a rush of sound, like the waters cutting around the boat in his video. What took over her senses was overwhelming, but in the right kind of way.

The control she could call forth when she was around a man she wanted had eluded her for two days. Now here it was, ready for her to grasp it with both hands. And he had his hands on the same controls, as if they were piloting that boat together.

"Ask me," he demanded.

"Kiss me," she ordered.

"Close enough," he muttered.

Hard muscle, heated man, cotton, bagels, coffee, warm, firm lips. A provocative tongue that teased her mouth, her lips, her own tongue. As she pressed herself to him, his arm banded even more securely around her. He used the hold to give her an additional heft, so strong, making it easy to leave the ground, wrap her legs around him.

He brought them back to the swing and settled them, her straddling him, legs folded on either side of his long thighs. A hum of approval teased her lips at the rigid pressure she encountered, pressing between her legs. When he tangled his hand in her hair, she liked the pull on her scalp, answered it with a press of her fingers into his T-shirt across his chest, burrowing into the muscle beneath. He smelled as good as the coffee.

The swing was moving, creating a friction between them she enhanced with a rock of her hips. Those eyes became even more intent, the muscles of his face showing the warrior fierceness he could bring to her bed.

A helpful reminder that they weren't actually in her bedroom. She couldn't fuck him on her backyard swing, but this...oh God, she could easily do this to orgasm, and he looked ready to let that happen, even if it left him hard and aching while she took her full pleasure.

She appreciated that in a man. Particularly a man who didn't easily relinquish the reins. Testing it, she flattened her palm on his chest, applied pressure.

His gaze flickered. Though he caressed her mouth with his own, he eased back, grip dropping from her hair to her waist, stroking her upper arm on the way there. Her hands spread out, curved over his biceps.

"You brought me bagels," she said. "And coffee."

"No, I didn't. That's all for me. But I might share." He gave her a slow, heated smile, his fingers flexing on her hips. The pressure created another small movement between their bodies, entirely intentional. The wave of sensation was powerful enough to have her lips parting.

"Come right here," he said. "I want to watch you."

His attention was overwhelming, logging her every tiny shudder, how she moistened her lips. The tautness of her body, the way she held onto him. But her dread of how she'd expected him to behave against the confusing reality, the questions it left, helped her keep control against the strength of his demand. It also reminded her she didn't take orders, even pleasurable ones. "Coffee first."

Those strong hands gripped her tighter, one more tempting stroke that called a gasp from her throat. But it was just a tit for tat thing, a reminder his will was as formidable as hers. His gaze glinted with satisfaction at her shudder of response, but it was chased by a pleasing dose of male frustration. He gallantly lifted and helped her move into a seated position on the swing next to him.

He touched her face, caressed a lock of hair. That momentary silence could have worried her, what he was about to say, but he turned toward the coffee in the cardboard holder, popped the top on one. "How many sugars and creams?"

"One sugar, one cream."

As she watched him open the small packets, his hands so competent, expression so relaxed, a lump caught in her throat. "You don't make this easy," she said.

"Good. I'm not in the mood to make things easy for you." He opened the bagel bag, fishing out her favorite, an asiago cheese so good it qualified as a sin. He pulled it in two, releasing an intense wave of that addictive, fresh-baked smell, and offered her half.

As she chewed, she put her knee up on the swing so she could turn toward him, gaze at his profile. He was eating his own bagel, sipping coffee. He looked as if he was merely studying her backyard landscape choices, Zenning out on a nice day. He rocked the swing slowly for both of them with his braced long legs. Her gaze lingered on the short beard that covered his jaw. It had been both soft and coarse under her hands when he'd kissed her. She put a hand out, grazed his cheek, a light stroke. "The bruise is mostly gone."

"Yeah. I'm hard-headed."

"Your multiple texts confirm it. Don't you have any prospects other than me, a fine, strapping lad like yourself?"

"I'd like to strap something." He dipped his gaze downward to her buttock, then brought it back up again. "Bastion said he'd be happy to show me the ropes—literally—if I was interested in switching teams. Is anyone who works in executive management at TRA *not* a top?"

"None that have come out of the closet."

"Probably afraid. Hostile work environment, lots of pervertibles. Rulers, letter openers."

"Stress balls make really good gags. We have some with the TRA logo. Big, squishy roses. Purple." She gave him a considering look. "How do you know kink speak without being out as a Dom?"

He gave her that lazy, toe-curling look. "If you think I'm not 'out' as a Dom, I'm doing something wrong."

She made a face at him. "You know what I mean. New Orleans is a great venue to play."

"I've always preferred the one-on-one private approach."

She took a sip of the coffee. The ecstasy of the caffeine made her hold onto the cup with both hands. He was being playful, attentive, relaxed. Aroused. Offering normal conversation, helping her be okay with him. He managed it so well, so naturally, she believed it was genuine, not an artificial comfort zone manufactured for her benefit.

That lump returned, and she swallowed over it, hard.

"Did you know about Lawrence before he was with Ros?" She managed to keep her tone light. "That he was a sub?"

"Oh, hell yeah." A quick grin. "Soon as we started hanging out, I could tell he was hankering for a Mistress. I could also see he felt uncomfortable discussing it, so I kept my own interests to myself around him. With Dale being an obvious Dom and our Master Chief at the time, I didn't want Munch to feel outnumbered."

She raised a brow. "How about Max?"

"Well, Max isn't a Dom, but he's not a sub, either. He doesn't fit any mold. He doesn't have to. He fits with Janet. They just work. Anyone who's around them knows that relationship was meant to be."

He cocked a brow. "You strike me as the type of Domme who's been in this long enough to know that a power exchange relationship has to do with the fit between the people doing it, not so much over the way they define themselves." His gaze sharpened. "Which tells me that you holding me at arm's length was never about that, was it?"

She took another bolstering shot of caffeine. "Took you a while to breach that door, sailor."

"Because what's behind it is too valuable to risk a forcible entry." He trailed his knuckles along her upper arm. Her thick ponytail had fallen forward over her shoulder, so he curled a crimson lock around his finger, tugged.

"When did Dale figure you out?" While she wanted to gravitate into the touch, get lost in it, she didn't give in to it.

"Pretty early, just like me with Lawrence. Dale had a conversation with me about it a lot earlier, though. He's been a practicing Dom most his life, so for him, talking about it is like a quarterback talking about game strategy. We'd discuss techniques, interests, preferences. Plus he wanted to make sure if I did anything with it, I knew what I was doing. Who he is as a Master Chief is pretty much who he is as a Dom. *Mentor* was stamped on his forehead at birth."

She wouldn't mind talking techniques, interests and preferences with Neil, learning more about how he'd discovered, pursued and developed his own. But it could wait. She wasn't up for anything that complicated right now.

His attention shifted to her house keys, still lying on the patio where she'd dropped them. "Where were you headed?"

"To the river," she said. "I liked your video with the boat."

"Good." He rolled the bag closed, paper rattling. "Let's head for my place. You can finish your coffee on the way."

"Neil..."

He cupped her face abruptly, his gaze direct. So direct she felt a flutter in her mind, a startling like birds. Birds flying into the sky. Her gaze lifted to see them. They were made of air, not flesh and blood, so in her imaginings, she only saw a hint of their outline. Ghost birds in a clear blue sky.

While her delusions were mostly auditory, her expanded senses could create some interesting visuals.

His touch gentled. He had his fingers under her hair, at her nape. Leaning in, he put his mouth on the pulse in her throat, lips stirring the nerves. She moved against him, need sighing out of her, answered by his own husky response.

His other arm wound around her, palm sliding down her back, over the upper rise of her buttocks and then back up. She dropped her head to her shoulders. The wind had picked up, turning her birds into blue-tinged translucent whorls. They could carry her up, let her dive and swoop at whatever pace she wanted. Hard and furious, driving. Gliding, somersaulting.

He tangled his hand in her hair, massaging tense muscles beneath.

"Are you with me, dream girl?"

"Are you in the dream?" she murmured.

"You tell me. I sure want to be."

She wanted him there, too. Slowly, she brought her gaze down, out of the skies, away from flying birds that weren't there, and found him. The piercing eyes came out of that distant place and back to here and now, his hands on her, his face so close. For one nice moment, it wasn't too close.

"Abby," he said. "Where I'm taking you today, on my boat, you can do and be whatever you want to be. So don't tell me what you don't want. Tell me what you do. I'm here to give you a good day. All right?"

He meant it. She sensed no hesitancy to him, how he was acting with her. He hadn't attempted to talk about what happened this week, or avoided the topic. Everything felt open to whatever way she wanted to go.

He wasn't following her lead. He'd figured out the direction she needed to go, taken her hand and led her there. Opened up the door and stood aside, so she could choose to step through. Or not.

Any mortification or awkwardness she'd felt was gone. The sadness and tiredness, still a weight upon her, felt a little less, because of it.

"Okay," she said.

CHAPTER SEVEN

His house was in one of the more rural parishes, southwest of New Orleans and nestled into a web of tributaries that fed into the Mississippi River Delta. The town he lived in had less than a couple thousand residents. Soon after they crossed its border, the two-lane highway became a route, and narrowed accordingly. When he left that, it was onto a gravel road bordered by a jumble of ground covers, old growth trees and ambitious saplings. As they bumped along, windows cracked, she could smell the bayou, telling her water lay close behind the screen of dense foliage.

They turned onto a driveway with no mailbox, just a couple of posts on either side with blue reflective stickers on them. She presumed it helped his visitors avoid ending up in the drainage ditch on either side.

They crunched across the gravel under a heavy lacing of live oak trees dripping with Spanish moss. Once he cut the truck's engine, the warbling of frogs and insects, an enthusiastic symphony, recalled the boat video.

Evocative paintings of the mysterious depths of the Louisiana bayou often featured scenes of winding grey-green watery pathways that disappeared among shadowy forests of cypress trees. Sometimes there was a house like this one in the picture, a tin-roofed, ramshackle-looking clapboard structure, perched precariously on the bank and tilted toward the water as if its goal was to slide right in and sink to the bottom. But she suspected it was more like a cypress knee, blending in, unassuming but solidly planted into the earth. Like the man it belonged to.

While she was looking, Neil had come around and opened her door. She hadn't noticed him exit the vehicle. The blank prompted a spurt of panic. Should she be doing this?

He'd made her feel so comfortable about the decision. Now, in a situation where she couldn't predict or plan for anything, she wasn't so sure. But as she stared at the house, struggling with her thoughts, she reached out to her right, without looking toward him. A wordless desire and one met by the man who read the cue. His larger hand closed over hers, fingers stroking her knuckles.

While not the prettiest belle at the ball, the house was well maintained. The screened porch, double the size of the actual house, had no rips or tears in the mesh. The tin roof's dark brown paint was less than a few years old. The same could be said for the visible portion of the pilings on which the house was perched.

Through the front porch screen, she could see buckets stacked by the door, next to several pairs of rubber waders. Fishing gear was hung up on the natural cedar siding.

She liked its simplicity. She could see him sitting on the porch in the evening, tipping back in one of the wooden chairs she saw there, one of his long legs bracing him on the porch rail as he listened to the night sounds.

It steadied her, and she slid out of the truck, holding onto his hand. He closed the door, then gestured her forward.

His yard was a wild natural area, a couple pots of herbs by the steps, probably for cooking, not landscape appeal. When he held the screen door for her, she noticed it opened silently.

"No squeak," she said. "And your truck door doesn't groan like a dying animal. You've broken the Southern good old boy code. How will your two a.m. bar hookup know you've rolled off her and bailed if she can't hear you leave?"

He flashed her a faint smile. "I'm trained for stealth. It's a hard habit to break, even for one-night stand protocols."

"So, before you became a SEAL, your parents knew when you dipped into the cookie jar?"

"Even SEAL training wouldn't have helped that. Whenever one of us was up to no good, our parents' detection range was better than a Mars probe."

So he wasn't an only child. Leaving that piece of information to pursue later, she shifted her attention back to the porch. By the door was a plaque displaying a bright red Twizzler candy stick. It had been animated with fierce brows and black dot eyes, and toted a pair of oversized guns. Bold black letters next to it declared, *"Forget 911. Body disposal handled out back."*

She knew his SEAL nickname, which suggested one of his brethren had given him the plaque. He turned the knob and pushed open the door. "No lock?"

He shook his head. "No point, isolated as I am, and most people around here are armed. Not much appeal to the casual thief, even a junkie. Plus, this way, if a neighbor needs something when I'm not here, they can come get it. You'll meet a couple of them today."

A living area and kitchen made up the main room, doors to a single bedroom and bathroom off to the side. "You're welcome to look around. Not much to it."

She liked it, for just that reason. The space was cozy-sized but not cluttered. The kitchen table and six chairs were well-made woodcraft, with straw-bottom seats. He had a fridge and stove, a microwave.

A bookcase in the living area was stuffed with books. The shelves were lined with things she thought might be souvenirs from his travels. As she approached to take a closer look, she noted photographs were positioned among them. She detoured to the bedroom.

His bed looked appealing, only not for the reasons she could have hoped. Tiredness kept coming in waves, wanting to drag her down into that darker place. She could burrow into his comforter, stack the pillows around her to form a perimeter.

He'd said whatever she needed or wanted today, he was okay with it. If she wanted him to lie down behind her, be part of that perimeter, hold her while she went down in that darkness, he might say that was okay.

He'd come up behind her. He wasn't touching her, but his hand was on the doorframe above her head. She could feel the heat of him.

"Tell me what made you turn away from the books."

"Photographs. Sometimes it's okay, but these days, not so much. Something happens to the faces when I look at them."

The eyes darkened, the faces started to melt and run. The voices would whisper to her, tell her they'd never been real, that they'd been pretend all along.

She'd packed away all the ones in her house, tucked them in drawers she had few reasons to open, so she wouldn't have to expend effort to avoid looking at them.

Telling him helped. Got it off her mind. Particularly when he didn't tell her how to feel, or ask her for more. The tiredness receded some, made her think of the other reasons one could use this room. Moving across the threshold, she sat down on the edge of his bed. She enjoyed the art of subtle teasing, and so was aware of the way his eyes followed the movement of her hand as she smoothed it over the comforter, thought of the man who lay here. "How do you sleep? Over the covers or below?"

"Mostly over."

"What do you wear?"

"Boxers. A T-shirt if it's cold."

He was still leaning in the doorway, watching her. Rising, she moved back to him, noting how his gaze coursed over the way she walked, the shift of her curves. She liked watching a man's hunger grow. Liked even more when he didn't try to take a bite until she told him he could. She controlled the pace. Decided if she'd allow him one bite, one course, or the full meal.

With a man who embraced submission, such compliance to her demands, his self-restraint, answered his deep need to serve a Mistress, please her.

Neil was a different animal, a more delicate line. He watched her the way she watched him. He didn't make his decisions the way a submissive made them. He was gauging her reaction as a Dom, same as she was with him. Figuring out what pathway between their preferences would answer what they each demanded—not asked—from a partner.

It held an intriguing appeal; a game where who won couldn't be predicted, and might change, round to round.

She recognized the contradiction. Her life of late went far smoother if she could keep it predictable, plan ahead. Nothing unexpected. Yet there was one part of her, struggling to survive, that craved that wild and free feeling, the right kind of unpredictability and spontaneity.

With Neil, a corner of her mind thought she could indulge the last scrap of herself capable of that. Was that what she'd recognized about him, why she was so drawn to him?

She'd reached him. He kept the one hand propped on the doorway, the other slipped into his back jeans pocket, making gray cotton stretch over his upper body. His T-shirt was worn untucked, so she slid a hand beneath to find heated man, a muscled abdomen, the line of hair down the center of it.

She slipped the button of his jeans, then let her thumb stroke the band of his underwear. Until she did that, she'd been watching the pulse in his corded throat. Now she dipped her chin to see the boxers were dark blue. If he were lying in his bed in nothing but them, she'd walk her fingertips under the leg openings, find the curve of testicles, the length of his cock.

He'd closed his other hand over her hip, was playing beneath the line of her own jeans, tracing the edge of cotton bikinis. She had sexier underwear, scraps of silk, sheer fabrics, but this was what she'd walked out wearing. A matching cotton bra was under her V-necked short-sleeved red shirt. The shirt had the outline of a pale pink heart printed on it, styled to look like it had been done with a paintbrush. He'd said what she was wearing worked for where they were going, what they'd be doing.

"We need to get some bug repellant on you before we head out," he said.

The message contradicted the intent of the erection pushing against denim. The resolve in his voice competed with a desire-infused roughness, but she could tell he wasn't going to give into the desire to go down that road.

Since he wasn't a sub trying to wait for her go-ahead, that meant he was determined to offer her something else first. Her own desires warred with curiosity, but she wrinkled her nose. "Not a fan of repellant."

"No one is, but the bugs especially aren't, and that's what's important. I don't want anyone biting you except me." His expression held humor and heat, the latter shimmering over her skin. "Plus, this stuff isn't too bad. It's a local blend. Persephone, she runs one of the parish's outfitting stores, started by selling it to the kayaking and fishing tourists. Works so well, she sells it online now, which gives MeeMaw some additional income."

"MeeMaw?"

"Yeah, it's her concoction. She's one of the neighbors you might get to meet today. We're cruising her way for lunch, if she'll have us."

She lifted her gaze to the strong jaw, the set of his lips. Laid her hand on his chest. "You won't be dissuaded from that plan?"

"I won't." He stared down at her. "That's what we're doing."

"Good. So if I was with a man whose self-discipline and will were less formidable, what would we do? Tell me."

She'd demanded an answer with the words he'd used earlier.

Tell me.

Neil dipped his head down, nudged her head to the right and put his mouth on her throat. As he held there, he scraped her with his teeth, let her feel the desire behind it, to bite harder. She still had her hand on his abdomen, fingers curled into the waistband of the boxers. Her other came to rest on his hip.

"I'd put you on my bed, remove your clothes. Take a good long moment to enjoy how beautiful you are."

He moved his mouth up below her ear, and told her a story, painted her a picture. "I have a couple old T-shirts, faded and soft. I'd cut them into strips, wrap them around your wrists and ankles, tie them to the posts. You'd be on your stomach, so you could nestle down in my bed, my scent, like a beautiful, red-feathered bird finding its home."

"Oh. I like that." She tilted her head against his lips. She'd closed her eyes. "Then what?"

"In an hour or so, when I'd looked my fill, and you were sleeping, because you felt safe, and knew you could sleep easy here, I'd decide it was time to wake you up. I'd put my knee between your spread legs, my mouth on the back of your knee. I'd work up from there, kissing, tasting, biting. I'd watch you wake up, start to move, then writhe."

A puff of heat as his voice moved from a low rumble to a whisper. "I wouldn't put my mouth on your cunt. That would come later. First, I'd worship every other inch of you. Until you're so wet and slippery that when I put my cock inside you, I'd have to go slow. Make sure I didn't slide into you too fast, hurt you."

"Maybe I like a little pain."

Fire sparked in his gaze, as she pulled her head back to look at him. His hand came up, cupped her face. Her lips parted, and she was leaning full into him. When she went on her toes, put her mouth on his throat and bit, she summoned a groan, a half curse.

Power flooded her. What he was describing was a scenario where he was in control, but he'd given her that image because she'd demanded to know what was in his head, what shape his hunger was taking. It was a delicious cliff edge to stand upon.

"I can give you pain, Abby." His voice came out of the darkness, because she'd closed her eyes again. "The right kind can drive demons away."

She knew that. She'd done it for enough of her submissives. Giving them that had simultaneously helped her hold her own monsters at bay.

Who gave and who took mattered, because receiving pain wouldn't offer her the same charge as giving it. However, since a lot of things were changing, maybe...

She shook her head at herself and drew back. Nothing lay down the 'maybe' road.

She offered a strained smile. "Time for that bug repellant."

Neil put a dollop of the whipped lotion in her palm and watched her rub it over her face, neck and arms as he'd instructed. "Close your eyes and I'll do your clothes with the spray version."

"They can get me through my clothes?" She complied, allowing him to turn her as he misted her T-shirt and jeans thoroughly, even the ankles of her socks above her tennis shoes. As he bent to do that, he rested a hand on her hip, hooking a thumb in her belt loop.

"The things that bite in this swamp can punch right through a T-shirt or thinner denim. I'd offer you thicker coveralls, but I like how your jeans look. I'd rather just lacquer you with repellant."

She came full circle and he gazed down at her, the light smile on her kissable lips, her thick lashes fanning her skin. Christ, she was impossibly beautiful. Fate really could be a sadistic bastard. He brushed a loose lock of her hair back. He'd recommended she braid it, and she'd done so, using a couple rubber bands he'd provided. "You can open your eyes."

She complied, surveying him. "You don't need any?"

"I'm tough-skinned, and the bayou recognizes its own."

He'd packed some basics, snacks, drinks and sandwiches, checking with her on her preferences. "I thought we were doing lunch at MeeMaw's."

"Not if she's not home. Plus, we're not on any set schedule. If we end up staying out longer than expected, I don't want you to get hungry. Water has a way of stimulating the appetite."

Which he hoped would happen. She'd noticeably lost weight since the day he'd seen her running at the park, and she'd sucked down the coffee he'd brought her far more eagerly than she'd eaten the bagel.

He took her out onto the back porch and walked her to his boat dock. He showed her where the life jackets and first aid kit were stowed, how to operate the radio. A safe boatman made sure his guest knew her options, in case something happened to him. Particularly when his cargo was this precious.

He guided her into the two-seat set up behind the wheel. She sat next to him when they first cast off, but he encouraged her to move up onto the flat and long front deck for a better view, and she took advantage of it. It gave him a pretty good view, too. She rested on her hip, her head turning this way and that, braid resting against the slope of her breast, as she took in the tangled forest of white oak, willow, cypress, bay and tupelo trees bordering their path.

Fallen branches and debris formed islands in the water, perches for a wide variety of wildlife. Her eyes widened at the sunning alligators, and her lips parted in pleasure when he pointed out a grey heron with purple tipped plumage perched on a white oak. The tree's trunk stretched ten feet into their path, the length of it poised inches over the water.

"What made it fall over?"

He indicated the green leaves. "It's not fallen. The forest is so thick, it grew that way to reach sunlight."

She started as a mature alligator, about eight feet long, dove off one of the debris islands. The wave of ripples rocked their craft. His head, the fixed staring eyes, remained visible as he seemed to float motionlessly past.

"Next time I'll introduce you to alligator wrestling," he said, poker-faced. "But this time around, you may want to keep your hands inside the boat."

She made a face, then scrambled back to the seat beside him when a snake crossed their path, sidewinding its way toward the opposite bank. "It's still early enough in the day we'll see some of them about," he reassured her. "But as the sun gets higher, you don't see them much. They like cooler temps."

She peered at the low sides of the craft. "Have any snakes ever tried to hitch a ride?"

"Depends. If I say yes, will you stay close to me like this?" He ran a hand along her back, squeezed her hip.

"I'll tell you to turn this boat around and get me the hell out of here."

He grinned. "It doesn't happen too often, and almost never an intentional thing. They get confused or fall off a branch when we're passing under it."

He pointed to a hook and a paddle, objects within easy reach, fastened to the inside of the craft. "Pushing them away or slapping the water with the paddle helps them change their course. Same with the alligators if they get too curious. If the snakes do get in, I can loop them with the hook and send them on their way." He winked. "Paddle's also useful if the engine conks out."

"I can imagine. Something to whack an amorous captain with, if that's the bayou version of 'the car ran out of gas.'"

He chuckled, appreciating her. She was listening to him closely, even as she kept her eyes on their surroundings. Her shoulder was pressed to his. While he had one hand on the wheel, his other rested on her thigh. She put hers over it, ran fingertips up and down his forearm. She had a nice touch, and he wanted more of it. He also wanted to move his hand up higher and stroke, but he kept it where it was. He was as comfortable here as in his own living room, but that was because he never forgot to pay attention.

Plus, though she'd made her interest way clear in his bedroom—enough to test his resolve—he saw hints that she wasn't a hundred percent. He'd keep things to an easy pace.

"The engine's not as loud as I expected," she noted.

"This boat is for casual cruising. I keep another boat with more horsepower stored at a marina when I want to go faster or farther afield. I figured you'd like the quiet, the slower pace."

"I do. You've been planning this."

"I told you I'd take you out on the boat."

"So you did."

Her hand stopped moving, stayed on his forearm, his on her thigh, the two of them just like that. The repellant's less pleasant scent was cut with a light vanilla. It made him think of something else.

"You had a man's shampoo on a shelf in your bedroom."

It had been grouped with several other seemingly disparate things. A shell, a piece of wide ribbon. A perfume bottle wrapped in a piece of cloth. A black glass cat, so small and light it had been secured there with a piece of double-sided foam tape.

She sent him a sidelong glance. "The shampoo is for the man chained in my basement. Don't worry. Ros will feed and water him while I'm gone."

"Good to know." He pinched her knee and she smiled.

She didn't explain it further. Instead, she seemed focused on water lapping over the clumps of debris and against the boat. When a heron took flight, passing over them, she lifted her hand as if she could brush the feet tidily folded against its body.

Her gaze came down, went out of focus. After a couple beats, it came to him. Touched base. Moved on.

He thought of how a person riding ocean surf got swept down below where he or she had left their beach chair. Each time they rode in a wave, they tried to make their way back to the starting point. That was what it reminded him of, watching her recognize she'd lost her focus, and making her way slowly back to him again.

"Tiger, one of my regulars," she said. "He has a scent that helps ground me. The other things, they also connect to strong sense memories. Taste, smell, sound. They help bring me back sometimes. I go through them like a rosemary."

He knew she meant rosary, but he didn't correct her, not wanting to fluster her. "How about the cuffs in your nightstand?"

"Oh, those." A fond smile touched her lips. "A farewell gift from my first solo submissive, back when I was in New York. He's a cop."

He grunted neutrally. While he thought he'd managed to project a casual reaction, her gaze suggested otherwise. The depths of the hazel color shifted with the alternating light and shadow coming through the trees.

"It's still bothering you, me talking about my sessions with submissives."

"Yeah. But I don't want you not to talk about it. It's part of you, isn't it? An important part."

"It was, yes."

"Was?"

She looked away. The ache in her voice was something he couldn't ignore, the tension that gripped her. "The last session I did...this started. I lost time. My words got mixed up. Not bad, I covered it, but I won't risk harming someone whose safety depends on me keeping my head straight."

Under other circumstances, he might be relieved, even selfishly thrilled, that she wasn't going to do any more scenes with male subs. But he thought of what Lawrence had said, and knew his preferences didn't honor something more important. Or what he wanted to be for her.

"You miss it."

"It hasn't been long enough for me to miss it. It's knowing I can't go back to it again that's difficult."

"What part of it will you miss the most?"

She turned toward him with an awkward jerk. He realized she was trying to answer him with a physical action, but hadn't been able to coordinate her movements the way she intended. She recovered, steadied herself. Then she gripped his wrist, looked at his other hand, employed with navigating the boat. "Any way you can give me both for a minute or two?"

"Yeah." They were in a good spot for it. He put the engine on idle, let her have his other wrist. She straightened his arms out to either side of him, as if she was pinning them to the air. Since his arm span was longer than hers, she slid her grip to the bend of his elbows.

"Hold them like that."

She trailed her fingertips from elbow to shoulder, back out again, as far along the inside of his forearms as she could reach.

He already knew her touch was something he wanted a hell of a lot more of, but the effect of it was unique, an impact on his attention and emotions he hadn't experienced before. Because he had to stay in tune with what was happening with the boat, he was aware of the drift. But it took an exceptional level of effort, making him glad for his familiarity with the waters.

Maybe it was the way she did it, with such an all-encompassing attention. Or how her nearness engaged his senses. From the moment she touched him, he was literally immersed in something. Like an element. Water. Air. Sunlight.

"I can feel how strong you are," she said, "and if I tell you to touch me, how to touch me, it's something that I keep feeling through your skin. Knowing all that strength is under my command. All that you are for that moment, centered on what I desire, where I want to take you. It's all mine."

He'd been telling her the truth, that he'd never felt the need to pursue his Dominant interests in a formal setting. Yet the more time he spent around her, seeing this side of her, hearing the way she experienced it, the more he thought he might change his mind about that. How she articulated it, how it came to her, stirred his interest in a familiar way.

Most women liked a man who took charge. In the privacy of the bedroom, he'd been able to take that where he wanted to go with it, because he chose his bedmates accordingly. He could tell with little effort which ones had a sexually submissive side, or even a full orientation for it. That woman might not have discovered or embraced it in herself when they first met, but by the end of Neil's time with her, she was tapped into a whole new sexual wonderland, one he'd had the privilege of revealing to her.

While Abby was all Domme, he thought he could use that same intuition to give her pleasure.

"May I?" At her nod, he reversed the position, gripping her wrists the same way. Only when he stretched her arms out, his were long enough that he could keep his hold there, his fingers sliding over pulse points. "What does this do to your mind? Where does it go?"

He'd done it slow, deliberately, keeping his gaze on her face, watching her lick her lips, her eyes lose focus. This time he was pretty sure it happened for different reasons than his ocean swimming metaphor.

He had a theory about that, too. It might be bullshit, but it was worth testing. Could her mind, her will, move into the protective shadow of his, not to submit, but to find reinforcements, a haven from the things that chased her?

He thought it could, because she looked like she'd figured it out herself. She appeared confused but thoughtful. "The two impulses don't have to be mutually exclusive," he said, reinforcing it. He took the wheel again, settling back into the seat. She did the same next to him.

"No. But...I miss it so much, holding the control. It helped. Pieces of yourself...they just start falling off."

"Why can't you keep doing it?" he asked. "Beyond the safety issue."

"A sub is there to get an experience, too. I can't trust myself to deliver that for them."

"But don't you and Skye share them, in a way?" Lawrence had told him how they tag-teamed.

"She has her own style. Her own desires to pursue in a session. I don't want her to alter that for me. Rosary," she said suddenly. "That's what I meant."

"I know." Even as he asked himself again why he wasn't leaving well enough alone, he still forced himself to keep on with it. "What if you had a spotter? Someone in the room who could watch for warning signs and step in, protect your sub if needed. No interference if everything is going well. I'd say someone to be your shadow, but that analogy seems problematic."

Surprise gripped her expression, then her lips curved. "Most people don't tease a schizophrenic about the crazy stuff they see or hear."

"There's no weapon in the world as powerful as a sense of humor. My teammate hurt on that last mission? When he woke up in the hospital, Dodge told him they were glad they didn't have to tell his girlfriend he was dead. Cedrick jumped right in to point out she wouldn't have noticed much difference."

Her smile stayed, wan but not forced. He returned to the subject. "Which sub would probably be most open to that idea?"

"You're serious."

"Why wouldn't I be?"

"Because watching me handle another male sexually would make you grind the enamel off your teeth."

"I have a good dentist."

"I'm changing the subject. Seriously. This is...too much right now."

"Okay. But think about it." He touched her neck, her shoulder, watched her gaze down at the water as he did. She was a sharp woman. Part of her mind would keep working it. "It's a way to keep doing something you love, not let it be taken from you."

The timing was good to leave it there naturally, because they were coming up on their first stop. As they rounded a bend in the estuary, a large houseboat came in view. Most people wouldn't think of it as a boat, since it was an anchored pair of metal buildings with decking built around and between them. The set up was two domiciles, giving Tommy and his son privacy when each wanted it.

Neil put his hand on Abby's shoulder, stroking the outline of her bra strap under her shirt. A gentle nonverbal warning before he bellowed a hail that echoed over the water. "Yo, Tommy. You there?"

The door on the shadowed screen porch opened. A wizened man baked to the color of month-old horse manure—his own description—stepped out. Lifting a hand in greeting, he rocked a bow-legged stride down the ramp to a floating dock. As their approaching boat sent a gentle wake under it, he held his footing easily. "Where you at, *cher*?"

"I brought you sunshine."

Abby sent him a bemused look while Tommy squinted, shading his eyes. Then he smiled broadly, revealing remarkably perfect teeth that gleamed. "So you did. I need a second wife. Doesn't look like you had to tie this one up or knock her out to get her here. Means she wants to be with old Tommy, right?"

"Depends," Abby responded. "What happened to the first wife?"

Tommy bent over laughing, slapping his knee, then straightened up with a jaunty twist of his lean body. "I like a smart woman. What's she doing with you, Neil?"

"Yeah. There are cypress knees that have a better chance with a woman than you, Neil. Particularly after she gets to know you."

Another man, his similar features suggesting he was Tommy's adult son, stepped out of his own house. The similarities ended at the face, though. Abby deduced that Tommy's wife must be a pro-wrestler, because their son had twice the shoulder span of his father and towered over him. He also had a long bushy beard and a bald head, whereas his father had a stubbled sharp chin and a close crop of springy black hair.

"Easy there," Neil advised. "Lady present."

"Plus, it once again depends on the cypress knee." Abby earned a grin from Tommy's son. "I don't believe in limiting my options without seeing it."

"If you don't want her, I do." Tommy's son braced himself against a piling with a hand the size of a catcher's mitt, using the other to catch the line Neil threw him. He nodded courteously to Abby. "Dobby. Short for Dobson Duet."

"Abby. Short for Abigail Rose. Nice to meet you."

"So what brings you here, boy?" Tommy asked.

"I was going to head up to MeeMaw's for some lunch and wanted to see if you thought that was a good idea." Neil propped the sole of his shoe against the dock edge as he held onto one of the pilings. With his other foot still in the boat, he demonstrated the same relaxed pose that Tommy did, proving how comfortable he was on unstable ground.

"Why, that'll just make MeeMaw's day. We'll follow you up. Grab my other hat, boy," Tommy told his son.

"I figure afterward I'll take Abby to the really scenic spots, give her a proper cruise."

Tommy winked at Abby. "He takes you deep enough into the delta, he thinks he won't have to worry about the tying up or knocking out part when you want to go home."

"But the tying up's the fun part," Dobby grinned, ducking away as his father swatted at him with his existing hat.

"Got that right," Abby murmured. Neil's sideways look, his wicked grin, contained a clear challenge.

Which of them would get their hands on the rope first.

His lack of concern over their shared Dominant preferences, as if that didn't make them incompatible at all, made the volleying easier to enjoy, no denying that. But what he'd proposed with Tiger had given her a jolt. Not an unpleasant one, just unexpected.

Considering the bigger obstacle to a deeper relationship, she hadn't spent much time on the shape it would have between two Dominants. Could have. But she had to admit, he'd intrigued her.

She'd known Doms who wanted to overwhelm her, prove to her

they could take the upper hand. Whether intentionally or through ignorance, it disrespected her own identity as a Domme. Those attempts left her flat. He didn't.

She liked the sexual mystery of a complicated man. And her own inexplicable reaction to it was intriguing as well.

"If we're dropping in for lunch, shouldn't we let MeeMaw know we're coming?" she asked, as Tommy and Dobby prepared to follow them.

Neil shrugged. "She always seems to know when she has company coming. It's why they call her the swamp witch."

"Yeah, don't cross her," Dobby warned. He held their camouflage-colored aluminum boat steady as his father clambered in and took a seat near the tiller. "Half the alligators in this swamp used to walk on two legs." He shot Abby a wink as he disappeared into the house.

When Dobby returned with a bill cap for his father, Abby was perplexed to see it was nearly identical to the one he had on, except for a different fishing logo.

"His going-to-visit MeeMaw hat," Dobby said, grinning at Abby while his father switched them out. "He likes to look stylish for her."

"I feel underdressed," Abby said.

"We can't have that." Neil reached over the wheel, hooking his fingers in a hole that let him lift a panel off a deck storage compartment. The mesh-backed bill cap he produced had blue fabric in the front, and an embroidered fish skeleton, wearing orange ZZ top style sunglasses.

Neil positioned it on her head, bringing the bill down level. After he made the adjustments, he slid his touch over her cheek, a thumb caressing her parted lips.

"The color brings out your eyes," he said. "Plus, you were starting to get a little too much sun, even with the block MeeMaw includes in the repellant."

She gazed at him. If she lingered too long, his features would distort like they did in the photographs. She didn't want to see his eyes become black sockets. But she didn't want to look away, either. So she shut her own eyes instead, holding the picture of him in her mind, keeping it safe.

He leaned in, his lips brushing the lid of each one. Then the boat rocked as he unwrapped the line and pushed off, giving Tommy and

Dobby room to start up their boat and take the lead. Neil kept the nose of his craft even with their mid-line, to make it easier to toss comments back and forth over the engine noise.

It was Laurel who had brought her and Ros to New Orleans. Though she'd been here for some years, Abby had never cruised the bayou. After learning that, Dobby and Tommy appointed themselves informal tour guides, offering tidbits about the passing scenery. Including some things she didn't want to know.

"If we're out here after dark tonight," Tommy said, "we'll shine a light out over the water. You'll see pretty blue specks. The eyes of bullfrogs, and they come in all sorts of sizes, from little fellows to ones it'd be hard to hold in two hands. But those blue specks can also be the eyes of the spiders that go bouncing across the water like skipping stones."

"How big are they?" Abby asked.

Dobby shrugged. "Depends. They can get as big as the palm of your hand."

"Your hand or my hand?" she asked. He grinned.

"If we're still at MeeMaw's by nightfall, I'm calling Uber," she informed Neil.

As he chuckled, Tommy drew his attention toward what appeared to be another clump of debris. "How about you bring old MeeMaw a gift?"

When Neil agreeably navigated that way, Abby saw the debris hid an entry to a cove, big enough for several small boats like theirs.

The men cut the boat motors, using the momentum to drift slowly into the space. Dobby and Neil had to duck beneath the low hanging branches of the trees on the moss-covered banks. Abby tried not to think about what Neil had said, about snakes falling from overhead.

The men used handholds on those branches to pull themselves further into the cove. Neil hooked their craft to a rock outcropping with the lines as Tommy and Dobby pulled up alongside. They tied themselves to Neil's boat fore and aft, inserting fenders between them to keep the boats from rubbing against one another.

Neil left the wheel, going up onto the forward deck and turning around to face her. As she watched, curious, he stretched his long frame out onto his stomach.

"Just keep your voice real low," Tommy told her.

"Why?" she whispered.

"You'll see. Don't want to ruin the surprise."

Fascinated, she watched as Neil put his arm over the side, immersing it up to his biceps. Dobby filled a large bucket with water and placed it on the deck of Neil's boat. Then he sat back down on his own.

Tommy's bench by the tiller had been augmented with a stadium chair, the kind used by football fans. Bolted to the bench, it gave him the back support he enjoyed now, lacing his fingers on his stomach. Dobby stretched himself out like Neil, only on his back. He put his hat over his face to shield his eyes from the flashes of sun coming through the branches overhead.

"It'll take about ten minutes," Tommy told her, in that same low voice. "Even though we tried to float in like logs, the fish have to get used to the boats being here. His arm has to equalize with the water temperature. This time of year, that won't take too long. Plus, lotta people, they might have to wait a half hour, or even longer. Not Neil. Your boy there, he has a knack for attracting pretty things to his hand." He smiled at her. "Just relax."

Then he let out a sigh and closed his eyes. Abby blinked at him, at his son. They had drifted into a cove and were now just...taking a nap.

She was used to the busy, noisy world of New Orleans, where there was always something happening and doing, even on the most normal day. It was why working at home had become her preferred choice. She needed the quiet, the control of variables, keeping sensory input to a certain level.

This was exactly that, so...okay, then. She propped her feet up on the console, linked her hands over her knees, and shifted her attention to Neil. It was a sight worth watching. His focus had sharpened, become more intent. The effect was...distracting. He was still looking in her direction, but he was concentrating on something else.

His expression was like hers when she was listening to things in her head, especially when they seemed more real than what other people saw around her.

She thought of what could be in those waters. Alligators, snakes, giant spiders. But Tommy and Dobby seemed perfectly fine with this, like Neil knew what he was doing.

And then...

She gasped as he flipped over, his hand clamped on the gill slit of a fish nearly a foot and a half long. The swift movement sent an arc of water splashing over him as he landed the fish on the center of the deck. She grabbed for the windshield as the boat rocked.

"Woohoo, never fails. You are the man, bro!" Dobby whooped as their boats bobbed together. He already had a long-handled net in his grasp. He used it to contain the wildly flopping fish, scoop it up with Neil's help. Together they deposited it into the bucket of water, Neil guiding it.

As the boats steadied, and her heart rate settled, Neil brought the bucket closer so she could stand up and look into it. The fish was swimming in a tight circle.

Slowly, Neil dipped his hands into the brackish water. The fish didn't seem alarmed when he cradled it, lifting it partially out to give her a better look. It had slick, speckled sides, the sunlight picking up colors that reflected off the shiny skin.

"You can touch him," he told her.

"How do you know he's a male?"

"See how his lower mouth has that hooked look to it? Plus males have bigger mouths than females."

"Big difference from the human species," Dobby noted. When Abby shot him a narrow look, he held up both hands.

"Your mouth looks nice and dainty," he assured her.

"Stop digging while that hole's only big enough for your dad," Neil told him.

The fish's mouth was opening and closing, the gills matching the rhythm. "He's trying to breathe," she said.

"Yeah. Here, I'm lowering him again. There you go, big fellow," Neil murmured. "It's all right."

"It's all right. You're going to die to be someone's dinner, but it's all right."

"There are worse reasons to die," Neil said.

"Said no one's dinner ever."

He gave her a searching look. Her hands were moving along the console edge. Back and forth. Tracing a nervous line. Her shoulder twitched. "You want me to let him go?" he asked quietly.

"Of course not. I'm not a vegetarian. It'd be very hypocritical to... Yes."

It had amazed her, watching Neil catch a fish with his bare hands. But it bothered her to see the fish caught like that, his life over and maybe not even knowing it. Or worse, maybe knowing it was, because suddenly his circumstances had changed, forces he couldn't control taking over...

"Hey. It's okay. Let's let him go." He touched her face. Tommy and Dobby had untied their boat, were floating a few feet away. Pulling the bucket over to the boat edge, Neil peered into it. "Here you go, fine fellow. You helped me impress the girl, so you win this round."

"Neil, you don't have to..."

He cocked his head at her, adjusted his weight back toward center so he balanced the craft. "You want to do it? Come up here. I'll tip it and you can just reach in there and help guide him out, so he doesn't hit the water too rough."

She did it, the fish sliding past her fingers, leaving an impression of oily slickness before disappearing. Into the darkness. She leaned over, watching, wondering what was there, what it was like, down in that deep void...

"Hey." Neil slid an arm across her chest and pulled her back against him. He settled her down between his thighs, in the center of the deck. "No mermaid kingdom down there, bébé. Remember the snakes."

He was teasing her, but his arm conveyed tension. He stroked a hand through her hair.

"You won't have anything for MeeMaw," she said. "To thank her for making us lunch."

He shrugged. "She always has an odd job for me. And I bring her supplies from places farther out than Tommy or Dobby usually go. She isn't on the beaten path for deliveries."

He touched her chin again, a light caress, and she pressed her nose against his jaw. She didn't need to look at him. His regard was there without eye contact, a sure connection. It might be a delusion, but it felt real enough to hold onto. He certainly was. As she curled her fingers over his forearm, she registered his heat and solidity.

He wasn't in any particular hurry, holding her like that, the boat rocking, drifting in the cove. She breathed him in, the calmness. By the time he gave her a little squeeze and helped her slide back into the seat next to him at the wheel, she felt settled again. When he engaged the motor and started out of the cove, she noted Tommy and Dobby had stayed at a casual but considerate distance, waiting for them.

After they had exclaimed over the fish the way they had, she'd expected a reaction that would make her feel awkward, uncomfortable, embarrassed. Instead, as they continued up the river, their banter with Neil resumed, and no one said another word about it. She suspected some kind of nonverbal communication she'd missed had made that happen.

When their path narrowed, one of them would take the lead. Otherwise, the boats cruised side by side. As they passed a pair of cypresses with a diameter likely wider than the span of her outstretched arms, Tommy pointed them out.

"Those are a couple of the older ones. They've found some in the Mississippi delta nearly a thousand years old. And they'll be here for longer. Water doesn't rot them."

He showed her those white teeth again. "Kind of like me."

She chuckled. "What did happen to your first wife, Tommy?"

"She moved upriver. Said I was a better husband at a distance. She's a smart, powerful woman. Needs a lot of space around her to breathe. That's fine by me, long as we're breathing the same air and I know if any man has a full claim on her heart, it's me."

Understanding dawned. "MeeMaw is your wife?"

"A lot of love stories in the world. No two of them look the same, and it's not always easy for folks outside of them to understand." Tommy spoke seriously. "But that's okay, as long as the people in love do. That doesn't just mean people in love, but the way we love one another in general. Family, friends, country, or just our piece of it."

Abruptly his squinted eyes twinkled in his creased face. "Why are you asking old Tommy about himself? You should be asking how many women Neil's brought out here to his love nest."

Neil snorted. "Yeah. Some love nest."

"I don't know about that. The fishing gear and rubber boots at the door were quite the romantic touch." She batted her eyes at him. "But slathering me with bug repellant was what really won me over."

She chuckled and ducked as he skimmed his hand in the water and sent a spray of droplets over her. He still had his other, non-driving hand draped over her thigh, that casual and distracting intimacy. She tapped the top of it.

"So how many women *have* you brought here?"

He gave her a pained look, though the underpinnings of laughter told her it wasn't real. "You think women are lining up to become the queen of my fishing shack?"

"I think plenty of women would be whatever was necessary, at least for as long as it took to get a SEAL in bed with them."

"Well, why didn't you say so? I'll turn around right now and head back to the house."

"I said plenty of women. Not me."

"She's got your number there, Neil. Won't be able to play that one." Dobby winked at Abby. "Now me, I respect a woman, treat her like a real queen. Keep that in mind."

"I will. You can count on it."

"You just mind yourself, before you end up gator bait," Neil advised a smirking Dobby. Then he jerked his chin, gesturing ahead of them. "Your mother's looking for you."

They'd drifted around a bend, bringing another waterfront home into view. A woman stood on the edge of the dock, waiting for them.

Abby had been right about Dobby's mother. MeeMaw was easily as tall as Neil, and as large-boned and solidly built as that thousand-year-old cypress Tommy had mentioned.

She looked like the human inspiration for Pachamama. The bright checkered brown, white and green tunic she wore over brown leggings reminded Abby of a mosaic she'd seen of the Chilean fertility goddess. Standing tall, bare feet on the earth, head of wild dark hair touching the sun. Her magnificent dark arms had been stretched out to touch the ocean waters on one hand, the swirling winds on the other.

The different square colors would add up to prime numbers. The image, chased by that random thought, was strong enough to blur the lines of reality. Fortunately, the docking of the boats, the bump against the rubber-buffered planking, helped sharpen them. MeeMaw watched, hands on hips, as Tommy and Dobby tied off their boat and Dobby stepped onto the dock to hug her.

Neil offered Abby a hand, holding the boat steady with his foot as she stepped off. His hand rested on her lower back, her hip. She put hers at his waist as she made the transition to solid ground. Or reasonably solid.

Now that she'd had a first impression of MeeMaw, her attention went to the house itself. Though Neil had indicated the place wasn't accessible by road, she bet it was a word-of-mouth kayaker attraction.

Closer to civilization, homes built along the water were pricey places, built with new and old money, part of or within a stone's throw of waterfront developments. But tucked back into the bayou, houses were more functional. A place like MeeMaw's represented the way people had lived out here for several generations. Even Neil's reflected the best fit for who he was and what home meant to him.

MeeMaw's house had some unexpected features, though. A rooftop deck shadowed the living quarters below and provided cover to the large screened porch. Built onto either side of the home were two castle-like turrets, only these were sized for a house. Made mostly of stone and some wood, they contrasted with the blue clapboard siding. An American flag was planted at the top of one turret, a Louisiana flag on the other, the blue field bearing the image of a mother pelican with spread wings and a cluster of fledglings around her.

"Is that..." Abby squinted at a wooden structure planted next to one of the turrets. She saw ropes and pulleys.

"It's a catapult," Neil said. "For stuff she can't compost, like fish heads and chicken bones, MeeMaw throws them to the opposite bank or way back into the water, far enough out she's not attracting critters to her place, teaching them to look to humans for food. Hey, there's a treat. Look there."

His arm around her waist, fingers wrapped over her hip, he used the other to gesture to a pile of dead trees about a hundred yards off. She saw a motionless trio of alligators. "There are two babies on the female's back."

Delight swept her as she saw them, just as motionless and with the same creepily passive stare as their mother.

Steppingstones cobbled the ground along the sides of the house. So plentiful and varied in design, they reminded Abby of tombstones in a graveyard. A forest of solar lights on sticks was planted between the stones, like those sold at dollar stores. Red, white and blue caps for the patriotic holidays, orange and black for Halloween, red and green for Christmas. Others had shapes, hummingbirds or butterflies. They'd been positioned to make the most of the sun, dappling the house and grounds through the trees.

"When I come up here to deliver stuff or help Dobby and Tommy with repairs, I usually bring her another handful of those things," Neil told her. "You have to replace the shit batteries the dollar store puts in them with good rechargeables, but once you do that, they last forever."

"I could learn how to do those repairs myself, but men must feel useful, or they get sulky," MeeMaw said.

Her greetings to her son and husband done, she was approaching them with strides that vibrated through the dock. "Give me a hug, tall sailor man."

As Neil complied, he nodded to the solar lights. "Looks like you have a bunch of new ones."

"Word has spread among the tourists," MeeMaw told him. "I think when they rent their stuff down at Penelope's, she tells them 'the swamp witch' might deign to offer a potion or entertain them with my witch woman advice, *if* they bring me a steppingstone or a new light for my garden. Or money." She winked. "A witch can't conjure payment for her generator fuel."

As she turned her attention to Abby, she continued speaking as if they already knew one another, no introductions needed. Perhaps Dobby and Tommy had taken care of that.

"But they have to give it thought," she said in a severe tone. "Think about what I might like, not just grab whatever trash they find to throw at me, like coins to a beggar. They do that, I'll send them scampering back to their boat with the threat of putting Gucci on their heels."

"Gucci?" Abby ventured.

MeeMaw pointed toward the farther side of her house. Abby saw nothing but several old trees, toppled together, an overgrowth of vines and foliage binding them together. Then she saw one unblinking eye. One of those "trees" was an alligator, easily fifteen feet long. His tail curved on the log beneath him.

"Course, he doesn't pay any mind to me," MeeMaw said. "Long as I leave him be, but those who come to see me don't know that, do they? If I throw something he likes toward the water..."

She used one of those plastic, long-handled ball throwers for dogs to scoop something out of a covered bucket. Abby thought the red dripping mass might have once belonged to a chicken.

MeeMaw's arm could rival the catapult. She tossed the contents well clear of the boats, into the middle of the narrow river where it bobbed, a pale lure.

Abby wasn't a faint-hearted person, but base survival instinct had her stepping back against Neil as that motionless log burst into movement. The alligator shot into the water, rocking the boats against the dock edge.

"They can sprint up to thirty-five miles per hour," Tommy mentioned.

Gucci scooped up the chicken like a shovel, and proceeded to cut lazy circles, looking for more. Neil stroked his knuckles along the center of Abby's back.

"What happened to not associating people with food?" she whispered.

"I think MeeMaw bends the rules to suit her," he answered, his chuckle feathering his breath over her skin.

His body's closeness was something she was finding more and more pleasant. It also made it harder for her to stop thinking about the things she wanted from it. From him.

Probably a good thing they were in mixed company, requiring her to restrain herself. Mostly. She'd curled her hand in the belt loop of his jeans, his loose T-shirt creasing into the motion, but now she dropped to his back pocket, hooking her thumb there as she ran fingertips over the curve of his ass. Since they had their backs to the water, no one could see what she was doing.

He brushed his lips over her ear. His hand's grip over her hip bone, the stroke of his long fingers along the inside of it, sent a frisson of feeling toward nearby areas. It was a promise with so many images attached to it she felt dizzy.

"Come get some lunch," MeeMaw said. "Corn bread, fried gator, white rice."

Neil's significant look reminded Abby of his comment that MeeMaw could anticipate lunch visitors. "Gucci doesn't get offended that alligator is on the menu?" Abby asked.

"Oh, *chère*, a male alligator will eat another one if he takes it into his head." MeeMaw shook her head. "Humans are a lot pickier than animals."

"Not me," Dobby said. "Anytime you want to fry up a tourist for lunch, I won't complain a bit." But he sighed with exaggerated drama and sent the next words to Abby. "Course, developing that indiscriminate pallet was a matter of survival. When I was a kid, she made me fight the gators and wild pigs for food."

"Yeah." Neil eyed him. "It obviously stunted your growth."

"Let's eat." MeeMaw was already headed up the ramp, waving at them to follow her.

She'd laid everything out on a wooden picnic table on the porch. Abby noted the table's slats were covered with carvings. Movie quotes, lines of poetry, even a couple of engraved pictures, an alligator, a heron. The center board of the table was painted red, with a song lyric on it.

Never time to save, paying by the hour. –Falling Awake, Gary Jules.

MeeMaw pointed to a stack of plates, inviting the men to help themselves to the fried and spiced food. Carrying aromas evocative of the day, it should have been appetizing, but nausea hit Abby, making her step back before she could stop herself.

Dismay spurted under her breastbone. She'd done it with such an abrupt jerk, the gesture couldn't be considered anything but offensive to a hostess.

The three men hadn't picked up a plate yet, either, but that was for different reasons. MeeMaw's attention was thankfully on them, approval creasing her broad face. She tipped her head toward Abby.

"Boys were raised right, waiting on the women first." But she shook her head at them, gestured to the food. "She's not going to eat that, and I'm still full from taste testing. Dig in."

She drew closer to Abby in a comfortably ponderous motion, so Abby didn't have to fight the reflex to step back, which was happening more often when people approached her too swiftly. Like something jumping out at her.

"I'm very sorry. It looks wonderful."

"Don't fret about that."

The woman's eyes, deep and soulful, gathered Abby in. "You've had a hard row of it these past few days, and it's a long river ahead of you, isn't it, bébé? You're already starting it out tired. Set yourself down by your man, take a rest and lean on him, while I get you something nourishing for the body and soul."

Her hand rested on Abby's shoulder, a bolstering touch. The nails were unexpectedly well manicured, polished a deep green like the shadowed swamp waters. She moved into the house, the screen door creaking behind her.

Unaffected by the exchange, Dobby handed his father a plate, and they started digging into the steaming bowls on the table. Neil offered her a hand to put a leg over the picnic bench and get herself seated. While he filled his own plate, she noted that Tommy and Dobby portioned themselves the same daunting amount of food, despite their size differences.

Neil took a smaller but still generous helping. When he sat down next to her, he broke off a piece of yellow corn bread, putting it on a napkin for her. "An appetizer," he said, nudging her knee with his. "If you're up for it."

The smell, when she brought it close to her nose, said she was. MeeMaw returned while she was on her second careful bite. The woman held a soup bowl, a pretty piece of pottery with a blue and rust-colored drip glaze. When she set it before Abby, a heavenly scent stirred Abby's sluggish appetite in a way she hadn't experienced in several days. Even the cheese bagel couldn't compare.

She didn't know what it was, didn't need to. Gratitude filled her, too much. The events of the past few weeks, the changes to her life she now faced, kept emotions churning just below the surface. She locked them down as much as she could, especially on a day like today, so she could have a chance to enjoy it, give herself a good time with Neil.

Unfortunately, all her decades of experience in closing down and channeling her fears and anxieties, dealing with the "what if" army invasion, meant nothing now that her mind was actually fragmenting. The locks had changed overnight, from steel to tissue paper.

Her hand shook so badly as she tried to pick up the spoon, it clattered against the lip of the bowl. Neil's hand closed over her other one, his grip warm and reassuring. MeeMaw sat down on her other side. Sliding an arm around Abby, she rubbed her with brisk, matter-of-fact care before Abby could mortify herself by falling apart.

"It's like that fish," MeeMaw said. "His fate was to die today, until it wasn't. Your choice changed his fate, or maybe that fate was always written. If he knew that, he wouldn't have felt fear, knowing today wasn't his day. But we don't know that. We can't live like that, can we?

Once we know the day and time, our possibilities, our view of everything, changes. Can become wider or narrower, that's up to us. There are things in the head that none of us understand. Or the heart, neither."

Abby stared at her. That gaze held her and didn't melt away. It just became more vibrant, a glow settling over MeeMaw's skin, as if she were a goddess in truth. But then she reminded Abby she was simply a woman. A very wise, kind woman.

She stretched her other hand out across the table to Tommy. It should have looked incongruous, the gnarled skinny fingers and her meaty grasp, but as he took it, Abby saw the strength in Tommy's.

When MeeMaw needed it, his strength surpassed hers. Abby saw that truth when he reached out with his free hand, caressed her face. MeeMaw's gaze softened in that way most women understood instantly. This was the man MeeMaw could depend upon when it mattered.

"You don't look at anyone's face too long," MeeMaw said, telling Abby she was speaking to her again. "But I can see you're the type of woman who prefers to look a man in the eye. You want to look at Neil, look inside him, explore all the worlds to see in there."

Acknowledging it, the loss of it, of everything she could no longer count upon, conjured that ache in her throat. "Yes. But it gets too overwhelming."

When it happened, it spread out from there, and everything became too much, visual information jumbled.

"That's all right." MeeMaw tapped the area next to her own eye. "When we go blind, lose one sense, look to the others. You're not looking at him now, but you feel everything about him. The way he's looking at you, how he's tuning into you, like you're traveling the same current." She sent Abby a playful look. "I know you also feel that fine body of his next to you."

"Maybe." The spurt of mischief was unexpected but a welcome answer to the turbulent emotions. MeeMaw beamed at her.

"Everything in life is common sense, girl, if we know when to call on it, put our fears and pride away. Laughter's one of the easiest ways to reach it. Eat up now."

Abby's mood steadied. Neil nudged her with the knee attached to that fine body, returned to eating. No expectations. Just sitting with her, enjoying being together.

"The soup is really good," she said, a few spoonfuls later. MeeMaw had made herself a small plate and resettled into a sturdy chair placed at the head of the table, Tommy to her left.

"Don't ask her what's in it," Dobby said. "It's far better not to know. Ever." He laughed as his mother leaned around Tommy to whack the back of his head. Dobby absorbed the affectionate blow with no recoil.

With her thigh pressed to Neil's, her shoulder brushing his, his distracting scent in her nose, along with that of the delectable soup and corn bread, Abby ate and listened to the back and forth between the loving family.

Like the lap of the water against the dock, the voices stayed low enough she could listen.

CHAPTER EIGHT

After the meal, they left Tommy and Dobby with MeeMaw. As Neil threw off the lines and they motored along the tributaries he wanted to show her, she rested on her hip on the flat front deck, watching the bayou world drift by.

A herd of spiky, black-haired pigs rooted on a muddy bank they cut up with their stubby hooves. Three deer crossed a narrow section of the estuary, plunging through the water and bounding up the opposite side. The water went from brown to a green so bright and unbroken, it looked as if it had been painted on the water with a brush.

Shades of green were everywhere. Giant elephant ears, lily pads dotted with thick-petaled white flowers. More delicate blooms grew up among the water plants in a variety of colors. Her favorite was a pale lavender blossom, nodding on a slender stem over ridged silver dollar leaves.

Frogs croaked from the crevices of logs, while turtles congregated on debris like the alligators, basking in the sun.

"I figured alligators would be like the snakes," she observed. "Preferring the cooler temperatures."

Neil shook his head. "A gator's back, the ridges, have blood vessels that act like solar panels. Their body temp has to stay above seventy to digest their food, or it will rot in their stomachs and kill them."

He pointed to an area they were passing. Beyond the cypresses planted in the deeper water was a marshy field of long tall grasses and more white oaks. "Female alligators make their nests in places like that and lay their eggs. They'll cover them up with the grass, and when that decays, it forms an incubator. If it stays above a certain temp, all the eggs will be males. Under it, they're all females."

He'd turned down a smaller tributary. "Where are we going?"

"There's something I thought you'd like to see."

She liked seeing his world through his eyes, the way he presented it for her enjoyment, without demands. No matter that she was tired again, and her face didn't want to move, a side effect to meds or the psychosis, or some of both.

As the day had progressed, her worries about what might happen that she couldn't anticipate had eased. Nothing had stirred or exacerbated her symptoms beyond what she could handle. But they were in a very controlled environment, weren't they? His ground, his comfort zone. She'd demonstrated an unsettling level of trust in that.

She thought of MeeMaw calling Neil "her man." Should that irritate her, the assumptions she'd made about the two of them? Would it give him the wrong impression?

"I'm not going to give you what you want, the response you want."

It wasn't the first time she'd said that to him, but this time there were far deeper layers of meaning to it. Layers that gave her voice an annoyed, anxious edge.

"You owe me nothing right in this moment, Abby. Look."

They'd seen cypress knees throughout the day, but now they were drifting into a lagoon that held a garden of them, in all sizes. The gloom that shrouded the place was soothing, peaceful, making her think of a cathedral.

"This place speaks to me," he said. "There's a communication in the silence, between me and it. I thought you might feel the same way. But I meant what I said. That conversation is between you and the place. You don't need to include me."

He cut the boat to an idling purr. Settled back in his seat, one foot propped on a bucket, his arm lying loosely over the seat next to him. His gaze slid over the area, eyes half closed as he relaxed.

From her position on the front deck, she saw what he was offering, but she couldn't let go of what was moving through her mind to grasp it.

"Why would you want to be here if you're not included?"

His response was a quiet rumble that fit the surroundings. "It's not like that. I can enjoy the sun and the wind, even if they're indifferent to my presence. But that's the thing. When I'm totally aware of them, I think they're aware. And they accept me. We connect, without any words having to be spoken."

"You and Vera need to have this conversation. She's the spiritual one." He was frustrating her, but the stubbornness she was feeling, the wall of resistance, had no target. She put her hands over her face, shutting out everything for a second, pulling it together. Then she found what was bothering her, and lifted her head again. "You're trying to make a point. Make it."

His voice betrayed no impatience, but she latched onto intent. He had more than a point. He had a purpose.

"You've got a lot happening in your head," he said. "You're trying to control it all, because that's what you're taught, what you feel. What you prefer. Staying in control."

"Everyone does."

"Yeah. But when that's not possible, there are other ways to find the same feeling. A different way. Are you willing to try one?"

"Tell me what you're asking."

"Lie down on your back. Feet toward me, flat on the deck, legs bent. Like if you were in your bed and I was standing at the foot of it."

What she heard beneath his even tone sent a ripple of reaction through her, disrupting the irritation. "I'm fully clothed."

"Did I say to take anything off?"

It was no longer beneath it. It had gripped his voice fully. Her gaze went to his, pulled there. What she saw in his eyes in that brief glimpse was familiar. Something she knew from his side of it, not this one, but she didn't reject it. "No. You didn't."

He cut the engine, hooking the boat to a pair of cypress knees to keep it still. Her gaze moved back to the deck, considering. Then she removed the hat he'd given her, handed it over the top of the steering console. He tucked it in a cubby beneath the wheel. His silence had become a weighted thing between them, a meaning that grew larger in that space.

She adjusted around so her feet were pointed in his direction. She lowered herself to her back, staring up at the sky through the trees.

Knees bent, feet flat. He touched her shin, telling her she was within his reach.

"Close your eyes. Palms on the deck on either side of you. Stretch your arms out in whatever way is most comfortable, but keep them that way."

As reactions built inside her, she knew if he stayed silent too long, the whispers would happen. She needed to tell him that. He spoke before it was necessary.

"Can you hear me breathing, Abby?"

"I wish I could. There'd be something to hear other..."

Than those other voices. Shadows outside were better than shadows inside, but it was past lunchtime. Not past three o'clock yet, her danger zone, but it was getting closer.

"Spread your knees."

That got her attention.

"They're already open."

"Spread them wider. I want to imagine putting my head between them, tasting you through the denim."

She complied, the image filling her mind. His arms coiling over her thighs, holding her open, the pressure of his mouth working on her through her jeans. When she'd ordered a man to perform oral sex on her, she'd felt the movement of his tongue as it danced over her flesh, as he figured out the best way to please her. With Neil, it would be different. He would please her, but the reasons, the intent, the control...it would have a different shape. Her body was clenching, opening. Wanting him.

All the sexual desire that had rolled between them throughout the day came back to heat her skin, fire her imagination. It had started with her first sight of him on her swing and carried them until now. Even at the ebb times, it hadn't fully vanished. Waiting to be called.

The rock of the boat told her he'd eased onto the front deck with her. "Now, no matter what I do to you, stay real still, bébé. Remember, there are alligators in these waters."

Her lips curved, a taut crescent. "There's one in the boat with me."

His hands settled on her legs, stroked, gripped. A small noise escaped her throat, her body reacting as if he'd touched her more intimately. It proved how strong that banked sexual desire had grown, just over the course of a few hours. From the thrumming energy in his touch, he felt it, too. But he kept the pace slow, deceptively relaxed.

"How do my hands feel?" he asked.

"Stronger. Warmer. Bigger.... Better than mine."

"I'd argue that from my side of things, but I'm happy to hear you feel that way." A pause. "I want to talk to Tiger. I want to be in the room, watch the way you handle a man at your feet, who wants to serve you as a sub."

"Why?" She kept her eyes closed. "What would that give you?"

"I like watching you eat a bite of cornbread. Sitting in the front of my boat, your hair soft around your face. I like listening to your voice, no matter what you're talking about. You think I wouldn't want to see you do something so important to you?"

The power of all the life around them had a pulse, and it was echoing in her own blood, calling to her. "Okay. Maybe." She was surprised her voice came out so even, let alone that she could chase it with humor. "But next time you go down range, I get to do a ride along."

"I'm sure Dodge will be cool with that. We hit some great tourist spots. You'll have your choice between Helltown, Death Alley, and my personal favorite, Shitholeville. There's a decent restaurant in Helltown. And a bowling alley."

"You never go anywhere beautiful?"

"We do. But there's nothing more beautiful than what I'm looking at right now." He gripped her calf. She thought of what MeeMaw said, about her ability to feel what he was looking at without needing to look at him. It might be a delusion, but she thought she really could.

He was gazing between her legs, up her torso, over her breasts, to her neck and face. It made her legs quiver, even though he stayed where he was, his hand resting on her ankle, playing with it under the cuff of her jeans.

The entire day, they hadn't talked about it. The way the words came to her now was as natural and inevitable as the water they drifted upon. They also possessed a risky, below-the-surface current.

"Most men wouldn't have reached out again. Not because they're assholes, but because it's too much to ask of a new relationship. Why did you?"

"Why do you think?"

"That's too much of a question for me to answer today. And I asked you the question."

He went under the hem of her shirt, fingers sliding along her waist, the base of her rib cage. A sigh whispered out of her. He kept up the caress, and it was a couple minutes before he spoke. Either because he wanted to focus only on touching her before responding, or he was gathering his thoughts. She was okay with either reason.

"Intel is important," he said. "But when intel fails, I have to rely on my gut. There've been plenty of times when my life, and the lives of others, depended on that. So I trust it. My gut told me to follow through with my offer to take you out on the boat. It didn't get into the why."

"Sure it was your gut? I've got a great body, and I'm not shy about taking a man if I want him." She cracked her eye open, let her gaze rove over his body, managed a brief touch of his face before she closed her eyes again. She settled her shoulders deeper against the deck. Though she didn't do it in a calculated way, it would draw his attention to her generous breasts. "You might only be home for a short time before you're called out again, and I'm thinking the options in Hellhole Town are limited."

Why not screw the crazy woman? Everyone thinks crazy women are freaks in bed.

She was glad she hadn't said that out loud, because even saying it in her head made things hurt. Since her teens, she had fought an uphill battle to claim self-worth, to recognize how much she deserved a good opinion of herself. Even now, she had to reaffirm it more often than she liked, but she could do it. Being a Domme helped a lot with that.

And yet, in a matter of weeks, what had been growing in her head had started tugging on that fabric, unraveling those careful triple stitches.

Worthless, useless...

She hadn't said it out loud. She knew she hadn't. But suddenly she sensed she'd stepped into uncertain territory with him. He shifted between her spread knees. Leaning over her emphasized the differences in their sizes. When he braced a hand by her shoulder, the heat and pure male animal pressed in on her, no matter the space between their bodies.

He lowered his mouth to her sternum, tasting her above the V-neck of her T-shirt with a brief flick of his tongue, an almost animal gesture. When her hands began to move, he spoke against her flesh.

"Be still."

She didn't usually take commands from men, but in this instance, she went motionless. He nudged the neckline of the shirt so he could put his mouth on the top of one quivering breast, tease it with heated breath, firm lips and questing tongue, and then he did it to the other.

"Oh..." How did the barest touch of his mouth do that, spread sensation like melted butter she wanted him to lick up, suckle from her skin?

He straightened the arm so he was over her again, staring down at her. She had her gaze on his chest, but moved it up to the pulse throbbing in his strong throat. When he touched her face, thumb going to her chin to lift it, she stiffened. "I...can't look at you...and see you. Sometimes."

"I know. You can see me without that. It's why you've gotten tense. You know you crossed a line. Close them."

She stiffened, but he'd kept his tone mild enough she complied. He leaned in again, pressed his mouth to her cheekbone, spoke against it. "The road you were going down, what you were going to insinuate? Stay away from that destination, bébé. Because when someone needs their ass strapped, I can see it, just as clear as you can. And I'm every bit as capable of doing it."

"You wouldn't dare."

"I'm way more old school than you might think, and I'm bigger, stronger, and more determined." He paused. "Okay, bigger and stronger."

That made her smile, her emotions loosening their tight hold on her insides. When he drew back, her eyes opened. For a painful heartbeat, their gazes locked. Then his expression eased, and he slid an arm underneath her, bringing her into a sitting position as he went to his heels. When her face rested against his shoulder, his jaw pressed against the side of her head, his beard brushing her cheek.

"I'm taking you home, to my place. So I can see all of you. Be inside you. Make my point."

His certainty of it, the way he had his hands resting on her, defied argument. Between here and there, her mind could do all sorts of things to sabotage the plan, but right now, her body was allied with him. That might be enough to make it happen. Her skin was tingling, her sex throbbing. She wanted his hands, his mouth, his cock. Every inch of him, she wanted to take possession. Call him hers without any arguments, even internal ones.

"We could do that right here. It's pretty quiet."

"You aren't wearing bug repellant under your clothes." She heard the rueful humor in his response. "I'm not exposing your pretty tender parts to the mosquitoes. Remember what I said. I'm the only one who gets to bite you."

Even her restless body couldn't argue with that. He gripped her hand, helped her shift from the front deck to come sit next to him again. Once she was seated and he put the boat in drive, he didn't say much. That was just as well, because he'd given her a lot to think about. She needed the time to shore up what her brain might try to dismantle between here and there.

Stressing about it would only make it a self-fulfilling prophecy, though. She hadn't been bragging on herself; it was a simple fact that she'd been blessed in the good looks department. She also knew a SEAL had no difficulty finding bed partners when he wanted to get off with a soft, willing body. If Neil was with her, he had other reasons. He'd made that clear in lots of ways today.

"I'm sorry," she said abruptly, keeping her gaze ahead of them. "Don't let me get away with that kind of shit."

"I don't believe I did."

He slanted her a glance, and just like that, it was fully okay between them again. She took a breath, let it out, smiled. "No, you didn't. And today is about being whatever I need or want to be. Or have to be."

"It sure is. No pressure, bébé." He bent close again, spoke against her cheek. It routed them around the eye contact issue, replacing it with intimate closeness. "I might want to plow you like a field, have you tear open my back with your nails, but if it happens, it will be because that's what I feel from you, too. That's what makes it feel so damn good, and I can wait for that for a decade if that's what you need. I have only one requirement that I won't negotiate."

His lips touched her cheekbone, her eye, her forehead. "I want to be as close to you as I can be, as you can let me."

He straightened, but he kept a grip on her hand. She laced her fingers in his, tightened that grip, put her other hand on top of it. She drew a deep breath. *Okay.*

It took a half hour to get back to his place. He pointed out more alligators. Herons taking flight, fish swimming alongside the boat. A large toad sprang three feet through the air and landed in the water with a giant splash. Sunlight shafted through the cover of the trees, grew sharper, longer, the day waning.

She pushed her worries about that to the back of her mind. Instead, she watched the water ripple out to the shores. The play of light and shadow. Listened to the quiet drone of the motor compete with the voices. Watched him handle the wheel one handed, the other resting on her knee, in her grasp. His gaze stayed moving over their course, and over her. The continuity of his regard, how it never truly left her, spoke of everything behind it.

She thought of the passionate heat of their greeting kiss this morning. Then how he'd taken her over on the deck of his boat. His suggestion about Tiger, the implication that she might be able to exercise a Domme's demands inside the protected shelter of his care.

His Dominance.

Neil's one inflexible demand was to be close to her. But she had her own demands, too. Reaching up, she caressed his face, drew his attention to her. Then she put herself on his knee, straddling it, and laid her mouth solidly on his. She slid her touch behind his neck, fingers moving over the slightly curling hair there, damp from sweat. He kept it short, but since special operators didn't do the conspicuous military high and tight, it was long enough she could grip it.

It was his job to make sure they didn't crash, so she didn't give that any thought. One of his hands stayed on the wheel, but the other curved around her waist, gripped with sure strength, that heady evidence of male desire.

When he eased back his mouth was taut as his body. "We're almost home," he said.

She shifted back into her seat so he could bring them up to the dock. The light in his gaze sparked through her, but the rush of desire had stirred up other things, too.

Damn it.

She'd always had to be linear, to stay in control. Now her thoughts moved like someone in zero gravity, going here, there, everywhere. They tugged her back in time, but not to the pleasantness of this morning.

Instead, they took her to when he'd found her half out of her head. He'd stayed calm. He'd helped her. Before he showed up today, before he'd sent her the boat video, she'd been absolutely certain they were done, that the only thing left was the obligatory, pathetic follow up to make sure she was okay.

Her practical side had no doubts; that would have been the best thing for him. And if it had happened? The not-practical side would have been hurt to the core, far out of proportion with what their relationship was at this point.

"Tell me the truth. How much did you really freak out, after you saw me like that?"

He'd tied off the boat, cut the engine. Now he sat back down in the captain's chair, touched her thigh. When his hand brushed her back, she twitched.

"You can't look at my face, but you can turn toward me," he said. "Do that, and I'll answer you. Don't shut me out with your body language, Abby."

"I'm not." But she was. He didn't say anything, and she finally turned on the rotating seat. She stared at his thigh, the column in faded denim. His fingers gripped his knee. He had a thin scar on his forearm, about six inches long. "What caused that?" she asked.

"Knife. From crabbing with my dad." Humor, a little forced, entered his voice. "Not all of my scars have an action-hero story. Does that make me less attractive?"

"Couldn't you hear my libido just wilting?"

An easier chuckle, but he gripped her hand. "It upset me, seeing you like that. I was worried as hell, and then, when I learned what it was, I was pissed that you're having to face that. You're an incredible woman, Abby, dealing with something unimaginably difficult."

No pity. Just kindness. And no obvious abatement in his desire or interest. How he conveyed that so clearly, she didn't know, but it held her in place, kept her sharp, defensive tongue muted as he continued. "I've seen women in places where their world has totally gone to shit, with no real hope it's going to get any better for them or those they love. I've seen them cope in ways that tell me just how strong a woman can be."

He paused. "When I was with you on your steps that day, I didn't yet know what was wrong. But I thought, if I was going through something like that, a day out on the boat might be a good way to get a break from all of it. Everything you're having to worry about." An edge entered his voice. "And before you get into trouble again, no, this is not a pity date."

"I don't think I ever really believed it was," she said honestly. "Even if I had, you've proven with everything you've done today that's not your motive. But there are plenty of fucked-up women out there, decently normal enough to challenge you in a relationship without dragging you into hell with them. So...why?"

"The only easy day is yesterday. That's a SEAL credo. Normal challenges bore us."

Just like that, her hackles were back up. "I don't want to be anyone's project."

"You're ignoring the answer I'm giving you, and putting your own spin on it." Though his tone stayed mild, it notably sharpened in response to the stiffness in hers. She imagined the look in his slate eyes would match it. "I'll go down a lot of roads with you, bébé, but again, not that one. I want to be inside you, and you want that, too."

He rose, stepped out of the boat, extended her a hand.

"You want to start a fight," he said conversationally, "be polite and wait until after we fuck each other. The way we've wanted to, all damn day."

The comment startled her enough her gaze rose to his set profile. His expression was so ornery, she couldn't help it.

She laughed.

~

As he stowed the gear they'd carried, she stood on the dock, gazing at the moving water. As dusk was closing in, the bayou sounds were getting louder, but it wasn't overpowering, because the warblings, chirps and cries fell against a thick pallet of such...stillness.

Unfortunately, she didn't have that buffer zone inside her. The afternoon sun still warmed her shoulders, but the shadows were deepening. Voices getting louder. She swayed, the ground tilting. Or maybe it was just her perspective.

We are coming for you. We're watching you now.

She jumped as he settled his hands on her shoulders, but it didn't make him draw away. He stroked, grounding her. Then his touch moved to her waist. "I'm going to take over for a while," he said. "All right?"

"This path is only going to bring you pain, Neil." Her voice had gravel in it, raw and scraping. "It will tear me into even smaller pieces to watch it happen, because I won't be able to do anything to stop it."

Her mother had said psychotic episodes came with one dubious mercy. When sucked down into one's own terror, euphoria, paranoia or mania, it temporarily removed the ability to see what it was doing to those she loved. When she hadn't been in psychosis, alcohol or illegal drugs had helped numb that agony. Kept her from digging out that excruciating ache with the sharpest thing she could find.

By her eighth birthday, Abby had begun locking up anything pointy in the house, watching her mother like a hawk when she had a pen or fork in her hands. Constant vigilance.

He knew what that was like, didn't he?

"Can't avoid pain in this life." His voice was floating around her. "Not if you're really living it. You haven't answered my question."

"Because you didn't ask one. Not really." She jerked, an involuntary movement, not an attempt to pull away. He didn't let go. "Sounds more like you're telling me."

"If it's easier." He paused, and when she said nothing, the flex of his fingers heralded his decision. "I'm taking control for awhile," he repeated.

"I'm afraid I won't want to take it back," she admitted.

His chuckle was relaxed, sending a counter surge of pleasure to war with her agitation. "That possibility doesn't worry me at all. You're not lazy and you're not weak. Just tired of carrying it alone."

His voice dropped to a rumble, the words implacable. "Turn to me, bébé."

Just like on the boat. He required a gesture that told him she was giving him her attention. Not shutting him out or pretending she didn't want this.

The touch of Cajun he put on the endearment, distinguishing it from "baby," sent a small electric current through her, helping her to move. When she turned, it was within the span of his hands on her waist, because he didn't retreat at all. She couldn't quite relax enough to lean into him, but her neck did bend enough to drop her forehead on his chest, rest against the heat and heartbeat there.

He bent and lifted her, keeping her so close as he did it, like she was something he'd scooped up in his palm. She imagined being that size, carried that way, and didn't mind it. If she was that small, she'd be ignored as the armies of demons galloped by. Nobody noticed a field mouse on a battlefield, or a bird flying overhead as guns roared and blood was spilled. Wind still lifted the bird beneath her wings, carried her aloft.

Unless a stray bullet caught her.

Neil carried her away from the dock, and into his house. It still had the scent of the bayou, marsh grasses, open air, sunlight and shadows. The quieter kind. The rough textured paneling offered a pine scent like the wood floors, which shone softly where the area rugs revealed them. The rugs were striped blue and brown. Colors of earth and water, with lots of screened windows to let in the light. He didn't have central air, but before they'd left, he'd switched on a mobile A/C unit set up in the bedroom.

For her comfort, she suspected.

Sitting her on the bed, he took his phone out of his jeans pocket. He scrolled with his thumb, his free hand resting on her shoulder. As he set the device on the table next to them, the notes of the song he'd chosen drifted out into the room.

He'd kept the volume low, Aretha talking about the way a man could make her feel. A natural woman.

She would have joked about him having a sex playlist, but another Dominant would recognize the tactic in an instant. Humor being used as a defensive shield. She had no energy for that. Defensive measures were for where you had walls to defend. Hers were crumbling into grains of sand in an hourglass, slipping away ever faster.

He was close enough that she was done waiting. She nuzzled his abdomen, hands slipping up his thighs as she bit him through the T-shirt, finding hard stomach muscle. He drew her to her feet again, held her against him. Her hands were under his arms, fingers digging into his back. He kissed her beneath her ear, along her cheek, as he gathered her hair up into one fist and moved it out of his way. His grip tightened, radiating sensation through her scalp. Then his mouth was at her throat. He locked his grip on her hair, tipped her head back, and bit her, giving her the edge of his own teeth.

I can give you pain, Abby.

Her body lifted to him, to the gift of it, as he held that grip, put his other hand beneath her shirt. He traced her lower back, the sensitive valley of her spine. He was moving them, a slow rock. Her foot was between his, the other on the outside, tangled in what seemed like the start of a dance, and she guessed it was.

He kissed the areas he'd bitten, and drew her T-shirt up. Dropping to a knee, he put his mouth on her upper abdomen, just below the joining point of her rib cage, an area she hadn't realized was that sensitive until his lips were teasing it. As he did that, he slipped the button of her jeans, opened them up for the stroke of his fingers between her hip bones, trailing an arch over her mound, leaving the folds of her flesh pulsing.

He was inhaling her, tasting her. Touching her as if he was exploring her reaction, one nerve ending at a time. She'd closed her eyes to keep the stimulation from distorting her surroundings into a distraction. She would hold them at bay, so she could feel as much of this as she could.

"Hold my shoulder," he said. When she did, he removed her shoes and socks, took her jeans down. She stepped out of them, her fingers exploring the broad strength of that support. She bent over, pressing her nose to his shirt, against his back, and he wrapped his arms around her hips, deftly lifting and turning her so he had her laid out on the bed, himself above her, hand braced by her head.

As he traced her face, she was aware of how she was staring at him. No smile, nothing, everything weighed down. Flat effect. A symptom that made people think someone with schizophrenia wasn't feeling anything, when the opposite was so vividly, bitterly true.

She tried to tell him, but only managed a few words. The explanation was like a bucket of water, threatening to dash the fire building within her, between them.

His answer was to trail a fingertip down her sternum, down to her shirt hem, and slide his hand under it again. Slow, his gaze on the movement of his hand beneath the fabric, until he reached her breast.

He surrounded it with his large grasp, bringing her heat, rubbing his calloused palm over her erect nipple so she bit her lip, rose to his touch.

"You think I don't know you've been inside a storm all day?" he said, low. Unexpected. When his gaze flicked up, she caught a glimpse of lightning in his eyes. "Weathering it, trying to keep the boat from capsizing? I'm standing inside you, Abby. I see the storm. I may not see all of it, because you're the captain, not me, but I'm a damn good first mate."

He was. How many ways had he said it today, that she could be and do whatever she had to be, and *that was fine*. It changed *nothing* for him. The more he'd proven he meant it, taking her into environments that supported that resolve, the more okay she'd become.

The more okay she became.

She could be here, doing this, even with the storm raging. It wasn't a comfort zone, but it was definitely something she wanted.

"A first mate like Gilligan." A rare sound passed her lips. A giggle. Inappropriate humor was a symptom. Recognizing that made her breath hitch, a startled reaction. However, amusement wreathed his features, paired with mock annoyance.

"I am *not* Gilligan," he said.

He took off her T-shirt. When she arched, his eyes followed the motion, rested on her breasts in the plain cotton bra, a bit of lace along the cups. He slid his hand under her, unhooked it, took the straps down her arms.

"Holy God," he murmured, making her smile. She had the kind of breasts no man could resist staring at clothed, let alone naked and quivering. She'd never appreciated that fact quite so much.

But now she was only in panties. And he was too overdressed.

She wrapped her hand in his T-shirt. "Off." A quiet demand. "Can you take orders from a woman, sailor?"

For this, apparently yes. He removed it, and her hand was on solid male flesh. He left the shirt on the bed, and her other hand nestled in the cotton, holding it, stroking. She wanted to bring it to her face and inhale. She'd seen him shirtless at the barbecue, and then closer up, at the park, but in this slower moment, more potent, she had a better chance to look and absorb. He *was* beautiful, sculpted to fight for everything that mattered.

"Holy God," she murmured, and made him smile.

Gripping her wrist, he kissed her palm, the pulse, his eyes growing more intent again. "I want to do things to you," he said. "Can you let me take control?"

A repeat of his earlier question. Not "may," the permission version, but "can," to see if it was possible for her to do it, to find pleasure in it. He was precise. As precise as she was.

"My inner Domme might break out and kick your ass."

"I like a good fight. Don't move."

He rose, went to his closet and came out with another gray T-shirt, though this one was so faded it was hard to tell what the logo over the left breast side had been. It also had a couple holes in it. "Remember what I told you earlier?"

She wasn't sure until he ripped it along the seams. He used a pocketknife to finish the job and divide it into strips.

"Hope that one wasn't a favorite." Her mouth was dry.

"It will be after I do this with it."

He sat back down on the edge of the bed. Keeping his attention on her reaction, he picked up her hand, wrapped one of the strips around her wrist. She put some pressure against his hold, a nonverbal cue he picked up on, letting her bend her arm so it was up against her face, and she could smell. His scent, strong and reassuring, just as she'd hoped.

"Good?"

At her nod, he lifted her arm out to the side and back, toward his headboard, which had useful wood railings. He attached the end to one. "You can pull loose with little effort. Do you restrain your subs?"

"Sometimes. Usually in a way where they can free themselves." Her heart was thudding in her ears. A couple weeks ago, she'd have known her reaction to this. She would have wanted to be the one doing the tying. Still wouldn't mind that, but now her feelings were in unknown territory.

She'd told him she couldn't go back to being the kind of Domme she'd been those same couple weeks ago. But she wasn't a sub, either. She had no judgments here. She was letting it happen, seeing how it felt. How her brain reacted. At the moment, it was still. Not listening to the mutterings in the shadows. It was intrigued enough to stay attuned to Neil, what he was doing. Trusting enough.

He did the other arm, then moved down and did the same to her legs. "How much self-control do you have, Mistress?"

"As much as I feel like having. Control *and* self-control."

He laid a hand on her leg. "Then keep your legs spread and your hands where I've put them. Until you can't stop yourself from touching me." His gaze heated. "When that happens, that will tell me you want me inside you."

Wicked laughter bubbled up, mixed with something far more explosive. "That's a broad interpretation of my response."

"When we get there, I'm thinking it will be pretty specific and difficult to misinterpret."

The fire in her leaped up in response to his. "I wanted to shred the T-shirt you were wearing," she said.

Pull at the cloth, reveal the resilient body beneath. No matter how much she yanked, he would have absorbed it like a rooted tree. One designed to shade her, nourish her, grow with her.

"If I'd known that, I would have put the old one on and let you do the job for me." His faint smile didn't reach his eyes. He brushed his hand along her throat, following her shoulder, the tender underside of her arm. Despite his obvious pleasure with her breasts, he took his time getting there, enjoying the way her arms were held out so he could stroke them, above and below, caress her wrists in the T-shirt strips as he leaned over her.

He trailed his fingers between her breasts, following the curves beneath, then between them again. Orbiting the peaks made them all the more sensitive, needy for his touch. When he finally let his fingertips graze them, reaction bolted through her, her breath sucking in.

She could counter his teasing with enticements of her own, particularly when it matched exactly how her body wanted to move. Arching up into his touch, eyes closed, legs spread, breasts offered and quivering. When he muttered a fervent oath, she was gloriously aware of her sexual power.

He captured her breasts in both hands, thumbing the nipples with a firm flick that shot electricity through her again. Arousal could be a race, the competitors pushing one another toward that finish line. But ultimately it was a team sport, the two of them bound to one another, unwilling to go over the finish line alone. Wanting the race to go on as long as they could, because every step of it was taken together, and the longer it took, the more amazing it could be.

He slid his hand down her abdomen, over her hips. "No scars."

The gods, in their capricious form of compassion, sometimes left the outer body alone when Fate intended to destroy the inside. At least in Abby's case. Her mother had carried burn scars from her own mother's violence.

She didn't want her mind to go there. Fortunately, he either anticipated it or just had really good timing. He put his mouth on her hip bone, almost reverent.

"So do you let your subs put their mouths on you? Other than when you command them to do oral?"

"Sometimes." A breathless whisper. She gazed down at him, watched his back curve over her, his thigh flex as he braced his foot next to the bed. He continued to explore her with his mouth, the crease between hip and upper thigh.

"Come up here." She moved restlessly against the bonds.

"In a bit."

She moaned, a hum in her throat, as rough stubble grazed the tender flesh above her mound. "You know," he murmured, "I enjoy watching a woman's every reaction when I have my mouth on her cunt. When I play over that slick flesh. Licking her, teasing her with my tongue, biting her. I love that moment when her eyes drop half closed, her head presses deeper into my pillow, and she arches her throat."

She was doing just that. She felt his head lift as he looked up at her, then his mouth settled on her upper thigh again. His breath feathered over her clit. "You know that churning, creamy kind of foam in ocean surf? How drops of it spray against your face when the wave crests? When it's warm in the summertime, it reminds me of that honey between a woman's legs. When she starts lifting up and down, like you're doing, I see her on the waves. Then comes the little moans and gasps, like you just made."

She'd described it that way to Tiger, a wave. No surprise that a SEAL would choose his sexual metaphors from the same element.

Neil's voice deepened, became more concentrated. In control. "I can feel you moving into my hands, trusting yourself to me. When you're fully there, you're all mine, resting in my arms like I've earned a gift from the gods."

Her gaze flicked down to see that smile that wasn't a smile at all, but a binding all its own, fully capturing her attention. "Or in this case, a gift from a goddess."

Her hand curled above the binding on her wrist. Uncurled. Curl. Uncurl. Fingers tightening, releasing. Her eyes moved to watch them as his mouth and hands moved on her. Incredible snapshots, while a billion upon billion other things, just as miraculous, happened in the universe, as the world whirled.

Whirled world.

They're watching. They want to scoop out your brain and put it on toast. With peanut butter. Butter with peanuts.

She pressed her head back into the cushioning of the pillow. The last time she'd masturbated, she'd imagined it as Neil's hand when her own moved between her legs. She'd thought of those steady eyes watching her. Then he'd turned into a tree, his roots curling over her arms and legs, but not to imprison her. They drew her to him. Into him.

His hand moved over her dampening flesh, caressing, dancing, playing. Her hips lifted, demanding more.

Asking more.

Desire stuttered, faltered, then caught again, rose. He was different. Something she didn't usually want. But her body, her heart and her soul said differently.

Her mind was being altered. Was the invader changing her heart and soul with it? Or were the heart and soul like the opposing army, marshaling the best weapon they could find to fight back? Telling her that the tactics, the field, had to change, because the mind sure as hell had the home court advantage. It knew everything. She had to go down a road it didn't know.

To do that, she needed a specific travel companion, but he didn't deserve an unfamiliar road, one that would end in darkness.

"That's the job I signed up for, bébé."

Her head jerked up. It was as if he was there, but he wasn't. The whispers swallowed the words, but they couldn't erase them from her mind. She couldn't open her eyes, wouldn't. The world would pounce on her, tear her apart. If her eyes stayed closed, she'd be right here, with him, in this room.

He was right. That was the job he'd signed up for. But not on domestic soil. Not at home. She couldn't be anyone's home. She wasn't even a home for herself anymore. That was the worst feeling of all.

"My job is to protect you from all enemies, foreign and domestic." *Including what's in your own head.*

How was he answering her? How was she talking aloud when she didn't hear herself doing it? Or was it his responses she was imagining?

Such confusion between reality and illusion normally sent her into a tailspin, destroyed desire, making it stutter out like a flickering candle. But she wanted this too much. She grabbed for the whole day, the easiness of it, the way he'd taken everything in stride, nothing allowed to raise an alarm. He reinforced it with his words now.

"Grip the T-shirt strips holding you, bébé. Feel the softness. I'm right here. We're riding the waves, no matter where they take us. We're riding them together."

His mouth was making her mind dance, sending light over the ceiling, cascading like a waterfall. Her eyes were open again. She could almost feel the mist, see the rainbow caused by the light coming through it.

Then his mouth was on her sex. She cried out, her body bucking up. Her hands flexed in the bonds, seized the soft cloth. She was being swept away, but she knew who and what she was. Was she losing that to this? She was going to lose too much. She couldn't afford pieces of herself to dissolve, as if there had never been any substance to them.

"Give me direction, Mistress." He pressed his mouth on the top of her thigh. "Here?" He moved down, to the inside, but closer to the knee. His hair brushed her sex, making her shudder. "Or here?"

"There," she said, and he lingered in that spot, his hand wrapping around her knee. Her hips lifted against the friction his hair, the pressure of his head against her inner thigh, was giving her.

Two messages being sent. Following her direction, but holding her at the same time.

"Tell me what you want me to do, Mistress," he repeated. "High level. Where do you want me to take you, and then you leave it to me to get you there."

"I want you to take me...where you're going."

He knew the destination, could see it without melting words or fog. He could get her there. She struggled to say more, but the words slipped away from her.

"Yes, ma'am."

Somehow he'd heard her. Or he knew. It didn't matter. He was working his way around her thigh, lifting her onto one hip to put his mouth on her buttock. "Fuck, you have an ass worth giving up Heaven for."

She pressed her face into her biceps as he teased, kissed, stroked her with his tongue, then he put her onto her back again. When he made his lingering way up her thighs, she was writhing. One part of her wanted to jerk free of the bonds, to tell him it was time for the taking, but she didn't. An act of will, pitted against his, in a sensual game she wasn't yet ready to concede.

She told herself she would much prefer him to cheat, take her regardless. But the truth was what she'd said. She wanted to tangle with him on the same ground, not knowing where it would go, but sure they'd both get there.

His breath was on her damp folds again. His tongue lazily tracing the swollen flesh, dipping in, compelling a range of responses from her that mounted in their intensity. Men who knew what they were doing down there were something every woman appreciated. But this...

He was enjoying it for his own purposes as well, aware of her every reaction, thriving on it, using it to decide what he wanted to do next. Fuck her deep with that clever tongue muscle, adding in a finger to share the space, driving her up higher as he stroked the front inner wall. Breathing on or licking her clit, sucking on it with his firm lips. Biting her, making her cry out. Every time she was close, he backed off, continuing to do the same things, but making her cries become shrieks. Writhing became full-on thrashing.

She wanted him inside her. This wasn't one of her club scenes, where the sex had strict rules and structure, mostly set by her. Neil wasn't going by her playbook, but he wasn't disregarding it, either. He pressed the heel of his hand against her, containing all those throbbing nerves. One leg kicked free of the bonds and curved over his back as she pushed up into his touch.

He didn't immediately follow up on his sensual threat. She guessed it was because he considered her hands the key to the decision. Leg movement was more unconscious, harder to control, when a man was dining on a woman's pussy. But the decision to put a hand on him... that was a different message.

In some tangled way, it worked. He was waiting for that blessing to take more, to take what he said he wanted. Much as a sub did. Only different. He kept his mouth going in between her legs.

"Neil...please..."

His head came up, eyes on fire, mouth damp. "You taste like everything," he said.

"Fuck me," she said, a low, raw order. *Take me where I want to go.*

Where I need to go.

While I can still go there.

He waited, not responding. She knew what he was waiting for. By setting it down as a rule, it straddled the line between asking and telling. She hadn't pulled her hands free, put them upon him. He was waiting until that tacit permission was there. Or did he view it as an order?

Her gaze slid over his shoulders, down to his bare chest. Unlike her, he was a map of scars. She could see at least five from here. Five ways the world had struck at him. And he'd struck back, survived to be here with her.

The spiral of need got tighter, faster, and it drilled down, breaking into that emptiness at her center. She knew what she wanted. He'd driven everything away but him and the music, another female artist in his playlist crooning out a woman's need, straight from the heart.

She didn't have to ask for it. He'd told her how she could demand it.

Her hand flexed against the T-shirt strip and then she'd pulled it free of the loose cuff. She put it on his face, dropped it to his shoulder. "Now," she demanded.

His lips twisted, eyes glinting. He rose, standing next to the bed. He'd taken off his shoes and socks already, so all that was left to remove were the jeans and dark blue boxers. As he freed his cock, the rigid shaft was flush with blood, the testicles heavy and tight. Her cunt contracted in a primal response.

He fished in a drawer, pulled out a condom, but she shook her head. It might not be true going forward, but at least right now she knew who she had and hadn't been with. "I'm clean," she said. "And I can't get pregnant."

He pressed his lips together. "You think it's a good idea to trust someone that much, someone you haven't known that long?"

"Which of us are you talking about?" Her gaze moved around him, following the outline of his body. A way to show he had her focus without meeting his eyes. "You aren't the type of man who risks a woman's health and wellbeing. You're not the type of man who makes impulsive decisions."

"Glad you noticed that. Hope you keep it in mind."

He left the packet on the nightstand. His attention slid to her other hand, still tied. Dropping his touch to her upper thigh, he traced a line there, a circle, widening the diameter, letting her feel the sensation ripple out from it. He knew how to turn a teasing tickle into a firmer stroke at the right moment. She wondered if it was something he'd practiced, or just intuitively picked up. Maybe both, since intuition evolved from skill. Because of that combination, she herself knew how to deduce things about a sub's state of mind from the slightest tension or shift of their body, their eye contact.

Or rather...she used to know how to do that.

Before she could get snagged there, he'd moved his hand up. Slow, her gaze following it. He teased the light down of curls, then his knuckle passed over her clit.

"Look at me, Abby. For three seconds. One Mississippi..."

Her eyes went to his. The colors were like those heron's feathers again, shifting with colors of purple, grey, blue, a touch of green, starting to swirl. She had to look away. She had to...

"Two Mississippi..."

While his gaze held hers, relentless, he slid three fingers inside her. With a gentle movement, one that showed the power of the man and how careful he was being with that strength, with her.

"Three Mississippi."

While his steady eyes stayed in place, riveted on her, her gaze shifted to and clung to his mouth, the press of his lips against one another, as she imagined them on her.

"Oh..." Her legs quivered, spread out for him. As he thrust his fingers inside her in that gliding rhythm, he laid an almost chaste kiss on the top of her thigh.

"Neil..."

His eyes were alive with so much, she shut hers again. His mouth touched her forehead, her eyelids, her cheeks and lips. She reached for him, gripping his back, his shoulders, as he stretched out on top of her. Reaching down, he guided her thigh over his hip, and she responded to the unspoken desire, wrapping both her legs over his hips and ass, holding him to her.

He guided her still bound wrist out of the T-shirt strip's hold. A quiver in her stomach registered the significance of him being the one divesting her of that final binding. He kissed her flesh, teasing her pulse. He didn't put himself inside her right then, but took his time as he had from the beginning, letting her feel their bodies together like this.

We fit, Abby.

"You are beautiful," he whispered again. She swallowed, tightening her arms around him. So was he. And she thought he meant his words the way she meant her thought. It meant something so much deeper than the physical, and had to do with everything they knew about one another so far. The complexity of who they were, as people, as souls sharing the same space in the universe.

He eased inside her, just the head of his cock, making it a slow thrust. Her body welcomed him, pulling him in. She hadn't had a man fully penetrating her for some time, but she had toys at home for that purpose. Even so, his girth and length were more ambitious than those. His fullness elicited a little sigh from her, a moistening of her lips. His gaze gleamed at her as he held himself back, not pushing all the way in yet. "That work for you, bébé?"

"More," she whispered back. "And I'm not delicate."

"Not true. You're delicate as glass, and sharp enough to cut a man to the bone." That gleam stayed in place, became a conqueror's flame as he slowly withdrew, then sank all the way back in, bringing fireworks of sensation.

"Oh," she breathed, holding onto him. "Yes. Just like that." She managed to tease, a little taunt. "What do you think, sailor? Can you keep that rhythm until the end?"

"I live to serve, Mistress. But careful what you wish for."

He held the rhythm. In, out, slow, deep, as the nerves danced, thrashed, pleaded for more, the sensation building and building.

Shadows began to talk, but the sibilant clicking she hated got absorbed in the roar of rising desire, like it had in the movement of the river against his boat, particularly when Neil opened up the throttle and sped up. She gave herself over to that, her nails scoring his back. He was so strong, never flagging, even as his skin dampened from the humidity, and their bodies moved slickly over one another, the bed rocking with them. She heard the cry of a bird, responding to her own cries.

"Neil...now..."

"I think this pace suits us," he said, his voice hoarse. "Watching you come apart, your body take fire...fuck...you're made of light, Abby."

He had his hands in her hair, was tightening his fingers there, a demand he matched with words. "Where do you want me to take you, Abby?"

The same question, same demand once again, with the same answer and same far deeper levels of meaning.

"Wherever you're going...as long as we go...together."

It was something she could do and feel down to the soul, in this moment, even if the truth beyond it would be far different. They couldn't move forward together indefinitely. But they had right now.

"Good. That's where we're going then. Hold on."

She did, as he worked them up to an impossible height, the near climax going on so long, her body became nothing but sensation. Then he put his hand down, gripped her buttock, squeezed and unleashed all that strength, starting to thrust harder. Her gaze flew up to his, and his was there, holding her, grabbing her.

"Yeah, I had more, just for you. Come with me, bébé."

She fell into his grasp, the climax shooting through her, setting off reactions in places she didn't know could experience a climax. She was screaming, and he was holding her, ass flexing under her calves as he shoved into her, released and laid a claim, took her with him, and bound them together.

If she'd been told the universe experienced a small earthquake in this one contained space, she would have believed it. It shattered the things holding onto her, that frightened her. For just a few blissful moments, she spun away, unafraid, because he had her. He was with her.

Together, just as he said.

~

As they slowly came back down from one of the most incredible climaxes he'd ever experienced, Neil knew he had his response to Lawrence's observation, his unspoken question.

Go out on your boat, think it over. When a relationship turns into a shit-show, most people have already invested enough time they're willing, for better or worse, to risk their lives, their heart and soul, to defend what they hold dear. Doing something that matters for the long haul takes a full commitment from all three of those things.

If Neil hadn't known the answer when he was with Lawrence, or later, when he'd gone out on the boat by himself, he knew now, from spending the day with her.

She was his country to defend.

CHAPTER NINE

Dr. Maureen Whisnant had green eyes the color of faded leaves and dark coffee brown shoulder-length hair. One dyed blonde lock twisted against the straight expanse of the rest like a curled ribbon. Her brows were articulate strips of silk, and she had a slim, sparingly curved body. It was clad in a tailored skirt and feminine cut jacket over an ivory blouse. Her stylish brown pumps had gold tips.

The look broadcast professionalism, while the ribbon of hair suggested a creative identity that embraced sensuality. Her voice projected authority, was threaded with warm patience, and she had the thoughtful expression of an active listener, paying attention to non-verbal body language as well as the words her patients spoke.

If she'd crossed her path in the business world, Rosalinda's impression would be that of a worthy opponent or valued ally, with the added bonus of a potential friend.

In this case, none of those things mattered but one. Ros hoped Maureen deserved the patient and family accolades Max said she'd accumulated.

Max's sister required institutional care due to a debilitating head trauma. Matt Kensington, Max's employer, had helped get her into a private care facility. A facility that had a neurology center annex built with foundation funds provided by Kensington & Associates and

Tennyson Industries. Tennyson's CEO, Savannah, happened to be married to Matt. The couple were Ros's friends as well.

Those interconnecting strands had brought Maureen to this meeting today. Ros never underestimated the value of networking. Or the influence of powerful friends.

Maureen offered polite nods and a firm handshake when greeting the other women. As they waited for everyone to get some coffee and take a seat, she didn't indulge in comments to highlight her credentials. Instead, she expressed seemingly casual interest in the décor of the room, the age of the building, the kind of work they did here.

Ros had taken her usual seat at the head of the table. When Maureen was directed to take a chair, she stopped at the one where Abby most often sat. Ros twitched, and Vera, across from that seat, leaned forward as if to speak. They squelched the reactions quickly enough they shouldn't have been noticed, but Maureen did. She chose the next chair over. She sat, crossed her legs, and turned toward Ros, Abby's chair in between them. Maureen's hand rested on the back of it, as if Abby were there, part of the conversation.

Please let her be as good as she seems to be.

"We're waiting for two more," Ros told her, when Maureen and Cyn reached a natural pause in a conversation. Cyn was providing highlights on their more interesting marketing projects.

Lawrence had texted her that Neil had arrived, and that they'd be up in just a few minutes. The short delay suggested Neil had some questions or reservations that Lawrence wanted to address first.

When she'd invited Neil to this meeting, Ros had known he'd have to wrestle with the ethical dilemma of attending without Abby's advance knowledge and express consent. He couldn't get either without revealing Ros's intent to do it that way for her own group. If he had a problem with Abby being out of the loop, even just temporarily, his only option was not to attend.

She wasn't worried that Neil would tell Abby regardless. Lawrence had confirmed it. Neil would respect Ros's decision, especially if she honored her promise to tell Abby soon after the meeting.

In the event he did choose to attend—which apparently was the case—she and Lawrence had agreed Lawrence's primary focus during and after the meeting was going to be Neil and his state of mind. Ros had a pretty good idea what his reaction would be to at least one of the things they would be discussing, and it wouldn't be pleasant.

She could relate. What Ros had hoped Abby would never have to face was here. Since the day she'd come back from Baton Rouge and seen Abby curled up on her bed like an exhausted animal, unshowered, muttering to herself, Ros had wanted to burn the world down, throwing the Powers That Be on top of it.

Powers That Be, her ass. Be what? Useless? Good for nothing but standing back and letting good people suffer? Or worse, being the ones that fucked with them to begin with?

Those were her emotions, taking the upper hand. That response had its time and place, but not when decisions needed to be made. Her whole life, she'd believed that whatever gods were out there simply helped people handle the shit that Fate threw at them; they didn't prevent it. Or orchestrate it. Why would they need to do that in a world where people were capable of creating such monstrous clusterfucks all on their own?

But they made a convenient scapegoat when one was feeling helpless and angry. Her team knew her mood. So did Lawrence. He hadn't crowded her this morning, but when she'd been standing in their sunroom, staring sightlessly at the yard, forgotten cup of coffee sitting on the window shelf, he'd come to her. Sliding his arms around her, pressing his lips to her shoulder, giving her the strength of his compact and resilient body. She'd quaked, one hard shudder from shoulders and hips, and his grip had tightened. A whole language between them without words.

I'm here. We'll get through.

Yes, they would. She didn't shrink from a fight. Even against an enemy playing hide and seek inside the head of the woman she loved most in the whole world. Even if half of the torturous battles had to be fought with Abby herself.

If the objective mattered, Ros knew how to be ruthless.

Just ask Lawrence.

~

When Neil arrived at TRA and was given access to park in the back lot, Lawrence was waiting for him at the break room kitchen entrance. As Neil headed toward the building, tension gripped him, a resurrection of what he'd wrestled with throughout the night. But it hadn't stopped him from being here, had it?

"For the record, I'm still not comfortable doing this without her knowledge," he said shortly.

"Then you shouldn't have come." Lawrence's green eyes showed a razor's edge. "Rosalinda and her team have been struggling with it for a lot longer. She's having this meeting because she loves Abby, and she thinks it's best. But it's still ripping up her conscience, no matter how she hides it. If you're going to give her shit about it today, get back into your truck and head out of here."

The reaction pulled Neil out of his head, told him how much of this Lawrence was carrying inside him.

"Sorry, man. After spending the day with her on the boat...it's made me a little possessive and tunnel-visioned."

The corner of Lawrence's mouth tipped up, and things evened out between them in a blink.

"I got that." Lawrence paused. "Abby doesn't have a great opinion of therapists. On the rare times her mom agreed to therapy, they were either burnouts on autopilot or complete idiots. That's another reason Ros is going this way. She wants to make sure this doc isn't one of those before even attempting to get Abby to meet with her."

"Makes sense. Should we head up?"

"Yeah. But one more thing." Lawrence's gaze held his. "Ros wanted to reinforce what she told you the other day. She's giving you access to the same info as the rest of us, but after getting it, if you don't think being with Abby is the right thing for you, then you should bow out."

Neil pushed down his immediate reaction, which was to get his hackles up and say fuck that. He could still feel Abby in his arms, her mouth against his. One moment she was so lost, and the next, she was helping him find himself, in a way he'd never experienced with a woman.

"Roger that." He cleared his throat. "In Ros's shoes, I'd say the same to someone relatively new in Abby's life."

"In Ros's shoes, your arches would be screaming."

"But I'd totally rock those four-inch spikes. Admit it."

"They'd make your butt look high and tight. You couldn't turn your back on Mount."

"Only down range. On base, I'd save them for our special private moments together."

They bumped fists, in accord again. Lawrence opened the break-room door and Neil followed him in. As he did, his mind went back to the memory of having her in his bed.

Specifically the aftermath, which had led to a conversation that had played through his mind ever since.

~

After that incredible sex, she'd fallen asleep.

When their day had started, he'd seen the shadows under her eyes. Throughout the boat ride, he'd detected other hints of that tiredness, but he should have picked up on the significance of it when MeeMaw noted it herself.

Her slumber was so deep, nothing roused her—not him getting up to make her a breakfast he covered and put back in the stove. Not him rinsing the boat on the dock or taking his shower. It was a small house, where every movement could be heard, every step resulting in a vibration through the pilings.

She was exhausted.

He'd figured the episode a few days ago had worn her out, but she'd successfully masked just how much, from him and apparently everyone but MeeMaw.

He'd need to pay closer attention in the future.

Before she'd dropped off into that sleep, she'd lain in his arms, her bare curves pressed back against him. As he kissed her shoulder and nuzzled her hair, he passed his hands all over her soft skin, learning her, connecting with her. She reached out and put her finger on the unopened condom packet he'd left on the nightstand. "So...since you left this off, is that because it's been awhile for you?"

He wouldn't lie to her, though he wished she hadn't asked. "Not so long. Maybe a couple months. In VA Beach, there are women who hang out at the watering holes where we are. Some of them are fine with the occasional hookup, no strings attached. But I was always safe with them."

He skimmed a hand along her side, to her hip bone, around to her backside. She pressed against him, and he let out a warning noise. "Keep that up, I'll be back inside you."

"Threat or promise?"

"Whichever way you like to take it, Mistress." He moved his hands to her breasts. Christ, she was made so beautifully, and her acceptance of that, without vanity or insecurity, just increased his desire for her. She was a woman with a confident grip on who she was, when her mind wasn't trying to shatter that grip, like a hammer turning bones to sawdust.

"You said you couldn't get pregnant," he said. "Don't go there if you don't want to, but what did that mean?"

"I had my tubes tied when I was in my early twenties."

She skated the condom package back and forth a few inches. A tense line straightened the area between her shoulders. He slid her hair away from it, put his mouth there. She shivered, pushed her lower body into the cradle of his hips, another rub against his rousing cock.

He might thrust inside her before they both fell asleep, but he was content to leave the potential within reach.

"My mother fooled herself into thinking she was going to escape this." Abby's voice became flat. "When she got pregnant with me, by accident—meaning when she was high or in the middle of an episode, with a guy whose face she doesn't even remember—I was her symbol of hope. The belief that wishful thinking would outrun statistics and biology. I'm not playing that kind of bullshit roulette with an unborn child."

She looked at him over a pale shoulder, her hazel eyes clear and unemotional. "The next question most people would ask me is if I ever regret it."

"What do you answer?"

"If I had somehow escaped the statistics, the world is overrun with kids who need parents. Blood doesn't matter; the heart does."

"No argument there." He tightened his grip on her. "At the rec center we all volunteer at, where Lawrence works, the kids prove that all the time. Having an adult they can count on, who cares about them; that's what matters. If not their parent, it can be someone else, but only if that person is willing to step forward and work twice as hard to make up the ground having an indifferent or shitty parent causes."

He could tell he had her close attention. Her hand slid up and down his forearm, fingers making small designs against his flesh. "If a kid doesn't have that kind of love," he continued, "it's a lot harder for them to choose the right path. Not much different from most of us, when we're going through rough things." He kissed her ear, held her closer. "Or having to make rough choices. I'm sorry you had to make that one alone."

"What makes you think I was alone?"

"Because you got that shut down look in your eyes, like people do when they had to do something tough on their own. And you have a generous heart. If someone had helped you, you would have mentioned them."

He stroked her hair away from her shoulder again, because the thickness kept it slipping forward, unless he gathered it up and held it, as he did now. "I could kiss your shoulders and neck for hours. I love how you respond to it. With soft little breaths, and pushing your hips against me." He slid his arm across her chest to cup her breast. "Nipples tight. Begging me to suck them."

"Or demanding."

He smiled. "Either way, it's my pleasure, Mistress."

"I think I might be ready for round two," she said.

Despite that, he'd noted how her eyes kept dropping half closed. He made a noncommittal noise, let his hand glide down to her thighs, in between them, and stifled a groan at the slippery heat there. Yes, her body was ready, but rather than imposing his own demands, he stroked her. Let her body rise and fall against his touch as her head dropped back to his shoulder, her cheek pressed into her pillow. Wondering, he watched desire wash over her.

"It's so warm here," she murmured, breath catching in her throat. "Oh...oh..."

He'd eased his fingers back inside her, his thumb passing back and forth over her clit, circles, easy pressures. Her body pushed into his more urgently, then her face turned fully into the pillow as the small climax took her. She clamped her thighs around his hand, rocking over it as her hand dropped to cover it, push his fingers more deeply into her.

"Oh..." Her voice softened.

He gave her a few minutes before speaking again. His cock was hard, but he kept his lower body still, wanting to make it about her. "So what would you do for a sub at this point?"

"It depends."

He cherished the sly, teasing tone, the quick glimpse of it in her hazel eyes, still dazed by the climax. She moistened her lips. "If he's the kind of sub who likes the denial of his own release in favor of his Mistress's pleasure, I'd leave him to suffer awhile. Balance that with telling him how much he pleased me, and that I like looking at how hard and thick he is for me." She nudged her backside against him, a little tease, gave him that smile again. "Then I'd reinforce those words with action."

As they spoke, he'd eased his fingers from her, moving his hand to her hip. His intent had been to let her segue into a drifting, post-coital sleep, giving her rest. Instead, she rubbed herself against him again. Christ, she was good at that, offering him a deft stroke as effective as a hand wrapped around his shaft.

She'd apparently found her second wind. Reaching for his hand, she captured it, drew it over and in front of her, up to the headboard. She molded his fingers over one of the wooden railings. Slipping her grip to his taut wrist, a firm cuff, she rotated against him, giving him a hint of that slippery orifice so close to his aching shaft. Her voice was barely a whisper.

"I'd tell him how wet I am for him, how pleased I am that he can be so close to my cunt, yet restrain himself. Even though the smallest shift would put him back inside it, thrusting to completion. But instead of all that pleasure rushing into one spot, released and gone, denial, restraint, spreads throughout him. It makes his whole body rigid with desire for me, hungry, needing. The power, the way that flows over me, it's a heat I can carry with me through the coldest, most lonely moments..."

She stilled and tipped her head back, breath along his jaw, her lips brushing him there. "Does that answer your question, sailor?"

"It does." Fucking hell, it did. He imagined her taking that kind of control over a man, how it would make him desire her. It made him want to abandon any thoughts about facilitating a session with her and one of her "regulars."

He pressed his face against her hair. In one decisive movement, he adjusted and drove slow but sure into those slick tissues from behind. A small moan broke from her, and he shifted his grip to her throat.

"You can make a man's dick impossibly hard for you with just words," he growled against her ear. "And those mysterious cat eyes."

Which demanded one response from him. This one.

He pushed in deeper, stroking her throat, hand moving up to her cheeks and mouth. She held her face against his palm as he cinched his other arm around her waist, bringing her down further on him. She reacted with another flexible undulation of her body, possessing a taut urgency that spun up his own.

He'd shifted their combined weight so she was pushed more toward the pillow, her hips tilted back and beautiful ass lifted. He knew when he was making good contact, because her gasps built, fingers curling into the pillow to claw and grip. He had his thigh pressed over the back of hers, holding her down even as her hips kept trying to move up against his, desire building.

He gripped her hand, took it down between her legs and molded it over her clit, over the spread labia where he was stretching her. He held his own hand over hers, adding pressure and friction as he stroked in and felt the blissful wet heat of coming back out, then in again.

A cry as the third climax he'd given her took her over. He kept going, not making it rough, but not making it too gentle either. He wanted her to know he'd been there. Hold onto it, maybe, against some of the other things.

The climax rose up and he spoke, fierce and husky against her ear. "Going to mark you inside, Mistress. Make you remember me there."

His hips jerked, his grip making the headboard groan as he drove harder into her. She cried out, his demand and hers twined together, coming to this.

When he was done, they were both sunk deep into the pillows, nested together like birds. The half lidded look at him, the tiny smile, was mixed with deeper, quieter things. As she turned toward him, he brushed his mouth over her cheekbone and covered the both of them with the sheet. Then he crossed his arms over her head, cocooning her fully inside the heat and shelter of his body.

"Sleep, bébé," he said. "I'll watch over you."

Her eyelids dropped, curtains coming down with finality. "I'll walk on the backs of alligators. Don't let the spiders turn me purple."

He pressed another kiss to her cheek. When he lifted his head this time, he could tell she'd gone fully under, leaving him studying her face in repose.

He wasn't sure if he had the right interpretation of those words, but he gave her more than the security of his arms. He tied a T-shirt strip around her wrist, binding it to his with a knot that wouldn't tighten while he slept, but would hold her to him securely.

"No walking on the backs of alligators tonight," he told his sleeping woman.

~

After she'd finally woken and he fed her breakfast, she'd needed to get home. He'd dropped her off. She hadn't removed the T-shirt strip. Instead, she'd twisted and wrapped it around her wrist like a bracelet.

As he came back to the present, Neil held onto his last image of her. A kiss pressed to his mouth, a light smile, a pinch on his ass before she danced away up her stairs, laughing. "See you later, sailor."

Lawrence had taken him up a back stairwell to the top floor. When they emerged, he saw the executive board room, the double doors open, the women's voices drifting out.

When he stepped inside, he registered the tension simmering beneath the surface of the seemingly social tableau, the cauldron of mixed feelings about why they were all here. Ros met his gaze and nodded to him. Bastion encouraged him and Lawrence to grab a coffee and something from a tray of afternoon snacks.

Neil chose a coffee. Lawrence slid into the chair next to Skye, leaving Neil the chair at the opposite end of the table, directly across from Ros. He wondered if that was significant, the two of them representing critical points around which everything else regarding Abby would orbit.

He didn't consider the thought hubris. After the past couple days, he believed the way he felt about Abby, and how Abby acted toward him, was a significant strategy point.

Maureen Whisnant looked intelligent, kind but not too touchy-feely. He got a good vibe off her, but time would tell if it was warranted.

"Since we're all here, let's get started," Ros said. "Just to confirm: Abby will know about this meeting shortly after it happens. I know that's not ideal, but this is about us, understanding how to help her the best way we can, no matter what choices she makes."

She swept her gaze over the assembled, lingering an extra beat on Neil, as if she knew he'd needed to hear it for the official record. Maybe she did, too. Vera gave Ros a reinforcing nod she seemed to appreciate. It made him remember what Abby had said, about Vera being the more spiritual member of their inner circle.

Ros glanced at Maureen. "You have the floor."

"Thank you." Maureen's gaze took in each one of them. Surprisingly, she paused on Neil as well, making him wonder what Ros had told her about him.

"Good morning," she said. "I expect you're all dealing with a lot of emotions right now. Anger, worry, a horrible sense of helplessness. So it might help you to know what I felt when I walked in. Hope. Because what I see is a committed and strong support network. Paranoid schizophrenia —if that is what Abby has—is an illness with a terrible prognosis. Without a support network, it can quickly become an unimaginable personal hell."

While warm, her tone was precise, her gaze as piercing as a Master Chief's. She wasn't blowing smoke, trying to make anyone feel better. She was laying it out.

"Your lives will continue," she said. "But from here forward, Abby's life will evolve and revolve around management of her illness. Even when a patient is doing all they can to help themselves, it's a difficult disease to manage. It can also derail the lives of those helping her with that. Which is why the larger network helps."

"You said 'if that's what she has.'" Cyn's dark eyes narrowed. "You don't think she has the same thing as her mother and grandmother?"

"I think it is very likely, because I've reviewed her mother's medical records. Her grandmother's illness was far less documented, but what's available matches. However, it's important to be sure."

Maureen stroked back a lock of her hair, revealing a silver hoop in her ear and a second hole for a small garnet stud. "Schizophrenia can mimic bipolar disorder. There are also different degrees of schizophrenia, like schizoaffective disorder, versus paranoid schizophrenia. When choosing treatment options, it's vital to confirm what illness we're treating."

Maureen paused, let that sink in. "But if she does have it, her situation is exceptionally rare. Late onset, female, and inherited from a direct line that has been passed through two generations. Most late onsets are also less severe than early onsets, and respond better to medication. Her mother and grandmother didn't fit either of those parameters."

"I gave Dr. Whisnant as much information about the other night as I could remember," Ros interjected. "Can you tell them what you told me?"

"Certainly. And if any of you are more comfortable with it, you may call me Maureen."

Maureen laced her hands on the table. Her nails were painted a glossy black. "The psychotic episode appeared to respond to the medication Abby had. In the prodromal period, when the person has been on no medication at all, such a quick response can be falsely encouraging. Her mother was ultimately resistant to most of the available medications. This doesn't mean all meds will be ineffective on Abby, because there are additional second-generation medications that can be tried in addition to, or in combination with, the first generation ones.

"Her mother also did not have the benefit of a psychotherapy approach," Maureen continued. "For many years, we spun our wheels, trying to get patients to delve into the *why* of their disease as if that would lead to a cure. Or we chose treatment options driven not by the patient's needs, but by the desired comfort level of bystanders, those outside looking in.

"It's a physical problem in the brain that we currently do not have the skill to fix. Only manage. So now many psychotherapists believe the better approach is helping the patient find the best ways to do that. Anticipate it, know what triggers the more challenging symptoms. Give them whatever levels of control they can access to handle its presence in their lives."

Her gaze swept the table. She had their full attention. Neil could tell even Ros, probably the hardest sell in the room, appreciated hearing information that didn't sound as if it were resting on guesses or ungrounded hopes.

"Most of you have read a great deal about this illness," Maureen continued. "That's helpful. Though hearing me talk about these things, when it applies directly to someone you care about, can still be as difficult as if you had no knowledge at all. Arriving on the heels of what was perhaps Abby's first full psychotic episode makes it far more real."

She sobered. "Schizophrenia is hard to understand, because it is a network of failures in different areas of the brain, hard to pin down with consistent treatment options. Most patients have to go through a variety of med adjustments during their first several years. While no treatment will likely remain 100% effective throughout their lifetime, it provides a baseline of understanding upon which a care team can build."

"I'm sorry." Vera's expression darkened. "Years?"

Maureen nodded. "Which is why a support network is vital. A person going through that will grapple with a mental isolation that can be terrifying and desolate. Debilitating depression is common, particularly right after psychotic episodes."

Her gaze shifted to Neil, an unexpected slight smile on her lips. "My understanding is you provided the antidote for that this time, by taking her out on your boat. You got her out of the house, helped distract her, lift her up again."

Neil glanced toward Ros, then back at the doctor. "She was tired, a little low when we started. At the end of it, she seemed happier, but she still slept pretty hard at my place."

"Physical exhaustion is preferable to the lethargy associated with depression," Maureen said. "Though sometimes it's difficult to separate the two."

"We had a pretty energetic day." Neil checked himself. "I mean..."

"No." Vera lifted a finger, her light gray eyes twinkling despite the seriousness of the discussion. "Don't fix that. A little levity might make this easier."

"Nothing will make this easier," Ros said shortly, quelling anyone else's reaction. "She seemed more even keel when I checked in with her this week. Preoccupied, and she has some of that slightly off behavior, but no different from what she's been displaying over the past few weeks." Bitterness touched her tone. "And off and on for months."

"That off-and-on period has fooled many family members," Maureen told her. "It's hard to convince yourself something is truly wrong when the patient demonstrates symptoms only some of the time. Even with that, you've tried to get her to consider treatment and diagnostic options many times throughout your friendship."

Vera sent Ros an *I-told-you-so* look, reached out and squeezed her boss's hand. Ros's responding expression could have been gratitude or weariness. She wasn't going to let anyone talk her out of kicking her own ass when she felt it was deserved.

Except maybe Lawrence. The way his gaze rested on his Mistress, Neil suspected he'd hoped she'd take the breather Neil's unintentional innuendo had provided. Abby would probably have laughed at it herself.

But she wasn't here.

"The episodes might get worse and more frequent as things progress. Right?" Skye spoke through her phone, a firm female tone with a light Southern accent.

"Without any kind of treatment plan, yes. It's almost a certainty," Maureen responded. "So I'd like to focus on what appears to be our biggest hurdle. Abby's attitude toward the diagnostic process and treatment. Ros says Abby is very pessimistic about her options. While that pessimism may be well-founded, for the reasons I stated, *any* chance of success rests in her willingness to try."

Her expression became grave. "We are dealing with a past that had a profound impact on her. With her mother, she had a front row seat to the often frustrating experimentation process with the meds, the repeat failures, augmented by her mother's alcoholism and drug abuse. Her mother was also hospitalized. Even under a managed treatment regimen, because of the variables in finding the right course, or the unpredictability of the illness over time, it's not unusual for a patient to need hospitalization more than once during their lifetime. Though treatment can help reduce the length of those stays."

"Abby has a deep fear of that happening," Ros said. "It didn't help that her mother's life ended at a hospital." Her gaze shifted to Neil. "She killed herself."

Shit. At an age when most little girls were thinking about Barbies and boys, Abby had been struggling to help a parent with an illness that could overwhelm even an adult caregiver. And though her mother's hospitalization had likely been the best thing for her daughter, Neil suspected that wasn't how Abby saw it. Especially when her mother had taken her own life there. If that kid had carried the roots of the overachieving, accomplished woman he'd met, she would have taken that as a personal, crippling failure.

Abby also had the heart of a Domme, a woman who loved the pleasure that holding control could give her and her subs. There was a link there, too. A more positive one, but it still connected.

"Ros has told me that Abby harbors a strong sense of responsibility for her mother's death." Maureen voiced his thought. "The opposite is far more likely to be the case. Abby helped her mother stay away from that course far longer than she might have, without her daughter's love and care. Death by suicide is statistically very high among those suffering paranoid schizophrenia."

She turned her gaze to Ros. An obvious wordless communication passed between them before Maureen spoke. "It's your choice."

Ros pressed her lips together at the cryptic message, her palms flattening on the table. Her gaze shifted to Vera. The curiosity in Vera's gaze told Neil whatever Ros and Maureen were talking about wasn't known by anyone else at the table.

When he saw the muscles tighten in Lawrence's shoulders, he amended that. Everyone but him.

Ros made her decision. "What I'm about to say is going to upset you all. I'm sorry I've had to hold it back, but the information wasn't mine to share. Abby made me swear not to tell anyone. The night of her episode, she finally gave me permission to go ahead, when I felt the time was right. I never believed it was right to keep it from you all, though I talked myself into it by hoping she'd change her mind, and this discussion would never happen."

She gripped her hands tightly together, stared down at them. Neil could tell Lawrence wanted to be right next to her, where he could reach out to her.

That would come later. For now, it was clear Ros needed to do this, say it, as a CEO, where she had that iron backbone and the sense of command that being the top of the pyramid gave her. Where she had to hold it together, get through it, get it done.

When her gaze rose, the blue eyes were flint, the emotions behind them making her voice hard.

"Years ago, Abby made a decision about what she would do, if and when she began to go down the same road as her mother and grandmother. She contracted with a place in Switzerland. At this point, she just needs to set a date and perform the last steps associated with that."

"Set a date for what?" The flatness in Neil's voice made the question not a question at all, but rather a demand for an answer.

Though he already knew it, felt it, in the painful thudding of his heart. Saw it in Vera's frozen expression, Skye's incredulous one, Cyn and Bastion struggling with different levels of denial, even as they anticipated the words. By talking about the fate of Abby's mother, Abby's fear of hospitals, Maureen and Ros had pointed arrows right at it.

He made himself stay silent, fighting the bucking inside his gut, the volatile reaction building there. He didn't want Ros to say it aloud, any more than the rest of them did, but he'd asked the trigger question, and she pulled it.

"To conduct an assisted suicide," Ros said.

Silence, heavy as a tsunami, then the wave broke, flooding the room with intense emotion. Murderous fury for Cyn, speechless shock for Bastion. Sorrow and anguish for Skye and Vera.

Ros's face had gone to stone, waiting them out. Maureen's expression was quietly passive, doing the same. Lawrence remained still as a statue, eyes on Ros.

Neil thought of the photo he was carrying in his wallet, a woman with the group but somehow not, disconnected. A woman who knew the date of her own death, because she intended to set it herself. Now it made sense, the undercurrent of fatalism about her.

"That's bullshit," he said. "That's total bullshit."

Ros met his gaze, then shifted it to encompass the group. "Where you are, where you all are. I've been there."

"Really?" He stood, body radiating aggressive tension. He was aware of Lawrence's alertness to the move, what it meant, but Neil didn't really give a shit. "You've been there? You've just met the person you want to spend your life with, but oh, sorry, that's got a short expiration date because she's planning to off herself?"

His temper didn't come out of the sheath often, but when it did, he knew the edge of it could dismember anyone stupid enough to get within range.

Ros flinched, but that blue flint became steel, a quick match for his own reaction. "I've been through the anger phase," she said. "I'm just farther down the road, where I've learned anger doesn't change anything."

"Who would do this without it being a terminal illness?" Cyn demanded. She looked almost as pissed as he did. Vera reached out to touch her hand, but Cyn jerked away.

"If the person passes their competency requirements, assisted suicide is legal in Switzerland, even in the absence of terminal illness," Maureen said.

"Which is why she doesn't want to wait too long," Vera realized. Her voice was strained, but her mind hadn't stopped working. "If it gets too far along, she believes the illness and any medications she takes could alter her mind, cause her to fail those requirements."

Ros nodded. "Before any of you get too lost in your heads, thinking of how to 'fix it,' you need to understand an important point. One I've run afoul of enough times that I can vouch for how serious she is about it."

She'd moved her knotted fists into her lap. Now she put them back on the table, knuckles pressed together. "This isn't a topic Abby is willing to debate. I can't tell you how to handle that, but if any of us push it too hard, give her too much shit on it, I guarantee she'll act on it sooner, in some misguided logic that it will save everyone more pain."

His heart was thudding in his ears. No one at the table could miss the deep anguish in Ros's voice, her lined expression. Done with the distance, Lawrence rose and came to stand at her side, just behind her so he could rest a hand on her shoulder. His green gaze met Neil's, sending the same clear message he had in the kitchen.

I get that you're pissed, but don't cross the line. She's mine to protect.

He knew the feeling. Except he'd just been told the biggest danger to the woman he wanted to protect was herself.

Ros looked toward Maureen. "You said lots of people miss the signs, but that doesn't make me feel better. I'm good at noticing things other people don't. But when she was calling me about the shadows, and then I saw other things, things I feared were early manifestations, I didn't take this step, and I should have. But I didn't want... She's lived so long with the dread of this, I wanted her to have as long as possible to believe...she still had her life."

Her voice broke. Lawrence's grip tightened, then eased to stroke. Ros shut her eyes, muttered a curse. When she opened them, her mouth was a firm line and her voice was strong again. "I didn't want to lose her. It was as much about me as it was her. I was selfish and afraid. That's why I'm blaming myself. All the time I was listening to her, watching her, I was reacting to this based on my interpretation. My feelings."

Tears were sliding down Skye's face. Bastion had gripped her hand, and the mute woman overlapped it with her other one. Vera again reached out to Cyn. Cyn ignored the gesture and rose. Her eyes snapped sparks.

"You should have fucking told us. I don't care what she said, what she made you promise. If she was going to do this to us, you should have told us, so we didn't..."

Cyn broke off the accusation and pivoted. She left the room, slamming one of the double doors so hard the glass rattled in the frame, a sound that echoed through the silent, emotionally charged room.

Lawrence had made that same choice, Neil recognized. He'd watched his friend fall for a woman he knew had every intention of taking her own life. But unlike Cyn, Neil couldn't hold that against him. In the world he and Lawrence had inhabited together, they understood just how finite life was. Not opening up to someone for fear of losing them made no damn sense at all.

Living like that was no way to live.

He stopped on that thought. There was something to it, a key, but he needed some space and air before he could examine it further.

"Excuse me," Neil said quietly. When he stalked from the room, he wanted to slam the door as hard as Cyn had, but he held back. For one thing, though she was strong and fit, he was a hell of a lot stronger. He'd likely shatter the glass in the frame.

Lawrence looked down at Ros. He knew she was still shaky deep inside, but she gave him her patented ballbuster nod. "Go with him. Let me know if he'll be back."

"He'll be back. Just give us a few minutes." He sent her a *hang in there* look, brushed his fingertips inside the collar of her blouse, along the tender skin of her throat.

Then he followed his friend.

~

Neil stood on the TRA front walkway, staring at a alabaster statue of Aphrodite in one of the natural areas. Her face was turned coyly to her shoulder, her robes outlining her graceful form. The intern Bastion had asked to cover the front desk was staring out the window at him, rather nervously. It suggested Neil hadn't looked all that friendly when he'd crossed the lobby and headed out the door.

Lawrence sent the intern a reassuring look before following his friend out. Neil losing his shit was a rarity. It was what made him the best team guy in the worst circumstances. But when that middle-of-the-earth deep calm was challenged, even a Master Chief like Dale would tread carefully.

If Neil decided to get into his truck and head for Abby's to confront her, Lawrence would have to figure out how to stop him. No way in hell should he see her until he'd defused what was radiating from him.

Fortunately, Neil went to one of the benches in the natural area. He sat down, bracing his hands on his knees as he stared at the flagstones. Lawrence took a seat next to him and waited him out. Neil was working the problem in his mind, and he'd go through the first reactions fast, before getting to what needed to be done.

"Stupid," Neil muttered at last. "Just stupid."

"She has the right to be stupid," Lawrence pointed out. "It's covered under the Ninth Amendment."

"Yeah." Neil scowled, then sighed. "No."

"No, it's not covered by the Bill of Rights?"

"No, she's not stupid. That's the last thing she is. It's what makes the whole problem such a bitch." Neil dug the toe of his shoe into the dirt under the bench. "She knows she's facing something that's going to dog her for the rest of her life. There aren't a hell of a lot of hypotheticals in her mind. As Dr. Mo said, she's watched it destroy two family members. She knows the impact it has on the people who love them, because she was one of them, with her mother. Evaluating suicide as an option is reasonable."

He spat the word out, the taste obviously not to his liking, but his brow furrowed. "Accepting it as the *only* reasonable option, shutting down an evaluation of any others, that's the problem to solve. If she's going to turn away from the suicide thing, she's got to believe things can be better for her. She has to have a reasonable expectation that life can be made worth living, no matter how rough the road gets."

Yep, he was working the problem. Lawrence suppressed a smile. Neil glanced at him, a cue he was ready for input.

"Did I stop the meeting?"

"You weren't the only one that stormed out. Cyn was as pissed as Cedrick was, that time a snake got into his pack and bit him. Good thing you were there, or the snake wouldn't have had a chance."

"Not the snake's fault. He was just looking for a shelter from the storm." Neil paused. "Spending the day with her, Munch...I see those pieces of her, and they're not broken glass, not to me. They're like stained glass. They form a picture. I can see the patterns, but even when I don't, it's still beautiful. Still her."

I'm all in. No turning back.

Neil couldn't have said it any clearer. Lawrence would let Ros know they no longer had to worry about Neil's awareness of what lay ahead, what their responsibility was for that. From here forward, those questions would be between him and Abby

"That snake." Neil was continuing, his eyes thoughtful. "That's the difference. We're trained to fight the storm, never even consider looking for a shelter while there's fighting still to be done."

"Because we have each other's backs. Not to get all Hallmark about it, but we are the shelter, for each other."

Neil's gaze turned to him. Lawrence still saw the pain, knew a part of Neil was consumed with the enormity of the news that had just been laid upon him. But the wheels were greased and turning again. "Yeah. Good point. But sorry, that was dead-on Hallmark. I've got a tear in my eye."

"And me without my handkerchief."

Neil's serious mouth curved. "Let's get back to it."

~

When Neil returned to the conference room, Cyn and Vera were absent. Ros and Maureen were talking, and Skye was doing something on her tablet, Bastion on his laptop. Everyone was occupying themselves until the absent members returned.

Neil headed to his seat. Lawrence went to Ros, dropped to his heels next to her chair. His hand covered her tense one on the arm as he spoke to her. Whatever he said had both her and Maureen looking toward Neil. He didn't pay attention to that. Instead, he picked up his coffee which, thanks to the insulated cup and the lid he'd put on it, was still warm. As he sipped it, he turned the chair from side to side, short strokes while he continued to mull.

A whole room inside his head was on fire, howling in denial, wanting to bust shit up. But he locked it up. Later he'd handle what was in there, the additional layers of truth this meeting had revealed. Right now, he kept his eye on what mattered.

He knew a lot about fear and anxiety, the primitive levels people had to manage under extreme duress. SEAL training spent significant time on it, since extreme duress was at the top of the job description.

Everyone had their process. He felt everything. He knew the dangers of trying to shut that down. The heart and soul, they were what kept a man open to the reasons for living, fighting, dying. But his mind was what sorted through all of it, made the decisions that kept those reasons clear. Or as clear as possible in a world that often made no sense at all.

Ironically, the pain of the others, a living, writhing thing, helped steady him. It was a reminder that he wasn't the only person invested in Abby.

Plenty of things were impossible for one person to accomplish by themselves. A team could change that.

And Ros...he gazed across the table at her. He'd been right, in what he'd felt, unlikely as it had seemed at the time. Ros knew it would revolve around the two of them, however this played out. She'd invited him here because she'd suspected what he hadn't realized until he'd said it aloud so forcefully.

You've just met the person you want to spend your life with...

Yeah, he and Abby hadn't known one another long. But that didn't really matter, did it?

If the worst happened, maybe it would hurt him less than it would the others who'd known her longer. And maybe that was bullshit, something else an arbitrary amount of time couldn't define.

Lawrence returned to the seat to Neil's left. He'd snagged a couple protein bars from the snack tray and pushed one at Neil now. As he did, Vera re-entered the conference room. She gave Ros a meaningful look. Whatever non-verbal message she sent translated into a slight easing of Ros's expression. About a minute later, Cyn came back. The dark eyes framed by the riotous waves of sable hair were still monumentally pissed, the calm around her a tenuous thing, but Neil suspected it would hold. Like him, she might be angry, but she was here, determined to help.

Cyn reinforced it with her sincere first words. "Sorry," she said to Ros. "I know this isn't easy for you."

"You handled it better than I did," Ros said. "When Abby first told me, it took me a week before I could even handle seeing her again, let alone discuss it."

"Tonight I'm beating the stuffing out of the gym punching bag," Cyn said. "You're paying for the damage I do to it."

"If you let me have a go at it first, you've got a deal." Ros glanced at Maureen. "I think we're ready to keep going."

The doc had remained quiet, still apparently unruffled, but Neil recognized the signs of a fellow trained human sponge, soaking up every bit of intel happening around her.

Lawrence appeared to be reading his thoughts. "Doc," he said. "Neil solved the question of what to call you. Dr. Whisnant doesn't feel right, and Maureen doesn't either."

"Oh." Her gaze moved between him and Neil. "So what was the decision?"

"Dr. Mo," Lawrence responded. "It's what we did, in our team. We gave nicknames to those in the trenches with us."

Neil sent Lawrence a bemused look. He hadn't even realized he'd called her that until Lawrence pointed it out. But it told him that she'd already earned a sufficient level of his confidence.

Seeing how the announcement sank into everyone here, somehow lightening things up a few degrees, confirmed he wasn't the only one who recognized it.

It worked that way down range, too.

Maureen inclined her head, her expression thoughtful, slightly amused. "All right. Accepted. I'll endeavor to live up to it. Let's continue."

Her expression sobered. "While undoubtedly united in your desire to turn Abby away from her decision, I see no reason at this time to doubt Ros's assessment. Pushing that agenda overtly is likely to have the negative results she described. But helping Abby recognize how much support she has, and how that support can enhance the quality of her life, is a different approach toward the same goal."

Maureen gestured at all of them. "Connections, friendships, family; anything to combat the isolation of what's happening in her head that she feels is separating her from everyone else. I spoke about that. But this is an illness than can also turn that perceived isolation into a reality, driving people away. Abby may become withdrawn, apathetic, unsociable. Even combative, manipulative, because she might be interacting with delusions that have mapped themselves onto the people around her, driven by the paranoia."

Neil translated that into what he knew, spoke it aloud. "She's fighting a battle in her head. When you're in the middle of a fight, that's where your focus is."

"A good way to frame it. Then there's the lack of filters, the hyper-awareness of her senses." Maureen surveyed the listening women. "You're telling Abby good morning, getting yourself a coffee, chatting about your night. Meanwhile, she is getting overwhelmed by stimuli. The colors of your clothing, the wallpaper, all the sounds of the office, the smells, they expand and fill up the space in her head. She has a smile pasted on her face, is struggling not to miss social cues, but on top of that, the voices in her mind are screaming like a barrel of monkeys let loose in her brain, distorting what people are saying to her."

"Goddess," Vera muttered.

"That's without meds," Maureen said. "It can still happen on them, but the goal is to find the right mix and dosage that keeps that effect down to something she can manage and maintain a more normal life."

"She's been dealing with some of that already," Neil said. "I think she's been masking a lot."

"I agree," Ros said unhappily.

"We've been aware of enough of it to take steps to help," Vera reminded her. "Encouraging her to work from home, reducing pressure and stress, the pace."

"So Ros has told me," Maureen said. "That's good. You should keep doing the daily check-in. Rotate the responsibility so she keeps those multiple connections, and make sure those interactions are simple, low-key. Stopping in for a cup of tea, for instance. It's not just a wellness check. Your presence in her lives not only reduces that isolation; it sends her the vital message that she has value. That she's worth it."

Cyn frowned. "Abby doesn't have self-esteem issues."

"Perhaps not in business," Maureen said. "Or in social settings with her close friends, those she trusts. But masking is a skill the mentally ill often master well and early. It's rare I don't find a patient suffering from self-destructive thoughts, hammered by insecurity, a hamster wheel that never stops. It's only when the illness overwhelms and breaks through the wall that friends, family and co-workers see it. It's a startling revelation, to recognize how much is happening inside the mind of a person with this illness."

She shifted, crossed her legs. "Loss of control is the common foundation to most human fears. Abby's prodromal period has proven to her she hasn't escaped the illness. The resulting stress is self-fulfilling, bringing on episodes, exacerbating those symptoms. It can unearth feelings that have been in her subconscious since childhood, where she was trying to save a mother who ended up not wanting to be saved. *I am unloved, I am worthless. I need to listen to the voices and be destroyed.*"

"And that in turn would make it hard for her to accept that her caregivers want to help," Vera observed. "She's terrified not only of becoming what her mother and grandmother did, but being that kind of burden upon us. She'd feel she wasn't worth that."

She's worth it, Neil thought. *She's worth the moon and more.*

Ros rose abruptly, moved to the wide bank of windows. She'd crossed her arms, emphasizing the ramrod straight lines of her back and shoulders. "Nothing could be further from the truth." Her voice was raw. "We love her so much."

Ros was a formidable personality, unapologetic and not given to public displays of sentiment. Today, though, the stress cracks were showing. But it made sense, didn't it? She and Abby had been friends for years. While Abby had probably held onto a slim hope the schizophrenia would bypass her, Ros would have nursed the same hope. Abby wasn't the only one grieving the loss.

"It fits her," Bastion said. The solidly built office manager had listened silently through most of the meeting, but the input he offered now, the way the others turned to him, told Neil he wasn't here as a notetaker. "You're the head of this family, the father, so to speak." He looked toward Ros. "Abby is the mother. She keeps her fingers on how everyone is doing, feeling, and how to help or fix things. If I ask her if she needs anything, a hundred percent of the time, the answer connects to someone else's well-being, not her own."

So could Abby see *herself* as the person who needed her help? Neil wondered. Turn a key portion of that strength of will, the caring and protectiveness that was part of her nature, that she extended toward others, toward herself?

Maureen tapped one of those nails on the table again. "You're all making excellent observations. But I feel I should again stress my viewpoint on Abby's situation is subject to change, because I've not yet had a chance to speak face to face with her."

"So step one is getting her to meet with you," Vera said.

"Ros has been trying to do something like that for years," Cyn said flatly. "Since we learned about it, we've all tried. So what will make her listen to the same thing she's been told a hundred times before? Without us doing what Ros says, triggering her into accelerating the timeline?"

A deep, booming voice came from Cyn's right, making most of the people around the table jump. Thanks to the plethora of television commercials—and the TV series *24* being a guilty pleasure—Neil recognized the trademark deep voice of actor Dennis Haysbert.

"Maybe she's never heard it suggested in a deep, sexy man drawl."

All eyes turned to Skye. She still had her fingers poised over her tablet's illuminated keyboard. Her bow-shaped mouth, glossed with a purple-tinged lipstick, curved in a humorless half smile, but the gaze she had fastened on Neil was deadly serious.

In the pause, the mix of ideas that had been ricocheting around the room came together in his mind. "We haven't walked in her shoes," he said slowly. "We haven't seen what she has. She believes she knows what lies ahead of her, and she's probably right about most of it. But the most important variable, one she's not considering, probably because of those insecurities and fears Dr. Mo mentioned, is herself. She might not be able to control the weather or the seas, but it's her hand on the tiller, not her mother's or grandmother's."

He moved his attention to Maureen. "Reminding her of that, in ways where she can have some control, even while dealing with this, might help. Right?"

Maureen studied him. "What are you considering?"

While he noted varying reactions around the table, Neil also felt a shift, an encouraging one. It was the energy that said a team was clicking, working the right way toward fixing a problem. Lawrence's expression said he felt it, too.

But first things first. He shifted his attention back to Ros. "Does the doc know everything about what Abby is?"

Ros immediately knew what he meant. Vera picked up on it, too. "It's a big part of how she defines herself," Vera said to Ros. "Seems a good idea to let Maureen in on it."

Ros glanced around the table, confirmed no one had an objection, then spoke to Maureen. "Abby is a sexual Dominant. So is almost everyone at this table. If you think you know what that means, I'll want to hear your thoughts on it, to be sure you really do understand it, in a way that's not counterproductive to your helping Abby. Too many health professionals have the wrong idea about it."

Maureen's green eyes had flickered with surprise, then interest. Neil couldn't pick up what flavor the emotions possessed, because the woman had a damn good professional mien. However, after a bated pause, she dipped her head toward Lawrence. "He's not a Dom. He fairly screams submissive. A handsome, protective and devoted one, an irresistible combination to any Mistress."

A moment of startled silence, exchanged glances, then appreciative female chuckles swept the table, laced with Bastion's low baritone. Neil shot a covert glance toward Lawrence. While his former teammate's ears were a little red, he took it in stride, grimacing and batting away Bastion's teasing punch to his shoulder.

"I apologize, Mr. Barrera." Maureen chose the formal address, probably to strengthen the sincerity of her words. "But I felt the most direct way to prove my knowledge was with an insightful comment."

"So it's not just your connection to the neurology center that brought you to Max's attention," Vera noted.

"Janet and I are also friends," Maureen said. "I prefer private group play in home dungeon settings, and she and I crossed paths in several of those environments."

She looked at Ros. "Janet gave me a heads up about you and your ladies, but I'm glad you volunteered the information. Every aspect of Abby's personality that she associates with her core identity will be important to helping with her therapy." Her gaze slid to Neil. "And it apparently relates to what you have in mind. Do you identify as a Dominant as well?"

"I haven't practiced in a formal way like these ladies, but yeah, pretty much." He was aware of Lawrence's attention. Even if was news to his friend, upon reflection he probably wouldn't find it that surprising. Just as it hadn't been a surprise for Neil, knowing Lawrence preferred the other side of the power exchange.

"Dominant personalities aren't always easy to mesh, especially if the two involved are expecting the other to switch," Vera said, her expression serious.

"Abby won't appreciate you pretending to sub for her," Ros added.

"Which is why I won't," he said firmly. "Whatever form a power exchange takes between her and me, there won't ever be any pretending or pressure to be what we're not, on either side."

While Ros was giving him the benefit of the doubt, he recognized the watchfulness behind her eyes as he spoke. Abby had her first loyalty. He wouldn't want it any other way. Which meant, considering what info Maureen had given them so far, he had to put another couple things on the table before he got into his idea.

"Some might say the way I feel about her, and her me, has lousy timing," he said.

"I'd say her illness has lousy timing." Bastion cocked a dark brow, his lips curving. "Seeing the cool and collected Abigail Rose's heart go pitty-pat was a miracle none of us ever expected to witness. Let alone happen the first time she laid eyes on you. Since we can tell she's done the same to you, we've been in your corner from day one."

The others nodded. Including Ros. Neil's momentary speechlessness was fortunately covered by some well-timed doctor-speak by

Maureen, though Lawrence shot him a look of good-natured amusement.

"Finding herself in a new relationship, one she enjoys, can also contain an important subliminal message. Life has not ended because of her illness. The fates have determined there is room for her to fall in love."

"But Neil is worried if things go bad with the relationship, it could have a negative effect on Abby's outlook." Skye was back to using her female Southern tone. Her dark eyes had a speculative look, emphasized by the arch of a pierced brow.

"Partly," he said. "With all the other factors involved, the ups and downs of a relationship concern me. But if I back down, use kid gloves, it would just piss her off. She likes to push boundaries between us."

"True." A gleam went through Ros's blue eyes, recognition of that side of her friend that yes, Neil found perversely appealing.

He forced out his next point, an even more difficult one. "Then there's my job. I can be called away at a moment's notice, be gone for weeks at a time. It's dangerous work. Every time I go there's a real chance I'm coming back in a box. Or injured enough to be a serious liability to a woman with more than enough on her plate."

He had to pause before saying the next words, because they carried pieces of his heart with them. Which he guessed was proof of how much of it was already invested in her.

"So does that mean I should bow out now? Is that what's best for her? If the feeling from the group and the doc is that I should back off...I'll do it."

Though he had no clue how he'd shut off what his heart, mind and body wanted, he couldn't allow his own desires to override the intuition of people who'd been in her life a lot longer. Plus the opinion of a brain doc who clearly had the chops to hold the attention of everyone at the table.

Maureen tapped her black painted fingernails on the table. The white streak in her hair made him wonder if she changed the power suit and doctor demeanor for a Goth Domme look on the weekends.

"You're right to have reservations," Maureen said at last, and his heart hammered his insides. Her pale green gaze held his. "But from what I've seen here today, my current answer is no. I wouldn't recommend anyone who is bringing value to Abby's life to bow out of it now, unless the person himself wants that, which I suspect is just the opposite for you."

"Yes, ma'am," he said, letting the fierceness of his emotions tag the words. "I'm a hundred percent committed. I wouldn't be here otherwise. Lawrence can vouch for that."

But he looked at Ros. "Do you agree with the doc?"

Yeah, she'd nodded at Bastion's comment, but it wasn't the same. He wanted it straight out from her.

She didn't speak right away, but when she did, the words rang true. "I absolutely do. I'm glad you're part of her life, Neil. Bastion wasn't exaggerating. I'm speaking for everyone here."

Bastion sent him a *told-you-so* look as Maureen picked up the thread. "A lot will depend on your intent, your will, and how you continue to feel about her as your relationship and her illness progress. But for now, I think the natural path of a romantic relationship can give her a sense of normalcy. As far as your job, you continuing to pursue what you love, alongside your interest in her, reinforces that message."

She gestured to the other women. "Plus, from what I can tell, Abby's support team won't experience attrition as her illness progresses. I feel far more certain of that than I usually do. Typically there are one, maybe two, primary caregivers, who bear most of the stress and worry. Which can compound the anguish and despair of the patient themselves, seeing the toll their struggle is taking on the ones they love."

When she met his gaze, Neil nodded. Let out a breath. "Okay, then."

"So," Cyn said, after a bated pause. "Are you going to keep us in suspense forever, or tell us what kind of kinky shit you have in mind to help her?"

Chuckles swept the table. Neil laced his fingers on the cool surface. At the time, he'd proposed it as an idea to help her feel better, not a strategy with this kind of import, one that would affect her decision to...

He couldn't make his head speak the thought and stay clear, so he moved past it.

"I need to talk to Tiger. I want to bring him into the loop and set up a session with him and her, with me in the room as a spotter, a safety net."

Surprise gripped his audience, followed by an exchange of startled looks and expressions, ranging from dubious to thoughtful.

Ros was the first to recover. She'd picked up on what he had in mind, and he was reassured by the approval that crossed her face. Then Vera and Skye figured it out. Though Cyn initially looked suspicious, dawning comprehension morphed into a wicked smile.

"I briefly brought it up with Abby," he said. "She gave me a tentative go ahead, but it wasn't definitive. By setting up a meeting with him, I'm taking a step out of bounds, but I'll take the slap for it when the time comes. Having whichever one of you is best to pave the way with Tiger, letting him know I'm not trying to disrespect her, might help the chances I can get him to do it."

"A good thought. He's protective of her. He'd likely punch you in the face if he got the wrong idea," Cyn said.

Neil met her gaze. "Protective and possessive?"

"Mostly protective," Vera interjected. "He's her first choice when she's choosing a session, but it begins and ends there. They're friends. They meet for lunch on occasion and sometimes do dinner, but that's usually an after-session thing, when she wants to keep an eye on him."

Neil grunted. "Good. So it's not likely I'll have to punch *him* in the face."

"Can I come along to watch this conversation?" Cyn asked.

"I'll talk to him." Ros sent her a narrow look, then shifted her gaze to Maureen. "You're thinking something."

Maureen was studying Neil. "I'm going back to what Skye so insightfully suggested. If Neil is successful in making this session happen, then Abby might become more receptive to meeting with me. While I wouldn't want to make it entirely dependent on the success of this, it will certainly help if it goes well. I assume you're planning to do it soon?"

"That was the intent."

Maureen directed her next words to Ros. "You indicated you were going to tell Abby about this meeting and what was discussed here. Does that include his participation?"

"Yes," Neil said, before Ros could respond. "Sooner rather than later. If I can be effective at all, she has to trust me. As the doc pointed out, I'm the newest variable, so I'm the one Abby'll be looking for any excuse to shake when things aren't going well."

"She might do that when she finds out you were here," Ros said. "Especially when she knows you're aware of the decision she's entertaining."

"She can try. But don't ever fucking use the word *entertaining* again when talking about her killing herself."

He hadn't meant to say it like that, tagged with a fury that set the words on fire. He dialed it back, managed a halfway apologetic nod, though he knew nothing about the rigid set of his face suggested regret.

Ros's gaze had registered an answering heat, but she tamped it down the same way. She knew it hadn't been personally directed. "Agreed," she said.

He cleared his throat, made his fingers relax. "Thanks. As I said, I can handle the heat. But anything you can say to her to make things smoother for me will be appreciated."

"I'll do it today. I told her I was going to stop in after work. She might not take your call tonight."

"I'm persistent."

Bastion sent Neil an approving look over his broad shoulder. "That's a good thing. If he can't hold his own, this group will run right over a man, leave him squashed into roadkill for the vultures."

Ros tossed her office manager a narrow look. "Don't make me regret inviting you to this meeting."

Bastion snorted. "Like you could have kept me away."

"Humor is good. You'll all need that." Maureen spoke to Neil. "If she does give you the opening, don't complicate it or overwhelm her. If she'll simply agree to one meeting with me, I'll take it from there."

"And if she doesn't agree, or reacts badly to my attempt?"

"Just back off of it. You and the others can seek out additional opportunities when changing circumstances present themselves. Abby seems to be a very strong and decisive personality. She's not going to be bullied, badgered or talked into something she doesn't agree with. So the key is presenting things that make sense to her, and hoping she still possesses enough of the one vital element that can overrule everything else."

"What's that?" Vera asked.

"Her desire to live." Maureen met her gaze. "Because to be honest, when a patient decides she's done, she very often is."

Neil's hands curled into fists again. "No. She's not there."

All eyes swung to him, but it was Ros's gaze he held. "I watched her on my boat. She wants to live. She just has to see a path where it's possible, which means she has to clear off some of the shit from the past she's piled up on that road. I will figure out a way to clear it."

"If there's a way to do it, he will," Lawrence confirmed. "I've seen him do it in far worse circumstances."

After a still moment around the table, Maureen nodded. "Neil, I'm going to give you my contact information, as I did Ros. Use email for things where information or less urgent guidance is needed, the phone for a crisis matter where you feel Abby's well-being is at immediate risk."

She turned back to Ros. "I think we have a game plan. Anything else you want me to address?"

Ros studied her. "Before this meeting, I was already planning my next step, if you fell short of expectations. If you'd heaped a bunch of authoritative bullshit on us, trying to make us believe you had all the answers, I would have written this up as a pointless exercise." She offered a tight smile. "Instead, you proved you know your stuff, and acknowledged what you don't know, without ego. Unfortunately, you also confirmed our worst fears about what could happen, and what Abby is facing."

"Yes. What you're facing with your friend, your sister, your lover," Maureen's gaze moved to Neil, "has the potential to be every bit as bad as you imagine it can be."

For the first time, her expression lost its warmth, assumed a peculiar flatness, masking the depth of emotion her next words likely represented. "My sister has paranoid schizophrenia. It started in her teens, but wasn't accurately diagnosed until her twenties. I watched it destroy my parents' marriage, alter my childhood and that of my siblings in traumatic ways. It took years to reach where we are now, but Sissy lives in a good group home. She works as a math tutor, a low stress job that nevertheless challenges her abilities and gives her a sense of accomplishment."

Her gaze flickered. "She attempted suicide twice, disappeared several times. Got addicted to heroin. Lived on the street. Even now, when my phone rings and I see it's a member of my family, my blood pressure spikes. I worry that the meds have failed, or Sissy has gone off them because of changes in her brain that have put her in psychosis again.

"I am disclosing that to confirm my personal insight into the challenges facing you. But it also will not cloud my professional judgment on the unique challenges facing Abby. I do not have all the answers, but you will have my dedicated effort, to help her find the best path possible."

Neil had come here with the same mixed feelings as Ros, but as Maureen concluded, he had the encouraging feeling they'd added another formidable weapon to Abby's arsenal.

Now, if they could just get her to use it.

When he saw Skye's gaze resting on him, he remembered that deep booming voice, and what she'd said using it. Knowing the ball was in his court, to convince Abby to consider something she hadn't been willing to do before, was a sobering thought.

He didn't mind having the ball, though. For a SEAL, failure wasn't an option.

CHAPTER TEN

"You did *what?*"

Abby stared at her friend, the woman she considered family. And no one could push a person to fantasize about murder faster than a family member.

"I invited a psychotherapist to sit down with the team, to discuss how best to support you in the coming weeks. I also told them about your Switzerland decision which, if you'll recall, you gave me permission to do when I felt the time was right. With your current symptoms, inviting an open discussion with a trained expert seemed to be prudent."

"You're using the voice you use when you're handling one of our difficult clients."

"I accept the literal 'handling' definition, not the way you're implying it. Wouldn't you agree it's better for you if we understand what you are handling, since, by extension, we will also be handling it?"

Her temper spiked. "They don't need to handle anything. That's the reason for Switzerland. So they won't have to."

"I think last week proved that not to be the case." Ros's blue eyes didn't falter. Despite that, Abby saw the signs of stress in the tightening of her mouth, the set of her shoulders. Yet the voices tried to put a different spin on it.

Another calculation. Manipulation. The sincerity of her motives are irrelevant.

"No matter your plans, Abby, you don't have to be alone in managing until then."

"You could have told me beforehand."

"Would you have wanted to come?"

"To be the target of an intervention, when you told them how I'm resolving this? Or give you a chance to evacuate the room and leave me with the head doctor? Not likely. You still should have told me."

After a long, tense moment, Ros inclined her head. "All that might be true. But Abby...they needed this. To prepare. To help, however they can. To have the chance to say good-bye. And I didn't want you to talk me out of it."

Honesty. She recognized it, had known Ros long enough to overrule the voices, shove them in their box. At least right now. Abby sighed, rubbed her forehead. "Since when have I ever been able to talk you out of anything?"

"If I can be talked out of a course of action, you're the person who has the best chance of doing it."

I wish I could do the same for you. Though Ros didn't say it, Abby felt the jagged edges of the unspoken words in her lower abdomen.

She wished she *could* let Ros do that. She'd made the decision long ago and had kept it locked up tight, so it couldn't be influenced. But as the importance of Ros and the others had grown in her life, it was like they'd set up a space in her mind, right next door to that contained room. She could hear them through that locked door, tempting her to turn the knob.

Fortunately, turning away from her present and staring at the scenes from her past always quelled that urge. The things she knew about her illness firsthand added mental deadbolts to the door locking the others out. Whatever delusions assaulted her, she'd hold onto that reality with double clenched fists.

Ros was right, about needing to prepare the group. It was a reassuring reminder of why Abby had chosen Ros to hold her power of attorney, her living will. Knowing the difficulties of the path ahead, she could count on two things from Ros. That she would honor the central core of Abby's wishes, no matter how she disagreed with them.

And that she possessed the backbone and sheer guts to make the hard choices. Even when they pissed Abby off.

So she'd let it go. "I'm not the only person who can change your mind," she managed. "Lawrence can. And he has far more persuasive measures than I do."

"Don't tell him that."

Abby was glad for the shift in her friend's voice, from tension to tentative humor. She really didn't want to fight with Ros. She'd spent the morning finalizing the figures on several projects, and she was tired. Sitting here with Ros at her kitchen table, sharing a glass of wine, Ros's heels tumbled on the floor while she braced her stocking feet on the seat of Abby's chair...this was a good moment.

"I'm going to give them a few days to think about all of it, sort it out in their own heads," Ros said. "Then I'll get us together at my house for dinner. Let them say whatever they need to say. If you can handle it, I think you should be there. Cyn might be a little tough, but Vera and Skye should be all right. I'll try to talk to Cyn before then, settle her down."

Abby noticed her friend's shoulders still looked rigid, and Ros was toying with her wine glass. Now those frank blue eyes lifted. "One more thing. Neil was at the meeting."

Her heart thundered up into her throat. Abby set her soda down before it could reach her lips. "What?"

"It was my decision to invite him," Ros said firmly.

"And he accepted, knowing I wasn't aware of the meeting?"

"He'll take responsibility for that, but it was tempered very much by my insistence that it was in your best interest for him to attend, and—"

Abby was out of the chair. As she left the room, she heard Ros curse and scrape back her own to follow her. Before she could join her in the living room, Abby had pivoted and met her in the open threshold. She stomped into Ros's personal space, her blood gone to full boil. Even knowing stress was not a good idea, she couldn't restrain herself.

"You had absolutely *no* right to do that, Ros. None. And he..."

"He plans to call you tonight to talk about it. He wasn't comfortable with the decision, and wants to clear the air with you as soon as possible."

"He is *not* part of this. He should not be part of this."

"So your plan was just to let the good times roll and then cut him loose?"

"Yes," Abby snapped.

"Well, I'm sorry." Ros slashed a curt hand through the air. "That plan got fucked when he saw you piling kitchen ware on your back porch, babbling in tongues, and bleeding."

Her friend was perilously close to having her ear slapped through her head.

"We haven't sparred in some time," Ros said, reading her body language. "Go for it, if it will make you feel better."

"It will make you feel better. I have no interest in that."

Abby crossed the room, started up her stairs. She was going to lock herself in her room, tell Ros to go to hell, to leave. Instead, on another surge of emotion, she spun around. Ros was already there, meeting her at the bottom of the steps. Her face was pale, but her eyes were still sparking with that fire.

Without her heels, Ros was still a couple inches taller than Abby, but Abby leaned into her face from the bottom step. The dissolving of Ros's eyes wasn't a worry when rage fought with a wailing despair. The two feelings came together in one hissed, helpless word. "Why?"

Ros had the grace to flinch, but she held her ground. "Because in all the time I've known you, you've never risked your heart. You do with him. No matter how hard you try not to."

Because Neil made it so easy not to try, not to guard herself. "So it's okay to use him against me?" Abby demanded. "Risk his heart like this?"

"If I am using him, it's with his full awareness. And I'm sorry, love." Ros closed her hands on Abby's shoulders, wouldn't let her yank away. "I will do and use whatever way I have to convince you that life is worth hanging around for."

"That's pointless, and you should know it by now. You had no right," Abby repeated.

"I'm your friend. A sister. And none of us made any decisions *for* you. The primary purpose of that meeting was exactly as I stated it. We wanted to know the best ways to help you. To be there for you."

Abby shifted her gaze to the wall. A month ago, she'd had an asymmetrical arrangement of photos there. A trip they all took together to

Belize. She could still see the faint rectangular outline, since the sun hit the wall and had faded the paint where the pictures didn't cover it. When she spoke, her voice was toneless. "How did he take it? When he learned...what I planned."

"He deserved to know, Abby," Ros said. "You know he did. You aren't talking about some guy you went to dinner with once or twice."

"We just had our first actual date."

"Which was kind of like four dates rolled up into one. And before that, you had the barbecue. You met months ago, when he and Dale helped get me and Lawrence out of trouble. So that's more than a first date."

"You didn't answer my question. How did he take it?"

Ros dropped her hands. "Quietly. Deep ocean quiet."

It sent a small quake through her lower belly. Abby gripped the banister. Her gaze was wandering around Ros, the trim outline of her body getting fuzzy. A paper doll, cut out with bad scissors.

Cut them all out. Hold onto the scissors. Protect yourself. They will come through the cracks. Enter your body through the soles of your feet. You can cut them out with the scissors.

She was going to start screaming to shut them the fuck up. They were delusions. Fantasies. A tiny part of her mind tried to tell her that, like a flower pushing out of a sidewalk crack. By midnight tonight, those delusions would rip it right out of her brain pan. As they stomped the life out of the tender petals, they would be snarling.

Does that feel like a delusion, bitch?

"I'm cutting him loose." She tried to hold her voice steady. "I'm done with him."

"If you still want him around, I think you should let him make that call. Since we brought him into the loop, you can't say he isn't making an informed decision." Ros's voice hardened. "If you want to get rid of him just to spit in my face, punish me, then that's the wrong reason."

Abby brought her fist down on the banister, pain singing up her arm. The impact sent an echo through the room that made her want to clap her hands over her own ears. She fought through the noise. "Why won't you understand? Or listen?"

"Why won't you?"

Ros reached out again but Abby jerked back. "Leave. I want you to leave."

Ros let her hands drop. Spoke with quiet firmness. "Okay. But I am listening, Abigail. And I'm walking a tightrope of respecting your wishes, being your friend, watching out for your well-being and the rest of the team. All while desperately wishing for a miracle that will keep me from losing another sister. So cut me some slack, goddamn it."

Abby gripped the banister as Ros returned to the kitchen. Ros took a bracing swallow of the wine, then poured the rest of it in the sink, rinsed out the glass and collected her purse. She'd turned toward the door before she stopped, spoke again, keeping her back to Abby. Her voice was rough. "Text me when you go to bed. Let me know you're okay. I'll see you tomorrow."

After the kitchen door closed after her, Abby stood on the steps for long minutes. Then sat on them, pressed against the wall, her cheek against the cool sheet rock. She wrapped her arms around herself, rocked a little. Let her feet tap restlessly on the wood. They developed a pattern. Back and forth, out a couple feet, then back together again.

Ros had said Neil would call. Her gaze slid to the clock, and she started, realizing she'd been sitting here over an hour and a half.

Maybe Ros was wrong. Maybe thanks to that meeting and the revelations it held, Abby wouldn't hear from Neil again. She told herself that was a good thing, a relief. It would solve the issue.

She had no desire to hear from him if he decided changing her mind was a mission. They'd definitely be done. But she didn't want it to get ugly like that. Not with him.

Yes. It was better for him never to call. To be done quietly. Let her hold onto that day at the park, the time on his boat, in his bed, exactly as it was.

She wanted to throw things. She wanted to scream. Ros's pain had been too difficult. How could she counter her friend's anger, when it was drawn from the same vat of anguish, helplessness and pain she herself was feeling?

Ros had acknowledged the moral dilemma of calling the meeting. She wasn't an impulsive woman, not on decisions like that. Even as Abby was hurt, angry, she knew Ros had managed the wrongness, taken care for most of it, not to step outside the lines without careful consideration.

On everything except Neil. She'd fully stepped over the line on that one, but being Ros, she'd freely owned it, and had shrewdly gauged why she could do it. She'd understood Abby's vulnerability toward him.

Abby would have ripped into her worse for it, but Ros's ballsy bitch side had slipped there at the end, revealing the hurting friend beneath. Abby couldn't bring herself to tear into her. Not right now. Maybe she'd do it later.

Yes, Ros "handled" clients. But that "handling" was driven by Ros's care for them, her professional pride in giving them the right strategy to meet their needs, the best outcome for their desires. She was looking out for them. Simple fact.

But one thing was for certain. Abby wouldn't meekly accept being handled, no matter the motive. She had her path, and she would follow it. She wouldn't lose that control, wouldn't allow herself to reach the point where her will vanished under the onslaught of her own cracking mind. A hurricane was coming, and she had her eye on its advance, its pace. She knew what to do before it got here.

She didn't need them to agree with or understand her decision. Merely to accept it, or keep their opposing views to themselves so she didn't have to devote any energy to dealing with them.

She had her phone on silent, she realized suddenly. Maybe Neil *had* tried to call. When she went to the kitchen and picked up her phone, her heart jumped. She had three missed calls from him. One voicemail.

In that perverse way that women had—not just the ones tumbling fast into the insanity pool—she felt a spurt of disappointment that he hadn't countered her silence by coming over to initiate face-to-face communication.

He hadn't overlooked other methods, though. He'd also sent a series of texts. If she opened a window, she'd probably get dive-bombed by SEAL-trained carrier pigeons.

Smiling was like tearing open a stitched wound. She moved away from that horror movie imagery fast, and opened the text stream. When she read the first one, she slid down the cabinets, backside thudding to the floor.

Shit. Shit, shit, *shit*.

Sorry, bébé. Got called back to VA Beach for training exercise; good news is I should be back in forty-eight hours. You can tear a strip off my ass then.

If only he meant that literally. The visual alone could warm her cold bed tonight. If she wasn't supposed to be pissed at him, she'd send him that titillating suggestion, see how he reacted. That mix of heat—anger and lust—was better than the sinking feeling that he was no longer nearby, that he was out of reach.

So the reason he hadn't come over was because he'd been called away. Okay. That felt better. Slightly.

When she read the follow up text, those conflicting emotions spiked. *Private room set up at Progeny, Tue 7pm. Tiger waiting for you, me as spotter.*

Thanks to the shock, she read it a couple times to be sure she understood it. Had she told him she was ready to do that? If he was going to fuck with her head, make her believe she'd said something she hadn't...no. He wouldn't do that. For one thing, he didn't know she was having difficulties parsing what she'd actually said and done with what she imagined. At least she didn't think he knew.

She would have laughed hysterically if she didn't fear what else that reaction would unleash.

What had he told Tiger? She couldn't imagine how that meeting had gone. Wait...Ros would have had to facilitate it. Tiger had never met Neil. Son of a bitch.

No, not son of a bitch. Just bitch. Teetotal bitch.

Hyperstimulation of her senses aside, her hallucinations were mostly auditory, not visual. Even so, she took one more careful look at the text to verify it was real.

Then she sent a text. *Coward. Slinking out of town after dropping that bomb.*

A pause. Her heart leaped traitorously as dots rippled across the screen, telling her he was typing a response.

Tactical, not cowardly. Gives you time to get over being mad at me.

Your place has no locks, she responded. *Fish heads will be rotting in your mattress when you come back.*

Gives me an excuse to sleep at your place.

She could hear the sensual tag in his masculine voice, imagine the look in his eyes. It brought her mind back to the two of them in his bed, her hands curling and uncurling against the softness of his cut T-shirt binding her so loosely, his lips resting on the inside of her thigh.

She'd kept the one strip she'd brought home, wrapped around her wrist. She'd worn it that way several times when she was by herself, though she'd tucked it away before Ros came over.

But what purpose did embarrassment serve anymore? For instance, she could be furious with Ros, embarrassed about Neil being at that meeting, but what did it matter, really? Her time was short.

She'd told him the truth. It hadn't been that long since that last club scene, but believing she'd never be able to do it again had increased the longing for it, the sense of loss. She wanted at least one more session to enjoy being a Domme without worry. Neil was offering her the chance.

She went to the voice mail.

"This isn't the way I wanted to do this, Abby." His deep voice vibrated through her, made her want to clutch it closer. "I was going to drive over when you didn't answer, figured you were probably dodging me because I went to that meeting. I'll say I'm sorry and mean it, but I still would have gone, because you matter. That day on my boat, I hope I proved to you that I don't see you as a charity case."

He paused. "You're a damn strong person and you're facing a bitch of a challenge. It was Ros's show, and I went along with it, because she and the others love you, she has a longer history with you, and I wanted the intel. Not a blameless excuse, but I hope you'll let me earn your forgiveness, Mistress."

His chuckle sent shivers up her spine. "Yeah, I figured that might perk your ears up."

His tone shifted to something less playful. More reserved. "There are other things we need to deal with. You owe me an apology. We'll get that sorted out. First things first. Check your texts, and I'll see you in a couple days. If you don't show on Tuesday, I *will* come find you."

She wrestled with herself. The whispering shadows had their own opinions. Telling them to go fuck themselves, working herself up over them, only made them worse. So she took more pills and tried meditating.

Her approach to meditation wasn't the conventional method of clearing her mind. For one thing, that ability had moved beyond her reach months ago. But she could sometimes carve out a small room in there. A closet.

In that closet, she imagined herself back on the boat with Neil. Only instead of his kind of boat, it was like Tommy's, where she could sit between his spread knees, her hand resting on his thigh, her head against his arm as he steered using the tiller. Leaning against the sturdiness of him, hearing the easy rhythm of his heart, she watched how he handled the boat, so comfortable navigating the waters ahead.

Fine. Decision made. She wasn't going to give Neil up. As Ros the Teetotal Bitch had pointed out, he was fully informed. Well, as much as anyone could be when what they had was the tip of the proverbial iceberg. Once he hit the full glacier, she'd insist he embrace the practical realist his career choice said some significant part of him had to be.

That's when they'd call it done. Even if she had to pit all her energy against his formidable will to do it.

~

When the night with Tiger arrived, she put everything else aside. To do this right, she had to have one primary focus. If she let in other issues and conflicts, she'd get overwhelmed, and this would be over before it started.

And she really wanted to do this. Not just for the proving-herself thing. Her sharp yearning tonight was infiltrated by grief for what the future held.

Her intuition, the portion of it that rested in the lower pit of her belly where anxiety liked to concoct its bubbling stews, said the ability to do this would soon be out of her reach. Even with a spotter, her mind wouldn't let her reach those levels she desired, where her sub's reactions could offer her the reciprocal pleasures of Dom-space.

Her last session with Tiger had been like a lung cancer patient not realizing their last cigarette had, in fact, been their last ever. So she was going to give everything she'd ever wanted to give to a scene, take it unforgettable places for her and Tiger. She wanted to defy a lot of things tonight, including the bitch slap of Fate.

Having Neil in the room made that charged potential even greater.

He'd made it back with a couple hours to spare, sending her a text to confirm he would be there.

Before her priorities had had to change, her preference for club wear had been sexier, more creative. But in recent weeks it had been easier to choose slightly softer versions of her corporate office style. Neil had been spot-on with that, the night he'd selected the flowing slacks and lace blouse. Even when Abby wanted to bring a man to his knees—more than usual—she would change up some details, but the basics would remain essentially the same.

Tonight she'd gone beyond any of that. She'd dressed and prepared herself with the intent of commanding a man who wouldn't be commanded.

Club Progeny had a coded side entrance for members who wanted to keep their headspace undisturbed by the lively social atmosphere at the main doors. The security person there watched as she ran her card through the reader. When it beeped green, he held open the door for her.

Abby had worn a hooded velvet cape, its taffeta overlay shimmering with a starfield of sparkling rhinestones. The cape swirled around her shiny black boots. They creased around her ankles like a supple second skin, inviting the touch of a man's hand, his lips. When she turned a half smile toward the security guard, letting him see her face, he did a double take.

"Holy shit," he murmured. "Knock 'em dead, Mistress. I'll help you hide the bodies."

Her smile deepened, a feral pleasure surging through her. Goddess, she felt so powerful tonight, something she'd acutely missed. She knew the euphoria was a warning sign. As were her expanded senses, which made her note everything from the subtle flaring of his nostrils at her scent to the flex of his fingers on the door latch, the unconscious lean of his body toward her.

She'd sometimes wondered if she'd been overly vain about her looks in a former life. Such that she'd foolishly made a devil's bargain for this one, exchanging a sound mind for an overabundance of physical beauty.

If so, she'd realized the error of that decision, well before she grew out of childhood.

In the changing area, she locked up her keys and purse, slipped another pill. The stiffness of her face hadn't affected the guard's reaction to it. That fairly mild side effect—like wearing a clay mask, her mother had called it—could be channeled into the Mistress persona she intended to project.

She checked the wall clock and headed for the private room. Neil had texted her again when he'd arrived, thirty minutes before she did.

When you're ready, we're here, Mistress. For you.

Her heart rate elevated as she approached the door, thinking of the two very different men behind it. Both capable of meeting her desires, as a Mistress and a woman.

How much had he told Tiger about her situation? Revealing the basics about her illness was a necessary evil; otherwise, Tiger wouldn't have agreed to the presence of another male in the room with them. In some ways, he was just as alpha as Neil. He wasn't into sharing.

She should have been in on that discussion. She was the Mistress here. Tiger was under her care.

Well, he was, and he wasn't. That was why Neil was here, because she couldn't guarantee she could keep Tiger safe.

They will overwhelm you. Pull your mind apart. Leave it on the floor and walk over it. Make it disappear into the cracks of the tile. You cease to exist after tonight.

She set her jaw. "Nothing ever ceases to exist," she whispered. *You can't destroy energy.*

Tonight, she'd put her whole will into becoming a being of pure energy.

She unlatched the door and stepped through.

This was her preferred room for private scenes. It had a wide and sturdy spanking bench, one mirrored wall that was currently screened by a curtain. Erotic black and white stills were framed in silver on the walls. Those walls were painted in large triangles of dark blue, black and white. The floor tile was black with deep blue grout. The light fixture, a geometrically balanced mix of metal circles with shaded lamps in their centers, could be adjusted to different illumination levels.

Tiger knelt on a padded square. Spreader bar between his wrists, one securely wrapped with Velcro, the other with the strap threaded into a loose loop, waiting for her to finish the binding. The bar braced his hands two feet apart, but it could telescope out to four feet. The black shorts, the only thing he wore, clung to his thighs, the curves of his firm buttocks, and his arousal.

He was a beautiful male. Sculpted by life, hard work, discipline, commitment, sacrifice. Much like the man in the corner. Neil had his arms folded as he leaned against the wall, silent but *so* present.

Why not one of the others? Cyn, Vera, Skye, or even Ros? Why did it have to be him?

But Abby knew the answer to that. It was the only way Neil was going to tolerate her being in the same room with a man there to serve her as a Mistress. A reaction that defied the idea that their connection was temporary, what they were becoming to one another.

A day ago, she would have said she and Neil weren't becoming anything because of that visit from Ros. But here they were.

Tiger's arousal wasn't as full mast as it normally would have been, waiting on his Mistress's pleasure. A likely side effect of his awareness of Neil and the unusual circumstances of the session. She would handle that.

Neil was here for oversight only. She could react to that however worked best for what she wanted to accomplish in the scene. So right now she didn't do more than note him in her peripheral vision. Tiger was her focus.

He'd assumed the formal posture of a sub waiting for his Mistress. No fidgeting, no looking around. She'd sent the instructions to his club account Monday. He was probably intrigued by the spreader bar, since she rarely employed restraints that he couldn't get out of himself with little effort. Once she secured that other cuff and finished what she intended to do to prep him, he wouldn't be able to get loose without her.

Or Neil.

She'd avoided such bindings, worried that what had finally happened during their last session would occur. She wouldn't dare fate or endanger her sub. Not with the monster lurking, biding its time her entire life, ready to jump out of the closet at the worst possible moment. No one would pay a price caused by foolish optimism.

Tiger was feeling her careful study. It was in the straighter line of his back, the deeper dip of his head. The press of his lips, the curl of his fingers. A ripple of energy over his muscles. She let him hear the deliberately spaced click of her boot heels as she moved closer. Air movement from the swirl of the cape would be feathering over his skin.

When she was close enough he could look at the boots, another ripple passed through him. The right boot was decorated with an anklet shaped like a set of handcuffs. A ruby red heart dangled from the chain.

"I want your mouth on the heart, Tiger," she said. "Don't speak, and don't move once your mouth is there."

He shifted to comply, though she could feel his desire to respond, "Yes, Mistress." He loved speaking those words to her. She'd deny him what he loved until he'd been punished for his transgression, earned her forgiveness.

When he leaned forward and put his mouth on the little heart, she dipped down over his bare back, propping her elbow on it to steady her as she tightened the looser cuff on his wrist, then checked the other, ensuring it wasn't tight enough to restrict circulation. It wouldn't be the last time tonight she checked, since she intended to have him straining against those bonds.

She slipped the throat and front fasteners of the cloak and slid it off her shoulders. Though she hadn't looked toward that corner again, she held it out in that direction and waited, her gaze on Tiger.

Neil would be looking at her now, at what she'd chosen to wear. Maybe that was why it took an extra beat before a strong hand closed over hers on the velvet. The caress of his fingers sent lovely sensation up her arm. No matter that it had been only a few days, her body had missed his touch, longed for it.

Maybe he'd also waited a beat to underscore the point that he wasn't here as her sub. Or her valet.

Maybe not, but she was going to show him the rewards of service and attention, until he was aching from the demonstration. Whether that ache came from the drive to reclaim her attention from another man, or consider the merits of being on the other side of a whip with a Mistress, it would serve her purposes, too.

She'd received a heavenly waft of his male scent, and granted herself a quick look as he turned away to hang up her cloak. He'd taken care with his appearance too. Belted jeans that made her want to spend far more time looking, and a black, tucked-in dress shirt with rolled up sleeves. Everything feminine in her gravitated toward the simple clean lines of his strong male presence. But by the time he turned, she had her attention back on Tiger.

Tiger wasn't by nature a brat, but he would test her. Particularly if she'd let her attention drift to another male. As she looked back down, she caught the subtle lift of his head that would have given him a glimpse of her body. The expulsion of a startled and reverent breath told her he liked what he'd seen. And that he knew he'd been caught.

"Did I say you could look at me?" She spoke in a tone of sensual menace.

The comment was of course directed to Tiger. However, when she looked toward the corner where Neil was leaning, arms once again crossed over his chest, she wasn't at all surprised by the reaction. When Tiger lowered his gaze, Neil raised his. The challenge there—and accepted.

It was more difficult for her to look at people's faces, their eyes, when they were looking at hers. Since Neil's gaze was passing over the rest of her, she had a measured opportunity to savor the heat in his expression. He started from her boots and worked up, though she noted the slate gaze paused on Tiger for a charged moment. Neil studied the way he had his mouth against her ankle, the cant of his body toward her, before moving onward.

She wore shimmering, sheer black stockings held by garters. The back seam was a tiny, embroidered chain of red roses, from ankle to thigh. The straps of the garters were visible in front because her short skirt was clipped to the tops. It formed a scalloping of fabric that covered her sex and a meager amount of her upper thighs. The skirt's stretchy fabric clung to her ass.

A decorative belt rested low on her hips, nipping in the line of her sheer white blouse, held by two buttons at the waist. The blouse's opening above revealed the high set of her breasts, cradled in a black bra with red satin lining. That red matched the crimson soles of the boots and the embroidered roses on the stockings.

The oblong silver pendant she wore on a slender chain was a gift from Ros when Abby claimed her identity as a Mistress. An orientation she'd hoped ran deep enough to overwhelm anything trying to define her against her wishes.

The engraving said it all.

Mistress.

"Not that anyone you ever top will need the reminder," Ros had said. "*But they'll love the reinforcement.*"

So did she.

"No, Mistress," Tiger murmured. "You didn't tell me I could look. But...thank you."

The gratitude arrowed through her stomach, because of what the words meant, for what his tone held, as well as what it didn't. Whatever Neil had told Tiger, it hadn't changed his behavior toward her, except for a deeper level of emotional reaction that only enhanced what they already had. It would make her cruel and demanding in a way he'd enjoy.

"You think I choose what to wear based on your desires, Tiger? On anyone's desires but my own?"

"Of course not, Mistress," he said quickly, fingers tightening. "I'm just thankful to be in your presence, allowed to look."

"But you stole that look, because you couldn't wait for permission. And you already started this evening with a punishment due, didn't you? Meeting with this man without my express consent."

Though her tone expressed her disapproval, he knew it was part of the scene. She'd already told him, through their club email exchange, brief but sincere, that she held no anger over it.

Not with him.

"Yes, Mistress." His fingers clenched. "I ask your forgiveness."

"Better than that; you'll earn it." She closed her hand on the wooden handle of the dragon tail. She'd tucked it into the back of the belt, where it couldn't be seen right away by the man who would be receiving its sting.

The triangular square of fabric was deceptively soft, but a dragon tail could hurt like hell when snapped, though she could modulate the impact to use it as a warm-up toy. On the nights they shared him consecutively, Skye was the one more likely to play to Tiger's pain threshold, but Abby knew exactly where it was.

"Stand up."

Tiger rose to his six-foot-two height. As she moved to a counter, a set of cabinets bolted above it, she was sure that two sets of eyes were on her swaying hips. She picked up the remote that controlled the chain dangling from the ceiling. When she returned to Tiger, she clipped the hook in the center of the spreader bar to the chain. She pressed the retract button, watching the chain pull Tiger's arms up over his head, keeping it going as his body stretched upward.

When his heels left the floor, pushing him onto his toes, she stopped, bumped it down an inch. Now his body was stretched to its maximum length, but his heels were in contact with the tile.

As she tucked the small remote into her bra, she enjoyed the view. The definition in his arms, his abdomen, the hollows between hip bones and the elastic waistband of his underwear. The erection was growing. He wasn't thinking about Neil so much anymore. It was starting to be all about the demands of the Mistress before him.

That was where she wanted his head, though her own awareness of Neil had tripled. It didn't diminish her focus on Tiger a bit, though. She knew this ritual. The beginning, the build-up, the leap and flight, the prolonged and reluctant circle back to earth, the languorous return to reality.

She'd loved it ever since Ros had introduced her to it, a way to enjoy sexual intimacy, vulnerability, in a controlled setting that hadn't set off anything troublesome in her. Not until recently.

Abby walked her fingertips along Tiger's torso, down to his lower abdomen. She circled him, her touch following the same path, so she could push the underwear down and get a view of his bare, muscular ass. She palmed it, brushed her lips over his back. It was an overlay, imagining Neil's body, experiencing the reality of Tiger's. Both of them available to her in different ways.

Tiger's now, Neil's later.

She was aware when Neil shifted restlessly behind her, but she kept her gaze on Tiger. Neil had set this up. If he was suffering, watching her enjoy another man, he had no one but himself to blame.

She might have fantasized about turning this into a threesome, but it would stop there, on the far edges of her mind. One primary focus. That didn't allow for a renegotiation mid-session. She didn't trust the facility of her mind to handle that.

Plus, Tiger was hard limit straight. Neil had indicated—and Tiger verified—Neil's involvement in this room would be interactions with her or watching. Nothing that involved direct contact with Tiger, unless Tiger was in some kind of physical distress that required Neil to intervene.

That info had confirmed for her that Neil had told Tiger about her illness. But that wasn't important. The recollection that Neil was here a hundred percent for her, to help her protect Tiger, was.

She let the dragon tail drift over the top of Tiger's buttocks, then she threaded it across his front, below his hips. She pressed herself against his back as she tightened the slack, let him feel her curves pushed against him above the bra, the cut of the metal studding her belt. "I can't wait to leave marks on this fine, fine ass," she murmured. "See you try to hold still. Tell me your safe word, Tiger."

"Motorcycle." His voice was gravel rough, his fingers flexing in the bonds.

"Good. Don't use it unless you mean it."

She backed off and slapped him with the dragon tail, a light-handed blow. She kept it up, a rotating movement, spreading out over back, ass, thighs, sides. Warming up the flesh, following up those slaps with caressing fingers, stroking. Then she landed the first pop, with a deft snap of her wrist. The point struck flesh with a sharp sting, causing his body to jerk, his breath to draw in.

"You gave me this moment, Tiger," she said, her voice a purr. "You gave me the ability to punish you. I'm very pleased you did."

"Thank you, Mistress."

She kept going, alternating strokes, slaps, pops. Some delivered a quick sting that shimmered across his skin, but as those strikes penetrated deeper, they sent a searing burn into the muscles. The sting and burn combination intensified things. He started arching up at each blow, sucking in a curse, the chain clanking.

Though she hadn't done pain like this often, it was a dance she enjoyed, building on what he could tolerate, what he could bear. She offered admonishments and encouragement to him with her whispers, her hands, the brush of her body against his. She was pushing him to the boundaries of his tolerance. If she did it right, she'd take him just the right distance beyond it. Proving his devotion, his desire to please her, which would please them both, showing her what he could bear for her. It would also show he accepted her punishment, her judgment on him, her control.

In the aftermath, the stings would settle into a delicious wave of soreness, a reminder of what he'd borne for her.

"Ah...*Christ*." She'd delivered the highest level of pain yet, with three successive blows that wrenched a hoarse cry from him.

She stepped back. "The whip has left kisses all over your skin. It will leave more, if you don't give me the apology I want, Tiger."

His voice had the right amount of rawness, of need, telling her where he was at. He also offered her the words that landed right in the part of her mind where she needed them most.

"I'm sorry for not respecting your authority, Mistress. Your control in here, which is absolute. I serve you."

"Yes, you do. And very well, too." She closed in to put her mouth on his shoulder blade. She caressed his ass, pinched a red spot, following it up with a scrape of her nails that had him hissing through his teeth. But he held still for her. With her this close, he would fight all movement to keep her there.

The flash of his gaze in her direction, showing heat, apprehension but lust for more, was what she wanted to see.

She moved around him several more times, absorbing everything. She smiled when she trailed the whip over his sensitized flesh from behind and he jerked, not anticipating the touch to be gentle. She let the fall slide over his neck, his shoulder, as she moved in front of him.

His eyes were glazed, in the zone. "You're so beautiful, Mistress."

"I'm still angry with you."

"You're beautiful when you're angry. You're beautiful all the time."

She used her fingertips to explore his chest and abdomen, tugged the line of hair running down to his cock. Yes, he was in the zone, but not as deep as she wanted him to go. She was in the mood to exercise her full power tonight, turn her captive into a mindless beast.

She touched the top of her breast, drew a circle over it, went down into the cup, playing with the nipple. Then she scooped out the weight of the curve, tweaking the tip. With the belted sheer shirt over it, he saw the temptation through that veil. The chain mount in the ceiling clanked harder as he reacted, shifting restlessly.

"You'd suckle me if I told you to, wouldn't you, Tiger?"

"Yes, Mistress."

She could tell he wanted to say it in a far rougher way. *Fuck, yeah, I'd suck on those tits.* But he knew better. She required her subs to behave like gentlemen. Until she commanded them not to.

She hadn't forgotten there was a third person in the room. Not in the least. She wanted to test his limits, the way she was testing Tiger's.

"Close your eyes. Let the pain sink into your muscles, and imagine how far you'll go to please your Mistress. What you'll let her do to you. Because I'm far from done."

She stepped behind Tiger, moving the few steps to her unzipped personal toy bag. She kept it checked in with the staff so they could leave it in the room for her as part of the prep, when she requested it.

Dropping to her heels beside it, she reached in and closed her hand on what she wanted. As she did, she tipped her head up to look at Neil. He was only a couple feet away. He'd shifted toward her, his thumb hooked in one belt loop, his shoulder against the wall. His foot was hooked around the opposite ankle, drawing attention to the long thighs, cradling a firm and aroused package.

The entire combination, head to toe, made her own breath draw in. It was the first time she'd looked square upon him since she'd started. His gaze was hot enough to burn, and it covered her with that heat. The cleft between her breasts, her throat, her skin beneath her clothes.

Everyone knew the saying, "undressing me with his eyes." Neil was burning away any covering she had.

Because she looked beyond lust, though, there was more than that, and it gave her pause. In his voice mail, he'd included that cryptic comment, that she owed him an apology. A fire wall existed behind the heat, guarding something important. She had his full support here, his male attention. But not knowing what was behind that wall made her uneasy, sensing he was holding things out of her reach.

It had to do with that meeting, she was sure of it. She didn't want her head to take her there. Not right now.

Then his gaze dropped to what she had drawn out of the bag and rested on top of the canvas folds. His eyes came back up to hers, locked. "Not happening," he growled.

A direct challenge was just the thing to drive that uneasiness away. Abby straightened, sauntered closer. Putting her hand boldly against his upper abdomen, she rose on her toes, speaking low so Tiger couldn't make out the words. The position brushed her thigh against Neil's. He immediately gripped her waist, holding her firmly.

"You're here to support me," she reminded him. "I'm in charge."

"Yeah. For sure. Turns me on beyond belief to watch it." His eyes were honed blue-gray steel. "You're in charge. But bébé, I'm in command. Touch him, enjoy him, enjoy yourself, even make him come, but I'm not watching you fuck another man in front of me."

The heat level mounted. Her fingers dug into his corded forearm. If he'd asserted anything different, or left it there, she could have argued it, relegated it to male petulance, but this was anything but, which his next words proved.

"Call that an extremely hard limit. You push it, I'll prove it to you."

"Tell me how."

The danger thrilled her. She wanted to tease both men, take them places none of them would ever forget. She moved in closer, resting her breasts against Neil's chest as he cupped her ass, fingers threading under a strap of the garter belt. When he discovered she wore no panties, his eyes darkened. She straddled his leg, rubbing herself against denim with a sinuous stroke. There was no limit to who she could be tonight. "Tell me how you'll prove it, sailor," she murmured. "Because his Mistress *is* taking his fine ass tonight."

A battle of wills, the two of them staring at one another. He wasn't going to concede this one, and she wouldn't put it past him to go caveman on her to prove it. She wanted that claim, that possession. But she also wanted to take Tiger down this road. Would he understand?

She'd learned to expect more of Neil, and he didn't disappoint her now. A light kindled in his gaze she thought Lucifer himself would recognize. A man who would let nothing, not even the promise of Hell, keep him from what he considered his.

"If you fuck him, you do it with me inside you."

"Deal," she said.

CHAPTER ELEVEN

She went back to Tiger. Walked her fingertips down the center of his back, watched the reactive flex of his buttocks above where she'd pulled down the shorts. She let her touch glide down the seam between them. She'd played there a few times, knew he was responsive in that area as most people were, once they got past any hang-ups over it. Pretty much every square inch of the body had been designed to feel pleasure, if a person cared to take the time to explore and learn how to bring it forth.

She thought of Neil, his hair brushing her skin, the rough feel of his jaw, the firm pressure of his lips, the heat of his breath, all bringing different sensations to her. He'd proven he had that kind of patience, desire, intent. What had added to its searing power—whether she thought of it now, or in whatever lifetimes were to come—was it had been about marking her, such that if sunlight or rain or the brush of clothes touched her skin, she remembered him. She would always remember.

She wanted to believe that, the way the tiny person in a tiny boat in a big sea believed, with the last breath of life in them.

"Tiger, I want to take you here." She pushed her fingers into his rim, just enough to feel the nerves clench, react. "When we started, it was a hard limit. Over time, as I showed you how you reacted to rim play, you felt differently."

Goddess, that had been a session. She'd put the broad head of a vibrating wand against his rim, offering slight movements for friction and to vary the sensation. He'd been bent over a bench, legs spread, and she'd made him hold open his buttocks for her so she could keep her hands free to manipulate the vibrator.

His hips had started to jerk and rotate in an asymmetrical dance, his powerful thighs trembling, shoulder muscles bunched. Rasping breaths had turned into hard grunts, groans, pleas like she'd never heard from him before. It had become a symphony of the male animal, his lust holding him by the throat, all through a Mistress's hand.

"Once rim play was no longer a limit, we talked about anal play. You told me, under the right circumstances, with a Mistress you trust, you might be willing to let a woman fuck you. As long as her dick wasn't bigger than yours."

The memory brought a smile to her face. She heard Tiger manage a strained chuckle. The humor was such a relief, the normalcy of it. Proof that, though the waves were rising and falling, and the shadows were there, she was still holding. At her center, she was still her, able to connect with a sub.

A glimpse of Neil's tight smile told her he'd appreciated the comment, too. Though they were different sides of the Dominant and submissive coin, he and Tiger had plenty of traits in common.

Tiger was still shuddering with the strength of his arousal. The reaction had only grown stronger as she'd laid her mouth on those places she'd stung him the hardest with the dragontail. She moved in front of him, used her knuckles to track a line down his center. His cock was erect and thick. Her spoken intent to fuck him hadn't withered any of that desire. Just the opposite. It was a welcome threat.

Everyone liked riding a perilous edge of desire, as long as the vital connection to the person riding it with them held. When it came to a Domme and a sub, that ride could climb high and fast, if the sub trusted the Domme to integrate his vulnerabilities into meeting both their needs.

Not a problem. Connecting to his vulnerabilities, Tiger's needs, fueled her power and pleasure with him.

Abby pulled Tiger's shorts down in front, so now the entire garment creased around his upper thighs. She climbed the substantial length of his cock with a spider walk of her fingertips, pressed a nail against the wet slit. He shuddered from the effort to stay still. He was a big man. Another reason he tried not to move when she was this close was knowing, if he jerked or bucked, he could push her back, dislodge her hand. So, like most big, powerful men who craved submission from a woman whose frame and weight were smaller, he'd learned how to contain the reaction, let it build in a confined space.

The explosive heat of it would emanate out in waves, bathing a Mistress with the glory of it. She'd feel it over her skin, see it swirling in the air. She saw it now, the energy dancing around them, electrified, flocks of beetles with iridescent wings that were lightning bolts of flashing color.

She swayed. Hands gripped her shoulders, strong fingers. "Ask him the question, Mistress."

Hadn't she? Perhaps not. That worried her, but the hands holding her were sure and steady. Neil's hands. They stroked her as he spoke against her ear, his breath on her neck. "He's all yours. Waiting for your direction. With impatience, yes, but only to serve your desires. He will wait for them forever, eternally patient for you to voice them. We're here for you. With you."

It was so much information and sensation, from so many directions. "You don't have to worry," he said. "I've got both of you. Just feel and enjoy, and we'll make sure everyone's safe. Together."

If the shadows spoke, if the walls turned to liquid gold, if the light became flashings words around them, she could be sure that somewhere, in all of it, he was there, understanding, knowing what was most important to her.

"Keep *him* safe. Above everything else. Promise me."

She felt Tiger shift, his head turn. Maybe he and Neil looked at each other.

"You got it," Neil said. "Now take you both where you want and need to go."

"How about you?"

"I'll take what I want when I'm ready." His tone promised it, in a way that made her body tighten in response.

The rest might not make sense. This did. This was where she was meant to be, the destination she'd intended to reach.

Some of the most brilliant artists, thinkers and creators were believed to have schizophrenia. The disorder dropped them into places where they created unforgettable art and wonders, made discoveries that transformed and elevated the lives of others. All while the artist suffered the torment, the consequences, of not knowing reality from illusion. They couldn't stop the voices or constant mood swings, fatigue, crazy distortions. They could paint masterpieces but be overwhelmed by a simple progression of tasks.

Brush your teeth, take a shower, get dressed.

But as she stood where such wonders could be found, she thought she probably felt as they did when they stood in their own version of such a place.

She was behind Tiger again. She put her hands high on his muscled back. "Lower the chain enough to ease the strain," she said to the void, because Neil was out there in it, hearing her. Like the god who responded when one tiny person on one tiny boat cried out in the center of a huge storm, far vaster and way more powerful and overwhelming than the pitiful blip of a human's existence.

But the soul was a powerful thing. *It* was a god. A goddess, able to prevail, persist. Endure. Triumph.

Sensations of omnipotence were also a trap, a way to rush the lemmings to the cliff edge. But it was as Neil said. She was in charge, but he was in command. The assertion he'd made, to confront her, challenge her...it was a comfort. A reassurance. It was okay.

He'd keep them safe.

Her touch had dropped to Tiger's hip. She dug into his flesh as she pressed her forehead to the middle of his back. He had a tattoo there, too. Thank God, it wasn't anything with eyes that could stare back at her. It was an infinity symbol made of razor wire. Crimson and black blood dripped from it.

If he'd shown her that the first time they'd met, she would have known they were destined to play together, people who understood that life always had two sides, light and dark. Shadows defined. But they also swallowed, hid monsters.

"Only one focus, Mistress," that voice said. "Him. Narrow it down. Like being in the boat."

Neil's hands were back on her shoulders, his lips moving to her nape. Tiger spoke.

"Yes. I want to do it, Mistress. I want to serve you." His rumbling voice was sunshine filtering through the trees on the bayou. Her on the boat, her body tight and full, wanting to give and receive pleasure, close that circle, feel its magic.

"You didn't ask him anything," Neil noted.

She loved him for knowing what was important to her as a Mistress. She didn't want to be carried through this. By either of them. Things came back into focus, sharpening with her tone.

"Are you trying to direct things, Tiger? There's only one person in charge here."

Only one person in command.

Neither of them Tiger.

"Are you trying to anticipate my desires?"

"No, Mistress." He corrected himself. "Just wanting to serve them."

"Good. Understand the difference. I don't want to have to hand out another punishment. I'm going to fuck your ass now, and only two things will stop me. My own whims, if I decide to deny you, to remind you who's in charge. Or you, deciding you need to get on your motorcycle and ride away."

"Not going to happen, Mistress." Raw lust saturated his voice like a strong whisky. "Want to make you happy. Give you pleasure."

"Lower his arms, please. Take off the chain."

She moved, as Neil's hands withdrew, disappeared. She didn't know which. Awareness could come and go like that. Tiger's arms had been lowered, the spreader bar resting on his shoulders, arms bent and fingers curved over the shaft. "Lift your hands, put the spreader bar in front of you."

When he did, she gripped it, used it to lead him to the bench. She put the bench between them, him bent forward so his palms rested on the firm cushion.

She placed her hands on top of the spreader bar and depressed the button that telescoped it out an additional two feet. It pulled him down closer to the bench, put his face just above her breasts, held high and quivering in the black bra. With amusement, she watched Tiger struggle not to let his face land right in her cleavage. Barely two inches separated his mouth from that valley between her breasts.

Fortunately, he managed it. Later she might dwell pleasantly on the severity of the punishment she would have handed out if he'd failed.

She secured the spreader bar to the bench with a pair of straps, holding him in place. His head was bowed, eyes down. A submissive posture, but he also looked ready to leap up and fight an army at her command.

Neil was looking through her toy bag to find what she would need. She didn't have to think about any of that. She could keep her focus on just this. Limit the factors, the stimulus. But not the sensation. Not the good stuff.

At the park, Neil had talked about isolating muscle groups to work out. He'd turned it into a metaphor for seduction, isolating and focusing on every part of her body.

She smoothed her hands over the upholstered bench. "I've watched you leave the club on your bike, Tiger. Throw your leg over the seat, get it started, all that power and vibration between your legs. Settle that fine, tight ass into the seat. I've imagined you bent over it, like now, while I strap that beautiful ass, or sink into it, press myself up behind you, play with and tease you until you spew all over it. Then I'd chide you for making a mess of your baby."

His fingers clenched against the red vinyl. His cock twitched, brushing against his belly as she spoke. His lips were pressed together into a line.

"I don't want your answer to a question I haven't asked, Tiger," she said. "I want you to say what's running through your head right now. Not a demand, but a wish you'll hope I'll grant, if I'm merciful. What is it?"

A hard breath, a shudder through the big shoulders. "I want you to fuck me against my bike, Mistress. Please. I need to give you that."

"Why?"

"Because you want that. You're demanding it of me, and I want to give you pleasure. Be your pleasure."

"Your body, my pleasure. Yes. You remembered the first lesson I taught you here. Good. You are a gift, Tiger. Such a gift...to any Mistress."

Blue waves of tears, swamping her, grabbing her throat, her words, wanting to own her.

Strong emotion, a trigger. A threat.

Come at you through the cracks, through the soles of your feet. Everywhere you're vulnerable. They're here to kill you, take you away, put you in a box. Red lights. Red, bloody red lights.

Desire was at risk of being flooded, quenched. She circled Tiger, seeking a spot where he couldn't see her. This was the way it worked, an ambush. Just when things were going right, the bike would hit the stone in the road that would fling the rider off and into a ravine. Branches would tear the flesh. Everything good and breathtaking about the ride disappeared.

That was what hell was. Proving how fast joy or anything good could be obliterated, no longer even within the grasp of memory, except as an instrument of torture.

"Mistress." She was against the wall, palms pressed to it.

"Fall foliage falling. Too fast, too many colors. Words on branches, separate, no sense."

"Slow it down, then. Take a breath. Put it together. It's a tree. It's all connected."

Yes. Yes, it was. Those words and thoughts, spread out on so many branches. She could tip them, pour them toward the trunk. They'd make sense again when she let them drop into Neil's hands. She groped for one, and it was there, large and warm. She bent her head, pressed her lips to his palm. Taking the words back into her, where they made sense.

He was stroking her with the other hand. It was okay. Tiger. She was here with him and Tiger.

They had a deal. A delightful, provocative one.

The world steadied. Neil's hands were on her arms, her sides and hips. When his fingers tapped the waistband of her skirt, a question, she nodded.

He hooked his thumbs in it, slid it down her legs, to the floor. Being naked beneath the garter belt made her feel way too vulnerable, but the belt and the skirt were merely being replaced, by the pair of shorts she kept in her bag. Clingy shorts, like Tiger was wearing.

Neil unhooked the anklet, unzipped the boots and let her step out of them. As he worked her stockings down her legs, he caressed her from thigh to foot. He folded and tucked the stockings into one boot, the anklet into the other, and set them aside.

She'd been having trouble getting air, anxiety driving up the need for oxygen, but in the filmy shirt, satin bra and shorts, she was in control, comfortable, but still sexy. Able to stretch, move, breathe. Fly.

Straps brushed her buttock, and he was buckling the strap-on around her hips, between her legs, so she didn't have to figure it out. When she dropped her hands toward the dildo threaded through it, Neil nipped her ear, a warning. "It's lubed up good."

She made a noise as he cinched it in, putting pressure on her clit. He pressed up behind her after he seated it, letting her feel his erection, as substantial as Tiger's—but not at her command. The contrast stole her breath.

"What do you want, Mistress?" Neil wasn't speaking from the shadows, but right up against her ear, her neck, so he drowned out those other murmurs.

In command.

In charge.

There was a push and pull there, a challenge. In a surge of reaction, she grasped it with both hands and tossed it back to him. "To fuck his brains out."

A husky chuckle, and he moved his hands to her hips, his grip flexing with formidable promise. "Whatever you take from him, I'm taking twice as hard from you."

She bared her teeth in a smile. "Good thing SEALs have stamina. Try to keep up."

Fireflies were in the air, the voices rising, but she was aware of Tiger, of Neil, of what was happening. Everything in sharp relief, intense, her senses drinking it in.

Neil had left her to draw back the curtain from the mirrored wall. Which meant as she moved toward Tiger, he could see her coming, her hips swinging just the right amount. A woman could turn walking in a strap-on into a mesmerizing dance, an animated work of art, and she was a Botticelli.

She couldn't dwell on images in the mirror for more than a moment; that could quickly go wrong for her. She would have liked to see the desire in Tiger's eyes flare, war with the trepidation over what she was about to do to him, but she could feed off of what the rest of his body told her.

The decision to let Tiger see her wearing the strap-on was a calculated risk. There were men who enjoyed being fucked by one, but they never wanted to see it. She saw the dip of his head as he considered it, watched her. And she saw his cock twitch again, pre-come spill out of the top.

He liked watching.

She stroked her hand down his back, over his flank, ran her knuckles along that expanse. "Are you with me, Tiger?"

"Yes, Mistress." Voice tight, but not in the wrong way. She reached her other hand behind her, and Neil clasped it, caressed, giving her the reassurance that he wasn't hearing any flags from Tiger, either.

"I've wanted to do this to you for a very long time, Tiger. I've lain in my bed and brought myself to climax, thinking of it. You remember, I told you I'd ask how far you'd go to satisfy your Mistress's demands. Is this too far?"

"No, Mistress." Husky emotion. "It's...thank you. I'm glad you want this from me."

She slid behind him, folded her hands over his shoulder blades, followed the wideness of his back to the taper of his waist, the bumps of his spine, and that gorgeous, lifted ass. Neil pressed the tube of lubricant into her hand. Though the strap-on was greased up, there was never too much lube for a virgin ass.

The strap-on that had been in her bag wasn't as large as Tiger's own equipment. It was appropriate for a first time, but it wasn't insignificant. He'd feel it. There'd be the right kind of discomfort, telling him he'd suffered for his Mistress, but she'd make sure it wasn't unbearable—and that he'd be wanting to do it again.

She could check out the mirror in her peripheral vision, enough to verify he was watching her intently. She didn't linger. If his face changed, the eyes becoming dark pits, she might not be able to understand what he was saying. Hear him if he safeworded.

Just the worrisome thought froze her momentarily, but she eased herself away from that, back to that one focus.

It didn't hurt that Neil was behind her, taking her hair down out of the twist she'd put it in. It made her smile, how much he liked her hair. He stroked his fingers through it, tugging on her scalp.

As he did that, she eased well-lubricated fingers into Tiger, stroked and stimulated, greasing up the rim and the channel. Sharp desire surged between her legs as he grunted in response, thighs trembling again.

"Mistress," he groaned, fingers clawing into the bench.

"Beg me to take your ass," she ordered. "Tell me it's mine to fuck."

"It's yours, Mistress. Please. Take it."

As Neil took the lube away, Abby fit the tip of the phallus to Tiger's opening. "Lift up to me, push out." Her mind went calm and centered, at the moment it was most important, and that alone made her grateful. She burned for the man who'd made it happen, at the same time she was greedy for the pleasures the man before her could give her.

Neil settled his hands on her waist, but stayed there. He understood it was important for her not to be distracted from Tiger's care at this key moment. But the reminder of his presence, the heat and strength of his body behind her, had her vibrating, her core readying itself for him, even as she prepared to take Tiger.

She was easing in, slow, slow, one hand on Tiger's back, feeling the vibration of his physical and emotional reaction as she guided the phallus. She kneaded his buttock, gave it a little slap and pinch because it pleased her to do it, hitting one of those red spots the dragontail had marked. He groaned again, and pushed back into her. She slid home.

He tightened up some then, because it would burn, this first time, no matter how carefully she'd proceeded. She'd stoked his lust and he'd pushed back into her, accelerating the full lock.

"Easy," she murmured, reaching around him to grip his cock, take possession of it.

Neil took her shirt off her shoulders with slow, stroking fingers, unhooked her bra. Straps off. Though he might have done that for his own purposes, she pressed her bare upper body against Tiger's back. He made another noise of pleasure and gratitude.

That was all he got, though. Neil's hand slipped around to her throat, easing her back so his other hand could cup her breast, fondle it. He didn't allow the stiff tip to brush Tiger's flesh. A message saying which man in the room had the top claim on her. A simple, straightforward missive she wouldn't argue with. Not right now.

She pushed back in, stroked Tiger's cock, captured his testicles, rolling them in her hand. As she established a rhythm, Neil pinched her nipples, squeezing both breasts. He let her feel the demand he'd gilded with that scorching heat when he'd looked at her. Her breath came faster too, a little moan breaking from her lips.

"Hold...back," she ordered Tiger. "Tell me when you think you're too close. You don't release until I say."

"Yes, Mistress. Always." He sounded as if he was fighting for that control now.

Each thrust into him pushed the strap-on against her. Neil slid his hand between her legs from behind. The dildo she wore had two straps that ran between her legs, framing the labia and leaving the area in between accessible.

Especially when he found the seam in the shorts and ripped it open.

Her hips jerked, causing a deeper plunge into Tiger that wrested another raw groan from him, a music she wanted to build into a heavy metal male crescendo of wild release.

Neil's fingers elevated that desire, gave it teeth. Then he brought his grip back to her throat. He exerted the pressure to put her head back against his shoulder. Since that arched her back, inhibiting her ability to keep up the same movement, he helped, the pressure of his pelvis against her backside pushing her into Tiger. Neil had moved the other hand to her hip, and he also used that hold to pull her back, push her in, for a few powerful strokes.

But then his heated palm slipped away from her hip. He had another urgent use for it.

She bit back a lung-filling gasp as he guided his cock into her from behind. She hadn't heard him open his jeans, but that had no relevance at the moment. He returned his hand to her hip and slid in deep, with a decisive thrust.

He was thick, piling-driver hard. It wasn't painful, but it wasn't entirely comfortable. She was certain he'd wanted her to feel his penetration that way. A reminder that she was taking her pleasure from Tiger while Neil was taking his pleasure from her.

The thought plus the sensation pulled another strangled moan from her. Tiger's hoarse groans were mounting, and she fought to concentrate on his pleasure, his needs. Fortunately, the way Neil was moving her against Tiger was carrying both of them. It helped her give Tiger what he needed, even as Neil was driving her higher. He put his mouth to her ear, his hand tightening on her throat.

"Same goes, Mistress," he murmured. "You don't go until I let you go. And I don't ever plan on letting you go."

White hot need ripped through her, and Tiger let out a deep snarl. "Mistress, I can't..."

"Come," she gasped, gripping his hips, thumbs pressing into his buttocks as she and Neil worked in and out, deep thrusts. When she wrapped a firm, stroking hand around Tiger's cock, his rough scream rocketed through her body, galvanizing the sensations between her own legs, the fullness, the friction.

"Please..." she whispered, and the voice in her ear, the hands on her body, the man buried so deep inside her, gave her what she needed.

As he had from the beginning of this night.

"Come," he said.

~

It had been an amazing scene. It had worked. It made her giddy, happy. At least at first.

Once they freed Tiger, Neil helped her remove the strap-on and encouraged her to sit down in a chair while Tiger rested at her feet, between her spread knees. She could stroke his hair, tend to his aftercare. Simple, easy things that gave her the chance to recuperate as well.

Neil brushed her face with gentle fingers, a quiet touch that conveyed approval of where she was, what she was doing. No territorial annoyance about performing the intimate care for Tiger. She liked that.

Her sex was sticky with Neil's release, the shorts damp, the torn parts sticking to the tender insides of her thighs. Neil wet a cloth with warm water from the sink of the room's small bathroom. When he returned, he stood behind her, putting his hand on her shoulder as he leaned forward, dropped his hand between her and Tiger. He pressed the cloth between her legs.

Tiger's head lifted despite his floating state. She would have murmured a quiet reproof, but when his gaze met Neil's, whatever he saw there made it instantly shift away, back down. But she still felt his intent awareness of what was happening.

She shivered under Neil's touch, her body lifting into it. Neil thoroughly rubbed and stroked the area, caressed her inner thighs, that tender pocket between them and her sex. Watching his fingers move was mesmerizing. She kept stroking Tiger's head as he did it, scraping her nails against the short-cropped scalp. It was a stirring intimacy, the three of them.

Neil finally withdrew the cloth. As he did, he pressed a kiss where her neck and shoulder joined, cupping the opposite side of her head in firm fingers as he did it. Then he straightened, tugging a lock of her hair. He'd left bottled water and crackers at her elbow in case she needed them for Tiger.

Mostly he just needed what they were doing, though. Letting him lean between her legs while she touched him, told him in those subtle, precious ways how much he'd pleased her.

While she tended to her exhausted sub, Neil cleaned up. He packed away the dragontail, and wrapped up the strap-on in a club-provided disposable bag, so it could be sterilized before re-use.

Eventually, she'd give it to Cyn. She'd give all her toys to the different women, according to their preferences.

She put that thought away. Instead, she ran her hands along Tiger's nape, his shoulders, murmured her approval. Encouraged him to sip at the water. When Tiger fumbled it, she steadied his hands, stroked his throat as he drank. Guided his head back down to her knee.

Caring for a strong man when he was vulnerable, in this circumstance...it never lost its value to her. Tiger could be a handful, was a formidable personality in the world outside this club. At his garage, no one dicked with the boss. They even called him that. Boss. And they respected him, because he was a great mechanic, a good businessman, and a generous member of his community.

Here, he laid the shields down, offered her his soul, took fierce pleasure in becoming everything she needed, fulfilling everything she demanded. It was a miracle, what was revealed in this room, in the relinquishing of power. It never looked the same, but the feeling, that rightness...she hoped she'd always recognize it, no matter how many broken shards her mind became.

Neil dropped to his heels next to her, placing a hand on her knee. He was studying her, doing the same thing she was doing with Tiger.

Assessing her state of mind, her physical well-being. A far more complicated analysis, she suspected.

She put her hand over his. "I'm gone," she said, then paused, shook her head. "I mean, I'm good."

His gaze flickered. "Yeah, you are. Skye texted she'd come take over aftercare for you in about ten minutes. You can get changed and then we'll talk."

Now that the sexual fire, the rush of power dynamics had crested and ebbed, she saw the wall behind his eyes that had been there at the beginning. Things unresolved, to be discussed.

"Neil."

"Later. This is your only job right now."

Despite the tension created by what wasn't said, she liked that he turned his attention to Tiger, bumped a fist lightly against Tiger's shoulder. Tiger managed a half smile.

"Make it thirty minutes," she said. She didn't want to rush this. She kept up a circular stroke of Tiger's back, over the infinity tattoo, letting her gaze rest there. "Thank you."

Though her attention didn't leave it, she was offering the words to both of them.

"You're welcome." A pause, then Neil straightened. He collected her toy bag and left the room, carrying it over his shoulder.

"Think he's pissed at you about something," Tiger said groggily. "Got that feeling at the beginning of the night, before you arrived."

"Probably."

"Let me know if you need me to...kick his ass. Give him an attitude adjustment. But he did okay in here. I thought it might not be so good, but he was...good."

He was slurring his words. She knew he'd drift in and out for a while. A half hour had been the right call. His boneless state of relaxation, the pressure of his head against her leg, the light curl of his fingers around her ankle, gave her a deep sense of satisfaction. She'd brought him to sub space before, but he didn't usually go this deep. Probably because she'd always held back. She loved being a Domme, but she'd put limits on herself, out of fear of what could happen.

Of what actually *had* happened tonight.

It had turned out okay. Better than okay. Her body was still vibrating, remembering Neil inside her. She dropped a kiss on Tiger's neck, ran her palms over his back and shoulders again. He was dozing with one leg folded, foot tucked under his hip, the other foot braced and knee raised. She'd let him pull the shorts back up, but the position gave her an excellent view of the cock and testicles under their snug confinement. She covered the braced foot with her own bare one, petted him with it.

"You did well tonight," she told him when he roused at her attention. "You've done all I need and then some."

He dropped his head back on her knee, wrapping his hand around her calf. Normally she would have said something about the uninvited gesture, but she was holding onto him, and he was holding onto her. Given the winds she could feel rising in her subconscious, she'd take the mutual grounding.

Tiger was right. Neil had done well. Though he'd told her he had experience and knew what he was doing, seeing it demonstrated, his comfort as Dom and helpmeet in a formal scene, had surprised her. Shocked her. Overwhelmed her. And he'd cared for her, given her something she wasn't sure she would have accepted from anyone else.

So what was his problem? It was a tiny barb in her general contentment, but by the time Skye arrived, it was starting to dig in and irritate.

Skye gave her a questioning look. *All good?*

Yes. Abby signed back, because she didn't want Tiger to hear the conversation. *He did exceptionally well, but he's out of it. Not sure he'll be good for anything else tonight.*

Skye lifted a shoulder, conveying that wasn't her purpose. This wasn't a night they'd arranged a consecutive session with the same sub. She was just here to take over aftercare, if Tiger needed some more time, which Abby knew he did.

Skye's appearance confirmed it. Jeans and a soft T-shirt, none of her usual scene trappings. With the longer side of her hair wisping around her round face, she looked exceptionally snuggle-able, if that was a word, but still in control of the situation. An appealing look to provide aftercare to a big, tough biker.

In the past, Abby had provided similar relief for some of Cyn's subs. Cyn wasn't always in the mood to stretch her limited nurturing side to the level her bottoms needed after she wore them out. But for

Dommes like Abby and Skye, aftercare brought its own deep satisfaction.

As Abby rose for Skye to take her place, Skye stroked her arm, a quick caress followed by a glance, saying a lot without saying anything. Abby acknowledged it with a nod.

After she donned her cloak and boots and reached the door, she looked back. Skye had Tiger's head on her lap. One broad shoulder was slumped, powerful arm limp and hand half curled on the floor.

Was it blasphemous, that this was the image that came to mind whenever she thought of Leonardo Da Vinci's La Pietà, the powerful-looking Madonna holding the limp body of Christ? A strong man finally letting go, the job done, willing to surrender to her care. Life beginning and ending with the mother, the Goddess. Earth.

Vera would approve of the spiritual drift of her thoughts. But drift was the key word. She was drifting. Time to go.

She headed for the changing room. Once there, she rinsed off in one of the private shower stalls before changing into the street clothes she kept in her locker. A skirt that flirted above her knees, paired with a knit shirt that clung to her breasts and had a V-neck that showed a hint of cleavage. After she put her scene outfit and the boots in a garment bag, she slipped on a pair of canvas sneakers. Finally, she brushed out her red hair, pulled it back with combs, and began to touch up her makeup.

She wasn't surprised that, as she made herself presentable, her pleasure with the evening's events started to change. She'd felt euphoria at the beginning, which had settled into a happy pleasure as the session unfolded well. Then she'd lost Tiger in the overwhelming sensations, and dread had threatened to grab her. Neil had made certain she didn't lose contact with Tiger. Her mood had gone up again. It had settled into a deep satisfaction while holding Tiger, appreciating the unforgettable experience they'd shared.

Yet without Neil's presence tonight, there was no denying she would have been swept away. She hadn't been able to control the tone and direction of her mind, not a hundred percent. A wall of delusionary, wandering thoughts would have divided her attention from Tiger's care, the most important job she had as a Domme, when a man was under her control.

Putting on makeup properly while simultaneously avoiding

looking at herself in the mirror, she remembered the several times her mind had been pulled away. Tiger could have safeworded and she would have missed it. Neil had made sure that didn't happen.

At the time, she'd felt reassured by that. It had kept the anxiety low, a stressor that could have made what was happening in her mind worse. Like now, thinking about this, the roller coaster ride of what was good and bad about tonight, what she'd thought was real that might not be.

Yes, that was why she'd brought Neil, but it confirmed it all, didn't it? She really couldn't be trusted alone anymore. He'd given her a gift, but also the curse of knowledge that couldn't be denied. She felt the finality of it.

Weirdly disconnected parts of her still kept clinging to the idea that maybe it was random, and things overall hadn't changed. She'd just hit a rocky period and she hadn't really run out of smooth road.

Because of that hope, the moments where she had to face the reality, the truth, were a punch in the face, times ten.

Had Tiger really gotten pleasure out of this? Or had he done it out of loyalty? Or worse, pity?

He didn't deserve to be called into service this way. This wasn't what their time here was supposed to be about. How had she let herself get talked into this?

Because they speak to you through the walls, out of the shadows. They come through the cracks and distract you while worms get into your head.

She had to leave. The walls were starting to close in.

CHAPTER TWELVE

When she left the locker rooms, she was surprised to see Tiger waiting for her. Then a check of the clock told her she'd been in the changing area for forty-five minutes. He was back in his street clothes, worn jeans, biker shirt, biker boots. His leather coat was hooked in the bend of his arm, his hands shoved into his pockets. Leaning against the wall, he looked every inch the badass he was, unless a Domme stared into his eyes, and saw the softness. The desire for raw vulnerability people wouldn't expect to find there.

His expression appeared relaxed and content, but she couldn't believe in it. Her feelings were buzzing through her brain. Guilt gripped her. This hadn't been fair to Tiger, to put him in this position. Of course he'd agreed to it, no matter how Neil had phrased it. He cared about her, had a deep need to serve a Mistress. Why had she said this was okay? She'd abdicated her responsibilities.

"This isn't why you're here," she told Tiger. "To deal with this shit. I'm so very sorry."

The ease died out of his expression. But rather than immediately questioning her, he gave her a long, thorough look. He straightened from the wall. "That's bullshit, Mistress."

Though his tone was mild, the look in his eyes wasn't. The set of his jaw reminded her how strong a submissive male could be.

"Can I have your card?" he asked.

"Excuse me?"

"I didn't realize you'd gone pro-Domme on me," he said evenly. "Here just to give me what I need, without any consideration of what you might need, too."

Her gaze skittered away from the force of his. The last thing she wanted in her head was the vision of Tiger's eyes melting and running down his face. Or darkening so she couldn't see anything in them but an abyss.

Neil was at the end of the blue and gold carpeted hallway. The gold toned prints on the walls were mounted against a semi-gloss paint of the same deep blue color. Below the metallic gold chair railing was clean white beadboard. The hallway did a dog leg into the private rooms.

Neil straddled a chair at that bend, a seat he must have borrowed from somewhere. He watched them, his arms crossed over the back.

He was giving them space, but staying close as well, in case she needed him. But she didn't want to seek his shelter on this. She'd stepped into it all by herself.

"It's why it's always worked," Tiger persisted. He shifted a step closer. Though he didn't touch her, it put her in his shadow. She shifted away from it nervously, putting a hand up to her ear to block a sudden burst of chatter, then forced herself to lower it again.

Tiger had stopped. She wondered if he'd received an encouraging sign from Neil, because despite her odd body language, he continued. His voice was calmer, though. Gentler. But he didn't let her off the hook, which saved him from the shot of annoyance she would have felt if he did.

"We give each other what we need, and that can change from session to session," he said. "You've always picked up on it when I had a shitty day, or was feeling rowdier. If I needed a stricter or looser hand, more freedom or less. You liked figuring that out, anticipating me. I liked knowing I was hitting all the checkboxes on what *you* looked for in a sub."

His frustration was palpable. "How is this different, Mistress? You needed me tonight, so you gave me the gift of helping you. The way you've helped me get to a zone a million times. And fuck, you took me a place I've never been with you before."

Somewhere in the middle of the diatribe she'd caught up. She held to his words, refused to let her mind sweep them away, lose them in a soup of other sensations. The walls weren't really closing in. That was structurally impossible.

She reached out to grasp his hand. Her stomach hitched, because she couldn't seem to manage it, the hand-to-eye coordination. Tiger moved his hand, clasped hers instead. She closed her eyes, tried not to fight and exacerbate things, while simultaneously holding her ground. His hand squeezed tighter, holding her. Helping.

"You're right, Tiger. I apologize for insulting you." Her eyes opened, her gaze sliding from his chest toward Neil's general direction, then back again. "And I thank you both, for honoring me as a Mistress in your own unique ways."

"Just remember who does the better job for you on his knees." When her gaze shot up, surprised, Tiger winked at her. That wicked mischief he did extremely well, and with good timing. "Oh, and by the way...the outfit? Warn a guy next time. I'll have a pacemaker put into my chest beforehand."

The world had steadied enough she could appreciate him. "Get out of here." She punched his arm. "Before I decide to unpack my dragontail again."

"Yes, ma'am. Don't have to tell me twice. I'll be feeling it this week when I'm riding. Which I expect was your plan." He grinned at her, but then his expression sobered. For a moment, he held her hand, didn't say anything. She stared at the contact, not really wanting to draw away. When he finally spoke, she realized he'd been sorting through his thoughts, deciding how he wanted to say what he did next.

"A buddy I grew up with, his sister's bipolar. Been that way a really long time. So I've seen how difficult that kind of thing is, for her and for him. Anything you need, Mistress. Don't hesitate. And I'm always up for this, whenever you want to go a round. But if you don't mind..."

When he paused, tension grabbed her, because she wasn't sure where he was going to go from there. "May I hug you, Mistress? Hold you, for just a minute? Just one friend to another, to say I'm sorry you're dealing with this shit, and hoping you know you can count on me if you need anything."

She didn't know if he said that last part for her benefit, or the watchful male a few feet away, but it was her decision to give. She nodded, but had to keep staring at his chest, because of the emotions swamping her. They choked the words she managed to say.

"I'm sorry I can't look at you, Tiger. I want to, but if I look at you, it will grab me, and pull me away, and I don't want it to pull me away. Not right now."

Babbling nonsense, but as if he completely understood, Tiger stepped up to her, closed his arms carefully around her, waiting until she relaxed before holding her more securely. She slid her arms up under his, wrapped them over his broad back, and it was okay.

"Thank you," she said again, trying to keep her voice steady. The overload was increasing the potency of the smells, sounds, visuals around her, but she tried to give as good a hug as he was offering, not flinch away or get stiff. She hoped she'd managed it when he slid away, squeezing her upper arms. Then he picked up his bag, and spoke, his voice warm. "See you next time, Mistress."

He moved down the hall. Someone called his name, and he lifted his hand in answer. Abby pivoted to watch him approach Sy, one of Cyn's regulars. Their sessions with their respective Mistresses done for the night, they would probably go hang out, have a drink somewhere.

People going through their lives, with their ups and downs. Few of them knew what it was like to have their head trying to shoot them on a permanent downward slope, where ups had to be actively reached for and grasped, with an unimaginable level of effort. Always fighting through anxiety, the foreboding of what lay ahead, exacerbated exponentially if everything wasn't planned for to the nth degree. And that planning was just a deception one did to get through, a mind game that could turn into a mindfuck in a heartbeat.

She turned away. The hall was skewed, wider here than it should be, narrow further down. Neil had risen from the chair and was waiting for her, standing against a tilted wall. She pushed past that, the audio and visual distortions, and focused on what his body language was telling her.

Time to confront that wall between them.

She suddenly wasn't in the mood. She was grateful, yes, but she hadn't asked for any of this from him. If he wanted to bitch at her for not telling him the things he'd learned in the meeting, he needed to get over himself. As Tiger had just pointed out, she'd faced this all her life, and Neil had only been part of it for a very short time.

So yeah, he'd happened to cross her path at the moment her life was passing the threshold into hell. Everything was slowing down so she could see the flames coming for her, inch by inch, and she couldn't move. Paralyzed, as if there were bonds holding her, and crazy laughter happening, people dancing behind her.

People in white quotes...coats. Or was it quotes? People not real to her, bracketed by something she didn't understand.

Like him. Seemingly so close, but the way he looked at her. Distant. He was holding himself apart from her. Mad at her for fuck knew what.

"I can get myself home," she told him shortly. "Thank you for setting this up." Then she pivoted and strode away, past Sy and Tiger, who glanced at her as she passed. From their startled expressions, she expected she didn't look quite right. So she managed a courteous nod, but she had a goal, and her feet were going to blur like a cartoon character's before she got there. People moved out of her way as she cut a swathe through them with her speed and intent.

Noise blurred too. A question shot at her by the hostess. Several people in the lobby, recognizing her, but she didn't know them. Not right now. Not when their faces couldn't be brought into focus.

Why hadn't she taken the private side entrance? Too late to change direction now. She went out the front double doors, so fast and aggressively she almost ran over the people coming in, though fortunately a security person drew them out of the way. She called out a sharp reproof, but Abby was already stepping off the curb.

A car hit the brakes. Going too slow through the parking area to be a danger to her, just not expecting her to step out, but she was past that, ignoring everything. It was too much. Too much noise, too much input, and none of it made sense.

Some part of her knew she couldn't drive herself, but getting to her car was all that mattered. She'd close herself in it. Maybe she'd sleep there. God knew, they'd found her mother in hers often enough. Usually in the driveway, because she hadn't gone anywhere—Abby had taken her keys away—but her mother liked the cocoon of it.

She remembered making her mother a tent fort in her bedroom with sheets, towels, a variety of brooms, mops and boxes. When her mother was in it, Abby would slip food and drinks under the towel that formed the flap. Coax her out to bathe. She liked the sound of a tent fort. She had some sheets that someone had given her, soft and dark...

"Hey. *Hey*!"

She had her hand on her car door. His voice was the one that penetrated when no other did, maybe because he'd added a force to it that turned it into a startling rifle shot. She swung around as he came striding across the parking lot, his expression like a thunder cloud. The shadows swallowed him, the noise of them like the crowd at a concert. A storm rolling toward her.

"No." She shrank back, almost bolted, but found some scrap of reality in the midst of all of it, maybe because he slowed down, came to a stop a few feet away. "Don't."

"Abby," he said, calmer. "It's okay. Take it easy."

She closed her eyes, opened them, and it was Neil. Standing in front of her. The voices muttering.

"No. Session's done. You...thank you. But you don't get to be nice now, not when I could tell you're carrying around...a madness. Being mad." She giggled at her turn of phrase, then sobered. As she stared at him, she registered his wary look, taking the place of his reserve, what he was mad about. It made her angry. She hated kid gloves. Hated being cared for like that.

"You're the problem. You were perfect during that session. Open, real. But it wasn't real. It was just...functional. You did what needed to be done."

"It was incredible, Abby," he said. "I had no idea it could go like that. If I had, maybe I would have tried this kind of thing a long time ago." He shook his head. "But I doubt it would have been the same. It was special, because you were there. You were part of it."

She was calming down at the sound of his voice, the sincerity in it, the appreciation. That warmth that could help steady her, even with other things between them. His knuckles stroked her upper arm, easy. "Hey there," he said, quiet. "You with me? You scared me, stepping out in front of that car. I was caught behind a mob of people. I may have trampled a fairy."

At her startled look, his lips curved. "She was wearing fairy wings. And a corset defying the laws of human anatomy."

She had her hand on his forearm, she realized, responding to his touch. "It's not good to piss off the Fae."

"No, it's not. But she'll have to forgive me. Like I hope you will." He paused as her brow creased in surprise. "I'm sorry you picked up on what I wanted to talk out with you. I didn't want that to interfere with the session."

He gave her a humorless smile. "I forgot how intuitive you are. After seeing how you are as a Domme, I'll never forget it again."

"It's about what you learned during the meeting, isn't it?" Just like that, her anger was back. She wanted to shove at him, push him back, but that was wrong, he'd done nothing to warrant the violence. It didn't stop the flood, fueled by her own frustration, by the emotions all of this had stirred up, the good and the bad. It didn't matter; it all ended up bad when she committed the crime of feeling too much.

"You knew I was fucked up," she said, before he could respond. "You've known it since you came to my house uninvited that day. So you had a meeting without me present to make it official. Did that change things for you somehow? You have *no* right to be angry with me. You all did the meeting without me. You arranged this thing with Tiger without my express consent, with just a grudging *maybe, okay* from me, and you ran with it."

"And you enjoyed it, and it helped you feel better."

A wash of blood red anger hazed her vision. "I'll have your medal for sainthood mailed to you."

When she turned back toward the door, she gasped as he grabbed her arm. He pushed her against the side of her car, holding her there with a hand at her waist, the other on the side of her neck, fingers along her jaw.

His swiftness had nothing to do with distortions in her head. He could just move that fast. A quick glance at his snapping eyes told her something else. That wall she'd sensed? It definitely wasn't there now.

"So you're pissed at me," he grated. "How about we call it even? You let it go that I set this up without your full say-so. I'll let it go that you intended me to be your last hurrah before you kill yourself."

She went pale, swallowed.

"You thought I wouldn't figure it out?" he asked silkily. "You haven't pursued a real relationship with anyone in years, and now these symptoms start happening. You realize 'Hey, that's it, time's up.

But I can at least have this. He won't get in too deep. There won't be enough time. Yeah, he might miss me for a little while, but low investment, low impact. We can have a good fuck before I choose oblivion.'"

She slapped him. He didn't dodge the blow, nor did he let go of her waist or the hold he had on her face. She stared at the red handprint on his cheek and jaw. It was easier to look at that than at the anger and other raw things in his expression.

Then her own emotions rose up, made her quiver under his hands, a noise of anguish caught in her throat.

"Damn it," he muttered. She shook her head, a sharp jerk.

"Don't be kind. I don't want kind." She found a resting place for her gaze on the stretch of black pavement, reflecting the parking lot light with a gleaming slash. "When Ros told me she included you in the meeting," she said slowly, over a tight and aching throat, "I expected you to make a straight line to my door, to give me a piece of your mind."

She remembered how Ros said he'd taken it.

Quietly. Deep ocean quiet.

At the time, she hadn't been sure how to interpret that, and Ros hadn't elaborated. But it had made her quake, as if something inside her knew. Quiet for Neil was comparable to a leopard lying in the grass—as a gazelle grazed her way toward him.

It had been waiting all night, circling her, lunging at her in small bursts. The effort of keeping it at bay, managing it, had taken its toll. She was so tired, and when she was tired it would break loose, roll over her.

Damn it, she knew...it couldn't...

She freed her arm from his grip, fumbled for her keys. Her head was starting to pound, her palms sweaty. She couldn't take the risk of losing it. She needed to get home. Get to where it was safe.

"Hey. Abby, stop."

No way, no way. Singsong, a singalong really. No, no, no. She wasn't going to become this in front of him again. She should have cut him loose. Cut him loose.

She couldn't drive. She couldn't.

"Not hiding. Not retreat, not surrender...not...faking. Going.

Trolley stop. Have to go because the angels are angry, and it's all my fault."

"Hey, stop. Shit, I'm sorry."

Her mood was like a churning sea, smooth and easy one moment, frothy and storms pending the next, and she was being tossed on the waves. She didn't want to be. She wanted to grab the tiller, find some way through it, but she couldn't find the damn thing.

"No being sorry," she snarled, slamming a fist against the window of her car. "Can't steer the boat. I can't steer the boat, goddamn it."

The asphalt was swirling, the sky was melting. She dropped down to her heels, tucked her head down, covered it with both hands. Her purse was somewhere else. Oh God, not here...

He covered her. Like he might cover one of his teammates in a fire fight. Just dropped down next to her, wrapped his arms over her, dipped his head down, surrounding her with heat and his scent. The voices from the shadows were trying to shove through the holes, get to her, but he was talking. His strong, even voice. She couldn't hear the words, but she grabbed for it like a life ring, strained to hold on as the cacophony rose.

The pills should have lasted longer than this. She was too upset. Stress zapped brain molecules, paralyzed them so they couldn't defend, stop the onslaught. Her mother had told her that.

Mother knows best, mother knows all. Mother is living in a hole in the wall.

Her mother had liked rhyming poetry. Dr. Seuss. It was coming back to bite Abby on the ass. Or give her a way to communicate when nothing else worked. But nothing was working right now. She couldn't find the energy to force the words through that small opening in her mind.

"She's okay," Neil was saying. Someone had come to check on them, was trying to get her to tell them she was okay, not taking his word for it. Of course not. It was the club, they had to be sure... consent...consensual...

So funny. The BDSM world was built upon permission, structure. You had to give your permission for things to happen. But no one gave their permission to have really fucking bad things happen to them. A disease happened, love happened, at the worst times possible...

The colors were coming apart, she was speaking her thoughts

aloud. Things were getting clearer, the tide ebbing a little. An eye of the storm. The people retreated, so she must have said the right thing. Neil touched her face, still sheltering her, holding her.

"I need to go home," she said wearily.

"Okay. I'll get you home. But I'm staying. Whether it's in your bed, on the couch or on the porch, I'm staying."

"I have to work tomorrow."

"So I'll make sure you get to bed. Give you cookies and milk. Read you a story."

That got through, made her chuckle. "I'm not into Daddy play."

He smiled and she saw his relief, that she was back. However temporary that would be.

He stroked a lock of hair back from her face again. "I'm sorry I lost my temper. I feel a lot for you, Abigail, so I thought holding it all in until we got to the right place to talk about it was the right thing. I didn't mean to shut you out."

He'd called her Abigail. Only Ros did that, when she was trying to make a particularly emphatic point. She liked how it sounded with his strong Southern accent.

"Damn it, if you're going to be mature, how can I be petulant and sulk? Tell you '*I'm fine*,' in that female tone that strikes dread in the heart of males everywhere?"

He pressed a kiss to her forehead, her nose, her lips. A lingering touch, his fingers caressing her face. The world steadied further. "You can say it. I promise to quake in my boots."

"You're not wearing boots. And you wouldn't know what fear is unless you googled it."

"I get afraid of stuff. Literally, the word 'stuff.' It's too vague. Ominous."

"Wise ass."

"Regarding Tiger," he said. "I'd apologize, but I wouldn't really mean it. I couldn't figure out a way to do it differently. You might not have agreed if I asked for confirmation to go ahead with it, and this is something I thought might help. Right? You saw how Tiger handled it, Abby. He considered it another way to serve you."

When she didn't respond, neither agreeing nor disagreeing, Neil persisted. "Didn't you sometimes do things for your mother that helped her, that you knew she wouldn't agree to?

"Yes," she said dully. "Which is maybe why it upsets me. It's just a reminder that I'm becoming like her."

"You have the same illness. You're not the same people."

She didn't want to think about that. Instead, she tapped the top of his hand, resting on her drawn-up knees, and tangled it with her own hands.

"I liked that you got mad, didn't act like I'd break. You were willing to fight with me."

She lifted her gaze to his bearded jaw and strong throat. When he leaned in and brushed his mouth over her temple, her eyes closed, absorbing his rumbling response.

"Damn straight," he said. "When you're under attack, I'll be in your corner. But if you want to fight, bébé, I'll give you a fight. I might be mad at something you did or said, but it will never change who you are to me. How I feel about you."

He drew back, held up her keys. When had she given him those? "How about we stop somewhere and get some coffee. A dessert?"

"I can't. Everything is too much right now. I need to be home."

"You got it. How about we pick up something on the way back to your place? I'm not done fighting with you, and I want you to have nourishment."

She was surprised enough to glance up at him. "Do we have something left to fight about?"

"Actually, I'm hoping it won't be a fight at all. I have some thoughts to share, and I'm hoping you'll listen. But we can do it in the morning if you need to go right to bed."

She considered it. "If you can get me home, give me an hour or so to just have quiet, then maybe we can talk. Okay?"

"Okay," he said.

His smile warmed her, even as she saw the stress at the corners that indicated how much he'd had to rein back, just to have the kind of conversation normal couples could have.

It made her sad, but she was tired of that, too. For now, all she knew was that she needed to be home.

And Neil could get her there.

CHAPTER THIRTEEN

They stopped and picked up some of her favorite Italian on the way to her place. Once there, she ate only a few bites though, then went up to her room, telling him she'd eventually be back, but he could go if she was gone too long.

She removed her clothes and makeup, put on a sleep shirt, and tunneled into her bed. The shadows closed in, but she rocked herself to sleep, talking to herself and to them, giving in to the exhaustion, knowing if she could just sleep, her head would be clearer when she woke.

She hoped.

She was pretty sure he came in at some point. She was aware of a hand smoothing across her brow, easing the muttering, someone clasping her fingers, a masculine thumb slowly stroking over them. When she woke, she could detect his lingering scent.

A glance at the clock showed her she'd been sleeping for two hours. It was nearly one a.m.

She was enough in her right mind to act like a woman with a handsome man in her house. Before she went down, she tidied her hair, applied moisturizer to her face, brushed her teeth. She left the sleepshirt on because it was comfortable and soft, the scoop neckline falling off of one shoulder. Though she doubted wild sex was in her immediate future, he'd like the way it looked, clinging loosely to her body, offering a hint of her nipples, the curve of her hips and movement of her breasts. She wore nothing under the shirt.

She found him on the couch, but he wasn't sleeping. He had his arm stretched out along the back, a foot propped on her coffee table, though he'd had the good manners to remove his shoes. He'd also removed his socks. Barefoot was a sexy look for him in his jeans. After their session, he'd traded out the dress shirt for one of his T-shirts. It had the same outfitter's logo on the breast pocket as on the hat he'd loaned her, a skeleton fish smoking and wearing sunglasses. She wondered if that was Penelope's place, where MeeMaw sold her bug repellant.

He had his head resting on a throw pillow. When she came down the steps, he adjusted so he could watch her advance, and tilted his jaw in her direction as she sank down next to him. She drew her feet up, and he rested one of his large hands over her bare toes. "Your feet will get cold, bébé."

"I'll be all right. You look deep in thought."

"Yeah."

She wondered at the things he was considering. About her, him, the two of them. Then she took a closer read. The struggle going on inside him seemed more volatile than those kinds of ponderings warranted, especially after the ground they'd already covered tonight.

"What is it?"

He used his foot to nudge his phone, resting on the coffee table. "I thought I'd have another day or so, but I've got to leave again in a few hours, Abby. I'll be gone...fuck all, I don't know how long. A week or two, maybe."

Her stomach flipflopped, her heart sank. Worse, an unexpected panic snatched at her. Damn it, it was wrong to react that way. He needed his head clear. She didn't want him worried about her. She schooled her expression to simple acceptance, putting the rest aside to deal with later.

She curled up against him, adjusting her legs over his lap, an arm over his chest, and sent him a tentative smile. She touched his face, smoothing a finger over his jaw, his soft clipped beard.

She'd caught his attention, which meant he logged her appearance. The tumble of hair over her bare shoulder, the lengths of her smooth legs under the drape of his arm.

"Not a lot of time for chit chat, then. So I guess whatever else you wanted to talk to me about, we better get it out of the way. Then we can have some hot departure sex. Unless there's a prohibition on sex before an op because it steals your strength or something."

"I think that only applies to sporting events." His lips tugged with a smile, then he sobered. "Can you tell me what it's like?"

"What?"

"In your head. Your mind. When things get like they did at your car. Help me understand."

The request surprised her. "Based on the way you react to it," she said carefully, "you've already figured a lot of it out."

"That's intuition and luck, and I'm just glad I wasn't completely off base."

"You were also at the meeting."

"I'd like to hear it from you. Your view of it. What interests me is the world through your eyes. If you feel like you can share it."

He had laced the fingers of his other hand with hers on his chest. Now they were in the air between them, the fingers tangling and untangling. His thumb brushed her palm in feathery strokes, moving down to her pulse before he closed his hand over it and brought it back to his chest, pressing it over the thud of his heart.

She'd tell him, because he'd asked. For no other obvious reason than he wanted to know. And because he'd told her she mattered.

"This..." she said, increasing the pressure over his heartbeat, the rhythmic thump. "That steady, even calm. It goes away. I'm okay, and then I start to notice things. I hear whispers. It makes me anxious. Everything starts to be...more. I can't stop it. Can't shut it off."

She stopped, taking a steadying breath. "Talking about it can bring it on, too, if I get too anxious about it."

"Keep going, but stop whenever you need to."

She nodded. "A person appears in my office, but I never see them cross my threshold. It's as if I black out for short periods, like a dropped cell signal, only instead of missing words, I'm missing transitions, movement around me, and suddenly they're there."

She gazed at their tangled hands. "The voices from the shadows are the worst. On a good day, they're just mutters, murmuring, maybe a conversation in a restaurant where you catch a word or two. But then, they get more specific, like a person who appears behind you and blurts something into your ear. They say fearful things, like the person in my office is there to hurt me, or is hiding a monster behind their eyes. Things are going to come through the cracks, burrow into me like parasites.

"I try to focus on what the person in my office is saying, but suddenly the words are clicking, wet. The numbers run away. I can't focus, can't do anything but pray that person leaves my office as soon as possible, before I lose it. They leave, and I shove away from my desk, run to the door to lock it so no one else can come in. But I'm uncoordinated, clumsy. I can't walk, I shuffle. If I hurry, I stumble, fall to the carpet. But I panic, scramble up, throw myself at the door, close it..."

She stopped. She was trembling. When he tried to move his arm from the top of the couch around her shoulders, she twitched away, warning him against it. At the car, him surrounding her had helped. Now she would feel trapped.

She shared that with him, that contradiction, the unpredictability of every response. "The dramatic stuff is only part of it. Organizing my thoughts, normal tasks, the day-to-day. The simplest stuff, bathing, putting on the right clothes, eating. I can't wrap my head around it, don't want to. Forget to."

She shook her head. "Fortunately, that hasn't gotten so bad yet, but I feel it closing in. My mother...eventually I had to make sure she took care of herself. On one of her meds, which failed spectacularly—probably because she was combining it with street drugs—she thought something would come out of the toilet to invade her body if she used it, so she used a bucket instead."

"Oh, Abby."

She reached toward him again. Smoothed her palm over the fish logo, the firm chest beneath. "It's like sitting on a trap door. You never know when the lever's going to be thrown and you'll drop into a hole. Or when you're going to get yanked back up, start it all over again. Stress can set it off, but as it gets worse, any major highs or lows can do it. I land a big account that I've worked hard to get. Ros wants to go out and celebrate. If I'm lucky, the trapdoor doesn't spring during the toasts, and I can make it home afterward and deal with the symptoms here."

"So this has been going on a while."

She paused. There was a weighted steadiness to his look, but she didn't hear a reproof. So she would give him honesty.

"What happened that day, with my kitchen, the appliances. Up until then, it hadn't been that unmanageable. I could keep it contained. The mild symptoms started some months ago. I wasn't sure at the time if they were real, or just my worries. They've gotten worse this past month. The early sins. Signs, I mean. Prodromal."

She grimaced. "Clinical terms. Like that helps, to call it something other than what it is. What it means is now I'm fully fucked. The trapdoor switch is being manned by a monkey on speed, who cackles every time he hits it."

"Ssh." He'd heard the rise in her voice, countered it with a soothing note. When he touched her face, her gaze flicked to his arm, but she didn't feel like pulling away this time. "Does it feel good, me touching you?" he asked.

"Yes. Some schizophrenics avoid touch all the time, or even lose their libido, thanks to the illness or meds." She tried to lighten her tone. "Lucky for you, it didn't seem to affect my mother's in the slightest."

"Don't do that." This time she did see a flash of reproof, though it was mild, and the squeeze of her shoulder was gentle. "You said you never met your father."

"No. But she used to run with other people who had similar issues. So if he was also a schizophrenic, it skyrocketed the genetic likelihood of passing it to their offspring." She spread her arms out, presenting herself like a game show winner. "Ta-da."

She sighed, shook her head. "I'm sorry. You're right. I'm being a bitch." She propped her elbow on the back of the couch, head on her hand to gaze at him. "Please don't, Neil."

"Don't what?"

"Don't waste any energy or time we have together trying to change my mind. That's what you wanted to talk to me about, wasn't it? You want to convince me to try psychotherapy, the newest meds. Ros would have put that on you, because she knows I'm not going to hear any more from her on it."

He pursed his lips. "Are you willing to explain to me why you're against considering any of that?"

"Are you going to argue with me about it?"

"I don't know enough about your heart and mind on it to argue. But I am really interested in understanding."

She gazed at him. "Okay, but if you argue, I'm stopping. I'll kick you out without giving you memorable sex before you go on your life-risking op, *and* I won't suffer a moment of guilt over it."

He touched her mouth, ran a thumb over her lips, slow, his gaze sliding down to her body in a way that said he was looking at it and seeing all the curves beneath. "Duly warned."

"Dealing with a man who knows his sexual appeal is a pain in the ass," she informed him.

It inspired a faint smile, but there was no humor in his gaze. "You matter to me, Abby. That's why I'm trying to understand. Please."

She sighed again, closed her eyes, dropped her head back on the couch. When she opened them, she stared at the ceiling. "Everyone has their opinion on what I should do, but I'm living inside the storm. All of you can take a boat to shore and get out at any time."

She rose, moved restlessly around the room. "It wears you down in ways large and small. Takes away everything, so you can't appreciate anything, think of anything, but keeping your life as simple and limited as possible, so everything doesn't overwhelm you, become too much. And it's always waiting to do that, no matter what you do."

An ache had started in her gut, was climbing, spreading. She would have to stop soon. Probably go back upstairs, go to bed again so she wouldn't know when he left. Or could pretend he hadn't.

So much for the wild sex. Thinking about all of this was as big a libido-killer as any medication.

She gave a despairing laugh. "I know what you'll think about it. Ros has been there too. 'Are we not worth the fight? Why are we not worth hanging around for?'"

She closed her hands into fists. "You are. You so are. You're worth all of it. I just...can't. I don't have the strength to stand in my mother or grandmother's shoes and turn into that. Surface from an episode and find I've hurt someone, or ended up wandering in the streets babbling."

She shook her head. "I give tons of money to homeless shelters and mental health centers, but when I see a homeless person talking to himself, I cross the street to avoid him. I'm so afraid I'm looking in a mirror."

He'd taken his feet off the table, had sat up, his hands clasped between his spread knees. He was a good listener, she gave him that. He was obviously thinking through her words, respecting her. He'd said he wanted to understand, and he obviously meant it. She'd give him her best effort.

"I know where this road goes, even with treatment. It never ends, it never stops taking its pound of flesh, not just from me, but from everyone I love, who has to watch me go through it."

He lifted a finger. "Okay, pause there just a second. If you get to make the call on what you can bear, why don't those who care about you get to make the same decision on what they're willing to handle? You can't factor that in when making a decision for yourself. Did you throw a party when your mom finally died?"

It jolted her, but she saw he wasn't trying to goad her. "I don't understand what you mean."

"Did you ever stop wanting to help her, care for her, love her? Up until the very end, you hoped she could get better, not have to suffer so much anymore, right? That she could enjoy her life more. Didn't you want her to keep trying?"

The words summoned the ache in her throat that thinking of her mother always did, but she'd answered these questions before. "She did try, Neil. It didn't work. She tried again and again, and yeah, she was fucking it up with the drugs and alcohol, but when those voices are in your head..."

She shook her head. "It's the chicken and egg dilemma. As I said, people who aren't dealing with it can't really get why someone would be willing to give up their life to get away from it."

He nodded thoughtfully and sat back, stretching his arm along the top of the couch again. As he did, he rested his ankle on his opposite knee. Heavens, the man had long legs.

"How do you blend in places where the average height is a lot shorter than you?"

His expression flickered at the abrupt segue, but his eyes twinkled. "Same thing we do when we go into areas with team members who are much browner than the local populace. They do a lot of the behind-the-scenes logistics, keep a low profile, and are ready with backup, while the others do the frontline stuff. Come sit with me again."

He held out a hand. She obliged, coming around the table to let him grasp her fingers, tug her down next to him. "Psychological methods are the most efficient forms of torture," he told her.

She blinked. "I'm feeling proud of acting casual about you going away for scary reasons. Are you trying to mess that up?"

"No, but it does confirm the whole depriving me of sex and not feeling guilty about it thing was a bluff."

She elbowed him. He fended her off, but tapped their clasped hands against his knee, a thoughtful punctuation for his next words. "Making a prisoner believe they've been forgotten, that no one is coming for them, that this is their life forever, not knowing what's going to happen to them from day to day...that combination of constant anxiety and mental isolation is worse than anything. Not being able to reach through all that and find a connection with those you care about."

Her hand tightened on his as she thought of his scars. "Have you been through that?"

"No. We've extracted those who have, and I've seen how it can shatter the mind, take the spirit. Even when they come back to the world, they may never pull themselves out of that pit."

She drew an unsteady breath. He'd wanted to understand, asked to understand. Connected with her understanding. She needed to stop talking. She'd make herself vulnerable to things she knew were pointless.

"So what do you think of that?" she said instead.

"I think there's a reason we're given a life to live. And it's not over until the sunshine goes away and doesn't come back."

He cupped her face, leaned in and put his lips on hers, tasting. When she pressed into him, twining her arms around his neck, he took the unspoken cue, pulled her closer. She felt that heat—the sunshine—roll through her as the kiss took her on a swirling ride. When he finally lifted his head, she was somehow in his lap, gazing up at him.

"Is the sunshine all gone, Abby?"

"Not yet," she admitted. But the number of dark days were growing.

"What if you could figure out ways to keep it shining?"

She shook her head, pushed off of him and moved to an easy chair. She rubbed her forehead, wondered why she was continuing to have this conversation with him. "The isolation gets worse over time, Neil. Trying to act and behave normally is like running a marathon on three days of no sleep. Your brain...it's like shards of a mirror, disconnected reflections only you can see, that you can pull from, get some meaning from, but what comes out of your mouth...no one understands, even though you're seeing it clear."

She'd lowered her head as she spoke, stopped rubbing her forehead to wrap her arms around herself. She was starting to rock, though she told herself not to do it. It was better if she hid it. Hid as many signs as she could.

When he came and knelt before her, she flinched at the touch of his hands on her knees, but he didn't take them away. "Please stop making me think about it."

"Okay. I'll stop. Hey." He brushed his fingers over her shoulder. "I promised I'd stop when you said stop. I'm stopping."

She nodded. He sat with her as she hummed, a calming technique that sometimes brought the voices back down. She concentrated on reducing the rocking motion. Sitting with the stillness and the humming.

She became aware he'd been rubbing her back, slow, massaging circles. When her hand dropped back over his and gripped, she was doing better. She lifted her head to show him that.

"When do you have to go?"

"Soon," he said. Paused. "I'd like to ask one more question. A short one, about your decision. This thing you plan to do."

The weight he gave the words told her what he meant. At her look, he shook his head. "I can't handle saying it. Or hearing you say it. But tell me how long."

The strength of compressed emotion in his voice startled her, hurt her heart. But he'd asked a fair question, for fair reasons.

"A few weeks from now."

His expression went rigid with shock. The hand over hers gave a slight jerk. She knew Ros had told all of them the final details were in process, but Abby herself hadn't had the date until two days ago, when she'd received the confirmation from the clinic.

Ros was the only other person that Abby had told directly. Long ago, in a weak moment, Abby had asked Ros if she would be with her, there at the end.

Before that, she'd considered giving those closest to her just the general timeframe, but not the exact date. In that naïve, ideal plan, she'd say good-bye in subtle, kind ways they'd remember later and understand the significance. Then she'd shut down her computer on a Friday, take a plane to Switzerland and cease to exist by the Monday morning staff meeting.

No muss, no fuss. She would manage those final days with grace, aplomb. Full control of her mind.

What a joke. She'd been fooling herself.

"A few weeks, meaning about a month and a half," she clarified. She'd get the chance to see him again.

Maybe it was cruel to him for her to be glad of that, but when his expression eased some, she realized it wasn't as unkind as she'd feared. He wanted the chance to see her again, too.

"Okay." His voice was still tight, but she could see him struggling to balance his reaction with her desire not to discuss it any longer. God, she needed coffee.

"How about I make you some breakfast?" she said. "Send you off with a good meal? I know it's early in the morning, but if we're both up..."

"Yeah. Sounds good." He rose, holding her hand to draw her up with him. When she moved away, needing the space, he picked up on it, letting her get past him to head for the kitchen. He followed at a slower pace, took a seat at her kitchen island. Whereas she'd have to hook her feet on the bottom rung of the high stool, his were flat on the ground. A good metaphor for the man himself.

He watched her pull out a skillet, break the eggs she'd removed from the fridge into a bowl, add sour cream to make the mix creamy.

"Abby," he said at length, "I want to put one other thing out there before I leave it. And it's not an argument. Just something for you to consider, think about. Are you okay with that?"

"Until the voices tell me to cut out your tongue to shut you up," she said lightly.

"I'll stay on this side of the counter. You're trying to manage your symptoms by self-medicating. I assume getting those meds without a prescription isn't easy."

"It's very easy. I just put on my ski mask, stick my nine-mil in my handbag and knock off the corner pharmacy. I think Rollins, the pharmacist, may have recognized me last time, because I forgot to change out of my blue pumps. Oh, and before I left, I told him that the pineapple upside down cake recipe his wife gave me worked out great. But so far he hasn't turned me in."

Neil shook his head at her, but she'd managed to dispel some of the tension around his mouth. "Smartass."

"All day long."

"Why *not* see that psychotherapist who met with us?" he said. At her stiffening, he lifted a hand. "As I said, I'm offering this as information, not an argument. She seems like a straightshooter, and she knows your plan. She could give you access to medications that might help you manage things, and you can talk about things with her. See what treatments are out there now, what behavior therapy she can help you with, to manage things until the date comes."

She noticed his gaze became a little more alert as she pulled out her bread knife to slice up fresh bread for the toaster. The corner of her mouth curled up. "Don't worry. A boning knife is far more practical for cutting out a man's tongue."

"Abby."

She shot him an even look. "The only reason you're suggesting it is you hope it'll help change my mind."

"Absolutely," he said without hesitation. "But it doesn't change the fact that it might make the next few weeks smoother for you, right?"

He was honoring what he'd said, his tone reasonable, not pushy. And he was being honest. Then he rose, came around the counter to her. With an amused look, he gripped her wrist, removed the bread knife, set it aside.

"Sorry. It's hard for me to focus around an untrained civilian bearing a big, nasty weapon."

"Who says I'm untrained? When I'm not knocking over pharmacies, I'm a ninja assassin. I can do blood curdling things with that bread knife."

"I'll bet."

He sobered, cupped her face, ran his fingertips under her eyes. "You're tired, bébé. It's wearing you out. Why shoulder it all alone?"

"Because if I do what you're suggesting, it will give Ros and the rest of them false hope."

"You're right. Losing you will hurt a lot less if we don't have false hope."

"Don't." Her voice thickened, and she looked away.

"Okay. Sorry, that was me being an ass. I get it." He gripped her upper arms in gentle hands. "You love them deeply. This is hurting them, and that pain is just one more burden for you to bear."

"There are days I wish I'd never told Ros," she admitted. "But part of the reason I'm doing it the way I'm doing it is because of my mother."

He had his head bent attentively over hers as she gazed at his chest. It was the first time she'd said it aloud. She hadn't even explained it to Ros.

"The way she took her own life. Garroting herself with her own bed sheet, giving no one time to prepare or say good-bye. If she hadn't been hospitalized, it would have been me who found her, or a neighbor. This way...it's more humane, planned. Civilized. Peaceful. It's not an act of desperation. It's my decision. One I've thought about for a long time."

"Okay." He stroked back a lock of her hair, caressed her shoulder where the sleepshirt revealed it. "Then here's the last point. What if the psychotherapist could not only make things easier for you, but help the others handle your decision?"

"How so?" She sent him a suspicious look.

"Spending time with the therapist reflects a willingness to understand your current options, and honors the way they feel about you," he pointed out. "It doesn't matter that you know so much more about all this stuff, or that you've been dealing with it for so much longer. Now that the time has come, it's different for your friends. If you give it a good faith effort, and the date comes, at least they won't feel so much like they didn't try hard enough."

She was tattooing the counter next to them with a closed fist, a sign of stress, but he picked up that fist, pried it open and put a kiss on her palm.

"You're strong and smart enough not to be influenced if you don't want to be. And in the meantime, the therapist can make the road you're taking a little easier for yourself. Which in turn could improve the quality of the time you have left with your friends."

No. No. She had her plan. But he'd known where to reach her.

Easing her friends' heartache, even if it didn't change anything for them. Damn him for pointing out things that were entirely reasonable. Even if he'd calculated her vulnerability in that area, it didn't make it untrue.

As she gazed at the counter moodily, he spoke again. "I asked you what it was like, and you told me. Facing a possible lifetime of that, even the struggle of how to make it better...I can't imagine that. However, I do know about coping with the uncertainty of life. Sometimes you have to give yourself the breaks that life provides to mitigate that stress. Have a beer after a day of unimaginable hell, and take the good that moment offers."

She lifted an incredulous expression. "Having a beer at the end of a terrible day can make life worth living? That's your sage advice?"

Hooking a thumb in his jeans while he kept holding her with the other hand, he pursed his very distracting lips. "Yeah. Abso-fucking-lutely. A silver lining may only be a sliver, but it distracts us from the storm cloud."

"You're still going to get drenched."

"And possibly struck by lightning. So enjoy that beer while you have it."

She sighed. "It doesn't change anything. Everyone needs to understand that. But...okay. I will meet with the therapist."

"All right. One more thing."

"Sailor, you are really pushing it."

"You'll be okay with this one. No more masking. Okay?"

His piercing look had a lot of stern Dom to it. While it almost made her smile, she couldn't deny the stomach flip. When it came from him, she wasn't immune to the sexual charge. "Don't conceal symptoms. Stop being a control freak. You're not alone in this, and you never have to be. You have a damn army, Abby, and you're the colonel of it."

"Not the general?"

"That's me. You're in charge, I'm—"

"In command," she finished.

He smiled, then sobered again. "I know it's really hard, but for the people who love you, being able to be in on this journey with you...it's a gift."

"It's the worst gift ever."

"But still a gift," he said firmly.

"Kind of like that saying you see on plaques. 'A bad day at the beach is better than the best day at work'?"

"Yeah, that kind of fits."

She eyed him. "This is a day at the beach where it hails, you get stung by a jelly fish, the flies won't leave you alone and, oh yeah, the water is too cold for swimming."

He grunted. "One time we had to do a dive off the coast of a country I can't name, where the only thing between me and instant hypothermia was a wet suit. Even then, my balls stayed blue for a week."

She chuckled; she couldn't help herself. With a sigh, she put her head down on his chest, closed her eyes. He stroked her hair again, toyed with it, curled it around his hand. She let herself feel that, enjoy it. Be comforted by it.

"Okay. I'll try. But I have a condition. Next time your balls are blue, you come to me for warming." She lifted her head and held up a hand. "I have very heated palms."

"I've noticed that."

As he bent, pressed his lips to her collarbone, sexual awareness rippled straight through her breasts and arrowed down her body. She moved a hand to his biceps, gripped, and she swayed against him. "I guess I'll have to tell Ros her special delegate got the job done."

"Skye said you just needed to hear it in a sexy male voice."

She pulled her head back to stare at him, then laughed. "Whose voice did she use?"

"Dennis Haysbert. The guy who does the insurance commercials and was in *24*."

"I have good friends. Now, where did you put that knife?"

His smile flashed again, but rather than retrieving it for her, he fished out his wallet, withdrew a card and propped it against her cookie jar, which held three flavors of cat treats for Freak's frequent visits. "Here's the appointment card. It's for Thursday, lunchtime. You can reschedule it if you want, but I thought if you had it already set, it'd be easier."

"You are way too prepared." She scowled. "Like with Tiger. I really should have given you more shit for that."

"Believe me," Neil grimaced. "Meeting with him to set it up was uncomfortable enough to be a punishment."

She snorted. "By the end of it, I'm sure you two were drinking beer and male bonding. You were too in sync."

He made a noncommittal noise, but gestured at the card. "I think you'll like her. She's a Domme, too."

"What?"

"Yeah. She and Janet are apparently friends."

Abby picked up the card. "Her office is in the Garden District."

"She said she'd come to your place if you want. Or you can take the trolley to her."

Hope was the most dangerous thing in the world. She replaced the card, stepped back, away from the temptation of his hands, his scent, his heat. "I'll meet with her at least once. But I won't change my mind, Neil. You need to accept that. So...if the longer we spend time together, the harder this is going to be on you...we can call it done now."

Saying it tore something inside her, but she forced out the words, straightened her back, let him see the resolve. "I know what this will cost them, but it's nothing next to what I'm sparing them, even if they don't see it that way. Yes, that's their choice, to bear that pain, but it's a never-ending circle. Their pain hurts me, mine hurts them, and it all comes back to me in the center."

Her voice thickened again. "I love Ros and my family. I love them so much. I won't put them through this, and I won't put myself through it. By the time my mother reached the end, all of who she wanted to be was gone, beyond her reach. I've had a magnificent life, with more blessings than my mother ever knew. I want to go out with all that clear in my head. It's enough. My body, my mind, my life. Got it?"

He touched her face, came away with a glistening tear she hadn't realized she'd shed.

"Got it," he said quietly. "So here's my decision, and I'm going to ask you to respect it, the way you want me to respect yours. I'm sticking. No matter how it tears me up, no matter how much it hurts. I'm telling you that straight, so you know you don't have to feel bad for me, feel guilt or apologize. My choice. Only way I go is if you tell me and really mean it. Not because you're trying to spare my feelings."

She pursed her lips. "Can you try not to talk me out of my decision every moment we're together?"

"I'll do my best, Abby."

"Say it to me."

His gaze flickered with heat, but he put his hands back on her shoulders, giving her his strength, the sense of his full attention. His voice, though still laden with combustible emotion, was steady. "It's your decision, Abby. Your body, your mind, your life."

His gaze sharpened. "But fair warning. My plan is to take your heart, and bet on it being strong enough to pull the rest of you away from the edge."

She framed his strong face with her hands, his beard soft under her palms. She fanned her fingers over the sun lines on his tanned face. "SEALs don't accept failure, right?"

At his surprised look, she cocked a brow. "You're not the only one who's done your research." But then she sobered. "My decision isn't a failure on your part, Neil. I really need and want you to understand that as well."

"What else do you want?" He tightened his hands on her, caressed her lower back, her hips. "Because whatever you want and need, bébé, that's what I am, as long as I have you."

She smiled, a painful thing, but there was good stuff in there with it. "When you can be here, when your job lets you...I'd like to be with you."

I'd like to fall in love with you. She didn't say that aloud. She wouldn't consciously make what she was asking of him harder than she already knew it would be. No matter what he'd said, about taking responsibility for his own decisions and pain, she knew her words drove nails into his soul.

Maybe the Powers That Be had sent her a SEAL at this point in life because they knew she needed someone who could bear the unbearable.

She could give him better things with her honesty, too. "I'd like to fully enjoy the man you are. See what kind of life you live."

"Careful what you wish for." He gave her a speculative look. "All right. When I get back, I'm taking you to a girls' softball game."

"A softball game?"

"Yeah. I'm a pretty hardcore fan of the sport." Though his eyes glinted with amusement, she could see he was serious.

"Just tell me it's not about looking at underage girls in snug uniforms."

"Some of the curvier ones do bring back fond teenage memories, but I assure you, my passion is for the game and how they play it."

"And how's that?"

"With pure determination, even when skill falls short. Which means sometimes they win, even when all other factors say they should lose."

She pinned him with a warning glance. "A little on the nose."

"Maybe. But I wanted to say it."

He hadn't moved back, was twisting a lock of her hair around his fingertips again. "Are you fantasizing about me in one of those uniforms?" she asked.

"Maybe. Are you imagining what I might do to you while you cook me breakfast?"

"I'm cooking me breakfast. I'm just being a courteous hostess, making enough for my guest."

She gave him her best dismissive sniff and head toss before returning to the stove and the waiting eggs. As she pushed down the toaster lever for the bread, she turned on the stove heat, then poured the egg mixture into the skillet.

She was aware of his regard, but he didn't seem inclined to say anything further. Which was good, because it took a little while for her to settle down from that conversation, let the mood turn toward something else. Proof of how he'd flustered her, she'd even forgotten to start the coffee, but he was on top of that.

He'd moved to the coffee maker and chosen her favored K-cup blend and one for himself, before reaching up into the cabinet above to find her mugs. Comfortable in her space.

As he waited for the coffee to brew, he leaned against the counter, watching her with those eyes that seemed to hold their own heat source.

Though she kept scrambling the eggs with deft movements of the spatula, she was aware of all the things in his attention. She closed her eyes as the coffee scent filled the room. He'd apparently been waiting on the progress of the eggs, because when they were almost done, he shifted behind her. Taking a generous handful of her hair, he held it to the side to put his mouth on her bare shoulder. And that was just his starting point.

Oh God. The man knew how to use his mouth. As he worked his way over her collar bone, to the base of her throat, his lips and tongue exercised the right amount of damp heat and sucking pressure. Arousal spiraled up through her like a vine coaxed from verdant earth. She leaned back into him, her eyes half closing as his hands ran down her sides, caressed her hips.

She'd talked about departure sex. It had been an attempt to handle things lightly, but she didn't want to think about him leaving. And he...

"Oh..." A breath left her as his hand dropped to her thigh, his knuckles stroking close to more intimate regions. He was kissing her throat more aggressively, giving her teeth, a pressure that sent more urgent reactions straight down her center. She could give as good as she got and proved it now, rotating her hips skillfully against his erection, putting her hands behind her to grip his hips, curve her fingers over as much of his taut ass as she could reach. It lifted and offered her breasts, nipples pushing against the sleepshirt fabric.

She'd laid the spatula somewhere, she didn't care where. She didn't have to. His arm slid around her, beneath her breasts, his hand curving up to palm the outside of the right one. As he did that, he shut off the stove and moved the spatula to a spoon rest, a safe proximity from the heat.

He turned her around, bent to slide his arm under her knees and lift her. "I like watching you make me breakfast. But I'm hungry for you."

She held his shoulders as he carried her up the stairs. Did it with barely a hitch in his stride, the strength taking her breath. When he reached her room, he didn't lay her down on her back. He set her on the bed on her hands and knees, and pushed up her sleepshirt to put his mouth between her legs from behind.

Had she worried he'd treat her like she was breakable? Not a problem right now. The forceful probe of his tongue, the suckle of her clit, drove her to her elbows, had her clawing at the covers. He spread her thighs wider with his hands. He wasn't giving her room to do anything, make any decisions. He took control in a manner and at a speed that overwhelmed her, while narrowing everything down to the sensations he was giving her.

As a Domme, her skill at reading a man was well-honed. A lot had been stirred up by their conversation, and he was taking out his frustrations on her body. He didn't want to accept the things she'd told him, but he'd agreed not to argue with her over it.

At least not with words.

How did he take it?

Quietly.

Neil was at his most dangerous when he stopped talking.

His mouth roused near-orgasmic pleasure on every inch of her flesh it touched. When he flipped her over again, he pulled off her sleepshirt so she was naked to his gaze, which left her covered with flame before he put his mouth back to work. Relentlessly stroking, thrusting, teasing and suckling her pussy until she gushed. A scream tore from her, and she grabbed his shoulders, seeking an anchor, scratching flesh. He caught her wrists, held them to her thighs as he kept working her, pushing the climax past its normal limits.

He didn't let her reach the ebb point. He had other plans.

Pushing himself up off the bed, he stripped off his shirt in an economical, almost pre-battle motion. Her gaze wanted to devour the smooth movements of his arm and chest muscles, the sinuous motion of his hips and lower torso, his erection straining against denim. He shoved the pants down and out of the way, put his knee on the bed. Her legs were still parted, but not as much as he wanted.

"Spread for me," he ordered her, his eyes relentless steel.

She did it, her heart knocking hard against her chest. No question in her mind who was holding the reins right now, and that he fully intended her to understand it. It wasn't a way to disrespect her Domme side, not exactly. It was a different, far more devastating message.

I'm falling in love with you, too. And I'm not going to let you be alone with this. I'm going to help you, hold you, carry you, however needed. And you can't push me away. You can't refuse me. I won't let go of your heart.

He stared at her body, her wet sex, quivering breasts, the aching limbs wanting to hold him. Her dry lips that needed the moisture of his.

"Yeah," he said. "You're mine. And bébé, I am all yours."

He bent over her, sliding one of those powerful arms around her waist, bracing his other hand beside her shoulder. "Try to look at me as long as you can," he said. And then he thrust into her, lodging himself deep.

The orgasm he'd started, the edge he'd taken her over, it was still close enough that the sensations looped back, pushed her up again with him, making her groan from the searing waves. He stroked, in, out, hand tight in her hair. She held his gaze as long as she could, which wasn't long, but she put her mouth to his throat, that intimate connection, telling him she was with him. She was here. God damn it, she was here, and at least in this single moment, the gods had been kind, didn't let her broken brain take it away.

"I want to put you on top of me, see your breasts bounce as you ride me, feel your pussy gripping my cock like it won't ever let it go. I'll take all that down range with me. It'll be the best damn reason to get the job done fast."

She had her hands on his back, his hips, that incredible, flexing ass. After those words, he rolled them, helped her push up so she was straddling him. He brought her down on him with those sure hands on her hips, his intent expression marking the quiver of her breasts from each impact. A hoarse sound broke from him as she did clutch him with her inner muscles, telling him she never wanted to let him go.

"I've never seen anything so fucking beautiful in my life. Inside and out." His gaze showed her how he saw her. Dwelling on her face, her eyes, the ripple of red hair over her pale shoulders. "Fragile and strong at once. You have my heart, Abby. You already have my heart."

CHAPTER FOURTEEN

He'd thought about waking her before he left, but in the end, he didn't. She was sleeping hard, and he wanted those circles under her eyes to be less deep.

Plus, he didn't think he could leave her while she was awake.

He'd done a lot of things that didn't thrill him. Swum in freezing cold waters. Carried heavy gear in ball-melting heat. Performed ops in the shittiest conditions imaginable.

Abby had picked on him when he grumbled about setting up the session with Tiger, but yeah, that had made the suck list, too. He wouldn't tell her she'd been right, about him and Tiger having a beer together.

That aside, she had zero appreciation for the effort it took, him setting up a sexual encounter for her with another man. When his feelings for a woman began to run this deep, it activated the exclusivity clause for him.

But he'd never expected to fall for a Domme. There were lines he could cross, but he had no switch side at all. Play was play, and they'd both proven they could deal with that, but this wasn't a woman who wanted to occasionally tie up her man with scarves in the privacy of their bedroom. For it to work for her, it had to be real and true.

Neil's possessive feeling hadn't gone away as she'd put her hands on Tiger. Once or twice he'd even indulged a leisurely fantasy of how many ways he could inflict lasting, crippling pain on Tiger's long, muscled body. But she'd been in her element. Lawrence had been right. Watching her draw a submissive male's arousal to heights any man would crave, all by feeding his soul-deep desire to serve and pleasure his Mistress, really had been a work of fucking art. A big neon sign that this was a vital part of her life, who she was.

The hard truth? Helping her reclaim that, watching what that meant to her unfold, surpassed his desire to call her his and his alone.

Caring about someone meant adapting.

The dreaded meeting hadn't been that bad. He'd set it up at a bar they both knew. Tiger had been waiting for him when he arrived, in a booth with a clear shot at the entrance. Ros had initiated the meeting as Neil had requested, her involvement ensuring Tiger would at least hear Neil out. However, from Tiger's wooden expression as he approached, Neil hadn't been surprised by the acrimonious tone of his first words, when Neil slid into the booth across from him.

"I respect the hell out of Ros, but I'm telling you this straight. I don't like this. If that feeling gets worse once you start talking, I'm out of here. And anything we talk about, I'll be telling Abby. I won't lie or hide things from her."

The man was as decent as Ros had told him he was. It helped Neil contain his entirely petty resentment that Tiger looked like every woman's bad boy biker fantasy.

"I plan to tell her myself," Neil said. "But I respect you wanting to give her your own take on it. None of us are comfortable telling her after the fact. But I don't see any other way to help her keep doing the Domme thing, and that's critical to her."

"Stepping into the submissive role beneath you?" Tiger met his gaze with flashing dark eyes. Yeah, he was ready to take Neil out in the parking lot and beat on him some. Neil understood the feeling, so he didn't let the goad to his temper stick. Instead, he met the other man's gaze squarely.

"I don't look down on you, man. I'm just not wired as a sub. When it comes to that...I'm not what she needs. And what matters to me is what she needs."

Tiger gave him a long look. Whatever he saw had his jaw easing a fraction. "So what's the deal? I'd rather get it up front before we order drinks, in case I decide to leave the conversation."

"I'm picking up the tab either way, but fair enough. Your last session with her, did you notice something a little off?"

Tiger lifted a shoulder. "Everyone has an off night."

"Her focus unexpectedly wandered, and she said some odd things. Things that sort of made sense, but didn't. Maybe her moods seemed to swing, becoming really emotional then flat."

Tiger's dark eyes met his, the truth revealed in the flicker. "What's the deal?" he asked. "Is she okay?"

The hardest part was saying it straight out. As he'd told Tiger, none of them wanted to impinge on Abby's privacy. But this was about her ability to hold onto as much of herself as she could, and Tiger could help with that.

"She has a mental illness. The symptoms started a while back, but they're getting worse. It's why she hasn't been there on her regular night lately."

Tiger's expression transformed to concern, protectiveness. Being a close cousin to possessiveness, it incited a growly reaction in Neil, but he remembered what Cyn had said. Protective, not possessive. Plus there was something more important at stake—having as many people as possible in Abby's corner.

"I suspected something was up," the man was saying. "Sometimes we grab a sandwich together for lunch, so I'd sent her a text about doing that. To touch base. She said maybe soon, but right now she was busy with work." Tiger's brow furrowed. "I don't want to overstep, but is she...getting the help she needs?"

As Neil opened his mouth to give a general, vague answer, an unexpected surge of emotions swamped him. He hadn't coped with the reality put in front of him, because he honestly couldn't figure out how to start. Not on top of realizing how deep his feelings for her ran, so deep that cutting his losses and backing away weren't on his radar. Not even as a passing thought.

Tiger swore. "So no. She's a stubborn, goddamn control freak, just like most of you Doms. Let's get that drink."

When they had their beers, Neil gave Tiger a few more details about the illness. The shock and chagrin in Tiger's reaction amplified Neil's own. But it also opened him up to what Neil was proposing. Before the second round of beers was ordered, he was on board, willing to do whatever was needed to help the Mistress he cared so much about.

Damn him.

~

Neil stopped by his place, got a shower, took care of some bills. He grimly stuck to his usual routine, though his mind was turning like a damn grinder.

Tell me how long.

A few weeks from now.

A few fucking weeks.

He'd talked her into meeting with Dr. Mo, yeah. But as a reasonable measure to make things easier on her friends, give her potentially more control over the symptoms. Not as an avenue to a different outcome altogether.

And now he had to go to work, goddamn it.

Her matter-of-fact shift away from that momentous decision about her life, as if they'd been discussing dinner plans, had planted a fear in his gut. Not only was she a woman whose mind was made up, she'd made peace with that decision, enough to put it on a shelf well beyond anyone else's reach.

Well, as she'd pointed out, he was pretty damn tall. And he had access to ladders. Climbing gear. A helicopter.

He texted Tommy, told him to send Dobby tomorrow to clear his fridge of perishable items. Then he walked down to the end of his dock and gazed out at the water, hand braced on a piling.

Unlike a lot of his teammates, he didn't bottle up volatile feelings left over from their ops. He compartmentalized during, aired and cleaned out those rooms after, when the op was done. He understood his place in the world, what he was meant to do, wanted to do, with his life. He didn't have a god or hero complex. He had a strong compass for the lines he would and wouldn't cross.

He understood that life fucked with them all, but getting hung up on that, making it personal, was a sure way to miss all the gifts. His ritual of going out on his boat, reconnecting to the rhythm of a natural world, understanding acts of simple survival and moments of tranquility, helped him deal with and remember that.

He'd experienced grief, despair. Rage. The full gamut of emotions that could destroy a universe, whether it was one person's or an entire planet's. But he'd never felt it like this before. So personal, his heart heavy enough to hold him to the dock, his feet unable to move. He couldn't leave her right now. He couldn't.

But he had to. It was his job, and lives literally sometimes rested on him doing it, and doing it well.

Did her life depend on the same? Yeah, he might not have a god or hero complex, but this wasn't that. This was a gut feeling about what had brought them together and why.

His head definitely wasn't in the right place. In a handspan of hours, he might be on his way somewhere it had to be focused. Straight.

He'd figure that out. Somehow.

Returning to the house, he shouldered his go-bag and headed to his truck. If he turned it around and headed down his bumpy drive with a little more aggression than usual, spun the tires when he moved onto an empty highway, well, that was just part of spilling off what he didn't need, in order to get the job done.

Fifty minutes later, he pulled into the airfield where he kept the Cessna. Usually there were no more than a few cars there. Today he recognized several. Lawrence's silver Charger. Ros's Mercedes. Dale's Dodge truck. An Audi Sportback.

The full delegation of drivers and passengers was standing around or leaning against the vehicles. Ros and Vera, Max, Lawrence, Dale and his wife Athena. He figured out the Audi's owner when he saw Dr. Mo resting against it. She was sipping from a bottle of water, those reassuringly calm eyes assessing the group with lively interest.

Then he saw Abby, and her presence submerged his curiosity into the whole vat of emotions he'd felt when standing on his dock.

She pushed herself off the hood of the Mercedes. She said something to Ros and Vera before walking toward Neil's truck, meeting him halfway. It provided them a semi-private bubble for conversation.

When he'd left her, he'd assumed she'd likely sleep half the day away. Instead, she'd mobilized a send-off party. His gaze slid over Ros and Vera, wearing unreadable expressions. If Abby's multi-tasking skills hadn't been up to this, he expected she'd drafted them to help.

He remembered what she said, about having to struggle to do the basics. He figured that might be the case here, because though she'd look beautiful rolled in mud, she didn't seem as if she'd had much leftover time to put herself together and get here. She had on a pair of worn jeans and a purple T-shirt with a startling picture on the front. A black cat with a blasé expression, holding a bloody knife. Below the knife was a bold, one-word declaration. *"What?"*

Apparently, people struggling with mental illness could draw from the same dark reservoir of humor that SEALs did.

Her canvas sneakers had no socks, and she'd scraped her hair up in a ponytail. No makeup, and she looked like she was running on fumes. But her determined expression said she had a mission, and she was damn well going to accomplish it.

When she reached him, he brushed a loose strand of hair away from her cheek. The hair felt like silk, her skin soft beneath his rough fingertips. He could touch her all day and never get tired of it. "You needed the sleep, bébé," he said, a mild reproof. "What are you doing here?"

She jerked her head left, toward Maureen. There was a grudging note to the movement. "We're going to go have coffee," she told him.

"Sorry, I don't have time," he said mildly. "But thanks for asking me to join."

She narrowed her gaze. "You're not invited. You have places to be."

"I wish I didn't."

Her lips pressed together, and she lifted her hand, closed it around his wrist, her slim fingers surprisingly strong. She stepped closer, putting her other palm on his chest.

"What's all this about?" he asked. He wound his fingers in the thick locks of her ponytail. He'd thought about the weight and heat of her hair, the way it felt against his flesh, a hundred times since he'd seen her, only a handful of hours ago. His mind had stayed full of her, and would, until the absolute last moment when he'd have to push out everything but what his job required.

Her fingers slid along his jaw, his beard. "You can't do it this way. I can see it in your face. You have to figure out how to get on that plane, go to work, and leave all this shit here. Have your head on straight, no matter how fucked up mine is. Get the work done and come home to me."

He stared down at her as she pretty much echoed his own

thoughts, then let his glance lift and pass over the others. "Why are they here?"

"To remind you of all the people I have in my life I can count on for anything. Well," she looked toward Maureen, "except her, but I wanted her here because it would help you to know I keep my promises. But all the rest will go to the wall for me. They'll take care of me while you're gone. You have to be okay with that. Accept that. Okay?"

Her voice had raised with the force of her emotions, and her eyes were doing that shifting left and right thing. She closed them, swallowed a curse.

"Don't take this as a sign I'm losing it," she said crossly. "Take it as a sign of how much I mean it, how much I need you to understand it. Fear of you not getting it is getting me worked up."

"I'm getting that. And I get it." As he reinforced it with a tug on her hair, a caress of her upper arm, he saw Dale move. His former Master Chief squeezed his wife's hand, their gazes meeting, before he headed toward Neil. Though Dale had a below-the-knee amputation on one leg, his prosthesis and adaptability to it meant no one would notice much difference in Dale's gait from any other superiorly fit man in his fifties. One fully capable of kicking the ass of someone three decades his junior.

Max and Lawrence had come with him. When they reached Neil and Abby, they formed a half crescent wall behind her.

"Abby, can we have a minute with him?" Dale asked.

Her gaze was fastened on Neil, the base of his throat. She answered Dale's question with a quick nod. But before she withdrew, her hand closed in a fist on his chest, pulling in some of his T-shirt in her grasp. She beat a light, brief tattoo against him. Her back was straight, her chin up when she turned away, joining Ros and Vera at Ros's Mercedes.

Ros spoke to Abby. Though Neil couldn't hear the conversation, he saw Abby give her a tight smile.

He'd heard her words, knew how strong she was. He didn't doubt that. But he also couldn't get a disturbing image out of his head, one that had come to him when he stood on his dock. His mother had an Italian vase of sky-blue glass, shaped like a twisted flower bud. She'd kept it on the mantel for years. People walked through the room, flopped down on the couch, opened and closed doors, windows. All the daily activities of a home with two adults and three kids, a couple dogs. All things that created vibration, such that the vase had moved in tiny increments toward the edge of the shelf, no one noticing as it got closer and closer.

Neil's father had an uncanny sense of where to be when he was needed. Neil's mother had always laughingly said it was one of the main reasons she'd married him. He'd been the one close to the mantel on the day the vase finally tipped. He'd caught it halfway to the floor.

He'd been there to avoid catastrophe, to save something precious to his mother.

He'd been there.

"Do you trust us?"

When a Master Chief spoke in that *listen up or my boot will be lodged up your ass* tone, an operator's attention would automatically snap to him. Though Dale was retired and usually dismissed the MC term, Neil wouldn't have answered any other way. "Yes, Master Chief. I do."

"Good." Max and Lawrence looked as serious as Dale did, and had closed in the space Abby had left behind, so they were right up in his grill. "Your head being half here, half there, that doesn't work." Dale gave Neil a hard look. "You love her."

"Yeah. I do."

"Which is why I didn't phrase it as a question." And also probably why Dale had asked Abby to give them a moment. He'd deduced Neil and Abby hadn't had that exchange. The first time a woman heard a man loved her shouldn't be through a third party.

"Then you have one job." Dale's blue-green eyes were as powerful as the ocean. "Keep your head where it belongs. Lock this shit up while you're down range."

He gestured to those gathered around the cars. "We'll take care of her."

"And remember what the doc said, about Abby's support network?" Lawrence said. "It goes for you, too. We have your back. We'll hold that lifeline, for both of you."

Neil met his gaze, as well as Max and Dale's. A buttload of history, of crazy things that most people couldn't imagine, passed between them. Behind those gazes were hearts and souls who would do just as Dale had said.

Take care of her.

The bitch of it was *he* wanted to be the one who cared for her, above and beyond anyone else. He was worried if she had an episode, they wouldn't understand her words as he had. They wouldn't know how best to help.

Time for his rational brain to man up. She stood with strong, accomplished women, her closest friends. And he faced three men who'd handled some of the craziest shit that a fucked-up world could manufacture.

Then there was the doc. She was going to meet with Abby—at least once—and if anyone in her profession could, he was putting money on her being able to click with his beautiful Domme.

Neil let all that info settle in, made himself examine the truth of it, balance it with his desire to be in charge, to control things.

...stubborn, goddamn control freak. Just like most of you Doms.

As he recalled Tiger's words, the tension died back. It didn't go away, but enough spilled off he could manage it. Plus Dale had reinforced it with a direct order, no matter that he was retired.

"Roger that," Neil said. Then he lifted his voice so Abby could hear. Her attention, her body language, had stayed pointed in their direction, even as the other women spoke to her. "Now, could you give me a little space to say good-bye to my girl?"

"Don't take too long," Lawrence said, deadpan. "She promised all three of us kisses after you get on the plane. With tongue."

"Yeah, yeah. Fuck off." Despite the mock warning, Neil gave them a simple nod of *thanks,* in that way that required nothing further. Lawrence bumped a fist with him while Max and Dale returned the nod, message received. They cleared out as Abby returned to him.

"You offered them kisses with tongue?"

She shrugged. "I had to offer them something. Though I expect treating them all to brunch was the deciding factor."

A reluctant glance at his watch told him what he already knew. He really had to go.

Everything disappeared but her, here where he could touch her, and he did, banding an arm around her waist and pulling her tight up against him, all those sweet curves, the slim columns of her thighs.

Her palm was on his chest, his heart thudding hard against the pressure.

"Okay, Mistress. You have my oath. I'll keep my head straight. But I need a promise from you."

She tensed, and he brought his hand up between her shoulder blades, to massage her nape. "Don't," he murmured. "Don't tighten up on me."

"What's the promise?"

"Shit can happen down range. Sometimes something that takes a few days can take longer. Be here when I get back."

When her resistance increased, he shook his head impatiently. "I'm not asking you to change your decision or your timeline. Just don't let it go down sooner, when I'm not here, under some bullshit that it's easier for me. Don't do that to me. Don't make me have to worry about that."

"Neil..."

"A promise for a promise." He drew back, met her gaze just a brief second before he shut his eyes. "Is it easier to look at my face when they're closed?"

She traced his eyelids with light fingers, his cheekbones, moving down to his lips, to stroke his beard. "Yes," she said wonderingly. "It is."

"I can feel your gaze like your touch." He put his forehead against hers. "Promise me, Abby."

"Okay," she said in that darkness. "But if I think you're starting an international incident or a small war just to screw with my schedule, all bets are off."

He chuckled. "Fuck, I'm going to miss you."

"I might think of you on occasion." But there was an unsteadiness to her voice. Her fingers curled against his chest again, that tight hold that said she didn't want to let him go. Now he detected what the show of support had been covering, keeping the focus on him and his head.

He had helped her, provided unexpected stillness in her world spinning out of control. And he was leaving.

"Abby..."

"No," she said fiercely. "I meant everything I said. You can't believe you're the person I need more than any other. No matter how crazy my head gets, we both know that's not my reality. The people here tell us that. You do your job, and I'll do mine."

"Okay." He wanted a way to hold her even closer as a shudder ran through her. "Stay with me, bébé. And by the way, don't freak out, but I love you, too."

He pressed his lips to the crown of her head, her face pressed to his chest. Her hands dug into it as if she was going to set up shop in his heart. He tipped up her face, and kissed her. A long and demanding kiss. Exploring lips, tongue, teeth. He'd be okay with some perverse god stopping time right here, in this moment.

She pushed back from him, broke the kiss, and he saw the determination in her face, her rigid jaw. "Okay, then. Get your ass on your plane and get going. You're late for work."

"Giving orders, Mistress?"

"It's what I do. What are you going to do about it?"

Despite the terrible ache inside him, and all the emotions he could feel from her, he gave them what they both needed. He swept a deliberately heated look up and down her curvy, cock-teasing body and smiled. "Come back and give *you* some orders."

Abby stood apart from the others, watching the plane become a receding speck in the sky. He'd piloted it to the runway, touching the brim of his cap at her as he trundled past. Though the shield of glass had obscured his features, she could feel the impact of his gaze. *I can feel your gaze like your touch.*

When he took off, the plane gaining speed, the wheels leaving the ground, her heart pounded in her throat, the noise overwhelming her, the wind stirring up loose tendrils of hair around her face.

He knew how to fly a plane. Navigate a boat in the bayou. Fight bad guys in remote corners of the world. He was sensitive, caring, strong. He'd engineered a session for her with one of her favorite subs, while making it clear he considered her heart his exclusive terrain.

He'd told her he loved her.

Fate had sent her a real-life romance hero when her life was going to shit.

Fucking, goddamned Fate.

She'd given Ros money and asked her to take the others to brunch, let them enjoy breakfast together. Now she heard them all leaving, teaming up in the different cars. She'd ridden with Ros and Vera, but that wasn't how she was getting home.

Pivoting as the cars pulled out, she faced the one person remaining. Dr. Maureen Whisnant, still leaning against her Audi as if she had all the time in the world.

Abby fought back the irrational fear of the woman. She wasn't going to act like a victim of her illness, manipulated by or accepting a doctor's input about what was happening to her own body, like words handed down from God.

Psychotherapists usually liked their home turf. But Abby had pulled herself out of bed fighting fatigue. She wouldn't be able to track Maureen's voice in a place where she was sorting a lot of unfamiliar input. So when Abby suggested her own place for coffee, like she was throwing down a gauntlet, the woman's response surprised her.

"I think that would be lovely," Maureen said.

As she sat down in the passenger side of Maureen's car, the woman surprised her again. "Since it's a bit of a drive back to the city and your place, you're welcome to recline the seat and take a nap, if you'd prefer to do that."

"As long as the meter's not running," Abby said. "I wouldn't want Ros's money to be wasted."

"I haven't accepted payment yet," Maureen said. "I wait until after the first meeting. To determine if I can provide any benefit to the patient."

"Have you ever wondered why they call someone under a doctor's care a patient? Maybe because they have to be ready to wait forever to see any benefit to it."

Maureen made a noncommittal noise as she pulled out onto the road. "You're a professional woman, Abby. When a client acts as if you're the enemy from the first meeting, how do you handle it?"

The car had a fresh linen scent to it, and was clean, no crumbs or excess dirt in the floor carpets. Maureen had a charm hanging from her rearview mirror, something with a pewter dove and several sparkling stones. It swung and made circles with the movement of the car. It was bugging Abby, a lot, making her feel queasy. She turned her attention to the window. Then she realized she hadn't answered

Maureen's question. While it took a moment to find it in her head, she had a ready answer for it.

"I would tell them they need to look for a different marketing firm. But it's not a valid comparison. There's not much chance I can get my clients locked up and force-fed anti-psychotics that do nothing or make things worse."

She was being a bitch. She'd told Neil she'd do this. She reminded herself it was for his and Ros and the others' benefit. She didn't have to take it out on someone just doing her job. She needed to shut up and take the nap.

Maureen gave her a sidelong look. "You can unhook that charm and put it in the glove box. My sister gave it to me. She chose the stones herself, each one meaning something different, but all of them about protection from chaotic forces beyond our control. Like New Orleans drivers." Her voice held humor. "I expect its effectiveness won't be reduced by temporary relocation."

Abby removed it, tucked it in the glove box. She saw a car manual, a tire key and a pair of Halloween socks, printed with black cats and jack o' lanterns.

"Oh, that's where those are," Maureen observed, surprised and pleased. "I've been looking for those. I go all out on Halloween decorating, and a friend sent those to me as a gag last year. I'd forgotten I'd tucked them in there."

She made a turn, putting them on the main highway toward New Orleans. "Back to your comment. I see no indication that you require hospitalization at this point. You're lucid, not in psychosis. But you're battling, aren't you?"

She sent Abby a steady look. "Even right now, there are things talking to you, and the input around you seems distorted, too much. It's in your speech pattern, the way you move, your eyes."

As Abby tensed, Maureen lifted a calming hand, her gaze back on the road. "It's subtle. Someone who doesn't know what it looks like wouldn't make much of it. Anyhow, let's not start talking now, unless that's what you want. How about I stop at one of the beignet places on the way into town and pick up a treat to go with our coffee?"

"Okay." Abby had enough to sort. Though she felt an itchy, anxious and irritating desire to keep the upper hand in the conversation, she didn't see anything in Maureen's manner designed to take it away from her. Just kind consideration for her weary state.

Whether calculated or not, her talking about a sister also reminded Abby the psychotherapist was a normal person, a woman with a family. "But if I wake up in a strait jacket and a padded room, you're getting a crappy online review."

Maureen's white teeth flashed, her pale green eyes glinting. "My daughter is always telling me she's going to give me a one-star review as a mother. I tell her that a one-star from a teenager equals a five-star review among my parent peers."

"What does she say to that?"

Maureen grimaced. "Depends on the day. Sometimes I get a slammed bedroom door. Sometimes a demand that I be less cerebral, more like 'normal' parents. Sometimes a bit of a smile. Those are the good days. Would you like to listen to some music?" She gestured toward the radio. "There are satellite channels, and programmed play lists by mood."

Abby shook her head, recoiling from the radio. "Nothing, thanks."

"Silence works better?"

"Most of the time. The car engine works."

"Okay then. Have a good nap."

Surprisingly, Abby did sleep. Despite the often rough state of Louisiana highways, she was lulled by the quiet purr of the Audi, the rumble under the wheels. She thought of Neil, the heat of his mouth, strength of his arms. His scent.

When she'd woken later in the morning, after he'd left, she'd pressed her palm to the part of the bed where he'd lain next to her, stroking her hair, her bare back.

As her thoughts had turned to his probable state of mind and where he was going, anxiety had speared her. It became a short panic attack as she tried to orient herself, figure out what to do. She boiled it down to one thing. She called Ros, told her what needed to happen, and asked for help.

Cyn and Skye had things they couldn't reschedule, but Vera had been able to join them, along with Neil's former teammates. Athena had come along with Dale for further female reinforcement. She was the definition of a Southern magnolia: soft spoken, gracious, and formidable as air support in a crisis.

When he finally took off, Abby had felt much better about where Neil's head was at. Though she couldn't help wishing it and the rest of him were with her.

She roused when Maureen pulled into Abby's driveway. The woman complimented the landscaping and look of the historic home in a genuine way, asking questions about the planting choices and how Abby liked living in the neighborhood. Once inside, Abby gestured her to the kitchen table. She asked Maureen her coffee preference, since Abby had several flavors for herself and visitors.

Because she'd been in a rush, throwing on her clothes, charging out the door to meet Ros when she pulled into Abby's driveway, it was only now she noted little details she'd missed. Neil had cleaned the breakfast dishes. He'd eaten some of the scrambled eggs and left her a portion in the fridge. A purple bloom cut from the pot on her back porch was on top of the container. He'd wrapped the stem in a piece of wet paper towel so it wouldn't wilt, and attached a post-it note to the lid.

Eat.

She brought milk and sweeteners to Maureen for her coffee. "I used to be as well put together and efficient as you are," Abby said. "It makes me hate you. I'm sorry."

"Everything I've read about you says you're an exceptionable businesswoman, and a generous member of the New Orleans community," Maureen responded. "I'm sorry this is happening to you."

Abby sat down at the table with her own cup of coffee. Maureen opened the box of pastries she'd picked up, and the scent of baked goods was soothing. The clock ticked on the wall and the fridge's ice maker was running. Voices on low right now. Nothing setting her off, and she was home, where she felt steadier. She needed to be clear, firm.

"I've agreed to one meeting."

"Then let's make it count." She could feel Maureen gazing at her and lifted her attention to the psychotherapist. Maureen put a beignet on a napkin in front of herself. "I understand you have an assisted suicide option in place."

"Yes. I'm meeting with you for them. My friends and Neil." Abby couldn't glean a single hint of what the doctor was thinking, what her opinion was about Abby's decision. But Abby knew all about the ability to mask, appear entirely normal, when a storm was raging.

Neil had seen through it, though. *I'm standing inside you, Abby. I see the storm.*

"It's kind of you to consider their feelings," Maureen said. "Do you think there's any chance you'll change your mind? Extend your timeline?"

Abby shook her head. "I'm already devolving, and if I'm not lucid, proceeding with the assist becomes far more difficult."

"Hmm." Maureen chose a different topic. "What you did this morning was interesting, and astonishing. Despite an obvious struggle with your symptoms, including fatigue, you mobilized your friends and Neil's to ensure he departed with the best mindset possible. It tells me a lot about your will. Your history reinforces it. What you made of yourself, despite being the child-aged caregiver of your adult parent, someone with severe, poorly managed paranoid schizophrenia. You—"

"Stop," Abby said. "You're not the first to try the 'you're so strong' argument to get me to change my mind. If Ros's agenda is driving you, then there's no point to this."

Maureen paused, but when she spoke again, Abby noted her resolute tone conveyed a streak of steel that somehow managed not to sound combative. "Likewise, if you are going to frame everything I say in terms of the motive you've assigned to me, you're correct. But I'm hoping you'll give me a chance to make my point."

Abby set her jaw. It was a valid observation, but she would make no apologies for being on the defensive. She wasn't here to make things easier for the psychotherapist. "Okay. Prove me wrong."

"This isn't a competition, my way versus yours." Maureen sent her a no-nonsense look. "You've had to repeatedly shut down discussion about your decision, with those you consider your family. Their motives, their perceptions, are through their own lenses. Because of their intense love, their attempts to change your mind have likely been difficult."

Another pause. "They can't focus on all that has gone into your decision, really listen, because they're so afraid of losing you. They feel empathetic listening is conveying acceptance, and they can't accept that outcome."

Maureen leaned forward. Despite Abby's resistance to the woman, she had her attention. "Our discussions on the topic, if we do discuss it, will be about *you*. Your thoughts, feelings, decisions. Past, present and future. One part of my role, an important one, is to be your sounding board, someone who can ask you objective questions to help you achieve a deeper understanding of why you're making the decisions you are about your illness."

"Why? To what end? To change my mind?"

"You have to be defensive with Rosalinda and your friends, because you are anticipating them attacking your reasoning. But Abby, you of course need to question and explore your decision, beyond the functional need to meet clinical competency requirements."

Maureen took a sip of her coffee. "Most faiths believe in counseling sessions for a couple about to get married. Not to challenge the decision, but to help the couple explore and discover a deeper meaning, grasp a wider understanding of what their commitment means. Don't you think it makes sense to do the same with a decision to end your life? To be certain that, if you do go ahead with it, you've made true peace with it? While your friends and family may never understand your reasoning, or agree with it, if you achieve that peace, then you will give them some measure of the same."

The silence after she said that drew out, surprisingly comfortable, before Maureen spoke again.

"Now, part two of how I view my role. When it comes to paranoid schizophrenia, I help people learn to manage the illness in ways that improve their quality of life. I've seen people accomplish that, quite well."

"People can manage to roll a boulder up a hill."

Though Maureen had said she had no ulterior motive, Abby couldn't help but be back on the defensive. "They can make it happen day after day after day. But eventually they start wondering why they're doing it. They get tired, knowing that damn boulder is never going to reach the top of the hill.

"But hey, they're 'managing' it, which makes everyone around them happy. The world is hunky dory, because they're not the one rolling it. The people who have to pick you up when it rolls over you, crushes you, who get you up to start the whole pointless process over again... As grateful as I am for their presence in my life, they still can't fully get it. Their hearts are too involved."

Maureen cocked her head. "What if we can make rolling that boulder up the hill easier more days than not? Or enough days to make life worth living? Is that something that's interesting to you? You've decided on a course of action, you're set on it, and you think I'm asking you to change mid-stream, which is jarring and hard, inciting resistance. Choices and options are what everyone struggling with mental illness is most afraid of losing, because your mind takes control away from you. I am another option you are exploring. That is all."

As Abby stared at her, Maureen pressed on. "What I'm asking is, since you have a little time, why not use me to pause at that crossroads? Look down the other roads to see what's currently there, before you press the gas pedal to go straight to your destination. At least let me make the drive smoother, less bumpy, if I can. Whatever road you take."

Abby sighed. "You're better at this than I wanted you to be. What if, when we talk about things, we disagree?"

"I'll tell you why I disagree with you. If you are lucid enough, you'll weigh whether my points are valid or if I'm full of shit." An amused smile touched Maureen's lips. "And if you tell me I'm full of shit, I'll tell you the same thing I tell my husband. You're crazy."

Abby chuckled, something she'd never anticipated doing in the presence of a psychotherapist. "I have trust issues. I think that's clear. But you've made enough sense I'm not quite ready to kick you out."

"Good. Because I am here for *you*. That's my priority. Keep that in mind." Maureen's tone became brisk. "Now, if you think you're up to it, I'd like to talk about where you are in your symptoms, and how you've been handling medication. If you'd let me conduct a formal diagnostic review, I can confirm your diagnosis. That will allow me to prescribe you any medications we discuss and agree might be a good idea for you to try."

"The one I'm on is the only one that halfway worked for my mother. It seems to do the same for me."

"But its effectiveness is already waning," Maureen pointed out. "You're having the occasional tremors, the flat effect to your face. The auditory hallucinations are still getting through enough to distract and disrupt you."

"Not as loud, the first few hours after I take it." Though that time range was diminishing.

"There are some newer medications," Maureen said. "They're worth a try, and we can use them in combinations."

Everything Maureen was saying made sense, but words like *diagnosis, hospital,* and *work-ups* dropped a ball of jagged ice in Abby's belly that rolled around in there, making her put her hand on it, knead. "First it's a diagnosis, then it's official. Then it's the med roller coaster. At least the medication I'm using, I know what it'll do or not do. Mostly."

Maureen tapped the table next to Abby's tense hand. "Abby, I'm not your parent or your dictator. This is a partnership. We can work together. Keep a diary of your symptoms for me so I can help you track how well the meds I suggest are handling things. We can alter them, ease them back or increase the dosage, depending on how effective you feel they're being, or how much you really need in conjunction with therapy methods."

"It's a partnership until it's not." Abby pressed her lips together. "Be honest with me. What happens if something goes wrong and I go into a full psychotic episode?"

"My understanding is that's already happened at least once on the meds you're already taking," Maureen responded. "But you and the others handled it."

"You would have put me in a hospital," Abby said.

"Not necessarily. There are many factors that go into that decision. Remember, in that instance, an additional dose of the meds brought you back to yourself." Maureen gestured with her cup. "But if you go into a full psychotic episode, where you could hurt yourself or someone else, you're smart enough to know someone you trust should grab the reins. Which I expect is why Ros has your healthcare proxy."

She cocked her head. "On a separate but related note, I find it very relevant that you, a lifelong Domme, are gravitating toward another Dom as a love interest at this time of your life."

It surprised Abby, that Maureen had chosen to go that way. But since the change of direction gave her the chance to think about Neil, Abby welcomed the digression.

"You aren't alone. I've never seen myself as a switch."

"No, I didn't think you were. But what Dom/sub relationships are can be remarkably fluid, when the people involved need them to be."

It matched her own thinking, and Neil had pretty much stated the same. "While I am a woman of science," Maureen added, "I'm a woman of faith as well. I think someone out there put you in the path of a man who can exercise that fluidity. At least from what I've seen of him so far."

Also echoing her thoughts on it. For form's sake, though, Abby frowned. "He can be more inflexible on other things."

Maureen's smile was pure female. "Rigidity isn't a bad thing in a man, in the right circumstances."

"Isn't there some kind of professional rule against doctors making sexual innuendo jokes?"

"I was actually referring to aspects of his personality, but I can go there, too, when the moment is appropriate for it." Maureen shot her an amused look.

"What I mentioned at the beginning, about your will," she continued. "Facing and managing paranoid schizophrenia is a matter of will. But you made a good point with your boulder analogy. It changes nothing about the illness itself, the toll it takes, the control it saps. But will shapes attitude, and attitude is the soul, the character of the person. You're in a relationship with a man whose profession is all about will. He won't meekly stand by while you tell him what you're going to do with your life. He's an obstacle, a conflict."

Abby bypassed Maureen's assessment of the relationship to focus on the part about the man himself. "I'm not sure Neil has ever meekly done anything."

"And he's a Dom to boot."

"He doesn't try to overpower or bully me with it, though. Not that way. He...spars. He likes the give and take, the combat, so to speak, of two Doms figuring it out together."

"He likes a challenging relationship."

"Yeah. Which means he won the lottery with me, didn't he? But he seems to seek peace when he's at home. What I'm dealing with isn't the least bit peaceful, to me or anyone around me."

"Maybe not, but your kitchen reflects the same contrast."

Abby blinked. "How so?"

"Your décor reflects someone who understands it's important to enjoy life in all its nuances. Not just the big excitements or changes, but the quiet routines." Maureen gestured to the features as she identified them. "The beauty of sunlight reflecting through a window decoration, fresh flowers on a ledge, cut from your own garden."

She met Abby's gaze. "You and Neil live lives straddling a line between two very different worlds. Only the darker side of yours is inside your mind, whereas his might be halfway around the world."

The psychotherapist took a tablet out of the computer bag she'd brought into the house with her. Placing it next to her, she rested her well-manicured hand on it.

"I know a great deal clinically and academically about mental illness, Abby. But my knowledge has to be tailored to you, your uniqueness. If you are willing to do the work-up, give me as accurate an accounting as you can manage about what's going on, I promise I'll do all I can to develop tools that might be useful to helping your journey go more smoothly. If you're on board with it, I'd need more than one session to do that. Your choice."

Abby looked down. She'd pulled the beignet into so many pieces it looked like a fluffy mound of cereal on her napkin. Her hands were sticky. She closed them into balls, thinking.

Your choice.

Slowly, she nodded her head. Once.

"Okay."

CHAPTER FIFTEEN

Neil rubbed his face. If he had to look at another set of detailed schematics with text so small a cockroach would need reading glasses to review it, he'd claw out his eyes.

The conference room they'd used for the briefing a couple hours ago wasn't going to win any beauty contests, but there was wall space to pin up data and a spot for the projector to run the slide show of intel. Most importantly, the room had provided a full coffee pot next to a heaping platter of hazelnut cookies. The cookies were gone, no surprise when the full team plus the support staff had been in the meeting. Only a pile of crumbs was left. Since they'd been really good cookies, he considered using the paper doily on the platter to funnel the crumbs into his mouth.

That said, he'd give up cookies forever if he could have what he really wanted to be tasting. As he twisted a pen over his knuckles, he thought of Abby lying on his bed, her body rising up to his hands and mouth. The fragrance of her skin, her breath, her sex, all that glorious red hair. Her fingers tangled with his as she slept, him behind her, the softness of her ass pressed against his groin. Supporting the smooth lengths of her thighs with his own spooned up behind them.

Close enough to absorb every twitch of her body, as he lay awake and listened to her muttering in her sleep. Stroked her hair as her brow furrowed and she jerked, fighting battles in her dreams.

Fuck, why was he here?

When one of the married team guys was frustrated because his wife or kids were having a problem and he couldn't be there to help, Neil had understood, peripherally. There was always shit happening on the home front. But it was the job, one of the things they all learned to accept. If you couldn't, you hung it up and worked for someone else.

"Knew I'd find you in here. Feel ready?" Dodge asked.

Neil pulled his thoughts back to the present as his chief entered the room. When Neil rolled his chair back so he could swivel around and look at him, it squeaked loudly enough an enemy could use it to target their location. Fortunately, they were still at the German base.

"Who's stepping in for Billy?" Neil asked.

"Wolfman. His team could spare him for a few days."

Neil grunted. He was familiar with Wolfman. While having all the usual team members for an op was ideal, having someone familiar, whose experience they knew and respected, was acceptable.

Dodge leaned a hip on the scarred table and nodded to the laptop screen Neil was studying. "You haven't given me an answer on taking over Mike's job, but you're sure as hell acting like it's a done deal."

"Whether I am or not, I'm most qualified to stand in on it until it's decided."

"Something holding you up on it, Twizz? Last time I asked, I could have sworn it was a no-brainer for you."

Neil laid it out honestly. "That woman I showed you. She's pulling me in deep."

Dodge's mouth creased in a smile. "Well, damn, brother. Congratulations."

At Neil's questioning look, Dodge lifted a shoulder. "You're pretty single-minded. We all knew if you ever showed signs a woman was getting under your skin, she'd likely be the one. Have you set a date yet?"

Neil lifted a brow. "I'd prefer not to scare her off, thanks. 'I just met you, let's get married.'"

"Yeah." Dodge pursed his lips. "Usually that only works if there's lots of alcohol involved. So what's the problem? You're not like one of these other young bucks. She wouldn't have a hold on you if she couldn't handle you being a SEAL."

"She's facing a serious problem. A mental illness. Far as I know, there's no caveat that says 'in sickness and in health, unless your job requires you to take off at a moment's notice.'"

"Love fits its own definition for the two people involved." Dodge shrugged. "Maybe the 'in sickness and in health' part means making sure she has what she needs when you're not there. Does she?"

Dodge's words reminded him of Tommy's similar take on it, what he'd told Abby. "Yeah. She does. Including a duo of former SEALs and a retired Master Chief."

Dodge's eyes glinted. "Always glad to hear Ack-Ack, Munch and MC are staying busy. Have you told her you have a promotion pending?"

"No. She's got a lot to deal with."

"Oh, sorry. Didn't realize she's a child."

Neil shot him a withering look. Dodge held up a hand.

"A woman interested in hooking up with an operator long term isn't the type who wants to be treated like porcelain. There's an unfortunate hypocrisy to being a SEAL, and we all have to make peace with it. While we're out super-heroing it, our families have to deal with the shit thrown at them, mostly on their own. If they do get our help, it's usually long distance, or in spurts, during whatever time we have between ops."

He shifted into the seat next to Neil, braced his foot on the support struts beneath the table. "There are challenges to it, beginning to end. But when the burn is new and hot, they can seem even more critical."

Neil knew he was right. It didn't make it easier to feel. When she needed her hand held, he wanted to be the hand within easy reach.

"The job is yours until we have to make the decision and you tell us no," Dodge said. "If you take it, it's likely you'll eventually lead your own team. If that's what you want. Or maybe you'll be a hell of a right hand to the team leader until your retirement comes. Either way, you have value here."

He straightened. "This life calls to a very few. The ones with families who can weather it with them are an equally elite group. It's a lot of variables to think about when making a decision. When in doubt, go with your gut. I've never known it to fail you. And listen to her, what she wants. What's her name?"

"Abigail Rose. Abby."

"I look forward to meeting her. Let's talk over the mission. I know you have some ideas about entry point."

When Dodge left thirty minutes later, they had the op squared away, and Neil had fifteen minutes to kill before he needed to find some chow and get his gear together for the plane ride.

Drawing out his phone, he scrolled through her photos, dwelling as always on the one where she sat by the pool. Sitting in the middle of a group of people who cared about her, but still somehow managing to look alone.

Yeah, he was just fucking with his head. But the last call he'd made to her had its barbs in him. She'd looked wiped out. The doc was trying a combo cocktail that used the existing medication plus one other. Abby had explained there were side effects that were supposed to disappear in a couple days. She seemed restless, fingers tapping, eyes darting around, but her smile for him had been genuine. She rose during the conversation to pace around the bedroom.

The nightgown she wore was a pale blue filmy thing that had a deep plunging V back. Her red hair rippled over her arms, the valley of her spine, the silk-clad nip of her waist and swell of her hips.

"So who're you wearing that for?" he asked, craning his neck as if to see who else was in the room.

She made an exaggerated waving motion at something off screen. "Thor, damn it, I told you and your giant schlong to stay hidden in the closet. It's a tight fit, but you can manage it. Suck in your twelve-pack abs."

He grinned. "You're wearing it for me. Admit it."

"I'll do no such thing. I'm wearing it for me, because I look damn good in it."

"No argument there, Mistress. Want to lift the hem, give me an ass pic?"

"Hard no."

"Well, fuck it, I'm going to bed then."

Though humor wasn't the main emotion he felt, he injected it into his voice, hoping he was providing a useful distraction while she fought not to jump out of her skin.

She'd sat back down and closed her eyes, adjusting the vanity chair so he was looking at her profile. She averted her head as they spoke, telling him she was having difficulty looking at the rectangular screen, the close up of his face, though she kept her hand on the side of the phone. As if she wanted to touch him, even if she couldn't look at him. The yearning line of her body, the way she had her chin tilted toward him, suggested he wasn't imagining that.

As her red silky hair fell forward on her pale shoulder, the scent of it lingered in his olfactory memory.

"Sing that song," she said.

"Which one?"

"I don't care. Whatever you think works."

He chose Tim McGraw's "Maybe We Should Just Sleep On It," because he knew all the words. When he reached the second verse, she rose, shoved the straps off her shoulders and let the nightgown fall to the floor.

As she braced her hands on the chair back, turning partly away from him, she was a heart-stopping pin-up, with all her erotic curves and that mane of fiery hair. But she wasn't teasing him. The light tracked perspiration on her back.

"The meds, side effect. Just sudden waves of heat. Like early hot flashes. Keep singing." She turned her chin toward her shoulder so he could hear her. She'd left the phone propped on a vanity shelf.

"Okay." He pushed away the automatic desire to reassure, comfort, ask questions. That wasn't what she wanted. He kept singing to her. Though his off-tune rendition would make Tim McGraw send out a cease-and-desist so Neil could no longer mangle his song, she didn't feel that way. She rocked to the rhythm, slightly ahead of the beat. As he finished what he could remember, she spoke again. While he heard the strain in her voice, there was pleasure, too. Plus a desire to tease him.

"For a Dom, you take orders well."

"Occupational hazard. But since I am a Dom, I can increase the scope." He let his fingers hover over the screen. Not touching it, but outlining the subject matter.

"I'm trailing my fingers down your back," he said. "A slow, easy glide. Your skin, slightly damp, so soft. Back up, under your hair, then back down again."

As he spoke in the soothing, sensual murmur, he noted her rocking slowed down. She was getting easier with it, less tense as he moved between words and humming a repeat of the song lyrics. "Over your shoulders, upper arms, back to the neck... Cupping my fingers over it, stroking. Gathering up your hair and then letting it go so I can watch it tumble down your back..."

Her body's movements now followed and responded to the suggested touch of his hands, increasing his desire to be there in person. She gathered up her hair and did what he'd described, dropping her head back as her hair cascaded down, almost reaching that tender seam between her buttocks.

"You're killing me, Mistress. My hand is sliding forward, around your throat, stroking your pulse, your chin, over your parted lips."

Her voice was throaty. Husky with need. "Keep touching me."

"Always, bébé."

Neil came back to the present. He was sliding his fingers back and forth across the table, imagining her skin, the same way he had on the phone. He thought of how her body had moved as he visually touched her with his voice.

He'd told Dodge he was in deep with her, that he wanted to be with her. He also knew he was a damn good operator.

The marriage thing hadn't been the joke he'd made it out to be. Neil was trained to make impactful decisions based on a rapid evaluation of all available factors. He didn't need traditional markers, or some arbitrary time range, to know what Abby "would become" to him. The bond was already set. Because of that, if Abby hadn't had that support network, no matter how Neil felt about his job, he would have resigned without hesitation. He didn't spit on Fate's choices. Not when they were that in his face.

But she did have a good support network. As Dodge had pointed out, him resigning might not be what she wanted—or needed. In a firefight involving his brothers, the first, primal urge was to run into it, to unleash hell. But taking that vital second to evaluate was critical. Did they need help, and if they did, where and how? What was the best way to get the mission done, and everyone back home safe?

Those decisions sometimes required locking down emotion, setting aside anyone else's definition of bravery, intelligence, expectations or standards. The decision had to be defined by the people involved in it.

That thought brought him to another possibility. The one he didn't want to consider, but to support her as he knew he should, it had to be faced. Neil needed to be prepared to do it, which meant he needed to prepare his team leader, too.

Pushing back from the table, Neil went to look for Dodge.

Each morning when she woke, Abby fought through the fog by latching onto a thought of Neil. This morning it was the memory of his last phone call, the one where he'd sung Tim McGraw to her, in that deep, sexy off-tune croon of his, his Southern drawl tagging the uneven notes.

Then there'd been the visualization he'd laid out for her, his voice rough with desire. She could feel his hand sliding along her back, stroking her hair. After their call had ended, she'd left the gown on the floor, gone to bed with her arms wrapped around herself, imagining his body behind her, his arm over her, heavy and strong.

She kept her eyes half shut, letting the morning light coming through her bedroom windows bring the features in the room into focus. She could predict what kind of day it was going to be by how she got out of bed. Sometimes she had to struggle, like she was swimming out of the deep end of a pool filled with molasses. Other times, she erupted from the mattress as if electric cables were wired to the springs.

Today was a molasses day. Once she was vertical, she took the requisite handful of pills and reached for her journal. In it, she documented the details Maureen used to guide any medication adjustments.

Those details included the day's rating. *One* meant Abby felt like she was squashed under a boulder every time she moved. *Ten* if she was a monkey on speed. *Five* was something approaching normal.

Today was a three, since it took about fifteen minutes to get headed toward the bathroom. She was going into the office today. She needed to meet with a couple staff members, show them things she couldn't via screen or phone call. She was the head of a department. She had to act like it as long as she could.

She really missed work. She missed being a part of the flow, rather than a fish thrown up on the bank, flopping, gasping to its death as all of them swam by, looking at her with pity. Or not looking at all, because they were focused on the current, not even seeing her. But if she had to choose, she'd go with that one. She didn't want to be the center of anyone's attention.

She'd been doing mostly drive-bys at the office since Ros had held "the meeting." Part of it was due to dealing with her symptoms and treatments. The other part was a suggestion from Ros, giving the others time to digest the information, work it out among themselves.

Because her energy level had plummeted and symptoms got hairy on the night Ros held the dinner at her house for all of them, Abby had told her to go ahead and do it without her. Another opportunity for them to talk things out without worrying about Abby's feelings or reactions.

But if Maureen could help stabilize her, Abby would ask Ros to have a second dinner, where she could meet with her friends, let them say to her what they wanted to say, no holding back. She had things to say, too, to give them what peace she could.

Reaching the bathroom, her gaze skated over the column of post-it notes stuck along the right side of the mirror. The top one was the title for the list, done in a vivid purple marker. *Things I must do every day, no matter what my mind tells me.* Her gaze ran down the other notes. *Shower. Brush teeth. Put on clean clothes that match. Eat meals. Drink water. Take meds on schedule.*

She'd always had an organized closet. But now she'd reduced her hung-up daily wear to about a dozen combinations, the sets separated by six inches so all she had to do was go in the closet and grab one, no thought necessary to picking out her clothes. Even so, she had more notes pinned up in there to help her stay on track.

Having watched the movie *Conspiracy Theory*, she wondered if her house would become like the apartment of Mel Gibson's character, Jerry, papered with notes that seemed like scribbled nonsense to anyone on the outside.

The outside of her mind.

As she took her shower, she thought about Neil's promise to take her to a girls' softball game when he returned. An unexpected adventure. She brushed her hair, pinned it up. Sat down on the tub edge, looked at the notes again. *Oh, brush teeth. Got it*. Back up in front of the sink.

This group of meds was making her feel...odd. Fuzzy. She didn't like that. She'd tell Maureen. But first she needed to go to work.

Neil had figured out looking at the screen was hard for her. Only a few weeks ago, that had to do with the same issue she experienced with photographs or looking at people's faces. Now there was an additional issue. Wi-fi.

If the device was connected to wi-fi, sometimes the voices told her someone would use that connection to come and get her. But when he'd been singing to her, and she'd been listening to his voice, imagining his touch, that feeling hadn't interfered. He was a SEAL, so the connection was very secure.

She had no meeting with Maureen today, because the psychotherapist was in Tennessee for a meeting. Abby would text her about the fuzziness, ask her if they could adjust the med when she returned.

She changed her mind about that once she boarded the quieter mid-morning trolley to get to work. Her energy changed direction, started to climb. Things started to come into focus. A little more sharply than needed, but it would help her prepare the numbers she needed to give Cyn this morning for her staff's client presentation.

Since she hadn't managed to get out of bed in time to do her morning run, she'd brought her exercise clothes so she could do it on the way home, rather than taking the trolley. She was fighting to maintain an exercise regimen. Endorphins and serotonin played a critical role in dealing with the debilitating drag of depression. Exercise might take a huge effort to get going on it each day, but it was a simple act. Any simple act that helped maintain focus and perspective was good.

Plus, when Neil got back, she wanted to go running with him in the park, give him a decent workout.

At some point, she'd have to decide what to do with her car. The most logical choice was to donate it to Laurel Grove, the domestic violence shelter she and Ros had founded after Laurel's death. They'd make sure it was put to good use. She should visit it once more anyway, before...

The sudden tight feeling in her chest reminded her of all the final decisions she needed to make. In planning for the big things, she'd overlooked how many details would pile up at the door during these final weeks.

Details that would have to be resolved by a woman using post-it notes to remind her to shower and brush her teeth. Without them, and that purple title note, ordering her to do them each day no matter what, she might not, especially if she was tired or spaced out.

When she arrived at the office, she entered through the staff's breakroom. The appetizing scent of coffee literally pulled her over the threshold. She'd always had a healthy love of caffeine, but lately it had become more important to her than life itself. No surprise. For her grandmother, it had been cigarettes, one practically lit before the other burned out. Her mother had mixed it. Coffee and cigarettes.

"Good morning, Miss Rose." The cheerful chirp came from Lindi, a promising intern in line to be a full hire when her schooling finished. If she still wanted to be here, that is. It was hard to anticipate what might change for Lindi, especially at her present age.

Right on the heels of what Abby hoped was a suitable greeting, Lindi rushed on, failing to mask the urgency behind her cheerful tone. "Cyn was just mentioning your numbers for the ten o'clock meeting. Can I make you a cup of coffee and bring it up to you while you get them printed?"

"Scuttle along, mini-Ros." Bastion's deep voice cut in. "That's my job, and you have work to do."

Something happened in Abby's peripheral vision, a hesitation, a brief flash of tension. By the time she turned in that direction, Lindi was gone and Bastion was standing by the pot of coffee, pouring some in Abby's preferred Mardi Gras World mug.

He was as handsome as always, in brown slacks and a shirt the rich color of palm tree oranges. It outlined his powerful shoulders. His belt had the same well-oiled shine as his brown oxfords, and his long, dark hair was combed back from his sculpted features. The braided tail fell to the middle of his back.

"Getting coffee for me isn't your job, either, Bastion."

"The scope of an admin's job is far beyond anything that can be written down, honey, and you were staring at the pot like you might toss in a straw and drink it straight from the carafe. You got those numbers?"

Abby frowned. "I moved them into the client's shared file before I went to bed last night." At three in the morning, followed by two hours of fitful sleep.

"Oh." Bastion's puzzlement turned into another easy smile. If she looked closely enough, she'd likely find his dark brown eyes assessing her in that way she didn't particularly enjoy, but it was to be expected now. Maybe there was a practical reason so many mentally ill people stopped looking directly into people's faces. "I'll re-check," he said.

"I'll get up to my office and make sure I transferred them." She sighed. "The little monkey men probably invaded my computer and took the spreadsheets to Saint-Tropez."

"You can't argue with their choice of vacation destinations."

During her "drive-bys," Skye, Vera and Bastion's methods of coping with her, at least in the office, had involved staying positive and upbeat. Initially their efforts had come off a little awkward. Today, though, Bastion's sincere humor worked, no matter the more contentious reactions she expected were moving through his mind.

Cyn had avoided her altogether.

"Nice to have you with us today," he added. It was as if he'd realized, at almost the same time she had, that this was the first time they'd had a mostly "normal" conversation since they'd found out. He handed her the coffee. "High test. You'll need it."

On this group of meds, her attention and energy levels could be like a staticky phone signal. Fortunately, his relaxed reaction brought clarity back, with such force it was like being slapped by an ocean wave.

She'd set her coffee down to add sugar, but now she straightened, frowning. "I'm the hold up. That's why Lindi is acting like she has fire ants in her underwear. You're waiting on my numbers to finalize the client packets."

"Don't stress. I have everything printed and laid out. Soon as you shoot it to me, I'll run the copies, slip it in and do the bindings. It'll be done, like this, this, and this."

He snapped his fingers on the first two utterances and executed a dramatic clap of his hands for the last.

The clap sounded like a shotgun fired into the Grand Canyon. It was still echoing through her when he approached, laid a hand on her arm. "Abby?"

She suspected he'd said her name a couple times. The meds must be exacerbating certain noises, sensory input. Obscuring others. It was okay. She gave him a shaky smile. "Glad I wasn't holding the coffee. Go into my shared file to get the numbers."

"I don't have your latest password."

"John Nash. All lower case, one word. Before I leave today, I'm going to give you all my passwords."

She squeezed his arm, gave him a direct look as difficult as staring into a sunlamp. The cloak on his emotions dropped, revealing his pain —and how much he cared.

"Thanks, Bastion." As she left him, she felt his hand on her back, a helpless caress but also a sign of support. Moving out of the kitchen took her to the back stairwell door. She knew how many stairs it was to her office, how many steps down the hallway. The blue and gray carpet picked up the wall and trim colors. Gleaming chandelier lights. She loved working in a place that had been a grand and graceful home from a previous century. Vera said sometimes she could feel the spirits of the families who had lived here, swirling in their dresses and coattails, living the lives they'd lived then.

She'd passed her office, and couldn't remember why. She looked down at her feet, realizing she'd stopped. A glance right told her she'd come to Cyn's office, and then the reason for her being here kicked back in.

Their senior account manager was standing, tapping something into her phone, probably a last-minute text to one of her staff regarding the meeting. She lifted her gaze at Abby's appearance.

"I have the numbers for Bastion," Abby said. "He's ready to put them in the packets for the client. You'll be all set for your meeting."

"Fine." Cyn's stare seemed a million miles away. Abby squinted to bring her into better focus.

Cyn had been raised and shaped in one of the roughest parts of New Jersey. While she demonstrated infallible professionalism with clients, she could also use her personality like a blunt instrument. Her diamond-hard beauty and intimidation factor as a Domme made for a surprisingly good fit with the account director position. Her sales staff were eager to please and impress her, because she rewarded initiative and intelligence as liberally as she shredded incompetence and carelessness.

Her particular knack for handling their powerful businessman clients was based in qualities the men themselves perhaps couldn't quite grasp, but the other four women certainly did, with no little amusement.

Amusement Abby didn't feel right now. Cyn's anger was overwhelming. The most overused and disliked word in Abby's vocabulary right now, because it applied to so many things.

Brushing her teeth, for God's sake.

She turned and walked away, toward her office. As she did, she thought of being in Neil's boat, just drifting through the bayou, him at the wheel, her lying on deck. Reaching back to link fingers with him as he steered one-handed.

She missed him. His quiet core. Would she want him as much if she didn't settle around him, feel a peace that was eluding her elsewhere? Why did it matter if that was the truth? When everything was on a dwindling timeline, what mattered started to become a much shorter list.

Maybe she'd start a new chain of post-it notes with that title. *List of what still matters.*

"Why do you care?"

The sharp comment drew her out of her head. She'd returned to her office, but hadn't yet crossed the threshold. Turning, she saw Cyn standing at the door of her own office. The account manager's sleek warrior body was clad in trim black slacks and a red plaid vest. It picked up the hints of auburn in the riotous tumble of her dark burnished hair.

"I'm sorry?" Abby responded, mystified. *Go, easy, Cyn. Go easy. I can only handle so much.*

She hated the thought, the weakness, but the alternative was worse. A volatile acid started to churn as Cyn stalked the few steps toward her. If she didn't have the doorframe at her back, Abby would have retreated, trying to prevent the invasion such a determined advance felt like.

"Why aren't you running off to an island? Doing a tour of Vegas? Spending your days eating ice cream, walking in a forest, whatever the fuck you do when you're about to die? Oh, wait, that's right." Cyn's sarcasm was sharper than a blade, slicing into Abby's center. "That's what a *terminally ill* person would do. You're not dying. You're a suicide. They don't pull their heads out of their asses to appreciate anything or anyone in their lives."

A schizophrenic mind could freeze. Stop, the consciousness gone somewhere else. Small gaps of time, enough to make a friend think she had no response to give.

Cyn gave her a disgusted look, then pivoted, returned to her office. Abby heard her on her phone. "Bastion, don't pick up the meeting pastries. I'll walk over and get them. I need to get out of here for a few minutes."

The phone slammed down and then Cyn was out of the office, keys in hand. She didn't look toward Abby as she passed her and strode toward the back stairwell. The door swung shut with a small whoosh of air, bringing the historic house scent that fresh paint, carpet and modern furniture could never completely conceal. The history of what had been here, what they'd built upon.

The medication was supposed to help with mood swings, the precipitous highs and abyss lows, keeping her on a more even keel. But this was a new cocktail. Untested by extremes.

Until now.

Abby put her laptop in her guest chair. She was aware of Skye coming down the hall, Vera standing in the doorway of her own office. They'd heard the exchange. Abby left them doing the silent ping pong game with their expressions, the way Bastion and Lindi had. Abby shook her head as Vera said something. She went through the back stairwell door.

Her lassitude really had vanished, energy riding that red wave. It felt good, mighty. She was ready to swing onto the back of a dragon, go to battle, set the world on fire. She flew down the stairs so fast she tripped once or twice, but she had a good hold on the rail.

Sparks rippled through her veins as she took the exit into the side garden, made her swift way into the back parking lot. Cyn was just reaching the door of her pickup truck. It was big enough to require a handrail to get up into it, and she had a gun rack in the back window. While Cyn did have a rifle, she didn't carry it in the truck. Instead, she had a stiff single tail whip resting there, one side coiled in a circle and bound with a red ribbon. A pair of handcuffs was threaded onto the whip, held to the center of the braided length by a piece of red Japanese bondage rope.

When men pulled up beside Cyn in traffic, ready to make some snarky comment, most of the time they swallowed it. Or they outright fled, recognizing that she looked more than capable of getting out of the truck and giving them a proper thrashing.

One that they might just thank her for.

"Hey!"

When Cyn turned, Abby strode toward her. "You know where I live. If you're this pissed, you could have come over, talked this out with me, asked whatever you want to ask. Instead of ambushing me here with attitude."

"You've made your decision," Cyn fired back. "Long ago, apparently. So why the fuck would I care to do that?"

The energy between them was popping with heat. When Cyn's eyes narrowed, Abby felt an alarming surge of jubilation that felt...so good. She couldn't call it back. And Cyn didn't stop talking.

"I told Ros I'd try to honor her wishes, about not pushing you too hard. I have that much respect for what you're going through. But you get in my face like this, and don't show respect for what this means to *us*? Fuck you. I'm not playing that shit. You don't want to deal with my attitude, don't fucking come to the office."

Cyn was getting too close, too loud, but Abby rode that wave, too, exultant. "Fine. Unleash the beast. Forget Ros. Stop being an emotionally constipated cunt. Don't hold back. Let me have it all."

Cyn's shock was replaced with full-on rage. Good. "How do you justify checking out and leaving us? Leaving Ros, after she had to lose Laurel the way she did? The way we all did?"

In terms of an emotional blow, it qualified as an upper cut, knocking her back a step. Abby knew it had been coming, but it still jarred her to hear it said out loud. She, Ros and Laurel had been so close in college they'd considered themselves a trinity. Until Laurel's abusive husband killed her.

She rallied. "Maybe you could try just listening, try to understand."

Something she'd told Ros plenty of times about Laurel, and then Laurel had ended up dead anyway. While Abby still wrestled with her own guilt over it, it was less than Ros's. Because Abby had always understood a person's right to make choices no one else remotely agreed with.

"No." Cyn made a slashing movement with her hand. "I'm not ever going to listen and understand what you're planning. I'm not giving you the easy out of telling you this is okay with me. Or with any of us, no matter what lies they tell you, or how they're dancing on eggshells to make *you* feel better."

A fitful breeze made the trees over them sway, drop a few cupped oblong leaves on the truck's hood. Cyn's dark hair scudded across her face, but the curls didn't obscure the fury in her snapping eyes. "I've lived through plenty of shit that makes people lie down and decide to die. I kept going, got to the here and now. You're every bit as strong as I am. Stronger. I didn't give up."

"Giving up? What do you think this is like? Holding onto a cliff edge until help arrives? Or finding the strength to pull yourself back up? There is no path out of this, Cyn. None. This is where I am, for the rest of my life."

"Screw this," Cyn muttered, turning away. "If you're going to do this to yourself, then you'll do it."

"I don't need anyone to lie to me to make me feel better, Cyn. I want *you* to feel better; that's all I've got left to give. So...hit me. Violence always helps level you out."

Cyn's head whipped around, her eyes widening. But Abby had already moved in, shoved her off the truck's step plate. Cyn fended her off, eyes narrowing. "Stop it, Abby."

"What?" Abby scoffed. "Don't want to hit a crazy person? Or is it because I've kicked your ass when we've sparred? You don't want it to happen here, with everyone pressing their noses to the windows?"

Cyn's fist snapped Abby's head back, made her stumble a few steps. She blocked the next punch, drove her fist into Cyn's abdomen. The muscles there were almost as resilient as Neil's.

While Cyn knew more advanced fight techniques than Abby, Abby was a classic fighter, methodical and even-tempered. Even today, when she was in a maelstrom, she held onto the center, backed off after they'd exchanged three good contact blows. Cyn's lip was bleeding. The ache in Abby's jaw said she'd have a bruise there by tomorrow.

"You're right." Cyn's bloody lip curled, her eyes on fire. "That did make me feel fucking better."

"Then do it again. Hit me until it eases your pain. Your confusion, your inability to make it make sense. If I could do it, I would. You're right. You've fought hard things. Your own reaction to them, your despair. But how do you escape the monster, the enemy, when it's permanently inside your head, when it's never going away?"

Abby's voice was hoarse, not as strong as she'd intended it to be. As she saw the light of battle die out of Cyn's eyes, a sure sign she finally had her friend's attention, she prayed for the ability to say what she needed to say. Fortunately, it seemed the gods had given her this crystal-clear moment. The clouds cleared, brightening an already sunny sky, putting that extra heat on her shoulders, light sharpening things around her.

"Don't ask me to live as a shadow of who I was, Cyn. Out of all of us, I know you understand what kind of hell that is. To have your choices taken away. I would never ask that of you, or anyone else."

Cyn had turned away, but she wasn't retreating. Abby closed the distance. She put her hands on Cyn's arms. But then Cyn whipped her head toward Abby. Their eyes were so close. The darkness of Cyn's yanked at Abby's, pulling them into their depths.

She let go of Cyn, stumbled back, clapping her hands over her eyes. She spun away, sought the light, the patch of sunlight that was clear of shadows. If she could find that...

"Abby?"

There. She dropped to her heels in that bright square patch, the heat resonating from the asphalt. She put her arms over her head. The colors, scents and sounds pelted at her, but she would get this out. She could. Pride wasn't as important as it once was, but Cyn needed her strength now. Her words.

"I can get it out. Let me get it out."

She sensed Cyn said things to her, but Abby didn't hear them. She felt Cyn hovering over her, though, all that anger mixed with helplessness, with fury and pain.

Welcome to my fucking world.

The words came tumbling out, a fast stream. Because she was rocking, her voice rose and fell as if she was trying to talk while running. "No escape from a battlefield when you *are* the battlefield. It's your own body and brain versus your heart and soul, and most of the strength for your heart and soul comes from the strength of your body and mind. You tell yourself none of it's real. Yet it feels so real, you can't stop yourself from reacting to it that way."

She dropped her head lower. Her breath was a harsh rasp. Everything was disintegrating. Shit, shit, *shit.* She was going to lose today. Was it the drugs? Was it the illness? She couldn't think straight. The fight was quickly moving to the negative number column in her journal. She needed to go home. But she had to get this out. Cyn, her extreme reaction, her extreme opposition, had brought forth the truth, in the rawest, most honest way Abby could voice it.

She needed Cyn to hear her, and anyone else who was listening. She hoped to God the words were coming out the way she heard them in her head.

"That fight goes on and on and on, every day. Sometimes it's okay, for just a little while, but just as you think you're going to have a good day, it jumps back out at you. There's no day completely without it, or anticipating it, or dreading it. You can't plan for it. All you know is it will probably come when you least want it to. It's exhausting."

So exhausting, she had no words for it. Death was a welcome sleep when you were that tired.

"It's not a fight, Cyn. If it was a fight, you're right, you're right about the fight. I have might, but it's not right..."

She hit the side of her head with the heel of her hand, three sharp blows, a reset. "It's not a fight. It's drowning, trying to keep your head above water in a whirlpool, trying to keep from being pulled down, knowing it's going to happen because the body has limits, even if the mind doesn't."

Cyn was down on the asphalt with her, her hands on Abby's shoulders. "Stop. You're surrounded by people with goddamn life jackets, a life raft."

"It doesn't work that way. It doesn't. Just...talk to me, Cyn. Get it out. Say it. I can take it. I just can't handle your silence."

Abby pushed away, tried to get to her feet. She swayed, and Cyn steadied her, though her friend's face was rigid, her touch cold. She stepped back once she was sure Abby could stand on her own.

These women were her friends. Even as she was acting so crazy in front of them, they saw her. Cyn was fighting with her. Arguing with her. She wasn't letting Abby become the disease, wouldn't give her any out like that. Not now or ever.

Christ, she'd chosen the strongest and best kind of family, of sisters.

For Cyn, Abby stood up straight in the storm, held onto this spot on the earth. No matter that it was ready to tilt and make her slide right off, her gravity connection gone. The parking lot was skewed, the fence at a forty-five degree angle.

Hold. Just hold until she says what she needs to say.

"Goddamn you," Cyn said, her voice choked. "While I was becoming your friend, you already knew your check-out date. I can never forgive you for that. I don't want...I just don't want to see you anymore, until it's over and done. It hurts too damn much. I don't want to. I love you too much to let you go, and I don't care if that makes me a selfish bitch. I've lost too many things I love."

Abby understood. She was okay with brutal honesty, more than Cyn realized. She was already bleeding out.

"Okay," Abby said. "Okay." She wanted to touch her again, but Cyn was staring at her from a football field away. Or maybe it was just a foot. It didn't matter. "I'll make this my last day. Do the rest of things from home. I hope...you know where I am, if you want anything from me."

She turned and started back toward the building. She made it ten unsteady steps before she heard a crunch of booted heels approaching. She started to turn, but a yelp broke from her as arms were abruptly wrapped around her, forcefully enough that it drove her to her knees. Cyn was holding her tight, face buried against her back.

"Damn you," the other woman was muttering. "I hate you so much. I didn't mean it."

Cyn was strong, and Abby couldn't get her arms free. It spiked a swirl of terror through her. "Cyn...let me go. Now. Please."

Fortunately, Cyn registered her reaction and released her immediately. Abby scrambled a few feet away, not caring that she was scoring the fabric of her slacks or scuffing her own heels. As she struggled to breathe, she saw Cyn was still where she'd let her go, on folded knees, her hands braced on them. She looked almost as wiped out as Abby felt. A reminder that she wasn't the only person having sleepless nights over this.

Only it was because of her.

"I know I'm a bitch," Cyn said, low. "I know the way I feel, that's about me, not you. Doesn't change anything, any more than you can change the way you feel. I get it. I love you, and I hate you, because I love you."

"And they say I talk crazy." Abby's chuckle sounded like a rusty door, but she won an answering flash of amusement in Cyn's eyes.

She'd take the small wins.

As they sat there, Abby closed her eyes, sifting through what was happening in her head. She'd worked on that with Maureen, the psychotherapy side of things. She was able to pull the voices back down, but that storm, the rumble of it through her...her anxiety level was rising, and that didn't bode well. Time to go home.

She realized Ros was there, and Vera and Skye. She struggled to say something...normal. "It's probably close to ten and nobody picked up the pastries."

"Yeah, I'm sure we'll lose the whole account over it." Cyn rose, approached her. Abby held out a hand, a slow up and down movement, the sign of keeping things low, slow. Cyn understood, dropping to a more sedate pace, though electric energy still sparked off her. Abby could see it. Pretty, pretty lights.

Not real. Delusion. *Focus*.

"I just can't deal with this, Abby."

"You don't have to. As I said, I'll—"

"No to that, either." Cyn's eyes were sad and tired. "You be whatever you have to be for all this bullshit. Come here as often as you need or want to. I don't want you to feel alone."

She dropped to her heels, and when she offered her hand, Abby turned hers palm up, left it on her knee. That was as far as she could coordinate while she was trying to manage everything else, but Cyn understood. She gripped Abby's hand, squeezed it with bruising strength. "I've said my piece for now. I fight, Abby. That's what I know. So there's nothing in me that will ever understand this. I believe what's after death is death. Oblivion. I'm not signing up for that voluntarily, no matter what."

"You can't approach life as a fight, because you'll tire out long before life does." Vera dropped to her heels next to the two of them. She rested a hand on Cyn's shoulder, giving it a light squeeze. "I'm not even going to discuss the HR nightmare of what just happened in this parking lot. I'll have to remind the staff of our zero-tolerance policy toward workplace violence."

"Blah-blah-blah and blah-de-blah. That's all they'll hear. I bet one of them videoed it on their phone. It will be on the Internet tonight."

Cyn wiped the blood off her lip and squinted up at Ros, who had drawn closer, Skye at her elbow. "She landed a good punch, boss. I'd forgotten how well she fights."

Abby lost the thread of the conversation as they talked around her. Over her. Through her. No, she was part of the conversation. But now that the adrenaline was settling, her jaw throbbing, the heat of the asphalt was penetrating. The voices were blurring, and then...

She was up and moving back. "What?" It was the breeze, the wind rising. Oaks creaking. She spun around at the wet, clicking noise behind her. Nothing. But she could hear them. The whispers, a sudden cruel laugh that sent fear threading through her stomach. She put the heel of her hand to her head again, a thump. *Get back. Move back. Leave some room in there.*

"Abby?" Ros was at her elbow. Ros's scent. "You okay?"

"Wet, clicking. Like...crabs. Crabs dancing in my body, in my grave. Crazy poetry. Numbers. Based on numbers. Bastion needed numbers... Pastries are the key. Don't."

She flung off Ros's touch and put her hand back to her head. "Ssh. Stop it. Stop it."

"How about I take you home, Abby?"

"Numbers. Always numbers. Waiting."

"We'll handle that. Bastion has the numbers. He got them off your computer."

"Abby." Cyn had spoken her name. Abby turned her way, registered the alarm. "Are you okay? I didn't mean to..."

"Recalibration. If only it was that easy." Abby laughed, hit herself in the head again. It kept the voices jumping, unable to grab hold, to start talking, so she kept doing it.

Hands were on her, trying to make her stop. She shrieked and moved back. Too quick and violent. She went down. Palms scraped. Smell of asphalt.

"It's all right. She came in looking pretty rough," Ros was saying, a low murmur, as if Abby couldn't hear her. That was how you knew you were crazy. People started talking around you.

Abby sat on the asphalt, feet braced. Hands on her knees. "Going home. Need to plant the wifi. Make sure it doesn't grow. Salt in the earth. Salty death."

"Did you take your meds this morning?" Vera was asking. Calm, relaxed. Not touching her. She'd drawn the others back. Abby latched onto the smoothness in Vera's voice. The others were emanating more volatile vibes.

"Fuzzy. Molasses brain. Yes. I think." Or had she imagined taking them? She ran down the column of notes on her mirror. Teeth, hair, shower...meds had been next. Or first? And breakfast. Had she done that? She wasn't hungry, but she didn't feel full.

"Do you want to go home?" Ros asked.

"Yes. Home. Plant wi-fi. And zinnias. Boat. Need the boat. Grow zinnias in the boat, in the bayou."

"Okay. We'll take my car."

There was some conversation happening around her, getting lost in the fog. That clicking, that horrible clicking, was getting louder.

She squinted again, trying to focus. Someone helped her up, but she pulled away fast. With dragging footsteps, she followed Ros. Screenshots passed by, rotated. Cyn's worried, painful expression, Skye's softer one. Vera, trying to look calm and even, but so much pain, the storm there beneath the surface, for all of them.

Ros was talking to Cyn, puzzle pieces...presentation.

"Tip, tilt...numbers. Tiptoe through the numbers."

"Yes, I'll make sure Sonja handles that." Cyn had understood her. Sonja Tiltwell was Abby's right hand in the finance area.

Her feet were getting leaden, the more she moved toward the car. Skye had drawn closer, was rubbing her back. Abby twitched away, but Cyn had the door open, was behind her. Why were they hemming her in?

"Move back...get away. Far away."

Vera was on Abby's other side as Ros took the driver's seat. The HR manager put a hand on Abby's arm. "It's okay, Abby. Can you get in the car?"

Get in the car, they will lock you up.

Momma, please get in the car. They'll take you somewhere to make you feel better.

Where your brain won't matter anymore. Where they'll forget you, where you'll forget yourself.

She nodded. "Okay."

When Vera stepped back, Abby shoved Cyn, hard, knocking her into Skye. They grabbed for her, confirming that was what they wanted. To hold her, take her. They disappeared. Just as she suspected, they weren't her friends. It was the things with clacking pincers and wet noises, tearing flesh, melting into the shadows where she couldn't see them, but she could hear them.

She ran.

She ran through the gardens, around the building. The gate, the gate was locked, but she got over it, though the pineapple shaped points on top hurt her arm. But she was free of the cage. She heard the screech of tires, horns, felt the heat of dragons blasting against her, but it didn't matter.

She was free. They couldn't put her anywhere. On a shelf, wrapped in cotton, unable to breathe.

But now she was in a world she didn't recognize. The monkey men were running with her, holding dead fish in one hand, flopping loosely. As they held her numbers in the other, their chatter and maniacal laughter surrounded her, choked her.

They took everything else away.

CHAPTER SIXTEEN

Neil drove straight from the airport to Thomas Rose Associates. The post-op briefing in VA Beach had concluded early. Recognizing the unpredictability of his schedule, Abby usually gave him a general idea of her day via text or email, for when he was able to check either. So he knew she'd intended to go into work.

When he saw the NOLA PD unit out front, he left the truck parked behind it and went over the gate rather than calling for a pass-through code. He was at the front steps in a heartbeat. The several staff members gathered on the porch looked startled by his dramatic entrance, but Bastion met him halfway down, crushing out a cigarette and tucking the butt into an empty soda can. The man looked serious and stern, someone not to be fucked with. Neil could hear raised voices behind the front door. Ros and possibly the officers. Maybe Cyn.

"Good timing," Bastion said. "Welcome home."

"What's going on? Where's Abby?"

"She ran off."

"What?"

Drawing him onto the porch, Bastion positioned them close to one of the tall windows flanking the front door. Through it, he could see a slice of the foyer, where Ros was talking to two cops, a man and a woman. Vera was at her side, though Neil noticed she seemed strategically positioned between Cyn and the officers. Cyn was leaning against the front desk, her gaze fixed on the police, her face a mask of barely suppressed anger. From the attentive posture of the male officer, who was closer to Cyn, he was aware of it. The partner was talking with Ros.

"Abby got into a fight with Cyn," Bastion said. "They resolved it, but then she had a bad episode. Started talking funny, acting out of it. They were going to take her home, and she bolted. She went over the gate like you just did."

Any emotion that wouldn't solve the problem shut down. As a result, Neil knew his voice came out flat. From the slight widening of Bastion's eyes, maybe on the wrong side of menacing as well. "How long ago?"

"About two hours. Skye, Lawrence, and several of the staff are checking all the places she might go. Her house, Ros's place, the parks and neighborhoods where she runs. She was on foot, but she could have grabbed a trolley or a bus. They've been texting me as they go." Bastion lifted his phone. "Nothing so far."

"Have they called Dr. Mo?"

"Yes. She's at a conference in Tennessee. After Ros described Abby's behavior, one of her recommendations was that we call the police." Bastion gazed unhappily through the window, watching Ros's strained body language, the impatience when they asked her something she obviously didn't consider relevant, an unnecessary delay. "They told us they can't treat a functioning adult as a missing person this early, unless other factors are involved."

Bastion's gaze turned back to Neil. "Dr. Whisnant told Ros to tell them her diagnosis. Cyn opposed that. Strongly."

Coldness entered Neil's gut as he realized why Cyn would have been against it. "She's worried the police will assume Abby's dangerous."

"Yeah." Bastion craned his neck to get a better view. "You can't tell through this wavy pre-Civil War glass, but Cyn's sporting a busted lip from the fight with Abby."

"It got physical?"

"Oh, it surely did." Bastion rolled his eyes. "These women are worse than boys in a schoolyard when they get their dander up. When the cops saw the lip, it put them on alert. Asking Cyn if she wanted to press assault charges was what set her off. She told Ros she was an idiot for calling them."

"Which didn't help."

"No. Cyn's temper is always a problem, but she's just worried, like all of us." Bastion gestured with the can. "I haven't smoked in a month. Abby... It was like she was a different person altogether. When the officer asked Ros if she could be a danger to herself or others, Ros said 'No,' but she said it so fast, it came off like she was just being loyal to her friend." Bastion paused. "I've never seen Abby like that. I don't think anyone has, not even Ros."

Ros had seen Abby that day at her home, with the appliances on the porch. Which meant this episode was worse. Just as Dr. Mo and Abby herself had predicted.

"Should I go in?" Neil forced himself to ask, when what he wanted to do was muscle in, take charge. Bastion's answer helped him sit on the urge.

"Hold off until the police are done. Emotions are kind of high. Plus, you know they always give the side-eye to a boyfriend when a woman is missing, even if she ghosted herself. They should be done in a few minutes."

Neil pulled out his phone, sent a text to Lawrence. *I'm at TRA. Where do you need me?*

The door opened as he was waiting for a response. When the two officers stepped out, he saw the woman was an older veteran, the man maybe a year or so past rookie.

"We don't want anything to happen to her," Ros was saying, her expression tight. She shot a glance over her shoulder at Cyn, who had stayed at the desk, glowering. Vera was with her, talking low.

"None of us do." The male officer, whose name plate said Rubin, spoke in a neutral tone. It held little reassurance, but it wasn't unkind. "We'll be putting the word out to all the units in the area, to keep an eye out for her."

"If you see her, what will you do?"

"We'll stop and ask if she needs assistance, evaluate from there. If you locate her in the meantime, please let us know."

Ros's lips pressed together. "Don't make me regret calling you."

"Your instincts were good, Ms. Thomas." Maersk, according to her uniform tag, reinforced her partner's guarded response. "If she is experiencing a psychotic episode, she needs help. You've alerted us to the fact she's mentally altered. That was a good call, because the more information we have about someone who may be in trouble, the better the chance we can react appropriately, keeping her and others safe."

She glanced at her partner, then added, "The department has given us some training for handling the mentally ill. We can't let her hurt someone else, but we know she's not a criminal."

Cyn shoved away from the desk. "You bet your ass she isn't. You hurt her, you do anything, I swear—"

Vera bodily put herself between Cyn and the door, kept speaking to her, with quiet urgency. Cyn shook off the hand Vera put on her arm, but when Cyn tried to get around her, Vera shifted, her tone sharpening. Though Neil didn't hear the words, he got the gist. Cyn was going to have to go through her.

The two officers exchanged a look, and then Rubin spoke, raising his voice to carry to Cyn and Vera. "If she's in trouble, ma'am, we want to help."

Cyn's expression said she had no confidence in that, but she pivoted and moved back to the desk. Vera threw a look to Ros, confirming she had this under control.

People responded to fear different ways. Some did it by getting pissed. Neil saw what Bastion did, that Cyn's guilt that their fight might have exacerbated Abby's current state, plus apprehension about how the police would handle a confrontation with Abby, were driving her current behavior.

Certain fears had their uses, but guilt dragged down response time. He curbed his impatience and hung back with Bastion as Ros finished with the officers.

As soon as they were headed down the walkway, Ros turned in the doorway, locked gazes with Cyn. "Do you really want to square off with me right now?" Her expression had gone glacial. "Because your anger is serving no fucking purpose. If you can't control it, get the hell out of my sight."

The harsh admonishment silenced all conversation on the porch. Her tone was a hundred percent alpha bitch, telling one of her pack that if she didn't stand down, she'd be knocked down, and she wouldn't get up for awhile.

Neil had seen team leaders do the same, usually toward someone less experienced, or, like Cyn, too spun up in their emotions to see straight. Knowing Ros had to be sick with worry, yet could shift gears so decisively, proved what Lawrence had told Neil about his Mistress.

You do not fuck with this woman, unless you come with serious firepower to back it up.

Cyn's eyes were still hot, her body rigid, but she didn't have that kind of firepower left. Helpless frustration flashed through her gaze, but she managed a tight nod. When Vera murmured to her, touched her arm, Cyn's shoulders slumped. She disappeared up the curved stairway to the upper levels, likely headed to her office. Staff members from the first level offices, gathered at the two archways on opposite sides of the foyer, watched the interaction with tense expressions.

Vera waved at them, a gentle nonverbal order to resume their tasks, then turned to Ros, but Ros cut her off.

"I don't have time to be her mother right now. I've got no time for that shit."

"I know, I'll handle that." Vera pointed. "I'm trying to tell you Neil is here."

Ros pivoted, surprise gripping her features. Possibly also some relief. "Neil. You're back."

"Yeah. Just now. Does she have her phone with her?"

"No. She left it here, with her purse. She typically carries a little money on her, in case she decides to jump on a trolley or bus. But I don't know if she's clear enough to figure that out." Ros's face crumpled, but only for a blink before she smoothed it, though with visible effort. "She was so messed up, Neil."

He gestured with his phone. "Munch is on his way back, him and Skye."

She moved to one of the porch chairs and sank down on it. Bastion made the same kind of gesture Vera had toward the several employees still milling on the porch. They dispersed, heading back into the building through the front or side entrances. Ros stared at the painted porch boards as Bastion came to her, put a hand on her shoulder. She covered it with her own, held it tight.

"I can't handle losing her, Bastion."

"Bullshit. You can handle anything."

"Okay. I don't *want* to handle losing her."

Ros's head came up as a vintage Mustang pulled up to the curb. The convertible had the top down, and carried Lawrence and Skye. Lawrence's gaze met Neil's.

"They've found out something," he told Ros. Though he didn't add that the news wasn't entirely good, not if they'd waited until they could deliver it face to face.

Skye preceded Lawrence up the stairs. Going straight to Ros, she dropped to a knee and gripped her friend and boss's hands, giving her an encouraging look.

"We might have a lead," Lawrence said carefully. "According to the guy at the QuikMart about a quarter mile from here, a stunning redhead in office clothes hitched a ride with a group of bikers. They happened to mention they were planning a stop at Tubby Mike's."

Neil knew it, a biker bar about fifteen miles outside NOLA.

"What?" Ros surged up from the chair. Skye rose with her, stood at her side, a hand on her back. Her own expression was somber but determined.

Lawrence held up a hand. "I called them. The bikers were there, but she wasn't. Not anymore. She came into the bar, but the noise of the place drove her back outside fast. She grabbed a ride with a local regular, driving an old light blue pickup truck with a white stripe. The bartender said while she was in the bar, she was talking a mile a minute, and kept saying 'I have to get to the boat.' They headed southwest."

Neil had been mentally mapping her progress. It sent a jolt to his center. "Christ. She's trying to get to my place."

Lawrence shifted his gaze from his Mistress. The steel calm Neil saw was the kind that had been trained into them, to deal with situations that could end up totally fucked. "Sounds like it to me."

"Let's go."

~

Ros updated Officer Maersk on the way. Lawrence took the wheel of her Mercedes and followed Neil's truck. Munch had probably suggested he drive so Ros could keep an eye out, and because of her worried state of mind. He'd also likely realized keeping up with Neil would require combat-driving skills.

As Neil left New Orleans and took the route to his place, he kept his gaze moving along the sides of the road. Just in case. He wasn't going to go into the red zone of how he'd react if something bad had happened to her. He wouldn't let his head get stuck on her being at the mercy of strangers on motorcycles or in pickup trucks, a beautiful woman out of her head. He had to turn that one over to God, to watch out for her, keep her safe. He'd seen enough to know God's job description didn't always include keeping shit from happening. But sometimes it did.

He'd tried Tommy and Dobby, but there was no answer from them. He'd passed the biker bar some miles back and had decided not to stop. Lawrence was confident they had whatever useful information they could get from that. But ten miles later, Neil hit the brakes, pulling off at a roadside dive bar that offered billiards. A battered blue pickup with a white stripe was in the parking lot.

He parked and got out, knowing Lawrence would be close on his heels. When he pushed open the door, the first thing he logged was Abby wasn't there. The couple pool tables were in better shape than anything else in the place. The plywood bar was built against the wall, and several mismatched tables for patrons looked as if they'd been pulled from a dumpster. A half-dozen men were playing a card game at one of them, while four others played pool.

All the patrons were male, and apparently the owner didn't really give a shit about the laws against smoking, because the haze was enough to make his eyes water.

The bartender sat on a stool, reading a People magazine featuring a celebrity divorce from three years ago. He sat next to a marine radio that crackled with the occasional communications between boaters, marinas and outfitters. This close to the bayou, most of the regular customers were involved in the fishing trade and related services, like Penelope's place. So it wasn't unusual for a bar or restaurant to keep a marine radio on, as a source of local news and communication.

At Neil's entry, the bartender slid off the stool, ready to take an order. They might not have ambiance, but customer service was prompt.

"Who drives the blue pick-up?" Neil asked brusquely.

"That'd be me." One of the billiard players spoke up. Grizzled-looking, probably in his late sixties, he might have been a biker himself before abuse of the bottle, obesity and age made riding a torture to his back and joints. "Am I parked illegally, officer?"

Guffaws circled the room. "Even if you aren't, Harvey," one of the poker players said, "that truck couldn't have passed a road inspection a decade ago."

"Good-looking redhead," Neil said sharply. "You gave her a ride. Where is she?"

The room stilled at Neil's tone. He was aware Lawrence had arrived, was at his flank. Then Neil took a closer look at Harvey.

"Hey!"

The man let out a shout of protest as Neil knocked the pool cue out of his hand and slammed him against the wall, one fist screwed into Harvey's T-shirt, his forearm against his throat.

"Why is your face scratched?" Neil snarled.

Chairs scraped, but he trusted Lawrence to have his back.

"I didn't do nothing to her," Harvey said, pushing against him. He paled as he realized he couldn't remove Neil's hold.

"He's trained to kill you in more ways than you can imagine, Harvey."

All gazes swiveled to the door, where Ros stood, a sleek and severe figure with her fixed expression, high heels, dark slacks and gold silk blouse. "So tell him why he shouldn't."

"Easy there, young feller. And ma'am." Harvey managed a credible nod toward Ros. He also sent a nervous look toward Lawrence, who Neil was sure looked as set on murder as himself.

"I gave her a ride. Nice way she was dressed, I figured her car was broke down somewhere. She didn't say so, but when I said I could get her to a good garage with a tow truck, she just nodded her head. We got about five miles past this place. She wouldn't talk to me, was talking to herself most of the ride, hunched against the door. I put on the radio, thinking that might help her relax, just chatted at her. I know a woman's got to be unsettled in that situation, no cell phone, out by herself."

Neil didn't step back, but he'd eased his hold, since Harvey wasn't having any problem talking. "I needed some gas, so I slowed down, turned into Nick's station, over by the old processing plant. You know the one."

He looked toward the others for reinforcement. "There's a neighborhood close to it, and the kids like to bring Nick those nickel return bottles they've collected from the drainage ditches to buy candy."

Neil heard some supporting grunts, comments, which reassured Harvey. At least until his gaze swiveled back to Neil's face. He swallowed. "Some of them had got their hands on firecrackers. They set them off, and she goes crazy. She's fighting to get out of my truck, and can't figure out the latch. It sticks, so I reach over her to let her out."

Harvey gave Neil an unhappy look. "She turned on me like a feral cat. I stumbled out of the truck just to get away from her, and she comes out after me, screaming about razors and blood. Monkey men. She ran off into the woods."

"It's acres of swamp there," Neil said. "You *left* her?"

"Neil." Lawrence's hand was on his biceps, pulling him back. "You're cutting off his air."

His arm had shifted, was bearing down on Harvey's windpipe. Neil recalled himself, let Harvey go, stepped back. Temper, letting loose the emotions he was feeling, wasn't going to help. Since he normally didn't need the reminder, it told him he needed to double down on the self-restraint.

"Me and the kids went a ways in, calling for her," Harvey said defensively. "Even Rick did. Then we figured, it's so boggy in there, she'd have no choice but to circle back out to the road. Wouldn't make sense for her to do anything else. She'd be okay."

He held out a hand that had tremors, probably a permanent result of alcoholism. "I was so shook up, I came back here to get a drink. I only stopped shaking bad a while ago. Ask these fellers, if you don't believe me."

He straightened up. Though he pulled a T-shirt that had seen better days back down over his belly, he did it with recovered dignity and a direct look. "Son, I might drink too much and get obnoxious with a woman in a bar, but that lady was in trouble. I swear to you on the Holy Bible and my momma's soul, I did not try anything with her. I was just trying to help.

"Ronnie, that's the boy with the firecrackers—he's Martha Linden's son—he got on Rick's radio and put out the notice on the public channel for the boat traffic, just in case. You know we take care of one another out here. They'll be looking out for her, make sure she gets help to fix her car."

Neil turned to Lawrence. "I know Rick's station. Let's go."

As he started to move toward the door, a familiar voice crackled over the radio, stopping him in his tracks.

"Sol's Watering Hole, Sol's Watering Hole, pick up for MeeMaw One."

Dobby.

The bartender had a wary look fixed on Neil, but he picked up. "Sol's Watering Hole here. Come back, MeeMaw One. What can we do for you?"

"We found Harvey's hitchhiker. Switch to 54 for a private channel."

"Switching to 54."

Neil was behind the bar already. Reading his body language, the intelligent bartender had the mike extended to him. Neil took it. "Dobby, this is Neil. Is Abby with you?"

"Well damn, son. God's good timing is what you got. Yeah, we have her. She's...something's wrong. We were going to get her to the local doc, but she got so worked up at that, she almost tried to jump out of the boat."

"Where did you pick her up?"

"This is the crazy part. We were gigging, and there she was, just squatting in the swamp about a quarter mile behind Rick's station. She looked like a toad herself, rocking back and forth, swatting at mosquitos. It was that red hair we saw. It...it was surreal, man."

Neil closed his eyes, sent a prayer of thanks to anyone listening. In his peripheral vision, he saw Lawrence go to Ros, clasp hands with her, a reassuring and hard squeeze. "Is she still with you?"

"Yeah. We radioed MeeMaw, and she told us to take her to your place, and that she'd come to us. So that's where we are now." A pause, a crackle of static that Neil cursed silently.

"Say again MeeMaw One. Missed that last part."

"Soon as we docked, she scrambled out of the boat and ran into the house. I'm still in the boat, and Dad's positioned himself in front of your place so we can make sure she doesn't try to leave."

"I'm on my way. I have female help with me, so if MeeMaw isn't far from her place yet, you can tell her we got it covered."

"Understood. Over and out."

Neil signed off. Turning, he saw Ros was white-faced, but relief was part of the million emotions in her dark blue eyes. Turning on one elegant shoe, she exited the building.

Neil nodded to the bartender. Though he still wasn't on board with Harvey leaving her, he knew the man didn't deserve the full dose of what he was feeling. "Thanks," he said stiffly. "Thanks for trying to look after her."

"Hope she feels better," Harvey ventured. "She seemed like a nice lady."

When Neil stepped out of the bar, he coughed out the smoke and moved toward his truck. Ros stood next to it with Lawrence. Her gaze was on the ramshackle dive, the thick woods behind it.

Everything in him wanted to go, go, go, but he had enough faith in Tommy and Dobby he could take a moment for a status check. "You okay?" he asked her. Lawrence's attention was on her, too.

"When Abby talked about her childhood, she'd tell me things like this." Ros's voice was brittle. "Stories that sounded too fantastic to be true. Her mother, a tax accountant, would end up in the dark corner of a crack house, or at a pond in the middle of nowhere, covering herself with mud to camouflage herself. No rhyme or reason. Abby was always too afraid to call the police, for fear they'd take her mother away where she couldn't care for her anymore. She'd go out to find her on her own, hitch rides with people, since she was too young to drive."

Ros's eyes glistened. "She said it was amazing, and heartening, how often people really did want to help, no matter who they were, where they came from. It made the ones who didn't, seem small and insignificant to her. One time, she hitched a ride with a man who tried to attack her. She jumped out of a moving car, ran. Limped back to the road after he was gone, hitched another ride."

Neil stared out over the back of his truck, but he was still listening. Maybe he was understanding more about why Abby looked away, couldn't meet gazes when she was feeling too much, was too overwhelmed.

"I don't want to get it," Ros said softly. "To understand why she feels the way she does. I don't. But seeing this... She's said to me, so many times, 'I don't want you to see me like that. I don't want anyone to go through that for me.'"

"We've got to go," Neil said, bringing his gaze back to them.

Lawrence nodded at Ros. "Tell him what Dr. Mo said first."

"I called her on the way here, told her what was happening." Ros sighed. "This is a full psychotic break, Neil. It can happen even when someone is on medication. Maureen said...she needs to go to the hospital, to the psych ward, so she can be monitored until she stabilizes. Maureen is on her way back, so she'll take over her supervision personally."

"Okay."

"No. Not okay." Ros snapped. The fierce frustration showed a woman at war with herself. "She made me swear. Never, *never* let her be put in a hospital."

Crap.

Lawrence said something and Ros replied, but Neil was sorting things out in his head, everything he knew of Abby so far. Maybe because he hadn't known her as long, it gave him more objectivity to see a possible path. Not an optimal one, but there were no great solutions for this scenario.

"What's the priority?" He broke into the conversation, but whatever the subject, they switched their focus to him.

Ros's brow furrowed. "What do you mean?"

"Her top reason not to want to be put in a hospital has to be a loss of control," he pointed out. "Like Dr. Mo said. The right to make decisions for herself. That's the deepest fear. If you have faith in the doc, and the doc knows getting her stabilized is what will give her back that control, then you break one promise to serve the more important one."

Ros stared at him. A single, stingy tear rolled down her cheek, and she swallowed. Though the struggle in her expression didn't ease, she stepped forward, cupped his face in manicured hands. Lifting onto her toes, she pressed her lips to his, a firm, brief kiss. "Thank you for proving why she's falling in love with you."

Stepping back, she gripped Lawrence's arm. Resolve was back in the set of her attractive mouth. "Let's go."

~

Tommy and Dobby were watching her, he reminded himself, probably for the tenth time. If anything changed, they would let him know. He didn't slacken his speed much, but he did avoid breaking the sound barrier, mainly because incurring police attention would delay them.

So many things could have gone wrong. Particularly in the swamp. That was the one getting under his skin. Even an experienced hiker or boater could get in trouble, which was why it was best to go in pairs. Yeah, he didn't, but the bayou's unpredictability was just another training ground, a really familiar one to him. But she wasn't familiar with it at all.

Snakes, alligators, bogs—hell, too many mosquito bites could make a person sick. In office clothes like what Ros was wearing, those bloodsuckers had made a meal of her.

Only when he bumped down the road to his place did his blood pressure drop. Tommy sat in a folding chair, whittling. He'd positioned himself far enough back from Neil's front porch to keep the sides of the house in view. Dobby would be covering the back in the boat, though Neil couldn't see the dock from here.

Tommy rose, raised his hand to get Neil to stop. Keeping his attention fixed on the front of the house, he backed toward Neil's open window.

"She's on the porch," he said, low. "She's kind of holed herself up there, pulled your buckets and gear around her like a barricade. A couple of the tourist boats have gone by, and the noise seems to set her off. So I'd keep your truck and its diesel engine back here."

When the Mercedes pulled in behind Neil, and Lawrence and Ros emerged, Tommy tipped his head toward them, continued to speak to Neil as they approached. His dark eyes showed concern. "MeeMaw says the girl has a brain sickness. That she felt it, that first day she came."

"Yeah."

Tommy gripped Neil's arm, unspoken support, and stepped back as Neil got out of his truck. "Dobby and I will stick around until we're sure things are okay. You going to take her to the doctor?"

Neil looked at Ros. Though she'd seemed to accept his logic, it didn't alleviate the struggle in her eyes, over betraying a friend's trust to do what seemed best for her. "Let's see how it goes," she said.

"Ask Dobby to hold his position," Neil told Tommy.

Tommy moved back to his chair, sat down and picked up his

phone to text his son. While his relaxed pose was reassuring, Neil knew the man would be watching close, ready to help.

As they approached the porch, he heard Ros's indrawn breath when she saw Abby. He felt a similar punch in the gut. He hoped Ros was as strong as Lawrence believed she was, because nothing about the next few minutes was going to be easy to bear.

Abby was crouched on her heels at the far corner. Her back was to the siding, but she was rocking against it, hands tucked against her body. Her hair was snarled, her eyes unfocused and she was muttering. Her nice clothes were torn, dirty and wet. She had scratches on her face and arms, smears of blood, where the mosquitos had gone after her.

Without the type of clothes she was wearing, she'd blend right in with the mentally ill homeless people routinely seen in downtown New Orleans.

So many emotions flooded him. But next time she was lucid, he'd be able to tell her that not a damn one of them was what she'd dreaded him feeling. Deep inside, he could *see* she was fighting. Fighting to hold onto herself, a ragdoll trying to stand and scream at a brick wall. One fragile human, bringing a persistent defiance to a challenge that would terrify anyone.

All he wanted to do was help her face it, carry as much of the load as was possible.

She shifted. Since it was his place, and he had the longest legs, he'd taken the lead onto the porch. Now he stopped, putting up a closed fist, the signal that would bring Lawrence to a halt, keep him and Ros where they were. Neil backed down the steps to them, kept his voice low.

"Stay here." He met Lawrence's eyes. "She has a weapon."

"Oh my God." Ros started forward, but Lawrence put a hand on her arm.

"Mistress," he said firmly. "Trust him. Look at her."

Ros was, and it was tearing her up inside. Abby put her free hand up on the siding, patted it, as she tipped her head up. She looked as if she were staring at something specific on the ceiling of the covered porch, tracking it. Then she ducked her head down again, huddled into herself. More rocking, more talking to herself.

As far as a weapon, Ros couldn't see what Neil could see. Abby had her other hand hidden against her lower abdomen, screened by a barrier of buckets, crab traps and a couple pairs of rubber boots.

Neil had shifted that steady blue-gray gaze to hers. "Stay here with Lawrence," he said. "No matter what."

Translation: Don't make me have to worry about another variable. She understood that, even as it was taking everything she had not to rush up there and protect her closest friend, her sister in every way that mattered. Figure out how to reach this version of Abby she'd never seen before. Hints of her, sure, but this...

This was what Abby had feared the most. This was why she wanted to take her own life. What Ros feared most was she was about to see her do it, right here and now.

Trying to hold onto calm, she remembered something else Maureen had said on the phone. "We need to find out if she took her meds today," she said, low. "She said it's important to know that."

Neil nodded. He gave his former teammate a look that Ros suspected covered a lot of things, then he mounted the porch steps again. As he did, tension flowed away from him. Within three steps, his body language was as casual and relaxed as if he was meeting her for a date.

Despite the vibration his movement across the porch had to be causing, Abby didn't seem aware of him yet, looking at things that they couldn't see, all around Neil, above him. Pointing, muttering. Humming a song Ros didn't recognize. Then ducking her head down again.

When he dropped to a squat several feet away, Abby shifted. Ros clutched Lawrence's arm. She was clutching a ten-inch chef's knife. As she started tapping the point of the knife on the ground, she kept humming.

"Hey, there," Neil said. "What's going on, bébé?"

Her eyes rolled around, moved over him, back, pause. Then away again. "They're there. They're here." She put the heel of her empty hand against her temple, tattooed it. "I'm going to cut them out. They won't stop whispering."

"What are they saying?"

"They're clicking, wet. I hate it. *Hate* it." Her hand tightened on the knife. Ros saw the muscles flex along Neil's back, preparation to move. Her fingers were pressing into the bones of Lawrence's forearm, her heart pounding as a one-word prayer went through her head. *Please...*

"Sounds awful. I think I can help. Want to dance? You're singing our song." He picked up what Abby was humming, gave it lyrics so Ros recognized it. Neil's warm and deep singing voice was off tune, but not unpleasant. "Maybe baby, I'll have you...maybe baby..."

Buddy Holly.

He'd dropped to one knee and was moving his upper body in a graceful rhythm. Ros saw Abby start to focus on that movement, her head tilted to absorb the words. The tapping of the knife began to follow the beat, the snap of his fingers, as he kept time with his singing.

Abby's head came up straight on her neck then, and she blinked, squinted at him, as if she were trying to see him through a fog.

"Home again. Away from battle. Away."

"Yeah. I came to your office to see you, but you'd already headed here. That's a nice surprise, finding you home and waiting for me."

"Home. Home." The rocking paused. Then she lunged.

Not at Neil. She leaped at something in the air around her, the knife slashing back and forth like she was stabbing at a flying insect. "Go away," she shouted, her eyes full of fear. "Get out. Stay away."

The knife sliced down toward her other flailing arm. Ros choked out a cry, was halfway up the steps before Lawrence could stop her.

Neil moved even faster. Faster than anyone she'd ever seen, and smooth, like an arc of water flashing through the air. With a lifetime of experience and muscle memory, he'd gauged his timing, a choreography of one opponent against another, and how to be the one that prevailed. Protected.

He clamped down on her wrist, pulled it out wide so the knife missed her other arm. Then he gave the wrist a sharp shake that dislodged the blade and sent it clattering to the boards. In another move, equally fluid, he'd pulled her to her feet, had a hand at her waist and turned her. Into an honest-to-God twirl under his arm that brought her back up against him in a dance pose, though his arm held her more firmly, her wrist still in his grasp.

During the distraction, Lawrence had released Ros, darted forward, secured the knife. Before Abby even noticed, he was back at Ros's side.

Their intuitive coordination told Ros how well Lawrence and Neil had worked together as active SEALs. Something that might spike her ever-present desire for her handsome sub later, but right now it translated to painful gratitude.

During the transition from knife-wielding to dance execution, Abby's face went through a horror movie montage of contortions. Rage, fear, confusion. Neil's proximity wasn't immediately taken as a good thing, but anticipating that, Neil backed off right away. He gave her some space, moving his hand to her hip, his grip on her wrist transferring to a loose hold of her hand. "I like dancing with you," he said.

Her eyes rolled back, and her knees buckled. He closed the distance again, this time lifting her and moving her out of the cluttered corner, back toward the steps. By the time he was there, she was already rousing, though she seemed strangely docile as he settled her into a seated position on the top step. Ros noted Neil remained alert, which was good, since she remembered Abby had acted quiet right before she bolted away from the car.

Abby drew her hands from him with a sharp tug. Sending him a suspicious look, she folded them back against herself, started rocking once more.

"You know who I am?" Neil asked.

Her gaze skittered over his face, out to the view of the woods. "Of course," she said impatiently. "Wind in the willow." Her face creased, struggling.

"Try again."

"'*Everything is part of me, Firmament and moving sea; I of all that is am part, Stone and star and human heart.*' Poems about oak for $500, Bob. William Henry Venable. I sought them out, all the poems, all the words of oaks. Seeking you. Neil." She fixed on him for a hard moment, then her eyes lost focus again.

While Neil's tone remained even, a light smile on his face, Ros thought if she touched him, she'd find every muscle drawn as tight as her own. "Double points for that one. How about them?" He looked toward Lawrence and Ros.

"He's her shadow killer. Ties him down, holds her up."

"Maureen is right. What she says makes sense," Ros murmured to Lawrence. Her hand rested on his broad shoulder, drawing strength, feeling it move as he nodded in agreement. The revelation provided little comfort, though.

"How about her?" Neil gestured at Ros.

"Magnolias. No! Roses. With thorns. Sharp, delightful thorns that make us bleed. Blood pure and clear."

"Clear is good."

"I need to bleed," she said to him. "Can I have your knife?"

"Maybe in a bit. I'd like to walk with you first. Will you take a walk with me, tell me more?"

Her face suddenly crumpled. "They're whispering again. I'm afraid. So afraid." She surged up, whirled around, going the opposite direction on the porch. It wrapped around on that side, followed the perimeter of the house.

Neil didn't hamper her movements, but stayed close as she moved from the back porch to the dock. Dobby sat in the captain's chair on his boat, silent, watching. He had a bottle of beer open in the cupholder and a bag of pork rinds on the passenger seat.

Abby spun so abruptly, the big man almost leaped out of the boat, as if he was ready to dive into the water and get her if she fell in, no matter that Neil was closer to her.

Abby's face went dark. She thrust a fist at Neil, as well as Lawrence and Ros, because they had followed him. She stabbed the air as if she still held the knife. "Stay back! I'll hurt you. It's not safe. Humpty dumpty. Humpty dumpty..."

She collapsed into a cross-legged position on the dock, so heavily Ros expected the impact vibrated through Neil's shoes. As Abby put her head in her hands, Neil knelt next to her. "Did you take your medications today, Abby? We need to know."

"Fur...molasses...fur. Freak has molasses on him."

"They're making her feel fuzzy," Ros guessed. "Slow."

"Abby, do you feel safe with me?" Neil asked.

She peered through strands of wet, dirty hair, squinting as if her head was hurting. "Do you feel safe with me?"

"Yeah. I do."

"Then why won't you give me your knife?"

"I'm afraid you might hurt yourself with it. It's pretty sharp. How about I cut something if you need it cut?"

Her face cleared and she thrust out her palms, hands bent back to expose her wrists. "Let them out." She said. "If I bleed, it will let them out."

The stark anguish that gripped Ros made her lean against Lawrence's supportive hand on her waist. She saw a similar look on Neil's face. But then it was smooth again. He closed a gentle but firm hand over Abby's wrist, thumb rubbing her pulse.

"I need your knife," she demanded. "To protect me. They're coming for me."

"I'll protect you," Neil responded. "No one's going to get you. I won't let them."

She pulled her hand away, closed it on her knee. "We need to cut them," she said softly, a plea. "Cut them now."

"Why don't we cut some wildflowers for MeeMaw? Put them in a vase."

"You don't have a vase." The sudden clarity in Abby's gaze was startling. As was the spurt of humor in her eyes. "Not even a coffee can." Then a shriek, and she shrank back from him, clutching her head again. "Shut up, shut up, shut up. Get out. Cut it out, cut it out *now*."

She was scrambling backwards, toward the dock edge. Neil caught her, and she kicked out, but not at him, though she landed a solid blow to his upper thigh. As he got her turned around, her back against him, she clawed at his arms, but she was doing it to hold on. She kicked out over the water, as if she had an attacker descending upon her from the air. Her terror was palpable, her pupils dilated and breath rasping in her throat as she cried out in fear.

Then the fight went internal. "Get it out, get it out!" She was hitting herself in the head, trying to claw at her eyes.

As Neil grabbed her wrists, pinned them against her, restraining his strength but using every bit of it necessary to contain her, he shot a look over his shoulder at Ros. A question demanding her answer.

Debate time over.

A hundred variables went through Ros's mind in a microsecond. Abby, trying to dig voices out of her head. The knife, which Lawrence had tucked out of sight beneath the steps. Abby wielding it wildly, almost slicing it across her own flesh. But what held the most weight was the abject fear in Abby's face. She was imprisoned by a terror none of the rest of them could see.

Never let them hospitalize me. Never.

She thought of Laurel. *It's my life, Ros. He's my choice.*

Abby was wailing, shrieking, bucking against Neil, but he had her. He'd sat down on the dock, had her in a secure hold.

Ros thought of the things she valued in her life, the choices she'd made, the paths she'd taken. How she'd feel if anyone thought they had the right to take those away.

But what if she was where Abby was right now, out of her head, not able to tell if someone was friend or foe? And there was a way to get that clarity back, though it would involve something she'd always said she wouldn't, couldn't do?

Abby would want to do it. What's more, she'd want someone to make sure that happened, if she couldn't make the decision herself.

That's why she had Ros.

When she surfaced, Abby likely wouldn't feel that way. Ros might be making a decision that could drive her friend away from her entirely. A friend who planned to depart this life only a few weeks from now.

This isn't about you, Rosalinda Thomas, she told herself fiercely. Loving someone meant sometimes doing things that would make them hate you forever.

She could waffle from now until the end of time. She had all the information to make the decision and knew what it had to be, no matter how much she wished it was otherwise. No sense in dicking around any longer.

She sent Neil a short nod.

As if the gods just wanted to fuck with her, Abby abruptly went limp, stopped fighting. When Neil eased his hold, she crumpled to the dock, her head resting against the sun warmed boards. She lifted one hand in front of her face, stared at her spread fingers. One by one she closed them, until just her ring finger remained. "I got a splinter."

"We'll get it out. Can you sit up?"

How Neil could sound so casual, as if he hadn't been locked in combat with her less than a minute ago, Ros didn't know. What was equally remarkable was seeing the same behavior in Abby, though Ros suspected her friend's calm was far less deliberate. She slowly pushed herself up to a sitting position, even let Neil stroke her snarled hair from her face. She dipped her head toward his touch.

"Tired." Her voice was muffled, her lips against the heel of his hand.

"I know, bébé. Give me your finger."

"I have to keep it. You can borrow it."

He smiled. He took a pair of fingernail clippers out of his jeans pocket. Though the gesture seemed nonchalant, Ros noted his attention never left Abby. Nor did Dobby's, still sitting close by on his boat.

Neil drew her hand up to pluck out the splinter. Abby watched, a little pain reaction crossing her features, then clearing as he removed it.

"Thank you." She looked around. "I like being at your place."

"Good. I like having you here. We need to go now, but we can come back later."

"Where are we going?"

As Neil paused, Ros suspected he was weighing the same thing she was. Tell her a lie to get her there as peacefully as possible? Or tell her the truth and risk the fight?

"We need to go to the hospital," Neil said. "So they can help you feel better. Dr. Mo said it was a good idea, and me, Ros and Lawrence agree. I think you would agree, too."

Abby started shaking her head during the first sentence, shooting apprehension through Ros's lower belly. "No, no, no. Curtains. Red blood. Red blood. Red lights...no. They swallow you and you're gone."

Just like that, the lull was over. Abby surged to her feet, Neil matching her movements. But she swung away from the dock, and stomped back toward the back porch, where Ros stood with Lawrence. Abby pointed at her, bared her teeth, uttered a saliva-spraying hiss. "Get out, get out, get out. You're not welcome here. You're not going to win. You're not going to turn me into this. You can't get in here, too. No room, no vacancy."

She started beating her head with both fists. "Too fucking much there already. You can't come in, too."

Neil closed his hands over Abby's wrists, crossed them over her chest and took her to the ground again, his body coiled tensely behind her.

Then hell really broke loose.

Abby started to scream, terrible noises like a wounded cat. She demanded they get out of her head, no red blood and curtains. She bucked and thrashed against Neil's hold without success. It was obviously not the first time he'd had to subdue someone on his own. He had his legs locked over hers, his hands holding her wrists while his arms kept her elbows pinned against her body.

But no way could he hold her like that for the long drive back to New Orleans. Not without restraints. Almost as soon as Ros had the unthinkable thought, Neil went there, too.

"Munch, bring one of my long-sleeved T-shirts," he called out. "And the handful of cloth strips in my nightstand." Abby was pleading now, crying. But the gaze that clung to Ros belonged to an enraged she-tiger, being imprisoned against her will. Ros was frozen by that accusatory stare. If she moved, she was afraid the pain striking her heart would shatter it into too many pieces to ever put it back together.

Lawrence moved swiftly into the house and returned with the items. The strips looked like they'd been torn from another T-shirt, worn and soft. "It's okay, Mistress," Lawrence murmured, touching Ros's arm as he passed her. "We've got this."

The two men worked together, using the strips to bind Abby's crossed wrists and hold her elbows close to her. Then they pulled Neil's oversized T-shirt over her head, worked it down and belted it below her arms with more strips.

Neil and Lawrence likely knew plenty of ways to render someone unconscious and leave them breathing, but Ros suspected none of those tactics were without risk. They wouldn't attempt it on someone they loved, particularly when that someone was thrashing, increasing the danger of the procedure.

Neil's training had surely taught him how to bind someone, but what Ros saw now was a different kind of skillset. The focus in Neil's eyes, the swift but careful way he handled every knot and cinch, came from a Master's experience in restraint, used to secure and protect.

When they finished, Abby's upper body was in a modified form of strait jacket, her arms bound against her in a way that would contain violent movements, make them less likely to cause her injury.

She was also lying on her side, crying. Speaking one word. "Please..."

As Lawrence sat back and looked her way, Ros somehow got her feet moving. She dropped to her knees by Abby. Neil knelt by her other side, his hand resting on Abby's hip. Though he spoke quiet words of reassurance, Abby stared into space, face streaked with tears, saliva, her nose running as she said that one word over and over.

Lawrence handed her a leftover piece of the T-shirt. Ros used it to wipe Abby's nose, her tears. Abby seemed disturbingly passive, but Ros used the lull to stroke her friend's tangled hair from her face, from the bruises and mosquito bites. As the hazel eyes rolled her way, Ros caressed her cheek.

"It's okay," she managed in a voice that somehow didn't tremble. "You're okay. We won't let anything bad happen to you."

Abby stared at her. "Too late. Go away. Get out of my head."

As she erupted again, Ros backed off with a strangled sob. If she stayed this close, she was going to tell them to untie Abby, all because she couldn't bear it, bear the responsibility that her friend had known she could handle.

She had to act. Ros straightened, left Abby in Neil and Lawrence's care. She returned to the porch and followed it around to the front.

Shutting everything else down, she listened to another voice mail from Maureen. She sent the woman a text. She couldn't trust herself to have a conversation right now. Tommy was sitting in his chair, leaning forward. She wondered if her expression looked as ancient as his. Everything that could cause pain in the world felt like it was crowded into this moment, overwhelming her with despair.

"S'okay," the man said. "You'll make it better for her."

Abby had said it wouldn't get better. For all her protestations and refusals to believe that, Ros found that certainty cast adrift. Witnessing the attack Abby's own mind had launched upon her couldn't help but make her doubt...everything.

But she managed a mute nod at the kindness, drew a couple steadying breaths. Footsteps on the porch heralded Neil and Lawrence, coming to join her. Neil was carrying Abby, cradled in his arms, swathed in his T-shirt. Her red hair draped over his elbow, her legs dangling past his hip as he strode toward their car.

She was quiet again, relatively. Muttering, angry, twitching, but not actively fighting or screaming.

"I'll ride in the back with her," he said to Ros.

She watched Lawrence open the door of her car, help Neil get Abby inside. Was this what Abby meant? Seeing everything from a distance, the pain keeping you from connecting to anything? Wanting to be numb, so you didn't have to acknowledge the unimaginable was happening to you?

She'd felt like that after Laurel's death. It had been easier to stay distant, disconnected, the grief too awful to be acknowledged, until time reduced the enormous size of it.

Lawrence was standing in front of her. Someone who could always bring her back to herself, because there was strength, comfort there. Someone to bear it with her.

In the midst of this, you feel all alone. Completely disconnected. You're moving in an alternate universe, where no one can see what you're seeing or feeling or hearing. Even if the people who care about you are standing right beside you.

Abby, telling Ros how her own mother had described it, in one of her clearer moments.

"Mistress." Lawrence touched her face. "It will be okay."

"That's what Maureen said," she answered woodenly. "She's called ahead to the psych ward at the hospital. We just have to get her there. She sounds absurdly calm and reassuring about something that is not the least bit fucking okay."

Lawrence put his hands on her upper arms, caressed her with his strong, intuitive touch. Knowing what she needed from him. "You are the only one Abby knew would be strong enough to make the right decisions when the time came, Rosalinda. This is the right one."

"If it is, it is the worst feeling, right decision in the world," she said. "I hate myself almost more than she ever could, and that's saying a lot. She didn't want this, Lawrence. She..." Her voice broke. "She didn't want this."

He pulled her into his arms, held her close. "She didn't want any of it," he murmured. "But she has the best friend anyone could ask for, to help her deal with it. I know it, and so does she. She expects me to tell you that, and not let you believe anything different. If I don't, she'll kick my ass."

That made her snuffle out a chuckle. "She didn't say that to you."

"Yeah. She did. Words don't matter. Feelings do. And I agree with her. C'mon." He pulled back to meet her gaze with his thoughtful green eyes. "We'll handle all of it together. We'll help each other—and Abby—get through it."

CHAPTER SEVENTEEN

She fought and fought. The fight was the thing. The monkeys surrounded her, cackled, waved torches, everything highlighted in flame. She screamed until her lungs seemed to seize up, her throat raw. She couldn't move her arms, couldn't protect herself. Then the smell of blood and antiseptic, clothes sterilized into bland nothingness. A monkey bit her arm, a sting, a poison puncture, which she resisted with more fighting, more screaming.

Nothing was familiar. Everything was real. And terrifying. No way to escape the fear.

Nothing was familiar. Except...

She had whipped her head down, back, down again, and her jaw brushed something soft. Her bindings. The thing binding her arms to her. It was soft, familiar. Safe. Oh, God. Safe. She latched onto that feeling with desperation, pulling in other senses. It smelled like something comforting, a shelter from the storm.

Then the storm howled into the shelter, blew it all away.

More screaming, vomiting...then at last, the monkeys vanished, and she drifted away on the clouds. It seemed she rolled around in them for a long time. It was tempting to stay there, but it still didn't feel right. She couldn't get rid of the low-level anxiety in the pit of her belly, that she would fall out of the sky. Plummet. She didn't want to come back to earth. She sensed there was too much to be afraid of there, but she wasn't given a choice. That was the worst part, always.

Inevitable should be the most hated word in any language.

Her lids lifted, though she told them to stay closed. They ignored her. Everything was fuzzy, and her tongue had turned into lead. Anti-psychotic, probably mixed with sedation. The voices murmured, a familiar rise and fall that was almost welcome. Much better than the roar of a mob. Slowly, as she rode the uncertain air currents, she pieced together what had happened.

She'd had a psychotic episode. A bad one. They'd brought her to the hospital. She'd struggled, screaming about how everything was wrong, about people with scary, melting faces, clicking, wet noises, monkey men, numbers. Ros's stricken visage, her resolute jaw. Lawrence's concerned eyes. Neil, holding her through it all.

Dobby and Tommy...they'd been there, too, but she couldn't remember how that had happened. It would come. She wouldn't get all of it back, though she probably didn't need or want to.

She saw walls painted the color of ice melting in lemonade, clean white trim. Placid, peaceful landscape pictures. No faces, not even of grazing sheep or cows. Good decorating choice for a schizophrenic's accommodations. Her gaze rolled over the pictures and up, to an acoustic tile ceiling, the dated choice of medical institutions everywhere. Always with the inevitable brown rust stain from a leaky pipe, though this one was missing that.

Someone was talking, an even, relaxed cadence. As her mind oriented itself to consciousness, it filled in the blanks, one descriptive at a time.

Male. Southern drawl. Pleasing. Neil. Neil's voice.

He was reading to her.

The words were familiar. Time passed, she wasn't sure how long, but eventually she was following the passages. It was one of her favorite childhood books, *Black Beauty*.

From where he was in the story, if he'd started from the first page, he'd been reading to her awhile. Was he using the copy from her house? She kept it in a bookcase in her bedroom. She'd read the book a lot, which he probably knew now, too, thanks to all the lines she'd highlighted in it. Her lips moved, dry, her voice a hoarse croak.

"Hey, let's get you something for that." Ice chips, rubbing against her lips, placed on her tongue. More time passing, eyes closing, lids weighted down again. But there were more ice chips. At last she felt like she could talk, though the words scraped against her esophagus like sandpaper.

He bent down, bringing his scent to her, clean and male. "What, bébé?"

"'We call them dumb animals...and so they are...they cannot tell us how they feel...but they...'" She swallowed a couple times, but the words were swimming by slowly, so she could catch hold of them again. "'They do not suffer less because they have no words.'"

Slowly she lifted her gaze. An unstable joy filled her. She could meet his slate-colored eyes, and didn't have to look away. It wouldn't last for long, so for now, her gaze clung to his, holding onto that connection she desperately needed. She wanted to cry, to scream for an entirely different reason. She wouldn't do it. There was no point. She thought of something better.

"So..." She croaked it out. "Best third date ever?"

His gaze flickered. "If you count the phone calls, I think we could call it our fifth."

Leaning forward, he pressed his lips to her forehead. Tears spilled out of her eyes, damn it. She started to shake.

He wound his arms around her, and she was in the shelter of his body. He was over her, pressing her down against the mattress. She couldn't hide from the things that tormented her, but he provided her a moment's haven, a respite she needed.

"But as a matter of fact, yes," he said, when she'd calmed somewhat. "It's going to be hard to top this one."

"Just tell your boss it's bring-your-girlfriend-to-work day. Maybe we'll get captured and tortured in Helltown. Then we can go bowling."

"Sorry, I did that with my last girlfriend. I want to be original. Don't worry, I'll figure out something even better."

He eased back but stayed close, stroking her face. She could only imagine how terrible she looked. She smelled like antiseptic, too, which meant she'd done something mortifying that called for a hospital soap clean-up. Her teeth needed brushing, stat. But her hair had been brushed and was braided.

As her awareness further returned, she realized she couldn't move her arms. Her wrists were cuffed to the bedrails. The immediate spike of fear was temporary, because he was unbuckling them as soon as she registered the restraint. He rubbed her wrists, easing the feeling.

"They'll get mad if you do that," she said. "They yell, take away your visitor privileges."

She hadn't been able to tell her mother no. Moments later, her twelve-year-old self had been screaming for the nurses, because her mother was trying to gouge out her own eyes to let the demons out.

Get them out, get them out... She'd screamed that. A flash of memory, of mother and daughter, layered images of past and present. Neil holding her wrists. He'd been stronger, better at it, than she'd been with her mother.

Oh, God. She wanted to dissolve again, but Neil was talking. She could focus on that, keep herself together.

"Dr. Mo told me it was okay to take them off when you woke up," Neil assured her. He'd pulled out his phone. The book rested on the covers next to her. It was her childhood copy. "I'm sending her a text now. She was here earlier. We're supposed to let her know when you're back with us."

"What time is it?" She laid her hand on the book, the glossy orange and black hardcover. The corners were frayed, the binding loose. Badges of honor, a book's way of showing it was well-loved.

"About two a.m." He put the phone back in his pocket. He wore those jeans that looked so good on him, and a long-sleeved white T-shirt with a colorful fishing tournament logo on the front. His bill cap rested on the foot of the bed. She saw an empty soda and half-eaten pack of crackers on a side table next to the foam pitcher of ice chips.

"Ros took the first shift with you, then Lawrence talked her into going home to get a shower and a few hours of sleep. I texted him, too."

"Tell him to let her get her rest. I feel odd. But okay."

"Yeah, they tried some other drug on you. Maureen said the side effects might make you feel wonky, but her hope was that it would break the psychotic episode, get you back to at least status quo."

"Good call. My head's mostly on straight. I can look at your face without it distorting. That's good. Voices still there, but low-level." A relief after the shrieking cacophony that had seemed to go on forever and ever.

"If Munch was here, he'd say that's not distortion. That's the way my face normally looks."

Though a smile took effort, and from his expression she thought it came out worse than weak, it still felt good to be able to manage it.

In a day or two, in between a few brief spurts of manic euphoria, she'd be hit by a solid wall of debilitating depression. Wash, rinse, repeat. Might as well enjoy her time on the bridge. "It's a good face. Lawrence can just keep his opinion to himself."

She paused. "I don't remember...a lot. A ride on the back of a motorcycle. A bar... Then you finding me at your house."

"Do you want me to fill in the blanks?"

"Maybe in a bit." She struggled to push herself up to a sitting position, and the world tilted. Neil slid an arm around her, helped steady her as he pushed the button on the bed adjustments. A low whir, and it elevated enough to support her back, cushioned by the couple pillows Neil adjusted behind her. "Where are my clothes?"

"They put everything in a bag, and gave it to Ros. She said she'd bring you clean stuff when she came back."

A wave of emotion rolled through her, pushing words out that she knew better than to say aloud. "I don't want to wait that long. I want to go home right now."

"Abby." Neil laid a hand on her wrist. She jerked back, a reflex, as the emotions did another spike. The problem was determining what was the illness and what was a true reaction, but she was pretty damn sure this one was real. She'd woken up exactly where she'd never wanted to be, and from his careful way of speaking, they weren't going to let her leave. She was trapped, imprisoned, and they had no right, no right at all.

"Mistress."

He caught her attention with the sharp word. She'd started to crawl back up the slope of the bed behind her, her legs bent up against her, elbows pressing into the mattress like she was an upside-down crab, preparing to scuttle.

Crabs. Clicking, wet.

"No," she said to her head sharply. "*No.*"

"Mistress."

"I want to go home. Let me go home."

He didn't try to touch her, but he did put his hand on the railing close to her, fingers moving lightly along it as if they wanted to stroke, touch. She stared at them as he spoke. Easy, firm. Honest.

"Your sub's just been through an incredibly intense session," he said. "You sent him into subspace like a rocket to the moon. He's come down, but he's disoriented as hell. He tells you he's going to drive himself home, you can't keep him there, and to give you his goddamn keys. What do you say?"

The ticking in her head was like a clock, but she followed its rhythm as it slowed down. She realized what she was tracking was her pulse. Her heartbeat, settling. Neil had a hand back on hers, was stroking her wrist, slow and easy.

"I tell him he'll keep his ass right where it is if he knows what's good for him," she said. "Because I'm still taking care of him. And if he honors his Mistress, he'll trust me to know when he's ready to go home."

"Yeah. Sounds about right." He rubbed his thumb over her palm, raised it to his face to put a kiss on it. He met her gaze, and she saw a rock-solid sternness there. "I promise you. No one has any intention of keeping you here. Just let Dr. Mo come and see you, check things out." His pocket buzzed, and he kept her hand while he pulled the phone out with the other, took a look.

"In fact, Dr. Mo says she can come right now, if you want her to. Or she can see you in a few hours, at breakfast."

Abby opened her mouth, fully intending to tell her now, now, and by the way, fucking now. But she closed her mouth. Flexed her hands. "Is the door locked?"

"No."

She stared at him, her lips pressed back together. She didn't want to be that person, but he read it in her face, and didn't show offense. Rising, he moved to the door, opened it for her, proving it.

She took a breath. "Will you...stay with me?"

She didn't want to be that kind of person either, but when a resolute smile crossed his face, glinted in his eyes, the surge of relief made that irrelevant. "No one's taking me from your side," he said. Another promise.

"Okay." She respected Maureen enough to let her get a good night's sleep, have time to see her daughter off to school in the morning. Particularly when she remembered Maureen had been at a conference. This had obviously brought her home early. "Breakfast, then."

After Neil sent that message, she took another breath. "So, I got to ride a motorcycle. That's something. Was the biker hot like Tiger?"

"Mess with me, and you'll get only hospital food, instead of the good stuff they're serving in the café downstairs."

The smile hurt, but not in a bad way. "Tell me what else happened."

"You sure?"

He had her hand again. She stared at his rough knuckles, ran her thumb over them. "Yes. Tell me all of it. What you all had to do. And Neil, I need honesty. Can you give me that?"

She closed her eyes as he leaned over, kissed her brow. "I can give you anything you ask me for, Mistress," he said.

As he told her, most of it did come back to her, but he was able to replace the distortions and hallucinations with the reality. When he told her the knife part, her heart started beating harder. She remembered going after those voices with it, but then the knife went away. So that was when he'd taken it from her.

She thought about what could have happened if Neil and Lawrence hadn't been with Ros, if Ros had tried to approach her on her own, thinking she could "get through" to Abby. Abby hadn't been seeing Ros. It had been shadows, swooping down like buzzards, trying to tear out her guts, a downed animal not completely dead.

As she had learned, from her mother and now from her own experiences, a schizophrenic seemed most dangerous when they were actually down-to-the-bones terrified, trapped in a nightmare they couldn't escape, believing they were fighting for their own survival.

She put her head in her hands, rocked, this time for self-comfort, wishing for no thoughts, wishing... She sighed, stilled. The meds were working, because she was able to stop that carousel, bring it to center. Stop the ride.

"On one of my visits to my mother in the hospital, she was lucid enough to tell me what happened when she tried to drown me in our bathtub."

You remember when we went to the neighborhood pool, and you and I held hands, dove under the water together? You were laughing at me like a mermaid, bubbles coming from your mouth, your eyes bright. It reminded me of when you were inside me, so safe. And then I saw the monster, trying to get you. I knew, if I held you under long enough, the monster would drown, and you'd be fine. It was so real...so real.

Her mother had such bad tics from her medication at that point, she'd been jerking while telling the story. Abby had wanted to hold her. At first her mother couldn't settle enough for her to do that, but when Abby removed the cuffs, before things went bad, her mother had sat up, leaned against her, their shoulders pressed together.

Then she started asking, *"Has the monster come? Has it come for you?"* And the eye gouging had happened.

Before her mother had strangled herself, she'd left Abby a note, scraped into the paint on the wall. The paint chips had been under her nails.

I took the monster with me, Abby. You're safe.

As she told him all that, in halting words, Neil had lowered the side rail and shifted a hip onto the bed. "That's messed up," he said.

"Yes, it was." She stared at the sheets, his thigh, the faded denim. His large, capable hand, braced on the covers. "But it was also an act of love. Even if she was psychotic, it doesn't change that. Your brain's a Picasso, but the pieces, you assemble them, and to you, they make so much sense."

She thought of the knife. "When I'm scared, I want to hold a weapon to feel safer."

He closed his hand on hers, drawing her attention to their linked hands. "You're holding a weapon, bébé," he said quietly. "Do you feel safer?"

She did. But she was also so tired. "There's this revelation moment," she said, staring at their linked hands. "When the road you're going down, you know you can't escape it. The anxiety and sadness and loss are too much."

She wanted to fold herself up like a piece of paper, into smaller and smaller sections, until she disappeared from sight. No longer part of that inevitable current toward crash or destruction.

He slid into the bed next to her. It was a small bed, and he was a large man, but she could burrow up against him, let him drape a leg over hers. He wrapped his arms around her, held her close to his beating heart. He didn't say anything, just being that oasis of calm and quiet for her. Her voices murmured, their volume held down by Maureen's drug choice. She'd take it, for however long it held.

"I said horrible things to Ros, didn't I?"

"Don't worry about that. You made up with her. When she was here, before I took over, she held your hand, kissed your head. You patted her arm, told her it was okay."

"I did?"

"Yeah, you did. You meant it. Helped her a lot."

That helped her, too. "Could you read to me some more? I like the part where Beauty and the cab driver spend the day in the country."

He kept one arm around her as he reached over and picked the book up off the rolling table where he'd moved it. He handed it to her so she could find the section, which she did easily, since it was her favorite part.

"Do you want to read it to me instead?" he asked.

She did, surprisingly. But her throat was still tender, so he tumbled some more ice chips into a paper cup, gave them to her, and took the book back to read to her again. She lay against him, holding the cup, sucking ice chips and listening to the words. As he spoke them, the vibration rumbled through his chest, under her ear.

When a nurse came in wearing blue scrubs, Abby tensed, but she was there only to take Abby's vitals and ask if she wanted a fruit cup or some Jell-O. Neil began to get up, to get out of the nurse's way.

"You can stay where you are," she told him with a smile. "She looks relaxed where she is, as any woman with half a brain would be."

Abby's anxiety dialed back some at the nurse's easy tone, the lack of anything that looked like it was intended to stab, poke, or prod.

The nurse's demeanor also confirmed Neil's reassurance that she wasn't an inmate. "You're not on a psych hold," Neil said after the nurse left. He'd apparently read her face. "If you truly wanted to leave, you could. But Dr. Mo advised you to wait until the meds had fully settled into your system and she saw you in the morning." He gestured with the book. "Keep reading?"

She nodded. "Unless it's wearing your throat out."

"No, I'm good."

He resumed, letting her settle, drift in and out. Neil eventually slid out of the bed, lowering it again for her, a better sleeping position. He adjusted the blanket over her shoulder before he took a trip into the bathroom. She didn't remember him coming back. Slumber had pulled her back into its embrace.

When she surfaced again, sunlight was coming through the window, filtered by the lacework of the metal screen over it. They'd painted it yellow like the walls, an attempt to make it blend with the cheerful décor. Not entirely unsuccessful, though the cover was an obvious precaution against a patient deciding to take a suicidal shortcut to the parking lot.

Neil was back in the chair next to the bed, one foot braced on the bed rail as he read a fishing magazine he'd gotten from somewhere. He had it balanced on his bent knee as he rested a hand on her shin. Despite the covers between his palm and her leg, she could feel the heat of his touch. The morning light showed the stubble above and below his clipped beard, the deep set of his eyes. He looked relaxed, not exhausted, but a closer look showed her the subtle signs of fatigue. Had he slept at all?

"What's the longest you've gone without any sleep?" she asked groggily. "Even a cat nap?"

His light smile showed his pleasure at her awake state. "Three and a half days, I think. Maybe four. Satisfying a sorority of randy college coeds requires stamina."

He chuckled when she swatted clumsily at him.

"Good to see smiles happening in here." A quick rap on the cracked door, and Maureen stuck her head around the edge. Her amiable expression was the same as it would have been if they'd met over coffee at Abby's house, rather than in a psychiatric ward where Abby had woken in restraints. It shouldn't have made Abby feel better, but it did.

Even better, she was carrying a cardboard tray of coffee.

"She's back and sharp, Doc," Neil said. "Quoted *Black Beauty* first thing when she surfaced."

"Without coffee? Impressive." Maureen put one of the cups on the rolling table and brought it within Abby's reach. She also deposited several packs of sugar and cream next to it. "I remember you like to doctor yours up a bit."

As Maureen offered Neil one of the cups, Abby popped the top of hers and added the cream and sugar. The craving for the hot caffeine was immediate and strong, and with it came some appetite. Fortunately, Maureen had thought of that as well.

She held up a brown bag with straw handles. "Egg sandwich and fresh fruit from that organic place you mentioned liking. Plus a chocolate croissant." At Neil's pained look, she put the bag next to Abby's coffee and pulled a smaller brown bag out of it, bearing the familiar golden arches logo. "Plus a couple sausage biscuits and potato planks, chock full of manly salt, fat and grease."

"You're a goddess, Doc." He winked, and took the bag with a nod of thanks.

Maureen turned her gaze back to Abby. Now Abby saw the professional doctor, assessing her patient. But as she had from the beginning, Maureen stayed aware of Abby's need for self-determination, particularly after the past few hours when she'd lost control of so much. "Abby, would you be all right if Neil gave us some time, just you and me?"

"I'm sure he has a sorority to visit." She shot him a mock narrow glance, a tacit okay.

He rose, stretching, a pleasing thing to watch. It amused Abby to see even the composed Dr. Mo get a little lost in it. Neil wasn't oblivious to his appeal to the opposite sex, but since that wasn't his focus right now, he seemed charmingly unaware. "I won't be far," he told her.

Abby knew she should tell him to go home, get some sleep. Even more because him leaving gave her a spear of panic. She needed him to stay close, to help her feel safe. That kind of dependence wasn't who she was. She cared for others, helped *them* feel safe.

Maureen had left the door standing open. A reminder that she was free to leave.

"If you want, after we talk, I can drive you home." Maureen was watching her face, how she was looking at Neil. The woman was perceptive, a blessing and a curse. "I told Ros you'd likely be home by mid-morning."

Neil wanted to take her home, she could see that. But that was driven as much by worry as desire. They'd taken care of her; now she needed to take care of them. Of him.

Let them know she was still capable of that.

"That'll work. Neil, go home. Get some sleep, shower, a shave."

"Giving orders, Mistress?" The tone was deceptively mild, a hint of dangerous waters. He spoke as if Maureen wasn't in the room. When he deepened that drawl, looked at her like that, Abby kind of wished she wasn't. But as much as Neil could stir her libido—and had won her heart ten times over by doing it now, showing his desire was genuine even when she was in this state—it wasn't going anywhere further than idle fantasy for either of them. She hadn't had a full shower or brushed her teeth. She might need to soak in a tub for half a day to feel like herself again.

"Just want you to refuel that stamina," she said lightly. "You still owe me a girls' softball game, after all."

Though those warring emotions remained in his gaze, he picked up on her vital need to feel in control again. She gave him points for reining back his natural inclination to protect, especially when the effort it took was obvious. "We'll go this weekend if you're up for it," he said.

"Better sooner than later."

She flinched as soon as she spoke the words, but the damage was done. A shadow crossed his face, the muscles tightening. However, after a bated pause, he nodded. Maureen received a polite version of the same.

Before he headed for the door, though, he picked up *Black Beauty*, opened it up to a page he'd marked with a napkin. "This is the part I like." His gaze rose, then lowered. "'My troubles are all over, and I am at home; and often before I am quite awake, I fancy I am still in the orchard at Birtwick, standing with my friends under the apple trees.'"

His gaze lifted to her again. "Makes me think of our day on the boat.'"

"You skipped to the end while I was out."

"Well, as you said, time can be short. I wanted to make sure it had a happy ending." He held her eyes. It really was a positive sign, that she was able to hold the lock a full, measured beat, and that some part of her fragile psyche responded to the challenge there. "I'll see you soon, bébé."

Picking up his hat, he tugged it down on his head, then reclaimed the McDonald's bag and his coffee. As he disappeared around the corner and she heard his footsteps recede along the tiled hallway, she grimaced. "I didn't need to do that."

"Remind him that his time with you is finite?"

She turned her attention to her shrewd psychotherapist. Maureen had settled into the guest chair Neil had vacated, her legs crossed, the toe of her slick-soled black flat resting against the bed rail. She was wearing a silver cross on a thin chain around her neck, a matching bracelet dangling from her wrist. She'd had a manicure since Abby had seen her last, her nails now a dark green that matched her scoop-necked shirt she'd paired with gray slacks.

"Yeah. Don't know why I did it, after what I've put them through."

"Maybe because of that," Maureen said. "A reminder they won't have to put up with it much longer, to make yourself feel better? Like a hostess apologizing for the house not being clean enough when she has unexpected visitors."

Abby ran a hand over her face, the limp strands of hair wisping free of the braid. Goddess, she did look like shit. "How do you manage that? Sound reasonable and informative, instead of patronizing?"

"I could flippantly say I took a course in it, but it's mostly painful experience. Which eventually brought me back to something one of my smarter professors told me, back when I was too full of the narcissism of youth to listen. I have the advice framed on the wall of my home office."

Maureen paused. 'First, listen. Second, ask the right questions. Third, listen some more.'" Her green eyes flicked up to Abby's. "'Because having *doctor* attached to your name only means you've been given more chances than most to fuck up people's lives.'"

Abby blinked. "I really don't want to like you. So stop saying shit like that."

Maureen chuckled, but then sobered. "How are you feeling?"

She'd let it go some with Neil, but Maureen had told her from the beginning, this was why she was here. Abby was the loaded gun, and the question was the trigger. All of it hit her. Everything Neil had told her. All the thoughts about her mother, herself, the journey she'd known was coming but had never wanted to take, Ros, her friends, her life...

She could send herself into some bad places if she cried too hard, got herself too worked up, but a long, quiet cathartic cry worked.

Maureen sat quietly by her, providing tissues, moving to sit on the edge of the bed, rub her shin much like Neil had.

When at last Abby slowed down, dried her eyes, blew her nose, she managed a wry look. "What was the question again?"

Maureen smiled. "You have a marvelous sense of humor."

"The best comedians have the most fucked up lives. Because that gives them their best material." Abby took a breath. "As far as how I am, I'm in the state I'd expect after an episode that bad. Wrung out. Dreading the depression phase. But I'll take the lull before the jitters come back in and the next cycle of circus fun house starts up."

She shook her head. "I appreciate your efforts, but I think I should go back to the one medication. I at least know what to expect from it, and I shouldn't be around long enough for it to deteriorate into total ineffectiveness."

Maureen gazed at her. "So is the date solid at this point?"

"Yes. About three weeks."

Abby waited to see how the psychotherapist would react. Maureen mulled for a few minutes, then leaned forward. "The medication I gave you to break this episode; I think you could pair a milder dosage of it with that existing medication. I've tried the combination with other patients, those who have a greater awareness of their symptoms and triggers, who are interested in doing more psychotherapy management with less medication. It works because they accept it's not going to decrease their symptoms to the levels most patients would prefer, or avoid more minor episodes."

Maureen gestured with her coffee. "Unless you're planning some bucket list trips, it also obviously works best if you continue the therapy with me while taking that mix."

Abby uttered a brittle half-laugh. "Unpredictability and spontaneity aren't really my friends now. My desire to hang glide the Grand Canyon will wait for the next life."

"So what *do* you want to do with those few weeks, then?"

She looked up at Maureen, then back at the coffee. She felt the heat of it through the sides, thought of the man who'd just left the room. "I want to make the most of the time I have left with the people who matter most, who want to be around me, even when I'm like this."

The finality of it all settled like a lead weight in her stomach. Decision-making from here forward would have a limited range. "It's been a great life. I have no complaints, except the very normal wish for more of the same."

She squared her shoulders. "So yes. Let's do the med combo with a lighter touch and psychotherapy. The next three weeks, I should be in pretty manageable situations. The most exciting thing will probably be that softball game, which hopefully won't set off a psychotic episode. But if it does, I'll be with Neil." She flashed Maureen a smile. "If a SEAL can't handle one crazy woman at a sporting event, then naval special warfare training really needs a revamp."

Neil sat in his truck at a remote spot in the hospital's parking lot, a position that let him see the upper story window of Abby's room. As he waited for Ros and Lawrence to arrive, he ate his biscuits, drank the coffee Maureen had brought. When Ros and Lawrence pulled into the empty slot next to him, he gave them the update on Abby's condition, being sure to include her humor and other evidence of her return to clarity.

Relief crossed Ros's face, but he expected the darker things in her mind reflected his own. He left them after that, pulling out of the parking lot, resisting the impossibly strong desire to go back to Abby's room, hover in the hallway. She'd asked him to go. He'd sensed her fear of his absence, the clamoring need for him to stay. He wanted to respond to that, not her unspoken message to respect her need to confirm to herself that she had things in hand. That she could handle this.

Him staying would serve his wishes, not hers. But he couldn't push away the memory, throbbing like a toothache, of how she'd worn herself out on the way to the hospital. Fighting the restraints he'd put on her, crying, pleading and screaming about monkey men and clicking noises. It had been the longest trip of his life.

Maybe he was the one more afraid of leaving her side.

But there were other things he couldn't forget, or stop going over, as if they held the key to solving the problem. Things that had happened when they'd arrived at the hospital.

As he drove, they filled his mind again, pages of a book he was determined to read in its entirety like that children's classic, until he figured it out.

~

Once they reached the hospital, they'd heavily sedated her, injected her with the meds that Dr. Mo had instructed them to use.

As Ros signed the paperwork, Neil could almost see the flesh-tearing flogging the woman was enduring inside. Lawrence stuck close, his hand on her back, massaging.

When the sedatives started taking effect, ending Abby's screaming and fighting, it brought visible relief to the three of them. Neil hated that undeniable truth, recalling Maureen's words.

Treatment decisions for the comfort of the bystanders...

This wasn't that. Dr. Mo was trying to help Abby for Abby's sake. Yet the flood of panic in her hazel eyes as she began to feel the effects of the meds had reminded Neil of a drowning swimmer. With him standing on a boat, right next to a fucking life ring he couldn't throw to her. It had destroyed him.

He'd taken sentry duty on one side of the bed, Ros on the other. Abby's hands were held to the rails in padded cuffs. As she'd calmed down enough for her to be okay with it, he'd had his hand on hers. Ros had stood by the bed, a hand on Abby's face, her hair, as she talked to her. Told her they were there, it was okay.

Abby's eyes vacillated between panic and calculating suspicion, helpless terror. But then slowly, slowly, she let go, her body relaxing enough that she slipped from consciousness.

He'd been through beatings that didn't leave him as battered as this.

He'd stepped out when a female orderly came to help Ros remove Abby's torn and dirty clothes, give her a sponge bath, get her into a gown. When he was invited back in, Ros was brushing Abby's hair.

He'd sat silently, watching her hands move over her friend with such excruciating love and care, Ros's sculpted face a rigid mask that spoke of the emotions dammed up behind her jewel-blue eyes. He'd had a rubber band in his pocket he gave to her to use when she braided Abby's hair. He'd pulled it off a file back on base in Germany and had tucked it there, forgotten it. It was bizarre, an inanimate object connecting the mundane to the terrible.

Then Maureen arrived. She talked to them about what happened, checked in with the nurses and doctor on call. Assuring them Abby would be out for a couple hours, she told them she wanted to speak to all of them for a few minutes, in a conference room just outside the ward. Lawrence had been dispatched to bring in the others, and they had arrived, were waiting in that room.

Earlier, he'd used his ability to set emotions aside to work the problem, resolve the crisis. That relief didn't exist in the aftermath. He didn't want to let her hand go until he saw her surface again. What rested in his gut, his chest, was a grenade. The pin was a jarring step away from falling loose.

He was distantly aware that his stare must have said all those things to Maureen and Ros, because Ros disappeared. A few moments later, Lawrence slipped into the room. He said something to Maureen, and she left as well. Then it was just him and Munch.

"This is getting to be a habit, her sending you to talk me down," Neil noted in a neutral tone, his eyes on Abby.

"It's a mutual sending. This is tough. You've never been through something like this."

"If you start talking about Valentina and comparing this to that, I'll hurt you. I'm a cold bastard right now."

"Not intending to do that. Hey. Look at me."

Neil turned his head, met Lawrence's sharp green eyes. "She'll be okay until we get back. Conference room is less than a hundred yards away, just outside the ward doors. Staff will come get Dr. Mo if anything happens at all."

Neil stroked a strand of hair from Abby's face. She frowned, twitched away from his touch. He closed his hand in a fist on her pillow as he gazed at her. "All the shit we've seen, I accepted it. Accepted that terrible things happen to people who don't deserve a damn bit of it. Being pissed is only useful if it helps get the job done. My job was to help. To make it better."

"Which is what you're doing here."

"Munch, I'm... I need to kill something for her. Destroy the monster in her head. Rip it into fucking pieces and let her dance on the corpse. I'd sell my soul a hundred times to give her that."

"Do you trust me, Twizz?"

It took him a second to pull himself out of that berserker haze, find their standard response. "Is that a real question?"

Lawrence squeezed his shoulder hard enough to make bones complain. "We need to go to the conference room. It's the best way to help her."

"Okay." He was leaning forward in the chair and now he looked down at his feet. Testing, he rocked forward on the balls of his feet, back. "It comforts her, when she does that. Sometimes. Other times, it seems to spin her up."

"Yeah, I've noticed that."

Lawrence didn't say anything further. He didn't need to. Neil rose, leaned over and pressed his lips to Abby's forehead. He wanted to let the touch linger, but she was restless. He settled for brushing one more loose tendril of that glorious red hair from her brow. "I'll be close by," he said, low. "Doesn't matter if I'm a Dom or sub, Mistress. I'm yours in every way you need me, until the very end."

When he straightened, Lawrence's gaze was full of understanding, ready to be in that danger zone right with him, no matter where it took them. Something Neil had always been able to count on.

He hoped Abby knew she had the same backup.

The small conference room had an oval dark brown table with six maroon-cushioned silver chairs around it. Neil and Lawrence chose to prop against a side table by the bank of windows, giving the five women and Maureen the seats. They declined Maureen's offer to have a couple more chairs rolled in. Since it was about five-thirty, Bastion was closing up the office for the day. Vera said she'd fill him in.

The first few minutes were a basic volley of conversation, bringing everyone up to speed. Neil logged any new information, but most of it he already knew, having had a front row seat. He wanted to get this done so he could get back to Abby.

Maureen paused, the initial update done. She looked as unhurried as always, but not in a frustrating way. Her professional calmness helped bring a touch of it to the rest of them. She'd arranged for there to be coffee, and the smell added to the comforting normalcy of an abnormal situation.

She wasn't playing airline hostess, though. The psychotherapist mantle was evident. Though she'd flown back from Tennessee on an emergency flight, come straight to the hospital to personally oversee Abby's care, her brown flowing slacks, blue blouse and tasteful jewelry conveyed a message of uncreased, tailored competence.

Her penetrating regard assessed their somber faces. Even Cyn looked too weighed down by her feelings to summon the fires of anger that seemed to be her fallback coping mode.

Comparing this meeting to the one at TRA, the contrast was bleak. Then, there'd been somber speculation, anger over Abby's decision, pain for the struggle their friend was facing. This was shellshock from a full dose of the reality, what it looked like, and knowing it was the tip of the iceberg.

"Before we proceed further, I want to say this to all of you," Maureen said. "Despite your lack of experience, you handled an incredibly difficult situation as well as any group of caregivers I've seen."

Ros lifted a quelling hand. Her blue eyes sparked with an animosity that betrayed her banked emotions. "All due respect, I'm not in the mood to be stroked."

Her raw tone reflected self-condemnation. "Personal choice. Willing consent and submission. There's nothing I respect more, and I crapped on all of that. Took it away from a woman who understands its value, maybe more than anyone in this room."

Maureen met Ros's gaze, one strong woman to another. "You did that as a temporary measure, because you saw it as the only feasible route. She was fully in the grip of a psychotic episode, a threat to herself and others. She could not make lucid choices."

Maureen's gaze turned to Neil. "Most people can't step into that foreign country and read the cues, make sense of what is happening. I believe Neil is an exception to that. Ros, can you tell the others what you told me?"

Neil, surprised, looked at Ros. "I told her how you anticipated her, understood what she was communicating," she said.

"Neil, I'd like you to explain your thought process," Dr Mo said. "What caused you to react the way you did?"

He had no idea where she was going with this. He was tempted to impatiently tell her it was just instinct, and stride from the room, go back to Abby. But he felt Lawrence's attention on him and remembered Dr. Mo wouldn't be asking him idle questions. She had a purpose.

So he looked for an honest answer, and when he found it, he got an inkling of where she was going. As a result, his answer wasn't framed as brusquely as it might have been otherwise.

"If she and I were facing an enemy, and I was fighting at her side, I'd match my actions to hers, counter them in the way that resulted in the best offensive and defensive tactics." He looked toward Ros. "It's her. Even in the very worst of it, she was *in* there. The illness doesn't shape her personality—it's integrated with it. That's why we can kind of follow what she's talking about. Because in her head, she's not talking nonsense."

"We discussed this at our first meeting, but now you have a deeper experience with it," Maureen confirmed. "Sylvia Nasar, who wrote John Nash's biography, a famous mathematician with this illness, pointed out that oral communications during delusions can be 'conscious, desperate and often painstaking attempts to make sense out of chaos.'"

She turned to Ros. "However, when the psychosis, the episode, worsens, it can go deeper than anyone can piece together, or predict the patient's behavior. Which is when a caregiver has to make the tough decision you did."

She covered Ros's hand. "Your strong desire to protect your friend's freedom of choice, make her a part of the decision-making process, highlights why Abby gave you power to make certain decisions for her. She trusted you not to let that desire outweigh your common sense, cause you to abdicate the very important responsibility she left you, which is making a terribly difficult judgment when she can't do it for herself."

Ros's mask slipped. Though her voice remained firm, Maureen curled her fingers over hers. "The fact you continue to challenge yourself with that decision shows your love and respect for who she is, who you know she is at her core."

As her attention turned to the rest of them, her hand slipped back to her lap, allowing Ros to regain her straight-backed and resolute-faced composure. "To keep supporting her, you have to be willing to forgive yourself when you make mistakes, missteps, and move forward. Otherwise, you cripple yourself and hamper your ability to provide her the best level of support."

"Not like we have to do it for long, right? If she's going to give up and end it all." Cyn had been watching Dr. Mo closely, listening intently. Her tone as she spoke now was sad, not angry. Neil preferred her anger.

Vera sent her a quelling look, though not an unkind one. "That's not helpful, Cyn."

"No." Surprisingly, Maureen shook her head. "Part of why I wanted to bring you together here is to give you a place to pause, regroup. That means a safe area to say whatever is in your hearts. Getting that out with each other keeps you all on the same page, which helps Abby, too."

Her gaze slid to Cyn. "Your feelings are legitimate, your anger and frustration. But it's also important that you recognize your words, 'giving up,' imply judgment, and are a personal opinion. While legitimate to feel and express here, it's likely not helpful to express it to Abby herself. Most things you've felt about this situation, Abby herself has reviewed and bludgeoned herself with, all while simultaneously facing the reality of her diagnosis."

"Spending half a day trying to figure out where she was, worrying she was going to be badly hurt?" Ros shook her head. "Seeing her completely unable to care for herself, to protect herself? I realized I might consider doing exactly as she's doing. Especially if I'd had not just a half day to see it play out, but years, with my own parent, and knowing I'd be facing the same fate."

"But you think it doesn't have to be that way." Skye spoke through her cultured Southern accent, directing the comment toward Maureen.

"I hope not." Maureen pressed her lips together. "You have your frustrations as her family. I have frustrations of my own. There are early treatment options now, that can be applied to those highly at-risk for inherited schizophrenia, well before symptoms manifest. Studies have shown a significant percentage of those who go that way have a better prognosis. Some of those options existed a decade ago. Would they have helped Abby? Maybe. If nothing else, they would have given us more time before the full onset."

Maureen lifted a shoulder. "But there's nothing I can do about that. She made the choices she made, and I have no way of knowing if my thoughts are wishful thinking, or if I would have hampered the life she chose to live so fully up until now. It all goes back to the same thing. We can't choose for her. We can only help her navigate the path ahead."

Though Maureen had shifted back to a smoother tone, Neil expected revealing the depth of her own feelings had served the purpose she'd intended; to show her genuine empathy with where they were all at.

"There are plenty more options for me to try with her," she said. "The question goes back to what else we discussed at the beginning. Her will and endurance, to find out if there is an option that will raise her quality of life, to a threshold where she's willing to fight for it."

"Not a fight," Neil said. "She said it's not a fight. It's riding in a boat, and deciding when you want to get out, when the ride is no longer worth it."

A thoughtful look crossed Maureen's face. "Perhaps. For a wide variety of serious illnesses, many patients find visualizing their treatment journey as a heroic battle works for them. Maybe not for Abby. She's seen that fight lost. And her mother saw her mother lose it. Abby's mother conceded 'the battle' and self-destructed with alcohol and street drugs. But...perhaps seeking a way into that boat, finding a way to 'ride' the illness, discover pleasure and moments of tranquility as an integration with it...that might be a better therapeutic approach for her."

She brightened, Neil's idea obviously gaining traction. "If the drug resistance is an inherited trait, we can also learn from the therapeutic roads taken by her mother that didn't work, or that weren't taken at all. Abby has a tremendous awareness of her disease, and that is a benefit, a strength. It's even harder when a person denies it, or in psychosis doesn't realize they're sick."

Ros was twisting a pen over her fingers, and stabbed it against the tabletop. "I want her to stay in the fucking boat. Let's go back to that original question, consider the problem again, with the new information. How can we support and respect her, yet help her get to where she could see staying in the boat as an option? Show her she's not on a one-way road, just because that's what she decided decades ago?"

When Vera opened her mouth then closed it, Maureen dipped her chin her way.

"Please say what you want to say."

"This isn't a marketing problem." Vera's gaze met Ros's. "We can't 'sell' Abby on the idea of staying alive. That argument is between Abby and herself. But we can have faith, and focus on the factors we *can* control."

"Like?" Ros asked.

"Make sure all of our actions for and toward her prove that having her in our lives has a value completely independent of her illness or the course it takes, the highs and lows. Take that factor out of the equation."

"Yeah." Neil nodded. "She's brought that up a lot. How it will impact all of you. Plus our relationship."

"Your value to those you love has a tremendous influence on your view of your own value," Maureen agreed. "And those who suffer from mental illness have multiple reasons to struggle with that feeling. If you're in a wheelchair or are blind, that's a difficult challenge, but it's one people can see, which makes them empathize better. A physically handicapped person often faces a struggle between getting more help than they need, and not enough sensitivity to what their real challenges are."

Skye raised a hand, palm to the air like she was at a church meeting. "Tell it, sister, tell it." Her phone spoke in a preacher's baritone.

"I wasn't being insensitive," Cyn told her. "I really thought you could win that singing competition last year. I'd heard the other contestants."

Unexpected chuckles, faint smiles, swept the room.

"A mental illness often receives far less understanding," Maureen continued. "Particularly when the obvious symptoms come and go, and the person's behavior causes embarrassment, or disrupts lives and rituals without warning. Then there's the fear factor, particularly for paranoid schizophrenics. The end result is too many with the illness end up shunned by all but a very small number of the people closest to them, who take the time to understand and effectively help with its management."

She gazed at them. "Which goes back to the very first thing I said to all of you, only now you possess a greater grasp of its significance.

This support network, people to reduce the isolation of what Abby's managing, is vital to her quality of life, both the actuality of it and her perception. It provides the buffer as well as the foundation on which she can stand, to absorb the blows that come from others' lack of understanding."

"And everything that shows life doesn't have to be a total suckfest means..." Skye had returned to the game show hostess voice. She punctuated it with a dramatic "now-you've-won-this" sweep of her hands toward Vera.

"Maybe she considers staying in the boat," Vera said.

"Control your fear of losing her and instead focus on carrying her to a better understanding of her possibilities. And it's my hope, through therapy, I can help her ask herself those questions, to take her to a better path as well."

Ros tapped the table. "The dinner Abby wants with all of us. I think she planned it as a way for us to get out whatever we want to say to her, good, bad, mad. But maybe instead we make it like all the other dinners we've had over the years. The laughter, the sharing of our stories, the pleasure we take in being in one another's company."

"Agreed. I just wish we could just inundate her with stuff like that." Vera glanced at Maureen. "But I get that wouldn't keep it easy, natural. We can't think about the deadline."

"Three weeks from tomorrow." Skye's Southern voice made the quiet statement.

It jolted Neil. He'd been gauging the possible date, based on her earlier declaration of 'a month and a half,' but now he knew it for sure. As he dealt with that, Maureen spoke again.

"It's not easy to stay 'natural' in your intent under that short timeline. But I believe Vera is right. You can only express how you feel to her, be there for her in whatever way she needs, without pressure."

"And in the end, it still might not work. Because sometimes the patient is right." Skye spoke again, eyes serious under the fall of spiky blond hair.

Neil wanted to say *fuck that*. He saw Cyn likewise bite back a protest, and Ros's fingers tighten on the tabletop, but they all got what Skye was really saying. Not that they thought Abby should kill herself, but that the ultimate responsibility for that decision was not theirs. Her life and how she wanted to live it, no matter how it connected to others, belonged to herself.

"When I'm around her, I just want to shake her," Cyn said. "Or tie her up until she changes her mind. I don't feel like she's in a boat at all. More like in a rip current, not able to turn back."

"But a rip current isn't trying to kill you," Lawrence said unexpectedly. "It's just a force of nature."

As all eyes turned his way, he looked at Neil. "You don't fight it. You go with the natural flow of it, let it carry you to waters that will let you get back to shore. Or in the boat."

Neil blinked. There was an idea there. Maybe Lawrence himself didn't know what it was, but deep in his gut, Neil felt a spark of response. He'd be thinking about that. He nodded to his former teammate.

"Our clients often bypass bigger firms to do business with us," Ros said, drawing their attention. Her gaze went to Vera, Cyn, Skye. "That happens because we never forget it's always about the people. Who they are, what they want and need. How we can best help them get where they need to go."

She looked at Neil. "So we'll each do what we can, and hope to God Abby changes her destination."

CHAPTER EIGHTEEN

As promised, Maureen had Abby checked out of the hospital by mid-morning. Neil was back by then. He hadn't gone home, but had taken advantage of Dale's house in the city for a shower and a quick nap.

At the hospital entrance, Abby told Ros she didn't want to wait to have the car brought around. She would walk with them to the parking lot. As she did, she kept stopping, squinting through her sunglasses, and staring around her as if she was looking for someone.

Neil glanced at Ros and Lawrence, a silent message suggesting they go ahead to their vehicle while he kept her company.

"What do you see?" he asked her.

"Nothing. It's just...skewed. Like walking sideways on an incline. Damn fun house effect." Her next dose, including the adjustments she and Maureen had discussed, would be due soon after they reached her place. Maureen had warned her and Ros about the side effects of what was cycling through her system. Since Neil had paid attention, he knew it included this one.

He proffered an arm. "Here. What good is having a big, strong boyfriend if he can't give you an arm for a stroll?"

"Good point. Make sure you don't get your arms blown off on a mission. Your boyfriend points will go down considerably."

"I'll just compensate with other appendages."

"I opened myself up for that one, didn't I?"

"Wide open, Mistress. Like a bass fish's mouth." He'd made her smile, and she put her hand around the crook of his elbow, fingers pressing into his biceps. When a car door slammed, she shrank against him, but then shook off the reaction irritably, straightening up again. She kept her hand on his arm, though.

"Hearing amplified," she explained. "That's the illness. Maureen has me journaling it, so she can track what's a side effect or the schizophrenia, though at times it's hard to tell."

As she spoke, her gaze focused to the left of his face. Her way of showing a person had her attention, when she couldn't manage direct eye contact.

In dealing with the loss of his leg, Dale had said that re-evaluating how he approached and did almost everything had been a bitch at first. But now, he'd adapted to it so well, Neil and the others rarely even thought about it.

Abby's schizophrenia might always have markers visible to those who helped with her care, and probably even to those who didn't. Or, if she hung around long enough, maybe she and Maureen would find meds that helped her feel and act more like who she was before the onset.

Almost as soon as he had the thought, Neil realized that kind of thinking might not be all that helpful. Dale had pointed out something along those lines.

You can't really go back to who you were. Just carry pieces of it forward. Evolved is the word I hung onto, because when I was frustrated, I wanted to call it just the opposite. Deteriorate, decline, incapable, handicapped. Settle for, resign myself to... Just no. Fuck no.

Evolved. Neil liked that word. "Here comes Ros."

As the Mercedes slowed beside them, Lawrence got out of the passenger side, holding it open for Abby. Ros leaned over. "How about we have the boys take Neil's truck and pick up a muffuletta from Central Grocery?"

A pause, Abby looking up at the sky. Then her gaze lowered, and she nodded. "That sounds good." Her hand slipped away from Neil, though he put a hand on her lower back as she slid into the car.

He pulled the seatbelt out, buckled it around her. As he brushed his lips across her cheek, he felt her hand find his side, curl into his shirt. "I know you can buckle your own seat belt," he told her. "But it made me feel better to do it."

She moved her fingertips to his jaw, stroked his beard. Her smile drew his attention to her soft lips. "Tell them not to go too heavy on the olives," she said.

"You got it."

Crazy how just a normal conversation with her, a light touch, made him want her more. He could tell just getting out of the hospital was making her feel better, and he wanted to celebrate that with a parade through the French Quarter.

He and Lawrence were early for the Central's usual long lunch line. Even if it had been peak time, the staff was efficient, though. He and Lawrence didn't talk much. While there'd been no indication Ros was trying to get rid of them, Neil assumed Abby was feeling self-conscious about her appearance. She hadn't wanted to take a full shower at the hospital. She wanted to get cleaned up at home. Which likely meant she was more comfortable in the close quarters of a car with another woman.

He didn't want her to be self-conscious around him, but he focused on the positives; self-awareness and clarity were good things.

Even if, upon their arrival at Abby's house, it became apparent the clarity had some quirks to it.

When they came in through the kitchen, Neil didn't see Ros, but he did see Abby, sitting in her living room. Her hair was damp, in a twist up on her head, so she'd taken the shower. She wore a light green cotton dress with a nipped waist and V-neck. The fabric outlined the beauty of her body, though there was a fragility to her posture that emphasized her collar bones, the thinness of her neck. She wasn't wearing makeup, but without it she was still as beautiful as a cluster of wildflowers, no embellishment needed.

Her feet were bare, propped against the lower rung of the straight wooden chair she'd apparently pulled into the living room from the kitchen. She had it facing the mantel, and was staring at the shelf and its contents with an odd expression.

Before he could investigate, there was a creak on the stairs, the tap of Ros's shoes. She had a thing about shoes, and today's pair were open-toed, low heeled, black with what looked like a yellow and green feather hand-painted along the back and sides of the uppers. They went with the yellow slacks and V-necked cotton shirt she wore, printed with a Paris café scene. The shirt emphasized her excellent figure and picked up the shoe colors.

Ros was always well put together. As Abby had been, before all this started happening. Neil wondered if Ros's meticulous appearance was one more thing reminding Abby of what often seemed beyond her grasp these days. Probably so, but his beautiful Domme would never want her friend to change because of that.

Ros had latched onto Abby's odd focus as well. She stopped at the bottom of the stairs. "What are you doing, Abby?" she asked.

"Watching. They'll hatch soon." Abby pointed to the shelf.

Neil moved to the mantel. Three candles were mounted in a diagonally sloped iron candle holder, painted white. Next to the lowest candle was a bird's nest, likely something Abby had found after a nesting season and placed here as a decoration. He saw a handful of the pills Maureen had given her, arranged like eggs.

"They'll give birth to maggots," Abby said. "Maggots they want to put in my brain. Plenty there already, you know? I'll take the pills once they hatch and wriggle away."

Lawrence had moved to stand by Ros at the stairs. Abby's back was to them, so he put his hand on hers, gripped as Ros's blue eyes shifted to him. Her face was expressionless, but she tightened her fingers in response.

"Hmm." Neil picked up one of the larger pills. He moved slow, in case she'd object, but she didn't, only watched with interest as he broke it in half. Coming to the side of her chair, he dropped to a knee, lifted his palm to show her. "Look. Nothing inside but more of the pill."

After a hesitation, her hands came up under his, cupped it. "No maggots."

"No maggots. I think maybe the illness is making you believe that. The pills might help. Make it easier to think clearly. What do you think?"

Maureen had told them when her head was clear enough, it was important for them to be straight with her like that.

Abby made a face. "You just said it's hard for me to think right now, and you're asking me to think."

He half-smiled. Yep, she was in there, his sharp Mistress. "True. It's time to take them. Want me to get you a glass of water?"

"I'd prefer a soda. One of the little cans in the fridge."

"You got it." He heard Lawrence move toward the kitchen.

Ros's expression had eased, making him glad Maureen's advice had been sound. If they could all figure out Abby's new way of communicating, moving through the world, they could help make that easier. Which in turn might take them closer to everyone's ultimate hope.

Keeping an eye on the prize without obsessing over it. Good trick.

Like a tightrope walk through gale winds. Fucking piece of cake. Something Mike was fond of saying, right before the team hit the most vital moment in an op.

Lawrence brought the soda and Neil opened it for Abby, handing it to her. "Thanks," she said. She tilted her head toward the stairs. "Ros?"

"Yeah, honey?" Her friend sank down on the sofa near Abby's chair. Abby dipped her head at her as she swallowed the pill.

"There's your brain, and then there's your mind. Your mind tells you who you are. But if your brain is having problems, it will try to tell you you're not what you thought you were. That your mind has had you standing on a rotting floor all this time, and the termites have almost eaten all the way through it. You're standing on nothing. Your footprints are all gone."

Ros opened her mouth, then closed it, cutting off the argument Neil was sure she wanted to offer. "I never thought of it that way," she said instead.

"Yeah. It's why so many geniuses are crazy. God's little joke." Abby sighed, dropped her head back. "I'm so tired. I don't want to eat right now. I'm going up to take a nap." But she stared at the ceiling, her body sagging.

"Why don't you let me take you to your bed?" Neil suggested.

She smiled at him, a gentle, easy gesture. "Are you asking permission? You don't do that. You're not made that way. You do you. I like you." Her gaze slid over him. "Though I admit it gives me a charge and lots of fantasies when you drop to a knee next to me."

Lawrence's low chuckle was echoed by Ros's smile. She stroked Abby's upper arm. "I've turned down your bed and put away your stuff," she told her, then glanced at Neil. "We'll be down here if you need anything."

"I'm going to sleep for the next twelve hours," Abby told her. "Eat the muffuletta, then go home, relax. Check in at the office. Don't let Bastion realize he can run everything fine without us. He'll stage a coup."

"I'm not worried. I have a pit bull. Cyn's volatile but intensely loyal." Ros shot her an amused look. "Though if you think Bastion doesn't know he could run the whole show without us, you *are* crazy."

Abby shot Neil a triumphant look. "She can be taught. How to joke with a crazy person, 101."

She looked toward Ros with a smile. "We need to get one of those calming pheromone plug-ins Bastion uses on his dog. For Cyn. Put it in her office."

"I'll add it to the office supply list."

"Okay. Come on then, woman." Abby's eyelids were drooping, so Neil rose and scooped her up, hefting her as she put arms around his neck, laid her head on his shoulder. Ros stood, leaned in and kissed Abby's cheek, nuzzling it. The dark-tipped blond strands of her shoulder-length hair brushed Neil's arm. "Sweet dreams, dear one," she murmured to her friend. "Glad you're home."

"Me, too."

Neil got a nod from Lawrence, a silent message they'd join him in a heartbeat if he or Abby needed them.

She felt good in his arms, soft and female, her lips near his throat. As he carried her up the stairs, Neil spoke. "Speaking of disappearing footprints, have you read that footprints poem, the one about Jesus?"

"Hmph." Her tone was amused. "If you're about to compare yourself to Jesus, you're confirming my theory."

"What's that? That I think I'm God?"

"No. That Jesus was totally hot. Great ass and hair, charismatic, gentle strength and compassion. Women followed him, men wanted to be him."

"You know, if you believe the God propaganda, an indoor lightning strike isn't beyond His ability."

"I could always walk so you'd be safer," she pointed out.

"I like carrying you."

"You can't carry me forever."

"You don't need or want me to do that," he responded. "But I can when you do. That's what made me think of the poem."

Her fingers curled against his nape, stroking. Her eyes had closed, but he thought she was focusing on how it felt to touch him. He was okay with that.

"I'm heavy," she said. "Especially going up stairs."

"Bébé, I've carried a hundred pounds of gear up a cliff. And that's dead weight." He shifted her. "You are not dead weight."

"Not yet."

He'd reached the landing and came to a full stop, arms tightening over her in quiet reproof. "Don't."

Yeah, they needed to avoid putting pressure on her, but he drew the line at death humor that wasn't remotely amusing. He wasn't putting up with that shit.

She got it, too, biting her lip, regret gripping her features. "You're right. I'm sorry, Neil."

"It's okay." He moved toward her bedroom. Ros had turned down the covers on the right side, next to the night table. A small lamp was turned on. He could still feel the steam from the bathroom, telling him Abby had taken a very hot shower, a restorative for a lot of things.

He thought of the times he'd done the same, letting the water roll over him, take away the dirt, the blood, cleaning off one role so he could step out and assume another. Find the strength to do so.

"If you're carrying me, who's going to take care of you?" she asked.

"You will. This is just my shift. You take over next. Maybe later tonight."

"Shifts," she murmured. "Shifting. Shift. Mood shift, tectonic shift..."

When he put her feet down, she turned. A mirror, a pretty antique framed in dark wood and standing on an adjustable base, was behind them. Though it was half covered with an artfully draped sheer scarf, she started back from the image. Then, realizing it was herself, she stopped, looked at it. Her hands dropped to her sides, opening and closing once before passing over her stomach, chest, throat. "I look...ghostlike."

"I don't think so. A little worn out, is all." Neil stood behind her, nodded toward the image. "Think of her as one of your sisters, like Ros or Cyn. You're going to help her. We're all going to help her."

She stiffened. That muttering about mood shifts had been a warning. Too late, he realized he'd screwed up on his word choice.

"You're all going to 'help' me. Help me the way *you* want. You want me to wait. You all want me to wait."

She pivoted, stepped back from him, her chin lifting. The hazel eyes frosted. "Waiting means I could get too far gone, not be able to do it. Though that would overjoy the rest of you, it's not what I want. As I was lying in the hospital, you know the question I kept thinking about? If it makes more sense to do it right now, even if I can't do it in Switzerland. Do it when I'm sure I'm in my right mind. Right side, right foot forward, right, right, right, nothing is right...nothing is right."

She turned away, tapped her head with the heel of her hand. Not as forcefully as she'd done it before, but he went on alert, ready to stop her from hurting herself. But he didn't get the impression she was moving toward an episode. She was juggling new variables as she talked, moved, or formulated thoughts, but she was adapting, working with it. She might be navigating in heavy fog, but she had the advantage of it being her own mind, home turf. She knew the waters.

She closed her hands into fists, and he could see she was struggling to scrape it all back into something meaningful again. He debated what he could say. Whether he should say anything at all. "You have the assisted thing set up," he said quietly. "If you do it before then, here, it will hurt your family."

More than your decision to end it already has. He wanted to tell her that. Tell her she shouldn't add to their pain, but *telling* her anything in this charged environment was obviously the wrong way to go.

It didn't matter. She was smart enough to pick up what was implied. Her eyes opened, glittering. "So reasonable. Best way to handle the pathetic little mental patient."

"That's not what I said." His temper spiked. She picked up on that too, sauntering closer. Fuck, she was deliberately taunting him.

"Do I look like I want to be handled right now?" she demanded. "Say what's in your head. Don't hold back."

"You need to back up off me," he told her. "You're trying to crack me open like one of your subs, to feel in control."

"And you want me to take orders from you." She pulled out the pins holding her hair, let the wild, damp mane spill over her pale shoulders, around her tense face. "Just say it straight out. Me planning to take my own life pisses you off. It offends your philosophy of fighting onward and forever. I'm shitting on the SEAL mantra of never give up, and 'the only easy day is yesterday.'"

She gave a wild laugh. "I get so sick of hearing the *don't give up* thing from people who have no fucking clue. It's like falling off the Empire State Building, and when you pass the tenth floor, someone leans out and yells, 'Don't give up!'"

Her gaze speared all the parts of him he'd compartmentalized, planning to deal with them later on his own, not take it out on her. When he was with her, he wanted her well-being to be his only focus.

She obviously wasn't going to accept that. She was showing that ability she had as a Mistress, that he'd seen with Tiger. She was drilling down to find out what was really going on inside him.

And he'd given her the opening. Maureen had warned them about using language like "giving up," words that could be translated to judgment, to accusation. Unfortunately, if he answered her, let his emotions have him the way she wanted, that's exactly where he'd end up.

Or...maybe what she was demanding was that he treat her as if he could trust her with his feelings. His pain.

The way she'd trusted him. She wanted balance.

He ran through a lot of scenarios in a blink. He wasn't sure if the one he chose was his gut's intuition, or the vat of feelings churning in it, but he went with it.

"Yeah, it pisses me off." He closed the distance between them, let her see it in his expression. The brief flash of surprise, the instinctive step back, told him he was successful. He maintained enough control not to follow, but she was still within arm's length.

"It's tough on all of us," he said. "We're all trying to respect you, cope with it. Then you up and throw out to me that you're thinking of upping your timetable, going to do it here?" He glared at her. "You need to pull your head out of your ass and think about that. You said you didn't want to be your mother. You'd make one of us find you? You'd make me watch you die?"

She whitened, but then she rallied, closed that step between them and jabbed a finger into his chest. "No one said you had to be there. Or even invited you, for that matter. My decision will save you all from a lot of pain."

Neil looked down at the finger. The nail was polished, but had a jagged scrape. Probably from when she was wandering through the swamp, where she could have died. Which would have made their current argument unnecessary and had the added benefit of ripping his fucking heart out of his chest ahead of schedule.

Dale had once told him Neil had internal waters so calm even a boulder couldn't cause ripples. Abby was doing her best to initiate a full tsunami, with herself in the wave path.

"I don't want to be goddamned saved," Neil said. "Any more than you goddamn want to be told what to do."

Her jaw jutted, eyes flashed, hazel fire meeting blue-grey flame. "How about when this progresses? Doesn't matter if it's the meds or the crazy, they can change the way I act, physically, emotionally. Twitching, shuffling, clumsiness. Getting lost in my head, disinterested in what's around me. 'Flat effect' where it's like I'm wearing a mask all the time, where I seem to have no emotions or feelings."

She obviously had no intention of slowing down for an answer. "Or how about when I'm doing well, so well that I make the mistake every schizophrenic does. Convince myself I'm better and can go off my meds? Escape the damn side effects. Then I run off to a swamp again. Trapped in my delusions and shadows, with nothing left over to offer you. No acknowledgement of what you're going through or dealing with, because raging self-absorption is the biggest side effect of all, one they don't print on the bottles."

Her brows raised, mouth in a thin, angry line. "Then there's how it changes you, Ros, all of them. You get to the point you dread a call or text when you're away from me. You're afraid to look, because you know it could mean I'm having a problem and you need to drop everything in your life to come dig me out of whatever shit I'm mired in."

"Abby."

She plowed onward. "Don't forget sex. Or rather, do forget about it. While my mother would fuck anything that moved, some of the anti-psychotics can kill libido. Then there's what will happen as I get older. About a third of us get dementia."

"I thought you wanted to know what was in my head," he said

sharply, giving her a steady, cold look. "But all I'm hearing is you talking, not letting me get a word in."

She put her hands on her hips, shot him a look of frustration, anger, empty triumph. "Fine. Tell me. How will you handle all that, Neil?"

"I guess you'd have to hang around to find out, wouldn't you?"

That was too far. He knew it. She went whiter, opened her mouth, closed it. As she turned away from him, he tried to act calm in a way he didn't feel. He was primed to detonate.

"Abby."

She shook her head, sat down on her vanity chair. Back straight, legs crossed, hands linked on her knee. She knew what kind of bear she'd poked, but she wasn't a coward. She inclined her head, a classic steel magnolia move.

Or the Bruce Lee *bring it* gesture.

"You're right," she said, in a tight, even voice, too much like her normal self. "Tell me what you're thinking, Neil." Her gaze flicked up. "I want honesty, not bullshit."

Okay. He could give her that. Would give her that. He sat down on the edge of the bed, facing her, his feet braced, hands on his spread knees.

He didn't yell. He didn't raise his voice. But he put everything he was feeling into the words. "This is how I see it. If you think it's possible to get one good moment just often enough, be able to find a laugh or smile, or create a good memory, then I think you should stick around and try to make that happen. Because I'm willing to stand with you, do that with you, and suffer through everything you're feeling at the other times. Take all of the terrible, for one moment, one memory, of good."

He continued, his voice as inexorable as an avalanche of rock. "I will hate to see you suffer, hate it worse than anything in the world, but that will make me all the more determined to help you find the moments where you don't suffer, where you can take the best in life and give it to yourself. And maybe because of that willingness, on both our parts, we'll be able to make a lot more of those moments than if we didn't try at all."

She'd started trembling when he was halfway through, and now she'd turned away, was staring at the wall. "Stop it. I mean it."

"Then you stop it. And I goddamn, fucking mean it." He rose, dropped to a knee next to her, braced a hand on the vanity and the other on her chair, at her hip, surrounding her so he had her full attention.

"I've told you before. You do *not* get to factor into your death equation what I or anyone else can handle, what you have the right to ask of us. Because when you try, that's based on your fears, your experiences. Not mine or anyone else's. You think I'm pissed about you making the decision about your life because of some high-level moral code that drives me as a SEAL?"

He scoffed, a harsh sound that made her flinch. "You don't know every damn thing, woman. The reason it pisses me off is far more selfish than that. I fell in love with you, harder and faster than I've ever fallen for anyone, and I don't want to lose that. That's the beginning and the end of the reason. The only one that matters, that decimates anything else in my life."

Shock gripped her expression, followed by anguish. Maureen's admonition was in his head, not to back her into a corner, but so was Abby's taunt, telling him not to treat her like she couldn't handle hearing what was going on in his heart and soul.

Abby's taunt won. He couldn't stop himself, couldn't stop the feelings from rushing forward, grabbing him by the throat and taking him down a destructive road. "I don't think you want to lose it, either. Damn it, Abby, us meeting when we did? These things don't happen randomly."

She shoved out of the chair, tripping over him but managing to establish distance between them. She turned when she reached the bed, her color high, her eyes snapping.

"No. They don't. Fate is a sadist. It likes to sucker punch you just to fuck with you worse. I am tired of people feeling like...that they can't understand...that they don't...how can you...how dare you tell me you fell in love with me like that, like I'm special...like that means something..."

He had risen to his feet as her emotions built. She flew at him, shoved at him. He took the blow, wanted to hold her, but she'd already spun away. She scooped up the footstool by the bed, grabbed it by one leg and flung it toward him. Her aim was off, but the power of the throw was laudable. A shot-put thrower would have applauded.

It went through the window with a loud crash, sending glass spraying out ahead of it. But as loud as that was, it was drowned out by the long, frustrated scream that boiled out of her.

She'd cried when she'd woken at the hospital, the sorrow, the grief pouring out, but he hadn't seen the rage. It was here and now, in that cry. All the anger she'd felt, waking up in the hospital, everything that meant.

It echoed through the house, through his heart, soul and bones. Neighboring dogs started howling.

"Stop." Neil had her as she crumpled to her knees by her vanity, as she tried to slam her head against the wooden edge. "No. *No*."

"Why. Why did you have to tell me that?" She was wailing at him, punching him. Grimly, he held on until she subsided, reversed her intent. Instead of pushing away, she was clawing to get closer, rocking against him. Her shuddering body, the strangled sobs, the way she spoke the words, all of it told him this wasn't a psychotic break. This was a woman's pain, so unbearable she couldn't contain it. And he'd triggered it. Whether that was good, for the dam to break free, or he was an insensitive asshole, he had no idea. But he could hold her.

She pulled at his arms, as if she was trying to make them wind further around her, as if he could help her escape everything with the strength of their embrace.

"It's okay, bébé," Neil said roughly. The heart he'd feared would be ripped out of his chest from her loss was already shredded, a match for the breakage in her mind. As her cries died away, the sobs lessening, he spoke against her hair. "I'm sorry. I'm sorry I upset you. But you wanted me to be honest. Nothing would be worse than losing you."

A horrible, hoarse half chuckle against his chest. "Not true. Seeing me suffer would be worse. You're lying to yourself, Neil, or you just don't realize it's the truth. I watched my mother suffer until I begged any god kind enough to let it end. To let it end... Please let this end... The gods didn't hear me, but she did."

"Ssh. Ssh. Please...don't." He gave her the agony in his own heart, let it lock together with hers, as close as they were physically. He held her, rocked her. Held on even as his body was rigid with the knowledge that she was slipping through his fingers. Through all their fingers.

Lawrence and Ros stood in the doorway to the bedroom. He didn't know how much of the argument they had heard or witnessed, but Ros's eyes were alive with the pain they were sharing.

She put her hand on Lawrence's arm, drawing him back. Lawrence gave Neil a short nod, his expression tight, then he turned. From where he was sitting, holding Abby, Neil saw Ros reach the top of the steps. She sank down, the strength of her legs leaving her. As she buried her face in her hands, her narrow shoulders began to shake. Lawrence had the presence of mind to pull the bedroom door closed so Abby wouldn't see. Neil heard his feet swiftly cover the ground between the door and the steps, as he went to comfort the woman who held his heart as irrevocably as Abby held Neil's.

~

She'd already been tired; this wore her out. While he and Lawrence figured out how to tape up the window for the night, using a clear drop cloth they found in her garden shed and duct tape, she disappeared into the bathroom, taking a sleep shirt with her she'd retrieved from her closet. Ros had gone downstairs.

"It's a good thing you have home repair skills," Lawrence commented as they finished. "Because when you and Abby get under the same roof, the need for them seems to crop up pretty frequently."

Neil sent him a narrow look, but then Abby emerged from the bathroom. The shirt she'd chosen had sleeping cats scattered across a pink field of cotton fabric. Lawrence gave Neil a supportive nod before he left the room, carrying the window repair stuff.

"I'm going to sleep," Abby told Neil. "Go eat some of the muffuletta with Ros and Lawrence. I'll get some when I wake up. They could use your company. Particularly Ros."

"I don't want to leave you up here alone."

She gave him a sad smile. "I'm okay, Neil. We're okay. Go make sure our friends are all right. I need that. Please."

He studied her, then nodded. "Okay. I'll be close."

He wanted to say more, but the intensity of their exchange seemed to require a respite, for both of them. They'd figure it out. They just needed a breath.

After she climbed into the bed and he pulled the blanket up over her shoulder, resting a hand on it for a frustratingly helpless moment, he forced himself to follow Lawrence down the stairs. He and Ros sat at the table, the muffuletta box unopened. Ros had a glass of wine and Lawrence had a beer. Abby kept a well-stocked fridge for guests.

Lawrence rose and brought him another beer, twisting off the top before sliding the bottle to him.

"She's going to sleep awhile," Neil said. "I'll get us some plates. We should eat."

"Yeah. I told her." Lawrence dipped his head toward Ros, who shot him a neutral look.

"I wanted the wine first. Call it an appetizer." Her eyes looked tired, too.

Neil went into Abby's kitchen. He noted the colorfully painted backsplash tiles on the wall above her stove, and suspected they were a gift from Lawrence and Ros. Lawrence's mother created interior design stuff like that. Lawrence had a similar set he'd brought to Ros's when he moved in with her.

A reminder of easier times, normal things.

They could all use a break, without going too far away from the woman occupying their minds. So when he returned from the kitchen, putting the plates down on the table, he chose a topic that seemed to fit that objective.

"She told me a little about how you and she connected over the Domme thing. But she didn't tell me how you met."

The easing of Ros's expression, the intelligent flicker in her eyes, told him she'd picked up on his strategy and agreed with it. "It seemed an unlikely pairing at first. She was a brilliant math geek. Had won competitions. But she'd minored in business, and we had some of the same classes."

Ros contemplated her wine glass. "She was shy and quiet, didn't form attachments easily, didn't seek out social situations with a lot of people and noise. She was far more likely to spend her time in the library with the mathletes. Her beauty covered up some of that awkwardness, helped her blend. She knew how to mask anxiety and discomfort.

"I felt drawn to her. The few times we'd talked, I could tell there was a lot there. She wanted to experience those social situations. She just needed a buffer. I became the buffer. When we started hanging out, I discovered how carefully she paid attention. She knew a lot of things, way more than numbers. She'd come up with solutions to problems, based on the people involved in them. I found she was a generous and warm-hearted person, not the least bit distant."

While they were talking, Lawrence had quartered the muffuletta and distributed three pieces onto their plates. "Thinking back on it," Ros continued, "I know some of her personality then foreshadowed or fed into what she is now. But a lot of it was having such a traumatic childhood. Nurture and nature both contributed to that reserved personality. But she was competitive, focused. When she channeled her strengths, didn't let doubts or worries, or the past, pull her down, she became a force of nature. And when she tried her hand at being a Domme, she really unlocked that part of herself on a lot of levels."

Neil lifted a brow as he chewed. He'd heard it from Abby, but he wanted Ros's perspective. "Really? How did that work?"

"She'd been watching me awhile, asking me questions, learning. One night I was with someone who liked being shared. I asked her if she wanted to take over. She knew the structure, the rules. I suggested she explore where she wanted to take herself, and him. See if it really was her thing, or just an interesting distraction."

Ros gazed into that past memory, her blue eyes going still. "I won't ever forget that scene. He was tied up. She traced every rope on his flesh, trailed her fingers over him as she circled him. She asked him what he was feeling. What he was thinking. It sounds so simple, but she got into his head because the way she spoke, the way she touched him...you could feel the energy of it. It was..."

She shook her head, gazing fondly at Lawrence. "Well, sometimes it's like that. You come home to it, if that makes sense. She found something in that room that was real and true to her core, that had nothing to do with the past, or the future she was facing. She put a pin in the present and created a whole garden in her soul, rotating on that one point."

She met Neil's gaze. "She's kept her scenes as uncluttered and straightforward as what you see in her decorating, but she still gets deep into their minds, just like she did with him. She had him eating out of her hand. Literally. She fed him, had him drink water from her palms like a cup. As she did it all, there was this look of wonder to her.

She'd watched, imagined, but taking the reins herself—that opened a whole new world to her."

They considered that for a few minutes, ate in companionable silence. Then Lawrence tapped Neil's beer with his. "When do you have to go back to VA Beach?"

"I took a month's leave. Shouldn't be interrupted unless something major hits the fan."

Surprise crossed Ros's face, but Lawrence nodded. "I figured you'd done something like that, when you got back earlier than expected."

"Yeah." Neil took a swallow of his beer. "I'm up for Mike's spot. Dodge is retiring and he'll become team leader."

"Congratulations," Ros said. "That's major, isn't it?"

"Sure is," Lawrence said. "You deserve it, bro." He gave Neil a second look. "You haven't accepted it yet."

"Nope. I'll decide in a month."

"If she changes her mind, would you leave the SEALs?" Ros asked, studying him carefully.

"It's not something I'm going to talk about now. For one thing, if she knew I was debating it, she'd just add that to her bucket of reasons to go to Switzerland. The decision, when it happens, will be mine, for my own reasons."

"But it will still be driven by her, and how you feel about her," Ros noted. "You wouldn't be considering it otherwise."

"True." He bit off another piece of muffuletta. "I can't imagine not being part of the teams. It's like deciding to give up a lung to save my heart." He met Lawrence's eyes. "But she is my heart. I can live without a lung, even if I have to relearn how to breathe. When I'm around her, I breathe easier."

"Just remember what Maureen said," Ros reminded him. "Over a half dozen of us, including you, will prioritize her care. Don't make the mistake she made with her mother. Say what we all hope will happen does, and she changes her mind. The guilt and fear, that she's asking too much of those she loves, won't just go away overnight. A decision like you're considering could send her into a tailspin again."

"And remember Max," Lawrence added. "He thought he had to be everything for his sister because of her brain damage, until Janet showed him how he could share the load. His sister is better off for it now. You can be Abby's everything romantically, her person, and still be a SEAL."

"Abby is a very accomplished woman," Ros said, meeting Neil's gaze. "One who believes that if you have the chance to do what you love, you do it. You never waste that opportunity, because so many never get it."

Neil raised a brow, looked between them. "Have you two ever considered tag team wrestling?"

"Only if it involves mud and him in a Speedo," Ros returned, a hint of her normal smile in her eyes. "And there are limits to what he will do for me."

Lawrence pursed his lips, a tacit agreement with the assessment. Neil chuckled, then sobered.

"I get what you're saying," he said honestly. "All of it. And when the time comes to make a decision, I'll weigh all of it."

He met Ros's gaze squarely then. "But whether it's today, tomorrow, or a couple years from now, if ever I know she needs me to be here full time, even with all of you caring for her, that's what I'll do. And I won't regret it. That's a promise."

Ros reached across the table to tap Neil's hand. "I hope if that time comes, before you do anything, you'll talk to her about it. And really listen to what she has to say. You're a protective man who obviously cares very much about her. But she's also a strong woman who needs to know you have faith in her strengths."

"I have faith in her," he confirmed. "At every level."

CHAPTER NINETEEN

After Ros and Lawrence departed for the night, Neil turned off the lights, locked up, and headed upstairs. When he peered into her room, he confirmed Abby was out in one of those semi-coma sleeps, curled up in the center of the bed, barricaded with pillows. His beauty wasn't used to sharing her bed. He didn't mind knowing that.

There was a guest room on the other side of the hallway bathroom, and he figured he'd set up there. He wanted to be in her room with her, but he was respecting her earlier not-so-subtle plea for space.

He discovered a basket of toiletries in the bathroom. He'd brought his go bag, so he had his own toothbrush, but he made use of the soap and shampoo, then donned a clean pair of shorts before cracking open a book he'd borrowed from a downstairs bookcase. She was an avid reader, and her tastes were eclectic; Pat Conroy, Pam Godwin and Mary Shelley sitting side by side. He went with the Godwin, because it was a historical adventure with a hot female pirate, a woman who kicked ass and had some pretty erotic encounters with two men. He figured it could stoke some good conversations with Abby.

At almost every base, there was a small repository of books. As a result, over the years, he'd consumed a diverse amount of reading material. Knowing he liked to read, his teammates and others would bring him books, if they found a random one on one of the ops.

He remembered how she could quote *Black Beauty* to him. For him, books were an oasis, a touchstone amid human chaos, where things happened that could never be forgotten. For her, it would have been an escape from the quagmire of her own mind—or to forget that quagmire awaited her.

He settled down with the book, made it through several chapters before he put it to the side and cut the light. He hadn't heard anything from down the hall, so quelled the urge to check on her once more. Their argument, painful as it was, had proven she was back in control of herself. He would treat her that way.

He was a light sleeper, with a sixth sense for change in his in environment. So when he woke an hour later, he knew someone was standing in his doorway.

He didn't give away his conscious state right away, orienting himself to his surroundings first. Then he realized only one person could be standing there. When he opened his eyes to see her, he thought he might still be dreaming.

She was no longer in the sleepshirt.

It was a pink satin nightgown with spaghetti straps, and a plunging neckline. The fabric slithered over her skin, outlining her nipples, the curve of hip and length of thigh. Her hair was artfully tousled around her face, her lips red and wet. Bold eyeliner deepened her gaze, contrasted with her creamy skin. She looked like a creature of the night, come to his bed.

Holy Christ.

She was still barefoot, adding a poignancy to the look that tightened the reaction in his chest, as well as lower down.

When she moved, he could smell a light perfume. She was coming toward him the way a Domme would, no uncertainty in her movements. She stopped at the bedpost at the foot, stared at him.

"Something I can do for you, Mistress?" he asked, his voice husky with sleep. Desire was there, too, building fast.

She trailed a finger over his ankle. The blanket was tangled around his thighs, showing he was wearing just the shorts. "Take them off. I want to see you."

The energy in the room was thick and heated, the emotions below it charged. Earlier, he'd questioned if he'd screwed up, laying it out for her unfiltered, offering too much about what the past couple days had done to him. But her next words suggested that was why she was here.

"It's my shift. You took care of me. I'm going to take care of you now. And you're going to let me."

Her gaze coursed over him again, slow. When she lingered on the shorts, the rising arousal beneath, it was just like what he'd said in the meeting. She spoke a different language. He'd thought he was just picking up patterns, that his training had given him a particular adeptness at it with her, but it was far more personal than that. It was her. Who she was with him, how they connected with one another. However, whatever way she spoke, with or without words, he understood her.

He hooked the waistband of the shorts, slid them off so there was no barrier between her eyes and his flesh. He thought her penetrating gaze went to even deeper layers, roving the nerves beneath the skin, calling them to respond to whatever she wanted.

"What do you want to do for me, Neil? Tell me."

"Worship you." He thought of pirates. "Plunder. Pillage. Take everything, leave nothing, give everything back. All of it. Cherish you."

"Show me."

She moved then, a goddess who came to the bed in darkness, stood close enough he could put hands on her. He clasped her hip, the silk moving under his palm. He sat up and turned, framing her with his knees as he inserted his fingertips under one thin strap, nudged it off her fair-skinned shoulder. As he watched the silk tumble from one breast, the proud and taut tip was there for his touch, his mouth. The lush curve fit into his hand as he leaned forward, nuzzled, then closed his lips over the peak.

She cupped his head, fingers stroking through his hair, a hum in her throat. An approving goddess. She put her other hand alongside his neck, moving her touch to his shoulder, exploring what was hers.

Her hair brushed his knuckles at her hip as she tipped her head back, rolled it. Her back arched, pressing her breast deeper into his mouth, her body responding to his suckling, the pressure of his lips, light bites of his teeth, as he showed her male demand and hunger.

Pushing him to his back on the bed, she straddled him, and he adjusted them both, so he was stretched out full length on the mattress beneath her. She leaned over him, her hair brushing his chest.

"Just let this...be this," she whispered.

His hands flexed on her hips. "What do you want, Abby? What can I give you?"

"How about surrender?" She collared his wrists with her hands, pushing his up to the iron rails of her headboard. When she gazed down at him, her eyes were dark pools, her mouth a lush promise.

"I want everything from you," she said.

He remembered the story Ros had told, how Abby looked at that first sub in a way that said, if he surrendered to her, he would find everything his soul needed.

He might not be on the sub side of things, but looking up at her now, he knew just how that other male had felt. It made him recognize something at a visceral level, something important. He'd hold onto it for later. Not now. Now there was only what his Mistress wanted for him.

His Mistress. Not how a sub called her that, but something that went from top to bottom, bottom to top, scrambled all of it, to have and to hold, to keep her, for better or for worse. His Mistress.

Hers.

She put her mouth on his chest, bit him, her hands following the same path, digging in with claws, caressing, demanding. Doing what he had said, giving and taking both. She traced his angles and ridges with her tongue, tested muscle with her teeth. His grip on the rails tightened as her body rubbed against his, her cunt moving, a slick, heated promise against his cock, holding it down, stroking it with the forward and back motions of her body.

He wanted to coil his hands in her hair, put that lush mouth to work on his cock. He told her that, in a rougher whisper, and she bared her teeth in a feral smile, her eyes glittering.

"Maybe if you ask nicely, sailor. Maybe by the time I'm done, you'll even beg me."

Her gaze coursed over him again, avid. "I've never wanted to chain someone down the way I want to do that to you. Shove my cunt against your mouth, make you serve me until I come, rub myself against you, keep you hard and aching until I bring forth the beast and you break loose."

Her total attention pinned him for one resolute second. "Prove to me no bond is strong enough to keep you from taking what you want except my demand. Or refusal."

He understood the message. Until he could bear it no longer, he should consider himself chained. And he needed the reinforcement, because she sure as hell wanted to test it.

Placing her hand on his chest, she pushed herself back up, sitting tall upon him. She cupped both breasts, the one bare, the other covered in silk, and played her fingers over the nipple revealed to his gaze, squeezed and fondled herself. He wanted to follow everything her hands were doing, only with the gentleness, strength, roughness, force, of his male grasp. A contrast he knew she ultimately would crave, because it was in the glow of her eyes, watching his response to what she was doing.

She was looking at him, he realized. Holding his gaze. A small miracle, a respite for her. It dedicated him to the challenge to restrain his impulses, immerse himself in the wondrous unfettered expression of hers.

"I have a fantasy," she purred. "Sparked by myths of knights who wander into the castle of a sorceress queen." As she tugged harder on her nipples, she caught her lush bottom lip in her teeth. His cock convulsed at the sight, a curse caught in his throat as his biceps flexed. The headboard rails creaked.

Her gaze went to them, slightly widened, and her mouth curved. "One of my generals sends me a gift from the battlefield, an enemy commander. One who fought so fiercely that only a lucky strike knocked him unconscious, allowed him to be captured. Otherwise, he would have fought to the death rather than be taken."

One hand dropped, caressed his throat, his chest, tracing his pectoral, moving down his sternum. She followed the line of hair between his abdominal muscles, until the track disappeared into the inviting, shadowed valley between her spread thighs. She reversed her course, came back to his sternum again. She tugged on his chest hair, caught between her knuckles.

Her other hand was still playing with her bared breast. His mouth was dry with the desire to cover it, suckle that nipple hard enough to make her moan. Make the damp cunt she kept moving in slow strokes over his pinned cock wet enough to slide over it like an oiled rail.

"He's brought to my bedchamber, chained to my bed. I've told them to leave him without a blindfold. I want him to look around, see the feminine trappings of the room, and think he won't face anything there that he needs to fight, surrounded by a woman's scent and softness. But it's not to disarm him, make him succumb. It's to teach him that weapons clad in silk and softness can still demand every ounce of his strength. The only difference is the degree of pleasure in the effort."

She shifted, turning her back to him, and straddled his cock again. Only now she shimmied her upper body, her hips, lifted the lingerie over her head. Her red hair fell out of the tunnel of its embrace, sending him the fragrance of the fabric, of her heated skin and shampooed hair.

Christ, she was good at this. He was fighting not to let go of the railing, enough he had the absurd wish that she *had* chained him, so he wasn't having to work so hard to honor the imaginary bonds.

Exactly what she intended, he was sure.

Before she sat down on his loins again, she leaned forward to drape the gown on the end of the bed. It gave him a generous glimpse of her heart-shaped ass, the sweet cleft, the folds of her sex. She stayed there an additional moment, caressing his ankle, his shin, trailing her knuckles along it. She went to her elbows to taste the arch of his foot, take a sharp bite that made him jump, even as his gaze never left the display of pink, damp flesh.

Fucking hell. His cock, without her sitting on it, was at the angle intended by nature to make it ready to slide into a woman's cunt. When she turned her head to look back at him, her attention slid over it, lingering over its thick length. Her hair covered one eye, the other glittering at him.

"Does he curse you, your captive?" he growled.

"Repeatedly. He calls me foul names." Cruel amusement glinted in those hazel eyes. "I let him see how unaffected I am by his words. He's there for me to use, to enjoy, because he belongs to me. His anger, his resistance, makes me hotter, wetter. Especially when his cock only grows more impressive in size."

He could relate.

"I watch his eyes, the hunger that builds in them as I tease him with slow strokes, with the brush of my fingers over his battle-hardened muscles, the scars he bears. The cuts that he incurred only hours before on a different field, I cut them back open again. He'll bleed on this battlefield, too."

She shifted her hips to pin his cock down again beneath her damp sex, which gave her access to his thighs. She dragged her nails along their inner track, hard enough to leave red marks. Neil bit back a groan as her cunt rubbed against him. She was slicker now, her words and his attention driving up her arousal. As for him, his whole body mirrored his cock, hard and ready, blood pumping strong.

She dropped her head back on her shoulders again, her hair sliding along the curves of her buttocks. The ends almost brushed his abdomen. He wanted to let go of the railings, take two handfuls. Pull her back against him, drive into her from behind with her lying on top of him like this. He'd put his hand on her clit, use his fingers to strum and stroke, pinch, as he worked her, displaying her beauty to the heavens. Let the gods see him take the work of art they'd made, as he brought her to violent release.

"I tease him with the threat of keeping him chained by my throne, a warning to my enemies, a trophy of strength to display to my people." She spoke again, her head turned toward him, chin to her shoulder, her eyes lowered in deceptive demureness. "But privately, it will be for the pleasure I take in having his cock, his mouth, within reach, whenever I demand their service to my desires."

She moved in figure eights on his own organ, strokes up and back, and hell, she was building his response.

"Don't..."

"You don't want to come outside my body?" Her gaze flicked up, a taunt, then down again. "But maybe that's what I want. To see you lose control like that. I want to strip away any self-consciousness about what's expected of you by your own definitions, by the definitions of your armies, your men, yourself."

Her eyes glimmered again in the semi-darkness. "All that matters is the enemy you are getting to know so intimately, whether you intended that path or not. All that matters is what your Mistress desires. What makes her wet, what satisfies her hunger. Let go of everything but that, and together we are free. Everything falls away but the pleasure I want to take, and you find yourself unable to deny me."

Wherever she was in her head, she'd taken him with her. He'd sure as hell fight armies to stay there with her forever.

"I want to be inside you."

Her eyes sharpened like swords in truth. "Then beg," she said. "Beg for me. For my cunt. For my mercy. For my ruthlessness. Beg for all of it, for everything I can give you."

"No," he said, though his cock wanted him to give in. Hell, it was fine with him putting on a tutu and doing Swan Lake if he could drive into her. But he managed to hold the upper hand on it. "Any man would be your willing captive," he said. "But you wanted a prize taken from the battlefield. Because you wanted the fight. You wanted to earn your victory."

Her mouth curved, her gaze intensifying, and she turned around to face him again. She curled her fingers around the base of his cock, slow, each of her polished fingernails settling into place against his turgid skin. His shaft pulsed hard against her tightened grip. She placed her other hand on his chest, over his heart.

"My captive would watch me just as you're doing," she said softly. "So dangerous and still, lips pressed together, moistening them, making me want to gag that foul mouth with my cunt, demand that he devour me with the same fervor with which he wants to destroy me."

"Somewhere along the way, he stopped wanting to destroy you," he returned, voice thick. "He wants to return the favor, capture you, take you home, but not to share you as a trophy. He wants to keep you, pleasure you, never let you go, because the purpose he's only found on the battlefield in blood, in conquering, he's now found in you."

Her expression told him she liked that he'd walked fully into the fantasy with her, and held his own. But the emotional flicker there told him she also heard the truth, the reality, fueling the words. The urgent need.

She angled his cock to mount it, adjusting herself so her tight curls brushed the full head. As she slid down on him, he resisted the urge to drive into her before she was fully seated, or directed him to move. Watching her sex slide down the pillar of his cock, inch by inch, was a hell of a consolation prize. She was holding herself back, drawing it out. His attention on her, her body, where it was joining his, her expression, was absolute.

She reached the hilt, pressed to his pelvis, and braced both her hands on his chest, staring at him, a remote queen. "I do like the fight," she whispered. "So fight me. You've been pulling against the chains, and then suddenly, the link breaks. What will you do, commander? Will you give in to your enemy, or will you find out how this warrior queen holds her own?"

She came off of him with a purposeful tight-muscled stroke that very nearly caused him to climax. By the time he'd brought himself under control, she was halfway across the room, standing in a ready position, gloriously naked.

All the TRA women had self-defense training, plus some offensive fighting skills. Cyn had the most, being proficient in several martial arts. The others had learned from her, or been inspired by her example to seek additional instruction.

He wasn't sure what Abby's level was. The boxing gym Cyn and Ros used wasn't her preferred workout space, where Lawrence's witnessing of it could have given him that intel. But from the condition of Abby's body, the athleticism she'd displayed at the park, plus the look of Cyn's busted lip, he wasn't dealing with someone whose capabilities were limited to hair pulling and slapping.

The medications and illness's impact on her motor skills, her energy level, would be a factor on what she could bring to the fight. But this was sexual play, not a challenge to the death.

That said, he expected she'd go all out with him, knowing he could handle it.

He could.

"Should I assume one hand is still chained? Give myself a handicap?"

A smile flirted around her mouth as she shot a significant glance at his erection, still full and aching. "I already took care of that."

His return grin was a baring of teeth. In one swift move, he was off the bed and lunged for her. She dodged, but he caught her arm. She swung around, using the momentum to twist under his grasp, slip his hold. It worked, because to hold on, he would have to wrench or even break her arm. He had no doubt she'd factored in his self-restraint, his unwillingness to hurt her. But he could adapt to the changing environment.

A straight-out soft wrestling match, then.

He beat her to the door, caught her around the waist. She threw her weight forward to unbalance him, an excellent self-defense tactic he countered with backward force. Damn if the little minx didn't use it to bring her feet up, push off against the door, hard enough to shove him backward and almost put him on his ass. He had to let her go to protect them both and regain his footing.

She was laughing, impossibly beautiful as she jumped up on the bed and crouched like a wild thing. Her fingers were braced on the covers crumpled between her spread knees, her red hair swirling around her face. "Not bad, sailor." Her voice held that sultry purr. "But I still intend to get in a lucky punch or two."

"Lucky for you, not so much for me," he told her. "Lawrence and Max will double up on my training. They're tougher on me than my BUD/S instructors."

Her gaze softened. "I'm glad. I'm glad they make sure you stay at your best. So you can always come home to...those who care about you."

They stared at one another. "To you," he said. "That's what you meant to say. I don't want you to hold back, either."

"I don't want to make things more difficult."

"There's nothing you can do that will change that. So you damn well say everything you feel, how you feel it, when you feel it."

She went to one knee on the bed. He could see her heart thudding in her throat. "Fine," she said. "Let's finish the story."

He moved as fast as he was trained to move. She scrambled back, but he caught her, his momentum sliding them across the bed. He rolled them, put her on her stomach and covered her, holding her arms to her sides, his cock firmly against her ass. She bucked, snarled, called him a few names that he diplomatically decided to call part of the role play. He bit her ear lobe, then her neck, more sharply, settling her down.

Because of how she'd reacted to being restrained by his shirt, and to the cuffs at the hospital, he watched for any signs he was distressing her. All he saw was arousal...and a humbling trust.

"Your guards come through the door at the sound of our struggle," he said, rough and low, setting softer things aside for now. "But they see I could break your neck before they could get to you."

Shifting to pin one of her arms with his knee, it freed his hand so he could wrap it around the back of her neck, his long fingers stroking. "As you said, I would have preferred death in battle to capture. So they know I'm not afraid to die, as long as I take my enemy with me."

He tightened his grip, watched her eyes darken with lust, her lips press together. Felt the arousal in the body beneath him. Helpless physically, maybe, but containing enough power to bring him back to his knees with a look. He had no doubt of it.

"But their queen laughs," he continued, low. "She's not afraid of death, either. She knows...there are worse things."

He firmed up his tone, made himself stay with the sexually-charged fantasy. "She tells them to get out." He paused. "What does she say then?"

She adjusted her cheek against the mattress to look up at him through her thick lashes. "You face two choices, commander. One easy, one hard. Kill me, and be killed. Or fuck me, and face the unknown future, bound to me, serving me, in ways you can't possibly fathom."

His lips curved. The surge of feeling through him was so strong, so layered, he couldn't have defined all of it, but it confirmed the thought he'd just had.

Her greatest weapon was the steel of her soul.

Slowly, he bent, put his mouth on the shoulder her hair wasn't covering. He adjusted so his hands held her wrists to the mattress, while his knees moved between her spread thighs. He pressed his cock against her heavenly soft ass. "Your captive never chooses the easy way. You know that. And I can fuck you as hard as I fight a battle, Mistress."

Her eyes flashed, and a shudder ran through her back, her buttocks tensing against his length.

He turned her in one flowing movement, so she was on her back but still under him. With an arm cinched around her waist, he moved them up, so they were at the headboard again. Holding her gaze, he deliberately reached up and gripped the railing with one hand. "One chain still holding me," he said. "Still in service to my Mistress."

Still hers, and as hers, able to take the reins when that was what she needed. Service came in a lot of forms. As did submission. Submitting to the moment, to the emotions, to the needs of the woman he loved.

"I trust you, Mistress," he told her. "What can I do for you? How can I please you? Worship you." He dropped down to put his lips on her throat, under her ear. "Tell me what you want."

"Your mouth...everywhere." As he drew back, her smile was a little strained on the edges. "But starting with my cunt. I want to come against your mouth. I want to come three times before I ride you, give you a release. I want to see you savage and mindless, Neil. I want to feel the warrior's full power. I also want to feel your trust, to know you let me have that. Let me hold your soul for a little while."

He would have told her she was going to hold his soul forever, but they'd already come too close to that darker shore. Now it was time for something different.

He released the rail, moved down her body. He paused just above the temptation of her breasts, but she gave him an imperious look, as much a monarch as her fantasies had portrayed. "I didn't say start there."

He shot her a heated look. "Roger that, but just for the record, you playing with your tits in front of me? I haven't been that hungry to put my mouth on a nipple and suck since I was born."

Desire suffused her features. "Then do as I order, and you might get the privilege."

He slid down her body. He loved the smell of her arousal, her readiness to accept him. He nuzzled the curls, then tasted, tracing his tongue over the labia, teasing her, making her lift her hips. Her hand dropped to grip his shoulder.

Here was where his Dom side could come into play, to drive her up even higher, to make her reach for what he could offer to her. But he wasn't kidding about his hunger to taste her, plunder. So when he thrust his tongue inside, sealed his mouth over her to suckle that sweet honey fully, he relished the way she cried out. Her hips bucked, pushing her against his mouth, asking for more of what he was giving her.

She latched onto the railings to give her leverage, and the sight indulged his part of the fantasy, a queen chained to his bed, his prisoner turning screams of rebellious rage and curses on his name to pleading cries of desire.

He gripped her thighs, shoved them out wider, opening her up further, holding them there, increasing the sensation. Her response built to shrieks as she thrashed, learned she couldn't fight his strength when he pitted it against her for her own pleasure. It was the best use of it he'd ever employed.

She was close to release, but he drew it out, loving how her needs escalated to sensual desperation, his name breaking from her lips.

Later, he'd admit to her just how close he'd come to begging for her mercy as well. But not right now.

He kept her thighs spread open as the climax crashed over her, pushing the ride to an excruciating edge that would leave her vibrating for more.

She had said three times, after all.

Her screams echoed against the walls, vibrated over his skin, made him bear down on his cock against the mattress to contain his reaction. He wanted nothing more than to shove himself inside her when she was still rippling with the strength of the orgasm he'd given her. Apparently, he wasn't alone in that thought.

"Neil...please." Her nails were clawing at him, and when he looked up, he saw the wild urgency of her expression had a different note. "Please. Don't let them...noises...voices..."

Fuck, the power of the climax. She'd warned him how extremes, even pleasurable ones, could be triggers, bringing despair to her instead of bliss.

Not on his watch.

He released her thighs, rose over her. Circling her waist with his arm again, tilting her hips up, he drove into her, the transition swift enough the climax kept rolling forward, taking her with it. Her gaze was fastened on his shoulder, not his face, and he cupped her head, brought it against his skin. Bringing intimacy, a haven, with the sexual drive. Her arms and legs wrapped around him as he thrust and withdrew, her cries muffled against his flesh.

"I'm here. Feel me, bébé. I'm right here. I'm inside you. I'm always inside you."

He'd never had anyone hold him so tight. Not since he'd had to carry a kid out of an active fire zone, explosions and bullets turning the six-year-old's world into a living hell. Neil had to have one hand free for his weapon, so he'd trusted the kid's survival instincts to power the clamp of his young limbs around Neil. He'd had his hand cupped over the back of the small skull like he was doing to hers.

War zones happened where they happened. And if you survived, what made you able to leave them behind was who you helped survive as well.

She knew that, because even as she fought the fight with her mind, her lips moved to his throat, spoke against his flesh. "Come with me, Neil," she gasped.

He followed her over the edge.

~

As their thundering heartbeats slowed, she lay in his arms. She reached up after a time, traced the iron length of one of the head-board railings. His strength had pulled it forward, into a convex line. He covered her hand. "I'll fix that later."

"Don't. I like looking at it." She'd liked how intensely he'd climaxed, the groans it had ripped from him, the rigidity of his body. How he'd bucked, shoved into her, had proven what he'd said. That he'd fuck as hard as he fought when he was pushed to it, and he'd definitely let her take the reins, push him to it. She was still quivering from the results. If her head wasn't tilted on its axis, she would have held to her resolve to have him bring her to climax two more times.

She pushed away any negative feelings about that interruption. It had worked out fine. Really fine. Her fingertips slid over his chest, down to the nip of his waist, his hip, the rock-solid buttock.

"I'd sleep with you for your ass alone."

"Same goes, bébé. That and your breasts. And your hair. Your smile, your hands...hell, even your pretty toenails."

She smiled, shifted her gaze to the ceiling, watched the fan rotate. The sheer curtain over her plastic-covered window rippled slowly from the movement. "I need to call a window repair company."

"I think Ros already did that."

"Hmm." The shadows murmured their constant conversation, but they were lethargic, half asleep like her. Things were too vibrant and detailed, but she could handle that. Like Maureen said. As long as she could walk the edge where things looked different, felt different, but she could still tell reality from illusion, hear herself think over the voices, it was okay.

He stayed quiet, but his hands continued to move over her, tracing the curve of her breast, following her throat, her upper arm.

"I'm detecting complicated brain wave activity," she noted. "A rare phenomenon in men after sex."

He grunted. "Don't alert the media just yet. The only thing I was thinking was I should go get your muffuletta and feed you."

"Your stomach growled a few minutes ago. Tell the truth. You're actually wondering if you can have the part I likely won't eat, since Central's muffulettas are so big."

He chuckled, trailed his fingers down her back, caressed the shallow valley over her buttocks, then smoothed over them, traced the crevice. It was distracting, but she still sensed something more important than muffulettas were on his mind.

"If you want to say something to me, I'd advise you just to say it. I spend too much time digging around in my own brain. It doesn't leave a lot left over to excavate what's happening in someone else's."

Another quiet grunt. "You wouldn't know it, when you bring the Mistress side out. You get right into a man's head."

"That's different. That's like planting flowers versus weeding. Much more fun."

When she tilted her face up to see his smile, she brushed questioning fingertips along his jaw. He answered by stroking her collarbone, her upper arm, finishing at her hand, lifting it to compare it to the size of his. "You're so delicate," he said quietly. "Which is why it awes me, how strong you are. The life you've made for yourself, knowing this was coming toward you, something you believed could demolish everything you've built yourself."

She heard the depth of feeling behind the words, his sincerity. The way he saw her, she couldn't hide from him.

"Most people know we're all on a time clock," she responded, trying to keep her voice steady. "It's conceptual, though. Nebulous. We bargain and barter with ourselves, waste a lot of time thinking we have plenty of tomorrows. I always knew."

She lifted a shoulder. "I wanted to make sure, when I reached the end, I could look back on a life well-lived. Not years wasted, worrying what would happen when I got there. As it was, I lost those first few years after my mother died. It took me time to pull out of the swamp of my childhood, get momentum going in a better direction."

"Like I said, a strong soul," he responded, hands tightening on her. He paused. "And then I think... No one is that strong, unless they have hope. Or faith, no matter how small a spark, that you'll find a way to weather the storm, hold onto the things that matter."

She tensed, but he stroked her shoulder again, made a soothing noise. "Just voicing my thoughts, Mistress. Not requiring a reaction."

He tipped up her chin again, framed her face, her throat, with one large hand. Leaning in, he brushed his lips over her cheek, her jaw. "It's not the size of the spark that matters. It's not even how bright. It's that it keeps burning. You burn with such a beautiful light, Abby."

"You should do greeting cards. Motivational posters." There was no denying his words affected her, though. Neil didn't come from a cushy life of empty platitudes. He'd been in situations where the truth behind the words had been tested. Tested harshly enough to reveal what part of them was actual truth, when matched against the will and soul of the one tested.

He shifted her to her back so he could nuzzle her, taste her. Her hand rested on his shoulder as she enjoyed the male attention, his version of a tender aftermath. His care of her stirred lazy desire in her lower belly. But then a thought intruded, a wound from their earlier argument. She wouldn't let it remain untreated.

"I didn't mean it. What I said earlier."

"About what?"

He lifted his head, his eyes so close. Too close. She turned her cheek to the pillow, stared past his shoulder at the window. Sometimes now, her timing was off, her sense of when to say things.

"Never mind. I don't want to...this has been nice, and my head's acting up. I don't want to take us to a bad place."

"Okay. As long as the reason you don't want to say it is to keep your headspace where you want it. Not to spare my feelings. Remember what I said. I meant it." He stroked his knuckles down her face, kissed it, laid another kiss in the sensitive crevice between her breasts. He cupped them, held them close together as he played his tongue in the tighter channel, sending sparks to her lower belly.

"Neil, I don't think I can..."

"You don't have to do a thing, Mistress. You're the queen, captive in my bed, my plaything to enjoy."

"I'm afraid another orgasm that strong might make me...lose myself. Not in the good way."

Something no woman said, ever. But he didn't let her feel the crushing despair, the sense of being less now than she'd been before. He just sent her a smile that carried heat all the way to her toes. "Then I'll make sure it's like lying on a lounge chair inside the tideline. Feeling the surf come and go, water rushing over your skin, through your fingertips, all while you lie there and soak in the sun."

The words stilled her, and then what she heard in his voice, his intentions, made her breath catch. "I've got two orgasms to go to serve my Mistress's orders." He dipped his head, licked the top of her breast, increased the pressure of his fingers. "Tell me what you didn't mean, Abby."

"When I go to Switzerland...I'd like it if you were there."

His head rose again. In that scant moment when their gazes met, she felt everything he was, how remarkable. How much he'd brought to her life when she'd least expected it.

It made her hate herself for the words she couldn't hold back. Being incredulous at how she could have reached the point, so quickly, where she wanted this man present at her life's end was one thing; inviting him to face it with her was another. It was a terrible thing to ask. But he'd told her to say what she meant, and even before this had happened, she'd never been the type of person to back away from something once she put it out there. Which meant she had to finish the thought.

"I would like it, if you and Ros are the last faces I see."

She braced herself for the regret she'd feel when he drew back, or his emotions shifted in a direction that would tell her how badly she'd ruined the rest of their evening.

Instead, he lowered his head again. This time he put his mouth on her right nipple, drew it in, began to suck. Tenderly, building desire in her as he'd said, like the gentle rush of surf over and around her while she reclined in its embrace. Nothing demanding, but still a deep, abiding pleasure, something she was loathe to leave, and he made no demand that she do so.

The words slipped away. Not ignored, but absorbed in what they felt for one another, physically and at far deeper levels.

He brought her to the second climax just by suckling and playing with her breasts, with his thorough attention to them. His body was lying between her legs, so she was rubbing herself against the conveniently taut ridges of his abdomen when that wave lifted her. It rode her out to sea and back again, no big highs or lows, just a deep wash of feeling that eventually deposited her back into that beach chair, leaving her limp and throbbing with the aftermath.

When he lifted his head, the intensity of his expression held her. All he felt, about where he'd just taken her, and what she'd asked of him, was there. He cupped her jaw, threaded his hand through her hair to tighten on it, let her feel the strength of his resolve. In her bed, in her mind, in the way he answered her question now.

"Yes," he said. "I will be with you, until and through the end, no matter what happens between now and then."

Her throat got too tight to answer him, but her hands were holding onto him as if she'd never let him go. "For your third climax, I want to be inside you again," he told her. Then he reminded her of her earlier words. "There are no restraints strong enough to keep me from taking you, except your word, Mistress. So what will it be?"

"No words," she whispered. "Just take."

CHAPTER TWENTY

Humping ten miles of hostile terrain after getting shot had taken less effort than leaving Abby that morning. In light of the diminishing time he might have with her, Neil wanted to be with her 24/7.

But his instincts, which had never failed him—not when he paid proper attention to them—told him obsessive hovering was the wrong way to go. It reeked of the wrong kind of desperation, the kind that wouldn't be helpful.

When Ros and Lawrence had arrived with coffee and breakfast, Abby was still in bed. She hadn't stirred when he'd pressed his lips to the corner of her soft mouth. After he came downstairs, Lawrence had nudged him toward the door. Thanks to the demands of the past couple days, his teammate knew what Neil needed to do to recharge.

It didn't make the decision any easier, though. Particularly as he passed Tubby's and Sol's, reminding him of those harrowing hours when they'd been looking for her, not sure if she was okay. They were currently closed, too early for them to be open.

It wasn't until he reached his place that Neil acknowledged how right Lawrence was. He'd started up his steps when a glint under them made him stop, return to the ground. As he pulled out his chef's knife that Lawrence had stashed under there, he wasn't seeing his wavering reflection in the blade. He saw Abby slashing toward her arm, the terror in her eyes. Her holding out her wrists, telling him to let the blood out.

He carried the knife inside, slid it with careful precision into the butcher block on his counter. Then he picked the whole thing up and stuck it on the very top shelf of his kitchen cabinet, putting it out of sight. Bracing both his hands on the counter, he took a deep, steadying breath.

He and Abby had expended a lot of good energy on one another last night, but when she finally gave in to exhaustion, he'd found himself waking every time she shifted. He'd stared into the darkness, wishing he could take that fantasy she'd had and paint it into their reality. Where he could be some kind of superhero army commander who vanquished every enemy to protect his queen, whether those enemies were spawned of man, or came straight from hell.

He threw together some food, a cooler, and strode out to the boat. All his nerves were drawn up tight. With her, in her presence and the presence of the others, he'd concentrated on everything he needed to be for her, for them, to serve the mission, however stated or unstated.

But once on the boat, it was a starting gun, letting everything rise. What could have happened to her on her journey to his place. If he hadn't been quick enough to get that knife from her. How he'd had to subdue her, take her somewhere she feared enough to fight everyone she loved as if they had become the enemy.

With her illness distorting everything, they had been.

Things were better now, he reminded himself. They'd made the right call. Even she'd thought so, once Dr. Mo's creative pharmaceuticals had helped break the episode.

As he pushed away from the dock and settled into navigating the bayou waters, things got steadier, his breathing easier. That was how it worked. The pain and regrets, the loss, the shit about the world a man couldn't figure out, they didn't go away. But this place had enough room to let them spread out, bring in more perspective.

Lotta pain in the world. Lotta pleasure too. That was what MeeMaw always said. Incomprehensible savagery and astounding gentleness. It all gave a man a sense of wonder.

Sometimes wondering what he'd done to deserve the gift of a front row seat. Sometimes wondering if the gods had checked out of the theater a long time ago. And sometimes a man just had to shut down the wondering part of his brain and let it all go. Let it be.

He forced himself not to take out his phone and check it every two seconds. It was against his thigh, and would chime and vibrate if anyone was looking for him.

He caught a half-dozen fish, took them to MeeMaw's. Tommy was there, having spent the night. The husband and wife were sitting on the dock in comfortable wood-framed canvas chairs. He brought them up to speed on Abby. Under Tommy's listening gaze and MeeMaw's piercing regard, he told them what was in his heart.

That he loved her. And dealing with losing her, of having to accept that as her decision, what she wanted, was the hardest thing he'd ever faced.

He respected her privacy, but knew it wasn't abusing it to tell two people he considered family what was weighing on him. They listened gravely. As he expected, they didn't push a lot of advice or suggestions. They said little about it until MeeMaw was wrapping up a slab of her cornbread for him.

"Give the world room to turn the way it wants to go, bébé," she said. "Do your part and see what happens."

It reflected her philosophy of the world, one he counted on. But he was feeling better enough to tease her.

"That's all the infamous swamp witch has for me? At least sacrifice a chicken in front of me. Read its entrails to predict a cryptic future."

She harrumphed. "I won't do that to a poor old chicken, but if I thought sacrificing one stringy old obstinate man would help..." She jerked her head toward Tommy.

Tommy puffed on a hand-rolled cigarette. "Sacrifice an old goat like me," he commented, "the gods will be insulted enough to strike you dead, old woman."

With a smile, Neil pushed off, leaving them to their good-natured bickering. When MeeMaw went back to her chair, he noticed Tommy was there to provide a steadying hand as she lowered her considerable bulk. She had bad knees, which was why she was rarely on a boat with him and Dobby anymore. Once she was settled, she clasped Tommy's hand and waved her free one at Neil.

He wanted what they had, and he wanted it with Abby. After a bunch of years of athletic sex, dancing under the stars, doing all the things they could do at their current age. He'd never had anything more than a nebulous sense of that toward any woman. Was it the gods' way of laughing at people, giving them such thoughts only when the exact opposite scenario looked probable? Not a lifetime of company, but a lifetime of mourning the person you'd been sure was the one you wanted to share that lifetime with.

If all the things she talked about came to pass, it wouldn't change how he felt. If her illness took away the ability to have the athletic sex or even dancing under the stars, they'd find other journeys and experiences with one another. Other avenues to that sense of wonder. The world offered an endless amount of them.

The only thing that mattered was being with her.

He headed down another tributary, where the cypresses were exceptionally old, standing like ancient giants in dark, shadowed waters. This part of the bayou had always suited him, particularly when he was having trouble calling his mind back from down range. This place was a bridge between there and home, because it held its own dangers. A person navigating these waters had to stay alert, but in a very different way from his job.

Once he spent enough time here, gradually he'd take himself to the more populated areas, nod courteously at the kayak tourists, the vacationing fishermen, some who knew the waters, some who didn't.

They weren't like MeeMaw, Tommy and Dobby, people who led lives on the fringes of nature's hand-in-hand beauty and barbarism. One moment revealing scenes of detached cruelty, an animal's struggle to survive and not become someone else's food. The next, that same soul finding a good sunning spot, or playing with a sibling or mate.

The bayou was a live-in-the-moment world, the passage of time irrelevant, except to mark when to take refuge from predators more active at one time of day versus another.

Down range, there was a similar live-in-the-moment feeling, the mission notwithstanding. If you got a breather, you took it, made the most of it.

Then you kept on. You did your part and waited to see what would happen.

~

As Abby sat on the top step of her back porch two days later, she had her face turned up to the sun, her eyes closed, arms braced behind her. She thought about a TV crime show episode she'd once watched, where a young woman had been sitting on the steps of a library, reading *Frankenstein* by Mary Shelley. She'd had a bomb strapped to her torso beneath her trim wool coat, a buffer against the New York winter chill. Her brown hair was floating against her cheeks, and when people walked past her, they stole a look at something pretty, something that made them smile. A lovely young woman reading a book.

"Being schizophrenic is like that," she'd told Maureen. "You don't know when you're going to go off, while the rest of the world walks by, oblivious to how easily it could be triggered, not only by the things you expect, but by what you don't."

That first orgasm with Neil had been so amazing and incredible. He'd deliberately built her up to that height, knowing how far she would soar, the power of the flight.

But it had also come with the precipitous fall, the brain's adverse reaction to excesses. He'd handled it just right. He hadn't left it alone, let her stew in it and castigate herself. He'd taken her on a different but equally incredible ride, his body moving with hers, holding her the way she held him.

She'd still been chewing on it the next day, which was why she'd had the conversation with Maureen. When all was said and done, yes, it was a limitation that came with the illness. They'd found a path through, one that brought its own joys.

She remembered a day her mother had been level enough to go on a picnic. She'd laughed and talked with her six-year-old daughter as they made sandwiches and deviled eggs. When they'd put a package of Oreos in the basket, her mother talked about baking cookies later. At the park, there'd been a group of college kids jamming out on flutes and guitars, a lively version of "Galway Girl." She and Momma had danced in a circle.

Two hours later, back home, her mother was tired, twitchy. Pushing at her temple with her fingers like she was trying to thrust them into bone. She asked Abby to run a bath for her. When Abby had it almost full, had knelt by it to test the temperature of the water, hands had grabbed her head and shoulders. Her mother had shoved her face under, so forcefully the edge of the tub had left bruises on her ribs.

"You won't take my child," she'd been screaming, the words garbled through the water and terror. "You won't steal her soul. I'll free it. You're free, Abby. Fly. Fly!"

It had been the first of the two times her mother would try to drown her. Fortunately, the second time, Abby had been older and stronger. The only thing that had saved her the earlier time was her mother was weak with fatigue, her hands shaking and slippery. When Abby managed to get away, she'd cut her lip open on the three sparkling rings her mother wore on her left hand.

Abby opened her eyes at the sound of the truck rumbling down the driveway. The lift of her heart, the way it thudded harder, made it hurt, but in a better way. She watched Neil cut the engine. He'd had his radio cranked up, playing Mellencamp who was rocking in the USA. His large hand, the capable fingers that had stroked her to climax, had been tapping the steering wheel.

He was displaying that surface casualness, which didn't conceal the alert and lethally trained warrior beneath, who could be called forth in a heartbeat. Like a bomb beneath an attractive young woman's coat. He was a far more stable weapon, though, the trigger controlled by him and his cool mind.

Only a handful of hours after that tub incident, her mother had evened out again, made the promised cookies. By that age, Abby had learned to shake off any horror that happened, so as not to miss the small moments of joy her mother could offer her. Such violent episodes were often followed by days of depression. If her mother left her room, it was only long enough to go to the kitchen, sit down and do her client's taxes, then go back to bed.

Abby learned early how to help check her work. She could itemize deductions as soon as she learned to read.

Recalling the swiftness of her mother's mood shifts, she shouldn't be surprised that, only a couple days after the hospital, she was ready to accept Neil's invitation to take her to the girls' softball game. Of course the fabulous sex with a gorgeous SEAL and some decent hours of sleep hadn't hurt.

But mostly she was just eager to see him again. Crazily eager, like the lovesick teenager she'd never had a chance to be. The closest she'd experienced to that was when Ros had introduced her to the pleasure of a Domme's power. Initially she'd been infatuated with the way it felt. Almost addicted, commanding a sub, seeing his responses. Spinning a pleasurable cocoon around him with her demands. Cause, effect, action, result. While the effect and result could be wondrously different for each sub, she controlled how the difference manifested.

It was a power she loved. And seeing how many intriguing ways it manifested with Neil, who wasn't a sub...it was a whole new chapter in the never-ending book of where a power exchange could go.

"Hey there." He was standing in front of her. She had missed him leaving the truck and walking along the paver path to her. Not too long ago, that would have unsettled her enough to send her back into the house to hide. Now, she accepted it as her current reality, one she could handle.

Because it was temporary.

She didn't much care for that thought or reminder, not while she was gazing at him. She had a single second to worry if she'd see something different in his gaze. He'd had time to come to his senses, realize the danger of spending any time with her. But she only saw a reflection of the same feelings she was having. Deep gladness that they were together again.

Maybe they were both crazy.

"I've figured it out, why you and I work," she said. "You're a Dom, but you're also a masochist. You like a woman who puts you through hell."

"We might share that trait. You're the one who fell for a man who'd make a lousy sub."

"Not so lousy," she said, staying where she was, not leaning forward toward him yet, though his eyes practically compelled her to do so. "Go to your truck and then walk back to me."

He arched a brow. Held a beat. But then he moved to the truck. He tapped it like a racer touching his mark, slanting her a wry look before he turned and came back to her. Not hurried, not a saunter, but something in-between, the confident movement of a man aware of his capabilities, down to the minutest tolerances. His strength, his flexibility, stamina.

With Neil, that confidence included what he believed was true or not, what he would fight for and what he would not. He'd fight every battle in a manner that ensured he'd achieve his objective, or make his opposition pay the price for denying him.

Or think about the rewards of letting him win.

Today's T-shirt was printed with a picture of an alligator, shadowing an oblivious kayaker who was navigating with a paddle that had a gator-shaped bite taken out of it. It was a favorite, because it was faded, soft, and stretched over his musculature in a nicely clingy way.

His thighs, the creases of denim over his groin and hips, held her attention, and made that longing in her increase. She imagined curling her hand in the front of the shirt, pulling him down upon her on the porch, having him brace his knees on the step below her spread legs and drive into her. She'd lie back on the porch boards and feel the heat of the man and the sun spin her away into a hazy, wet euphoria.

"Come here," he said.

She'd given him an order. Now that he'd obeyed it, he'd demand parity. The firmness of his voice sent another ripple of pleasure through her. He stood on the ground, one foot braced on the bottom step, his hand out to her. While he looked as if he were patiently waiting, there was a restlessness in the energy around him that thrilled her, too. When she put her hand in his, he tugged her to her feet and right against him. He kept her on the step just above his foot, so they were even in height as he took her mouth in a demanding, heated kiss. The other hand dropped to her ass to knead, press her against him, so she felt a very ready arousal that made her quiver in the hold of his arms.

"I've missed you," they said at almost the same time, against one another's skin, because neither wanted to move back, allow an inch of space to separate them.

Being away from him almost two days had been unimaginably difficult. Telling him she needed those two days was even worse. They were both aware of her time clock. But she'd needed the time to perform tasks she couldn't inflict on him or her friends.

She'd finalized the transition of certain projects to Sonya Tiltwell, her right hand in her department. Abby told her and the rest of her staff she was planning an extended sabbatical at her Indiana family home.

She and Ros had agreed the staff would be told after the event itself. Abby could only handle a certain amount of emotional recoil over it, so she'd limited those in-the-know to the TRA executive circle.

She'd written up a letter that could be read to the staff later to explain things. Crafting the right words took time and required a lot of reflection. Many of them she considered friends as well as coworkers.

She'd started on her estate planning months ago, and perhaps because it *had* been months ago, it hadn't been as draining then. It had been mostly about numbers, handling transfer of property, distribution of funds.

In contrast, the final loose ends to be tied up, the more emotional decisions, planning and executing them, weren't as easy.

She'd considered when to end the sessions with Maureen, but Maureen said she'd be available to Abby, even up to the day she left for Switzerland. Since Maureen was helping Abby mostly hold her own against her symptoms, it made sense. There'd been moments over the past couple days they'd howled like barbarians at the gate, trying to beat through the barrier the meds and psychotherapy results had provided. Thin, but holding.

The sessions with Maureen also helped her clarify the things she wanted to say in her final communications. Choosing the words that she hoped would help ease any pain her decision would cause was difficult. Writing those missives could send her to bed for several hours.

But it was done. The individual letters to her closest friends formed a small stack in her secretary, next to the folder holding the important papers Ros would need for the estate processing.

In the closet, Abby had stored individual packages she'd put together for each of them, items she thought would be good remembrances. There was also a basket of treats and toys for Freak, Ros's three-legged cat. She knew Ros would get a smile out of that. Abby hadn't brought him over since the symptoms had gotten worse, but she had visited him at Ros's house. She'd miss the little frog-sounding feline, his imperious manner, the way he'd adapted to being practically a timeshare cat between her and Ros's home when Ros had to travel for business.

While they were apart, she'd asked Neil to do whatever he normally did when he was home. Work out, go to the rec center where he, Dale and Max volunteered, and Lawrence worked as a coach. Spend time on the bayou, fishing with Tommy and Dobby.

Yes, time was short, but she'd thought it through a long time ago. Life and schedules would proceed exactly as they would if she wasn't leaving for Switzerland. It was best for no one to act as if she was. Particularly for her, and not as a selfish thing. Well, not selfish in that way.

It took pressure off of everyone. It allowed her friends to continue to work, which helped distract them, and kept her from being destabilized by an overdose of emotionally intense attention. It was better to plan it in the proper doses and distribution.

She'd have the dinner with her TRA sisters at Ros's house two nights before she departed. Going to Switzerland would be a big enough change in her routine to likely cause a psychotic breakdown in the middle of the airport. She'd reserve the final day before travel to relax, be mostly alone. Maureen had agreed to give her additional sedatives to help her with the flight.

She had one last communication to write, and it was proving more problematic than expected. She'd put *Dear Neil* at the top, but couldn't go further. She'd put it away.

Later. She'd do that one later.

She hadn't been completely on radio silence with Neil these past couple days. Since she was sending Ros texts on her status, he'd insisted on being on the same distribution.

Which she'd done, but she'd also given in to the temptation to send him separate texts, which he responded to in ways that had her smiling, both then and later, while she was doing her tasks. Often, she'd slide her arms around herself in comfort, imagining it as his arms. Touch her mouth in sensual remembrance. Fight the urge to throw all her tasks aside and just be with him 24/7.

But she knew how important this stuff was. So she'd held firm, and now she faced her reward.

He touched her face. "Got done what you needed to get done?"

"Yes. All but one thing, and it can wait. I want to spend today with you. And tonight."

"Good. Saves me having to get bossy and insist." He took her hand, and she smiled at him as they walked to his truck.

"You'll be disappointed if you can't be bossy," she observed. "I'll change my mind a couple times today so you can do that."

"I still have a really good fantasy of spanking you. Sounds like a win-win."

She chuckled as he opened her door and gave her a hand up into it. "Did you fish with Dobby and Tommy?"

"Yep. Mostly slept on the boat deck while they fished, though. Until Dobby dropped a juvenile alligator on my chest, the crazy bastard."

"Actually, crazy would have been dropping one of the adult ones on you. He's big enough to pull it off."

"Thanks for putting that out into the universe for him to snatch up and do next time. I'm never closing my eyes around him again."

As he drove them to the sports park, their hands stayed clasped on his knee. She leaned against the console, close enough to brush her lips over his shoulder, inhale the scent of his shaving lotion off his throat, his laundry detergent. She slid her other hand over the crease of denim at his thigh, and over, across his testicles, up higher.

"Abby."

She slipped the button of his jeans and pushed her hand under the waistband to grip him, give him another stronger stroke as he bit back a curse.

She stretched up to bite his ear, whisper into it with a playful, deeper Southern drawl. "I'm so wet right now, you could slide into me as easy as a gator into bayou water."

He one-handed spun the wheel, bumped off the main road into a narrow alley between a bank, closed for the weekend, and a bodega that didn't open for another hour. "Get rid of the shorts," he said tersely.

She shimmied out of them, dropping them on the floorboards. When he brought the truck to a stop, he left it running but put it in park and set the brake. With the other hand, he dropped the seat back, then took her by the waist, pulling her over him.

The man had fast reflexes. She'd never appreciated that as much as she did right now. He pushed his jeans open, while she closed both hands over him, humming at his size and stiffness.

"I've missed you too much to wait," she breathed. "I've missed you inside me."

"I'm getting that, bébé. And same goes." He hooked the crotch of her panties with long fingers, holding it pinned to the tender pocket between thigh and cunt, his thumb pressing into her upper thigh. "Put me inside you," he said. "Your pussy better be as wet as you claim, because I don't plan to be gentle."

She guided the head in. No matter what he said, she saw him gauge the truth of it first, pausing to take in the slickness, the way her sex closed over the broad head as easily as her mouth. She gasped as he lived up to the threat then, putting his other hand on her hip and shoving her down onto him.

Oh, Goddess. It felt so damn good. She held on as he thrust into her, a hand on her hip, the other moving up to caress her throat, her nape, thumb running over her mouth, pushing into it so he penetrated both places as he worked her on his groin.

"How many times did you come while you were away from me?" he demanded, his voice hoarse.

"Only twice. My yard guy isn't...as good at this as you are. But he looks pretty...jeans...no shirt. Lots of tattoos... Nipple piercing."

When he smacked her buttock, she laughed over the breathless words. She dug her claws into his chest, and when he brought her down to kiss and bite her throat, her lips, she was already climaxing on him, crying out her pleasure into his mouth. His growl of response heralded his own release, his seed jetting into her.

They *had* wanted one another. Badly.

She held his gaze as long as she could, finishing with her forehead pressed to his, the two of them drawing shuddering breaths in the confines of the truck. The A/C blew a light draft along her lower back.

"Jesus," he murmured. "That was almost worth the wait."

"Almost?"

"I would trade any level of pleasure for spending every minute of my time with you. That's a pleasure that beats out any other, even this." He brushed back a strand of hair that had loosened from the comb holding it and caught in the corner of her damp lips.

She stared down at him, pressing those lips together. As she'd said, it was never just empty words with Neil. He meant it.

She'd told herself she'd push away any regrets, any weight that would try to gather on her heart about her decision. No way to go but forward. She was glad she'd gotten enough of those details handled that she could do this. What she'd told Maureen she wanted to do. Spend her last days enjoying and doing whatever she wished, whatever her symptoms would allow, with the people who mattered.

"Same question," she said, giving him an appraising look. She teased the softness of his beard, his clean-shaven throat beneath it, with her own touch. "How many times did you take yourself in hand, sailor, thinking of me? And you better not count the times you were thinking about someone else."

He chuckled, hands tightening on her as she bit his ear again. "I lost count. Couldn't stop myself from doing it wherever, whenever, I was thinking of you, which was all the time. Only you." The sudden intensity of his look speared her low in the abdomen.

"Come to think of it, maybe that was why Dobby dropped the alligator on me. Kind of a rude thing to be doing in front of him and his dad."

He laughed, catching her hands as she tried to pinch him. His gaze shifted to the mirror. "Oh, crap."

In as swift a move as he'd pulled her over him, he had her settled back on her seat and put her shorts in her lap. Only then did he tuck himself back in, pull the jeans in place without fastening them, and put the truck in gear. She glanced back to see a NOLA PD cruiser had turned in to take a closer look at what the truck was doing, idling in the alley. Neil gave the officer a friendly wave and eased out onto the street on the other side.

"You are trouble, woman." He flashed her a smile. "The good kind."

~

When they arrived at the sports park, a lot of the parking spots were full. "It's game day for the league," he explained. "There are five fields, so there will be ten teams playing."

The park was packed with softball players and their families, a scene of organized chaos, noise and enthusiasm. At her worried expression, he squeezed her hand.

"I've got a quiet space for us to watch, but if it gets too much, we'll go. No big deal. Don't get stressed over that. We don't have to leave because you're afraid something *might* happen. Trust me, okay?"

"Okay."

She gazed at his profile, watching him seek out the best parking spot. The other night, when they'd been together in her room, she'd thought what she was thinking now, in a nebulous sort of way. Ever since then, the thought kept coming back to mind, more and more significant each time. It was something she couldn't say to him. At least not now. If she did, it would be in that final moment, when hearing it would be a *thank you,* rather than a slap in the face.

He was the best gift a woman could receive at the end of her life.

His feelings about her decision had come spilling out that night in the bedroom, when they had their argument. But he'd not yet stinted on any of the emotional support she needed. When he held her, and passion became fierce, she might see a glimpse of the pain in his eyes, know deep in his soul there was a howling, wounded animal. But for her, he would keep it contained. Whatever emotional surfeits he had about it were being handled elsewhere, no suppressed resentments or pressures spilling from him.

She would have loved him for that near miraculous accomplishment alone, knowing just how tremendously difficult an effort that would be for anyone. Let alone an alpha male used to fixing things, working the problem, coming up with a solution.

He cut the engine, slid out and circled around to give her a hand out of his truck. But rather than backing off, he tugged her up against him, sliding his arm around her waist to lift her off her feet as he kissed her. He pressed her against the side of the truck, cupping the back of her head. She slid an arm under his to press her palm against his broad back, barely resisting the urge to drop it down and enjoy the firmness of his ass in the just-right-fit jeans he was wearing. It was a family park, after all.

And they had just had sex. It should be able to hold them for a couple hours.

Theoretically.

He surveyed her neat pair of light blue denim shorts, paired with a snug V-necked white T-shirt embellished with blue ribbon at the neck and sleeve hems. She also wore canvas sneakers.

"You match every fantasy of a woman I've ever had." Fishing in the back of the truck, he came up with one of his bill caps, one conveniently in a sky-blue color. He adjusted the tab in the back so it would fit her head better, and then snugged it down over her brow, giving the bill a tap. "I have a shady spot for us, but just in case. Got to protect that fair skin of yours. I think you're a vampire. What Southern girl doesn't tan?"

"One with a lot of Irish in her. I burn a pretty shade of rhubarb. When it sinks in, I manage pasty golden. Like French vanilla ice cream."

"Now I'm going to want to watch you lick an ice cream cone." He tossed her a suggestive look. "If this wasn't an important game day for the girls, requiring full fan support, I'd have talked you into staying in bed with me all day."

A few days ago, he'd had to pluck her screaming and raving off his porch, take her to a hospital. Yet he was treating her as a fully cognizant, independent woman, one he desired. Someone with whom he had all the time in the world to spend.

She had no idea if that contributed just as much as the potency of his kiss to the weakness of her knees, the giddy flipflops in her stomach, but she was fine with all of it.

She thought back to when she'd expected the two Dominants thing to be the obstacle that would keep him at arm's length. But the other night, the fantasy that had played out into her directing him to go down on her, to follow her orders to bring her to release again and again, it had worked out right. Her, commanding a Dominant captive, not a sub. The challenge had been exciting...fun.

Circumstances and the people involved sculpted the way the power exchange worked, but she expected their situation was a little unusual, even for that. It was as Tommy had said, right?

A lot of love stories in the world. No two of them look the same, and it's not always easy for folks outside of them to understand.

"You wouldn't have succeeded in keeping me in bed," she lied. "You promised to prove your interest in softball has nothing to do with nubile young women in snug uniforms."

"I didn't say it had nothing to do with it. I implied it wasn't my primary interest. I strive to be honest with you in all things."

"You can be a little less honest about that."

He shot her a wicked grin. He'd opened the door behind her seat to retrieve a picnic basket, cooler and a pair of stadium chairs. As he did that, she moved a couple steps away, to give him room to maneuver the items out of the truck. There was a grassy strip alongside the parking area, and her attention was caught by the sprinklers making their chit-chit-chit noise. The arcing lines of water caught the early sunlight, shimmering as they glided across one another's paths, then back again. The spray of drops turned different colors, depending on how the light struck them, where she was standing.

"I can see each one," she murmured. "Separate but moving together. It's beautiful."

He'd come to her side as she spoke. When she glanced up, she was likewise caught by his gaze lingering over her face, how he absorbed her words.

Recognizing the shift in her emotions, he put down the picnic basket, took her hand. "What is it?"

She hesitated, then told him. "Over the past few months, when the details got too vivid like that, it made me afraid, because of what it meant. I'd turn away, run from it. But the way you look, listening to me, the way I can show it to you through my eyes... If there are good things about the way my brain is set up, if it's not all bad, why not appreciate those things?"

She mulled it for herself, shook her head. "I hadn't thought about that. Denying those good things isn't going to change anything, and it balances the not-so-good things."

"Well, you told me a lot of great artists might have had schizophrenia or illnesses like it. And mathematicians."

"I'm definitely the latter. I can't draw a passable flower." She gazed at the moving water. "Numbers came so easily to me. Laying out a business plan, projections, juggling the variables. Seeing what we needed to do to get the business off the ground. Ros said I drew the outline, and she brought the crayons."

"Sounds like her," he said.

She fell silent, watched the sprinklers for another moment or two. He waited for her. No rush, emphasizing how nothing today needed to stress her out. He was here, and everything was okay. That thought, the way it connected to what could happen while they were here, didn't worry her as much as it once would have, either.

When she returned her attention to him, Neil offered her his free hand. He held the cooler, stadium chairs slung over his shoulder. The picnic basket was at his feet. "Ready?"

She took the picnic basket, sharing her part of the load. "Ready."

CHAPTER TWENTY-ONE

More cars were pulling in. Rear hatches were opened, players and parents removing chairs, coolers, softball gear. Teenage girls were everywhere, wearing uniform shirts and white pants with a side stripe that matched the shirt. The girls stretched, adjusted their shoes, and snugged caps down on their heads. Those with long hair threaded the tail through the opening in the back of the cap.

Unlike most teens, none of them were looking at a cell phone, or even seemed to be carrying one. When she shared that with Neil, he nodded.

"These are serious players, advanced teams. They play like the fate of the free world depends on the outcome. If I ever need a civilian militia, I'm coming here first. Most would just pick up a rifle and ask me to point them toward whoever needed their ass kicked."

At her look, he gave her a grin. "Of course, that would be after we made sure the targets were *really* bad people."

"Of course."

The bleachers near the dugouts were filling up. When a ball cracked against a bat, a coach hitting grounders to the players for warm up, she jumped.

Neil squeezed her hand. "We won't be sitting over there. I leave those spots for the players' families."

That relieved her of one concern. He wasn't giving up his

preferred observation point because of her limitations. Veering away from the sidewalk leading into the fenced playing field, he took her toward the mown expanse of grass behind one of the outfields. The ground rose toward a grove of established oaks and pines. As they reached the trees, the branches creaked, leaves whispering from the breeze.

All the sounds blended with her voices, but not in a bad way. The meds were doing their job on the auditory hallucinations today. So far, so good.

Several outfielders were firing the ball back and forth, the ball making a crisp *plock* as it hit the palm of their leather gloves. Neil pointed to the pitcher, a solidly built girl with a sassy cut to her black hair, and a set of rings along the shell of her ear. She reminded Abby of a young Vera.

"That's Tessie," he said. "I'll introduce you after the game. She's a great pitcher and a tough player. Says she intends to be a SEAL. Sometimes she joins me and Max at the park so we can put her through her paces."

"What are her chances?"

Neal lifted a shoulder. "She keeps on her current track, she'll make a good accounting of herself. Can't predict if she'll make it all the way through or not. Right now, she's a kid full of zeal. Which isn't much different from the guys who do it just to prove they can get through one of the toughest training programs the U.S. military offers. That's fine, but most will be knocked out."

"Why?"

The look he gave her showed the experience of a seasoned operator. "Because to stick with it, and see it through, you have to have a reason greater than that. During the training, there's a breaking point. That's where you decide the real reason you'll keep going, see it through. Or you'll call it done. Being a SEAL is a calling, a personal decision at the deepest level of your soul. It's a conversation you keep having, however many years you stay in it, because that resolve gets tested a lot, in ways no one anticipates."

"You'll never leave it."

His hand brushed her hip, and she felt the weight of his gaze on her. "When it's time, I will. As I said, it's an ongoing conversation."

"I'm glad you do something you love. That's important." She

assumed a more teasing expression. "And you're such an adult about it."

She liked that half smile he did, balanced between serious intent and amusement. "Don't sound so surprised. Depending on the day, I do a credible imitation of one."

She returned her attention to the girls, impressed by their energy. And this was just warm up. "Ever get some creeps who come here to watch for the wrong reasons?"

"Sometimes. Not too often. The Internet's easier, and New Orleans' heat can be a little brutal." His eyes twinkled. "Sometimes we have retirees, the ones who've reached the age they can indulge their dirty-old-man permission slip to hang out and watch, but they just like looking at pretty girls and dreaming of younger days. Plus, they're the first ones to notice the real creeps and drive them off.

"Another reason I'd come here for that militia," he added. "They'd make themselves useful, too."

He'd brought her to the crest. Beyond the tree line, it sloped back down. She saw walking trails that wound off toward other areas of the park.

Neil spread a doubled-up blanket at the base of a tree, set the two chairs to one side of it, the cooler in between them. He didn't direct her toward the chairs, though. He sat down on the blanket, braced his back against the tree's trunk, and tugged her down to sit between his knees.

"Oh yeah." He grunted, tightening his arms around her. "This is the way to enjoy the game."

With a smile, she leaned against him, her back comfortably nested against his chest, her arm looped over his bent knee. He pressed his lips to her hair, inhaled her. "Girls smell so good."

"Even sweaty and dirty?" She motioned to the field.

"Compared to boys, absolutely." He twined his fingers in her thick red curls that wound around his wrist as if they were holding him, instead of the other way around. An intriguing act he probably did on purpose, knowing what the hint of it would do to her. "I could sit like this forever."

"I doubt it. You'd get bored, always having to do quiet things with me. Everything planned, no spontaneity."

Avoiding crowds, figuring out ways to keep the stimulus low, not trigger her symptoms. Like what he'd said about Tessie and the SEALs. The novelty of it, the challenge, could be altered by the reality.

She was glad she didn't say any of that aloud, but she was admonishing herself for saying as much as she had. Why did she do that? She knew how much effort it took him to contain his reactions, to try not to pressure her, and she appreciated the hell out of that. And yet these comments kept slipping out, as if she had to keep shoving proof at him, why he was better off without her.

He'd given so much thought to how to make this day pleasant for her, and all of a sudden, with those damn mood swings, she was lashing him for it in an indirect way he couldn't help but recognize.

No, that wasn't her illness. That was her being perverse. Bitchy. So it didn't surprise her at all that he didn't let her get away with it.

Neil could tell himself he'd thought it through before he reacted, because there was a lot of need for that with Abby. But if time was short, he wasn't going to put up with passive aggressive bullshit, let that lock doors between them.

He was good at kicking in doors, in a variety of ways.

He tightened his fingers in her hair, a strong enough grip he made her pupils dilate in reaction, her lips part. He brought her head back on his shoulder and to the side with the pressure, so he could put his mouth on her throat. He gave her his teeth, a strong enough bite that if he hadn't had her full attention, he won it then, the sudden stillness of her body proving it.

"You forgot our deal," he murmured. "So let me remind you. I don't put pressure on you about your decision. You don't use who and what I am to justify that decision."

She stiffened, but he didn't ease up. He also didn't say anything else, because sometimes words were overrated. He let his mouth cruise over her throat, sucking and nipping the erratic pulse, taking his time. He kneaded her waist with the other hand, fingers sliding along the inside of the waistband of her shorts. He caressed her with a possessive ownership intended to be blatantly challenging.

She could have shoved at him, gotten pissed off, and he would have been ready for that, too. But after a long, quivering moment, tension ebbed out of her, along with a throaty chuckle. He caught the rueful light in her eyes, tinged with sadness, and it changed the tone. His grip gentled in her hair, became a massaging touch.

"All right, bébé?" he said quietly.

"All right. And I'm sorry." She cleared her throat, curled her hand over his larger one. "You're right."

He nudged her face up, put a kiss on her mouth. Tasted sugar, because after their too-brief stop in the alley, they'd split a beignet. He'd probably pay for that with an infestation of ants in the truck, from the powdered sugar that had landed on the floorboards or seats. But that was fine. He'd use a leaf blower to blast the little varmints out later.

He put his hands to her waist. "Tell me."

"Tell you what?" Her little flash of alarm made him give her another reassuring squeeze.

"You didn't miss anything, bébé. I just wasn't clear. Sometimes it feels like you're in my head."

"Oh." She took a breath, but that flash became a softer shine, reflecting pleasure with his comment. "I feel that way about you sometimes, too. What do you want me to tell you?"

"You've told me what it's like in your head. What you see, hear, feel. But tell me what daily life is like with a schizophrenic. When you're worried, you do the hit-and-run comments, like now, but I'd like a real picture, painted by that practical mind of yours."

She studied the pine needles scattered across the ground to her right. Her fingers slid along his forearm. "Why do you want to know that?"

"In case my next girlfriend has it."

At her narrow look, he held up a hand. "Hey, I'm really attached to this one, so it might be my favorite future dating pool. I've already contacted the dating sites about adding it as a check box."

She elbowed him. "You're such a wiseass."

"I know. Dale told Lawrence to shoot me once. I think us standing in a Starbuck's in VA Beach was the only reason Lawrence didn't do it. They couldn't figure out how to write that up as a friendly fire incident."

A smile quivered around her lips, despite her obvious efforts to conceal it. He ran a knuckle across her abdomen, making her squirm as he tickled her. "Yeah, I'm picking on you, but the question is serious. Will you tell me?"

She considered, then sighed quietly. "Okay."

It took her a couple minutes to put her thoughts together, so he leaned past her, pulled the cooler over. He drew a couple drinks out of it, popped the tab of her soda for her. Then he settled back, stroking her hair, her hip, watching the players below until she was ready to talk. If she didn't want to, if it stressed her out, he'd let it go. But she finally spoke.

"I've always been an obsessive planner. I had to force myself to trust spontaneity, never really comfortable with it. Ros helped me with that, once we met. Maybe it was because of always having to anticipate my mother's next move, or maybe it's something that foreshadows the illness. It's a skill that comes in handy, though, once it manifests. There's a reason they call it 'managing' the disease.

"You've seen it at my house. My day is planned out to a level of detail most people don't require or need. Same for travel or new events. The more I can anticipate, the less likely I am to get stressed. Everything has to be taken into account, to anticipate or avoid triggering symptoms."

She was drawing straight lines on his arm. "If you joined your life to mine, there are a lot of things you'd probably have to do on your own, or with other people, because it would be too much for me, not enjoyable."

She paused, her gaze resting to the left of his face. Her way of saying she wanted to be looking at him. He tightened his arm on her, captured the hand drawing on him, stroked her knuckles before releasing her to continue the self-soothing movement.

He waited to see if she would go on, let her see that she had his full and open attention. He didn't point out she was talking about the two of them, rather than in hypothetical third person.

"Say you had a friend coming into town for a couple days," she said, "and you really wanted me to meet him."

"I doubt that would be true if the friend was female."

She pinched him, hard. "Shut up."

"Shutting up, ma'am."

She shook her head at him, but continued. "We set it up at a restaurant where it's hard to get reservations, and boom, because it's too much excitement, or too many things to juggle, or none of that, just some crazy snap in my head, putting it in the wrong space for no reason at all, things would change. I'd have to excuse myself from the dinner, maybe right in the middle of it. And maybe I'm showing too many flag symptoms for you to trust that I could take a cab home on my own, so you'd have to tell your friend you'd be back, or cut the night short."

She paused again. Eyes now on a nearby tree. "Tell me what you're thinking," she said softly.

He tipped his head so his jaw pressed against her temple. He gazed down at her lovely breasts, watched her hand, curling and uncurling over his, where it now rested on her bent knee. He stroked her fingers one at a time, straightening them, then curling them under the shelter of his again.

"Cedrick, one of my teammates, has a couple kids. Several years back, he and his wife planned his daughter's tenth birthday party. It was a big deal. They put all kinds of effort into it. Eight hours before it happens, we get called into a time-sensitive op that lasted three and a half weeks."

When she swallowed, her gaze flickering with an emotion he recognized, he tightened his hands on her. "I'm not saying it's apples to apples, Abby. I'm telling you that plans changing when it's the last thing you want to happen isn't unfamiliar to me. Anybody who knows anything about the life a SEAL leads will tell you marrying one is batshit crazy."

Watching her profile, he saw a rueful half smile cross her face. "Did you just imply my craziness is what drew me to you, sailor?"

"Hey, you said it, not me. I thought it was just hyperbole, but..."

He'd pushed the humor too far. Her amusement disappeared. "Making jokes can't change the truth, Neil," she said tightly.

"No. It's not intended to. But finding humor in the craziest shit can loosen up the tension, make us step back and see it differently. Find a different way. Give us some breathing room from fear, the *oh, shit, we're fucked* moments. Believe it or not, that ability has saved me and my team from some pretty bad situations."

Case in point? It had just put enough distance between him and his emotions to do what he might have missed.

It had pointed him toward a window.

When she'd suggested his life would be permanently limited with her in it, he'd wanted to snap at her, but something else had occurred to him, biting that feeling in half. What MeeMaw had said.

Give the world room to turn the way it wants to go.

He'd interpreted her passive aggressive comment as something she was trying to prove to him, why he was better off without her. But what if that wasn't what was happening at all? Why was she trying to warn him off, to justify a decision she'd already made?

What if some part of her, even unconsciously, was exploring what it might be like if she stuck around?

For herself.

If he leaped on that hint like a starving dog on meat, he might knock it off its axis. The hope for it was too fragile a thing to be acknowledged. It had to stand hidden and off stage, glimpsed by peripheral vision alone.

A voice in the shadows. Yeah, the irony wasn't lost on him.

"This event was planned, but you've never done it before," he pointed out. "And you are never boring, bébé." He gave her hair a more playful tug. "Change of subject. When you were at my place, did you notice that bucket of rocks by my back door?"

She was still rigid, but she cocked her head, attentive. He took advantage of the shift, placing his lips on her throat again while he gripped her waist. He enjoyed the increased pressure of her buttocks against his groin, the insides of his thighs. "My dad was a geologist with an oil company. We moved around a lot when I was a kid, to monitor different locations, drilling sites. Then I became a SEAL, and it was more of the same."

"So each rock represents a place you've been?"

"You're anticipating, Mistress."

Her gorgeous lips curved. "Good thing I'm exempt from a sub's punishment."

"Pity. You might enjoy what I'd have in mind for that."

Her gaze was back on the field below. The girls were done with their warm-ups and had gathered around their coaches. Now she tipped her head back on his shoulder, sought his mouth. His touch was having the intended effect, because the kiss was heated, drawn out, inspiring an arousal he could push against her lower back and let her feel what she was doing to him. What power she had with him.

Like the night after she returned home from the hospital, that power pushed back the tide of worries that inhabited what either of them were feeling. It focused them on what they wanted from each other, in the here and now. He wanted to slide his hands up under her T-shirt, find his way beneath her bra to cup her breasts. Hell, he'd get rid of the damn thing entirely, let the lush curves fill his hands, those breasts that were God's gift to men. To him in particular.

Since he doubted that would meet the approval of the parents in the bleachers below—and he had no interest in sharing the view with any male who felt differently—he reined himself back and gave her a look. "Now you're trying to get me into trouble."

"Maybe. And maybe you'd enjoy what *I'd* have in mind for that."

"Maybe so." From the flare of heat and surprise in her eyes, he thought it might end up being an interesting evening.

But that connected to her point. No matter how worked up they became, by the time they were home, it might have to be tabled because of how she was feeling, how her meds were working today.

But that also supported *his* point. He not only lived an unpredictable life—he'd chosen one, and knew how to find balance in it, adjust for different paths. That was what he needed to help her understand. Believe.

"Rocks?" she prompted.

He pulled himself back to the context of the conversation. Despite her own arousal, her catlike hazel gaze told him she was well aware of his...and smug with it. But he could match that. He stroked her abdomen beneath the shirt, absorbing her quiver of response. When her lips parted, moist, heated breath touching his flesh, he thought he could spend a lifetime challenging—and being challenged—by the woman in his arms.

Softball game. Casual. Fun. Relaxed.

Rocks.

"Yeah. While you're right, that they did come from places I've traveled, I picked them up specifically from spots I found to center myself, stay steady, keep hold of who I am, the part of myself I don't want to lose."

He took it further, letting her inside to see what that meant.

"There are things I do, places I've been, that can take big pieces of who I am, who I always thought I'd be, and just make confetti out of them. Fate laughing its ass off at your vision of yourself, your plans."

She stilled, but he continued. "Early on, I had to figure out that core part of me that I wouldn't compromise. That would always be me, no matter what other things I had to adapt and change. When I go out on my boat, when I seek out those places on my travels, it's to honor that part, care for it, touch base with it and make sure it's still doing okay."

A faint smile touched his lips, but there was no humor to it. It was an offering, an acknowledgement to the gods for their sparing but precious kindnesses.

"Somebody on base growing a small vegetable garden, where I can go sit, pluck a tomato, smell all the things a fresh tomato means. An alley in a town torn up by violence, but someone has set up a shrine to the fallen, so it's quiet there, oddly beautiful, with all the flowers and mementos. Respectful, remembering what's important.

"My two favorite times at base camp are right before sunrise, and at dusk. Those crossover moments. They pull me back in my head to the bayou, what I find there, even in the middle of violent places. I just have to look for them, but it's an important message, how I manage to find such a place, every damn time, in every damn place, even if I only get to hold onto it for a moment."

A thought Neil didn't allow to snag him, though it was there, a pin he was sure his mind would come back to later, the precious moments he had with her.

Every one of them.

"It balances that adrenaline junkie in me in a way I need." When he turned his gaze back down to her, he made sure what she saw there would blast that damn elephant out of the room, once and for all, no matter what lay ahead of them. "We fit, Abby. I haven't seen a reason to doubt it yet. How about you?"

She closed her eyes, but she twisted to put her arms around his shoulders, her face against his throat. He held her close, put his mouth against her hair. "Don't answer that. It was a rhetorical anyway. Ask me about the game. The players. Anything to help me not think about how much I want to be inside you and stay there until the end of time."

She stayed where she was for another few heartbeats, then she spoke against his chest, voice barely a whisper. "Okay." She adjusted her head so she was looking toward the field again, even as she continued to hold him and he kept moving his hands over her sides, her back, down to her hips, endless circles.

"So is Tessie's team your favorite? Is that why you chose this spot?"

"Yeah. The Swamp Rats haven't won as much this year, because they lost several of their best players to graduation."

"How inconsiderate of them."

"Yeah, I know. Least they could have done was repeat a grade to increase the team's chances of getting a championship."

He noticed she was pressing her lips together, swallowing, a sign her mouth was dry. He wasn't caring for his Mistress the way he should. He picked up her soda, handed it to her, a reminder she accepted, taking several swallows. "Hey, looks like they're about to start."

Another reminder, of his primary goal for today. For the next couple hours, the focus would be on enjoying themselves.

Because just like everything in his life had taught him, including and especially with her, life was meant to be lived moment by moment.

~

Softball was played in seven innings, not nine, Abby learned. In fast-pitch softball, the girls were allowed to steal bases, though Neil said they couldn't lead off. The pitch, while underhanded, was sizzling and impressive, especially in Tessie's capable hands.

Abby looked forward to the other team being at bat, just to watch the steely-eyed girl evaluate each batter. Neil had declared she could do a dynamite windmill pitch, or throw a screw or curve ball that could spin a batter into a circle. Abby noted how Tessie kept command of things, and she didn't lose her cool when a batter connected with her pitch. She'd make an impressive Domme.

Passion was contagious at a softball game, particularly in Neil's company. As he schooled her on the nuances of the game, she found herself leaning forward, anticipating when a ball was hit or caught, cheering when it happened. Being up here, the noise didn't overwhelm her, and each time she leaned back into Neil's embrace, it increased that cocooned sense of shelter. If his backside was going numb, he didn't say so. They'd pulled the picnic basket closer, too, so they could fish in there for snacks as needed. The cooler had cup holders on the top for his beer and her soda.

Over the past few months, as her mind had been consumed by the advance of the schizophrenia, the fragmenting of her brain, and she'd tried to hold it all together, she'd lost this. What Neil had talked about, finding the small part of herself that was inviolate, that couldn't be lost if she protected it.

As she was pulled into the escapism of watching a game, being part of its energy, she realized her awareness of that part of herself was something he'd given back to her, with almost every moment they'd spent together. Racing him and Max in the park, the session with Tiger. Every flirtation that had escalated into an erotic intensity so strong the universe could be falling around them—or her brain could be falling apart—and it wouldn't matter so much.

She'd done the clichéd melancholy gazing at a sunrise, or watching children play in a schoolyard, feeling the full punch of the ephemeral nature of her existence, tangled in a salt-baked knot of appreciation for the wonders of life. But that appreciation was not, and never could be, the same as losing that awareness to have fun, get lost in what the world was offering. Letting go of her poor brain, dropping it to the ground to grab joy by the hand. Simply to go run and play for awhile.

Funny thing about joy is that you only really find it when you are too busy having fun to go looking for it. Skye had a magnet with that quote on her fridge.

Crack!

When they'd pulled out their sandwiches to have a light lunch, they'd moved to the stadium chairs. So now she jumped out of hers, whooping as the current batter, a short, dark girl with squinted eyes that tracked the ball like a laser beam, connected. She sent the ball on what Neil called the sweet spot trajectory, right between the pitcher and third baseman. Or woman in this case. The ball bounded into the outfield, rolling fast.

Now she egged on the outfielders. "Get it, get it, get it! Nail second base, nail it, nail it!" She cheered as they stopped the runner, but also whooped for Frankie, the girl who'd made the hit. She was on first base, already eyeballing second, formulating her strategy to get there.

She sat back down in the chair to find Neil grinning at her. "What?"

He shook his head, handed her the soda she realized she would have punted into a spinning arc away from her spot. Last time she'd taken a sip, she'd left it by her foot instead of in the cup holder. As she took a swallow and put it back on the cooler, he feathered his distracting fingers over the humidity-damp tendrils of hair on her neck. "They're going to be wondering whose side you're on."

She was enthused enough to be rooting for both teams, and unapologetic for it. "Oh, all the parents are yelling so loud, mine just blends in. We should sign these girls up for business internships. Employ all that drive and self-discipline, give them some useful empirical knowledge."

Neil chuckled. "You sound like my dad. He griped all four of the years Della pursued a degree in women's studies. He said he'd pay her the same amount to go to plumbing school. Said the thousands more dollars she'd make doing that could help care for him in his old age."

"Sounds like a smart man."

Neil grinned. "Except for the day he asked why he was paying tuition for a major she was biologically equipped to know everything about. In a house where the females outnumber the males, that didn't go over well."

As Abby laughed, Neil turned his attention back to the field. "Here comes Tessie. She's not as good a batter as she is a pitcher, but she does well enough. Every once in a while, she finds the power to send it into this tree line, so watch your head. She may aim for me."

Tessie didn't do that, but she did pull off a decent grounder that went toward that same sweet spot, though not as quickly as Frankie's hit. She squeaked onto first base with an impressive slide and was deemed safe. Frankie had made it to third. The crowd's enthusiasm ramped up, since the other team was ahead by one run.

"Yeah!" Neil shouted through cupped hands. "Hooyah!"

His echoing baritone was impressive. Tessie tipped her hat in his direction, a girlish smile escaping before her impassive game face returned.

"Her dad's a Marine," Neil told Abby. "She usually comes up to talk to me a few minutes after the game. And to see if I brought any of MeeMaw's cake."

"So that's not for us?"

"Some of it." He winked. "She'll also want to check you out."

"She scope out all the women you bring to her games?"

"All of them," he said. "Which, including you, will make...one."

"You better be telling the truth. I'll be asking her."

Neil gestured to the bleachers. "Her mom's that lady in purple with the straw hat. Her dad's currently stationed in Germany. When he's home, he's parked right there with her. The fat kid next to Mom is Tessie's brother, Benito. The one absorbed in his tablet video game. Mom drags him here to ensure he doesn't forget what sunlight is. Or walking. Tessie loves him to pieces, though. She says he'll be the next big computer genius mogul."

"What do you say?"

Neil grimaced. "I think his mom and dad will have to kick him out at eighteen to force him to get a job. But I think Tessie will help straighten him out."

She cocked her head. "You definitely sound like someone who has siblings."

"Two sisters, including Della. Amy has an engineering degree and works for a big aerospace company. A tradeoff with her childhood dream of becoming an astronaut, the first one to paraglide the rings of Saturn."

"And Della? Where did the women studies major end up?"

His eyes sparkled. "Psych counselor for a teen group home, a ranch of sorts. Tough love, rehab place. Not too far from where my parents live in Sedona. During all those early travel years, Mom developed a fondness for the area. It's artsy and relaxed. Air's good and she has terrible allergies. Whenever she visits here, she has to load up on the antihistamines, so I go to visit them there whenever I can."

He paused. A spot of dead air where she imagined he might have said, "I'd like to introduce you sometime." Or "You should go there with me one day."

The reason it wouldn't happen was too close to be overlooked or forgotten. He took her hand in an overly firm grip, kissed it. Then they were back on their feet as Tessie's teammate hit a ball in a high arc over the fence.

The crowd erupted, parents and fans jumping to their feet to cheer as Tessie's team took the lead.

As they settled back down, Neil had jogged down the slope. He retrieved and tossed the ball back to the crestfallen-looking outfielder, though Abby noted he said something encouraging to her that inspired a half-smile.

"They've only got one more inning," he told her as he returned. "If they get them out before they can make up those two runs, that'll be game."

"Do you have a picture of them?" she asked. "Your family?" She remembered the photos he'd had scattered around his place, the ones she hadn't looked at. She wanted to take a quick look now, imagine his family in her head.

Withdrawing his wallet from his back jeans pocket, he flipped it open and pulled a photo out of a clear sleeve.

"I expected you to show me on your phone."

"Yeah. I like to have a hard copy. Something to touch."

It was an informal shot against a backdrop of the red rock formations associated with Arizona. Two laughing young women were in the foreground, holding onto their mother, their father's head interjected into the top left of the picture. His arms were draped over their shoulders, encompassing all of them in his embrace. "He's tall like you."

"Yeah. Mom's short and so is Della. Amy got more of his height, but stopped at about five-ten and she doesn't have his arm span. Which is good, because Della said monkeys would think she was a mostly hairless family member."

Della was plump, with a round, sincere face and firm chin, framed by abundant blond hair, similar in thickness and color to her mother's shorter sassy style. Amy was thinner, angular. She had the expression of someone figuring out how the mechanical things of the world fit together. Della had a similar look, though her job as a teen counselor meant her focus would be on how to put a human heart back together. She reminded Abby of Maureen.

Neil had his father's strong features, though his eyes had the same blue-grey color as his mother's laughing ones.

They looked like what a family should be.

"Never met two families that were alike, but they all seem to have their hurdles in figuring each other out. When Della was a teenager, in the I-hate-my-parents phase, she declared that the bonds of family were as unbearable as the chains holding Prometheus to his rock. You just had to figure out how to endure having your guts torn out regularly."

Abby laughed, even as her own gut twisted. In her case, Della's teenage melodrama had been accurate. "You can't choose your blood family. And no matter what, they influence your course. Whether toward them or away, you always loop back around."

She glanced at Neil. While she didn't want to incite a flood of destabilizing emotion, she had to say the words that suddenly ached to be said. "I loved my mother. Even when I didn't understand everything she was going through."

He put his hand over hers. "She was lucky to have you. I'm sure it tore her up, that she couldn't be a better mom to you. But she shouldn't have left you that way."

She didn't hear anything in his voice that tried to connect that to her, so she didn't get hung up on it, and answered him honestly. "She got tired. I understand that. She had no one really, no one she'd let help her, except me. And a child, even when I became a teenager...it wasn't enough."

"No. But you fought the good fight. She needed a bigger army, but it sounds like she wouldn't let anyone in."

Abby handed the picture back. She didn't want to go there in her head. Old regrets. "Do your sisters give you a lot of grief?"

"Do they ever." He rolled his eyes. "I asked Mom if I could use Della for target practice."

"When you were kids?"

"Actually, I think it was last month."

She laughed. Neil flipped his wallet back open to slide the picture into its sleeve, but before he could, Abby's hand landed on his knee, next to the open billfold. Though obscured by the double layer of plastic, she recognized herself in the picture below the empty sleeve. Turning it over, resting her hand on top of his relaxed one, she saw it was from the barbecue, when she'd been by the pool. She wasn't looking at the camera, but off at someone or something else, an absent half-smile on her face. Strands of hair wisped around her cheeks in a light breeze, most of it held back by the sunglasses she'd pushed on top of her head.

"Lawrence sent it to me. I like having you with me, even when we're apart."

He'd carry it always. It was implicit in his tone, the way he touched her face, looked at her. He didn't say it, because she knew he refused to do any of the finality shit.

Not while there was a single scrap of hope left.

She pulled her gaze away. "Tessie is coming." But she caressed his hand, his wrist, before she withdrew her touch so he could close up the wallet, return it to his back pocket.

While they were talking, Tessie's team had struck the other team out, through Tessie's strikeout of one batter, and her teammates catching the two hits that her pitching skill had likely kept from having much power to them.

The girls had finished the handshake with the opposing team, and Tessie was jogging toward the back fence. She climbed over the chain link with easy grace, dropped to the ground and loped up the hill.

"Good game," Neil said as she reached them. He'd pulled a bottle of water out of the cooler, cracking it open before he offered it to the sweaty girl. She had dirt on her uniform from her slide. The face that had been so somber throughout the game bore a broad smile, her dark, thick-lashed eyes sparkling with the victory.

"Yeah, the Rockets are a tough team. It's a good win." She sat down on the ground, waving away Neil's offer of his chair. Her knees were up and bent as she sipped at the water and eyed Abby. Then she shot Neil a look.

"You born in a barn or what?"

Neil grinned and made a formal bow. "Teresa Sanchez, who goes by 'Tess' or 'Tessie,' this is Abigail Rose. Who goes by Abby."

"So are you and she a thing?"

"No. Abby is actually my Master Chief. While you've been dicking around with the whole being-a-teenager schtick, she already got into the SEALs and achieved senior rank. Stole your thunder entirely."

"You're full of crap," Tessie responded, making a face at him. She dipped her head toward Abby. "Even if it were true, I've got no problem with someone paving the way for me. Gives me some company among all those testosterone-laden fools once I get there."

Abby smiled. "A practical and smart female."

Neil sighed. "Another male institution under siege. Where will we poor men go?"

"Would you like a suggestion?" Tess laughed and ducked as Neil tried to grab for her cap. "So how long have you been putting up with him?" she asked Abby. "He's never brought you before."

"Has he brought others?"

"Not many. A couple Saints cheerleaders. The waitress who works late nights at the Waffle House. I think that was a hookup thing. He just didn't have time to drop her off before our game. I thought the cheerleader thing might turn into something, but it ended up being all about the pompoms. Hey, hey, hey..."

Neil chased her around the tree a couple times as she giggled and evaded him. Though Tessie was pretty fast, Abby could tell Neil let her slip past him, though he did manage to snatch the hat. The girl got it back when he defended himself from a gut punch and she leaped up, retrieved it.

As she returned to her seated position and bottle of water, she winked at Abby. Sent Neil an amused look as he dropped back into his chair, eyeing her. "Seriously, you're the first woman he's ever brought here," Tessie said. "So when did you two get together?"

"We met a few months ago, but we've only been spending more time together recently." Abby would have made a joke about not having to put up with him much longer, but she didn't feel like going down that road. Not after the exchange they'd just had. "Do you have time to show me how to pitch?"

Tessie's brows rose. She sensed Neil's surprise as well. Tessie tossed Abby the ball she was carrying in her glove. It was an easy throw, thankfully, since Abby's hand-to-eye coordination was iffy on her meds. When Abby caught it two-handed, she realized Tessie's purpose was to see her hands.

"You don't keep your nails long," she said approvingly, "but that polish will get chipped. If you're okay with that, then hell, yeah, I can show you. I'm riding my bike home to get an extra workout, so I've got some time. Let's head back down to the field. We'll let Neil bat, see if he can do a halfway decent job. Though my dad says you can't expect much out of a Navy guy."

"Except for saving a Marine's bumbling ass."

"Aren't the Marines part of the Navy?" Abby asked.

"Sort of. We tolerate them. Like an annoying tagalong kid brother." Neil shot her a wink.

As Tess preceded them down the hill and Neil folded up the chairs, he leaned down to speak in Abby's ear, hand closing over hers on the ball. "My back says your nails are just long enough, Mistress."

She nudged him with a reproving smile, though she was sure the heat that coursed through her didn't escape his notice. He went down the slope ahead of her, his backward glance indicating he was preceding her as a bulwark, in case she lost her footing.

With her uncertain brain, pieces of past dialogue were like a boomerang, returning at random moments. When they did, their significance could make her come to a full stop. Like now.

"Wait."

He half-turned, his brow raised.

"That comment, about a woman being bat shit crazy to marry a SEAL. Was that a proposal?"

His blue-gray eyes gleamed with amusement, heat and other toe-curling things. "You tell me, bébé."

When he started back down the hill again, she fired the ball at his back.

It didn't surprise her—but it did impress her, with an annoying little tingle—when he pivoted before it reached him and caught it one-handed, despite the stuff he was carrying. That heat in his eyes showed an additional burst of flame at the challenge. When she reached him, she gripped his sides and lifted up onto her toes. She placed a suggestive kiss on his mouth, nipped the bottom lip. Since he had both hands occupied, he couldn't put them on her, and she liked the functional restraint. But she retrieved the ball, teasing her fingers along his palm, and then also took the picnic basket.

"You don't have to carry everything, you know."

"Same goes, Mistress."

~

They circled around to the gate to access the playing field, though Abby was sure Neil could have easily hopped the fence like Tessie had. She met Tessie on the mound as Neil retrieved the bat, Tessie's own, that she'd left leaning against the fence inside the dugout.

"When you're learning to fastpitch, it's easier to break it down, and then put it together in one fluid motion." Tessie was all business again. She held the ball in one hand, extending both arms before her. "Hands out like this, like Superman flying. Then the leg kicks out, and the arm comes around in a full vertical circle, like a Popeye punch in the cartoon."

Abby was focusing, but trying not to do it so strenuously she didn't lose any of the sentences. It was a delicate line to walk, but she managed it. When Tess gave her a studied look, she wondered if the flat effect or her wandering gaze might be sending the wrong message, but Tess continued.

"That's the rough breakdown," she said. "First you practice that for awhile, until you can smooth it out. Then you refine your technique, making sure your head, shoulders, hips, are all lined up like this..."

Even the basics had more complicated nuances. After going through the pitch form with her a few times, making sure Abby had a decent grasp on it, Tessie concentrated on her grip. "The 4-seam C grip is a good one, lining your fingers up with the seam of the ball."

Tessie folded her fingers over it, showing her, then let Abby do the same. Tess's brown fingers moved patiently over hers, adjusting. "See how the seams form kind of a C here? Okay, yeah, that's good."

While they were doing that, Neil had moved to the plate, swung the bat a few times to warm up. "Give it a shot," Tessie told her.

Abby's first attempt went high. Neil would have had to be ten feet tall to connect with the ball. "Level hips, head and shoulders." Tessie reinforced the form again, adjusting Abby's stance with her warm, strong hands. "Don't try to throw it hard or fast. Just focus on getting it over the plate with the right form."

It took five more tries, Neil standing ready for each. He connected with the sixth one, a gentle impact that bounced the ball across the dirt and rolled it to a stop between first and second base.

"All those muscles for show?" Abby teased him as Tessie jogged over to retrieve it. "You can hit harder than that."

He grinned. "Send me a pitch worth my time, bébé."

"I'll pass that honor on to her." Abby waved Tess back to the mound. "Strike his smug ass out."

"Be nice to get something by him. Doesn't happen often. Reminds me a lot of my daddy." Tessie gave Abby a speculative look. "I might have a shot at it today, though, because you make his head spin."

As Abby blinked at that surprising statement, Tess's teeth flashed. Then her eyes went sharp. "Step back into the outfield," she instructed Abby. "Behind second base. If he hits it, we still want to get him out."

Abby took up the position Tess advised, and Tess threw. She and Neil judged it a ball, outside the strike zone over the base. Then Tess's arm did that fast, Popeye rotation, and the next two balls were strikes, clanging into the chain link fence behind the batter's mound.

Abby did a victory dance, and Neil glared at Tessie, tossing the ball back to her. "Tell your teammate no victory dancing until the job is done."

"She's psyching you out, which is fully acceptable," Tessie retorted. She caught the ball with the graceful light-footed movement of a backward dance step. "Just be glad I'm not having her record this so I can share your strikeout on the Marine chat boards."

Despite their banter, Neil wasn't patronizing the girl. Abby saw two warriors, Tessie as determined to get the ball past him as Neil was to hit it. As she watched him in the batter's crouch, his capable hands gripping the bat, his shoulders set, his gaze focused like nothing in life mattered as much as that ball, she lost herself in him.

Her vibrating body, the thump of her heart, told her she'd never in her life wanted a man as much as she wanted this one. She'd shove him against the chain link fence with a loud metallic clang, tear his shirt away from that irresistible body and climb him like a tree. She'd savor the strength of his arms, helping her as she pulled open his jeans and slid her way down his thick, rigid length. If she was that highly aroused, she knew he'd be ready for her, a guaranteed chemical reaction when two elements were brought that close together.

The wanting was deeper than sex, though all of it would rise and channel through the act of giving, taking, releasing. She wanted him in too many ways to list. And on the top of that list, absurd and pointless as it was, was the desire to have the time to become the person he could want, rely on and need.

Crack! The thought shattered at the slapping thud of the bat connecting.

The ball shot toward the outfield, a few feet to Tessie's left.

Though she dove for it, it was going fast enough to just make it past the reach of her glove.

"Abby, get it, get it. Cut him off," Tessie shouted joyously.

Abby was already bolting for it. Neil had passed first, brashly intending to go for a full home run. Lord, the man was a beautiful runner. Abby cursed when she stumbled—damn coordination—but she regained her footing, reached the ball and threw it to Tessie. Tessie had anticipated her inexperienced arm, closed the gap and caught it on the first bounce. Then she was headed for home plate, fast as a cheetah. Abby ran toward it as well.

Tessie reached home, put her foot on it and braced herself to block Neil's charge. He dodged her, playing keep away, trying to lure her from the plate. Abby got there then, and the two females worked together, trying to corner him as he danced around them.

"Tag him out," Tessie said, tossing Abby the ball, but when Abby lunged for him, Neil caught her arm and waist and hefted her, dumping her over his shoulder, arm securely around her thighs. He stomped on home. "Safe."

"Think again, sailor," she said, tattooing the ball against his firm ass. "Tell him, Tessie."

"Since there is absolutely nothing legal about running circles around the plate to make the catcher too dizzy to tag the runner, you are *out*." They were all laughing, Tessie gasping over her giggles. A young woman who could still embrace being a girl.

Neil put Abby on her feet, but held onto her, his arm over her shoulders. Then his watch beeped. Without glancing at it, he gave Abby a squeeze. "I'm going to go get you a bottle of water. You're sweaty from all that pitching work. You want another, Tessie?"

"If you won't give me one of the beers."

"Don't make me tell your daddy you said that."

Neil jogged away. As Abby had suspected, when it was just him, he took the short cut, scaling and dropping over the back fence with barely a pause and a nice ripple of shoulder and arm muscles.

His watch was programmed to alert him when it was time for her next dose of meds. She hadn't overlooked it consciously, but the urge had been there, to let the time pass by, put off taking them. It was such a good day today, she felt like she could get away with it this once.

But that was what her mother had done, far too often. And, as she'd told him, it was a common urge for many schizophrenics. The desire to feel normal when they were having a good day. Not to be reminded how different they were with meds, or a renewal of the side effects each dose brought.

Neil was helping her, she reminded herself. He'd anticipated her needs. Covered it so she could take them without it being a big deal. Maybe even anticipated her reluctance, dragging her feet.

It would still be her choice, but he'd take her all the way to the doorway, not letting her practice willful aversion.

"I hope you come with him again." Tessie broke into her borderline irritable thoughts. "You help his darkness."

The frank words surprised Abby, raised her curiosity. "He has darkness?"

"It's what my daddy said." Tessie glanced after Neil. Though it was just a flash, Abby saw the hero worship mixed with a girl's crush. Because Tess *was* a girl, and that was what girlhood was supposed to include. Abby suspected someone as disciplined and practical as Tessie would recognize it for what it was, but still feel it, indulge it, albeit in a relatively sensible way.

"Heard him talk to my mom about it. Said Neil's walked right up to the darkness, stood with it. He doesn't fear it, because he always holds onto the light that's in it and around it. Never loses his way. My dad says you could follow Neil into any storm and know, even if he can't get you where you're going, he'll never not be there, standing at your side."

Tessie shrugged. "I don't know about the kind of things Neil has seen, but the words feel right." Her attention came back to Abby, speculative. "I'm thinking someone like Neil wouldn't mind having someone stand by him, too."

Abby thought of her earlier thoughts, the kind of person she wished she could be for Neil. Someone he would look to when he needed someone to cradle his soul, reinforce all the good of who he was, be a listening ear, spend time with him.

The person who would keep his center solid, that darkness at bay... his entire life.

~

After Tessie left them, with a generous portion of MeeMaw's cake for her and her family, Abby and Neil went back up the hill. Though he'd put the picnic basket and chairs back in the truck, he'd left the cooler and blanket up there. They settled onto the latter, resting on their hips and facing one another.

"So why don't girls play baseball instead of softball?" she asked as they split the piece of cake he'd saved for them. He said it was a walnut yellow cake, possibly one of the best cakes she'd ever tasted.

"That's a loaded question." Neil swallowed his last bite. "It's a long and convoluted history, but to meet the equal opportunity sports laws in schools, most offer softball to girls and baseball to boys. There are some places they've overcome that, but this isn't one of them."

He gestured to the field. "Softball may be a consolation prize, but the girls own it. Even with their less experienced players, this team fights for the win a hundred percent, every time. A lot of that is Tessie's leadership. Her example. They make the other teams work to beat them. While they don't have as much natural aptitude as the last set did, they practice hard, and they listen to their coach. I think eventually they're going to build back up to a top team.

"You remember the one in the outfield, Monica? In a game a couple weeks ago, a catcher got in her way when she was running for home. I've seen battering rams hit with less force. Nothing makes them quit. They reinforce each other, keep each other going, even when the scoreboard says they're going to lose. So they're always winners in my book."

Abby gazed at the field. Told herself not to say it, and did so anyway. "So what does that make me, in your book?"

"Hey," he said. "Look at me."

She couldn't. She was starting to tire. The side effects of the next dose were setting in, making things painfully brilliant and fuzzy on the edges at the same time. It would pass, but she had to give it time, deal with that roller coaster of feelings that would kick up during the first part. Hope that it didn't leave her even more exhausted on the back end.

She closed her eyes tight, and her body jerked. If only things had been different, but they weren't. During the past fifteen years, she'd made herself a promise. That when this point in her life came, she'd not confuse it or cloud it with anything, but instead focus only on the present. What she could experience and enjoy before it was done.

He pulled her closer. Bracing his head on his hand, his elbow planted near her arm, he leaned in to kiss her forehead, cup her skull, bring her closer.

"Just settle against me. Relax, bébé."

She could do that. He stroked her hair, held her. The birdsong was too loud. It was time to go home.

"Is it the gap from here to there?" he asked, low.

"What do you mean?"

"Just be easy. Keep your eyes closed." He stroked her hip, her upper thigh, drew a figure eight there and came back, sliding his fingers under the hem of her shirt to caress her lower back, bring her even closer to him. She'd gotten rid of her sneakers and had a foot between his calves, curling against the denim.

"You know how Dale has a prosthetic leg? He told me once that he could handle losing the leg. It was the physical therapy, learning how to do everything differently, that made him want to go back and let that explosion finish the job. Dealing with all the in-between shit of figuring out how to get from here to there. One step forward, two steps back."

"While everyone else does twenty laps around the track past you, before you manage the next step."

"Yeah. Dale said it also sucked, being looked at differently because he'd lost a limb."

"Losing your identity to an illness. Being seen as that, nothing else."

She'd seen her mother become that. Had been around enough of the mentally ill in the hospital where her mother had been placed to know how often it happened. Being in her own head, when there were days it could consume her, the dealing with it, meant Abby sometimes did it to herself. She hated that most of all.

"There's always this question in your mind," she said. "Once it's bad enough, and I've been this long enough, who will remember who I was? Who I really am, inside all this shit? Will I even know?"

She shouldn't say those kinds of words aloud, because they took her to a dark place she didn't want to go today. Her brain might take her there anyway, but she didn't have to open the door for it.

But sometimes when she was with Neil, it was too easy to open up her soul and let out what was there.

She was now fully in his embrace, their bodies flush to one another. She'd slipped her leg fully over his. He spoke against her hair. "I know who you are. I told you that. I'm standing inside you, bébé. I see you."

"Earlier... I want to say...thank you. For honoring your promise. Not trying to talk me out of it, even when I can feel it in you, how much you're against it."

He rolled them, so she was on her back, and he was leaning over her. She could feel the war of emotions in him, in the tension of his body, where she ran her hands over his back, down to his waist. "It's your decision," he said roughly. Then he gave her a pained smile.

"That's all I can say about it, except what I've said before. We can't take your decision, but we all want to make damn sure no part of that decision is taking one from us. I'm in this with you. I want to be here. And so, as you go along, when the moment of decision comes, make sure the only thing you're basing it on is yourself."

She could have left it there, not challenged it, but being honest with him also seemed to be something she couldn't stop herself from doing. Maybe because he was the only one, other than Maureen, where she felt she could do that. Where he wouldn't jump in, try to force his will upon her. She loved Ros and the others, but they'd been her friends too long.

Or maybe she talked to him because she needed to be sure he understood as much as he could. As hard as it would be for the others, that history with one another, with her, would help them in the aftermath, be shared. He had others to support him, but what was between her and him, it was something only they experienced, and she'd be leaving him alone with those feelings.

"I can't base the decision only on myself," she said.

"Why not?" He gave her a hard look. "Didn't you feel like your mom took that decision from you, when she strangled herself? Didn't you ask yourself why you couldn't convince her that, no matter what she was going through, you could handle it and be there for her? That she could lean on you?"

Abby pushed him back, scooted away to put some space between them on the blanket. "Who told you that?"

"Ros. Don't give her shit for it."

"For giving you the ammo to get into my head?" Her jaw set. "No, I won't give her shit for that, because I understand. I don't retract what I said. You've been...you've been way better about this than I ever could have expected. So I know it's not fair to say this, but when you do try an underhanded punch like that...it makes me feel more alone."

"Abby..."

She shook her head, held up a hand when he would have closed the distance between them again. "I know what I'm doing to all of you, what I'm asking you to accept. And I know that's not fair, asking you to leave it alone, just enjoy what time we have. I really, truly understand that, Neil."

She emphasized the words, tried to put the full force of her feeling about it in the tone. "Having you honor it, respect it, and try not to cross that line, as best you can? It has meant so much to me. I hope you understand that, too."

Hoped he would continue to understand it, when she was no longer here to say it. Because she knew now she never would write that letter to him. He was the one she'd let inside, let read her soul until the very end. There weren't any words that could be put on paper to reflect that.

She rose and moved away, looked down the slope behind the tree line. She saw a man and woman jogging together on the path, laughing. The pain rose up, threatened to overwhelm her. The volume of the voices increased, enough that she gripped her upper arms harder to stop herself from pushing her palm against her head, to try to quiet them.

He was there, his hands resting on her shoulders.

"I'm only human, Abby. I'm doing my damnedest to find the right balance between what I want, and what you've asked of me."

"I know. I know." She crossed her arms over her chest, overlapped his hands on her shoulders, and bowed her head toward the one on her left, pressing her cheek to it.

"What you said, about my mother. Maybe I did feel that way, after she died. But over the years, I realized that was the guilt. Guilt for all those days when I didn't think I could stand it another moment. Or any time I'd let it creep into my consciousness, thinking what life would be like if she was gone and I was no longer spending every day mired in it."

"Abby, you were a child. We're adults, a whole group of adults who have each other for support, to help each of us help you. It's different. You know it is. Damn it, I'm sorry. Don't pull away. I'm stopping."

He wrapped both arms over her, nipped her ear. The struggle against saying more, that fight she'd told him she could detect in him, to try to persuade her, coax her, maybe even beg her, surrounded her like a momentary intense storm. Then he let her go, let it go, and stepped back.

She turned to look at him, but he was already headed for the cooler, his face concealed. "Need another soda?" His voice was rough.

She studied his broad back. By the time he'd flipped up the cooler, straightened with the soda in hand, she'd closed the gap between them. Taking the can from him, she put it aside, and framed his face with both hands. Though she was gazing into his eyes, she managed to hold the lock by turning her mind inward, focusing all her energy on what her expression was giving him. A Mistress's understanding of the make of a man's soul. A man who'd given her everything and asked for nothing but to care for her.

With a watch beep. With the comfort of his arms. Taking her to a softball game.

That was as long as she could hold it. After that silent, potent moment, she dropped her hands, wrapped her arms around his waist. Put her face to his shoulder. Whatever limitations she had, she'd still work her ass off to give him as much strength as he was offering her.

"I love you," she said. "Fiercely, eternally, forever."

Death wouldn't change that.

CHAPTER TWENTY-TWO

Two and a half weeks later, Abby had her last session with Maureen. A couple days from now, she'd be on a plane to Switzerland.

That meet took place at Abby's home, just as the first one had. She'd picked up a box of Maureen's favorite coffee and a tin of Pirouline cookies, which she knew the psychotherapist liked. She put them in an attractive keepsake basket on her kitchen table, tying a lavender bow with a sprig of silk forsythia to the handle. A low-key thank you to someone who'd made the last few weeks far smoother than they would have been otherwise.

When Maureen arrived, she thanked Abby for the basket, and gave her a light hug. As she took the coffee Abby had made her, she eyed the plateful of cookies Abby had set out. Big as small pancakes, they were a sinful indulgence from the local bakery.

"I can tell you think you're headed somewhere calories are no longer a concern."

"If they are, I'll know I landed in hell."

When Maureen laughed, Abby's smile faded away. Plenty of times, she'd thought through how these final days might feel. What mix of emotions she might expect. So she wasn't surprised that it took her a second to speak in an even voice, and not just because she'd rated today a three in her journal.

"Thank you. I'm very glad for my friends' love, for Neil's. But having someone to help me through this, who could be my objective sounding board...you were right. It was invaluable." She gave a half laugh. "Neil's been the most willing recipient of my poor taste humor, but even with him, there are some things that go too far."

"Like what? Lay one on me." Maureen gazed at her expectantly, bringing Abby's smile back.

"Telling him he won't have to come up with creative ways to say I'm not getting fat, saggy or wrinkly. And that I won't be around long enough to nag him about his bad habits."

"Does he have any? I can't get past the whole heroic SEAL and fabulous ass thing."

"Okay, I'll amend it. I won't be around long enough to discover *and* nag him about his bad habits." Abby sent her a mock glare. "And don't stare at his ass."

"Sorry, you won't be around to stop me."

Another shared chuckle, then they sobered together, a rise and fall, like all the emotions Abby had been feeling this week. She gazed down at her coffee. "It's gotten worse, my feelings about what I'm asking them. Neil and me, we're a separate category. But I'm having a particularly hard time about Ros. Because of Laurel. Because of how damn much I love her, love all of them." Her voice faltered. "Sometimes my heart hurts so badly I almost can't bear it."

"I've seen that, in our last couple sessions. Many people in your situation would have simply packed up and left, taken a far-away vacation until your time clock ran out. You've shown a great deal of courage and strength, staying. It's a lot."

"Neil getting me to do this, the steps you've taken me through, told me I owed it to them, particularly if I couldn't give them anything else they want." She took a breath. "So I've dealt with it the usual girly way. I've cried a lot, by myself. And I've cried while Neil held me. The first time it happened, I was afraid he'd use it as leverage to change my mind, but he hasn't done that. None of them have."

She sent Maureen a shrewd look. "I know you've been meeting with them. Were you responsible for that?"

"I've pointed them toward methods to manage their pain, their anger, frustrations and fears. I encouraged them to express those things to one another. I also suggested ways for them to convey how much you mean to them without heavy-handed acts of persuasion that could morph into guilt. Or expressions of anger that wouldn't accomplish anything except driving you away from them during these last days."

Gratitude was going to drown her. So Abby pulled herself away from that deep end and directed Maureen's attention to an envelope in the basket.

"I've written you a check that I think would cover about a dozen group sessions with them, plus a few more if they need you, one-on-one." She thought specifically of Ros. She would have Lawrence, yes, but she still carried too much about Laurel's death. Maybe Maureen could help with that.

She also thought about Cyn. Cyn carried so much about so many things, Maureen would have to become a one-patient practice to handle them all. If Cyn would see her, which Abby knew she wouldn't.

"Can you be there for them, afterward? They might not reach out, but maybe you could, encourage them to talk to you, come in to see you."

"Of course. That's very generous, Abby. And very kind."

"If they don't take advantage of it, or you have any left over, use it however you see fit. Take a vacation yourself, or donate it to a mental health facility."

Maureen made a noncommittal noise. She picked up a cookie, broke off a bite and inhaled the scent of oats, chocolate and pecans. The scent filtered over to Abby.

"Have you ever thought about how a submissive finds his way to subspace?"

The segue didn't take Abby off guard. Maureen often chose seemingly unpredictable paths that broadened Abby's perspective on her illness. But she'd mostly stayed away from the Domme orientation they shared. If she wanted to talk about power exchange on their last session, Abby was game. It beat being choked up and sniffly the whole damn time.

"Somewhat. What are your thoughts on it?" Abby asked. "If I'm not stealing your line."

"You are, but I'm happy to answer." Maureen winked at her, then became serious again. "BDSM, Dominant and submissive power dynamics, are a fascinating psychological study, because outside that world, our emphasis is on self-determination, self-reliance. We view dependence or letting go of control, with suspicion. In our day-to-day, secular world, those qualities are associated with weakness. Surrender is associated with defeat."

"It's anything but, when a sub does that for a Domme."

"It's a thing of beauty," Maureen agreed. A dreamy look went through her green eyes, an expression Abby recognized as a recollection of past sessions where that synergy had been achieved with a sub.

"You know, in a couple days, I won't be able to tell your secrets. Share any lurid details you want."

"I'll bear that in mind." Maureen slanted her an amused glance before she continued. "What I find particularly interesting is there's another world where letting go, in the right way, is considered the ideal. Spirituality. Our faith, our belief in powers greater than ourselves, who may know more than we do about how our lives are supposed to go."

Abby kept her tone light, though her stomach stirred in warning. "You're using a convoluted analogy as a last-ditch Hail Mary."

Maureen lifted a brow. "You're perceptive, but off the mark. I told you when I started, Abby. My job, my role with you, as I perceive it, is to be sure you are at peace with your decisions. In a way that will illuminate that path and possibly bring comfort to those who care about you. You stand on the edge of your final decision, so I will give you deeper questions to answer. It's what all the previous work has done, pulling back those layers to get here, to help you manage your situation better, no matter where it takes you."

Maureen's eyes twinkled, an unexpected shift. "You thought I was making our last time together a Domme gab session? I have to earn my fee to the end."

Abby snorted. "Money has nothing to do with it. You're as much of a workaholic as I am. Or was."

"You still are," Maureen said, more seriously. "You took on a second job. Managing your illness. That discipline and drive, your appreciation of hard work, has served you well. It will carry you as far as you need it to."

Abby shifted, glanced over her shoulder. Light was flickering against the wall. She adjusted the chair so she didn't have her back to it anymore, but she was still looking at Maureen. The voices rose, drawing her attention toward the other side of the kitchen. Maureen waited her out, relaxed. Patient.

The sounds were a discordant song, but low enough. Abby could handle that. The meds were doing their job, even though she was twitchy. Not unexpected on a three-rated day. She reclaimed the thread of their conversation.

"How do you think that mindset affects him? The sub?"

In answer, Maureen removed a bag of foil-wrapped candies from her laptop case. "At the risk of sending us both into a sugar coma after that cookie, I want you to try one of these. I remember you mentioning you like toffee. These are a transcendent experience. Put one on your tongue, but don't chew or swallow."

Abby sent her an intrigued look, but complied. Closed her eyes. "Wow."

"Yes. Keep your eyes closed, if you can. What if you resisted that taste, chewed it up, sucked it down, ignored its impact on all your senses, refused to let it take over? How much enjoyment would you get out of it? If you spit it out before finishing it, it would be easier to do that. You'd remove the temptation to experience it fully."

"A little on the nose there, Doctor. You're not usually obvious." But she kept her eyes closed.

"Still off the mark," Maureen said, a gentle reproof. "I want you to apply that analogy to a submissive. What is he doing in that room with you? In the very best sessions you've had, what occurs inside him?"

"I'm not a submissive."

"But you know." Maureen's tone intensified, Domme to Domme. "You and I know the most important parts of it, because it lies within all of us, both sides of that coin, the essential soul of it. What is surrender to a submissive?"

Abby remembered Tiger, Sy, all the subs she'd had the pleasure of having sessions with. Fun, intense, some of them emotional, stretching her and the man himself to the full extent of his emotional and physical endurance, until he reached...

"What is surrender to a submissive?" Maureen repeated softly.

"It's not failure or weakness," Abby said. "It's strength of heart, of soul. It's trust and hope. A willingness to accept those things fully."

"Okay. And what is that surrender to a Domme?"

The words came even more easily. "A gift. A chance to take that journey together, to the best destination possible."

Abby opened her eyes. Maureen was as calm and placid as always, like a lake, letting her patient sail the waters without telling them where to turn the wheel.

"I recently had a short meeting with Neil," the woman said, surprising her. "Well, he tracked me down at my favorite coffee shop, bought me a fattening beverage and sat with me. I have no idea how he knew where I was, but I expect SEALs have access to some unsettling tracking technology."

"Or Lawrence held one of your scarves under his nose," Abby said dryly.

Maureen suppressed a smile. "He was quiet in that way of his. Just sat there while I drank my coffee. Then he said when people call sailors superstitious, they don't get it. A sailor never forgets the wild card. Nature."

Maureen held a toffee wrapper between two of her fingers as they tapped the table. She never speared Abby with her gaze, kept her regard soft. Her gestures conveyed the significance of her words. "He said it throws things at a captain that he doesn't expect. Sometimes they're things he straight out can't handle. Experience helps him weather that better than never preparing for it at all. But luck and faith have to play their part, too."

She pursed her lips. "He said a sailor falls in love with the sea because of that. For every storm they weather, the sea also gives them beautiful sailing days, remarkable things that seem like gifts. He says they feel like rewards for being willing to trust themselves to Nature's mercies and cruelties, never losing faith by leaving the boat."

Maureen rose. Though she did it smoothly, Abby was deep enough in her whirling mind that the movement made her start. The psychotherapist squeezed her shoulder, moved past her. "I need to use your bathroom. Would you like to do the last half of our session in your backyard when I get back? It's such a pretty day." She gave Abby a wink. "Maybe if you're up for it I'll stay past that, and we'll do that Domme gab session."

As Maureen reached the hallway, Abby marshalled her thoughts enough to make a statement. "He meant for you to tell me that."

Maureen glanced over her shoulder. "He never said so. But I think he's a very single-minded man. He's devoted to being what you need. He's almost as remarkable an individual as my patient."

Another smile, then the psychotherapist disappeared down the hall.

Abby drew on her table, following the wood grain lines. Odd thoughts mixed with her emotions. She'd begun packing for her trip. Pajamas, toiletries. It was strange to think of the last time she'd brush her teeth, put on deodorant. Make-up. She'd packed the post-it notes so she'd remember to do those things, but Neil would help her with that too if she asked him. No dying with bad breath.

They'd only be there forty-eight hours, but she'd brought a nice outfit in case she, Ros, Neil and Lawrence wanted to have a last dinner together at a five-star restaurant. Her treat, of course. She'd also chosen what she'd wear to the clinic. The place had a beautiful, open-air resort style. Gardens, fountains, lots of sunshine and open windows. A calm and peaceful setting for her "transition."

On the morning they left the hospital for the clinic, she planned to leave her suitcase at the hotel desk, tell them to give all the contents to a charitable organization. Whatever Switzerland's version of a Salvation Army or Goodwill was. She didn't want Ros to have to worry about it. She'd be cremated in Switzerland. All Ros would bring back were her ashes.

Abby left the kitchen and moved onto the back porch. From there to the steps, so she could tip her head up, look for the sun. She noted the vast sky, how far it stretched. She imagined she was in Neil's boat, floating along, leaning against him, his hand resting on her knee.

Faith. Hope. Such simple, pointless things she'd never, well, had faith in. She and Maureen had explored her deep love for her mother and the struggle she'd faced. Her fears and despair. Abby thought about what Neil had said. If she could have her mother back, if she'd had even the slimmest chance of a better life than what she'd lived, would Abby wish her back? Want to beg her to try? To have faith?

She stood on that edge, looking out into the world ahead. She imagined the ocean from a goddess's view. The storms the boats would sail right into, the debris, the unknown. Those tiny boats, in all that vastness, doing what it would seem crazy to do. When he'd taken her out in the bayou, he'd shown her what he'd described to Maureen.

A bond to the elements, to what they could reveal to sailors, where they could take them.

Maureen had also shed light on other parts of Abby's soul. Journeys she'd taken, separate from her mother's, in ways she hadn't let herself explore before those sessions.

In one of them, Maureen had asked her a question that initially Abby had rejected, but it had come back to her several times, and it came back now.

"Do you feel you have to die because you couldn't save your mother? You don't feel you deserve to prove yourself stronger?"

"It's not a matter of being stronger. You know that, if you know anything about this illness."

"Every parent of worth hopes their children will surpass them. I know you've done a lot of comparisons between yourself and your mother, your grandmother. Spend some time thinking about the differences. You're the woman who had the strength to care for your mother as a child. You're the one who went to New York, became an accomplished businesswoman. Who found an outlet for your desires through being a Domme. Your path will have overlaps with your mother and grandmother, but you are a different story being written."

"I don't know how to believe that. And that path isn't followed in a vacuum. Everything I do, every stumble, every relapse, every progress of the disease, will have a ripple effect on those I love."

Throughout her life, Abby had thought a great deal about history. Political chaos, massacres, people thrown in dark places where suffering and fear were the only guarantees.

They'd survived, come out on the other side, but many hadn't. If the ones who'd survived had known for sure dealing with the horror would never be over, would they have even tried?

She'd struggled with the question of whether she was weak for choosing this course. Long before they'd known about it, she'd taken herself down every road her friends, her family, had used to reason with her, plead with her, argue with her. She'd come to terms with it.

But she hadn't really made peace with it, no matter what she'd told them. Maureen had shown her that. And somehow planted the seed that if Abby couldn't make peace with it, something wasn't right.

She could smell the bayou. The warmth of Neil's shirt against her face, his skin. His laughter. She loved her friends so much, but she'd told herself they had each other. Ros had been the hardest, as Abby had told Maureen, because Abby knew how Laurel's loss had impacted her.

But Ros had Lawrence. Abby believed in the strength of their relationship. It could weather those inevitable ravages of guilt Ros might feel. If it ever crossed her mind that her falling in love with someone had made it "easier" for Abby to choose this course, Lawrence could steer her away from that. Truthfully. Because it hadn't made it any easier.

But Neil... What if Neil was her person and...she was his?

These things don't happen randomly.

Her bitter response to him had been yes, because Fate liked to fuck with people. She wasn't a believer in a cosmic pattern of good, or things working out the way they were supposed to. Nothing she'd seen had supported that, unless Fate was exactly what she'd called it, a fucking sadist.

But...she didn't have words for it, an explanation. However, the feeling spreading through her...it changed something. She closed her eyes again, imagined his arms around her.

She wasn't willing to give that up.

Oh, God.

The revelation made her shudder, come up short. She'd moved into her backyard, which was fortunate, because when she lost her balance, she folded onto a garden bench. She gripped it as the world spun. A full octane injection of stress turned everything to glitter, showering around her, the sun a spinning dial.

"Help..."

"I'm here." Maureen was next to her on the bench, touching her wrist. "Just breathe. Easy. It was close to time for your meds." She folded Abby's hand around a paper cup that didn't seem solid or real. But Abby managed to swallow the pill. Maureen's shoulder pressed to hers. "Here's your coffee."

Abby took it, sipped. Maureen kept her from spilling it on herself, her hands slipping away only when Abby lowered the cup and set it aside. She rocked, kept her eyes closed. She waited for the darkness to close in, the wet clicking to get louder, mocking her choice, her willingness to believe in something that wouldn't get better, but would somehow be good enough to give her the will to endure.

To live.

She heard all those things. But she kept feeling Neil's hands on her, too. Feeling the rock of the boat.

It's your choice, Mistress. You're in control. She could hear the Southern drawl of his voice, so clearly it was possible it had now joined her delusionary shadow whisperers. If so, his was the only welcome one in the macabre choir. Maybe he could bring a couple of his guns along and take care of the others.

Saying the words aloud, the courage to do it, might have defeated her, except she was sitting here with Maureen, who was accepting everything, judging nothing, giving her space.

"Changing of the guard. New Direction. Band. No. That's One Direction. Cool Change."

"Little River Band. Sailing on the cool and bright clear waters." Maureen hummed the tune a little. "Got something in your kitchen where I can whip you up a quick lunch? Put something on your stomach that isn't sugar, so the pills won't come back up. I'm a good cook."

"Happy meal." Abby thrust the words out, a sudden spill, like something breaking through a clogged drain. "Have it your way."

"Okay." Maureen pressed a hand to her shoulder, went back into the house. The kitchen had a window view through the screen porch to the backyard, so though Abby appreciated the space, she knew Maureen was likely keeping an eye on her. She kept rocking, her body twitching, her mind whirling. Whirling like a dance she thought she'd known, but which now had a bunch of new steps.

Seeking a lower point of gravity, she stretched out on her hip, placing the coffee mug on the ground beneath the bench. She absorbed the sun's warmth, and folded her hands under her cheek. Watched the flowers nod. But the scene before her shimmered, and she was in the boat, remembering Neil's hands on her as she lay on the deck, his mouth on her inner thighs, his hair brushing her skin.

Her SEAL. Her Dom. Not in the sense that he was *her* Dom. But he was a Dom, and he was hers. Hadn't he said something similar about calling her "his Mistress?"

~

In the kitchen, Maureen kept a sharp eye on her patient, already formulating plans if Abby should go into full psychosis, lose her grip on reality and try to take off.

The medicine's first effects took about fifteen to thirty minutes. Abby's reaction to it was still not completely predictable, but for the last three days, with the psychotherapy and symptom management techniques she'd developed over the past few weeks, it had been able to steady her.

She'd just had a major jolt to her system of some kind, though. Maureen wasn't sure what it was, but she knew what she hoped it was.

Reminding herself to be a therapist first, she applied herself to putting together a chef salad with the items she found in the refrigerator. And waited to see what the turning of the clock, and her patient's mind, would bring.

~

When Abby opened her eyes again, she realized she'd drifted off. Something felt different. She pushed up, evaluating her surroundings, inside and out. Like Neil. Whenever he woke, she could tell he did a blink of recon on his immediate environment.

Maureen was sitting on the porch swing, working on her laptop, glancing at her phone on occasion. As Abby ran her hands over her hair, tidying it, waking herself up by rubbing her palms briskly over her face, she settled into the drug's expected effects. Dry, heavy tongue, the world a little fuzzy and slow moving at first. The voices had died down again. Though the details of the world around her were still a little more hi-def than most people experienced it, they weren't blinding, and the edges were clearer. It was manageable. More manageable.

She turned her mind to what had set her off. Examined it from a few different sides. "A conscious paradigm shift is as terrifying as jumping out of an airplane on purpose," she said. "No parachute."

Maureen closed the laptop, set it and the phone aside, showing she'd been giving Abby time to orient to whatever jumble her mind was in, sort it out.

"If I had any doubt you were in full command of your faculties, that very articulate and true statement confirms it. Want to come up on the porch, or should I come to you?"

"I'll come to you." Abby made it to her feet, swayed. It took her a few minutes to get going in the right direction, but at length she was sitting on the top step.

Maureen had put a pitcher of ice water on the side table. As Abby stared at the glittering movement of every individual ice cube behind the clear glass, Maureen poured her some, brought it to her and sat down on the opposite side of the step. Abby downed about half of it, unstuck her throat, her tongue.

"You're probably way over your hour. I'm so sorry. You should have called someone to watch over me."

"I had a feeling you had more to say to me. Do you?"

She thought she did. Maybe. "It's not wedding jitters."

At Maureen's look, Abby managed a smile. "You remember our first conversation? About the counseling for engaged couples?"

"Oh, of course. Yes." Maureen's smile was brilliant. "What's not wedding jitters?"

"Turning around. Calling it off." Abby watched the words drift like mist over her garden, become the whimsical wake of bees, words that loop-de-looped behind them. "My life is a roller coaster in a horror-filled fun house. That's not going to change. It'll get worse, then better, then back to worse again. No matter what, it'll likely be that way, far more often than I want it to be...none of that has changed. But I have."

Abby drew in a breath, let it out. It made a sighing noise inside her head that distracted her for a couple moments, but she didn't let go of the other thoughts. She took them with her, so she could speak them aloud.

"I want to wake up and see that suncatcher in my window. I want to hear Neil's heart when my head is on his chest."

She brought her gaze to Maureen's because it was important, even if she could only hold there a second, speak the words. Neil's words, her truth.

"I want to live the life I've been given."

There it was. Words spoken in a soft voice in her quiet garden, with her quietly listening psychotherapist. The world didn't falter in its rotation, not even by the slightest millionth of a fraction. But her world, the world of those around her...

She'd dreaded having schizophrenia her whole life. Now, these past few months, it had arrived. It had happened. She'd been hospitalized, had psychotic breaks, had done some of the things she'd handled with her mother. And it could get even worse.

But during that same time, she'd gone to a softball game. Met a wonderful man. Learned just how deep and strong her friendships with Ros, Cyn, Vera and Skye were. Maureen was helping her find the right treatment path, and Abby *was* feeling better. Even if the voices, the symptoms, the pitfalls, were all still there, she could truly say she kept having moments worth living for. Erratic, nothing she could count on, and yet the possibility of it, experiencing the reality when it happened...somehow, that made the rest more bearable.

If Maureen was doing a self-congratulatory touchdown dance in her head, a fist bump with all her peer psychotherapists, she didn't show it. Her smile was as serene as always, her first comment as simple a response as Abby's declaration—and just as momentous. "I'm glad to hear it. I enjoy our sessions, and I would have missed them."

"Me too." She meant it. Maureen helped. Had helped, and would continue to help.

"I made you a salad. I went ahead and ate mine, but can keep you company while you eat yours."

"No, thanks. I appreciate you making me lunch, but I want to go. I want to go tell him. But...can I ask a favor?"

Tonight was her dinner with Ros and everyone. They'd be coming to Abby's place, because she'd intended to give them her gifts. She'd wanted to see how they reacted to them. Which reminded her that she'd planned to ask Maureen for sedatives to manage the flight. She might still need them to handle her friends' reactions to her decision, though that thought brought a smile as concentrated as a million zillion angels dancing on the head of a pin.

Whoa. That was a distracting image.

"What was the favor, Abby?"

"Can you let them know? Ros and the others?"

"You don't want to tell them yourself?"

She shook her head. "I can't handle a huge wave of it. It's just too new. I'm certain, but kind of shaky over it." And now she understood Maureen's quiet reaction. Because she got it.

"It was a big decision," Maureen agreed. "You could take an extra dose before seeing Neil, if you want. It will help manage any stress triggers."

"I don't want to numb myself. The meds...you know, they do that sometimes. When I tell him, I want to feel his reaction, a hundred percent, even if the emotional wave sets me off." The frustrating limits to what she could feel would also always be part of this, but the good thing? She spoke it aloud. "He can handle it."

"Sounds like he's a keeper."

Abby laughed and rose, steadying herself on the railing. "He is."

Maureen gave her a critical look. "I'm a little concerned about you heading to his place on your own. I'll drive you."

"That's way too far and I know you like to pick up your daughter after school. I'll take the trolley down to the casino and pick up a cab. They'll appreciate the monstrous fare. I'll text you once I'm in the cab and once I get there. I think...I'm going to be okay for this, Maureen." She smiled at the woman. "You know my risk of having an episode is lowest during the first hour or two of the meds."

"All right. But please do text me."

"You got it. See you Friday?"

"See you then."

Abby went back into the house with Maureen. While she put together a quick overnight bag, Maureen covered up the salad, kindly said she'd take care of the dishes and lock up after she placed the call to Ros. Abby wanted to hear her friend's reaction, but she couldn't. Not now. She had one goal, and she had to keep her eye on it, or she wouldn't manage any of it.

What she wanted and needed most right now was a too-lengthy cab ride away.

When Abby bid Maureen a warm good-bye and stepped out onto her back porch, her zinnias were blooming in vibrant colors, the air was clear. Birds were chirping.

A bolstering sense of relief gripped her, like after a fearful medical diagnosis hadn't come to pass, or a dreaded confrontation had been dealt with. A burden laid down. Those colorful flowers were brighter than they should be, the tree branch tips too sharp, the porch board cracks too wide. The shadow voices giggled and whispered on the edges of the sunlight, made their clicking noises, but that was the same as yesterday, and likely tomorrow. Their volume would go up and down.

Some days they'd win, and she would be overwhelmed. But her will was strong. So were the people who loved and watched over her.

She wanted to live *this* life. It was hers, and no one else's. Maybe in Fate's lottery, there'd been tickets with different lives on them, and she'd taken this one, because she knew she could handle it, keeping someone else, like her mother, who couldn't, from having to go through it.

Such things were likely just a way to make sense of the insensible, help a person sleep at night. But Abby had always known life made very little sense. Even with that, it still seemed to hold a lot of things worth living for, if she tuned those senses—however often they were fucked and distorted—toward noticing them.

Like now. She'd reached the bottom of the steps, was walking along the side of her house, down her driveway. When she happened to look up into the kitchen window, she stopped, stared, and started laughing.

The cool, collected, unflappable Dr. Maureen Whisnant was doing a fist pump, touchdown style dance, including a short giddy-up gallop. Complete with self ass slapping.

When Maureen twirled toward the window, she came up short, seeing Abby standing there. The flash of embarrassment, the professional behavior warring with what had inspired the reaction, was a short battle. Abby helped make it so by grinning widely at her and blowing her a kiss.

"You slap that ass, girl," she murmured, continuing on. "You deserve it."

A lot of factors had come into play, not the least being Abby herself. Yet she had no doubt that Dr. Maureen Whisnant had helped Abby in multiple ways, with her fears, her worries, the self-destructive grasp of her past.

She'd helped save Abby's life.

The shadow voices might take her hostage plenty of times in the future, but Abby had a good chance of making sure they'd never be able to hold onto her. As Neil had noted, she had an army standing by.

Hers to call whenever she needed them.

CHAPTER TWENTY-THREE

Neil lay on the deck of his tied-up boat, watching the clouds drift through a blue sky, feeling the craft rise and fall beneath him as things elsewhere in the river caused the wakes. Maybe an alligator, disembarking from his haystack of debris. Or a boat upstream, a fisherman or kayaker.

He'd packed. Abby's sisters, as he thought of them—Cyn, Vera, Ros and Skye—were coming to her place tonight to say their good-byes. Per her plan, she'd spend her final day on her own, to finish up her details, get herself together. Then Ros would drive Abby to the airport with Lawrence, and Neil would meet them there. They'd get on the plane together. They'd show their passports, their ID.

He imagined customs in Switzerland. *"Is the purpose of your trip business or pleasure?"*

"It's to sit by the bed of the woman I love, a woman in perfect health except for a broken mind, and watch her die. How would you *classify that kind of trip, asshole?"*

Yeah, he had to get a handle on this. Lawrence had let him know Ros was in seriously bad shape. Neil had told him if Ros needed to beg off, he'd go with Abby on his own.

Abby had reached the same conclusion a week ago, told Ros she didn't need to go. Now that the time was upon them, Abby had recognized the full weight of what losing another sister, having to watch it happen, would cost her friend.

Ros had told them both no, separately. "I promised her," she said, with weary finality. "Besides, we'll need each other to get through it."

As the chosen two, he and Ros had done a session with Maureen, because they'd wanted guidance on what Abby would need from them during the unimaginable. Dr. Mo had counseled them on methods to manage their emotions until it was over.

"Afterward," she'd said, "vent them in whatever healthy ways are possible."

So blowing up Switzerland was out. Since he actually knew how to get his hands on the weaponry to blow shit up, the *possible* criterion was met, but he figured Maureen wouldn't classify a mass casualty event as *healthy*.

He'd lived through death, caused it himself. But in terms of a strategy against an enemy, or visiting an aunt with end-stage cancer. There was no fight here, no inevitable end.

I can't do it.

I can't bear it.

I won't fucking let her do it.

He kept pushing the declaration to the back of his mind, because if he spoke the words aloud, they would scald his throat, ignite a reaction he couldn't stop. God help him, he'd do exactly what Tommy and Dobby had teased her about. Carry her away, set her up in a cottage so deep in the bayou she couldn't escape. She could be lucid, rage at him, or babble and get lost in her head. He'd be there with her, live off the land, keep her safe and alive, two crazy people. She'd see that what he felt for her, the will he had to love her, keep her, was goddamn stronger than anything.

He wasn't a man who resorted to childhood wishes or behavior. Even as a kid, he'd handled with a methodical calm the things other kids reacted to with tantrums or impulsive acts. He weighed variables in ways even older teenagers or adults didn't do as consistently.

So part of him understood what it was to have a mind that didn't fit the norm. But his had been an advantage. Through the cruel capriciousness of life, hers wasn't.

More proof that they'd been brought together, because of who he was and who she was. He'd come back to that thought, over and over, and knew it was part of why he was having such a problem with this conclusion to the story, this end that shouldn't be an end. A rusty spike driven straight into his gut couldn't match the agony.

He'd had that injury. A lanky, pale, vampiric-looking kid, jumping out of an oil drum and throwing himself on Neil. He'd taken Neil down like a rabid eight-armed monkey, stabbing at him with the spike. Max had pulled him off Neil, but not before the kid had landed the lucky gut shot. He'd take that, ten times over, to avoid the way this felt.

Because that was a wound that had been able to heal.

Life was too complicated to have one formula for living. Maybe that was part of it, too, his desire that she keep seeking, looking for the one that would work, rather than...this. A final solution with no room for more options.

Fuck, maybe it was what she knew was best for her. But he couldn't accept it. He loved her. Loved her so much that the hardest thing for him wasn't living with her illness, as she thought. He knew he didn't know all of it, hadn't lived it, couldn't say if she was right or wrong about the toll it would take on those she loved, on their relationship.

But no matter how bad any of that could get, he'd rather find out, have the chance to meet the challenge. He'd rather be given the shot, the choice, to let love prevail, to prove it could make anything worth it. That it could help her, him, all of them.

But it wasn't his choice.

The hardest five words in the world, and the ones he would have to accept, at least for the next several days, to be what she needed him to be.

The person who would hold her as she died.

He sat up, took a deep breath. Put his hands on his face and discovered the tears that had squeezed through, run down into his beard, dampening it.

"I saw the Swamp Rats lost last night, four to six." Her voice wafted to him along the dock, echoing across the water. "Is that what's got you adding to the water table? I know you're their biggest fan. After their parents, of course."

He twisted around. She'd had her hair and nails done this week, and she wore one of her classy outfits. Black slacks, red blouse, her fire-touched hair clipped back on the sides. Low heels. The bra she wore under the modestly sheer blouse was a distracting red with lace. She'd had a session with Maureen. She preferred to dress for those like she was going to work.

With those kinds of outfits, she usually wore simple jewelry, like a silver chain necklace and matching hoops. Maybe a bracelet on her slim wrist. Never any rings.

The pendant on her necklace drew his gaze. A Trident, the SEAL emblem, crafted in gold and silver.

"Vera gave it to me," she said, noting his attention. "Her card said, 'A talisman of ownership. Mutual, though sometimes hotly contested.'" A light smile touched her lips.

She stopped a few feet away. He saw the emotion in her gaze, a reaction to seeing the tears on his face, he was sure, despite her attempt to save them both embarrassment by gently teasing him about it. Her gaze touched his, before she did her necessary shift of attention elsewhere. To the water this time.

She closed her arms over herself, rubbed her biceps. Then she twitched, tossed her hair, shifted to the other foot. She was a little agitated, which made him suddenly wonder how she'd gotten here and whether he should give her shit about doing it by herself, even if she'd taken public transport. She would have finished her session with Maureen, right before she came.

As all those puzzling pieces hit him, she brought her hazel eyes back to meet his gaze once more. Then she told him why she was making that effort.

"I'm not doing it, Neil. I've called the clinic, told them to cancel my appointment. Permanently."

Now it was his turn for his gaze to wander away, slide around her, as if seeking something from the air. Her brow creased as she noted it, stepped closer. "What?" she asked.

"Just seeing if I fell asleep. Trying to see something that tells me I'm not dreaming."

"Seeing me standing here isn't enough?"

His smile was slow, painful. "You are the dream, bébé. Whether I'm awake or asleep."

He rose to step from the boat, back onto the dock. And then Neil

Shepherd did something no frogman would ever admit to doing, even under the worst of tortures.

Thanks to legs that had become too shaky to carry him to solid ground, he fell off the boat.

~

"Neil!"

Abby lunged forward, too late. Fortunately, he hadn't fallen between the dock and the boat, where he could have cracked his head on any number of hard surfaces.

He surfaced a few feet away, sputtering, wet, his eyes a little dazed from the unexpectedness of it, but they cleared and lasered in on her fast, reassuring her. She was on her knees at the edge of the dock, her hand stretched out to him.

"The things I have to do to get you to kneel," he observed, stroking over to her.

"Keep talking like that and I'll push your head under when you get close enough."

Despite the tartness of the response, she kept her gaze on Oliver. She'd been the one to recently give him the name, a far-too-large alligator whose favorite sunning spot was a pile of branches and dead foliage about fifty yards away from Neil's dock. Though alligator eyes didn't seem to move much, they had an eerie way of looking like they were watching a person. As such, he seemed to be marking Neil's location with too much interest. She also kept her attention on any telltale ripples that might suggest he had brethren about. While Oliver looked like he was enjoying the sunshine too much to be disturbed, she remembered just how fast they swam.

As Neil approached, she was distracted from the alligator by the speculative gleam in her SEAL's eyes. Deciding the high emotions of the moment might be impeding his intelligence, she speared him with her best Domme glare.

"Try to pull me in with you, and I *will* make sure you drown and become Oliver's lunch."

He clasped her hand, his other gripping a dock cleat. But he didn't pull himself out. Instead, her heart lurched as he pressed his face hard into her palm, his shoulders going rigid. She bent over him, wrapping an arm over them, her head resting on his, absorbing his dampness into the sleeve and front of her blouse, and minded not a bit.

When he raised his head, she saw him realize he could look down the front of her blouse, see curves cradled in lace. Then the look in his eyes became something else. Her own flood of emotion joined hands with the physical pleasure of what it meant to have a man desire her. Pleasure that could be explored in endless ways.

"Back up, city girl," he said. "No way for you to pull me up without going in headfirst yourself."

As she complied, it was her turn to appreciate the view, a man who could heft himself out of the water with upper body strength alone, his T-shirt plastered to all the muscles that managed it, slick and wet. Drops ran down his corded throat and bare arms. He sat himself on the dock edge, legs still in the water. While denim couldn't provide the same definition, she was intimately familiar with the long thighs beneath the hold of the thicker fabric, and what he could do to a woman with what was between them.

His attention went back to the pendant resting against her damp cleavage. "When did she give that to you?"

"Yesterday. A going away gift of sorts. I hope she won't want it back." She fingered it. "I think the gift had ulterior motives, a reminder of what I was leaving behind."

He took her hand and pulled her down into his lap, no care for getting both of them soaked, and she was all right with that, too. He kissed her, giving her the flavor of the bayou and the man.

Despite the dizzying force of it, she realized she might have to be the one to look out for both of them right now. She put a hand on his chest, pushed back. "I'd feel far better if you pulled your feet out. Oliver has left his spot."

Neil shifted his gaze, saw the telltale V-shaped wake of the alligator's track in his direction. "Oh, shit." On a chuckle, he rose, pulling her up with him but not letting her go.

Instead, he clasped her in his arms again, held her flush to him. A little breath shuddered through her at his embrace, almost too tight, but that went on the same list of things that were okay right now.

He eased her back, stared at her, his hands rising to frame her face, run wet thumbs over her lips. "What happened?"

She pressed them together, absorbing his touch. "Several things.

I'm not really sure myself, but I think it happened over time. Others dated from the beginning, the past. They were already there, waiting to be noticed, or for me to have the ability to notice them."

Her gaze lifted, dwelled on his lashes, the water clinging there, then descended again, to where she had a hand placed on his T-shirt, over his heart. His hands had gone to her hips, her waist, were still holding her so surely and firmly. Not wanting to let her go. "But there was a catalyst for those things," she said. "You asked me to open my mind, my heart, in a way I didn't expect."

She shook her head. It was simple, and she wanted to say it simple, so he could hold onto it, for whenever the road forward took them straight into hell. And it would.

"You, Neil. It was you. Just as I said, when I backed away before, only now it's the reason I'm not. You are what helped me change my mind. The way you made me feel."

He took a deep, shuddering breath, his eyes glistening, this big, strong, calm man. Who loved her so much. She had no doubt of it. Even if every day her mind tried to take her certainties away from her, juggle them like plates that would dash to pieces if dropped—and they would be dropped—she would add that certainty to the lists of things she wrote down, posted around her house and office.

Get up. Brush teeth. Shower. Remember that Neil loves you beyond all definitions of sanity. Or insanity.

She told him that, loving his responsive smile.

"Speaking of sanity, you're going to do something crazy for me, right now."

She noted his eyes were a little wild, a startling look for him, one that told her he was a bit out of control right now, getting his mind around things.

Being a Domme, she actually delighted in seeing that, knowing she'd caused it. But she affected a wary look.

"What? I am not going bull frogging with you and Tommy at night. Not now, not ever. Not until you can assure me that every single giant hopping spider is eradicated."

"Yeah, you'll go with me. I'll talk you into it. But that's not it." He stepped back, but kept one hand linked with hers. "You in that wet blouse is more than I can handle. Leave it on, but take off the pants, shoes and socks. Definitely leave this on." His fingers brushed over the Trident.

"You're giving me orders, sailor."

"Yeah, I am." That wildness suddenly concentrated in twin points of fierce heat. "Do it for me, bébé."

So she did. She slipped out of the shoes, unzipped and dropped the silk lined slacks. He took them, carefully put them aside. Then he pulled a bucket out from under the bench bolted to one side of this part of the dock. He turned on the adjacent water spigot which had an attached hose, mainly for washing his boat.

The way his eyes never left her as he did all that kept her silent. Things had grown large between them, pushing words back into hearts that contained everything they needed to say. She could tell what he was going to do. It was rather obvious, but his expression said it wasn't about being playful.

When he shut off the water, he came to her. "Put your hands on my hips and tip your head back. Eyes closed. Water won't be bad cold, because it's from the well, but the sun will warm you up anyway. So will I."

She put her hands where he'd directed, hooking her fingers in the belt loops of his jeans, feeling the resilience of the man beneath.

He was right. It wasn't too cold, but enough of a contrast she swallowed a gasp. She kept her face turned upward, though, let it stream over her face, her hair, down her throat. Over and under the front of her blouse, down to her panties and bare legs, her toes gripping the dock.

He put the bucket back down, then his hands followed the water. Over her face and hair, her shoulders, and then he was plucking open the buttons of her blouse. His expelled breath made her open her eyes.

He was gazing at the glistening tops of her breasts, quivering over lace. His hunger wasn't like anything she'd ever seen in a man's face. Not even the submissives she'd driven to the pinnacle of their cravings for her dominance.

This was a hunger from everything he was, heart, body and soul, targeted toward another heart, body and soul. Hers. Everything about her, good, bad, dark, light, shadows, sanity, insanity. He wanted all of it, now and always.

And what made her sure of it was feeling the same way about him.

He has his own darkness.

Thank God. Because it understood hers.

He bent his head, and she shuddered, clinging to him, relying on his strength to hold her up as he suckled beads of water off her throat and breasts. His hand dropped, fingers pushing down into her panties to cover her between her legs. He used the heel of his palm to massage her with sure pressure and skill. "Come for me. Right fucking now," he growled. "Against my hand."

She was already bucking against his touch, the friction catching her on fire, surging over her skin. He'd been right. He'd warmed her in no time.

It should have been impossible, but she couldn't refuse the command. The climax swept her as she dropped her head back to cry out the pleasure of it, hold onto him so he could steady her through the sensations. They carried her like a swirl of rainbows, dancing through the sky during the storm, not waiting for it to pass or the sky to clear.

She was floating, still spinning, when he picked her up, increasing the feeling. "I don't want you to get splinters in your feet," he muttered.

A flash image, of him holding her hand, removing a splinter. A memory he'd brought back to her. The good among the bad.

She pressed her painful smile against his damp shirt. He was striding up the dock, onto his back porch. He shouldered the screen door open. As he did, she felt a tremor in his arms, or perhaps that was from her. As they entered the more dimly lit space, she touched his face. The kinetic energy within her generated its own heat.

She'd made the decision. She couldn't think about it now. As she'd told Maureen, it was too large a shift. Over the next few days, she'd digest it in small pieces, knowing even with that prudent plan she'd likely be overwhelmed by it. Her mind had nowhere to put such explosive bits. It would pack them all together and set off a fireworks show that would make her wonder if the decision was true insanity.

But every other part of her that wasn't her broken brain would know it wasn't. Because Neil and the others would reinforce it with her, be there with her, even if her brain sucked her down for a while where she couldn't see or feel anything but a reality entirely detached from theirs.

The lifeline was there. Here.

He sat her on her feet in the bedroom. At the press of her hands, a nonverbal demand, he removed his wet clothes. Then he removed the rest of hers. Blouse off, bra straps pushed down her arms, the back fastener unclasped. Wet panties skimmed down her legs as she held onto his bare shoulders.

When he straightened, she wound her arms around him, and he lifted her against him, putting a knee on the bed, taking her down beneath him slow. She felt his gaze on her face as she spread her hands out on his chest. She stretched up, put her mouth to his throat, her nose against his pulse. He locked a hand around the back of her head, holding her there.

Her hands slipped around, under his braced arms, down to his hips. She lifted to him and they came together, a slide and lock that had her lips parting, his eyes darkening. He bent, put his mouth on her breast, her sternum, as his hips moved, buttocks flexing to delve deep, savor the feel of her slick sex as he moved back, then in again.

The sound of water lapping against the dock intensified, the shards of light, shadows becoming even more precise, like knife blades. The voices rose, but their wet clicking was lost in those sounds, a part of it, manageable. Immersed.

"I can tell when those different parts of your mind rise," he murmured, voice husky. "Tell me where you are. Describe it to me. Take me there until I make it hard for you to talk, and then keep talking anyway."

She told him of the shadows, the water. The scents. "I can smell you, the water on your skin. The trees, the sky has a scent, mixed with the wood on the dock, and I hear things...birds. Frogs. Their whispers during the day as they wait for night to fall. So many things live in the shadows."

He cupped her face as her voice became strained, sensation rising with those images, impressions. "Stay with me," he said, a low demand. "I'm on the boat with you. In the storm together. Hold onto me."

Another soft cry broke from her. Pleasure radiated through her lower abdomen as he drove in deeper, rubbed her just the right way.

She lifted her hands to his face again, made her own demand. "Come for me, Neil. Let me see you get lost with me."

~

She was in a half-dream state when Neil slipped from her arms, murmuring something about being back in a while.

She drifted, content, but a memory came to her on those clouds. A day when Neil had taken her by the rec center, because he had to drop off a box of items with the director. Dale had been there. While Neil was occupied, Dale kept her company, leaning against the open window of the truck. He'd mentioned how helpful Neil had been the previous week, when Neil accompanied Dale on a trip into one of the poorer parishes. They'd been clearing a lot for a family whose home had been damaged by flooding. The unstable ground had brought down half a dozen old, large trees.

She remembered when she saw Neil the next day, he'd seemed sore and stiff. She'd teased him about getting older, slowing down.

He went at those trees with a ferocity that would have sent an army into full retreat. Dale had said it with an oddly intent look in his blue-green eyes.

He swirled away into the ether and Tess appeared, her dark eyes spearing Abby.

He needs you.

She came fully awake. He wasn't back. Finding his shirt, she put it on, slipped her feet into a pair of canvas sneakers she'd brought along in the overnight bag. Night had fallen, but there were lights on the dock and on the front porch. She caught a flash of movement in her peripheral vision. When she came to the front screen door, she discovered the movement wasn't her brain playing tricks on her. He was in his side yard.

It looked like he was doing a nighttime work out. He had a punching bag on a chain he apparently kept wrapped around the thick branch of a live oak for that purpose.

Her pulse accelerated, hand going to her throat as she watched him pound and kick the bag with a force that should have knocked it off the chain, or busted open the thick covering. His face was stretched in a mask of fury. A storm that had escalated into hurricane strength.

She'd suspected how much she'd been asking of him, but here it was at last, plain for her to see. Everything he'd been carrying—the pain, worry, the anticipation of loss.

Maybe this was a version of what he did when he went into the bayou to purge everything about his job that might poison him. Tonight he'd had to do that here, because he wouldn't leave her alone. But it had built up in him so strongly, it had driven him from their bed. He'd had to leave her arms to let it go. And that wasn't acceptable.

He was pushing himself beyond what she thought he should. She knew the signs of that, a man who'd let the emotions take him too far, too deep. Then she noted he was pounding on the bag with bare fists, and blood had bloomed against the leather.

Definitely unacceptable. She came to the end of the porch, the steps there. Gripping the rail, she moved down to the bottom one.

"Neil. *Neil.*"

He spun. He hadn't realized she was there, another startling flag. His eyes were feral, every muscle in his upper body above the loose hold of the faded jeans etched out. He stood staring at her, chest heaving, bloody fists clenched.

There were tears streaked on his face, into his beard, moistening his lips. A harder, stronger reaction than the few stingy tracks he'd allowed himself earlier in the day, when she'd come to find him. Those had been overflow, from a pain he'd still been struggling to contain.

These tears were catharsis.

Mutely, she opened her arms. He had no lawn, just natural areas of foliage and trees clustered around his home. Yet though his feet were bare, he didn't seem to notice the rough terrain he was walking through.

On that last step, he lunged at her, wrapping his arms around her like he was capturing her. Her breath left her. She was enveloped in an embrace that held hints of the violence his enemies had experienced, but she was the eye of the storm, surrounded by it but safe.

Unless she unwisely chose to deny the words he spoke against her bosom, his lips and tears pressed against the curve of her breast.

"I won't let you go again, bébé. I don't give a shit what we call ourselves. Master. Mistress. You belong to me. If anyone tries to take you from me, even you, I will fight harder than I've ever fought anyone or anything. Tell me you understand."

"I do. I'm yours. You're mine." She paused, and though it seemed an odd moment for it, she found herself smiling, staring up at the sky, the trees, at everything in her crazy, fragmented universe.

Crazy and fragmented, yes. But also hers. Like the man in her arms. "I feel you, and everything. I'm broken. Afraid and lost, but not so afraid of being lost anymore. I choose you, Neil. I choose surrender. To you."

He held her tighter, if that was possible. "Broken, maybe, but not needing to be fixed. You're perfect."

~

After she doctored his hands in the kitchen, they had a late-night snack—a pack of Oreos they split. Then they returned to the bed. He held her, and she felt him steady, reclaim that center once more.

"Sorry about that," he murmured against her hair, while he stroked it, twined it over his fingers in that way he liked to do. Binding her to him, him to her. It worked both ways.

"No sorries to be said. It was my shift. My turn to take care of you." She paused. "I'm not going to change my mind, but even now, I'm afraid to believe, Neil. Afraid to let go and fall without knowing where I'll land."

"You know where you'll land. Right here." He toyed with the pendant, then brushed the cleft between her breasts. "Did anyone else give you gifts?"

"Cyn was going to bake me a cake. She's a crappy cook, but she's a fabulous baker. I think it was going to say *Bon Voyage, You Bitch, Fuck You,* but even so..."

"Oh, well. That changes everything." Neil drew back. "Call Switzerland. You have to go through with it. It would be selfish to deprive the rest of us of that cake. Or to miss the miracle of Cyn demonstrating domestic skills."

He chuckled as she elbowed him. She liked that he had that ability, to find humor even in the shadow of something that could tear apart the soul.

"She has domestic skills. Other ones. She says she's a hell of an ironer. She's had lots of practice, using the backs of her subs. We think she's kidding."

Neil winced. "She might be more sadist than Domme."

"Jury's still out on that. But her subs always come back for more. They're addicted to her."

"Yeah. Like to a cult leader with the cyanide Kool-Aid. Did you hear from Maureen? Did she tell the others?"

“My SEAL has been keeping me busy.” Still smiling, she twisted toward the night table, pleased when he merely adjusted his hands so he could keep holding her waist. He brushed her hair aside to spread kisses between her shoulder blades, making her shiver.

She'd texted Maureen as promised when she arrived, but she hadn't looked at her phone since then. But at Neil's question, she found herself anticipating what she'd find. She wasn't disappointed.

She had a voicemail from Ros. Turning back around to balance the phone on Neil's bare hip, just above the folded sheet, she hit the speaker button so they could both hear it.

“Abby!” Ros's voice blasted into the small room, making her jump, but also making Neil's eyes twinkle at the unleashed enthusiasm in her friend's voice. Ros's New York accent came through with emphatic force.

“We're having a party at your house. Dr. Mo's here. She may be table dancing with Cyn before long. There's been some drinking. A lot, actually. We raided the ABC store around the corner. It's okay. We won't trash things.”

Abby was smiling, even as tears were running down her face. Neil's large palm cupped it, fingers stroking her.

“We know it's too much for you tonight, but we just wanted you to know. We love you so damn much. And thank you.” Ros's voice choked. “Damn it. Well, okay. See you tomorrow. Bitch.”

She was right, it was too much. Abby's laughter turned into more tears. But getting that kind of voicemail while in Neil's arms, letting him hold her as she shed a few happy tears? It was perfect. For this moment, it was just right.

She didn't know what tomorrow would look like. But even if she was lost to her shadows, she knew this would be here, waiting. A man standing in the dark at her side, never letting her forget she didn't fight alone.

Knowing she wasn't alone, that there was someone real and true, who understood, helped, lifted her up, asked more of her, that never stopped expecting her best effort, no excuses, but also never abandoned her—that was love's true, purest form.

The greatest gift life could give anyone.

EPILOGUE

"I think you have a knack for this," Celia Shepherd said, peering at the neat twists of dough on the pan. They would go into the oven and emerge as braided cinnamon twists, which would be topped with cream cheese icing. One of Neil's favorite homemade desserts.

"It's mathematical," Abby told her. "Two plus two equals four, four by four equals more before we're out the door."

"True enough." Celia glanced at Neil. He was playing a card game with his two sisters at the antique pine wood table in the spacious kitchen. The bank of windows behind them bathed the area in light. They also displayed a wooded ravine backed by the red rock formations that punctuated so many views of Sedona's skyline.

Neil rose from the table to come to Abby's side. He rubbed her back with a firm palm. "She's fine," he told his mother. "Getting close to time to take her next meds."

"Everything she said makes sense to me," Della said, fanning out her cards and shooting Abby a conspiratorial look. "She's making sixteen rolls, more than enough for all of us before you guys head out to Tlaquepaque for lunch. If Neil doesn't gobble them all up."

"Della's pretty smart," Neil told Abby. "She would have been smarter, but she was dropped on her head several times as a baby."

"Yeah, he did the dropping when Mom wasn't looking. Don't listen to him, Abby. I gave him all his smarts. You didn't think the SEALs trained him to be that intelligent, right?" Della arched a brow. "I'd be a great SEAL, if they weren't such misogynist bastards."

Neil snorted. "If the women can pass the training, they can get in. And we have women involved in the logistics and planning. Us brawny types who can carry our own body weight for ten miles are a dime a dozen. Gotta keep the brains back behind the front lines so they can get our dumb brute asses out of trouble when we need help."

"See how he did that?" Amy grinned at Della. "He'd make a decent diplomat."

"Yeah, if he wasn't such a know-it-all asshole," Della said. However, the comment was wrapped in such familial affection, Abby knew it held no heat.

Though they teased one another mercilessly, Neil's gentleness with them was readily apparent. He was the oldest, and had a good dose of protective big brother.

While they'd been bantering now, Neil had tapped out her pills, left them next to the glass of iced tea Celia had made fresh this morning.

A day or two ago, her getting her words mixed up would have flooded Abby with anxiety about having an episode in front of Neil's family. But now, Celia's reassuring wink as she slid the tray into the oven merely reinforced there was nothing to get worked up about.

She and Neil had been together for nearly a year. At eight months, Neil had started talking about a two-week road trip to Sedona to meet his family. Given the depth of their relationship, it made total sense that he'd want her to do that. Even so, she might have kept hedging against it, except her SEAL approached it like planning for an op.

He'd gotten the leave time approved, and then pulled her into the decision-making process. He'd also involved Ros, Maureen and whoever was needed to handle every contingency. Addressing her worries, one at a time.

What if I can't travel as far as you expect each day? He'd allowed for four days of travel, but had rented an RV for it. They'd decided together the attractions they'd see along the way. Art museums, hiking locales, restaurants.

What if something goes wrong with my meds because of all the new environments? Or I have a major psychotic episode? He'd learned every recommended psychiatric facility, hospital and professional along their route. Plus Maureen was on speed dial if they needed her.

Ever since Abby had known her, Skye had worn a medical ID bracelet to explain her muteness. She'd made one for Abby that fit Abby's unique style. Rose gold, with a three-tiered chain, one with alternating small and large links, one with straight beads mixed with pearls, and one threaded with stones, the birthstones of each of her friends, a reminder of her family support.

The medical ID cross was stamped on the oblong tag, embellished by a lacy rose gold border. On the back, her condition was listed, along with contact info for Maureen, Neil and Ros, as well as TRA's office number. Skye had employed a jeweler in their BDSM world to create it. It was well made and key locked. Abby had the key tucked in her toiletry bag.

Another layer of protection for their travels, in case she got separated from Neil.

What if I start displaying symptoms in front of your parents? Abby had learned to speak frankly with most people about her illness, help them understand her lack of eye contact, prolonged pauses in conversation. And to expect last minute changes in plans, or her abrupt retreat from a meeting or social event to a quieter environment, so as not to exacerbate her symptoms.

With some trepidation, she'd also started doing group therapy Maureen had recommended, spending time with other people diagnosed with schizophrenia, finding solidarity and insights in shared experiences.

Like the anxiety over meeting a lover's family.

Therapy sessions with Maureen had also helped her, walked her through worst case scenarios of a family audition. Neil had discussed with her what he would tell them in phone conversations ahead of time, how to prepare them for her behavior, same as she did clients or others.

In so many ways, he'd proven he could figure out how to work with her, help her manage her illness. And he never lost sight of who she was, even when things were bad.

And they had had bad. Psychotic episodes still came and went. A couple med regimens had crashed and burned, one so badly she'd ended up hospitalized for a week.

With Maureen's dogged perseverance and creativity, her outreach to others in her professional community, they had arrived at a medical and therapy balance that, for the past five and a half months, had helped Abby get ahead of the triggers for episodes, manage her life in a way that made the times between those episodes stretch out longer.

Her mother had never been stable for that long.

She had no illusions. She'd never be an ideal candidate for the existing crop of anti-psychotics and other drugs for mental illness, but combined with the methods learned in psychotherapy, she was living life in a way she found acceptable.

On the days she lost the individual battles, having the fierce and unwavering love of a man and a core group of loyal friends helped her. They showed her the good things about every day, wouldn't let the bad things or the struggles to win the war wear her down.

Whatever routines or environments helped her, that was what Neil prioritized, and he helped her do the same. He often kept her from unwisely backing away from those priorities in the misguided idea that it was more accommodating to her friends or work circumstances. Or because she got so damn frustrated with it and worn out with the constant vigilance, the ups and downs.

"You taking care of you. That's what matters to us." He'd made that clear a thousand ways. So had Ros and the rest.

On her side of things, she firmly reinforced that he should keep doing his job. When he was in New Orleans, they jumped between spending the evenings at her home, or at Neil's. She liked both places, and he said he saw no reason they shouldn't keep both.

They'd also rented a place in Virginia Beach, a waterfront cottage in the Chick's Beach neighborhood. Located on Chesapeake Bay, it was only a short walk along the shore to the perimeter fence and a watchtower for the military base. Now she often accompanied him when he had to be in VA Beach for an extended period. She loved flying with him, almost as much as she liked his ability to come right home to her at the end of his workday.

When he was called down range, she returned to New Orleans. She was determined to show him she didn't need his constant vigilance to do what was necessary to care for herself. Ros, Maureen and the others would help her with that.

He had an extended deployment coming up at the turn of the year which worried them both, but she knew they'd handle it. He was proving every day they could make this work; she wouldn't let down her side of things. She'd prove it to him as well.

However, he'd made one thing clear about his job. The night he had, they'd had an argument. He'd let Dodge know he wasn't going to take Mike's position. "My job already takes me away from you enough. I'm going to stick with what I have."

Nothing she said could change his mind, to the point she threatened to throw something at his stubborn head. She got past that, but later that night, when they were in bed together, her lying in his arms, she'd been determined to try again.

He wasn't wearing his watch, so he put her hand over his wrist, over the small cross tattooed there. He told her its significance, the ritual he did. *Faith first, country second, family forever and always.* Then he told her what was in his heart.

"This is the compromise. I stay an operator, but I don't put more on me there than I already have. And I need you to understand something, bébé." There was a set to his jaw, a look in his eye she now recognized. "If I ever decide you need me home fulltime with you, that's what I'll be doing. I'll end my time with the SEALs, find a job here. It will be my decision, not yours."

"My opinion won't count?"

"It always will, but you're first for me." He gazed down at her. "If I make that decision, you won't need to worry I've given up something I can't live without. You're the only thing that fits that definition."

He respected her, as a woman and as a Domme, but when his alpha and Dom sides locked together, he wouldn't be crossed.

If she'd had any doubt of it from that night, the message had been reinforced the day she tried to back out of the Sedona trip.

Neil had stopped by her office to take her to lunch. She only went into work one day a week now, on staff meeting day. Sonya came to the house, worked with her there. Sometimes the other members of her department did as well, which they all seemed to like.

Despite that, she'd been in a fractious mood. They were only a week away from the trip, and her anxiety over how his family would react to her had overcome her for the dozenth time that day. "I shouldn't go. I'm not going. There's no point. Your mother is going to be horrified you're with someone who needs this much care. Who can't give you anywhere as much as you can give me."

She should have had enough sense not to say that, but it didn't matter. He would have picked up the nuance.

"You shouldn't make assumptions about a woman you've never met." The stern response was backed up by a physical one, as he bracketed her up against her wall in her office. The borderline sensual menace in his expression jerked her out of the mood. He had a threshold of tolerance far more remote than most, but it was always clear when she'd crossed it.

She had.

Those steel eyes flickered with fire. "You said yes. You're going. And you are worth everything to me, Abigail Rose. You give me more than I ever thought any woman could. I know that. You're the one who keeps questioning it."

He tipped his head toward the six-foot wide white board she kept in there for calculations. "So I'm thinking I should close the blinds, make you strip down and write 'I'm worth it,' a hundred times on your board. Then you'll hand me the marker and I'll write it over your pretty ass. Before I put you over my knee and blister it."

He hadn't done it, but the threat had served its purpose. Steadied her, brought things back into perspective.

And yes, it had made her hot, him unleashing his Dom side on her like that. They'd done several more sessions with Tiger at Club Progeny. Even if Neil didn't like her touching another male, he liked who she was in those sessions. And reinforcing who had top claim on her afterward.

The explosive sex they had told her so.

They'd had a leisurely trip to Sedona. The breaks to visit tourist attractions they'd picked had worked out well. It should have built her confidence, but despite all her efforts and his, she still internalized a lot of trepidation, the closer they drew to Neil's family home. Neil had told her they'd be there in time for dinner. His mother had suggested they go to a favorite local restaurant.

Of course she'd been erratic, spun up, the voices too loud, her paranoia fighting with her medications. Neil simply parked the RV at a nearby campsite, called his mother on the cell. Told her they'd be a couple hours late, that Abby needed rest right now, and he was going to stay with her. Then he'd calmly coaxed her to lie down with him, helped her work through some exercises Maureen had taught her, followed by a short nap.

When she roused, they drove the last few miles to the house. Instead of the restaurant plans, Celia was finishing up a lasagna to have a family dinner at home. Afterward, they played board games at the kitchen table. Through it all, Abby sat quietly at his side, in a state of wonder at how they put her at ease, even got her laughing and participating. While they'd asked her some things about herself, the questions were easy and spaced out in a flow of conversation liberally laced with stories of Neil's childhood.

They'd taken her behavior in stride—lack of eye contact, occasionally mix-up of words, loss of focus. When she'd reached her limit and needed to go to bed, she and Neil retired to a guest room Celia had set up for them. A towel sculpture of a swan was on the bed—something she'd learned to do on a past Alaskan cruise.

"I think I'm in love with your mother," Abby said, staring at it.

As if summoned, there was a light rap on the open door. Celia beamed over a stack of towels. She handed them to Neil. "Will you put those in your guest bathroom, son? I want to talk to Abby. Give us a minute."

Neil sent Abby a reassuring look as he passed behind his mother. Celia came to her, extended her hands. "May I?"

Abby put out her hands tentatively, and Celia closed hers over them. They were cool, smooth. She wore a gold wedding set on one hand, a turquoise and silver ring on the other. "We're so very glad to have you here with us."

Pure sincerity. There was no way to mistake it, because Neil had the same delivery method. Abby stared at their hands, that ring. "Thank you...I'm really glad to be here."

"Good." A squeeze. "When Neil finally gave his heart to a woman, I wasn't sure what it would look like, but I knew it would be obvious. It was, from the very first call he made to us about you."

Abby's surprised gaze flicked up to catch Celia's smile. Her tone became more conspiratorial, woman to woman. "In the beginning, I admit, I listened the way a mother would, with my radar on full alert for any flags, anything that would bring my son heartbreak, but I also knew Neil. From everything he told me, I knew he'd found a woman who'd have a great care for his heart. Meeting you tonight confirmed it, just watching the two of you together."

Abby couldn't look away from their hands, the way Celia held her. Like a mother. She was in her thirties now, when she didn't really need one, and hadn't had a functioning one at the age when she did. But that touch reminded her forcefully what it was to want one. Deeply.

As she fought not to overreact to it, she accepted, like everything else, that it was okay to sometimes not succeed. "I didn't think I'd ever be what any mother would want for her son," she said, her voice thick. "I'm not an easy road, but I will do my very best to love him the way he deserves."

"You'd be wrong about that first part," Celia said, rubbing a brisk hand along Abby's upper arm. "He told me you've insisted he stay with the SEALs until he reaches his twenty year mark. The kind of woman who does that understands what being a SEAL means to most of them. To him in particular. He's never wanted an easy road. He wants one worth taking, that will challenge him. He seeks the value in things."

She stepped back as Neil returned. Celia brought him down for a hug, patting his broad shoulders, and planting a kiss on his bearded cheek. She rubbed her lips, wiggled them at the ticklish sensation. "I'll never get used to that. My tall son with a beard. You two sleep in long as you want in the morning."

She looked toward Abby. "We'll plan some shopping with the girls if you're up to it tomorrow, but I don't want you to worry about any of it. Part of why I love living here is how laid back it is. We traveled so much before Neil Senior retired, and technically, our native soil is Alabama and Texas, respectively, but we kept coming back to Sedona for vacations, and I thought, why not? Let's retire here. We haven't regretted it yet."

Abby had learned Neil's full name was Neilson. She'd also discovered where he'd acquired his distracting way with a woman. Neil Senior, a silver-haired version of his son, had sat by his wife during the board games, his hand often stretched behind her chair, or occasionally massaging her shoulder. While the gesture showed simple but deep affection, the look in his eyes when they exchanged teasing words was impossible to mistake.

Celia was the center of his world.

"See you in the morning," Celia said. "And remember, we take life like a riverboat around here. We'll go where the current takes us tomorrow, and enjoy the journey."

After Celia disappeared down the hall, Neil closed the door, turning toward Abby. "She doesn't mind that you love a broken woman," she told him wonderingly.

"Broken doesn't mean it needs to be fixed," he reminded her. He rubbed the bridge of his nose. "Broken twice. Says something about me. Something I want it to say."

He gripped her wrist, a pointed reminder of the handmade bracelet she wore, paired with the medical ID.

Abby had recently volunteered to tutor a girl at the rec center who needed math help. Imene had been bright as a star; her main shortcoming was valuing herself. Her mother worked two jobs, the father was long gone, and Imene cared for younger siblings. She questioned why she should strive for academic excellence when her home life was under siege. Abby had taken every opportunity to shine a light on the girl's value, what she owed to herself.

When Imene landed in the school's STEM program, she'd made Abby a friendship bracelet. The tiny white letter blocks she'd used, flanked by jeweled beads, formed three words.

I'm worth it.

The first time he'd seen it, Neil had closed his hand over her wrist the way he did now. The look in his eyes had taken Abby back to that day in his office, inspiring deeper emotions and a healthy dose of lust.

"Now I don't have to have it tattooed on your ass," he noted.

So here she was, in the present, making cinnamon twists with his mother, and engaging in lively conversation with his sisters. Neil Senior would be back in a couple hours. He was on the board of their neighborhood association, and they had a morning meeting.

"I'll take over here," Celia told her, giving her waist a pat. "You need to get to Tlaquepaque, so you have time to look around before you do Rene's for lunch. I was surprised Neil was able to get a reservation."

"I made the reservation in person," Neil said. "It made all the difference."

Amy rolled her eyes. "He blitzed the hostess's hormones with his hot SEAL mojo."

"Host," Neil corrected her. "The fact he'd prefer looking at my ass flex instead of any of yours doesn't figure into it."

"Right," Della said.

"And don't forget, we're staying overnight at Junipine," Neil reminded his mother, brushing an affectionate hand over her shoulder.

"I won't. That will be such a wonderful way to celebrate...I mean, appreciate, why we live here."

Abby noted Della and Amy making a face at Neil, one laden with a conspiratorial quality. Neil sent them a warning glare as he drew Abby out of the kitchen.

"What's that about?"

"My sisters, begging me to trounce them in front of you."

"Like you could," Della called after them.

Neil told her the name Tlaquepaque meant "the best of everything." The adobe-style architecture of the arts hamlet and shopping area was inspired by the ideal features of a rural Mexican village. "The guy who came up with this place wanted a living arts community," he told her as they walked up to the entrance closest to where they'd parked.

The inviting archway was covered with ivy. A courtyard with a center fountain was just beyond it. "So there are artists who live here," he continued. "And do their art stuff, where people can watch."

Many of the decorative and functional elements—iron grillwork for the upper terraces, pottery for the lush flower arrangements—had come from the creator and architect's travels in Mexico, collecting the pieces to add to their vision.

"Look at the trees," she said wonderingly. Smooth-barked sycamores, decades old, had been left undisturbed, galleries, restaurants and courtyards built around them. Inside the buildings, the thick branches appeared to be threaded through openings in the ceilings.

"They promised to preserve the sycamore grove on the original building site," Neil confirmed.

Flower arrangements and plants that thrived in the arid environment were everywhere. Lush desert blooms mixed with more delicate perennials and annuals, carefully tended. Endless numbers of fountains and solitary pieces of sculpture populated their wanderings through the open spaces.

"It can get busy," he said, "but not so much in the middle of the week, this time of day. I thought you'd like it."

She did. Immensely. Because of its design, she suspected even during busier times a visitor could find a semi-private nook in the shade to call their own. To people watch, get lost in the flow of a fountain, the details of a sculpture or enjoy the lively combinations of bright flowers.

There was a tranquil feel to the place. A core of quiet beneath the hum of activity that she latched onto and found pleasing. Calming.

He wasn't done showing her other things that pleased her. In the Andrea Smith gallery, she was amused to find the actual theme of the place *was* peace and tranquility, reflected in colorful paintings and sculptures. From there, they wandered into Esteban's, a mecca of local artisan pottery. She liked touching and handling the earthen pieces. She bought a print from the Smith gallery for Vera, a pottery piece from Esteban's for Skye.

Only a year ago, she would have been buying these things for her "good-bye" baskets. Now she'd be around to watch Skye and Vera enjoy them. See where they put them in their homes.

Neil also took her into the galleries and shops where the sycamore trees were growing, so she could stroke the smooth trunks and thick sprawling branches, study the cleverness of the openings that had been made for them so they could reach the sun and sky.

The next gallery they visited was about wildlife art, and the artist was sculpting a beautiful bobcat out of clay. While he did, he shared travel anecdotes about photo studies of his subject matter. Abby sat on a wooden bench to listen, Neil at her side, arm around her shoulders, her hand over his.

The gallery light sparkled on the sculptures, bringing them to life, their whiskers twitching and eyes gleaming. The shadow whispers became punctuated by mating growls, warning hisses, playful yips and howls. She tightened her fingers on Neil's, laid her head on his shoulder. She and Maureen had worked on low level distortions and auditory hallucinations, how to let them flow through her, identify if they were escalating, in danger of taking over her reality.

So far, so good. She closed her eyes as Neil put his mouth against her temple, held there.

"Want to go over to the brewery?"

"You've done a full hour and a half of the girly stuff. I guess you've earned a beer."

"Mistress, you are too good to me."

She elbowed him, but slid both hands into the crook of his arm as they wandered back out into the interior flow of the village. Everywhere she looked had something new to see. Neil didn't rush her, letting her amble and turn, tip her head back to study the eaves of the buildings. She touched the petals in a pot of flowers, spun in a slow circle at a fountain before tossing a coin in, where it flashed copper and silver with all the others. Then his arm was around her waist, hand curved over her hip, and they walked onward.

On its back deck, the brewery had a tree-framed view of an impressive distant red rock structure. Cathedral Rock, Neil called it, and it did look like a domed church, with columns flanking it. Abby had a soda while Neil got a beer. They held hands on the table, talked about the things they were seeing. Before she knew it, tears were running down her face.

"It's that new med. It makes me emotional," she reassured him. And the emotions felt good. Pure. Like a waterfall that ran clear, not a churning cesspool.

Neil also showed signs of what she was feeling. Soon after they left the brewery, they passed a bronze of an Indian woman pouring water from an urn. Her pensive face, the grace of her form, arrested them. "She reminds me of you," Neil said. "So beautiful."

The thickness in his voice had her turning in the curve of his arm to look up at him, caress his bearded jaw. "Neil?"

He squeezed her hand, his slate-colored gaze roving over her face, all of her. "I'm glad to be here with you, bébé."

He paused, then put his mouth on her forehead as he spoke

against her skin. "I love you, woman. Whatever made you change your mind, I just want you to hear me, know it's true, every damn day. You would have left a hole in my life I couldn't replace, in my heart, my soul. You can call that bullshit, and I'll forgive you for it, because I know what's true for me. And I don't mind spending the next few decades proving it to you."

She moved further into his arms, and they embraced there, while the fountains gurgled, the mountains surrounded them, the tree leaves rustled. She knew what he was feeling, because she was feeling the same way.

She remembered what he'd said, about being content to take one good moment, no matter how many bad ones there were. Every day, he was proving he meant it. And it was helping her be okay with it. She'd take those good moments. Even if a big chunk of today got lost to a turn in her mind or an unpleasant side effect of the drug, having someone with her who wouldn't let the harder moments take away the good things or overshadow the bad ones...it made it work.

It made life a beautiful thing.

They ambled through winding pathways in natural areas, under more of the sycamores, and across plazas cobbled with red brick pavers. She stopped to look at intricate windmill sculptures with leaf-shaped paddles, crafted in multiple shades of metal. They were too dizzying for her to watch for long, but she liked how they turned in the breeze. She liked how the fountain waters, when one stood close enough, cooled the breeze against the skin.

In places the adobe walls were lined with colorful blue and yellow tiles, slick and silky under the touch. They reminded her of the ones Lawrence and Ros had given her, and made her wonder if Lawrence's mother had supplied any of her work to Tlaquepaque.

So much sensory input. While it fed her heightened senses, she worked to maintain a balance, not get carried away with it into that euphoria that could eventually take her over the edge of reason. However, she drank in as much of it as she could. Whenever it started to become too much, Neil figured out a way to give her mind a rest.

Like suggesting lunch.

The courtyard at Rene's was filled with purple flowers. The inside eating area had well-spaced tables. He'd somehow swung reserving a table for a larger group, but when she saw the space, she understood why he'd done it. It was in a quiet corner, naturally secluded with the help of a bank of lush plants. As they ate, they kept their hands linked on the tablecloth.

Their waitress gave them a fond smile as she tended to them. "You two are nice to watch," she said. "Like a postcard for the perfect romance."

Perfection didn't have to be perfect. Sometimes, that was what made it even more so.

"There's a liveliness to everything in New Orleans," Abby told Neil, as the final dishes were taken away. "And I love it. But this place, the way they laid it out...it's special."

"My parents brought me here when I turned ten. Made me feel like I was a man, them taking me to an adult restaurant. My dad gave me some of his wine." Neil squeezed her hands and rose. "Stay here. I'll pay the bill and then we can go walk around some more."

As he disappeared around the wall she assumed took him to the cashier, music wafted to her from the courtyard outside. Rising and moving to the exit, she didn't see him. Deducing he might have visited the restroom, explaining why he'd chosen to pay for the check up front, rather than letting the waitstaff handle it, she wandered out to listen.

A trio of musicians was playing a Latin American tune. The romantic poignancy of the guitar notes, the lead singer's smooth voice, inspired her to make a couple turns, her light print skirt flowing around her. The man playing the guitar blew her a flamboyant kiss that made her smile.

The music flowed into the other colors and sounds, a river that drew her into its currents. She wandered past the shopfronts, occasionally executing another spin and tipping her head back, humming the tune that went with her.

Ahead was a trio of tall archways, the adobe wall from which they were cut thick with ivy. The walkway built over them had three aligned but smaller arch-shaped openings to allow crossing shoppers on the second level to pause and enjoy the elevated perspective. While they did that, they could lean against the weathered, waist-high stone wall, which had key-shaped openings to form railings.

Moving into the secluded, shaded area beneath the middle archway, Abby found a bench that gave her a view of the courtyards on either side. Fountains bubbled, surrounded by planters of colorful blooms and bright greenery. Her gaze moved to the upper mezzanine stores bordered by the lacy iron grillwork.

The spot felt special, containing a quiet significance that kept her there, soaking in the energy.

She was still doing that when she realized the small crossbody bag she carried was buzzing. She pulled her phone out.

Where are you, bébé?

She'd stopped worrying that Neil would freak out or panic if her mind disconnected like this and she did something unexpected. Her man didn't panic or freak out.

She looked around her. She'd lost sight of the restaurant and couldn't figure out what direction it was in. While a directory might be available somewhere close by, she recognized the fuzziness in her brain would make that useless to her. She settled for a text. *I'm under a walkway, and the wall has ivy and three arches. It's quiet here. Come sit with me.*

Stay there. Which he punctuated with a couple of purple rose emojis. And a Dom smiley face wielding a snapping whip, which made her smile.

She resumed her enjoyment of her surroundings. One of the sycamores had a thinner tree twined into it, its branches displaying bright red flowers. The fountain waters mesmerized her, the sun playing in the droplets.

About ten minutes later, her phone buzzed again.

Still there?

As ordered, O lord and master. She sent him a raspberry. Then her brow creased at his next message.

There's a blindfold folded in your purse. Put it on. Just for a couple minutes. I'm close.

Purse rummaging is a violation of privacy.

I didn't rummage. I planted something in it.

She found the blindfold, a purple satin. Based on what her illness could make her do around other people, strangers and friends alike, putting on a blindfold in a lightly populated public area barely hit her self-consciousness button.

Still, it made her a little nervous. Putting her in darkness in this environment could make those fragments of her brain uneasy. She opened and closed her hands on her knees. Her phone rang, the tone telling her it was Neil. She used voice command to answer it.

"Is it on?" he asked.

She relaxed at the reassurance of his voice. "It is. You have me curious."

"I'm looking right at you, only about fifty yards away." His faint background sounds, birds she herself could hear chirping, confirmed it. "I had them pack up an extra dessert," he added. "It was too good to only have one. We'll share it tonight at Junipine."

He'd told her the hotel had breathtaking views, good hiking trails. Still... "Are you sure it's not going to bother your mother, us doing an overnight? You don't get out here to see her that often."

"We'll come back for a couple more nights before we head home. And if Mom has any objections, it's because of you. She'd send me home in a heartbeat and let you stay forever."

"I would not. I—"

A quick cut off and gasp. Abby's lips curved at Celia's indignant voice, but her stomach spawned butterflies. His mother was here. Neil was having her wear a blindfold. Then there'd been that silent exchange between Neil and his sisters. Plus Celia's odd self-correction about Junipine.

Abby's heart started to pound harder. Was this... But how...what was he doing? Planning?

Thirty seconds passed. "Neil, what are you doing?" Her mouth was feeling dry, her palms damp. Anxiety level going up. A good anxiety, but when did that matter? *Don't you dare*, she told her brain fiercely. *Please don't.*

It was with her all the time now. It never went away. Not a single moment where she felt a hundred percent the way she had before it had manifested. But she knew the degrees of keeping her head above water. She was okay. She was.

Then his hands were on her face, mouth on hers, kissing her so slow and deep, and she was even better. She sank into the sensation of his firm lips, the touch of his tongue, his beard brushing against her more tender skin, a reminder of how it affected other parts of her.

She could still hear the music. It sank into her, too, along with the feel of the dry, cool air, the murmur of people, the colors and textures, waiting to be seen when the blindfold was removed. But she wasn't in a hurry. She didn't want all that to sweep any of this away, being enclosed in a space in the universe reserved just for them, this kiss.

"You look incredibly tempting, sitting here with a blindfold on," Neil whispered against her mouth. "I'm going to put it back on you when you're wearing nothing else, and eat that dessert off any part of your body I want to taste."

"Neil." She gripped his hand with her own. If he'd just shared that with his mother beside him, she was going to murder him. But when he took the blindfold off, Celia wasn't there. Had she imagined her voice?

"Your mom..."

"She went back to the restaurant. She'll wait for us there." He'd knelt beside the bench, his leg pressed against hers, her hands resting in the clasp of his. "This part is just us. And them."

He smoothed back her hair and nodded to her left. She looked in that direction. Jumped.

Ros, Cyn, Vera and Skye stood a few feet away, a semi-circle of anticipatory smiles.

She turned back to Neil. "What are you...oh my God."

His smile was brilliant, but there was a seriousness, too. "I had this all set up in the restaurant. Everyone was waiting on the back patio, including my dad. Rene's staff cleared it out to make it semi-private for about ten minutes. Great view of Cathedral Rock. Then I came to get you and you were gone."

That was why he'd reserved such a large table. "Oh my God, Neil... I'm..."

"Don't you dare say you're sorry." He looked at their surroundings, the courtyards, the arches they sat beneath. The nearby sycamore twined with the red flower tree. Fountain water continued to chuckle, and the potted plants moved in the light breeze.

His expression said nothing in the world was bothering him, not when he had his hands on her, and they were together. Since he'd spent the last year proving his sincerity on that score, she had no reason to doubt it now. No matter the extraordinary circumstances.

"That day I was here with my parents," he said, "we saw a couple get married, right at this spot. I doubt they were the first. There's something about it."

"Yes." She gazed at him. "You're doing what I think you're doing."

"I sure am. Since you're not trying to run, can I assume you're not going to refuse me?"

"I don't know." She rallied enough to sniff, toss her hair back. "No one's asked me anything yet."

She heard Ros's throaty chuckle, could feel the smiles and emotions of her sisters like damp sunbeams on her skin.

"You know I'm not going to ask." He gripped her hands, gave her a straight-to-the-heart look. "Marry me, Abby. Be my wife, let me be your husband. Let's make it every bit as hard to get rid of each other as we want it to be."

She swallowed, trying to give her lips, her tongue, the moisture to reply. It came out a hoarse whisper, but she thought the light in her eyes was powerful enough to burn.

"Yes."

His mouth was back on hers again, and she clasped his wrists, held on, kissed him back. So crazy, it was all so crazy, where she'd expected to be this time last year, a place she hadn't wanted to be but had accepted. And here was where she was now, a place she very much wanted to be, with a man she loved more every day. Who possessed her every bit as much as she possessed him. As he'd said. They would never let one another go.

But he wasn't done. He eased back, his hand on her neck and shoulder, the other resting on her knee. "I didn't pick out a ring. I want us to do that together." He glanced down at himself. "Doing this while I'm kneeling has a particular significance for us, doesn't it?"

"It works for me."

"I'll bet." His lips tugged. "Not too long ago, I became aware that there's an agreement among you and your sisters. That the man who binds himself to one of you, binds himself to all of you, and that his Mistress comes up with a way to confirm that binding among the group."

Abby blinked. In Lawrence's case, the first time they'd acted on that agreement, it had happened in their board room. It had occurred in a very physically intimate way which fit Lawrence's orientation as a sub, and as the man who understood what Ros needed from him.

"I'm not a sub, but I don't think that's what it's about." Neil nodded to Vera. "Would you mind stating it out loud, the way you explained it to me?"

"Certainly." Their half circle moved closer, arranging themselves behind Neil. Vera's eyes were full of emotion as she spoke to Abby, said the words that Abby already knew, but had never expected to hear applied to herself. "When a man becomes yours, one you want to keep, then we confirm that he understands you the way he should. Every level. Body, heart, mind, soul. While a full knowledge of that is something only time can provide, he projects the committed desire to serve you, care for you, treat you as you deserve to be treated. As a Mistress, a woman, a person. A soul."

Abby let the words soak into her, her gaze resting upon Neil's chest, staring at his heart, his center. Her center. She was aware of the scrape of Ros's heel, the rustle of a tunic Skye was wearing. The gleam of Vera's earrings and the lemon cream scent Cyn carried.

All of it so vivid. Too vivid. The colors, scents and sounds of the village pressed in. She put her hands on either side of her face, trying to reduce it, stay focused as her heart thundered. She'd taken the meds, she couldn't mess this up, it was too important...

"Abigail." Neil had his hands over hers, his touch an anchor, his voice a landmark. "Easy, bébé. Just breathe."

"What you arranged at the restaurant. On the back deck. It would have been quieter. Less input. A better setting for this. I messed it up."

"No, you didn't. Not at all." He cupped her neck, brought her head forward to rest on his shoulder, close it all out as he stroked her back. He hummed a few bars she recognized. "Have a song for me, bébé?"

"Maybe baby, baby...I'll have you."

"No maybe about it." He spoke against her ear. "I want to marry you. I will marry you. I want to have you, too. Have, hold, for better or worse, sickness, health, richer, poorer. Top, bottom, switch. All right?"

He pulled back enough to run his knuckles along her jaw. "Say yes again."

"Yes," she said, touching his face, kissing his palm. "Yes."

"Good. Because what you did? Coming here? It was perfect. You gave me an answer I was looking for, that I hadn't found, until just this minute."

Still holding her, Neil looked at Ros and the others. "After Lawrence told me about it, I thought about not doing this part of it with all of you. I protect her, look after her, and that's in my blood, my first and foremost job, over anyone else's. But then I thought of how you support her, love her, watch after her, just as much. Especially when I can't be here. To not acknowledge that, particularly for this, would be dishonoring that, your right and privilege to care for her, an act of trust."

He turned his gaze back to Abby. "You thought you messed up. You didn't." He looked at the ivy-covered arch. "We'll get married here, as an enduring reminder that when things happen we can't control or anticipate, we adapt, we change, we do whatever we have to do to hold the center." His hands closed on her waist, a firm grip. "This. Us. We're the center. The way we feel about one another. Everything else can change. That holds."

He leaned forward, pressed his mouth to her sternum, then her throat, and spoke against it. "Tell me how you want me to acknowledge that bond, that oath, to your sisters."

It was that peculiar combination he did so well. An order wrapped around an oceans-deep willingness to serve. Being asked to respond to such an important question should have made her go blank, the pressure too much to answer right away. But an image came to her mind as if it had been there waiting in her subconscious all along.

As if she'd known this moment was coming.

She rose. Her knees were shaking. It wasn't the illness. She was sure it wasn't, willed it so. The world steadied, even as it kept kaleidoscoping, the views rising and falling. Like ocean surf, pouring over her hands.

She moved behind him. The others adjusted to the other side of the bench so she could face them. She gazed at Ros, Cyn, Vera, Skye. Their expressions were still filled with joy, but also the gravity of what was happening, what Neil was putting out there.

When she'd cupped her hands on either side of her face, narrowing things down, it had helped cocoon her and him into one moment. Now this, the arrangement of their bodies, the language they projected, the expressions on their faces, turned this circle into the same, as intimate a space as one carved out on a dungeon floor.

"He's who I want," she said. "Sitting in my soul, streaking across my sky. Carrying me when my footprints are lost, holding my hand when I walk on my own. Staying at my side, or following or leading. He belongs to me."

She curled her grip around his shirt collar so she could trail her fingertips along his nape. "I want your knife, sailor. Your pocket knife."

~

Neil had an idea of what she had in mind, but he was also conscious of how unexpectedly her mind could shift. He removed the knife from the pocket of his cargo pants, but held it closed in his hand as he gazed at her. "You tell me what you want cut, bébé."

Ros had drawn closer. "His palm?"

"No." Abby closed her hand over his holding the knife, a protective gesture that touched him. "We can't hurt his hand. He needs his hands."

She leaned forward, hair falling against his shoulder. He turned his head, noting her lips curve as his breath feathered her cheek. She slipped several buttons of his dress shirt with her always distracting fingers. She caressed his chest with them as she put a hand over his heart, then slipped her other down the back of the shirt. Her palm was cool on the inside of his left shoulder blade, aligning with the pressure she was putting on his front. "Here," she said, nodding to her hand on his back.

"May I?" Cyn slid the shirt off Neil's shoulders, let it gather at his elbows. Her nails scraped him, perhaps unintentionally, but it was Cyn. Fabric creased below the now bare area Abby rested her palm against.

As Abby drew back, Vera moved in to survey the area, her sure fingers passing over it.

Their touch conveyed the confidence of women who knew a man's body so well they could see inside, possess his senses. And if the man became theirs, even his heart and soul.

In this moment at least, Abby was offering them that ownership. So was he.

Skye and Ros had filled in and tightened the circle around him. The few people passing by couldn't really see what was happening, but even if they could, it was an artistic community. They'd probably think a performance was being practiced or planned.

Abby showed no consciousness of that. She was letting her people, her family, take care of it. For once, as part of the pledge he was making to her, Neil let the Mistresses handle situational awareness while he kept his full attention on her.

"I'll make her cut when the time comes," he told Ros.

"All right." When Ros took the knife, she put her hand on his shoulder, leaned over him. Her finger notched the place Abby had marked. The starting point.

"An asterisk," Ros confirmed, speaking to Abby. "To represent a rose."

Abby nodded. She stood by Neil, hand on his other shoulder.

"How big?" Ros asked.

As Neil gazed at her, he saw Abby's eyes were luminous, focused on the bare expanse of his flesh. She lifted her free hand, opening it up. "Maybe as big as my palm. Like a regular rose."

Ros tested the blade edge and tip with a finger, glanced down at Neil. He nodded.

When Ros set the tip to his flesh, Abby reached out with her free hand. The weight of the blade against his skin increased slightly. Though he couldn't see, Neil realized she'd rested her hand on top of Ros's. Not to take control, but to be part of the act.

Ros made the slice decisively, but not too deep. The intent wasn't to leave a scar, just mark him for this important ritual.

Abby kept her other hand on his shoulder, but she did the same overlapping touch when Vera stepped in, took the blade, crossed Ros's line. Then Skye.

He was either impressed or concerned that not one of them hesitated or had difficulties making the cut. He could be grateful for it, though, since the sting was mild and quick. Until Cyn. When a much sharper pain stabbed him, rippled out from the area, he guessed she'd done a little twist of the blade tip as she made her mark. Maybe even snagged it with a flourish at the finish. She shot Abby a wicked grin. "Gotta make sure he remembers it."

Abby made a face at her. Stepping back to clear the field for her, Cyn offered Abby the blade.

She'd forgotten.

Neil didn't want to ruin the moment by taking a choice from her, so he stopped himself from immediately intervening. Instead, he watched his woman, this amazing, strong soul, stare at the offered weapon. Watched the wheels of her mind turn. Ros started to step forward, but he made a subtle gesture at her, forestalling the movement.

Slowly, Abby's eyes lifted and held with his, a precious second. "Help me," she said.

"Always."

Abby dipped her chin toward him, a message to Cyn. The other woman's dark eyes were full of emotions hard to decipher, but she returned the knife to Neil, handle first.

He bent his arm back so he could locate the knife in the general area. Abby shifted more fully behind him, her hand still on his shoulder. Her other hand closed over his. "Position it at the low point," he told her. "Then draw it upward."

She adjusted it accordingly. "It's all you," he told her, an encouragement.

Wanting to feel it, be fully there with her in the moment, he shut his eyes. The way she did, to close out anything else.

"It's all us," she corrected, her voice soft. She tightened her grip over his, used his hold on the knife to move it.

It hurt the most, because it was moving over the other marks, but it was bearable, and outweighed by what it meant, the binding it enforced. As she said, an asterisk, a rose. A star, fueled by the light of the five Mistresses who marked him, sealed the bond.

When she let go of him, Abby stepped back. Looking over his shoulder, he saw her staring at the mark. Her pulse was hammering, her eyes full of a million things.

Vera had disappeared and was back. She carried paper towels, one of which he used to swipe the blade clean before he folded it up, pocketed it. He let her tend him, with an alcohol wipe that made him grimace, followed by a gauze pad she taped over the area to hold pressure on the cuts. "Every shopping center has a first aid station, if you know where to look," Vera confirmed at Ros's questioning look.

Abby wet one of the other paper towels with a water bottle Skye gave her. She sat on the bench, had him adjust so she could clean the thin rivulets of blood that had seeped down his back, making his skin twitch.

"We got blood on your pants."

"The shirt will cover it." Her touch felt good, but he was concerned about how she was handling the surfeit of emotion.

Her smile reassured him. The others had stepped back so only she was in his view when she slid his shirt back onto his shoulders. It was an intimate gesture, holding that dual mix they both enjoyed. Something a sub might do for him as a Master, when he ordered it. Or what a Mistress would do, as her right, to enjoy the feel of the man who belonged to her, kneeling quietly under her fingertips.

He covered her hands with his, but then he looked to his right, where the four women were standing, watching them. Skye had taken a picture or two of them. Hopefully one with his shirt on, so he could share it with his mother.

"I will care for her and protect her," he told them, bringing it full circle, making it official. "She has my heart and soul, every part of me that's worth anything. You can count on it."

He shifted his gaze back to Abby when she touched his face, feathered her fingers over his throat. Looking at her, his throat thickened with emotion.

"Goddamn," he murmured. "You said yes."

Joy. That was what she heard in his voice. Sincere, real, precious as a shower of gold sunlight that washed through her. Joy to be with her, exactly as she was, and would be, no matter how and where that took them.

Ros's expression held a boundless love, and some of that same joy. For different reasons, but ones that didn't affect Abby any less. Then her friend's attention went to Neil, answering what he'd just said to them.

"Your gesture today confirms you honor what we are, and how we care for one another. And not that we minded making it formal, but you proved yourself to us a long time ago, Neil."

Ros met Abby's gaze, then shifted it back to Neil. "A Dom's job is to guard the wellbeing of whoever is under his care," she said thoughtfully. "But it's also about helping her embrace who and what she is, find the beauty and wonder in it. And then—sometimes the hardest thing—convincing her that you cherish those things, too."

She smiled, tipped her head toward Abby. "We'll go share a celebratory drink at the restaurant. Join us when you're ready."

However, as the others moved away, Ros stopped beside Abby. Abby rose and gripped her hand, hard, then the two women were embracing, Abby holding Ros as much as she was being held.

"I love you," Ros whispered. "Thank you. Thank you for staying a part of our lives."

"All she needed was a fine-looking SEAL to make life worth living," Cyn commented. "Seeing as you're tapping the fine ass of a SEAL regularly, boss, seems like that should have been a no-brainer for you."

Vera chuckled and Skye grinned, while Ros sent Cyn a mock glare.

"No," Neil said, drawing their attention. He'd risen to stand next to Abby, and when her hand curled around his, he knew she agreed fully with his next words. "It wasn't all she needed. She needed everyone. She'll always need everyone. And I'm the one most grateful that she has that."

"Not the most. No." Abby still had her other hand wrapped around Ros's and squeezed it. They shared another embrace, then Abby nudged her. "Go. You're all making me cry."

As they complied, moving away with their arms around one another, a united sisterhood, Abby watched them, feeling their contentment. And her own.

Then she turned her attention to her own fine SEAL. He stood just behind her now, hand resting on her hip. Her gaze moved to the arch.

"Your mother will be happy we'll get married here."

"My mother would be happy if I married you in a pigsty, as long as I marry *you*."

He tightened his grip. "I meant what I said. I don't ever want you to apologize for leaving that restaurant. You gave me the perfect way to pledge my forever to you, and to them. And prove you'll always be able to count on my ability and willingness to follow you down any road life throws at us."

She was crying, damn it, but that was okay. He was turning her toward him, brushing the tears from her face, Kissing them. He let her dip her chin to press her face into his throat as he stroked the back of her head.

"Abby, I wish I could command you to never again consider leaving all of us."

She stilled, but he kept stroking her, letting her know he didn't need her to reassure him. He was trying to tell her something, the import of it in his voice. "I know things may get pretty bad for you at times. And when that happens, you might wonder if it would have been the right choice. So I need to say this, in the hopes that you can hold onto it.

"I trained to adapt when adapting is needed. But there are things you can never prepare for, no matter how much preparation is made. That's life, for all of us." A pause, ensuring he had her full attention. "I think that's why we're given love. It's the only thing that makes it bearable, that can guide us back out of darkness."

"What about when darkness takes that knowledge away?" she asked softly.

"The binding is still there," he said, the conviction in his voice. "Everything that's happened to us tells me you can't shake it, and I can't let go of it. No matter how far you fall or how deep, I won't lose sight of you in the darkness. Even if sometimes you can't see me, I'll be there, holding onto you."

She lifted her face, managed to let her gaze travel over his face, touch on those intent, beautiful slate-colored eyes. All the things behind them, deep inside him. She remembered what Tessie had said.

"You can count on me for the same. Any darkness that either of us face, this is here." She moved her hands to grip his. "A binding that never lets go. No matter the darkness."

~

The End

AFTERWORD

In early 2021, I ran a contest on my social media pages, asking my readers to give me their favorite "real life romance hero" moment. Kristin H shared this one:

~

My husband (then boyfriend) took me out to dinner at one of our favorite romantic restaurants in Sedona. It was a Saturday and really busy, so tables were coveted, especially on the patio where we were.

We had finished and he paid, then excused himself to go to the bathroom, so I got up and went to the front so they could clear our table.

He was a little surprised, but we ended up walking around Tlaquepaque (a beautiful outdoor market there). We found a beautiful archway covered in ivy, surrounded by fountains and secluded, where he blew my mind by proposing.

Turns out, he had wanted to do it at the restaurant! He had set it up with the servers and everything.

We both thought it turned out even better than he had originally planned. In fact, we thought it was such a perfect spot that, eighteen months later, we returned to that exact archway and said I do.

Five years after that, we took our children back and showed them where their mom and dad pledged forever to each other.

It's one of my favorite places in the world now, because [it shows] my man has the perfect ability to adapt to change.

My contest prize was having one of those "real life romance hero" moments integrated into a scene in one of my upcoming books. When I saw Kristin's entry, I knew I had my winner. At the time, I didn't exactly know how it would work with Neil and Abby, but my muse is really good about pointing me toward vital pieces of a story, even before I know how they'll fit.

After fifty-plus books, that faith in the muse has proven itself a million times over, so no surprise, Kristin's story was a perfect mesh. Especially that final, important line about adapting to whatever the world throws at us.

Every love story I write is inspired by my belief in the many real-life ones out there. So I thank Kristin for sharing hers with me.

And thank you all for taking the journey with Neil and Abby. It was a truly special story to me and I'm so glad to share it with you.

WANT MORE?

The Mistresses of the Board Room series is a spin-off from Joey's popular Knights of the Board Room series. Would you like to spend time with the Knights and see exactly how inspiring they are?

Board Resolution, Book 1, is a **FREE** download. It's Matt Kensington's story, how he won the heart of CEO Savannah Tennyson. Both were mentioned in the book you just read.

You can find their story at your chosen vendor by clicking the cover below, or use this BookFunnel link for easy download to your preferred device:

---

https://dl.bookfunnel.com/ns4cw7rwsr

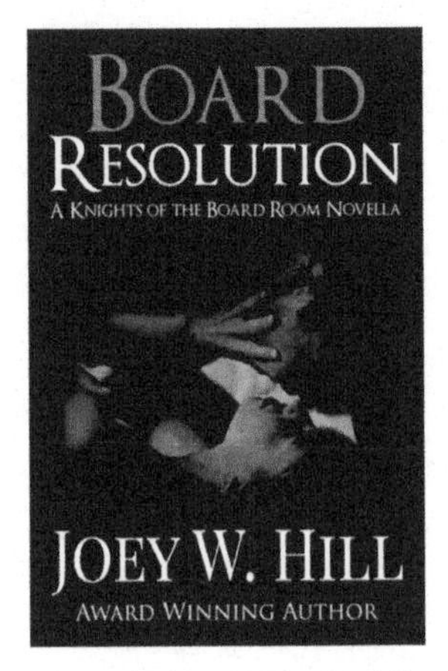

Find out more about the entire series at storywitch.com/series-kbr.

If you haven't read the first book in the Mistresses of the Board Room series, *At Her Command*, about Rosalinda and Lawrence, click the cover below or navigate to your vendor and check it out.

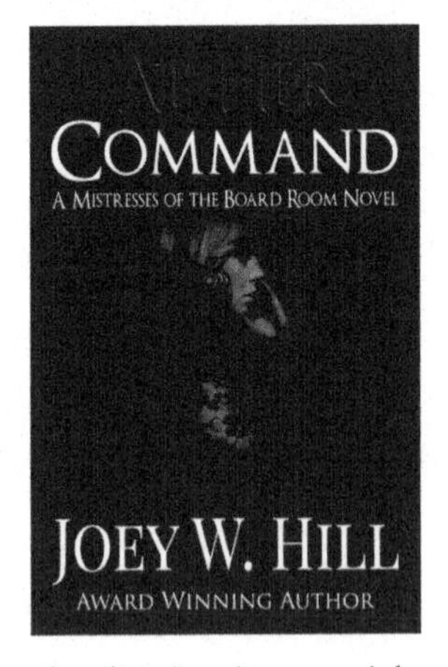

Find out more about the entire series at storywitch.com/series-mbr.

YOUR NEXT READ TEASER

From ***Board Resolution***, Book 1 of the Knights of the Board Room, **FREE** as noted earlier:

EXCERPT FROM BOARD RESOLUTION

Among all the offers of sympathies, the unwelcome press of strange hands and bodies near her – acquaintances, hangers on, a few genuine friends of her father's who had little to offer to her beyond their formal support as she stepped into her father's corporate shoes – Matt had been close. Savannah remembered the heat of his body near her throughout those long several days. The supporting touch of his hand, the only contact she had welcomed, at the small of her back.

After the funeral and memorial service, deep into the third or fourth hour of the never-ending wake at her father's sprawling estate, she had escaped to her room for a few minutes. Burying her face into her pillow, she'd screamed, beating the mattress, wishing for tears that never came. Though she stayed in there a good thirty minutes, trying to compose herself, she'd been undisturbed. It was only when she took a deep steadying breath, checked her hair and makeup and stepped back out in the hallway, that she'd found out why.

Matt sat on the top stair, with a brandy loose in his hand and a plate of untouched funeral food. Keeping watch. Keeping them at bay, the barbarians away from the gate.

"I don't need a watchdog, Kensington," she said uncharitably, frightened of how relieved she was to see him there.

He lifted a shoulder, took in everything about her at one glance. "Humor me. It gives me an excuse to stay away from them." He picked up a carrot from the plate, took a bite. "God, I hate these things."

"The vegetables?"

"No. When I die, I'm going to have a fast cremation and leave instructions for Lucas to throw a street party in my honor for a few thousand drunken revelers who have no idea who I am and could care less. They'll toast my memory because I bought the drinks, and the people who love me won't be put through a dog and pony show."

"Nobody loves you, Kensington."

He smiled. "You do." He patted the step beside him. "At least the food's good. Come have a taste."

She found herself quite willingly moving toward him. "Is Morris Johnson still downstairs?"

"Of course. He and his executive staff. Trying to schmooze up to the CEO of Bank of America and eating as much free food as he can get his hands on."

"If we slip a laxative into his crab dip, I'll bet we get a great interest rate on our next six month cash loan from BoA."

"How diabolical, Miss Tennyson. Remind me not to eat anything you've provided next time we're having an important meeting."

"I thought that's why you employ Ben. To be your official royal taster."

"Cute."

She lowered herself beside him, in the small space his large frame and splayed knees allowed, but it felt good, not crowded. She absorbed his warmth with a welcome shiver.

"Cold?"

"A little. It was overcast at the graveside."

"I'm sure Geoffrey arranged it. He did like the appropriate setting for all occasions. Here."

"I can go get a sweater." Her words died as he shrugged out of his coat, bringing a whiff of his cologne to her delicate nostrils, and laid it around her shoulders.

"There."

Suddenly, she was struggling not to weep. Why did she want to weep now, when she'd felt nothing in her room except rage? She made a snort that sounded suspiciously to her own ears like a sniffle. "I guess if we were in high school, you'd ask me to go steady now. Give me a broken coin and we'd each wear half."

A corner of his mouth lifted in a smile, and he reached over, tugged free a tendril of her hair trapped under the collar. "I was on the wrestling team. You're the football quarterback type. You'd have snubbed your nose at the likes of me."

"Wrestling?"

"Absolutely. You know how punishing football is on the adolescent bone structure? At least, that's what my mother told me, over and over again, *ad nauseum*, when I whined to sign up. We compromised with wrestling."

"Matt Kensington, whining?" She leaned back against the opposite wall, which made her knee brush his. The contact felt right, so she didn't take it away and he didn't seem to notice.

"Like the proverbial girl. But something tells me you never whined."

She gave a half laugh and some of the coldness returned. She crossed her arms over her breasts, gripped the edges of the jacket closer to her, letting go of the ball of tissue in her hand so it fell into her lap. The coat smelled of him. She pictured a closet of such suits, all smelling like this, and her falling into them, holding on in the quiet, tranquil darkness of his closet.

"Geoffrey didn't believe in it. He taught me that if you want something, you strategize how to get it. You never beg. And if you fail, you accept the failure, analyze it, go back and win what you lost back."

He nudged her knee with his own. "What's that in your lap?"

"Just a tissue..." She looked down at his puzzled expression and instead of the tissue, she saw a tiny ragdoll, little bigger than the length of her hand. She'd left it on her bed earlier, hadn't realized until this moment that was what she had clutched in her hand as she screamed into her pillow, and apparently had held onto when she left the room. "Oh." She lifted a shoulder, tried for a casual look, even as her hand settled protectively over it under his shrewd gaze. "At my father's corporate Christmas party, one of his business associates brought a little gift for me as the 'lady of the house'. When I was six," she added, at the twinkle in Matt's eyes. Her eyes couldn't linger on his face, so she looked back down, fingered the doll. "He knew nothing about me of course, was just trying to win favor with my father."

He had no clue that fawning on Geoffrey's child meant nothing to Geoffrey.

"But I liked it." Extraordinarily liked it. Kept it with her that night, slept with it hidden under her covers where her father couldn't see. But Geoffrey had known. "One night, I was tired over something, and I whined, I guess as children can do, and he punished me by taking it away. I found it in his closet when I was looking for a suit for him...for this."

"He never gave it back?" Matt raised an eyebrow.

She shrugged. "Of course not. As I said, he'd told me whining didn't get you anywhere. It meant the things that mattered got taken away from you, and when you lose things from your own actions, you must learn from them." Savannah shook her head. "Don't look at me like that, Matt. I know it sounds dysfunctional, and maybe it is, but you know, kids from good income brackets get about everything they want these days, and for the most part, they *are* whiny, self-indulgent, spoiled brats whose parents don't know how to say no to them. Geoffrey may not have been a loving, affectionate father, but he taught me everything I know about how to be successful. How to be hungry only by choice."

Reaching out, Matt put a hand to her face, startling her. She was immobilized by how good it felt, that human contact freely offered, pressed against her skin. "You were the best thing that ever happened to him," he said quietly. "He had all the money in the world, and he got his most valuable acquisition the day you were born. And not just because you could run his company better than he could run it himself."

Savannah didn't know what to say to that. She looked toward the bottom of the stairs. "It's odd no one's walked by here to disturb us."

"I told them there was free food in the main courtyard. It drew them off. Here." He offered her his plate. "As I said, the food's quite good."

"Of course." She shook her head at it. "Geoffrey already had his menu planned out. It wouldn't be less than perfect. Hungry by choice, remember?"

"The best kind of hunger there is," he said. Suddenly, she knew exactly where his knee pressed against hers, and what hunger he was talking about, because it had her lower extremities in a perilous grip.

"I want to give you something for later." He broke the charged silence between them. Withdrawing the handkerchief from the breast pocket of his jacket, he folded it into her hand, his own remaining over it.

"What, is my makeup running?"

"No. It's for when everything about this day hits you, and you finally cry, even if it's for no other reason than you don't feel like crying and *that* breaks you down." He rose. "Keep the coat until you're warm. I'll get it back later." Then he leaned down and kissed her forehead, just a gentle brush of lips, his hands holding the lapels so she was in a light embrace within the jacket. "I'm here if you need me, Savannah. I'm always here. Come down when you're ready. Lucas and Jon are in the foyer hallway, keeping people from coming this way. You don't have to come down at all if you don't want to."

"Of course I do." The dangerous temptation of such an image broke the spell. She rose to her feet, slid the jacket off her shoulders and handed it back to him. "I don't need this." But she kept the kerchief. It was a gift, after all.

She was on the step above him, so their positions put them at eye level. His expression had hardened with an emotion she couldn't read as he studied her face. In a surprising move, he suddenly slid an arm around her back and legs, swung her up in his arms and turned, carrying her down the steps.

"Matt," she hissed. "What are you doing?"

At the bottom, he let her feet touch the floor, but he held her elbow another moment. "That was to remind you that someday, you might need someone else to carry the load for awhile. And you can trust me to get you where you need to go, no matter how steep the hill is. Up or down."

He left her there, amazed, speechless. Oddly happy and hurting at once. And that was when she used the handkerchief for the very first time.

She'd kept it folded under her pillow ever since.

ABOUT THE AUTHOR

Joey W. Hill has books about vampires, mermaids, business executives, cops, witches, angels, housemaids...and the list goes on. If it's a good love story, she'll write it. She's penned over fifty acclaimed BDSM contemporary and paranormal titles, which includes six award-winning series. She's also been awarded the RT Book Reviews Career Achievement Award for Erotic Romance.

She is grateful for the support of a wonderful and enthusiastic readership, which allows her to live on her beloved Carolina coast with her even more beloved husband and menagerie of animals.

- On the Web: https://storywitch.com
- Twitter: https://twitter.com/JoeyWHill
- Facebook: https://facebook.com/JoeyWHillAuthor
- Facebook Fan Forum: https://facebook.com/groups/JWHMembersOnly
- MeWe: https://mewe.com/i/joeywhill
- GoodReads: https://www.goodreads.com/author/show/103359.Joey_W_Hill
- BookBub: https://bookbub.com/authors/joey-w-hill
- Amazon: https://amazon.com/Joey-W-Hill/e/B001JSCIW0

ALSO BY JOEY W. HILL

Arcane Shot Series

Something About Witches

In the Company of Witches

The Problem With Witches *(A Knights of the Board Room Crossover)*

Daughters of Arianne Series

A Mermaid's Kiss

A Witch's Beauty

A Mermaid's Ransom

Knights of the Board Room Series

Board Resolution

Controlled Response

Honor Bound

Afterlife

Hostile Takeover

Willing Sacrifice

Soul Rest

Knight Nostalgia *(Anthology)*

Mistresses of the Board Room Series

At Her Command

At Her Service

Nature of Desire Series

Holding the Cards

Natural Law

Ice Queen

Mirror of My Soul

Mistress of Redemption

Rough Canvas

Branded Sanctuary

Divine Solace

Worth The Wait

Truly Helpless

In His Arms

Naughty Bits Series

Naughty Bits

Naughty Wishes

Vampire Queen Series

Vampire Queen's Servant

Mark of the Vampire Queen

Vampire's Claim

Beloved Vampire

Vampire Mistress *(VQS: Club Atlantis)*

Vampire Trinity *(VQS: Club Atlantis)*

Vampire Instinct

Bound by the Vampire Queen

Taken by a Vampire

The Scientific Method

Nightfall

Elusive Hero

Night's Templar

Vampire's Soul

Vampire's Embrace

Vampire Master *(VQS: Club Atlantis)*

Vampire Guardian *(VQS: Club Atlantis)*

Non-Series Titles

If Wishes Were Horses

Virtual Reality

Unrestrained

Medusa's Heart

Snow Angel

Novellas

Chance of a Lifetime

Choice of Masters

Make Her Dreams Come True

Threads of Faith

Submissive Angel

Made in United States
North Haven, CT
21 November 2021